PENGUIN  CLASSICS

OLD MORTALITY

Angus Calder lives in Edinburgh, where he works as a professional author and as a part-time teacher for the Open University. He has published *The People's War: Britain 1939–1945* and *Russia Discovered: Nineteenth Century Fiction from Pushkin to Chekhov*.

SIR WALTER SCOTT

OLD
MORTALITY

EDITED WITH
AN INTRODUCTION BY
ANGUS CALDER

PENGUIN BOOKS

Penguin Books Ltd, Harmondsworth, Middlesex, England
Viking Penguin Inc., 40 West 23rd Street, New York, New York 10010, U.S.A.
Penguin Books Australia Ltd, Ringwood, Victoria, Australia
Penguin Books Canada Limited, 2801 John Street, Markham, Ontario, Canada L3R 1B4
Penguin Books (N.Z.) Ltd, 182–190 Wairau Road, Auckland 10, New Zealand

—

First published in 1816
Published in Penguin Books 1975
Reprinted 1980, 1982, 1985, 1987

—

—

Made and printed in Great Britain by
Hazell Watson & Viney Limited,
Member of the BPCC Group,
Aylesbury, Bucks
Set in Linotype Granjon

CONTENTS

CONTENTS

SIR WALTER SCOTT

WALTER SCOTT was born in Edinburgh on 15 August 1771. His father, a strict Calvinist with a special interest in church history, was a Writer to the Signet, i.e. a solicitor. His mother, the daughter of a professor of medicine at Edinburgh University, less austere in her attitudes than her husband, had an interest in poetry. Scott's early life was passed mainly in Edinburgh and at Sandy Knowe in Roxburghshire. In the period 1779–83 he attended the famous Edinburgh High School; afterwards, from 1783–6, he took classes at Edinburgh University. In 1786 he began an irksome apprenticeship in his father's office, and in 1789 he began to read for the Scottish Bar, to which, after another three years at Edinburgh University, he was duly called in 1792. Subsequently, despite his literary triumphs, he never entirely gave up the legal profession. He became Sheriff-Depute of Selkirkshire in 1799, and he remained Clerk of the Court of Session in Edinburgh from 1806 to within a year or two of his death.

Scott's private life went less smoothly than his professional one. While still a baby he suffered a severe illness which left him lame for the rest of his life. In 1785 he again fell seriously ill and only recovered after a protracted convalescence. In 1792 he fell in love with Williamina Belsches, daughter of a Scots baronet. His suit was unsuccessful, and the affair was brought to a close by Miss Belsches's marriage in 1796. In 1797 Scott married Margaret Charlotte Carpenter, or Carpentier, the daughter of a French refugee.

Scott's earliest literary efforts were translations of German poems and plays; a translation of a work by Goethe was the first publication to appear under his own name. His first major work, however, reflected his interest in a literary tradition nearer at hand: the collection of popular ballads called the *Minstrelsy of the Scottish Border* (1802–3). From this point on Scott's literary career was fantastically full and varied. He edited an amazing variety of literary works, including the works of Dryden and Swift; contributed regularly to periodicals; and, beginning with *The Lay of the Last Minstrel* in 1805, wrote the series of long, narrative poems that swiftly brought him fame and fortune. In 1814 *Waverley* appeared and soon it and its successors pushed that fame and fortune to still greater heights. The first nine novels drew on Scottish settings and on recent Scottish history, but after the appearance of *Ivanhoe* in 1819, Scott turned increasingly for his subject matter to England and Europe of the Middle Ages and the Renaissance.

For most of his life Scott was accepted as an outstanding luminary of the literary establishment. In 1813 he declined the offer of the Poet Laureateship. In 1818 he accepted a baronetcy. He stage-managed George IV's kilted state-visit to Edinburgh in 1822 and was himself lionized in Paris in 1826. In 1830 he declined the offer of a state pension and a Privy Counsellorship, and during his prolonged final illness he sailed to the Mediterranean aboard a naval frigate.

Since 1804 Scott had maintained a Border home at Ashestiel in Selkirkshire. In 1811 he bought Abbotsford, rebuilding the house and later adding substantially to the estate. These land investments were expensive and not entirely judicious. Since 1805 Scott's finances had been deeply involved with the printing firm of James Ballantyne with whom he had entered secretly into partnership. In 1813 the company got into financial difficulties and was helped out by the publishing house of Archibald Constable. But in 1826 disaster struck with the financial collapse of both the companies of Ballantyne and Constable. Scott's fortune was swallowed up in the crash and for the rest of his life he struggled heroically to earn enough by his writings to redeem the losses of his creditors, who were finally paid in full from the proceeds of the sale of his copyrights after his death in September 1832.

INTRODUCTION

IF you have never opened this novel before – and especially if you have never before read one of the Scottish novels of Walter Scott – you should certainly not bother yet with this introduction. You should vault over the intervening pages, ignore, besides myself, the rather tedious Cleishbotham and perhaps even the interesting Pattieson, and begin at once with Chapter 2, resolved to pay no heed to the notes or the glossary, which may be interesting, but aren't indispensable.

'In a single stroke,' writes Georg Lukacs, Scott 'sets us in the midst of a decisive action.' And the narrative which follows belies Scott's reputation for dawdling and strained invention. It is one of the leanest, swiftest and starkest constructions in the whole of fiction.

2

Old Mortality is a book written about an abortive revolution by a man who lived in a period which historians now often call the 'Age of Revolution'. Based on events in late seventeenth-century Scotland which, without it, would never have been widely known outside that country, and which, in spite of it, are now mostly forgotten, it yet remains painfully vivid. As a 'model' of how popular uprisings well up and fail, Scott's Covenanting army still seems relevant. And *Old Mortality* asks us more questions about the relative merits of 'enthusiasm' and moderation, of extremism and consensus, than Scott (or we) could ever finally answer.

The American War of Independence began when Scott was a little boy. The French Revolution flared up and raged at the decisive stage of his young manhood. In 1798, Ireland was swept by an unsuccessful but bloody rebellion in which, as Scott would have known, cultured Protestant gentlemen were caught up with much-abused and heartily vindictive Catholic peasants into situations much like those of Morton and the Bellendens in *Old Mortality*. By the time this story appeared, peace (with attendant economic problems) had been won at Waterloo after twenty-two years of almost incessant struggle between Britain and Revolutionary France. But Scott, owner of Abbotsford, sheriff of Selkirkshire, was deeply disturbed by the real promise of rebellion at home which was given by the resentments of textile workers who were products and victims of the world's first Industrial Revolution.

On 13 June 1815, in the hills where the little battle of Drumclog had been fought in 1679, 'an assemblage of people ... marched to the field of action, with military ensigns and music, for the purpose, as they said, of "Commemorating the Victory obtained by their Ancestors, the Covenanters, over the King's Troops, Commanded by Captain Graham".' There were thousands of them, and according to the frightened and scornful Sheriff-substitute of Hamilton, William Aiton, whose description I have quoted, they were 'democrats' – the textile workers and the free-masons of the near-by industrial villages wished in this way to demonstrate their approval of Napoleon, who had escaped from Elba and had raised the French once more against their lawful king.* It wasn't only Walter Scott for whom those old, unhappy, far-off things had lively current meaning.

Chill winds in the post-war economy threatened Scott as well as agitating artisans and farmers. The Waverley novels were not the least of the new inventions of that inventive age, and they sold while other speculations came to grief. But Scott needed money for his own favourite little Napoleonic project – he was in 1816 keenly buying land which by the end of November brought his estate by the Tweed up to 'about 600 acres', and planning the extensions which would turn his farmhouse there into what he referred to around this time, in a letter, as 'Conundrum Castle ... this romance of a house': Abbotsford, that charming and revealing combination of antiquarian detail and gentlemanly comfort. And meanwhile the printing business in which he was a partner

---

* Aiton, 7–8, 98–101. The full title of this book, as of others cited, will be found in the Bibliography.

with James Ballantyne had not so long ago been in serious trouble, and needed copious outflow from his study to support it.

Waverley and *Guy Mannering* had done marvellously well, and in May 1816 *The Antiquary* appeared, to increase yet further the fame and profit of its anonymous author. But this success, while it spurred Scott on to write more by gratifying the vanity of a man far lonelier and less sure of himself than he seemed to his wide circle of admirers, also opened up hopes of still more money. And early in April, even before *The Antiquary* was off the presses, Scott had commenced indirect negotiations with William Blackwood and John Murray regarding the forthcoming work of a second unknown author of Scottish novels. The publishers guessed that this was Scott himself and accepted the very stiff terms he demanded. To the rage of Archibald Constable, the publisher of the 'author of *Waverley*', whose reluctance to place printing orders with Ballantyne's press had annoyed Scott, *Tales of My Landlord* went to these rivals.

What Scott planned was four volumes, each to consist of one tale. The four separate tales would illustrate four different districts of Scotland. (There was rather more curiosity about Scotland in the England and Europe of those days than most people seem to feel about the Moon now.) The first tale, *The Black Dwarf*, set in the Borders at the start of the eighteenth century, hardly augured well. Admirers of Emily Brontë will notice the windswept setting, the name of the hero, Earnscliff, and the misanthropical rhetoric of the dwarf himself and will infer that it has perhaps some power; while it is one of Scott's weakest productions, it is far from boring. But Scott confessed to a friend that he had grown weary of the familiar ground of Border lore which he had trodden so often before, and had found that a single volume wasn't long enough for his wayfaring inventiveness. 'So I quarrelled with my story, & bungled up a conclusion as a boarding school Miss finishes a task which she had commenced with great glee & accuracy.' But *Old Mortality*, it seems, went well from start to finish, and flowed on to fill up the remaining three volumes. As Scott told the same correspondent (one of the few in the secret of his authorship, though most acute people easily guessed it) '. . . there are noble subjects for narrative during that period full of the strongest light & shadow, all human passions stirr'd up & stimulated by the most powerful motives, & the contending parties as distinctly contrasted in manners & in modes of thinking as in political principles. I am complete master of the whole history of these strange times both of persecutors & persecuted so I trust I have come decently off for as Falstaff very reasonably asks is not the *truth* the *truth*.' (*Letters* IV, 292–3). His other letters after he had finished display a similar, just satisfaction. He told another old friend that he thought *Old Mortality* was the best story he had executed, 'although written by snatches and at intervals'.

In fact, its writing seems to have been the work of a few weeks in the autumn. But since Scott always wrote fast, the dynamic concision of the narrative, which is hardly matched elsewhere in Scott's works, can't be attributed to exceptional racing of mind. Other factors must explain the power of *Old Mortality*.

The *Tales* appeared on 1 December 1816 and did well – though not well enough for Scott, who before long fell out with Blackwood in turn, over the relative slowness with which the four volumes moved. Of course, *Old Mortality*, though yoked with *The Black Dwarf*, was very popular; almost everything Scott ever wrote was popular. But in the nineteenth century it seems not to have been loved as *Waverley* and *Guy Mannering* and *Ivanhoe* were loved, and in the mid-twentieth it has shared in the general, perverse underrating of Scott's other fiction by comparison with the monstrously uneven *Heart of Midlothian*. Perhaps there is too much raw moorland air in it, too much of the severity of High Art and too little of Scott's characteristic easy humour. It has what T. S. Eliot might have called the 'unpleasantness' of great fiction. Its world is violent. To borrow Scott's own judgement (*Letters* XI, 59), two sets of 'cruel and bloody bigots' without 'the least idea either of toleration or humanity' oppose each other in ruthless conflict. One side, the stronger, uses torture and extortion and bad law. The other sees massacre as God's justice. And the moderation of the hero forced to choose between them, while it is seen as amply justified, brings him no palpable happiness. It is a book about rebellious, heroically active life, but also about death; 'old death', 'Old Mortality'.

I think we can find the explanation of Scott's achievement partly at least in an anecdote which his son-in-law and biographer, Lockhart, had from Joseph Train, the Galloway exciseman who supplied Scott with many tales and touches for his fiction. Like several of Lockhart's best episodes this story cannot be uncritically accepted as 'the truth'. (In fact, my own report of what was said ignores Lockhart's 'improvements' on his source and follows Johnson 552). Train was remembering a conversation years after it had happened, and had every reason to exaggerate his own role in inspiring a writer whom contemporaries freely compared with Shakespeare. It is odd if what follows is true that Scott writing to Train after the tale's completion should pretend not to be its author (*Letters* IV, 323). But Train's story seems 'true to' Scott; it seems to expose the way his mind worked.

Train, by his own account, visited Scott in Edinburgh in May 1816. He brought gifts, relics for Scott's antiquarian collection, including a purse alleged to have belonged to Rob Roy; also 'a fresh heap of traditionary gleanings which he had gathered among the tale-tellers of his district.' One was a letter from a schoolmaster named Broadfoot who signed himself as a joke 'Clashbottom' Flogarse. Scott received Train very hospitably, and before breakfast next morning they chatted in his library.

There on the wall was Scott's favourite picture; a copy of the best portrait of John Graham of Claverhouse, Viscount Dundee. The face (it was not just Scott's fancy) does combine pride with sadness, almost feminine beauty with a hint of cold-blooded cruelty. This was the man Scott was later to call 'Bonnie Dundee', stealing a nickname from the town to pin it to the man, with a song which has now become part of the repertory of folksingers who forget that it ever had an author.

Train was surprised. Tradition in the south-west had made Graham a monster – 'Bluidy Clavers' – the slaughterer of the pious poor in the 'Killing Time' of the 1680s. It was odd, he remarked, that such a man should have such a face. Scott replied that no man had been more traduced by the historians. Train suggested he might be made the hero of a 'romance'. 'He might,' said Scott, 'but your western zealots would require to be faithfully portrayed to make the picture complete.' And why not, the inspired Train suggested, use a device which Scott had employed in his poem *The Lay of the Last Minstrel*? Why not have the story told as if from the mouth of Old Mortality?

'Old Mortality! Man! who was he?' And Train reminded him of the aged Cameronian who had made it his life's work to keep sharp and clear the inscriptions on the tombs of Covenanting 'martyrs'. Scott as a young man had seen him and talked to him (he always talked to all manner of people). The preserver of tradition was now dead, himself a part of tradition. Tradition was threatened by the march of time into a new age of industrial mass-production; threatened more indirectly, but more finally, by the writing of men like Scott. Once written down, a ballad lost its freedom; a tale would be transplanted to the bookshelf.

Scott had first become famous as the editor of the *Minstrelsy of the Scottish Border*, the product of his 'raids' into the southern hills in search of ballads. He had found two in which Claverhouse appeared. I print them as an appendix. They are the basis of *Old Mortality*, the clue to its essential simplicity.

One presents the whig hero, 'noble Burley', in quasi-epic terms. 'Bold and stout' he vanquishes at Loudon Hill (Drumclog) the 'wicked Claver'se'. The second makes young Earlstoun accept fate's burden and set off to lead the whigs at Bothwell Bridge. But the whigs are slaughtered and, so the ballad says, when the Royalist commander Monmouth tries to check the carnage, 'wicked Claver'se' obeys reluctantly, only to make this the occasion for securing the execution of Monmouth as a traitor. 'Claver'se's' motive is simple; the rebels have killed his Cornet. In the Borders, where the Graemes (not relatives, in fact, of the historical John Graham) had been a notorious riding clan of robbers, blood asks for blood. The real people named in the songs swim with ease in the ballad tradition.

And what the ballads give Scott is the basic feature of his novel, its three contrasted heroes: Burley, less prominent in history than in folklore; Morton, developed out of the nobly pathetic Earlstoun, whom Scott took to be a 'moderate'; and

Claverhouse, whom Scott motivates partly as in the second ballad, by revenge.

But the impracticality, for a novelist, of displaying folk tradition as it stood was illustrated in 1818, when Scott's friend James Hogg, the 'Ettrick Shepherd', a devout believer in the legend of Bluidy Clavers, published his own botched Covenanting tale, *The Brownie of Bodsbeck*. Hogg's Claverhouse is a monster, with an eye which 'more than the eye of any human being resembled that of a serpent'. While it has moments of melodramatic force, Hogg's novel has no real historical foundation. Even if Scott had been willing to accept the whigs' diabolical Claverhouse, he knew that the only place for him in modern literature was in a story told in the folk manner, like the one into which he put him, 'Wandering Willie's Tale' in *Redgauntlet*.

In any case, Scott had a Jacobite heart, warmed by the stories he had heard from old men in his youth, not so much in the Borders as in the Highlands. There John Graham's legend was very different. Dundee, Ian Dhu Cean, Black John the Warrior, had led a host of clansmen to complete triumph over the lowland army at Killiecrankie in 1689, dying Homerically in the arms of victory, fighting the first battle for the cause of the Stuarts which was to meet its final check at Culloden in 1746. Hence his portrait in Scott's study, staring poignantly towards a doomed ideal.

Moreover, Scott was not simply a 'minstrel'. He moves the mode of his battles from ballad to epic, and the content of his story from folklore towards history. From boyhood he had collected printed 'sources'. He owned, beside a vast collection of relevant pamphlets, all the extant major 'secondary' studies of late seventeenth-century Scotland, and he knew several important manuscripts. His historical interests, wide ranging as they were, had tended to concentrate in this period. And good historians have been enormously impressed with what he did with his knowledge in *Old Mortality*.

One of these, Hugh Trevor-Roper, in the broadcast which commemorated Scott's bicentenary in 1971, called it Scott's 'first purely historical novel', seeing it as the first prose fiction in which Scott stepped back beyond the reach of living memory to work in a period where only printed sources could sustain him. This is true only up to a point. Scott never wrote so good a novel when he went back further. The best of his other fictions deal with the eighteenth century. Without the living force of vivid tradition (which for Scott did not amply exist for the reign of Charles I) this book, I believe, could not have worked so well.

It is, after all, explicitly based on folk traditions which its purported author, Peter Pattieson, claims to have collected. That this claim implies contact at only second hand with the events described can be confirmed by a passage from one of Scott's letters written soon after the publication of *Old Mortality*, and referring to it:

My father's grandmother who lived to the uncommon age of 98 years perfectly remembered being carried when a girl to these field-preachings with her mother where the clergyman thundered from the top of a rock, and the ladies sate upon their side-saddles which were placed on the turf for their accommodation while the men all stood round armed with swords and pistols and watches were kept on each neighbouring eminence to give notice of the approach of the soldiers. I mention these minute circumstances in order to make your Ladyship aware how nearly our oral and family traditions connect themselves with these disorderly times. (*Letters* IV, 342–3)

Old Mortality, to whom Scott had actually spoken, was 'old' enough to have spoken himself with veterans of the battle of Bothwell Bridge.

But Professor Trevor-Roper is wholly right to stress the importance of what Scott did in breaking away from the 'whig' account of the period which had been established, above all, by the industrious Reverend Robert Wodrow in his *History of the Sufferings of the Church of Scotland*, published in two heavy folio volumes in 1721–2, given official approval by that Church itself, and dedicated to King George I, who made the author a handsome cash present in return. This densely documented, uniquely tedious, deeply prejudiced book has never been superseded, and in it the character of Claverhouse is dyed stickily red with blood. Wodrow's tone however, is cautious and scholarly, unlike that of Daniel Defoe who had shown himself in his *Memoirs of the Church of Scotland* (1717) to be a propagandist

never excelled, one fears, by any of Goebbels's or Stalin's hacks –
vivid, circumstantial, and utterly unreliable. A much better-
looking source, and a favourite of Scott's was the *History of His
Own Time* by Bishop Gilbert Burnet, of which the relevant first
volume came out in 1724. But this specious and splendidly
written book is also grinding an axe for the whig cause, though
the moderate episcopalian position of its author was very much
like the one which Scott himself had adopted in his own
religious life.

Besides these, still on the whig side, Scott knew the pamphlets
of the period itself and the collections of 'dying testimonies' of
Presbyterian 'martyrs' collected in *Naphtali* (1667) and in *A
Cloud of Witnesses* (1714). And he was oddly attracted by the
very unpleasant but much reprinted *Scots Worthies*, by John
Howie of Lochgoin, a figure comparable to Old Mortality, who
had, in the late eighteenth century, concocted from various sound
and bad sources, biographies of many leading Covenanters.

Let us pause for a moment with the coprophilous old bigot,
Howie. When this Cameronian farmer brought out the second
edition of his book in Glasgow in 1781, the list of subscribers
showed where Covenanting tradition thrived. There were in
Paisley, for instance, fifty-seven; thirty-one of them were weavers,
and the only non-manual worker was a single merchant. As
Scotland entered its spectacular industrial revolution, the class
which bore the brunt of it was, in the west of Scotland, still
largely ready to curse with Howie the gentlemanly persecutors of
a hundred years before, and still ready, it would seem, to give
some pious credit to his superstitious anecdotes. Wodrow,
Howie's main quarry, was entering through him the very
marrow of nineteenth-century Scotland, that dedicated land of
industry whose pioneers, farmers, mechanics and missionaries
took their narrow, but energizing faith over the growing
colonized world. In Canada and Malawi, the ghost of Ephraim
Macbriar marches on. But what, we must now ask, was the
historical basis for the very important myth of the Covenanters?

A really curious reader must go to the excellent brief summary of the period in Rosalind Mitchison's *History of Scotland*, and beyond that to Gordon Donaldson's magisterial *Scotland: James V to James VII*. Both correct (with, I would suggest, a new 'centrist' bias of their own) the notion which later historians borrowed from Wodrow of the years from 1638 to 1689 as a phase marked above all by incessant, bloody religious conflict. Such current historians can point to the end, in the 1660s, of the Scottish tradition of building fortified houses, to a great systematization of Scottish law, and to early stumbling steps away from the Scotland of feuds and famine towards the Scotland of advanced industry and of super-excellent agriculture which came to birth in Scott's own lifetime. They dislike the Covenanters very much indeed. But the broad patterns of facts they display don't differ much from those which Scott knew.

There were two Covenants. The first was the 'National Covenant' signed in the Greyfriars churchyard in Edinburgh early in 1638 by representatives of the various classes, and later subscribed, willingly or unwillingly, by most of Scotland. This essentially conservative document expressed the reaction of nobles to the attempts by Charles I to reduce their social and economic power, and of people in general to the King's attempts to impose an Anglican type of church service on Scotland. It pledged its signatories to defend the true reformed church of Scotland against innovations.

That true church had had bishops for the previous twenty-eight years. But in the struggle between King and nobility which followed, the Presbyterian minority within the church was able to assert itself to such effect that the bishops were expelled and the notion that the Scots were a chosen people, uniquely bound to each other and to God by their Covenant, began to dominate the political life of the country. The result of the first Covenant was a revolution in Church and State. The king, whom the Scots had successfully defied, then had, in 1642, to face the challenge of the English parliament. The English rebels wanted Scottish help.

They subscribed, in return for it, a second Covenant, the 'Solemn League and Covenant' of 1643, which was proposed by the new rulers of Scotland. Both parties swore to preserve the reformed church in Scoland and (so the Scots thought) to impose Presbyterianism on England and Ireland as well. This programme, bullying and unpractical though it was, was still, it should be noted, supported by the Covenanters of 1679.

James Graham, Marquis of Montrose (1612–50) rallied the opposition in Scotland itself. In 1644–5, as general for the king, with a force of wild Highlanders and Irish, he fought a daring guerrilla campaign in the north. In August 1645 his victory at Kilsythe made him briefly master of Scotland. But his tribesmen melted away. On 13 September 1645, he was surprised at Philiphaugh in the Borders by a Covenanting army. The massacre which followed his defeat disgusted even hardened mercenaries present; but had not God delivered Jericho to Joshua?

The Scottish nobility, now much alarmed by the zealous plebeian ministers who claimed the right to interfere with the private morals of the mighty, saw that their only chance of retaining their ancient power depended on a deal with the king. Their 'Engagement' with Charles I broke the (relative) unity of the nation. After the 'Engaging' Army had been defeated at Preston in August 1648, the radical south-west, scene of *Old Mortality*, made its decisive entrance into history and gave the word 'whig' to the English language. The 'Whiggamore Raid' on Edinburgh hoisted the extreme Covenanters back into power, and a reign of the saints, or a reign of terror, depending on one's viewpoint, followed. Sinners were scourged by the civil authorities. The kirk was purged. The Act of Classes in 1649 excluded from the army, as from all public service, everyone except committed Covenanters.

The results of this devotion were seen in 1650. After his father's execution, Charles II reluctantly subscribed the Covenants in order to give himself Scottish support. This was in June; on the 3 September, Cromwell's invading army lay at Dunbar, at the mercy of a Scottish force which outnumbered it two to one and had all the advantages of position. But the ministers appointed to advise him overbore the able Scottish general, David Lesley.

The host, inflamed with Scriptural analogies, came down from the hills and the grateful Cromwell duly slaughtered them.

Scott's mother in her girlhood had known and talked with an old man who claimed to remember the battle of Dunbar and the entry of Cromwell's troops into Edinburgh. This was the furthest reach of memory.

Philiphaugh and Dunbar are a generation behind the events which Scott described in *Old Mortality*. But his novel is not 'true to' the few weeks in 1679 and few days in 1689 in which its action is set so much as it is 'true to' the entire period. Scott could no more forget the murderous, fatuous zeal of the Covenanters on those occasions where they had been on top than Major Bellenden can in his novel. For him the persecuted saints of Wodrow's pages were also, by tradition and in potential, persecutors.

Yet he took a harsher view of the government which the restored Charles II put over Scotland than modern historians seem to accept. Against the cruel Presbyterians, he set the cruel Cavaliers. This will surprise those who are used to regarding him as the besotted praiser of old aristocracies. But Scott wasn't by birth an aristocrat, nor by upbringing a gay dog. His own father, a lawyer, was a deeply serious Presbyterian who made Sunday a day of uncomfortable devotion for his children. One of Scott's more notable ancestors had been outrageously fined and lengthily imprisoned by the authorities in the Restoration period because his wife was a Covenanting woman. The fundamentals of Scott's own personality owed as much to the faith of his father as they owed to his genteel, Episcopalian, Jacobitty reaction against that grim and whiggish form of worship. And like most men of his class, whig or tory, in his own day, he saw the Revolution of 1688 which had put an end to the attempt of the Stuarts to assert the Divine Right of Kings as unquestionably Glorious. The rights of property had been established. The rule of law had been restored. The way had been opened to the island's fat commercial greatness. In cold blood Scott was always Hanoverian. It is not at all inappropriate that his head should now adorn one sort of Scottish pound note.

So Scott, once Charles II has, by 1662, renounced the Covenants and restored a moderate Episcopalianism, becomes a sympathizer with Charles's opponents. In the radical south-west – uniquely an area of small lairds and owner-occupying peasants whose view of the world was best represented by presbyterian concepts of self-government – most of the ministers refused to conform with Charles's settlement and were ejected. From among these came the illegal field-preachers whom the 'whigs' of this knobbly land preferred to follow. The Government responded by quartering troops on them to make them pay fines for nonconformity. Under the command of Sir James Turner, the oppression became intolerable. In 1666 the south-west burst out with the so-called 'Pentland Rising', which was defeated not far from Edinburgh and followed by the execution of thirty-three 'martyrs'.

Led by the relatively tolerant Lauderdale, who now made himself effective master of Scotland, the Government tried conciliation. The 'Indulgences' of 1669 and 1672 gave some 132 of the ejected ministers the right to preach again, but on the State's terms. Illegal open-air conventicles continued under those who refused such terms, not only in the south-west, but also, to a lesser extent, in the Lothians and in Fife. From 1673, repression was renewed. The 'Highland Host' which Lauderdale quartered on the recalcitrant westland men in 1678, in an attempt to bully the area into conformity, manured the soil for a new rising.

Scott's novel begins just after the act which sparked off the rising, the murder of Archbishop Sharpe on 3 May 1679. The notes at the back of this book will show how Scott's handling of the events of that year departs in detail and in general from what he knew from his sources. Few reproaches against him, however, are really worth making.

Old Mortality simplifies, compresses and synthesizes. It draws its 'history' not from one year alone but from the whole fifty-year period which closed in 1689. In form it is not and cannot be a work of scholarly 'history'. It is, precisely, a 'historical novel', and it has few equals in this genre. Scott created the 'historical novel' as a mixed form, like Shakespeare's 'history play'. *Old Mortality* modulates from analysis through comedy into epic, and back again. It combines a basic 'ballad' simplicity with additional and deliberate overtones of Homeric epic and of Renaissance

'Romance'. It is, in short, for all its starkness, a complex work of art.

Yet it is a work of art, deeply concerned with important events which actually happened, and it may well seem still to define better than any other single book the broad essential features of the period which it portrays. Scott, like all profound historical thinkers, knew that processions of dates and 'facts' may form in the end merely a drab fabric of useless illusion; the more one looks at the sources, the more firm statements dissolve, the more complexly and elusively human everything becomes. In this novel, Scott strikes out to reach the human truth, and raises an image of man's nature more unhappy but far more exalted than any which could have been derived from the neo-classical Edinburgh he worked in. But this image is not arbitrary, nor mainly itself a neo-classical fiction like the poems of 'Ossian'; it inhabits a real, an almost directly remembered, violent past.

For Scott, that the past had happened was a painful, highly personal truth. Hazlitt wrote of him, 'He is a learned, a literal, a *matter of fact* expounder of truth or fable . . . He has either not the faculty or not the will to impregnate his subject by an effort of pure invention.' To look at Scott's sources is to discover how commonly he makes memory serve the role of invention; of course, in a sense every novelist does, but every novelist does not have to confine himself to subject matter of which he has had, and could have, no direct experience. Scott rearranged freely the details the sources gave him, but almost never strayed outside their scope. Two instances of 'invention' stand out – the superb scene at Drumshinnel (Chapters 33 and 34) and the man who arrives to dominate it, Claverhouse himself. The 'historical' Claverhouse is as much of an 'invention' as the 'romantic' Morton;* no character in his fiction could better be cited against Hazlitt's friendly jibe, 'With reverence be it spoken, he is like the man who having to imitate the squeaking of a pig upon the stage, brought the animal under his coat with him.' Yet there is no doubt that Claverhouse squeaks uncommonly like the authentic pig; he goes beyond the 'factual' yet he is 'real'.

* For the 'factual' hints Scott found for Morton's character, see my 'General Note on Sources of Localities and Characters'.

Against the cannon of Wodrow and the volleys of Defoe, the Cavalier side gave Scott only a few pistols to pop off in defence of Claverhouse. He knew the wild little pamphlet, *Memoirs of the Lord Viscount Dundee*, from the second decade of the eighteenth century, and the more attractive, but not much more weighty, memoirs of the Royalist Captain Creichton, as 'ghosted' by Jonathan Swift some fifty years after the 1679 uprising which they describe.

Scott had to invent his own Claverhouse out of probabilities, polishing up the hints of dry irony found in the quaintly spelt letters he knew in manuscript, using his general judgement of the times to balance the propaganda of the whigs. It is, I think, to his credit that while the heirs of the Covenanters, and even his friend Hogg, protested that he had whitewashed Claverhouse, the biographers of Claverhouse accuse him equally firmly of maligning him. (One, writing in 1859, complained that Scott's 'temporising caution' had driven him to 'make a plum pudding of virtue and vice, and call it the character of Graham of Claverhouse.' [Napier 167–8].)

The known facts of Claverhouse's life, as his best biographer C. S. Terry assembled them early in this century, are still scanty. He was born, probably, in 1648, and took his name from the estate which he inherited near Dundee. Like scores of thousands of Scotsmen in that century, he left his poor homeland behind him to seek wealth in the service of foreign kings. In 1677 he quit the army of William of Orange to return to his native soil, and in September 1678 was appointed Captain of a newly formed troop of horse intended to help suppress the westland whigs. In February 1679 he was commissioned as Sheriff-Depute over Galloway. When some of Sharpe's murderers had reached the south-west, he set out after the conventicle they had joined, rashly attacked it at Drumclog, and was defeated.

While he commanded his troop at the Battle of Bothwell Bridge which ended the rebellion on the 22 June, his role there was essentially subordinate, though he was one of two commanders entrusted with the pursuit of the fleeing rebels. In 1682 he appears again. The south-west was still restive; while internal dissension and bitter defeat had disillusioned the more 'moderate' conventiclers, a small minority, followers first of Richard Cameron, and hence called 'Cameronians', still fostered illegal religious gatherings. Claverhouse seems to have worked effectively to keep the area calm. In December 1682 he was appointed Colonel of a newly formed regiment of horse, and next year he became a Privy Councillor. In 1684, he married into a well-known family of Presbyterians, though he dissociated himself altogether from what he called 'that plaigue of presbitry'.

The events and alleged events which made him a byword for cruelty are dated in the so-called 'Killing Time' of 1684–5. The Cameronian rump, led by the preacher James Renwick, published in November 1684 a declaration in which they proclaimed their right to 'punish' those who opposed them. The Government had long failed to distinguish clearly enough between quietist Presbyterians and militant extremists, and whether matters got very much worse now that the Council was thus provoked into extreme action against the Cameronians is not altogether clear. But it is in this phase that reports concentrate of Claverhouse making summary execution of men not permitted to finish their prayers, of small children tortured, of men shot down on the merest suspicion. Defoe accused him of slaying over a hundred men in cold-blooded cruelty. But the accusers are surprisingly short of circumstantial details – even Howie can only cite ten cases of people killed by Claverhouse or at his orders in cold blood, and Terry, carefully sifting the facts, found that no well-attested case clearly supports the charge of arbitrary, sadistic slaughter; Claverhouse merely executed the laws against men whose actions defied them.

Scott never made such a sifting. But he knew the laws themselves to have been cruel and bad, and he had no patience with the argument, now so often tacitly accepted by others as well as by Adolf Eichmann, that those who obey evil orders are not culpable. Scott's favourites among all his sources, however, gave him, from the whig side, licence to assume that Claverhouse was far from wholly evil. Burnet, though a bitter opponent of James

VII, described Dundee as a man 'of good parts, and of some very valuable virtues. But, as he was proud and ambitious, so he had taken up a most violent hatred of the whole Presbyterian party, and had executed all the severest orders against them with great rigour'. (Burnet 1.805). And Scott had long loved the biographies of Covenanting preachers published between 1724 and 1732 by one Patrick Walker. This was the quirky opinionated veteran on whom Scott was to model Douce Davie Deans in *The Heart of Midlothian*. To read Walker after Wodrow and Defoe is to breathe again the inhabitable air of a real world – for all his uncontrolled style and unattractive opinions, he writes from personal memory like a man about fellow human beings. When Walker notes that Claverhouse 'hated to spend his time with wine and women, which made him the more active in violent unheard-of persecution', it is a complex man, not a demon who is suggested; and Scott makes what Walker calls that 'mocking manner wherein he exceeded all persecutors' a cardinal feature of his portrait. (Walker 2.64).

But Scott's digestion of his sources was clearly not pedantically laboured; his Claverhouse flowed easily, enhanced by touches – his friendship for Sharpe, his love of Froissart – for which he had only faint and hearsay warrant. The result is the finest, surely, of all his characterizations of 'real' historical figures. Hazlitt conveys in a passing remark the ambiguous excitement which this 'fawning Claverhouse, beautiful as a panther, smooth-looking, blood-spotted' awakens in the reader.

But we meet not the in fact obscure Captain of 1679, but the Colonel of the Killing Time; not the rash inexperienced man whose flight from Drumclog on his maimed half-crazy horse finalized the rout of his small troop, but the cool Commander of a future Killiecrankie, exposing himself bravely, in Scott's superb and fictitious account of the skirmish, with such memorable composure in the face of danger, striving to bring honour out of a situation made desperate by the recklessness of his juniors. But equally it is not the Claverhouse who seems to have used force, in 1682, with a nice sense of selection, but the executor of still crueller orders three years later. It is Claverhouse at his best and at his worst, Claverhouse distilled not only into the essence of the two opposed legends of Bluidy Clavers and Black John the Warrior, but into the quintessence of all the cavaliers of fifty years of violent civil dissension. At one extreme he touches the gallantry of Montrose, at the other the viciousness of Dalzell. He is, as the great Russian novelists understood the term, a superb and definitive 'type'. His hands are bloody, his demeanour suave. His chivalry is acute, his class-consciousness candidly bitter. The rhythms of his speech are those of the age of Dryden; his be- haviour at Bothwell Bridge, where he shouts 'Kill Kill !', is that of a Highland chieftain, of the 'noble savage' Scott had called him in a letter to the poet Southey nine years before he wrote the novel.

But in that letter Scott had added, 'the beastly covenanters against whom he acted, hardly had any claim to be called men, unless what was founded on their walking upon their hind feet. You can hardly conceive the perfidy, cruelty and stupidity of these people, according to the accounts they have themselves preserved.' (*Letters* I, 400–401). It was easier for him to make a hero out of a gentlemanly Graham than to achieve what he saw, if we accept the essential truth of Train's account, as the necessary counter-balance – 'your western zealots would require to be faith- fully portrayed to make the picture complete'. For the risings of 1666 and 1679 exemplified the first movement in Scottish history which had made do without aristocratic leadership. As Professor Donaldson puts it (and as Scott himself knew) 'after the covenant lost its appeal to the magnates, it survived as the rallying point of the humbler folk, and it was the "very mean persons" who were most obstinate'. (Donaldson 367).

6

No admirer can avoid remarking, however reluctantly, that as Scott presents them in this novel, the Cavaliers are people one might find amusing company, whereas the 'western zealots' are so dour and devoted that (with the crucial exception of Bessie Maclure) only distant admiration and perhaps a small measure of intellectual sympathy are at best available to the reader. Scott's hero Morton, while he fights beside the humble Covenanters, is obviously most at ease among their adversaries. (We are told in Chapter 35 that talking to the remorseless Claverhouse, 'the hours' for him flow 'less anxiously than at any time since his having commenced actor in public life'.)

The novel provoked an immediate response from the Reverend Thomas M'Crie, a very considerable scholar from one of the Scottish dissenting sects which claimed descent from the 'martyrs' of the Covenant. His article, published in three instalments early in 1817 in the *Edinburgh Christian Instructor*, is itself the length of a book, and displays its author as a surprisingly shrewd literary critic. Scott replied through a counter-review in the *Quarterly*, part of which he wrote himself. An extract from it is given as an appendix to this volume, and all that need be said here is that M'Crie accused Scott of wilfully travestying the Covenanters, and that, while some of his individual points strike home, many go far astray, and anyone who has had the chance to set the actual sources known to both Scott and M'Crie against the novel itself, will confirm that Scott's view emerges as altogether more balanced and accurate.

Scott certainly handles the events of 1679 with great freedom. Just as he inflates the importance in that year of Claverhouse, so he makes his 'zealots' into men who sum up the common features shared by the triumphant theocrats of 1648–50 and the persecuted Cameronian 'remnant' of the Killing Time. Macbriar embodies the oratorical power and the intellectual strength of the movement over fifty years, as well as the courage shown by many 'martyrs'. In Kettledrummle Scott represents, not unfairly, the bumbling formalistic style of the less inspired sermons. Mucklewrath isolates the strains of bloodthirstiness and prophecy inevitable in a militant movement which was saturated in the less benign books of the Old Testament. And Burley is the archetypal lay Covenanter to set against Claverhouse. He too appears with blood sticky upon him. And Claverhouse himself readily admits the affinity between them.

Details are rearranged or imported to make the confrontation between the two violent causes an epic one. Dalzell is summoned by Scott to Bothwell Bridge, although in fact he wasn't present.

Lauderdale is likewise made to appear in order to confront
Cuddie and Macbriar with the chief man of the state. And whereas in sober fact (Cowan 48) the preachers themselves were mostly
'moderate' and only 'two or at most four of the eighteen ministers
present with the insurgent army' supported the extremist line of
the commander, Hamilton (whom Scott simply banishes, except
for one casual reference, altogether out of the novel), Scott gives
to extremist preachers the kind of dominance they had had at
Dunbar.

The moderate leader, the preacher John Welch, disappears
altogether. 'Indulged' ministers appear in the rebel camp to be
'moderates' in Welch's place; there were in fact none there. In
this way the pattern of right-left-centre is simplified. Two principles are set into collision. The Cavaliers represent Loyalty,
Order, Aristocracy. The extremist Covenanters rage against the
King, admire the understanding of mean people, see rebellion as
altogether lawful and are, in effect, republicans.

But there is a third party, and in Morton, Scott gives it a leader
no less brave than Claverhouse and Burley. The aims of the rising
of 1666, as its apologists had expressed them, had been 'moderate'.
When Morton talks in Chapter 14 of this novel about the 'rights
of the meanest Scotchman' he represents currents of opinion
which were already moving towards the settlement after the
Glorious Revolution which drove the 'Divine Right of Kings'
out of Britain. Scott himself was to write that Britain owed to
the 'revolutionaries' of 1689 'the inestimable blessing of a con-
stitution, fixed on the decided and defined principles of civil and
religious liberty'. (*Tales*). Whether or not the view of 1688-9
which Scott's kind of Tory shared with the Whigs (and with the
American rebels of 1776) can still be seen as historically 'correct'
need not detain us here. But we must notice that this was one
of the world's most significant and creative historical 'myths'; and
that in Scott's novel the victor – formally, not emotively, as we
shall see – is Morton, the fanatic of the centre, the unbending
advocate of 'civil and religious liberty', the man of 'moderate'
synthesis squeezed out of the dialectic of 'extremes'.

Scott accelerates the Bothwell Rising. *Old Mortality* opens, very
precisely, on the 5 May, two days after Sharpe's murder. Scott
moves the battle of Drumclog back from 1 June to the 8 May.
Not until Chapter 26, three-fifths of the way through the story,
when Scott first withdraws us a little from the direct shock of
events and begins to generalize to cover over the time between
Drumclog and Bothwell Bridge, do we reach the morning of 11
May. The 'revolution' in Morton's character is confirmed in less
than a week. The 'slender' attractive boy of the opening scene has
emerged as a leader of insurrection.

Movement is what the novel is about – movement of minds,
movements of men. From that third chapter where Morton and
Evandale gallop their horses to fire at the popinjay and the
anarchic ride of Goose Gibbie precipitates indirectly Morton's
involvement in rebellion by causing Lady Margaret to expel
Cuddie and Mause from their cottage, the novel rides on horseback at a pace wholly beyond the Duke's fatuous 'leathern
vehicle'. Gentility itself is left behind.

Yet such speed does not prevent Scott from establishing fully
the social scene. After the wappenschaw has drawn together the
contrasting parties of Cavaliers and 'Puritans', Niel Blane's
survey for his daughter of the people at his howff deepens and
sharpens our sense of the basic social conflicts while at the same
time characterizing the speaker. This is a novel where great
quantities of essential information are exposed in dialogue : what
we heard from Gilbertscleugh's mouth in Chapter 3 regarding
Morton's genteel but dependent status, is confirmed more vividly
from Niel Blane's, here.

Speech moves the story on. Speech exposes implicitly the contrasts and conflicts which it makes explicit. The jolly, bullying
Bothwell whose language is that of jokers in seventeenth-century
plays, confronts Burley, whose speech is constantly pointed by
references to the Bible, which Scott himself had known almost by
heart since childhood.

This is the first epic moment of the novel. Notice how Burley himself casts Bothwell as a representative, as 'type', of all the rapacious troopers of the epoch : 'I will forthwith make thee an example to all such railing Rabshakehs.' Both men, though full of faults, are larger than life-size, generously open to each other and to the world – Burley scorns to evade a conflict in which, even if victorious, as an intercommuned fugitive he puts his life at risk.

Chapter 4 ends with Cornet Grahame calling the troopers to horse to pursue Burley and Morton. Chapter 5 begins with a conversation on horseback, the first of several in the novel. And Morton confronts the first of that series of dilemmas which have encouraged R. C. Gordon to call this 'the most Racinian novel in English'. In his loyalty to his father's memory, Morton is a fanatic – yet as a man of the centre he must respect the authority of his uncle as head of the house. The two principles cannot (till 1689) be reconciled, any more than can the principles of tolera-tion and royal authority which they point towards, and both of which Morton accepts. He has to choose. And the more heroic principle triumphs. Morton *is* a hero in a far more complete sense than those 'very amiable and very insipid young men', as Scott himself candidly called them, who fill the hero's role in most of his other novels. Morton accepts the possibility of punishment (in fact, as we learn later, of execution without trial) and harbours Burley.

The force of his father's example, always, we must assume, latent, is only now triggered. 'Was not the cause of freedom, civil and religious, that for which my father fought,' he asks himself as Burley rides away in Chapter 6, 'and shall I do well to remain inactive, or to take the part of an oppressive government, if there should appear any rational prospect of redressing the insufferable wrongs to which my miserable countrymen are sub-jected?' This heavy language is suitable for the expression of general principles; but Morton's soliloquy speeds up, and even becomes choppy, as he considers his own particular case. His impulse is to escape to military service in Europe – but this will deprive him of his meetings with Edith. His love for a Scottish girl binds him to Scotland; it is part of the authentic complexity of Morton's character that we cannot separate his faith in civil liberty from filial piety and from patriotism, nor his patriotism from romantic infatuation. What gives him truly heroic force is his capacity to act firmly in spite of the tortoise-like style with which he irreproachably formulates his dilemmas and in spite (or because) of the rash impulses which Scott represents by a vehement rhetoric.

The high tone achieved by now must, however, modulate downwards as Morton confronts old Milnwood who, like Niel Blane, displays for us the meanness of 'moderation' in a time of great causes. Milnwood resists the epic mode and the romantic mode alike; he belongs to comedy. But the clash between Lady Margaret and Mause in Chapter 7 rises back from comedy towards epic. As in the case of Morton, latent heroic principles now become actual. Each of the two old ladies is ridiculously formalistic in the expression of a faith which is nevertheless deeply felt. Lady Margaret is obsessed with etiquette, Mause with doctrines she cannot bend and texts she will not deny. But each achieves a pathetic dignity in this parting.

Chapter 7 ends with speech and with a movement which takes us directly (as it were) into the great Chapter 8, in which comedy and suspense are so richly blended and Bothwell's relative good nature only serves to expose, by contrast, still more sharply the arbitrariness of the government's rule. Alison's parting diatribe against Mause drops us straight (barring the usual motto) into Chapter 9 and the opening remarks of another conversation on horseback. The ride of Bothwell and his prisoner Morton comes to a halt at Tillietudlem, but Scott has no time to describe the castle's setting yet – we plunge straight into more dialogue, and Chapter 10 is almost purely 'dramatic', centring on Edith's meeting with Morton in disguise, in which the energy and resourcefulness of Jenny Dennison (and her sexual vitality) are contrasted so markedly with the near paralysis of her dilemma-ridden mistress – 'For two or three minutes Edith stood as motionless as the statue of a saint which receives the adoration of a worshipper.'

Guse Gibbie's chaotic journey to Charnwood brings Major

Bellenden riding in at the start of the next chapter, to Tillietud-lem, where we are now ready for Scott's first sizeable 'set-piece' description since the wappenschaw. The setting of Tillietudlem, one of contrast and transition, symbolically apt, is described to us so that we can appreciate the ironically 'imposing' entry of Claverhouse and his force : ironic because today these 'glimmer-ing ranks' will be routed by peasants armed with scythes.

But Claverhouse does 'impose' himself upon us in Chapter 12. The 'polite trifler' in my lady's best room exults when Evendale comes with word that rebels are up in arms :

'Unpleasant news call you them?' replied Colonel Grahame, his dark eyes flashing fire, 'they are the best I have heard these six months. Now that the scoundrels are drawn into a body, we will make short work with them. When the adder crawls into daylight,' he added, striking the heel of his boot upon the floor, as if in the act of crushing a noxious reptile, 'I can trample him to death . . .'

It is characteristic of Scott to bring his main 'historical' personage into a novel only when we are equipped with the means of judg-ing him. 'Reptile' refers to Mause, amongst others. Even Burley has been shaken with remorseful dreams of Sharpe's murder. No character so far in the novel has been so attractive in manners as Claverhouse; now we discover that none has been so cruel.

And only now, with each opposing force supplied with a definitive leader, with the countryside crossed and recrossed, does Scott settle down to establish by flashback the story of Morton's love for Edith, and to introduce the 'Racinian' (or perhaps we had better say 'Cornelian') moral and psychological drama of the Edith – Evandale – Morton triangle. The term 'romantic' applies with more precision than usual to this material, which points back to the gallantries of medieval and Renaissance 'romance', to those 'metaphysical' (Scott's word) French stories which Edith reads so keenly. Scott is not merely giving the Martha Buskbodys of 1816 what they expect from a novel; the motivations of these young people belong to a very specific period, like those of the Germans who during Scott's own childhood had imitated Goethe's Werther even up to the point of suicide.

This kind of exalted if stilted 'romance' does not deprive its participants of their capacity to act at the level of the epic mode as a less pallid and more 'sentimental' passion like Werther's might. Evandale is all too easily summarized by Scott's very first description of him – 'a handsome exterior, sedulously decorated'. But his 'race of generosity' with Morton transfers to the private sphere the noble extremism of war and politics.

As he sees, so he thinks, the success of a socially superior rival, Morton experiences 'a singular and instantaneous revolution in his character'. His personal despair and resentment do not cow him but turn his passion outward, from self to society :

Desperate himself, he determined to support the rights of his country, insulted in his person. His character was for the moment as effectually changed as the appearance of a villa, which, from being the abode of domestic quiet and happiness, is, by the sudden intrusion of an armed force, converted into a formidable post of defence.

This image brings Morton's case, and the heroic world of the novel, uncomfortably home to Scott's Regency readers. What it suggests is exciting but frightening; as if the pretty houses of Ann Street, Edinburgh (begun in 1817) were to become outposts against the French in a siege. Thinking of Belfast, 1974, the image may well be disturbing even for us. And such things had happened in Ireland only eighteen years before Scott wrote his novel. To the inhabitants of the world's most comfortable nation, Morton's predicament made available for the imagination modes of feeling, thought and behaviour less secure and more noble than their own. And whether one should prefer salaries, routine and artificial lighting, to dangerous canters upon wild moors is not perhaps always clear, even now, to people in modern Britain and America, for whom westerns provide so much of what Scott offered their ancestors.

Morton, defying Claverhouse, consciously takes on 'typicality'; his own person represents 'the charter of my country'. And he shares the epic fatalism which links his opponent with Bothwell and Bellenden, Burley and Macbriar (how all those Bs thrust themselves out of the mouth !). But he cannot share Claverhouse's casualness about the taking of human life – in this instance, Morton's own. Claverhouse sees in Morton not exactly a whig zealot but something more dangerous still, a moderate like his father, 'cool, resolute, soldierly, and inflexible in his cursed principles'; principles which defy utterly those of 'divine right' which Claverhouse himself invokes when he says 'I *must* do my duty to church and state'. But Claverhouse, like Burley, is a political animal, and for political reasons he doesn't do what he considers his duty.

With Morton saved, the hurry begins again. The soldiers are pressed at hot pace towards battle. Yet another dialogue on horseback, between Morton and Cuddie, establishes the hero's human fellow feeling and (through Cuddie's admiration) his power to lead men. We pause for another set-piece as the battlefield is described. Then the soldiers are flung into battle by the noble rashness of Cornet Grahame and Evandale, and cannot be saved by that 'coolness' with which Claverhouse matches Burley's 'stern and gloomy deliberation'. In the epics, prophecies come true. The wild words of Kettledrummle and Mause have in fact predicted the rout of the troopers. And Claverhouse is proved right; Morton becomes a leader of the rebels.

The Covenanters he joins are presented selectively so as to achieve a 'higher' tone than Kettledrummle and Mause have so far offered. Except for Cuddie's, little humour appears in their camp, though Scott's sources (especially Patrick Walker) display plenty of it. The reader must decide whether the effect achieved is one of travesty or of dignity; for my own part, while I regret the absence of more engaging minor characters to balance them, I am convinced that, granted Scott's objectives, Macbriar and Mucklewrath are as they should be; and it is worth pausing here to praise the ventriloquist's gifts which enable Scott to move from the thick Lowland speech of Cuddie and Niel Blane, through the lightly Scotticized language of Lady Margaret and her brother, to the deftly differentiated idioms of Mause, of Kettledrummle, and of Burley, Macbriar and Mucklewrath. I think he participates to a remarkable degree in all idioms alike, and that only the Bible-saturated son of Scott's own dour father could have brought Burley so shockingly to life or have created the magnificent rhetoric of Mucklewrath, a triumph of neo-classical sublimity.

Perhaps the reader's first doubts about the success of Scott in integrating character with essential history will come with Burley's decision to maintain the (wholly fictitious) siege of Tillietudlem for reasons which include, indeed, military expediencies, but are perhaps insufficient to withdraw the cardinal Covenanting hero from the forefront of action and dispute. Yet vindictiveness and secular ambition are crucially part of Burley's character. And the balance of the novel demands that the fanaticism of Major Bellenden, who says he would be happy to see Morton hanged 'were he my own son', should be demonstrated by his fight against odds here, along with the corrupt and riotous character of the Government troops. The veterans of the 1640s are set into opposition, and their natural victims are a younger generation growing up to be weary of murderous causes.

There was a pause in the action between Drumclog and Bothwell Bridge too well-known for Scott to disregard, and in any case a lull is needed to set out the basis for a new climax. Morton must establish his military prowess, and forge his alliance with the moderate Poundtext. All historians agree that the Covenanters' chronic internal disputes were the chief factor in turning what was already almost certain defeat into total rout; what is striking in Scott's adaptation is how much epic dignity he is able to salvage for Burley from the affair, and how appalling he now makes seem the Royalist zeal of Claverhouse and Dalzell. Their behaviour, so much like that of tribal chieftains, counterbalances the suggestions worked into both landscape and action at Drumclog that the Covenanters themselves resemble an ancient tribe – a tribe like the Children of Israel whom they professedly imitate. In the absolute climax of the novel, the scene where Morton is bound at Drumshinnel to provide a ritual sacrifice, these suggestions are taken up with terrible force. It must be realized that Scott never condemned out of hand the customs and ethics of cultures and groups unlike his own; but first Claverhouse and then the Covenanters are made to seem like the Highlanders as he later portrayed them in *The Fair Maid of Perth* – adherents of violent codes incompatible with civil society.

Chapters 33 and 34 are possibly unsurpassed in all Scott's prose. 'Composed' as ever, Claverhouse expounds to Morton the ethics implicit in that famous motto which heads Chapter 34:

> One crowded hour of glorious life
> Is worth an age without a name.

The prim but sturdy, taut yet flowing rhythms of his great speech advance to what the reader perhaps knows already to be a prophecy of his own death:

> When I think of death, Mr Morton, as a thing worth thinking of, it is in the hope of pressing one day some well-fought and hard-won field of battle, and dying with the shout of victory in my ear – *that* would be worth dying for, and more, it would be worth having lived for!

And then Habbakuk Mucklewrath, equally a fanatic careless of human life, whose rhetoric, however, is at the farthest extreme from Claverhouse's own, rises up to foretell, with adequate accuracy though in a speech combining echoes from Jeremiah, Hosea and the Psalms, the final defeat in the coming whig century of the Stuart cause Claverhouse supports.

After such a confrontation of extremes, the quality of Morton's fanatical moderation must seem to the reader more attractive. Claverhouse lets his prisoner 'retain his sword, the wearing which was, in those days, the distinguishing mark of a gentleman'. Morton has been saved, and will finally be spared, because he comes from a class acceptable to Claverhouse. But he himself boldly argues against his saviour's contempt for the lower orders (a contempt which Claverhouse extends to his own troopers) and expounds a principle which is implicit both in the New Testament and in the most likeable thought of Scott's own lifetime. All men are ends in themselves; 'God gives every spark of life – that of the peasant as well as that of the prince.' We are only a step away from the easy inversion of that doctrine which under-lies all modern humanism, that these sparks of life are in themselves 'God', that is, what we must most respect and cherish.

But how, we wonder, was this compatible with the attitudes of Scott himself, who was always willing to endorse the use of severe force against working-class rebels in his own Scotland? The point is that Morton's rhetoric, *because* it is generalized and formal, is able to transcend Scott's own political commitments. As Crane C. Brinton pointed out many years ago, Scott's conservatism would have shocked those earlier tories, Swift and Johnson, because it was based on complete acceptance of the Revolution of 1688. What Scott wanted to conserve was the *status quo* of a very rich and successful trading nation which had emancipated itself from royal absolutism in the name of general liberty a hundred years before the French Revolution, and which in Scott's own day (this cannot be stressed too much) represented fairly fully, in actual embodiment, the political ideals of liberal 'revolutionaries' in other parts of the European world, except for the USA, which had taken the principles of 1688 still further. So it is really no paradox that Scott should make Morton express, as he does here, ideas one associates with the democratic revolution. Scott's, to borrow Brinton's phrase (121) is 'the Conservatism of the triumphant Revolution' – and it owes something to Fox as well as to Burke.

The British ruling class to which Scott hung on, presiding over the world's first industrial revolution and busy conquering opulent India while beating off the challenge of France, was perhaps the most effective the west had ever seen. Morton, like all Scott's heroes, uses its language, and so do Edith and Evandale. No feature of Scott's novels so puts off the modern reader as the colourless jargon of his virtuous young people. Yet we must not underestimate the usefulness of that jargon. It has behind it the achievements of the Enlightenment. It represents an attempt, which, regrettably, had sufficient success, to harmonize the contradictions within a society which combined advanced liberal principles with the dismal repression of the poor represented by those allied facts, the Game Laws and mass transportations of convicts. Without such a language, the class which used it could not have lived with itself or prospered. To succeed, the language had to be abstract; it dared not admit, by vivid suggestion, the possibility that the actual poor had social and political as well as legal rights which they might actually realize. But it had to be plausibly humane; its tone and judgements had to be convincing to thinking artisans as well as to rational ironmasters. Its hypocrisies had to be palatable.

Scott expressed and at the same time outflanked the centrism of his day in his novels. What happens in them, and what people like Claverhouse say in them, take us beyond efficient proprieties into a raw world of feelings, actions and impulses which defy moderation. He dashes his readers beyond the point where their favourite platitudes stop working, while remaining in touch with the very real strengths of the public voice of his time, which save him from merely picturesque or morbid 'romantic' excess and give him a common language (for that matter) with the radical Hazlitt.

The talk he puts into the mouths of his people brings into the view of the literate public modes of idealism, ethical standards, manners and customs which expose the limitations of its own; their lack of certain attractive kinds of human vigour. To be more concrete; the building of Gothic churches in early nineteenth-century Britain – there was one going up a bow-shot from Scott's house in Edinburgh while he was writing the novel – revealed, like the response to Scott's fiction, the quest of a culture for moral vitalities somehow denied by its graceful town houses and public buildings in rectangular good taste.

For Scott himself, neither past nor present can provide a whole and acceptable image of man. Hence the force of his fiction is critical, Utopian. Scott's heart was with Claverhouse's 'enthusiasm' for chivalry, even with the religious 'enthusiasm' of Burley, as much as it was with Morton's rational decency. His head was firmly committed to Morton; but the effects of novels upon their readers are not the same as those of judicious essays.

Morton's conversation with Claverhouse rides us into Edinburgh, where, with a speed not confirmed in the historical records, Covenanters are brought to trial. The composure under torture of Macbriar matches Claverhouse's own; but the reader must surely see the sense of the latter's ironic attitude when

Morton, whom Macbriar would have sacrificed to his God, praises his 'Wonderful firmness and gallantry!' Morton cannot have his moral cake and eat it. The 'self-devotion and heroism' of Macbriar are inseparable from what Morton calls 'the fiercer features of his sect'. Certain kinds of dignity, and certain kinds of security, are incompatible. When the search of oppressed classes for dignity overthrows what their oppressors call 'security' we call the result, as in China and Cuba, 'revolution'.

8

It is easy to misread *Old Mortality* so that its last eight chapters seem to dissipate the stern 'historical' strength of the rest of the novel in a series of striking but, as it were, arbitrary and 'romantic' scenes. There is still a great deal of rapid movement, but not towards, or away from, major 'historical' confrontation. Claverhouse dies off-stage while Burley plays the role of a crazy man meddling (beneath his dignity?) in relatively petty affairs of property. Morton returns like Ulysses, it is true, but since his Argus is only a yapping spaniel, the epic hints are now ironic. And this lonely, indeed almost despairing man is hardly more than the ghost Edith takes him to be.

But in fact this strange final movement is essential. Scotland must be shown as a country in which the epic mode of life is now, for better or worse, impossible, where violence is occasional and random rather than the main motive force of history – because this state of affairs is what the Glorious Revolution (in Scott's view) achieved.

Both violent causes have been defeated. Yet, by troublesome irony, the 'moderate' Evandale who might have been expected to concur, like Scott and Morton, in their defeat, is now moved to revolt not, as Morton had been, by direct oppression, but by a kind of whim – fidelity to a defeated king. Morton for all his busyness cannot save him, and it is Evandale who, by uniting the hands of the immobile Edith and the speechless Morton, alone displays heroic energy in the novel's final paragraph. When he dies, the novel dies with him. Morton and Edith, both now about thirty, have survived ten intervening years always tormented by their love for each other, which has had all this time no physical outlet at all. Whatever they may seem to represent at the end (and the formal triumphs of moderation and of principle are involved in their marriage) it is not warm-blooded, positive 'happiness'.

If the reader is left feeling that it has all been worth it, this must be because of warm affirmations made elsewhere in these last chapters. The vitality which an abstracted, mind-governed 'moderation' like Morton's can display only in moments of heroic outburst or intense moral dilemma, is given now to the lower orders in their daily lives. The real victors, as our affections as readers tell us, are not the neurotically self-repressed young genteel lovers, but Cuddie and Jenny and Bessie Maclure and that vivid little granddaughter of hers who trips so lightly over the dangerous moor.

Early in Chapter 37 the first *relaxing* set-piece description of the novel is given us. Though it includes the battlefield of Bothwell Bridge, the scene is as 'placid and quiet' as a landscape by Claude. It is idyllic. And the inmates of the idyll are Cuddie and Jenny, who, after their confrontation with the spectral Morton, tumble cheerfully into bed together as Scott would never have let his upper-class characters do.

Both Cuddie and Jenny are, if we must define them politically, 'moderates'. Some critics are oddly censorious of Jenny's 'selfish' concern for her own interest when she wishes Edith to marry a rich peer. And it is in the abstract very hard to separate her from the time-serving Niel Blane, the grasping Milnwood, the ease-loving Poundtext and the altogether unprincipled Basil Olifant who are, in this novel which *formally* extols moderation, representatives of moderation in action. But we feel – we are bound to feel – that what Jenny has and wishes to hold on to is real and good – husband, home, children, a fertile landscape. Since Morton and Edith are too refined to be happy, why should she defer to their exalted feelings?

And Morton is too intellectual, too genteel, to express the kind message of the New Testament as vividly as Bessie Maclure does. Her presence in these last pages tilts the balance of the novel towards the Covenanters, and towards the poor; no other character in the book can command so fully the reader's sympathy and moral approval. Her readiness to forgive without forgetting, to accept as her brethren both Burley and Evandale, assists in the important process of modulating 'history' into 'tradition' which occurs in these final chapters; but above and beyond that we see she is committed without being inhumane – indeed, she is committed to humaneness.

If the peasants triumph, so in a different way does Burley. The scene at the Black Linn and his final, fatalistic, heroically strong and typically vindictive struggle with the Dutchman in the Clyde, are used to integrate Burley with nature itself. He becomes in simile the 'tortured demon of the stream', the spirit of that wild moorland landscape which Scott in Chapter 41 invites us to regard both with distaste for its barrenness and with love for the freshness and vivacity of its stream. This landscape Scott associates with the 'tribal' past of the nation itself. It is typically, vestigially, tenaciously, emotively 'Scottish'. Yet it is hostile to man, or at least to his comfort, illustrating, as Scott puts it in Chapter 15, 'the omnipotence of nature, and the comparative inefficacy of the boasted means of amelioration which man is capable of opposing to the disadvantages of climate and soil.'

The prosperity of Cuddie exists in defiance of the past; yet it is in the fertile lowlands into which the Clyde falls from 'savage' hills that Burley finally submerges in the river. And Cuddie's imagination has already worked to soften the heroic past into folk tradition; Habbakuk Mucklewrath, he says, was 'a braw preacher for a' that.' Burley will have in the prosperous new Scotland an after-life denied to the virtuous moderates whose apotheosis must solely be found in that Heaven to which Morton glumly refers as an 'awful and boundless succession of ages'. Cleishbotham's footnote translates Burley directly into the very tradition which a figure we have almost forgotten – Old Mortality himself – sustained, by keeping clear and clean quaint, generous words like those on Burley's fictitious memorial. It is an ironic coming-down, in or out of the world, but it does mean that Burley defies destroying time, at least for a while.

In that first chapter which must not, ultimately, be skipped, a general meaning for the novel is predicted. The dying Pattieson will give us the stories of the dead Paterson, Old Mortality, whose frail white horse is like the ghost of the black steeds of Claverhouse and Burley. The novel is not 'tragic' in any useful sense of the word, but it is profoundly concerned with death.

Dead men ride through it – the gallant Montrose, Lady Margaret's husband, tough old Silas Morton – determining the conduct of men in the novel's present. Major Bellenden recalls old Corporal Raddlebanes; Cuddie pays the tribute of folk memory to the martyred preacher Rumbleberry who 'fought and flyted like a fleeing dragon'. Already within the novel's period, people are attuned to the idea that giants have passed away leaving puny successors. And then, through the novel, the heroes fall – Bothwell, Mucklewrath, Macbriar, Claverhouse, Burley, Evandale – while Major Bellenden dies broken-hearted. The heroes live in memory but within a tradition which is now itself dying, and in the minds of men like Pattieson and like Scott and like his readers who are themselves under the common sentence of death.

The Enlightenment had discovered that the gratitude of posterity might replace for a sceptical generation the Christian heaven, and even, as in the French Revolution, fuel exceptional heroism in the interests of drastic change. The Victorian religion of progress, harnessed to what George Eliot would call 'the growing good of the world', was already in formation in Scott's lifetime and he himself intellectually went some way towards accepting it; this would deprecate heroism and pin its faith on gradual advancement brought about by a multitude of small virtuous acts.

Scott offers us two modes of living well which are almost alternatives, almost incompatible. Frankly heroic action may be powered by Claverhouse's kind of fatalism :

It is not the expiring pang that is worth thinking of in an event that must happen one day, and may befall us on any given moment – it is the memory which the soldier leaves behind him, like the long train of light that follows the sunken sun . . .

The moderate's commitment, however, is to secular, this-worldly, current happiness; the reward of virtue is simply a happy family or a prosperous economy. Macbriar may hope to soar straight to heaven, but Cuddie's sphere must be this earth, and William's revolution is Cuddie's justification.

As it is Morton's. But Morton is a *heroic* moderate, to whom the Revolution brings (within the narrative's emotionally effective scope – I set aside the conclusion) no personal happiness at all. In Chapter 39, it is only conscious moral effort which seems to hold him back from actual suicide, and Scott comments at that point, grimly, that 'virtuous resolution and manly disinterestedness seldom fail to restore tranquillity even where they cannot create happiness.'

In a society where appetite and contentment are the highest principles, Basil Olifant (if the law's on his side) is as just a man as Cuddie. The Bible is not about prosperous tenant farmers (nor were the saints and martyrs accustomed to take their holidays on the Costa Brava). Morton's iron-grey moral idealism, awakened in a phase of heroic conflict, becomes the sustained pain of persistent moral choice in an amoral environment. It has no reward, since its Heaven is so grey, except, in effect, its own grey self. The tense and disembodied Edith brings nothing to marriage but similar moral pain (if we exclude her extensive property.) *Old Mortality* is not a pessimistic book, but its tenor is alien to easy hope.

And Scott's final modulation is into direct satire, teasing but not altogether without prickles, of his own readers. Pattieson, poor fellow, merely to please Miss Buskbody, gives them their 'happy ending' but in such a way that we cannot take it seriously. His final touch – suggesting that Goose Gibbie may have been 'whipped through Hamilton for stealing poultry' not only suggests, faintly but disturbingly, the continuous cruelties of civil society, but also, because it pretends to be 'documented', reminds us that the details uncovered by historical research rarely permit us to judge of the 'happiness' in general of those to whom they refer. History is not about happiness; it is about 'Old Mortality'. Its traces are mouldering tombstones and yellow papers. Its product is our own problematic lives.

family in a prosperous economy. Macbriar may hope to soar
straight to heaven, but Candide's efforts must be this earth, and
Willjm's revolution is suddenly in transition.

As it is Morton's. But Morton is a near-modern, to whom
the Revolution brings (within the narrative's emotional effective scope – I leave aside the continuing) no personal happiness at
all. In Chaptet 39 it is only conscious moral effort which seems to
hold him back from actual suicide, and Scott comments at that
point, saying that 'virtuous resolution and manly disinterestedness seldom fail to restore tranquillity even where they cannot
create happiness.'

In a society where appetite and contentment are the highest
principles, Niall Quiroz (freebooter, son, his etc.) is as real a
menace Cuddle. The Bible is not about prosperous men of fortune
(nor were the saints and martyrs accustomed to take their holidays in the Costa Brava). Morton's non-grey moral idealism,
awakened in a phase realistic conflict, becomes the self-doomed
pull of persistent moral choice in an amoral environment. It has
no reward, since in Heaven is to grey except in this—its own
grey self. The bare and disembodied faith brings nothing to
mitigate but similar moral pain. If we exclude non-existent
prophecy, Old Mortality is not a pessimistic book, but its result is
often to stay hope.

And Scott's final modulation is into direct satire, relieves but
not altogether, without prejudice, of his own feeders, Patinson,
poor fellow. And here please. Miss Buskbody gives them their
happy ending that in such a way that we cannot take it seriously.
His final touch – suggestion that Goose Gibbie may have been
whipped through Hamilton for stealing poultry, not only
suggests family but flittingly the continuous realities of old
reality, but also because it reminds to be 'documented' reminds
us that the deaths discovered by historical research rarely permit
us to judge of the happiness in general of those by whom they
were. History is not about happiness as it is about Old Mortality.
Its figures are the mouldering tombstones and yellow papers. Its
plot is our own problematic lives.

NOTE ON THE TEXT

THIS text is as exact a reprint as I can make of the one published in 1830 in the collected edition of the Waverley Novels which Scott called his 'Magnum Opus'. (I will refer to it as 'MO' hereafter.)

Scott revised it, added an introduction (which is printed as an Appendix here) and notes (which are incorporated with my own, so as to save the reader the distraction of their black little bodies in the novel itself.) It was the last printing he scrutinized in his lifetime, and he did make some not very significant changes to the text.

A revised text would have to be based on collation of the manuscript (which is in the Pierpont Morgan Library, New York) with the first edition and with numerous other editions between 1816 and MO, in which Scott probably made small corrections which were not all repeated in MO, as well as with MO itself. It would also have to take wary account of two later editions, the 'Centenary' of 1871 and the 'Dryburgh' of 1892, which differ from each other in detail, but were both prepared for the publishers, A. & C. Black, with the help of an interleaved copy of an 1822 reprint of *Old Mortality* in which Scott had entered corrections not all of which (we gather) were finally incorporated in MO. The interleaved MO set of 'Waverleys' disappeared in the most impertinent manner after 1939, when it was last heard of on sale in New York.

Discussions with Dr G. A. M. Wood of Stirling University and with Mr Tony Inglis of Sussex University, both of whom are working on revised texts of other Scott novels on the taxing basis I have outlined above, and both of whom most generously gave me a great deal of their time, convinced me that such a task is best left to specialists. I believe that a carefully revised text would differ from MO strikingly only on relatively few points, where the manuscript would yield clearly preferable readings. But the job ought to be done. Those curious about the difficulties involved should see G. A. M. Wood, 'The Great Reviser; or the Unknown Scott', *Ariel*, vol. 2, no. 3, July 1971.

I must also thank Mr Alan Bell of the National Library of Scotland, who showed me the materials relating to the missing interleaved set which are held by that very pleasant library, and Dr N. T. Phillipson, who made some extremely helpful comments on my introduction and notes. All errors, of course, are my own fault.

Facsimile of the title page of the first edition, 1816, Old Mortality *also ran to Volumes III and IV of this edition.*

TALES OF MY LANDLORD,

COLLECTED AND ARRANGED

BY

JEDEDIAH CLEISHBOTHAM,

SCHOOLMASTER AND PARISH-CLERK OF GANDERCLEUGH.

Hear, Land o' Cakes and brither Scots,
Frae Maidenkirk to Jonny Groats',
If there's a hole in a' your coats,
    I rede ye tent it,
A chiel's amang you takin' notes,
    An' faith he'll prent it.
      BURNS.

IN FOUR VOLUMES.

VOL. II.

EDINBURGH:

PRINTED FOR WILLIAM BLACKWOOD, PRINCE'S STREET:
AND JOHN MURRAY, ALBEMARLE STREET, LONDON.

1816.

Ahora bien, dixo — Cura, traedme, senor huésped, aquesos libros, que los quiero ver. Que me place, respondió el, y entrando, en su aposento, sacó dél una maletilla vieja cerrada con una cadenilla, y abriéndola, halló en ella tres libros grandes y unos papeles de muy buena letra escritos de mano. — DON QUIXOTE, Parte I. Capitulo 32.

It is mighty well, said the priest; pray, landlord, bring me those books, for I have a mind to see them. With all my heart, answered the host; and, going to his chamber, he brought out a little old cloke-bag, with a padlock and chain to it, and opening it, he took out three large volumes, and some manuscript papers written in a fine character. — JARVIS's *Translation.*

TALES OF MY LANDLORD

> Hear, Land o' Cakes and brither Scots,
> Frae Maidenkirk to Jonny Groats',
> If there's a hole in a' your coats,
>   I rede ye tent it;
> A chiel's amang you takin' notes,
>   An' faith he'll prent it!
>   BURNS[1]

INTRODUCTION

As I may, without vanity, presume that the name and official description prefixed to this Proem will secure it, from the sedate and reflecting part of mankind, to whom only I would be understood to address myself, such attention as is due to the sedulous instructor of youth, and the careful performer of my Sabbath duties, I will forbear to hold up a candle to the daylight, or to point out to the judicious those recommendations of my labours which they must necessarily anticipate from the perusal of the title-page. Nevertheless, I am not unaware, that, as Envy always dogs Merit at the heels, there may be those who will whisper, that albeit my learning and good principles cannot (lauded be the heavens) be denied by any one, yet that my situation at Gandercleugh[2] hath been more favourable to my acquisitions in learning than to the enlargement of my views of the ways and works of the present generation. To the which objection, if, peradventure, any such shall be started, my answer shall be threefold:

First, Gandercleugh is, as it were, the central part – the navel (*si fas sit dicere*) of this our native realm of Scotland; so that men, from every corner thereof, when travelling on their concernments of business, either towards our metropolis of law, by which I mean Edinburgh, or towards our metropolis and mart of gain, whereby I insinuate Glasgow, are frequently led to make Gandercleugh their abiding stage and place of rest for the night. And it must be acknowledged by the most sceptical, that I, who have sat in the leathern armchair, on the left-hand side of the fire, in the common room of the Wallace Inn, winter and summer, for every evening in my life, during forty years bypast, (the Christian Sabbaths only excepted,) must have seen more of the manners and customs of various tribes and people, than if I had sought them out by my own painful travel and bodily labour. Even so doth the tollman at the well-frequented turn-pike on the Wellbrae-head, sitting at his ease in his own dwelling, gather more receipt of custom, than if, moving forth upon the road, he were to require a contribution from each person whom he chanced to meet in his journey, when, according to the vulgar adage, he might possibly be greeted with more kicks than halfpence.

But, secondly, supposing it again urged, that Ithacus,[3] the most wise of the Greeks, acquired his renown, as the Roman poet hath assured us, by visiting states and men, I reply to the Zoilus[4] who shall adhere to this objection, that, *de facto*, I have seen states and men also; for I have visited the famous cities of Edinburgh and Glasgow, the former twice, and the latter three times, in the course of my earthly pilgrimage. And, moreover, I had the honour to sit in the General Assembly,[5] (meaning, as an auditor, in the galleries thereof,) and have heard as much goodly speaking on the law of patronage, as, with the fructification thereof in mine own understanding, hath made me be considered as an oracle upon that doctrine ever since my safe and happy return to Gandercleugh.

Again – and thirdly, If it be nevertheless pretended that my information and knowledge of mankind, however extensive, and however painfully acquired, by constant domestic enquiry, and by foreign travel, is, natheless, incompetent to the task of re- cording the pleasant narratives of my Landlord, I will let these critics know, to their own eternal shame and confusion, as well as to the abashment and discomfiture of all who shall rashly take up a song against me, that I am NOT the writer, redacter, or compiler, of the Tales of my Landlord; nor am I, in one single iota, answerable for their contents, more or less. And now, ye generation of critics, who raise yourselves up as if it were brazen serpents, to hiss with your tongues, and to smite with your stings, bow yourselves down to your native dust, and acknowledge that yours have been the thoughts of ignorance, and the words of vain foolishness. Lo! ye are caught in your own snare, and your own pit hath yawned for you. Turn, then, aside from the task that is too heavy for you; destroy not your teeth by gnawing a file; waste not your strength by spurning against a castle wall; nor spend your breath in contending in swiftness with a fleet steed; and let those weigh the Tales of my Landlord, who shall bring with them the scales of candour cleansed from the rust of prejudice by the hands of intelligent modesty. For these alone they were compiled, as will appear from a brief narrative which my zeal for truth compelled me to make supplementary to the present Proem.

It is well known that my Landlord was a pleasing and a facetious man, acceptable unto all the parish of Gandercleugh, excepting only the Laird, the Exciseman, and those for whom he refused to draw liquor upon trust. Their causes of dislike I will touch separately, adding my own refutation thereof.

His honour, the Laird, accused our Landlord, deceased, of having encouraged, in various times and places, the destruction of hares, rabbits, fowls black and grey, partridges, moor-pouts, roe-deer, and other birds and quadrupeds, at unlawful seasons, and contrary to the laws of this realm, which have secured, in their wisdom, the slaughter of such animals for the great of the earth, whom I have remarked to take an uncommon (though to me, an unintelligible) pleasure therein. Now, in humble deference to his honour, and in justifiable defence of my friend deceased, I reply to this charge, that howsoever the form of such animals might appear to be similar to those so protected by the law, yet it was a mere *deceptio visus*; for what resembled hares were, in fact, *hill-kids*, and those partaking of the appearance of moorfowl, were truly *wood pigeons*, and consumed and eaten *eo nomine*, and not otherwise.

Again, the Exciseman pretended, that my deceased Landlord did encourage that species of manufacture called distillation, without having an especial permission from the Great, technically called a license, for doing so. Now, I stand up to confront this falsehood; and in defiance of him, his gauging-stick, and pen and inkhorn, I tell him, that I never saw, or tasted, a glass of unlawful aqua vitæ in the house of my Landlord; nay, that, on the contrary, we needed not such devices, in respect of a pleasing and somewhat seductive liquor, which was vended and consumed at the Wallace Inn, under the name of *mountain dew*. If there is a penalty against manufacturing such a liquor, let him show me the statute; and when he does, I'll tell him if I will obey it or no.

Concerning those who came to my Landlord for liquor, and went thirsty away, for lack of present coin, or future credit, I cannot but say it has grieved my bowels as if the case had been mine own. Nevertheless, my Landlord considered the necessities of a thirsty soul, and would permit them, in extreme need, and when their soul was impoverished for lack of moisture, to drink to the full value of their watches and wearing apparel, exclusively of their inferior habiliments, which he was uniformly inexorable in obliging them to retain, for the credit of the house. As to mine own part, I may well say, that he never refused me that modicum of refreshment with which I am wont to recruit nature after the fatigues of my school. It is true, I taught his five sons English and Latin, writing, book-keeping, with a tincture of mathematics, and that I instructed his daughter in psalmody. Nor do I remember me of any fee or *honorarium* received from him on account of these my labours, except the compotations aforesaid. Nevertheless this compensation suited my humour well, since it is a hard sentence to bid a dry throat wait till quarter-day.

But, truly, were I to speak my simple conceit and belief, I think my Landlord was chiefly moved to waive in my behalf the usual requisition of a symbol, or reckoning, from the pleasure he was wont to take in my conversation, which, though solid and edifying in the main, was, like a well-built palace, decorated with facetious narratives and devices, tending much to the enhancement and ornament thereof. And so pleased was my Landlord of the Wallace in his replies during such colloquies, that there was no district in Scotland, yea, and no peculiar, and, as it were, distinctive custom therein practised, but was discussed betwixt us; insomuch, that those who stood by were wont to say, it was worth a bottle of ale to hear us communicate with each other. And not a few travellers, from distant parts, as well as from the remote districts of our kingdom, were wont to mingle in the conversation, and to tell news that had been gathered in foreign lands, or preserved from oblivion in this our own.

Now I chanced to have contracted for teaching the lower classes with a young person called Peter, or Patrick, Pattieson, who had been educated for our Holy Kirk, yea, had, by the license of presbytery, his voice opened therein as a preacher, who delighted in the collection of olden tales and legends, and in garnishing them with the flowers of poesy, whereof he was a vain and frivolous professor. For he followed not the example of those strong poets whom I proposed to him as a pattern, but formed versification of a flimsy and modern texture, to the compounding whereof was necessary small pains and less thought. And hence I have chid him as being one of those who bring forward the fatal revolution prophesied by Mr Robert Carey,[6] in his Vaticination on the Death of the celebrated Dr John Donne:

> Now thou art gone, and thy strict laws will be
> Too hard for libertines in poetry;
> Till verse (by thee refined) in this last age
> Turn ballad rhyme.

I had also disputations with him touching his indulging rather a flowing and redundant than a concise and stately diction in his prose exercitations. But notwithstanding these symptoms of inferior taste, and a humour of contradicting his betters upon passages of dubious construction in Latin authors, I did grievously lament when Peter Pattieson was removed from me by death, even as if he had been the offspring of my own loins. And in respect his papers had been left in my care, (to answer funeral and death-bed expenses,) I conceived myself entitled to dispose of one parcel thereof, entitled, 'Tales of my Landlord,' to one cunning in the trade (as it is called) of book-selling. He was a mirthful man,[7] of small stature, cunning in counterfeiting of voices, and in making facetious tales and responses, and whom I have to laud for the truth of his dealings towards me.

Now, therefore, the world may see the injustice that charges me with incapacity to write these narratives, seeing, that though I have proved that I could have written them if I would, yet, not having done so, the censure will deservedly fall, if at all due, upon the memory of Mr Peter Pattieson; whereas I must be justly entitled to the praise, when any is due, seeing that, as the Dean of St Patrick's[8] wittily and logically expresseth it,

> That without which a thing is not,
> Is *Causa sine qua non*.

The work, therefore, is unto me as a child is to a parent; in the which child, if it proveth worthy, the parent hath honour and praise; but, if otherwise, the disgrace will deservedly attach to itself alone.

I have only further to intimate, that Mr Peter Pattieson, in arranging these Tales for the press, hath more consulted his own fancy than the accuracy of the narrative; nay, that he hath sometimes blended two or three stories together for the mere grace of his plots. Of which infidelity, although I disapprove and enter my testimony against it, yet I have not taken upon me to correct the same, in respect it was the will of the deceased, that his manuscript should be submitted to the press without diminution or alteration. A fanciful nicety it was on the part of my deceased friend, who, if thinking wisely, ought rather to have conjured me, by all the tender ties of our friendship and common pursuits, to have carefully revised, altered, and augmented, at my judgment and discretion. But the will of the dead must be scrupulously obeyed, even when we weep over their pertinacity and self-delusion. So, gentle reader, I bid you farewell, recommending you to such fare as the mountains of your own country produce; and I will only farther premise, that each Tale is preceded by a short introduction, mentioning the persons by whom, and the circumstances under which, the materials thereof were collected.

JEDEDIAH CLEISHBOTHAM

OLD MORTALITY

CHAPTER 1

PRELIMINARY

> Why seeks he with unwearied toil
> Through death's dim walks to urge his way,
> Reclaim his long-asserted spoil,
> And lead oblivion into day?

LANGHORNE[1]

'MOST readers,' says the Manuscript of Mr Pattieson, 'must have witnessed with delight the joyous burst which attends the dismissing of a village-school on a fine summer evening. The buoyant spirit of childhood, repressed with so much difficulty during the tedious hours of discipline, may then be seen to explode, as it were, in shout, and song, and frolic, as the little urchins join in groups on their play-ground, and arrange their matches of sport for the evening. But there is one individual who partakes of the relief afforded by the moment of dismission, whose feelings are not so obvious to the eye of the spectator, or so apt to receive his sympathy. I mean the teacher himself, who, stunned with the hum, and suffocated with the closeness of his school-room, has spent the whole day (himself against a host) in controlling petulance, exciting indifference to action, striving to enlighten stupidity, and labouring to soften obstinacy; and whose very powers of intellect have been confounded by hearing the same dull lesson repeated a hundred times by rote, and only varied by the various blunders of the reciters. Even the flowers of classic genius, with which his solitary fancy is most gratified, have been rendered degraded, in his imagination, by their connexion with tears, with errors, and with punishment; so that the Eclogues of Virgil and Odes of Horace are each inseparably allied in association with the sullen figure and monotonous recitation of some blubbering school-boy. If to these mental distresses are added a delicate frame of body, and a mind ambitious of some higher distinction than that of being the tyrant of childhood, the reader may have some slight conception of the relief which a solitary walk, in the cool of a fine summer evening, affords to the head which has ached, and the nerves which have been shattered, for so many hours, in plying the irksome task of public instruction.

'To me these evening strolls have been the happiest hours of an unhappy life; and if any gentle reader shall hereafter find pleasure in perusing these lucubrations, I am not unwilling he should know, that the plan of them has been usually traced in those moments, when relief from toil and clamour, combined with the quiet scenery around me, has disposed my mind to the task of composition.

'My chief haunt, in these hours of golden leisure, is the banks of the small stream, which, winding through a "lone vale of green bracken", passes in front of the village school-house of Gandercleugh. For the first quarter of a mile, perhaps, I may be disturbed from my meditations, in order to return the scrape, or doffed bonnet, of such stragglers among my pupils as fish for trouts or minnows in the little brook, or seek rushes and wild-flowers by its margin. But, beyond the space I have mentioned, the juvenile anglers do not, after sunset, voluntarily extend their excursions. The cause is, that farther up the narrow valley, and in a recess which seems scooped out of the side of the steep heathy bank, there is a deserted burial-ground, which the little cowards are fearful of approaching in the twilight. To me, however, the place has an inexpressible charm. It has been long the favourite termination of my walks, and, if my kind patron forgets not his promise, will (and probably at no very distant day) be my final resting-place after my mortal pilgrimage.*

'It is a spot which possesses all the solemnity of feeling attached to a burial-ground, without exciting those of a more unpleasing description. Having been very little used for many years, the few hillocks which rise above the level plain are covered with the same

* Note, by Mr Jedediah Cleishbotham. – That I kept my plight in this melancholy matter with my deceased and lamented friend, appeareth from a handsome headstone, erected at my proper charges in this spot, bearing the name and calling of Peter Pattieson, with the date of his nativity and sepulture; together also with a testimony of his merits, attested by myself, as his superior and patron. – J.C.

short velvet turf. The monuments, of which there are not above seven or eight, are half sunk in the ground, and overgrown with moss. No newly-erected tomb disturbs the sober serenity of our reflections by reminding us of recent calamity, and no rank-springing grass forces upon our imagination the recollection, that it owes its dark luxuriance to the foul and festering remnants of mortality which ferment beneath. The daisy which sprinkles the sod, and the harebell which hangs over it, derive their pure nourishment from the dew of heaven, and their growth impresses us with no degrading or disgusting recollections. Death has indeed been here, and its traces are before us; but they are softened and deprived of their horror by our distance from the period when they have been first impressed. Those who sleep beneath are only connected with us by the reflection, that they have once been what we now are, and that, as their relics are now identified with their mother earth, ours shall, at some future period, undergo the same transformation.

'Yet, although the moss has been collected on the most modern of these humble tombs during four generations of mankind, the memory of some of those who sleep beneath them is still held in reverent remembrance. It is true, that, upon the largest, and, to an antiquary, the most interesting monument of the group, which bears the effigies of a doughty knight in his hood of mail, with his shield hanging on his breast, the armorial bearings are defaced by time, and a few worn-out letters may be read at the pleasure of the decipherer, *Dns. Johan --- de Hamel*, --- or *Johan --- de Lamel ---* And it is also true, that of another tomb, richly sculptured with an ornamental cross, mitre, and pastoral staff, tradition can only aver, that a certain nameless bishop lies interred there. But upon other two stones which lie beside, may still be read in rude prose, and ruder rhyme, the history of those who sleep beneath them. They belong, we are assured by the epitaph, to the class of persecuted Presbyterians who afforded a melancholy subject for history in the times of Charles II and his successor.* In returning from the battle of Pentland Hills,[2] a party of the insurgents had been attacked in this glen by a small

---

* James, Seventh King of Scotland of that name, and Second according to the numeration of the Kings of England. – J.C.

detachment of the King's troops, and three or four either killed
in the skirmish, or shot after being made prisoners, as rebels
taken with arms in their hands. The peasantry continued to
attach to the tombs of those victims of prelacy an honour which
they do not render to more splendid mausoleums; and, when
they point them out to their sons, and narrate the fate of the
sufferers, usually conclude, by exhorting them to be ready, should
times call for it, to resist to the death in the cause of civil and
religious liberty, like their brave forefathers.

'Although I am far from venerating the peculiar tenets
asserted by those who call themselves the followers of those men,
and whose intolerance and narrow-minded bigotry are at least
as conspicuous as their devotional zeal, yet it is without depreciat-
ing the memory of those sufferers, many of whom united the
independent sentiments of a Hampden with the suffering zeal of
a Hooper or Latimer.[3] On the other hand, it would be unjust to
forget, that many even of those who had been most active in
crushing what they conceived the rebellious and seditious spirit
of those unhappy wanderers, displayed themselves, when called
upon to suffer for their political and religious opinions, the same
daring and devoted zeal, tinctured, in their case, with chivalrous
loyalty, as in the former with republican enthusiasm. It has often
been remarked of the Scottish character, that the stubbornness
with which it is moulded shows most to advantage in adversity,
when it seems akin to the native sycamore[4] of their hills, which
scorns to be biassed in its mode of growth even by the influence
of the prevailing wind, but, shooting its branches with equal
boldness in every direction, shows no weather-side to the storm,
and may be broken, but can never be bended. It must be understood that I speak of my countrymen as they fall under my own
observation. When in foreign countries, I have been informed
that they are more docile. But it is time to return from this
digression.

'One summer evening, as in a stroll, such as I have described,
I approached this deserted mansion of the dead, I was somewhat
surprised to hear sounds distinct from those which usually soothe
its solitude, the gentle chiding, namely, of the brook, and the
sighing of the wind in the boughs of three gigantic ash-trees,

which mark the cemetery. The clink of a hammer was, on this occasion, distinctly heard; and I entertained some alarm that a march-dike, long meditated by the two proprietors whose estates were divided by my favourite brook, was about to be drawn up the glen, in order to substitute its rectilinear deformity for the graceful winding of the natural boundary.* As I approached, I was agreeably undeceived. An old man was seated upon the monument of the slaughtered presbyterians, and busily employed in deepening, with his chisel, the letters of the inscription, which, announcing, in scriptural language, the promised blessings of futurity to be the lot of the slain, anathematized the murderers with corresponding violence. A blue bonnet of unusual dimensions covered the grey hairs of the pious workman. His dress was a large old-fashioned coat of the coarse cloth called *hoddin-grey*, usually worn by the elder peasants, with waistcoat and breeches of the same; and the whole suit, though still in decent repair, had obviously seen a train of long service. Strong clouted shoes, studded with hobnails, and *gramoches* or *leggins*, made of thick black cloth, completed his equipment. Beside him, fed among the graves a pony, the companion of his journey, whose extreme whiteness, as well as its projecting bones and hollow eyes, indicated its antiquity. It was harnessed in the most simple manner, with a pair of branks, a hair tether, or halter, and a *sunk*, or cushion of straw, instead of bridle and saddle. A canvass pouch hung around the neck of the animal, for the purpose, probably, of containing the rider's tools, and any thing else he might have occasion to carry with him. Although I had never seen the old man before, yet from the singularity of his employment, and the style of his equipage, I had no difficulty in recognising a religious

---

*I deem it fitting that the reader should be apprised that this limitary boundary between the conterminous heritable property of his honour the Laird of Gandercleugh, and his honour the Laird of Gusedub, was to have been in fashion an *agger*, or rather *murus* of uncemented granite, called by the vulgar a *dry-stane dyke*, surmounted, or coped, *cespite viridi*, i.e. with a sod-turf. Truly their honours fell into discord concerning two roods of marshy ground, near the cove called the Bedral's Beild; and the controversy, having some years bygone been removed from before the judges of the land, (with whom it abode long,) even unto the Great City of London and the Assembly of the Nobles therein, is, as I may say, *adhuc in pendente*. – J.C.

itinerant whom I had often heard talked of, and who was known in various parts of Scotland by the title of Old Mortality.

'Where this man was born, or what was his real name, I have never been able to learn; nor are the motives which made him desert his home, and adopt the erratic mode of life which he pursued, known to me except very generally. According to the belief of most people, he was a native of either the county of Dumfries or Galloway, and lineally descended from some of those champions of the Covenant, whose deeds and sufferings were his favourite theme. He is said to have held, at one period of his life, a small moorland farm; but, whether from pecuniary losses, or domestic misfortune, he had long renounced that and every other gainful calling. In the language of Scripture, he left his house, his home, and his kindred, and wandered about until the day of his death, a period of nearly thirty years.

'During this long pilgrimage, the pious enthusiast regulated his circuit so as annually to visit the graves of the unfortunate Covenanters, who suffered by the sword, or by the executioner, during the reigns of the two last monarchs of the Stewart line. These are most numerous in the western districts of Ayr, Galloway, and Dumfries; but they are also to be found in other parts of Scotland, wherever the fugitives had fought, or fallen, or suffered by military or civil execution. Their tombs are often apart from all human habitation, in the remote moors and wilds to which the wanderers had fled for concealment. But wherever they existed, Old Mortality was sure to visit them when his annual round brought them within his reach. In the most lonely recesses of the mountains, the moor-fowl shooter has been often surprised to find him busied in cleaning the moss from the grey stones, renewing with his chisel the half-defaced inscriptions, and repairing the emblems of death with which these simple monuments are usually adorned. Motives of the most sincere, though fanciful devotion, induced the old man to dedicate so many years of existence to perform this tribute to the memory of the deceased warriors of the church. He considered himself as fulfilling a sacred duty, while renewing to the eyes of posterity the decaying emblems of the zeal and sufferings of their forefathers, and thereby trimming, as it were, the beacon-light, which was to warn future generations to defend their religion even unto blood.

'In all his wanderings, the old pilgrim never seemed to need, or was known to accept, pecuniary assistance. It is true, his wants were very few; for wherever he went, he found ready quarters in the house of some Cameronian[5] of his own sect, or of some other religious person. The hospitality which was reverentially paid to him he always acknowledged, by repairing the grave-stones (if there existed any) belonging to the family or ancestors of his host. As the wanderer was usually to be seen bent on this pious task within the precincts of some country churchyard, or reclined on the solitary tombstone among the heath, disturbing the plover and the black-cock with the clink of his chisel and mallet, with his old white pony grazing by his side, he acquired, from his converse among the dead, the popular appellation of Old Mortality.

'The character of such a man could have in it little connexion even with innocent gaiety. Yet, among those of his own religious persuasion, he is reported to have been cheerful. The descendants of persecutors, or those whom he supposed guilty of entertaining similar tenets, and the scoffers at religion by whom he was some-times assailed, he usually termed the generation of vipers. Con-versing with others, he was grave and sententious, not without a cast of severity. But he is said never to have been observed to give way to violent passion, excepting upon one occasion, when a mischievous truant-boy defaced with a stone the nose of a cherub's face, which the old man was engaged in retouching. I am in general a sparer of the rod, notwithstanding the maxim of Solomon,[6] for which school-boys have little reason to thank his memory; but on this occasion I deemed it proper to show that I did not hate the child. – But I must return to the circumstances attending my first interview with this interesting enthusiast.

'In accosting Old Mortality, I did not fail to pay respect to his years and his principles, beginning my address by a respectful apology for interrupting his labours. The old man intermitted the operation of the chisel, took off his spectacles and wiped them, then, replacing them on his nose, acknowledged my cour-tesy by a suitable return. Encouraged by his affability, I intruded upon him some questions concerning the sufferers on whose monument he was now employed. To talk of the exploits of the Covenanters was the delight, as to repair their monuments was the business, of his life. He was profuse in the communication of all the minute information which he had collected concerning them, their wars, and their wanderings. One would almost have supposed he must have been their contemporary, and have actually beheld the passages which he related, so much had he identified his feelings and opinions with theirs, and so much had his narratives the circumstantiality of an eye-witness.

"We," he said, in a tone of exultation, – "*we* are the only true whigs.[7] Carnal men have assumed that triumphant appellation, following him whose kingdom is of this world. Which of them would sit six hours on a wet hill-side to hear a godly sermon? I trow an hour o't wad staw them. They are ne'er a hair better than them that shamena to take upon themsells the persecuting name of bludethirsty tories. Self-seekers all of them, strivers after wealth, power, and worldly ambition, and forgetters alike of what has been dree'd and done by the mighty men who stood in the gap in the great day of wrath. Nae wonder they dread the accomplishment of what was spoken by the mouth of the worthy Mr Peden,[8] (that precious servant of the Lord, none of whose words fell to the ground,) that the French monzies* sall rise as fast in the glens of Ayr, and the kenns of Galloway, as ever the Highlandmen did in 1677.[9] And now they are gripping to the bow and to the spear, when they suld be mourning for a sinfu' land and a broken covenant."

'Soothing the old man by letting his peculiar opinions pass without contradiction, and anxious to prolong conversation with so singular a character, I prevailed upon him to accept that hospitality, which Mr Cleishbotham is always willing to extend to those who need it. In our way to the school-master's house, we called at the Wallace Inn, where I was pretty certain I should find my patron about that hour of the evening. After a courteous interchange of civilities, Old Mortality was, with difficulty, prevailed upon to join his host in a single glass of liquor, and that on condition that he should be permitted to name the pledge,

* Probably *monsieurs*. It would seem that this was spoken during the apprehensions of invasion from France. – *Publishers*.

which he prefaced with a grace of about five minutes, and then, with bonnet doffed and eyes uplifted, drank to the memory of those heroes of the Kirk who had first uplifted her banner upon the mountains. As no persuasion could prevail on him to extend his conviviality to a second cup, my patron accompanied him home, and accommodated him in the Prophet's Chamber, as it is his pleasure to call the closet which holds a spare bed, and which is frequently a place of retreat for the poor traveller.*

'The next day I took leave of Old Mortality, who seemed affected by the unusual attention with which I had cultivated his acquaintance and listened to his conversation. After he had mounted, not without difficulty, the old white pony, he took me by the hand and said, "The blessing of our Master be with you, young man! My hours are like the ears of the latter harvest, and your days are yet in the spring; and yet you may be gathered into the garner of mortality before me, for the sickle of death cuts down the green as oft as the ripe, and there is a colour in your cheek, that, like the bud of the rose, serveth oft to hide the worm of corruption. Wherefore labour as one who knoweth not when his master calleth. And if it be my lot to return to this village after ye are gane hame to your ain place, these auld withered hands will frame a stane of memorial, that your name may not perish from among the people."

'I thanked Old Mortality for his kind intentions in my behalf, and heaved a sigh, not, I think, of regret so much as of resignation, to think of the chance that I might soon require his good offices. But though, in all human probability, he did not err in supposing that my span of life may be abridged in youth, he had over-estimated the period of his own pilgrimage on earth. It is now some years since he has been missed in all his usual haunts, while moss, lichen, and deer-hair, are fast covering those stones,

---

* He might have added, and for the *rich* also; since, I laud my stars, the great of the earth have also taken harbourage in my poor domicile. And, during the service of my hand-maiden, Dorothy, who was buxom and comely of aspect, his Honour the Laird of Smackawa, in his peregrinations to and from the metropolis, was wont to prefer my Prophet's Chamber even to the sanded chamber of dais in the Wallace Inn, and to bestow a mutchkin, as he would jocosely say, to obtain the freedom of the house, but, in reality, to assure himself of my company during the evening. – J. C.

to cleanse which had been the business of his life. About the beginning of this century he closed his mortal toils, being found on the highway near Lockerby, in Dumfries-shire, exhausted and just expiring. The old white pony, the companion of all his wanderings, was standing by the side of his dying master. There was found about his person a sum of money sufficient for his decent interment, which serves to show that his death was in no ways hastened by violence or by want. The common people still regard his memory with great respect; and many are of opinion, that the stones which he repaired will not again require the assistance of the chisel. They even assert, that on the tombs where the manner of the martyrs' murder is recorded, their names have remained indelibly legible since the death of Old Mortality, while those of the persecutors, sculptured on the same monuments, have been entirely defaced. It is hardly necessary to say that this is a fond imagination, and that, since the time of the pious pilgrim, the monuments which were the objects of his care are hastening, like all earthly memorials, into ruin or decay.

'My readers will of course understand, that in embodying into one compressed narrative many of the anecdotes which I had the advantage of deriving from Old Mortality, I have been far from adopting either his style, his opinions, or even his facts, so far as they appear to have been distorted by party prejudice. I have endeavoured to correct or verify them from the most authentic sources of tradition, afforded by the representatives of either party.

'On the part of the Presbyterians, I have consulted such moorland farmers from the western districts, as, by the kindness of their landlords, or otherwise, have been able, during the late general change of property, to retain possession of the grazings on which their grandsires fed their flocks and herds. I must own, that of late days, I have found this a limited source of information. I have, therefore, called in the supplementary aid of those modest itinerants, whom the scrupulous civility of our ancestors denominated travelling merchants, but whom, of late, accommodating ourselves in this as in more material particulars, to the feelings and sentiments of our more wealthy neighbours, we have learned to call packmen or pedlars. To country weavers travelling in hopes to get rid of their winter web, but more especially to tailors, who, from their sedentary profession, and the necessity, in our country, of exercising it by temporary residence in the families by whom they are employed, may be considered as possessing a complete register of rural traditions, I have been indebted for many illustrations of the narratives of Old Mortality, much in the taste and spirit of the original.

'I had more difficulty in finding materials for correcting the tone of partiality which evidently pervaded those stores of traditional learning, in order that I might be enabled to present an unbiassed picture of the manners of that unhappy period, and, at the same time, to do justice to the merits of both parties. But I have been enabled to qualify the narratives of Old Mortality and his Cameronian friends, by the reports of more than one descendant of ancient and honourable families, who, themselves decayed into the humble vale of life, yet look proudly back on the period when their ancestors fought and fell in behalf of the exiled house of Stewart. I may even boast right reverend authority on the same score; for more than one nonjuring bishop,[10] whose authority and income were upon as apostolical a scale as the greatest abominator of Episcopacy could well desire, have deigned, while partaking of the humble cheer of the Wallace Inn, to furnish me with information corrective of the facts which I learned from others. There are also here and there a laird or two, who, though they shrug their shoulders, profess no great shame in their fathers having served in the persecuting squadrons of Earlshall[11] and Claverhouse. From the gamekeepers of these gentlemen, an office the most apt of any other to become hereditary in such families, I have also contrived to collect much valuable information.

'Upon the whole, I can hardly fear, that, at this time, in describing the operation which their opposite principles produced upon the good and bad men of both parties, I can be suspected of meaning insult or injustice to either. If recollection of former injuries, extra-loyalty, and contempt and hatred of their adversaries, produced rigour and tyranny in the one party, it will hardly be denied, on the other hand, that, if the zeal for God's house did not eat up the conventiclers, it devoured at least, to imitate the phrase of Dryden,[12] no small portion of their loyalty, sober sense, and good breeding. We may safely hope, that the souls of the brave and sincere on either side have long looked down with surprise and pity upon the ill-appreciated motives which caused their mutual hatred and hostility, while in this valley of darkness, blood, and tears. Peace to their memory! Let us think of them as the heroine of our only Scottish tragedy[13] entreats her lord to think of her departed sire :—

> "O rake not up the ashes of our fathers!
> Implacable resentment was their crime,
> And grievous has the expiation been." '

CHAPTER 2

Summon an hundred horse, by break of day,
To wait our pleasure at the castle gates.
                                                    Douglas[1]

UNDER the reign of the last Stewarts, there was an anxious wish on the part of government to counteract, by every means in their power, the strict or puritanical spirit which had been the chief characteristic of the republican government, and to revive those feudal institutions which united the vassal to the liege lord, and both to the crown. Frequent musters and assemblies of the people, both for military exercise and for sports and pastimes, were appointed by authority. The interference, in the latter case, was impolitic, to say the least; for, as usual on such occasions, the consciences which were at first only scrupulous, became confirmed in their opinions, instead of giving way to the terrors of authority; and the youth of both sexes, to whom the pipe and tabor in England, or the bagpipe in Scotland, would have been in themselves an irresistible temptation, were enabled to set them at defiance, from the proud consciousness that they were, at the same time, resisting an act of council. To compel men to dance and be merry by authority, has rarely succeeded even on board of slave-ships, where it was formerly sometimes attempted by way of inducing the wretched captives to agitate their limbs and restore the circulation, during the few minutes they were permitted to enjoy the fresh air upon deck. The rigour of the strict Calvinists increased, in proportion to the wishes of the government that it should be relaxed. A judaical observance of the Sabbath – a supercilious condemnation of all manly pastimes and harmless recreations, as well as of the profane custom of promiscuous dancing, that is, of men and women dancing together in the same party (for I believe they admitted that the exercise might be inoffensive if practised by the parties separately) – distinguishing those who professed a more than ordinary share of sanctity, they discouraged, as far as lay in their power, even the ancient *wappen-schaws*, as they were termed, when the feudal array of the county was called out, and each crown-vassal was required to appear with such muster of men and armour as he was bound to make by his fief, and that under high statutory penalties. The Covenanters were the more jealous of those assemblies, as the lord lieutenants and sheriffs under whom they were held had instructions from the government to spare no pains which might render them agreeable to the young men who were thus summoned together, upon whom the military exercise of the morning, and the sports which usually closed the evening, might naturally be supposed to have a seductive effect.

The preachers and proselytes of the more rigid presbyterians laboured, therefore, by caution, remonstrance, and authority, to diminish the attendance upon these summonses, conscious that in doing so, they lessened not only the apparent, but the actual strength of the government, by impeding the extension of that *esprit de corps* which soon unites young men who are in the habit of meeting together for manly sport, or military exercise. They, therefore, exerted themselves earnestly to prevent attendance on these occasions by those who could find any possible excuse for absence, and were especially severe upon such of their hearers as mere curiosity led to be spectators, or love of exercise to be partakers, of the array and the sports which took place. Such of the gentry as acceded to these doctrines were not always, however, in a situation to be ruled by them. The commands of the law were imperative; and the privy council, who administered the executive power in Scotland, were severe in enforcing the statutory penalties against the crown-vassals who did not appear at the periodical wappen-schaw. The landholders were compelled, therefore, to send their sons, tenants, and vassals to the rendezvous, to the number of horses, men, and spears, at which they were rated; and it frequently happened, that notwithstanding the strict charge of their elders, to return as soon as the formal inspection was over, the young men-at-arms were unable to resist the temptation of sharing in the sports which succeeded the muster, or to avoid listening to the prayers read in the churches on these occasions, and thus, in the opinion of their repining parents, meddling with the accursed thing which is an abomination in the sight of the Lord.

The sheriff of the county of Lanark was holding the wappenschaw of a wild district, called the Upper Ward of Clydesdale, on a haugh or level plain, near to a royal borough, the name of which is no way essential to my story, on the morning of the 5th of May, 1679, when our narrative commences. When the musters had been made, and duly reported, the young men, as was usual, were to mix in various sports, of which the chief was to shoot at the popinjay,[2] an ancient game formerly practised with archery, but at this period with fire-arms. This was the figure of a bird, decked with party-coloured feathers, so as to resemble a popinjay or parrot. It was suspended to a pole, and served for a mark, at which the competitors discharged their fusees and carabines in rotation, at the distance of sixty or seventy paces. He whose ball brought down the mark, held the proud title of Captain of the Popinjay for the remainder of the day, and was usually escorted in triumph to the most reputable change-house in the neighbourhood, where the evening was closed with conviviality, conducted under his auspices, and, if he was able to sustain it, at his expense.

It will, of course, be supposed, that the ladies of the country assembled to witness this gallant strife, those excepted who held the stricter tenets of puritanism,[3] and would therefore have deemed it criminal to afford countenance to the profane gambols of the malignants. Landaus, barouches, or tilburies, there were none in those simple days. The lord lieutenant of the county (a personage of ducal rank) alone pretended to the magnificence of a wheel-carriage, a thing covered with tarnished gilding and sculpture, in shape like the vulgar picture of Noah's ark, dragged by eight long-tailed Flanders mares, bearing eight *insides* and six *outsides*. The insides were their graces in person, two maids of honour, two children, a chaplain stuffed into a sort of lateral recess, formed by a projection at the door of the vehicle, and called, from its appearance, the boot, and an equerry to his Grace ensconced in the corresponding convenience on the opposite side. A coachman and three postillions, who wore short swords, and tie-wigs with three tails, had blunderbusses slung behind them, and pistols at their saddle-bow, conducted the equipage. On the foot-board, behind this moving mansion-house, stood, or rather hung, in triple file, six lacqueys in rich liveries, armed up to the teeth. The rest of the gentry, men and women, old and young, were on horseback followed by their servants; but the company, for the reasons already assigned, was rather select than numerous.

Near to the enormous leathern vehicle which we have attempted to describe, vindicating her title to precedence over the untitled gentry of the country, might be seen the sober palfrey of Lady Margaret Bellenden, bearing the erect and primitive form of Lady Margaret herself, decked in those widow's weeds which the good lady had never laid aside, since the execution of her husband for his adherence to Montrose.

Her grand-daughter, and only earthly care, the fair-haired Edith, who was generally allowed to be the prettiest lass in the Upper Ward, appeared beside her aged relative like Spring placed close to Winter. Her black Spanish jennet, which she managed with much grace, her gay riding-dress, and laced side-saddle, had been anxiously prepared to set her forth to the best advantage. But the clustering profusion of ringlets, which, escaping from under her cap, were only confined by a green ribbon from wantoning over her shoulders; her cast of features, soft and feminine, yet not without a certain expression of playful archness, which redeemed their sweetness from the charge of insipidity, sometimes brought against *blondes* and blue-eyed beauties, – these attracted more admiration from the western youth than either the splendour of her equipments or the figure of her palfrey.

The attendance of these distinguished ladies was rather inferior to their birth and fashion in those times, as it consisted only of two servants on horseback. The truth was, that the good old lady had been obliged to make all her domestic servants turn out to complete the quota which her barony ought to furnish for the muster, and in which she would not for the universe have been found deficient. The old steward, who, in steel cap and jack-boots, led forth her array, had, as he said, sweated blood and water in his efforts to overcome the scruples and evasions of the moorland farmers, who ought to have furnished men, horse, and harness, on these occasions. At last, their dispute came near to an open declaration of hostilities, the incensed episcopalian bestowing on the recusants the whole thunders of the commination,[4] and receiving from them, in return, the denunciations of a Calvinistic excommunication. What was to be done? To punish the refractory tenants would have been easy enough. The privy council would readily have imposed fines, and sent a troop of horse to collect them. But this would have been calling the huntsman and hounds into the garden to kill the hare.

'For,' said Harrison to himself, 'the carles have little eneugh gear at ony rate, and if I call in the red-coats and take away what little they have, how is my worshipful lady to get her rents paid at Candlemas, which is but a difficult matter to bring round even in the best of times?'

So he armed the fowler, and falconer, the footman, and the ploughman, at the home farm, with an old drunken cavaliering butler, who had served with the late Sir Richard under Montrose, and stunned the family nightly with his exploits at Kilsythe and Tippermoor,[5] and who was the only man in the party that had the smallest zeal for the work in hand. In this manner, and by recruiting one or two latitudinarian poachers and black-fishers, Mr Harrison completed the quota of men which fell to the share of Lady Margaret Bellenden, as life-rentrix of the barony of Tillietudlem and others. But when the steward, on the morning of the eventful day, had mustered his *troupe dorée* before the iron gate of the tower, the mother of Cuddie Headrigg the ploughman appeared, loaded with the jack-boots, buff coat, and other accoutrements which had been issued forth for the service of the day, and laid them before the steward; demurely assuring him, that 'whether it were the colic, or a qualm of conscience, she

couldna tak upon her to decide, but sure it was, Cuddie had been
in sair straits a'night, and she couldna say he was muckle better
this morning. The finger of Heaven,' she said, 'was in it, and her
bairn should gang on nae sic errands.' Pains, penalties, and
threats of dismission, were denounced in vain; the mother was
obstinate, and Cuddie, who underwent a domiciliary visitation
for the purpose of verifying his state of body, could, or would,
answer only by deep groans. Mause, who had been an ancient
domestic in the family, was a sort of favourite with Lady
Margaret, and presumed accordingly. Lady Margaret had herself
set forth, and her authority could not be appealed to. In this
dilemma, the good genius of the old butler suggested an expedient.

'He had seen mony a braw callant, far less than Guse Gibbie,
fight brawly under Montrose. What for no tak Guse Gibbie?'

This was a half-witted lad, of very small stature, who had a
kind of charge of the poultry under the old henwife; for in a
Scottish family of that day there was a wonderful substitution of
labour. This urchin being sent for from the stubble-field, was
hastily muffled in the buff coat, and girded rather *to* than *with*
the sword of a full-grown man, his little legs plunged into jack-
boots, and a steel cap put upon his head, which seemed, from its
size, as if it had been intended to extinguish him. Thus accoutred,
he was hoisted, at his own earnest request, upon the quietest
horse of the party; and, prompted and supported by old Gudyill
the butler, as his front file, he passed muster tolerably enough; the
sheriff not caring to examine too closely the recruits of so well-
affected a person as Lady Margaret Bellenden.

To the above cause it was owing that the personal retinue of
Lady Margaret, on this eventful day, amounted only to two
lacqueys, with which diminished train she would, on any other
occasion, have been much ashamed to appear in public. But, for
the cause of royalty, she was ready at any time to have made the
most unreserved personal sacrifices. She had lost her husband and
two promising sons in the civil wars of that unhappy period; but
she had received her reward, for, on his route through the west of
Scotland to meet Cromwell in the unfortunate field of Worcester,[6]
Charles the Second had actually breakfasted at the Tower of

Tillietudlem; an incident which formed, from that moment, an important era in the life of Lady Margaret, who seldom afterwards partook of that meal, either at home or abroad, without detailing the whole circumstances of the royal visit, not forgetting the salutation which his majesty conferred on each side of her face, though she sometimes omitted to notice that he bestowed the same favour on two buxom serving-wenches who appeared at her back, elevated for the day into the capacity of waiting gentlewomen.

These instances of royal favour were decisive; and if Lady Margaret had not been a confirmed royalist already, from sense of high birth, influence of education, and hatred to the opposite party, through whom she had suffered such domestic calamity, the having given a breakfast to majesty, and received the royal salute in return, were honours enough of themselves to unite her exclusively to the fortunes of the Stewarts. These were now, in all appearance, triumphant; but Lady Margaret's zeal had adhered to them through the worst of times, and was ready to sustain the same severities of fortune should their scale once more kick the beam. At present she enjoyed, in full extent, the military display of the force which stood ready to support the crown, and stifled, as well as she could, the mortification she felt at the unworthy desertion of her own retainers.

Many civilities passed between her ladyship and the representatives of sundry ancient loyal families who were upon the ground, by whom she was held in high reverence; and not a young man of rank passed by them in the course of the muster, but he carried his body more erect in the saddle, and threw his horse upon its haunches, to display his own horsemanship and the perfect bitting of his steed to the best advantage in the eyes of Miss Edith Bellenden. But the young cavaliers, distinguished by high descent and undoubted loyalty, attracted no more attention from Edith than the laws of courtesy peremptorily demanded; and she turned an indifferent ear to the compliments with which she was addressed, most of which were little the worse for the wear, though borrowed for the nonce from the laborious and long-winded romances of Calprenede and Scuderi,[7] the mirrors in which the youth of that age delighted to dress themselves, ere Folly had thrown her ballast overboard, and cut down her vessels of the first-rate, such as the romances of Cyrus, Cleopatra,[8] and others, into small craft, drawing as little water, or, to speak more plainly, consuming as little time as the little cockboat in which the gentle reader has deigned to embark. It was, however, the decree of fate that Miss Bellenden should not continue to evince the same equanimity till the conclusion of the day.

CHAPTER 3

Horseman and horse confess'd the bitter pang,
And arms and warrior fell with heavy clang.
Pleasures of Hope[1]

WHEN the military evolutions had been gone through tolerably well, allowing for the awkwardness of men and of horses, a loud shout announced that the competitors were about to step forth for the game of the popinjay already described. The mast, or pole, having a yard extended across it, from which the mark was displayed, was raised amid the acclamations of the assembly; and even those who had eyed the evolutions of the feudal militia with a sort of malignant and sarcastic sneer, from disinclination to the royal cause in which they were professedly embodied, could not refrain from taking considerable interest in the strife which was now approaching. They crowded towards the goal, and criticized the appearance of each competitor, as they advanced in succession, discharged their pieces at the mark, and had their good or bad address rewarded by the laughter or applause of the spectators. But when a slender young man, dressed with great simplicity, yet not without a certain air of pretension to elegance and gentility, approached the station with his fusee in his hand, his dark-green cloak thrown back over his shoulder, his laced ruff and feathered cap indicating a superior rank to the vulgar, there was a murmur of interest among the spectators, whether altogether favourable to the young adventurer, it was difficult to discover.

'Ewhow, sirs, to see his father's son at the like o' thae fearless follies!' was the ejaculation of the elder and more rigid puritans, whose curiosity had so far overcome their bigotry as to bring them to the play-ground. But the generality viewed the strife less morosely, and were contented to wish success to the son of a deceased presbyterian leader, without strictly examining the propriety of his being a competitor for the prize.

Their wishes were gratified. At the first discharge of his piece the green adventurer struck the popinjay, being the first palpable hit of the day, though several balls had passed very near the mark. A loud shout of applause ensued. But the success was not decisive, it being necessary that each who followed should have his chance, and that those who succeeded in hitting the mark, should renew the strife among themselves, till one displayed a decided superiority over the others. Two only of those who followed in order succeeded in hitting the popinjay. The first was a young man of low rank, heavily built, and who kept his face muffled in his grey cloak; the second a gallant young cavalier, remarkable for a handsome exterior, sedulously decorated for the day. He had been since the muster in close attendance on Lady Margaret and Miss Bellenden, and had left them with an air of indifference, when Lady Margaret had asked whether there was no young man of family and loyal principles who would dispute the prize with the two lads who had been successful. In half a minute, young Lord Evandale threw himself from his horse, borrowed a gun from a servant, and, as we have already noticed, hit the mark. Great was the interest excited by the renewal of the contest between the three candidates who had been hitherto successful. The state equipage of the Duke was, with some difficulty, put in motion, and approached more near to the scene of action. The riders, both male and female, turned their horses' heads in the same direction, and all eyes were bent upon the issue of the trial of skill.

It was the etiquette in the second contest, that the competitors should take their turn of firing after drawing lots. The first fell upon the young plebeian, who, as he took his stand, half-uncloaked his rustic countenance, and said to the gallant in green, 'Ye see, Mr Henry, if it were ony other day, I could hae wished to miss for your sake; but Jenny Dennison is looking at us, sae I maun do my best.'

He took his aim, and his bullet whistled past the mark so nearly, that the pendulous object at which it was directed was seen to shiver. Still, however, he had not hit it, and, with a downcast look, he withdrew himself from further competition, and hastened to disappear from the assembly, as if fearful of being recognised. The green *chasseur* next advanced, and his ball a second time struck the popinjay. All shouted; and from the outskirts of the assembly arose a cry of, 'The good old cause for ever!'

While the dignitaries bent their brows at these exulting shouts of the disaffected, the young Lord Evandale advanced again to the hazard, and again was successful. The shouts and congratulations of the well-affected and aristocratical part of the audience attended his success, but still a subsequent trial of skill remained.

The green marksman, as if determined to bring the affair to a decision, took his horse from a person who held him, having previously looked carefully to the security of his girths and the fitting of his saddle, vaulted on his back, and motioning with his hand for the bystanders to make way, set spurs, passed the place from which he was to fire at a gallop, and, as he passed, threw up the reins, turned sideways upon his saddle, discharged his carabine, and brought down the popinjay. Lord Evandale imitated his example, although many around him said it was an innovation on the established practice, which he was not obliged to follow. But his skill was not so perfect, or his horse was not so well trained. The animal swerved at the moment his master fired, and the ball missed the popinjay. Those who had been surprised by the address of the green marksman were now equally pleased by his courtesy. He disclaimed all merit from the last shot, and proposed to his antagonist that it should not be counted as a hit, and that they should renew the contest on foot.

'I would prefer horseback, if I had a horse as well bitted, and, probably, as well broken to the exercise, as yours,' said the young Lord, addressing his antagonist.

'Will you do me the honour to use him for the next trial, on condition you will lend me yours?' said the young gentleman.

Lord Evandale was ashamed to accept this courtesy, as conscious how much it would diminish the value of victory; and yet, unable to suppress his wish to redeem his reputation as a marks-man, he added, 'that although he renounced all pretensions to the honour of the day,' (which he said somewhat scornfully,) 'yet, if the victor had no particular objection, he would willingly embrace his obliging offer, and change horses with him, for the purpose of trying a shot for love.'

As he said so, he looked boldly towards Miss Bellenden, and tradition says, that the eyes of the young *tirailleur* travelled, though more covertly, in the same direction. The young Lord's last trial was as unsuccessful as the former, and it was with difficulty that he preserved the tone of scornful indifference which he had hitherto assumed. But, conscious of the ridicule which attaches itself to the resentment of a losing party, he returned to his antagonist the horse on which he had made his last unsuccessful attempt, and received back his own; giving, at the same time, thanks to his competitor, who, he said, had re-established his favourite horse in his good opinion, for he had been in great danger of transferring to the poor nag the blame of an inferiority, which every one, as well as himself, must now be satisfied remained with the rider. Having made this speech in a tone in which mortification assumed the veil of indifference, he mounted his horse and rode off the ground.

As is the usual way of the world, the applause and attention even of those whose wishes had favoured Lord Evandale, were, upon his decisive discomfiture, transferred to his triumphant rival.

'Who is he? what is his name?' ran from mouth to mouth among the gentry who were present, to few of whom he was personally known. His style and title having soon transpired, and being within that class whom a great man might notice without derogation, four of the Duke's friends, with the obedient start which poor Malvolio ascribes to his imaginary retinue,[2] made out to lead the victor to his presence. As they conducted him in triumph through the crowd of spectators, and stunned him at the same time with their compliments on his success, he chanced to pass, or rather to be led, immediately in front of Lady Margaret and her grand-daughter. The Captain of the popinjay and Miss Bellenden coloured like crimson, as the latter returned, with embarrassed courtesy, the low inclination which the victor made, even to the saddle-bow, in passing her.

'Do you know that young person?' said Lady Margaret.

'I – I – have seen him, madam, at my uncle's, and – and elsewhere occasionally,' stammered Miss Edith Bellenden.

'I hear them say around me,' said Lady Margaret, 'that the young spark is the nephew of old Milnwood.'

'The son of the late Colonel Morton of Milnwood, who commanded a regiment of horse with great courage at Dunbar and Inverkeithing,'[3] said a gentleman who sate on horseback beside Lady Margaret.

'Ay, and who, before that, fought for the Covenanters both at Marston-Moor and Philiphaugh,'[4] said Lady Margaret, sighing as she pronounced the last fatal words, which her husband's death gave her such sad reason to remember.

'Your ladyship's memory is just,' said the gentleman, smiling, 'but it were well all that were forgot now.'

'*He* ought to remember it, Gilbertscleugh,' returned Lady Margaret, 'and dispense with intruding himself into the company of those to whom his name must bring unpleasing recollections.'

'You forget, my dear lady,' said her nomenclator, 'that the young gentleman comes here to discharge suit and service in name of his uncle. I would every estate in the country sent out as pretty a fellow.'

'His uncle, as well as his umquhile father, is a roundhead, I presume,' said Lady Margaret.

'He is an old miser,' said Gilbertscleugh, 'with whom a broad piece would at any time weigh down political opinions, and, therefore, although probably somewhat against the grain, he sends the young gentleman to attend the muster to save pecuniary pains and penalties. As for the rest, I suppose the youngster is happy enough to escape here for a day from the dulness of the old house at Milnwood, where he sees nobody but his hypochondriac uncle and the favourite housekeeper.'

'Do you know how many men and horse the lands of Milnwood are rated at?' said the old lady, continuing her enquiry.

'Two horsemen with complete harness,' answered Gilbertscleugh.

'Our land,' said Lady Margaret, drawing herself up with dignity, 'has always furnished to the muster eight men, cousin Gilbertscleugh, and often a voluntary aid of thrice the number. I remember his sacred Majesty King Charles, when he took his disjune at Tillietudlem, was particular in enquiring' –

'I see the Duke's carriage in motion,' said Gilbertscleugh, partaking at the moment an alarm common to all Lady Margaret's friends, when she touched upon the topic of the royal visit at the family mansion, – 'I see the Duke's carriage in motion; I presume your ladyship will take your right of rank in leaving the field. May I be permitted to convoy your ladyship and Miss Bellenden home? – Parties of the wild whigs have been abroad, and are said to insult and disarm the well-affected who travel in small numbers.'

'We thank you, cousin Gilbertscleugh,' said Lady Margaret; 'but as we shall have the escort of my own people, I trust we have less need than others to be troublesome to our friends. Will you have the goodness to order Harrison to bring up our people somewhat more briskly; he rides them towards us as if he were leading a funeral procession.'

The gentleman in attendance communicated his lady's orders to the trusty steward.

Honest Harrison had his own reasons for doubting the prudence of this command; but, once issued and received, there was a necessity for obeying it. He set off, therefore, at a hand-gallop, followed by the butler, in such a military attitude as became one who had served under Montrose, and with a look of defiance, rendered sterner and fiercer by the inspiring fumes of a gill of brandy, which he had snatched a moment to bolt to the king's health, and confusion to the Covenant, during the intervals of military duty. Unhappily this potent refreshment wiped away from the tablets of his memory the necessity of paying some attention to the distresses and difficulties of his rear-file, Goose Gibbie. No sooner had the horses struck a canter, than Gibbie's jackboots, which the poor boy's legs were incapable of steadying, began to play alternately against the horse's flanks, and, being armed with long-rowelled spurs, overcame the patience of the animal, which bounced and plunged, while poor Gibbie's entreaties for aid never reached the ears of the too heedless butler, being drowned partly in the concave of the steel cap in which his head was immersed, and partly in the martial tune of the Gallant Græmes, which Mr Gudyill whistled with all his power of lungs.

The upshot was, that the steed speedily took the matter into his own hands, and having gambolled hither and thither to the great amusement of all spectators, set off at full speed towards the huge family-coach already described. Gibbie's pike, escaping from its sling, had fallen to a level direction across his hands, which, I grieve to say, were seeking dishonourable safety in as strong a grasp of the mane as their muscles could manage. His casque, too, had slipped completely over his face, so that he saw as little in front as he did in rear. Indeed, if he could, it would have availed him little in the circumstances; for his horse, as if in league with the disaffected, ran full tilt towards the solemn equipage of the Duke, which the projecting lance threatened to perforate from window to window, at the risk of transfixing as many in its passage as the celebrated thrust of Orlando,[5] which, according to the Italian epic poet, broached as many Moors as a Frenchman spits frogs.

On beholding the bent of this misdirected career, a panic shout of mingled terror and wrath was set up by the whole equipage, insides and outsides, at once, which had the happy effect of averting the threatened misfortune. The capricious horse of Goose Gibbie was terrified by the noise, and stumbling as he turned short round, kicked and plunged violently as soon as he recovered. The jack-boots, the original cause of the disaster, maintaining the reputation they had acquired when worn by better cavaliers, answered every plunge by a fresh prick of the spurs, and, by their ponderous weight, kept their place in the stirrups. Not so Goose Gibbie, who was fairly spurned out of those wide and ponderous greaves, and precipitated over the horse's head, to the infinite amusement of all the spectators. His lance and helmet had forsaken him in his fall, and, for the completion of his disgrace, Lady Margaret Bellenden, not perfectly aware that it was one of her warriors who was furnishing so much entertainment, came up in time to see her diminutive man-at-arms stripped of his lion's hide, – of the buff-coat, that is, in which he was muffled.

As she had not been made acquainted with this metamorphosis, and could not even guess its cause, her surprise and resentment were extreme, nor were they much modified by the excuses and explanations of her steward and butler. She made a hasty retreat homeward, extremely indignant at the shouts and laughter of the company, and much disposed to vent her displeasure on the refractory agriculturist whose place Goose Gibbie had so unhappily supplied. The greater part of the gentry now dispersed, the whimsical misfortune which had befallen the gens d'armerie of Tillietudlem furnishing them with huge entertainment on their road homeward. The horsemen also, in little parties, as their road lay together, diverged from the place of rendezvous, excepting such as, having tried their dexterity at the popinjay, were, by ancient custom, obliged to partake of a grace-cup with their captain before their departure.

CHAPTER 4

At fairs he play'd before the spearmen,
And gaily graithed in their gear then,
Steel bonnets, pikes, and swords shone clear then
        As ony bead;
Now wha sall play before sic weir men,
        Since Habbie's dead!
        Elegy on Habbie Simpson[1]

THE cavalcade of horsemen on their road to the little boroughtown were preceded by Niel Blane, the town-piper, mounted on his white galloway, armed with his dirk and broadsword, and bearing a chanter streaming with as many ribbons as would deck out six country belles for a fair or preaching. Niel, a clean, tight, well-timbered, long-winded fellow, had gained the official situation of town-piper of — by his merit, with all the emoluments thereof; namely, the Piper's Croft, as it is still called, a field of about an acre in extent, five merks, and a new livery-coat of the town's colours, yearly; some hopes of a dollar upon the day of the election of magistrates, providing the provost were able and willing to afford such a gratuity; and the privilege of paying, at all the respectable houses in the neighbourhood, an annual visit at spring-time, to rejoice their hearts with his music, to comfort his own with their ale and brandy, and to beg from each a modicum of seed-corn.

In addition to these inestimable advantages, Niel's personal, or professional, accomplishments won the heart of a jolly widow, who then kept the principal change-house in the borough. Her former husband having been a strict presbyterian, of such note that he usually went among his sect by the name of Gaius[2] the publican, many of the more rigid were scandalized by the profession of the successor whom his relict had chosen for a second help-mate. As the *browst* (or brewing) of the Howff retained, nevertheless, its unrivalled reputation, most of the old customers continued to give it a preference. The character of the new landlord, indeed, was of that accommodating kind, which enabled him, by close attention to the helm, to keep his little vessel pretty steady amid the contending tides of faction. He was a good-humoured, shrewd, selfish sort of fellow, indifferent alike to the disputes about church and state, and only anxious to secure the good-will of customers of every description. But his character, as well as the state of the country, will be best understood by giving the reader an account of the instructions which he issued to his daughter, a girl about eighteen, whom he was initiating in those cares which had been faithfully discharged by his wife, until about six months before our story commences, when the honest woman had been carried to the kirkyard.

'Jenny,' said Niel Blane, as the girl assisted to disencumber him of his bagpipes, 'this is the first day that ye are to take the place of your worthy mother in attending to the public; a douce woman she was, civil to the customers, and had a good name wi' Whig and Tory, baith up the street and down the street. It will be hard for you to fill her place, especially on sic a thrang day as this; but Heaven's will maun be obeyed. – Jenny, whatever Milnwood ca's for, be sure he maun hae't, for he's the Captain o' the Popinjay, and auld customs maun be supported; if he canna pay the lawing himsell, as I ken he's keepit unco short by the head, I'll find a way to shame it out o' his uncle. – The curate[3] is playing at dice wi' Cornet Grahame. Be eident and civil to them baith – clergy and captains can gie an unco deal o' fash in thae times, where they take an ill-will. – The dragoons will be crying for ale, and they wunna want it, and maunna want it – they are unruly chields, but they pay ane some gate or other. I gat the humle-cow, that's the best in the byre, frae black Frank Inglis and Sergeant Bothwell, for ten pund Scots, and they drank out the price at ae downsitting.'

'But, father,' interrupted Jenny, 'they say the twa reiving loons drave the cow frae the gudewife o' Bell's-moor, just because she gaed to hear a field-preaching ae Sabbath afternoon.'

'Whisht! ye silly tawpie,' said her father, 'we have naething to do how they come by the bestial they sell – be that atween them and their consciences. – Aweel – Take notice, Jenny, of that dour, stour-looking carle that sits by the cheek o' the ingle, and turns his back on a' men. He looks like ane o' the hill-folk, for I saw him start a wee when he saw the red-coats, and I jalouse he wad hae liked to hae ridden by, but his horse (it's a gude gelding) was ower sair travailed; he behoved to stop whether he wad or no. Serve him cannily, Jenny, and wi' little din, and dinna bring the sodgers on him by speering ony questions at him; but let na him hae a room to himsell, they wad say we were hiding him. – For yoursell, Jenny, ye'll be civil to a' the folk, and take nae heed o' ony nonsense and daffing the young lads may say t'ye. Folk in the hostler line maun put up wi' muckle. Your mither, rest her saul, could pit up wi' as muckle as maist women – but aff hands is fair play; and if ony body be uncivil ye may gie me a cry – Aweel, – when the malt begins to get aboon the meal, they'll begin to speak about government in kirk and state, and then, Jenny, they are like to quarrel – let them be doing – anger's a drouthy passion, and the mair they dispute, the mair ale they'll drink; but ye were best serve them wi' a pint o' the sma' browst, it will heat them less, and they'll never ken the difference.'

'But, father,' said Jenny, 'if they come to lounder ilk ither, as they did last time, suldna I cry on you?'

'At no hand, Jenny; the redder gets aye the warst lick in the fray. If the sodgers draw their swords, ye'll cry on the corporal and the guard. If the country folk tak the tangs and poker, ye'll cry on the bailie and town-officers. But in nae event cry on me, for I am wearied wi' doudling the bag o' wind a' day, and I am gaun to eat my dinner quietly in the spence. – And, now I think on't, the Laird of Lickitup (that's him that was the laird) was speering for sma' drink and a saut herring – gie him a pu' be the sleeve, and round into his lug I wad be blithe o' his company to dine wi' me; he was a gude customer anes in a day, and wants naething but means to be a gude ane again – he likes drink as weel as e'er he did. And if ye ken ony puir body o' our acquaintance that's blate for want o' siller, and has far to gang hame, ye needna stick to gie them a waught o' drink and a bannock – we'll ne'er miss't, and it looks creditable in a house like ours. And now, hinny, gang awa', and serve the folk, but first bring me my dinner, and twa chappins o' yill and the mutchkin stoup o' brandy.'

Having thus devolved his whole cares on Jenny as prime minister, Niel Blane and the *ci-devant* laird, once his patron, but now glad to be his trencher-companion, sate down to enjoy themselves for the remainder of the evening, remote from the bustle of the public room.

All in Jenny's department was in full activity. The knights of the popinjay received and requited the hospitable entertainment of their captain, who, though he spared the cup himself, took care it should go round with due celerity among the rest, who might not have otherwise deemed themselves handsomely treated. Their numbers melted away by degrees, and were at length diminished to four or five, who began to talk of breaking up their party. At another table, at some distance, sat two of the dragoons, whom Niel Blane had mentioned, a sergeant and a private in the celebrated John Grahame of Claverhouse's regiment of Life-Guards.[4] Even the non-commissioned officers and privates in these corps were not considered as ordinary mercenaries, but rather approached to the rank of the French mousquetaires, being regarded in the light of cadets, who performed the duties of rank-and-file with the prospect of obtaining commissions in case of distinguishing themselves.

Many young men of good families were to be found in the

ranks, a circumstance which added to the pride and self-consequence of these troops. A remarkable instance of this occurred in the person of the non-commissioned officer in question. His real name was Francis Stewart, but he was universally known by the appellation of Bothwell, being lineally descended from the last earl of that name; not the infamous lover of the unfortunate Queen Mary, but Francis Stewart, Earl of Bothwell, whose turbulence and repeated conspiracies embarrassed the early part of James Sixth's reign, and who at length died in exile in great poverty. The son of this Earl had sued to Charles I for the restitution of part of his father's forfeited estates, but the grasp of the nobles to whom they had been allotted was too tenacious to be unclenched. The breaking out of the civil wars utterly ruined him, by intercepting a small pension which Charles I had allowed him, and he died in the utmost indigence. His son, after having served as a soldier abroad and in Britain, and passed through several vicissitudes of fortune, was fain to content himself with the situation of a non-commissioned officer in the Life-Guards, although lineally descended from the royal family, the father of the forfeited Earl of Bothwell having been a natural son of James VI.[5] Great personal strength, and dexterity in the use of his arms, as well as the remarkable circumstances of his descent, had recommended this man to the attention of his officers. But he partook in a great degree of the licentiousness and oppressive disposition, which the habit of acting as agents for government in levying fines, exacting free quarters, and otherwise oppressing the Presbyterian recusants, had rendered too general among these soldiers. They were so much accustomed to such missions, that they conceived themselves at liberty to commit all manner of license with impunity, as if totally exempted from all law and authority, excepting the command of their officers. On such occasions Bothwell was usually the most forward.

It is probable that Bothwell and his companions would not so long have remained quiet, but for respect to the presence of their Cornet, who commanded the small party quartered in the borough, and who was engaged in a game at dice with the curate of the place. But both of these being suddenly called from their amusement to speak with the chief magistrate upon some urgent business, Bothwell was not long of evincing his contempt for the rest of the company.

'Is it not a strange thing, Halliday,' he said to his comrade, 'to see a set of bumpkins sit carousing here this whole evening, without having drank the king's health?'

'They have drank the king's health,' said Halliday. 'I heard that green kail-worm of a lad name his majesty's health.'

'Did he?' said Bothwell. 'Then, Tom, we'll have them drink the Archbishop of St Andrew's health, and do it on their knees too.'

'So we will, by G—,' said Halliday; 'and he that refuses it, we'll have him to the guard-house, and teach him to ride the colt foaled of an acorn,[6] with a brace of carabines at each foot to keep him steady.'

'Right, Tom,' continued Bothwell; 'and, to do all things in order, I'll begin with that sulky blue-bonnet in the ingle-nook.'

He rose accordingly, and taking his sheathed broadsword under his arm to support the insolence which he meditated, placed himself in front of the stranger noticed by Niel Blane, in his admonitions to his daughter, as being, in all probability, one of the hill-folk, or refractory presbyterians.

'I make so bold as to request of your precision, beloved,' said the trooper, in a tone of affected solemnity, and assuming the snuffle of a country preacher, 'that you will arise from your seat, beloved, and, having bent your hams until your knees do rest upon the floor, beloved, that you will turn over this measure (called by the profane a gill) of the comfortable creature, which the carnal denominate brandy, to the health and glorification of his Grace the Archbishop of St Andrews, the worthy primate of all Scotland.'

All waited for the stranger's answer. – His features, austere even to ferocity, with a cast of eye, which, without being actually oblique, approached nearly to a squint, and which gave a very sinister expression to his countenance, joined to a frame, square, strong, and muscular, though something under the middle size, seemed to announce a man unlikely to understand rude jesting, or to receive insults with impunity.

'And what is the consequence,' said he, 'if I should not be disposed to comply with your uncivil request?'

'The consequence thereof, beloved,' said Bothwell, in the same tone of raillery, 'will be, firstly, that I will tweak thy proboscis or nose. Secondly, beloved, that I will administer my fist to thy distorted visual optics; and will conclude, beloved, with a practical application of the flat of my sword to the shoulders of the recusant.'

'Is it even so?' said the stranger; 'then give me the cup;' and, taking it in his hand, he said, with a peculiar expression of voice and manner, 'The Archbishop of St Andrews, and the place he now worthily holds; – may each prelate in Scotland soon be as the Right Reverend James Sharpe!'

'He has taken the test,' said Halliday, exultingly.

'But with a qualification,' said Bothwell; 'I don't understand what the devil the crop-eared whig means.'

'Come, gentlemen,' said Morton, who became impatient of their insolence, 'we are here met as good subjects, and on a merry occasion; and we have a right to expect we shall not be troubled with this sort of discussion.'

Bothwell was about to make a surly answer, but Halliday reminded him in a whisper, that there were strict injunctions that the soldiers should give no offence to the men who were sent out to the musters agreeably to the council's orders. So, after honouring Morton with a broad and fierce stare, he said, 'Well, Mr Popinjay, I shall not disturb your reign; I reckon it will be out by twelve at night. – Is it not an odd thing, Halliday,' he continued, addressing his companion, 'that they should make such a fuss about cracking off their birding-pieces at a mark which any woman or boy could hit at a day's practice? If Captain Popinjay now, or any of his troop, would try a bout, either with the broadsword, backsword, single rapier, or rapier and dagger, for a gold noble, the first-drawn blood, there would be some soul in it, – or, zounds, would the bumpkins but wrestle, or pitch the bar, or putt the stone, or throw the axle-tree, if (touching the end of Morton's sword scornfully with his toe) they carry things about them that they are afraid to draw.'

Morton's patience and prudence now gave way entirely, and he was about to make a very angry answer to Bothwell's insolent observations, when the stranger stepped forward.

'This is my quarrel,' he said, 'and in the name of the good cause, I will see it out myself. – Hark thee, friend,' (to Bothwell,) 'wilt thou wrestle a fall with me?'

'With my whole spirit, beloved,' answered Bothwell; 'yea I will strive with thee, to the downfall of one or both.'

'Then, as my trust is in Him that can help,' retorted his antagonist, 'I will forthwith make thee an example to all such railing Rabshakehs.'[7]

With that he dropped his coarse grey horseman's coat from his shoulders, and, extending his strong brawny arms with a look of determined resolution, he offered himself to the contest. The soldier was nothing abashed by the muscular frame, broad chest, square shoulders, and hardy look of his antagonist, but, whistling with great composure, unbuckled his belt, and laid aside his military coat. The company stood round them, anxious for the event.

In the first struggle the trooper seemed to have some advantage, and also in the second, though neither could be considered as decisive. But it was plain he had put his whole strength too suddenly forth, against an antagonist possessed of great endurance, skill, vigour, and length of wind. In the third close, the countryman lifted his opponent fairly from the floor, and hurled him to the ground with such violence, that he lay for an instant stunned and motionless. His comrade Halliday immediately drew his sword; 'You have killed my sergeant,' he exclaimed to the victorious wrestler, 'and by all that is sacred you shall answer it!'

'Stand back!' cried Morton and his companions, 'it was all fair play; your comrade sought a fall, and he has got it.'

'That is true enough,' said Bothwell, as he slowly rose; 'put up your bilbo, Tom. I did not think there was a crop-ear of them all could have laid the best cap and feather in the King's Life-Guards on the floor of a rascally change-house. – Hark ye, friend, give me your hand.' The stranger held out his hand. 'I promise you,' said Bothwell, squeezing his hand very hard, 'that the time will come when we shall meet again, and try this game over in a more earnest manner.'

'And I'll promise you,' said the stranger, returning the grasp with equal firmness, 'that when we next meet, I will lay your head as low as it lay even now, when you shall lack the power to lift it up again.'

'Well, beloved,' answered Bothwell, 'if thou be'st a whig, thou art a stout and a brave one, and so good even to thee – Hadst best take thy nag before the Cornet makes the round; for, I promise thee, he has stay'd less suspicious-looking persons.'

The stranger seemed to think that the hint was not to be neglected; he flung down his reckoning, and going into the stable, saddled and brought out a powerful black horse, now recruited by rest and forage, and turning to Morton, observed, 'I ride towards Milnwood, which I hear is your home; will you give me the advantage and protection of your company?'

'Certainly,' said Morton; although there was something of gloomy and relentless severity in the man's manner from which his mind recoiled. His companions, after a courteous good-night, broke up and went off in different directions, some keeping them company for about a mile, until they dropped off one by one, and the travellers were left alone.

The company had not long left the Howff, as Blane's public-house was called, when the trumpets and kettle-drums sounded. The troopers got under arms in the market-place at this unexpected summons, while, with faces of anxiety and earnestness, Cornet Grahame, a kinsmen of Claverhouse, and the Provost of the borough, followed by half-a-dozen soldiers, and town-officers with halberts, entered the apartment of Niel Blane.

'Guard the doors!' were the first words which the Cornet spoke; 'let no man leave the house. – So, Bothwell, how comes this? Did you not hear them sound boot and saddle?'

'He was just going to quarters, sir,' said his comrade; 'he has had a bad fall.'

'In a fray, I suppose?' said Grahame. 'If you neglect duty in this way, your royal blood will hardly protect you.'

'How have I neglected duty?' said Bothwell, sulkily.

'You should have been at quarters, Sergeant Bothwell,' replied the officer; 'you have lost a golden opportunity. Here are news come that the Archbishop of St Andrews has been strangely and foully assassinated by a body of the rebel whigs, who pursued and stopped his carriage on Magus-Muir, near the town of St Andrews, dragged him out, and dispatched him with their swords and daggers.'[8]

All stood aghast at the intelligence.

'Here are their descriptions,' continued the Cornet, pulling out a proclamation, 'the reward of a thousand merks is on each of their heads.'

'The test, the test, and the qualification!' said Bothwell to Halliday; 'I know the meaning now – Zounds, that we should not have stopt him! Go saddle our horses, Halliday. – Was there one of the men, Cornet, very stout and square-made, double-chested, thin in the flanks, hawk-nosed?'

'Stay, stay,' said Cornet Grahame, 'let me look at the paper. – Hackston of Rathillet, tall, thin, black-haired.'

'That is not my man,' said Bothwell.

'John Balfour, called Burley, aquiline nose, red-haired, five feet eight inches in height' –

'It is he – it is the very man!' said Bothwell, – 'skellies fearfully with one eye?'

'Right,' continued Grahame, 'rode a strong black horse, taken from the primate at the time of the murder.'

'The very man,' exclaimed Bothwell, 'and the very horse! he was in this room not a quarter of an hour since.'

A few hasty enquiries tended still more to confirm the opinion, that the reserved and stern stranger was Balfour of Burley, the actual commander of the band of assassins, who, in the fury of misguided zeal, had murdered the primate, whom they accidentally met, as they were searching for another person against whom they bore enmity.[9] In their excited imagination the casual rencounter had the appearance of a providential interference, and they put to death the archbishop, with circumstances of great and cold-blooded cruelty, under the belief, that the Lord, as they expressed it, had delivered him into their hands.[10]

'Horse, horse, and pursue, my lads!' exclaimed Cornet Grahame; 'the murdering dog's head is worth its weight in gold.'

CHAPTER 5

Arouse thee, youth! – it is no human call –
God's church is leaguer'd – haste to man the wall;
Haste where the Redcross banners wave on high,
Signal of honour'd death, or victory!

JAMES DUFF[1]

MORTON and his companion had attained some distance from
the town before either of them addressed the other. There was
something, as we have observed, repulsive in the manner of the
stranger, which prevented Morton from opening the conversation, and he himself seemed to have no desire to talk, until, on a
sudden, he abruptly demanded, 'What has your father's son to do
with such profane mummeries as I find you this day engaged in?'

'I do my duty as a subject, and pursue my harmless recreations
according to my own pleasure,' replied Morton, somewhat
offended.

'Is it your duty, think you, or that of any Christian young man,
to bear arms in their cause who have poured out the blood of
God's saints in the wilderness as if it had been water? or is it a
lawful recreation to waste time in shooting at a bunch of feathers,
and close your evening with wine-bibbing in public-houses and
market-towns, when He that is mighty is come into the land
with his fan in his hand, to purge the wheat from the chaff?'[2]

'I suppose from your style of conversation,' said Morton, 'that
you are one of those who have thought proper to stand out against
the government. I must remind you that you are unnecessarily
using dangerous language in the presence of a mere stranger,
and that the times do not render it safe for me to listen to it.'

'Thou canst not help it, Henry Morton,' said his companion;
'thy Master has his uses for thee, and when he calls, thou must
obey. Well wot I thou hast not heard the call of a true preacher,
or thou hadst ere now been what thou wilt assuredly one day
become.'

'We are of the presbyterian persuasion, like yourself,' said

Morton; for his uncle's family attended the ministry of one of those numerous presbyterian clergymen, who, complying with certain regulations, were licensed to preach without interruption from the government. This *indulgence*, as it was called, made a great schism among the presbyterians, and those who accepted of it were severely censured by the more rigid sectaries, who refused the proffered terms.[3] The stranger, therefore, answered with great disdain to Morton's profession of faith.

'That is but an equivocation – a poor equivocation. Ye listen on the Sabbath to a cold, worldly, time-serving discourse, from one who forgets his high commission so much as to hold his apostleship by the favour of the courtiers and the false prelates, and ye call that hearing the word! Of all the baits with which the devil has fished for souls in these days of blood and darkness, that Black Indulgence has been the most destructive. An awful dispensation it has been, a smiting of the shepherd and a scattering of the sheep upon the mountains – an uplifting of one Christian banner against another, and a fighting of the wars of darkness with the swords of the children of light!'[4]

'My uncle,' said Morton, 'is of opinion, that we enjoy a reasonable freedom of conscience under the indulged clergymen, and I must necessarily be guided by his sentiments respecting the choice of a place of worship for his family.'[5]

'Your uncle,' said the horseman, 'is one of those to whom the least lamb in his own folds at Milnwood is dearer than the whole Christian flock. He is one that could willingly bend down to the golden-calf of Bethel, and would have fished for the dust thereof when it was ground to powder and cast upon the waters.[6] Thy father was a man of another stamp.'

'My father,' replied Morton, 'was indeed a brave and gallant man. And you may have heard, sir, that he fought for that royal family in whose name I was this day carrying arms.'

'Ay; and had he lived to see these days, he would have cursed the hour he ever drew sword in their cause. But more of this hereafter – I promise thee full surely that thy hour will come, and then the words thou hast now heard will stick in thy bosom like barbed arrows. My road lies there.'

He pointed towards a pass leading up into a wild extent of

dreary and desolate hills; but as he was about to turn his horse's head into the rugged path, which led from the high-road in that direction, an old woman wrapped in a red cloak, who was sitting by the cross-way, arose, and approaching him, said, in a mysterious tone of voice, 'If ye be of our ain folk, gangna up the pass the night for your lives. There is a lion in the path,[7] that is there. The curate of Brotherstane and ten soldiers hae beset the pass, to hae the lives of ony of our puir wanderers that venture that gate to join wi' Hamilton and Dingwall.'[8]

'Have the persecuted folk drawn to any head among themselves?' demanded the stranger.

'About sixty or seventy horse and foot,' said the old dame; 'but, ewhow! they are puirly armed, and warse fended wi' victual.'

'God will help his own,' said the horseman. 'Which way shall I take to join them?'

'It's a mere impossibility this night,' said the woman, 'the troopers keep sae strict a guard; and they say there's strange news come frae the east, that makes them rage in their cruelty mair fierce than ever – Ye maun take shelter somegate for the night before ye get to the muirs, and keep yoursell in hiding till the grey o' the morning, and then you may find your way through the Drake Moss. When I heard the awfu' threatenings o' the oppressors, I e'en took my cloak about me, and sate down by the wayside, to warn ony of our puir scattered remnant that chanced to come this gate, before they fell into the nets of the spoilers.'

'Have you a house near this?' said the stranger; 'and can you give me hiding there?'

'I have,' said the old woman, 'a hut by the way-side, it may be a mile from hence; but four men of Belial, called dragoons, are lodged therein, to spoil my household goods at their pleasure, because I will not wait upon the thowless, thriftless, fissenless ministry of that carnal man, John Halftext, the curate.'

'Good night, good woman, and thanks for thy counsel,' said the stranger, as he rode away.

'The blessings of the promise upon you,' returned the old dame; 'may He keep you that can keep you.'

'Amen!' said the traveller; 'for where to hide my head this night, mortal skill cannot direct me.'

'I am very sorry for your distress,' said Morton; 'and had I a house or place of shelter that could be called my own, I almost think I would risk the utmost rigour of the law rather than leave you in such a strait. But my uncle is so alarmed at the pains and penalties denounced by the laws against such as comfort, receive, or consort with intercommuned persons,[9] that he has strictly forbidden all of us to hold any intercourse with them.'

'It is no less than I expected,' said the stranger; 'nevertheless I might be received without his knowledge; – a barn, a hay-loft, a cart-shed, – any place where I could stretch me down, would be to my habits like a tabernacle of silver set about with planks of cedar.'[10]

'I assure you,' said Morton, much embarrassed, 'that I have not the means of receiving you at Milnwood without my uncle's consent and knowledge; nor, if I could do so, would I think myself justifiable in engaging him unconsciously in a danger, which, most of all others, he fears and deprecates.'

'Well,' said the traveller, 'I have but one word to say. Did you ever hear your father mention John Balfour of Burley?'

'His ancient friend and comrade, who saved his life, with almost the loss of his own, in the battle of Longmarston-Moor?[11] – Often, very often.'

'I am that Balfour,' said his companion. 'Yonder stands thy uncle's house; I see the light among the trees. The avenger of blood is behind me, and my death certain unless I have refuge there. Now, make thy choice, young man; to shrink from the side of thy father's friend, like a thief in the night, and to leave him exposed to the bloody death from which he rescued thy father, or to expose thine uncle's unworldly goods to such peril, as in this perverse generation, attends those who give a morsel of bread or a draught of cold water to a Christian man, when perishing for lack of refreshment!'

A thousand recollections thronged on the mind of Morton at once. His father, whose memory he idolized, had often enlarged upon his obligations to this man, and regretted, that, after having been long comrades, they had parted in some unkindness at the

time when the kingdom of Scotland was divided into Resolutioners and Protesters;[12] the former of whom adhered to Charles
II after his father's death upon the scaffold, while the Protesters
inclined rather to a union with the triumphant republicans. The
stern fanaticism of Burley had attached him to this latter party,
and the comrades had parted in displeasure, never, as it happened, to meet again. These circumstances the deceased Colonel
Morton had often mentioned to his son, and always with an
expression of deep regret, that he had never, in any manner, been
enabled to repay the assistance, which, on more than one occasion, he had received from Burley.

To hasten Morton's decision, the night-wind, as it swept along,
brought from a distance the sullen sound of a kettle-drum,
which, seeming to approach nearer, intimated that a body of
horse were upon their march towards them.

'It must be Claverhouse, with the rest of his regiment. What
can have occasioned this night-march? If you go on, you fall
into their hands – if you turn back towards the borough-town,
you are in no less danger from Cornet Grahame's party. – The
path to the hill is beset. I must shelter you at Milnwood, or
expose you to instant death; – but the punishment of the law
shall fall upon myself, as in justice it should, not upon my uncle.
– Follow me.'

Burley, who had awaited his resolution with great composure,
now followed him in silence.

The house of Milnwood, built by the father of the present
proprietor, was a decent mansion, suitable to the size of the
estate, but, since the accession of this owner, it had been suffered
to go considerably into disrepair. At some little distance from
the house stood the court of offices. Here Morton paused.

'I must leave you here for a little while,' he whispered, 'until
I can provide a bed for you in the house.'

'I care little for such delicacy,' said Burley; 'for thirty years
this head has rested oftener on the turf, or on the next grey stone,
than upon either wool or down. A draught of ale, a morsel of
bread, to say my prayers, and to stretch me upon dry hay, were
to me as good as a painted chamber and a prince's table.'

It occurred to Morton at the same moment, that to attempt to introduce the fugitive within the house, would materially increase the danger of detection. Accordingly, having struck a light with implements left in the stable for that purpose, and having fastened up their horses, he assigned Burley, for his place of repose, a wooden bed, placed in a loft half-full of hay, which an out-of-door domestic had occupied until dismissed by his uncle in one of those fits of parsimony which became more rigid from day to day. In this untenanted loft Morton left his companion, with a caution so to shade his light that no reflection might be seen from the window, and a promise that he would presently return with such refreshments as he might be able to procure at that late hour. This last, indeed, was a subject on which he felt by no means confident, for the power of obtaining even the most ordinary provisions depended entirely upon the humour in which he might happen to find his uncle's sole confidant, the old housekeeper. If she chanced to be a-bed, which was very likely, or out of humour, which was not less so, Morton well knew the case to be at least problematical.

Cursing in his heart the sordid parsimony which pervaded every part of his uncle's establishment, he gave the usual gentle knock at the bolted door, by which he was accustomed to seek admittance, when accident had detained him abroad beyond the early and established hours of rest at the house of Milnwood. It was a sort of hesitating tap, which carried an acknowledgment of transgression in its very sound, and seemed rather to solicit than command attention. After it had been repeated again and again, the housekeeper, grumbling betwixt her teeth as she rose from the chimney corner in the hall, and wrapping her checked handkerchief round her head to secure her from the cold air, paced across the stone-passage, and repeated a careful 'Wha's there at this time o' night?' more than once before she undid the bolts and bars, and cautiously open the door.

'This is a fine time o' night, Mr Henry,' said the old dame, with the tyrannic insolence of a spoilt and favourite domestic; – 'a braw time o' night and a bonny, to disturb a peaceful house in, and to keep quiet folk out o' their beds waiting for you. Your uncle's been in his maist three hours syne, and Robin's ill o' the rheumatize, and he's to his bed too, and sae I had to sit up for ye mysell, for as sair a hoast as I hae.'

Here she coughed once or twice, in further evidence of the egregious inconvenience which she had sustained.

'Much obliged to you, Alison, and many kind thanks.'

'Hegh, sirs, sae fair-fashioned as we are! Mony folk ca' me Mistress Wilson, and Milnwood himsell is the only ane about this town thinks o' ca'ing me Alison, and indeed he as aften says Mrs Alison as ony other thing.'

'Well, then, Mistress Alison,' said Morton, 'I really am sorry to have kept you up waiting till I came in.'

'And now that you are come in, Mr Henry,' said the cross old woman, 'what for do you no tak up your candle and gang to your bed? and mind ye dinna let the candle sweal as ye gang alang the wainscot parlour, and haud a' the house scouring to get out the grease again.'

'But, Alison, I really must have something to eat, and a draught of ale, before I go to bed.'

'Eat? — and ale, Mr Henry? — My certie, ye're ill to serve. Do ye think we havena heard o' your grand popinjay wark yonder, and how ye bleezed away as muckle pouther as wad hae shot a' the wild-fowl that we'll want atween and Candlemas — and then ganging majoring to the piper's Howff wi' a' the idle loons in the country, and sitting there birling, at your poor uncle's cost, nae doubt, wi' a' the scaff and raff o' the water-side, till sundown, and then coming hame and crying for ale, as if ye were maister and mair!'

Extremely vexed, yet anxious, on account of his guest, to procure refreshments if possible, Morton suppressed his resentment, and good-humouredly assured Mrs Wilson, that he was really both hungry and thirsty; 'and as for the shooting at the popinjay, I have heard you say you have been there yourself, Mrs Wilson — I wish you had come to look at us.'

'Ah, Maister Henry,' said the old dame, 'I wish ye binna beginning to learn the way of blawing in a woman's lug wi' a' your whilly-wha's! — Aweel, sae ye dinna practise them but on auld wives like me, the less matter. But tak heed o' the young queans, lad. — Popinjay — ye think yourself a braw fellow enow;

and troth!' (surveying him with the candle,) 'there's nae fault to find wi' the outside, if the inside be conforming. But I mind, when I was a gilpy of a lassock, seeing the Duke, that was him that lost his head at London [13] – folk said it wasna a very gude ane, but it was aye a sair loss to him, puir gentleman – Aweel, he wan the popinjay, for few cared to win it ower his Grace's head – weel, he had a comely presence, and when a' the gentles mounted to show their capers, his Grace was as near to me as I am to you; and he said to me, "Tak tent o' yoursell, my bonny lassie, (these were his very words,) for my horse is not very chancy." – And now, as ye say ye had sae little to eat or drink, I'll let you see that I have no been sae unmindfu' o' you; for I dinna think it's safe for young folk to gang to their bed on an empty stomach.'

To do Mrs Wilson justice, her nocturnal harangues upon such occasions not unfrequently terminated with this sage apophthegm, which always prefaced the producing of some provision a little better than ordinary, such as she now placed before him. In fact, the principal object of her *maundering* was to display her consequence and love of power; for Mrs Wilson was not, at the bottom, an ill-tempered woman, and certainly loved her old and young master (both of whom she tormented extremely) better than any one else in the world. She now eyed Mr Henry, as she called him, with great complacency, as he partook of her good cheer.

'Muckle gude may it do ye, my bonny man. I trow ye dinna get sic a skirl-in-the-pan as that at Niel Blane's. His wife was a canny body, and could dress things very weel for ane in her line o' business, but no like a gentleman's housekeeper, to be sure. But I doubt the daughter's a silly thing – an unco cockernony she had busked on her head at the kirk last Sunday. I am doubting that there will be news o' a' thae braws. By my auld een's drawing thegither – dinna hurry yoursell, my bonny man, tak mind about the putting out the candle, and there's a horn of ale, and a glass of clow-gillie-flower water; I dinna gie ilka body that; I keep it for a pain I hae whiles in my ain stamach, and it's better for your young blood than brandy. Sae, gude-night to ye, Mr Henry, and see that ye tak gude care o' the candle.'

Morton promised to attend punctually to her caution, and requested her not to be alarmed if she heard the door opened, as she knew he must again, as usual, look to his horse, and arrange him for the night. Mrs Wilson then retreated, and Morton, folding up his provisions, was about to hasten to his guest, when the nodding head of the old housekeeper was again thrust in at the door, with an admonition, to remember to take an account of his ways before he laid himself down to rest, and to pray for protection during the hours of darkness.

Such were the manners of a certain class of domestics, once common in Scotland, and perhaps still to be found in some old manor-houses in its remote counties. They were fixtures in the family they belonged to; and as they never conceived the possibility of such a thing as dismissal to be within the chances of their lives, they were, of course, sincerely attached to every member of it.[14] On the other hand, when spoiled by the indulgence or indolence of their superiors, they were very apt to become ill-tempered, self-sufficient, and tyrannical; so much so, that a mistress or master would sometimes almost have wished to exchange their crossgrained fidelity for the smooth and accommodating duplicity of a modern menial.

CHAPTER 6

Yea, this man's brow, like to a tragic leaf,
Foretells the nature of a tragic volume.
                                SHAKSPEARE[1]

BEING at length rid of the housekeeper's presence, Morton made a collection of what he had reserved from the provisions set before him, and prepared to carry them to his concealed guest. He did not think it necessary to take a light, being perfectly acquainted with every turn of the road; and it was lucky he did not do so, for he had hardly stepped beyond the threshold ere a heavy trampling of horses announced, that the body of cavalry, whose kettle-drums[2] they had before heard, were in the act of passing along the high-road which winds round the foot of the bank on which the house of Milnwood was placed. He heard the commanding officer distinctly give the word *halt*. A pause of silence followed, interrupted only by the occasional neighing or pawing of an impatient charger.

'Whose house is this?' said a voice, in a tone of authority and command.

'Milnwood, if it like your honour,' was the reply.

'Is the owner well affected?' said the enquirer.

'He complies with the orders of government, and frequents an indulged minister,' was the response.

'Hum! ay! indulged? a mere mask for treason, very impolitically allowed to those who are too great cowards to wear their principles barefaced. – Had we not better send up a party and search the house, in case some of the bloody villains concerned in this heathenish butchery may be concealed in it?'

Ere Morton could recover from the alarm into which this proposal had thrown him, a third speaker rejoined, 'I cannot think it at all necessary; Milnwood is an infirm, hypochondriac old man, who never meddles with politics, and loves his money-bags and bonds better than any thing else in the world. His nephew, I hear, was at the wappen-schaw to-day, and gained the popinjay, which does not look like a fanatic. I should think they are all gone to bed long since, and an alarm at this time of night might kill the poor old man.'

'Well,' rejoined the leader, 'if that be so, to search the house would be lost time, of which we have but little to throw away. Gentlemen of the Life-Guards, forward – March!'

A few notes on the trumpet, mingled with the occasional boom of the kettle-drum, to mark the cadence, joined with the tramp of hoofs and the clash of arms, announced that the troop had resumed its march. The moon broke out as the leading files of the column attained a hill up which the road winded, and showed indistinctly the glittering of the steel-caps; and the dark figures of the horses and riders might be imperfectly traced through the gloom. They continued to advance up the hill, and sweep over the top of it in such long succession, as intimated a considerable numerical force.

When the last of them had disappeared, young Morton resumed his purpose of visiting his guest. Upon entering the place of refuge, he found him seated on his humble couch with a pocket Bible open in his hand, which he seemed to study with intense meditation. His broadsword, which he had unsheathed in the first alarm at the arrival of the dragoons, lay naked across his knees, and the little taper that stood beside him upon the old chest, which served the purpose of a table, threw a partial and imperfect light upon those stern and harsh features, in which ferocity was rendered more solemn and dignified by a wild cast of tragic enthusiasm. His brow was that of one in whom some strong o'ermastering principle has overwhelmed all other passions and feelings, like the swell of a high spring-tide, when the usual cliffs and breakers vanish from the eye, and their existence is only indicated by the chafing foam of the waves that burst and wheel over them. He raised his head, after Morton had contemplated him for about a minute.

'I perceive,' said Morton, looking at his sword, 'that you heard the horsemen ride by; their passage delayed me for some minutes.'

'I scarcely heeded them,' said Balfour; 'my hour is not yet come. That I shall one day fall into their hands, and be honourably associated with the saints whom they have slaughtered, I am full well aware. And I would, young man, that the hour were come; it should be as welcome to me as ever wedding to bridegroom. But if my Master has more work for me on earth, I must not do his labour grudgingly.'

'Eat and refresh yourself,' said Morton; 'to-morrow your safety requires you should leave this place, in order to gain the hills, so soon as you can see to distinguish the track through the morasses.'

'Young man,' returned Balfour, 'you are already weary of me, and would be yet more so, perchance, did you know the task upon which I have been lately put. And I wonder not that it should be so, for there are times when I am weary of myself. Think you not it is a sore trial for flesh and blood, to be called upon to execute the righteous judgments of Heaven while we are yet in the body, and continue to retain that blinded sense and sympathy for carnal suffering, which makes our own flesh thrill when we strike a gash upon the body of another? And think you, that when some prime tyrant has been removed from his place, that the instruments of his punishment can at all times look back on their share in his downfall with firm and unshaken nerves? Must they not sometimes even question the truth of that inspiration which they have felt and acted under? Must they not sometimes doubt the origin of that strong impulse with which their prayers for heavenly direction under difficulties have been inwardly answered and confirmed, and confuse, in their disturbed apprehensions, the responses of Truth itself with some strong delusion of the enemy?'

'These are subjects, Mr Balfour, on which I am ill qualified to converse with you,' answered Morton; 'but I own I should strongly doubt the origin of any inspiration which seemed to dictate a line of conduct contrary to those feelings of natural humanity, which Heaven has assigned to us as the general law of our conduct.'

Balfour seemed somewhat disturbed, and drew himself hastily up, but immediately composed himself, and answered coolly, 'It is natural you should think so; you are yet in the dungeon-house of the law, a pit darker than that into which Jeremiah was plunged, even the dungeon of Malcaiah the son of Hamelmelech, where there was no water but mire.³ Yet is the seal of the covenant upon your forehead, and the son of the righteous, who resisted to blood where the banner was spread on the mountains, shall not be utterly lost, as one of the children of darkness. Trow ye, that in this day of bitterness and calamity, nothing is required at our hands but to keep the moral law as far as our carnal frailty will permit? Think ye our conquests must be only over our corrupt and evil affections and passions? No; we are called upon, when we have girded up our loins, to run the race boldly, and when we have drawn the sword, we are enjoined to smite the ungodly, though he be our neighbour, and the man of power and cruelty, though he were of our own kindred, and the friend of our own bosom.'

'These are the sentiments,' said Morton, 'that your enemies impute to you, and which palliate, if they do not vindicate, the cruel measures which the council have directed against you.

They affirm, that you pretend to derive your rule of action from what you call an inward light, rejecting the restraints of legal magistracy, of national law, and even of common humanity, when in opposition to what you call the spirit within you.'

'They do us wrong,' answered the Covenanter; 'it is they, perjured as they are, who have rejected all law, both divine and civil, and who now persecute us for adherence to the Solemn League and Covenant between God and the kingdom of Scotland, to which all of them, save a few popish malignants,[4] have sworn in former days, and which they now burn in the market-places, and tread under foot in derision. When this Charles Stewart returned to these kingdoms, did the malignants bring him back? They had tried it with strong hand, but they failed, I trow. Could James Grahame of Montrose, and his Highland caterans, have put him again in the place of his father? I think their heads on the Westport[5] told another tale for many a long day. It was the workers of the glorious work – the reformers of the beauty of the tabernacle, that called him again to the high place from which his father fell. And what has been our reward? In the words of the prophet,[6] "We looked for peace, but no good came; and for a time of health, and behold trouble – The snorting of his horses was heard from Dan; the whole land trembled at the sound of the neighing of his strong ones; for they are come, and have devoured the land and all that is in it." '

'Mr Balfour,' answered Morton, 'I neither undertake to subscribe to or refute your complaints against the government. I have endeavoured to repay a debt due to the comrade of my father, by giving you shelter in your distress, but you will excuse me from engaging myself either in your cause, or in controversy. I will leave you to repose, and heartily wish it were in my power to render your condition more comfortable.'

'But I shall see you, I trust, in the morning, ere I depart? – I am not a man whose bowels yearn after kindred and friends of this world. When I put my hand to the plough,[7] I entered into a covenant with my worldly affections that I should not look back on the things I left behind me. Yet the son of mine ancient comrade is to me as mine own, and I cannot behold him without the deep and firm belief, that I shall one day see him gird on his

sword in the dear and precious cause for which his father fought
and bled.'

With a promise on Morton's part that he would call the
refugee when it was time for him to pursue his journey, they
parted for the night.

Morton retired to a few hours' rest; but his imagination, disturbed by the events of the day, did not permit him to enjoy
sound repose. There was a blended vision of horror before him,
in which his new friend seemed to be a principal actor. The fair
form of Edith Bellenden also mingled in his dream, weeping,
and with dishevelled hair, and appearing to call on him for
comfort and assistance, which he had not in his power to render.
He awoke from these unrefreshing slumbers with a feverish
impulse, and a heart which foreboded disaster. There was already
a tinge of dazzling lustre on the verge of the distant hills, and
the dawn was abroad in all the freshness of a summer morning.

'I have slept too long,' he exclaimed to himself, 'and must
now hasten to forward the journey of this unfortunate fugitive.'

He dressed himself as fast as possible, opened the door of the
house with as little noise as he could, and hastened to the place of
refuge occupied by the Covenanter. Morton entered on tiptoe,
for the determined tone and manner, as well as the unusual
language and sentiments of this singular individual, had struck
him with a sensation approaching to awe. Balfour was still asleep.
A ray of light streamed on his uncurtained couch, and showed
to Morton the working of his harsh features, which seemed
agitated by some strong internal cause of disturbance. He had not
undressed. Both his arms were above the bed-cover, the right
hand strongly clenched, and occasionally making that abortive
attempt to strike which usually attends dreams of violence; the
left was extended, and agitated, from time to time, by a movement as if repulsing some one. The perspiration stood on his
brow, 'like bubbles in a late disturbed stream,'[8] and these marks
of emotion were accompanied with broken words which escaped
from him at intervals – 'Thou art taken, Judas[9] – thou art taken
– Cling not to my knees – cling not to my knees – hew him
down! – A priest? Ay, a priest of Baal, to be bound and slain,
even at the brook Kishon.[10] – Fire arms will not prevail against

him – Strike – thrust with the cold iron – put him out of pain – put him out of pain, were it but for the sake of his grey hairs.'

Much alarmed at the import of these expressions, which seemed to burst from him even in sleep with the stern energy accompanying the perpetration of some act of violence, Morton shook his guest by the shoulder in order to awake him. The first words he uttered were, 'Bear me where ye will, I will avouch the deed!'

His glance around having then fully awakened him, he at once assumed all the stern and gloomy composure of his ordinary manner, and throwing himself on his knees, before speaking to Morton, poured forth an ejaculatory prayer for the suffering Church of Scotland, entreating that the blood of her murdered saints and martyrs might be precious in the sight of Heaven, and that the shield of the Almighty might be spread over the scattered remnant, who, for His name's sake, were abiders in the wilderness. Vengeance – speedy and ample vengeance on the oppressors, was the concluding petition of his devotions, which he expressed aloud in strong and emphatic language, rendered more impressive by the Orientalism of Scripture.

When he had finished his prayer he arose, and, taking Morton by the arm, they descended together to the stable, where the Wanderer (to give Burley a title which was often conferred on his sect) began to make his horse ready to pursue his journey. When the animal was saddled and bridled, Burley requested Morton to walk with him a gun-shot into the wood, and direct him to the right road for gaining the moors. Morton readily complied, and they walked for some time in silence under the shade of some fine old trees, pursuing a sort of natural path, which, after passing through woodland for about half a mile, led into the bare and wild country which extends to the foot of the hills.

There was little conversation between them, until at length Burley suddenly asked Morton, 'Whether the words he had spoken over-night had borne fruit in his mind?'

Morton answered, 'That he remained of the same opinion which he formerly held, and was determined, at least as far and as long as possible, to unite the duties of a good Christian with those of a peaceful subject.'

'In other words,' replied Burley, 'you are desirous to serve both God and Mammon [11] – to be one day professing the truth with your lips, and the next day in arms, at the command of carnal and tyrannic authority, to shed the blood of those who for the truth have forsaken all things? Think ye,' he continued, 'to touch pitch and remain undefiled? to mix in the ranks of malignants, papists, papa-prelatists, latitudinarians, and scoffers; to partake of their sports, which are like the meat offered unto idols; to hold intercourse, perchance, with their daughters, as the sons of God with the daughters of men in the world before the flood [12] – Think you, I say, to do all these things, and yet remain free from pollution? I say unto you, that all communication with the enemies of the Church is the accursed thing which God hateth! Touch not – taste not – handle not! And grieve not, young man, as if you alone were called upon to subdue your carnal affections, and renounce the pleasures which are a snare to your feet – I say to you, that the Son of David hath denounced no better lot on the whole generation of mankind.'

He then mounted his horse, and, turning to Morton, repeated the text of Scripture, 'An heavy yoke was ordained for the sons of Adam from the day they go out of their mother's womb, till the day that they return to the mother of all things; from him who is clothed in blue silk and weareth a crown, even to him who weareth simple linen, – wrath, envy, trouble, and unquietness, rigour, strife, and fear of death in the time of rest.' [13]

Having uttered these words he set his horse in motion, and soon disappeared among the boughs of the forest.

'Farewell, stern enthusiast,' said Morton, looking after him; 'in some moods of my mind, how dangerous would be the society of such a companion! If I am unmoved by his zeal for abstract doctrines of faith, or rather for a peculiar mode of worship, (such was the purport of his reflections,) can I be a man, and a Scotchman, and look with indifference on that persecution which has made wise men mad? Was not the cause of freedom, civil and religious, that for which my father fought; and shall I do well to remain inactive, or to take the part of an oppressive government, if there should appear any rational prospect of redressing the insufferable wrongs to which my miserable countrymen are subjected? – And yet, who shall warrant me that these people, rendered wild by persecution, would not, in the hour of victory, be as cruel and as intolerant as those by whom they are now hunted down? What degree of moderation, or of mercy, can be expected from this Burley, so distinguished as one of their principal champions, and who seems even now to be reeking from some recent deed of violence, and to feel stings of remorse, which even his enthusiasm cannot altogether stifle? I am weary of seeing nothing but violence and fury around me – now assuming the mask of lawful authority, now taking that of religious zeal. I am sick of my country – of myself – of my dependent situation – of my repressed feelings – of these woods – of that river – of that house – of all but – Edith, and she can never be mine! Why should I haunt her walks? – Why encourage my own delusion, and perhaps hers? – She can never be mine. Her grandmother's pride – the opposite principles of our families – my wretched state of dependence – a poor miserable slave, for I have not even the wages of a servant – all circumstances give the lie to the vain hope that we can ever be united. Why then protract a delusion so painful?

'But I am no slave,' he said aloud, and drawing himself up to his full stature – 'no slave, in one respect, surely. I can change my abode – my father's sword is mine, and Europe lies open before me, as before him and hundreds besides of my countrymen, who have filled it with the fame of their exploits. Perhaps some lucky chance may raise me to a rank with our Ruthvens, our Lesleys, our Monroes,[14] the chosen leaders of the famous Protestant champion, Gustavus Adolphus, or, if not, a soldier's life or a soldier's grave.'

When he had formed this determination, he found himself near the door of his uncle's house, and resolved to lose no time in making him acquainted with it.

'Another glance of Edith's eye, another walk by Edith's side, and my resolution would melt away. I will take an irrevocable step, therefore, and then see her for the last time.'

In this mood he entered the wainscotted parlour, in which his

uncle was already placed at his morning's refreshment, a huge
plate of oatmeal porridge, with a corresponding allowance of
butter-milk. The favourite housekeeper was in attendance, half
standing, half resting on the back of a chair, in a posture betwixt
freedom and respect. The old gentleman had been remarkably
tall in his earlier days, an advantage which he now lost by stooping to such a degree, that at a meeting, where there was some
dispute concerning the sort of arch which should be thrown over
a considerable brook, a facetious neighbour proposed to offer
Milnwood a handsome sum for his curved backbone, alleging
that he would sell any thing that belonged to him. Splay feet of
unusual size, long thin hands, garnished with nails which seldom
felt the steel, a wrinkled and puckered visage, the length of
which corresponded with that of his person, together with a pair
of little sharp bargain-making grey eyes, that seemed eternally
looking out for their advantage, completed the highly unpromis-
ing exterior of Mr Morton of Milnwood. As it would have been
very injudicious to have lodged a liberal or benevolent disposition in such an unworthy cabinet, nature had suited his person
with a mind exactly in conformity with it, that is to say, mean,
selfish, and covetous.

When this amiable personage was aware of the presence of his
nephew, he hastened, before addressing him, to swallow the
spoonful of porridge which he was in the act of conveying to his
mouth, and, as it chanced to be scalding hot, the pain occasioned
by its descent down his throat and into his stomach, inflamed
the ill-humour with which he was already prepared to meet his
kinsman.

'The deil take them that made them!' was his first ejaculation,
apostrophizing his mess of porridge.

'They're gude parritch eneugh,' said Mrs Wilson, 'if ye wad
but take time to sup them. I made them mysell; but if folk winna
hae patience, they should get their thrapples causewayed.'

'Haud your peace, Alison! I was speaking to my nevoy. – How
is this, sir? And what sort o' scampering gates are these o'
going on. Ye were not at hame last night till near midnight.'

'Thereabouts, sir, I believe,' answered Morton, in an indifferent tone.

'Thereabouts, sir? – What sort of an answer is that, sir? Why came ye na hame when other folk left the grund?'

'I suppose you know the reason very well, sir,' said Morton; 'I had the fortune to be the best marksman of the day, and remained, as is usual, to give some little entertainment to the other young men.'

'The deevil ye did, sir! And ye come to tell me that to my face? *You* pretend to gie entertainments, that canna come by a dinner except by sorning on a carefu' man like me? But if ye put me to charges, I'se work it out o' ye. I seena why ye shouldna haud the pleugh, now that the pleughman has left us; it wad set ye better than wearing thae green duds, and wasting your siller on powther and lead; it wad put ye in an honest calling, and wad keep ye in bread without being behadden to ony ane.'

'I am very ambitious of learning such a calling, sir, but I don't understand driving the plough.'

'And what for no? It's easier than your gunning and archery that ye like sae weel. Auld Davie is ca'ing it e'en now, and ye may be goadsman for the first twa or three days, and tak tent ye dinna o'erdrive the owsen, and then ye will be fit to gang between the stilts. Ye'll ne'er learn younger, I'll be your caution. Haggie-holm is heavy land, and Davie is ower auld to keep the coulter down now.'

'I beg pardon for interrupting you, sir, but I have formed a scheme for myself, which will have the same effect of relieving you of the burden and charge attending my company.'

'Ay? Indeed? a scheme o' yours? that must be a denty ane!' said the uncle, with a very peculiar sneer; 'let's hear about it, lad.'

'It is said in two words, sir. I intend to leave this country, and serve abroad, as my father did before these unhappy troubles broke out at home. His name will not be so entirely forgotten in the countries where he served, but that it will procure his son at least the opportunity of trying his fortune as a soldier.'

'Gude be gracious to us!' exclaimed the housekeeper; 'our young Mr Harry gang abroad? na, na! eh, na! that maun never be.'

Milnwood, entertaining no thought or purpose of parting with his nephew, who was, moreover, very useful to him in many respects, was thunderstruck at this abrupt declaration of independence from a person whose deference to him had hitherto been unlimited. He recovered himself, however, immediately.

'And wha do you think is to give you the means, young man, for such a wild-goose chase? Not I, I am sure. I can hardly support you at hame. And ye wad be marrying, I'se warrant, as your father did afore ye, too, and sending your uncle hame a pack o' weans to be fighting and skirling through the house in my auld days, and to take wing and flee aff like yoursell, whenever they were asked to serve a turn about the town?'

'I have no thoughts of ever marrying,' answered Henry.

'Hear till him now!' said the housekeeper. 'It's a shame to hear a douce young lad speak in that way, since a' the warld kens that they maun either marry or do waur.'

'Haud your peace, Alison,' said her master; 'and you, Harry,' (he added more mildly,) 'put this nonsense out o' your head – this comes o' letting ye gang a-sodgering for a day – mind ye hae nae siller, lad, for ony sic nonsense plans.'

'I beg your pardon, sir, my wants shall be very few; and would you please to give me the gold chain, which the Margrave gave to my father after the battle of Lutzen' –[15]

'Mercy on us! the gowd chain?' exclaimed his uncle.

'The chain of gowd!' re-echoed the housekeeper, both aghast with astonishment at the audacity of the proposal.

– 'I will keep a few links,' continued the young man, 'to remind me of him by whom it was won, and the place where he won it,' continued Morton; 'the rest shall furnish me the means of following the same career in which my father obtained that mark of distinction.'

'Mercifu' powers!' exclaimed the governante, 'my master wears it every Sunday!'

'Sunday and Saturday,' added old Milnwood, 'whenever I put on my black velvet coat; and Wylie Macktrickit is partly of opinion it's a kind of heir-loom, that rather belangs to the head of the house than to the immediate descendant. It has three thousand links; I have counted them a thousand times. It's worth three hundred pounds sterling.'

'That is more than I want, sir; if you choose to give me the third part of the money, and five links of the chain, it will amply serve my purpose, and the rest will be some slight atonement for the expense and trouble I have put you to.'

'The laddie's in a creel!' exclaimed his uncle. 'O, sirs, what will become o' the rigs o' Milnwood when I am dead and gane! He would fling the crown of Scotland awa, if he had it.'

'Hout, sir,' said the old housekeeper, 'I maun e'en say it's partly your ain faut. Ye maunna curb his head ower sair in neither; and, to be sure, since he *has* gane doun to the Howff, ye maun just e'en pay the lawing.'

'If it be not abune twa dollars, Alison,' said the old gentleman, very reluctantly.

'I'll settle it mysell wi' Niel Blane, the first time I gang down to the clachan,' said Alison, 'cheaper than your honour or Mr Harry can do;' and then whispered to Henry, 'Dinna vex him ony mair; I'll pay the lave out o' the butter siller, and nae mair words about it.' Then proceeding aloud, 'And ye maunna speak o' the young gentleman hauding the pleugh; there's puir distressed whigs enow about the country will be glad to do that for a bite and a soup – it sets them far better than the like o' him.'

'And then we'll hae the dragoons on us,' said Milnwood, 'for comforting and entertaining intercommuned rebels; a bonny strait ye wad put us in! – But take your breakfast, Harry, and then lay by your new green coat, and put on your Raploch grey; it's a mair mensfu' and thrifty dress, and a mair seemly sight, than thae dangling slops and ribbands.'

Morton left the room, perceiving plainly that he had at present no chance of gaining his purpose, and, perhaps, not altogether displeased at the obstacles which seemed to present themselves to his leaving the neighbourhood of Tillietudlem. The housekeeper followed him into the next room, patting him on the back, and bidding him 'be a gude bairn, and pit by his braw things.'

'And I'll loop doun your hat, and lay by the band and ribband,' said the officious dame; 'and ye maun never, at no hand, speak o' leaving the land, or of selling the gowd chain, for your uncle has an unco pleasure in looking on you, and in counting the links of the chainzie; and ye ken auld folk canna last for ever; sae the chain, and the lands, and a' will be your ain ae day; and ye may marry ony leddy in the country-side ye like, and keep a braw house at Milnwood, for there's enow o' means; and is not that worth waiting for, my dow?'

There was something in the latter part of the prognostic which sounded so agreeably in the ears of Morton, that he shook the old dame cordially by the hand, and assured her he was much obliged by her good advice, and would weigh it carefully before he proceeded to act upon his former resolution.

CHAPTER 7

From seventeen years till now, almost fourscore,
Here lived I, but now live here no more.
At seventeen years many their fortunes seek,
But at fourscore it is too late a week.

As You Like it[1]

WE must conduct our readers to the Tower of Tillietudlem, to which Lady Margaret Bellenden had returned, in romantic phrase, malecontent and full of heaviness, at the unexpected, and, as she deemed it, indelible affront, which had been brought upon her dignity by the public miscarriage of Goose Gibbie. That unfortunate man-at-arms was forthwith commanded to drive his feathered charge to the most remote parts of the common moor, and on no account to awaken the grief or resentment of his lady, by appearing in her presence while the sense of the affront was yet recent.

The next proceeding of Lady Margaret was to hold a solemn court of justice, to which Harrison and the butler were admitted, partly on the footing of witnesses, partly as assessors, to enquire into the recusancy of Cuddie Headrigg the ploughman, and the abetment which he had received from his mother – these being regarded as the original causes of the disaster which had befallen the chivalry of Tillietudlem. The charge being fully made out and substantiated, Lady Margaret resolved to reprimand the culprits in person, and, if she found them impenitent, to extend the censure into a sentence of expulsion from the barony. Miss Bellenden alone ventured to say any thing in behalf of the accused, but her countenance did not profit them as it might have done on any other occasion. For so soon as Edith had heard it ascertained that the unfortunate cavalier had not suffered in his person, his disaster had affected her with an irresistible disposition to laugh, which, in spite of Lady Margaret's indignation, or rather irritated, as usual, by restraint, had broke out repeatedly on her return homeward, until her grandmother, in no shape imposed upon by the several fictitious causes which the young lady assigned for her ill-timed risibility, upbraided her in very bitter terms with being insensible to the honour of her family. Miss Bellenden's intercession, therefore, had, on this occasion, little or no chance to be listened to.

As if to evince the rigour of her disposition, Lady Margaret, on this solemn occasion, exchanged the ivory-headed cane with which she commonly walked, for an immense gold-headed staff which had belonged to her father, the deceased Earl of Torwood, and which, like a sort of mace of office, she only made use of on occasions of special solemnity. Supported by this awful baton of command, Lady Margaret Bellenden entered the cottage of the delinquents.

There was an air of consciousness about old Mause, as she rose from her wicker chair in the chimney-nook, not with the cordial alertness of visage which used, on other occasions, to express the honour she felt in the visit of her lady, but with a certain solemnity and embarrassment, like an accused party on his first appearance in presence of his judge, before whom he is, nevertheless, determined to assert his innocence. Her arms were folded, her mouth primmed into an expression of respect, mingled with obstinacy, her whole mind apparently bent up to the solemn interview. With her best curtsey to the ground, and a mute motion of reverence, Mause pointed to the chair, which, on former occasions, Lady Margaret (for the good lady was somewhat of a gossip) had deigned to occupy for half an hour sometimes at a time, hearing the news of the county and of the borough. But at present her mistress was far too indignant for such condescension. She rejected the mute invitation with a haughty wave of her hand, and drawing herself up as she spoke, she uttered the following interrogatory in a tone calculated to overwhelm the culprit.

'Is it true, Mause, as I am informed by Harrison, Gudyill, and others of my people, that you hae taen it upon you, contrary to the faith you owe to God and the king, and to me, your natural lady and mistress, to keep back your son frae the wappen-schaw, held by the order of the sheriff, and to return his armour and abulyiements at a moment when it was impossible to find a suitable delegate in his stead, whereby the barony of Tillie-tudlem, baith in the person of its mistress and indwellers, has incurred sic a disgrace and dishonour as hasna befa'en the family since the days of Malcolm Canmore?'[2]

Mause's habitual respect for her mistress was extreme; she hesitated, and one or two short coughs expressed the difficulty she had in defending herself.

'I am sure – my leddy – hem, hem! – I am sure I am sorry – very sorry that ony cause of displeasure should hae occurred – but my son's illness' –

'Dinna tell me of your son's illness, Mause! Had he been sincerely unweel, ye would hae been at the Tower by daylight to get something that wad do him gude; there are few ailments that I havena medical recipes for, and that ye ken fu' weel.'

'O ay, my leddy! I am sure ye hae wrought wonderful cures; the last thing ye sent Cuddie, when he had the batts, e'en wrought like a charm.'

'Why, then, woman, did ye not apply to me, if there was ony real need? – but there was none, ye fause-hearted vassal that ye are!'

'Your leddyship never ca'd me sic a word as that before. Ohon! that I suld live to be ca'd sae,' she continued, bursting into tears, 'and me a born servant o' the house o' Tillietudlem! I am sure they belie baith Cuddie and me sair, if they said he wadna fight ower the boots in blude for your leddyship and Miss Edith, and the auld Tower – ay suld he, and I would rather see him buried beneath it, than he suld gie way – but thir ridings and wappen-schawings, my leddy, I hae nae broo o' them ava. I can find nae warrant for them whatsoever.'

'Nae warrant for them?' cried the high-born dame. 'Do ye na ken, woman, that ye are bound to be liege vassals in all hunting, hosting, watching, and warding, when lawfully summoned thereto in my name? Your service is not gratuitous. I trow ye hae land for it. Ye're kindly tenants[3]; hae a cot-house, a kale-yard, and a cow's grass on the common. – Few hae been brought farther ben, and ye grudge your son suld gie me a day's service in the field?'

'Na, my leddy – na, my leddy, it's no that,' exclaimed Mause, greatly embarrassed, 'but ane canna serve twa maisters; and, if the truth maun e'en come out, there's Ane abune whase commands I maun obey before your leddyship's. I am sure I would put neither king's nor kaisar's, nor ony earthly creature's, afore them.'

'How mean ye by that, ye auld fule woman? – D'ye think that I order ony thing against conscience?'

'I dinna pretend to say that, my leddy, in regard o' your leddyship's conscience, which has been brought up, as it were, wi' prelatic principles; but ilka ane maun walk by the light o' their ain; and mine,' said Mause, waxing bolder as the conference became animated, 'tells me that I suld leave a' – cot, kale-yard, and cow's grass – and suffer a', rather than that I or mine should put on harness in an unlawfu' cause.'

'Unlawfu'!' exclaimed her mistress; 'the cause to which you are called by your lawful leddy and mistress – by the command of the king – by the writ of the privy council – by the order of the lord-lieutenant – by the warrant of the sheriff?'

'Ay, my leddy, nae doubt; but no to displeasure your leddyship, ye'll mind that there was ance a king in Scripture they ca'd Nebuchadnezzar, and he set up a golden image in the plain o' Dura,[4] as it might be in the haugh yonder by the water-side, where the array were warned to meet yesterday; and the princes, and the governors, and the captains, and the judges themsells, forby the treasurers, the counsellors, and the sheriffs, were warned to the dedication thereof, and commanded to fall down and worship at the sound of the cornet, flute, harp, sackbut, psaltery, and all kinds of music.'

'And what o' a' this, ye fule wife? Or what had Nebuchadnezzar to do with the wappen-schaw of the Upper Ward of Clydesdale?'

'Only just thus far, my leddy,' continued Mause, firmly, 'that prelacy is like the great golden image in the plain of Dura, and that as Shadrach, Meshach, and Abednego, were borne out in refusing to bow down and worship, so neither shall Cuddy Head-rigg, your leddyship's poor pleughman, at least wi' his auld mither's consent, make murgeons or Jenny-flections, as they ca' them, in the house of the prelates and curates, nor gird him wi' armour to fight in their cause, either at the sound of kettle-drums, organs, bagpipes, or ony other kind of music whatever.'

Lady Margaret Bellenden heard this exposition of Scripture with the greatest possible indignation, as well as surprise.

'I see which way the wind blaws,' she exclaimed, after a pause of astonishment; 'the evil spirit of the year sixteen hundred and forty-twa[5] is at wark again as merrily as ever, and ilka auld wife in the chimley-neuck will be for knapping doctrine wi' doctors o' divinity and the godly fathers o' the church.'

'If your leddyship means the bishops and curates, I'm sure they hae been but stepfathers to the Kirk o' Scotland. And, since your leddyship is pleased to speak o' parting wi' us, I am free to tell you a piece o' my mind in another article. Your leddyship and the steward hae been pleased to propose that my son Cuddie suld work in the barn wi' a new-fangled machine[6] for dighting the corn frae the chaff, thus impiously thwarting the will of Divine Providence, by raising wind for your leddyship's ain particular use by human art, instead of soliciting it by prayer, or waiting patiently for whatever dispensation of wind Providence was pleased to send upon the sheeling-hill. Now, my leddy' –

'The woman would drive ony reasonable being daft!' said Lady Margaret; then resuming her tone of authority and in-difference, she concluded, 'Weel, Mause, I'll just end where I sud hae begun – ye're ower learned and ower godly for me to dispute wi'; sae I have just this to say, – either Cuddie must attend musters when he's lawfully warned by the ground officer, or the sooner he and you flit and quit my bounds the better; there's nae scarcity o' auld wives or ploughmen; but, if there were, I had rather that the rigs of Tillietudlem bare naething but windle-straes and sandy lavrocks[7] than that they were ploughed by rebels to the king.'

'Aweel, my leddy,' said Mause, 'I was born here, and thought to die where my father died; and your leddyship has been a kind mistress, I'll ne'er deny that, and I'se ne'er cease to pray for you, and for Miss Edith, and that ye may be brought to see the error of your ways. But still' –

'The error of my ways!' interrupted Lady Margaret, much incensed – 'The error of *my* ways, ye uncivil woman?'

'Ou, ay, my leddy, we are blinded that live in this valley of tears and darkness, and hae a' ower mony errors, grit folks as weel as sma' – but, as I said, my puir bennison will rest wi' you and yours wherever I am. I will be wae to hear o' your affliction, and blithe to hear o' your prosperity, temporal and spiritual. But I canna prefer the commands of an earthly mistress of those of a heavenly master, and sae I am e'en ready to suffer for righteousness' sake.'

'It is very well,' said Lady Margaret, turning her back in great displeasure; 'ye ken my will, Mause, in the matter. I'll hae nae whiggery in the barony of Tillietudlem – the next thing wad be to set up a conventicle in my very withdrawing room.'

Having said this, she departed, with an air of great dignity; and Mause, giving way to feelings which she had suppressed during the interview, – for she, like her mistress, had her own feeling of pride, – now lifted up her voice and wept aloud.

Cuddie, whose malady, real or pretended, still detained him in bed, lay *perdu* during all this conference, snugly ensconced within his boarded bedstead, and terrified to death lest Lady Margaret, whom he held in hereditary reverence, should have detected his presence, and bestowed on him personally some of those bitter reproaches with which she loaded his mother. But as soon as he thought her ladyship fairly out of hearing, he bounced up in his nest.

'The foul fa' ye, that I suld say sae,' he cried out to his mother, 'for a lang-tongued clavering wife, as my father, honest man, aye ca'd ye! Couldna ye let the leddy alane wi' your whiggery? And I was e'en as great a gomeral to let ye persuade me to lie up here amang the blankets like a hurcheon, instead o' gaun to the wappen-schaw like other folk. Odd, but I put a trick on ye, for I was out at the window-hole when your auld back was turned, and awa down by to hae a baff at the popinjay, and I shot within twa on't. I cheated the leddy for your clavers, but I wasna gaun to cheat my joe. But she may marry whae she likes now, for I'm clean dung ower. This is a waur dirdum than we got frae Mr Gudyill when ye garr'd me refuse to eat the plum-porridge on Yule-eve, as if it were ony matter to God or man whether a pleughman had suppit on minched pies or sour sowens.'

'O, whisht, my bairn, whisht,' replied Mause; 'thou kensna about thae things – It was forbidden meat, things dedicated to set days and holidays, which are inhibited to the use of protest-ant Christians.'

'And now,' continued her son, 'ye hae brought the leddy her-sell on our hands! – An I could but hae gotten some decent claes in, I wad hae spanged out o' bed, and tauld her I wad ride where she liked, night or day, an she wad but leave us the free house and the yaird, that grew the best early kale in the haill country, and the cow's grass.'

'O wow! my winsome bairn, Cuddie,' continued the old dame, 'murmur not at the dispensation; never grudge suffering in the gude cause.'

'But what ken I if the cause is gude or no, mither,' rejoined Cuddie, 'for a' ye bleeze out sae muckle doctrine about it? It's clean beyond my comprehension a'thegither. I see nae sae muckle difference atween the twa ways o't as a' the folk pretend. It's very true the curates read aye the same words ower again; and if they be right words, what for no? A gude tale's no the waur o' being twice tauld, I trow; and a body has aye the better chance to understand it. Every body's no sae gleg at the uptake as ye are yoursell, mither.'

'O, my dear Cuddie, this is the sairest distress of a',' said the anxious mother – 'O, how aften have I shown ye the difference between a pure evangelical doctrine, and ane that's corrupt wi' human inventions? O, my bairn, if no for your ain saul's sake, yet for my grey hairs' –

'Weel, mither,' said Cuddie, interrupting her, 'what need ye mak sae muckle din about it? I hae aye dune whate'er ye bade

me, and gaed to kirk whare'er ye likit on the Sundays, and
fended weel for ye in the ilka days besides. And that's what
vexes me mair than a' the rest, when I think how I am to fend
for ye now in thae brickle times. I am no clear if I can pleugh
ony place but the Mains and Mucklewhame, at least I never tried
ony other grund, and it wadna come natural to me. And nae
neighbouring heritors will daur to take us, after being turned
aff thae bounds for non-enormity.'

'Non-conformity, hinnie,' sighed Mause, 'is the name that
thae warldly men gie us.'

'Weel, aweel – we'll hae to gang to a far country, maybe twall
or fifteen miles aff. I could be a dragoon, nae doubt, for I can
ride and play wi' the broadsword a bit, but ye wad be roaring
about your blessing and your grey hairs.' (Here Mause's exclamations became extreme.) 'Weel, weel, I but spoke o't; besides,
ye're ower auld to be sitting cocked up on a baggage-waggon wi'
Eppie Dumblane, the corporal's wife. Sae what's to come o' us I
canna weel see – I doubt I'll hae to tak the hills wi' the wild
whigs, as they ca' them, and then it will be my lot to be shot
down like a mawkin at some dikeside, or to be sent to heaven
wi' a Saint Johnstone's tippit[8] about my hause.'

'O, my bonnie Cuddie,' said the zealous Mause, 'forbear sic
carnal, self-seeking language, whilk is just a misdoubting o'
Providence – I have not seen the son of the righteous begging his
bread, sae says the text;[9] and your father was a douce honest
man, though somewhat warldly in his dealings, and cumbered
about earthly things, e'en like yourself, my jo!'

'Aweel,' said Cuddie, after a little consideration, 'I see but ae
gate for't, and that's a cauld coal to blaw at, mither. Howsom-
ever, mither, ye hae some guess o' a wee bit kindness that's atween
Miss Edith and young Mr Henry Morton, that suld be ca'd
young Milnwood, and that I hae whiles carried a bit book, or
maybe a bit letter, quietly atween them, and made believe never
to ken wha it cam frae, though I kend brawly. There's whiles
convenience in a body looking a wee stupid – and I have aften
seen them walking at e'en on the little path by Dinglewood-burn;
but naebody ever kend a word about it frae Cuddie; I ken I'm
gay thick in the head, but I'm as honest as our auld fore-hand

ox, puir fallow, that I'll ne'er work ony mair – I hope they'll be
as kind to him that come ahint me as I hae been. – But, as I was
saying, we'll awa down to Milnwood and tell Mr Harry our
distress. They want a pleughman, and the grund's no unlike our
ain – I am sure Mr Harry will stand my part, for he's a kind-
hearted gentleman. – I'll get but little penny-fee, for his uncle,
auld Nippie Milnwood, has as close a grip as the deil himsell.
But we'll aye win a bit bread, and a drap kale, and a fire-side
and theeking ower our heads, and that's a' well want for a
season. – Sae get up, mither, and sort your things to gang away;
for since sae it is that gang we maun, I wad like ill to wait till
Mr Harrison and auld Gudyill cam to pu' us out by the lug and
the horn.'

CHAPTER 8

The devil a puritan, or any thing else he is, but a time-server.

Twelfth Night[1]

IT was evening when Mr Henry Morton perceived an old
woman, wrapped in her tartan plaid,[2] supported by a stout,
stupid-looking fellow, in hoddin-grey, approach the house of
Milnwood. Old Mause made her courtesy, but Cuddie took the
lead in addressing Morton. Indeed, he had previously stipulated
with his mother that he was to manage matters his own way; for
though he readily allowed his general inferiority of understanding, and filially submitted to the guidance of his mother on most
ordinary occasions, yet he said, 'For getting a service, or getting
forward in the warld, he could somegate gar the wee pickle sense
he had gang muckle farther than hers, though she could crack
like ony minister o' them a'.'

Accordingly, he thus opened the conversation with young
Morton:

'A braw night this for the rye, your honour; the west park will
be breering bravely this e'en.'

'I do not doubt it, Cuddie; but what can have brought your
mother – this is your mother, is it not?' (Cuddie nodded.) 'What

can have brought your mother and you down the water so late?'

'Troth, stir, just what gars the auld wives trot – neshessity, stir – I'm seeking for service, stir.'

'For service, Cuddie, and at this time of the year? how comes that?'

Mause could forbear no longer. Proud alike of her cause and her sufferings, she commenced with an affected humility of tone, 'It has pleased Heaven, an it like your honour, to distinguish us by a visitation' –

'Deil's in the wife and nae gude!' whispered Cuddie to his mother, 'an ye come out wi' your whiggery, they'll do daur open a door to us through the haill country!' Then aloud and addressing Morton, 'My mother's auld, stir, and she has rather forgotten hersell in speaking to my leddy, that canna weel bide to be contradickit, (as I ken naebody likes it if they could help themsells,) especially by her ain folk, – and Mr Harrison the steward, and Gudyill the butler, they're no very fond o' us, and it's ill sitting at Rome and striving wi' the Pope; sae I thought it best to flit before ill came to waur – and here's a wee bit line to your honour frae a friend will maybe say some mair about it.'

Morton took the billet, and crimsoning up to the ears, between joy and surprise, read these words: 'If you can serve these poor helpless people, you will oblige E. B.'

It was a few instants before he could attain composure enough to ask, 'And what is your object, Cuddie? and how can I be of use to you?'

'Wark, stir, wark, and a service, is my object – a bit beild for my mither and mysell – we hae gude plenishing o' our ain, if we had the cast o' a cart to bring it down – and milk and meal, and greens enow, for I'm gay gleg at meal-time, and sae is my mither, lang may it be sae – And, for the penny-fee and a' that, I'll just leave it to the laird and you. I ken ye'll no see a poor lad wranged, if ye can help it.'

Morton shook his head. 'For the meat and lodging, Cuddie, I think I can promise something; but the penny-fee will be a hard chapter, I doubt.'

'I'll tak my chance o't, stir,' replied the candidate for service, 'rather than gang down about Hamilton, or ony sic far country.'

'Well; step into the kitchen, Cuddie, and I'll do what I can for you."

The negotiation was not without difficulties. Morton had first to bring over the housekeeper, who made a thousand objections, as usual, in order to have the pleasure of being besought and entreated; but, when she was gained over, it was comparatively easy to induce old Milnwood to accept of a servant, whose wages were to be in his own option. An outhouse was, therefore, assigned to Mause and her son for their habitation, and it was settled that they were for the time to be admitted to eat of the frugal fare provided for the family, until their own establishment should be completed. As for Morton, he exhausted his own very slender stock of money in order to make Cuddie such a present, under the name of *arles*, as might show his sense of the value of the recommendation delivered to him.

'And now we're settled ance mair,' said Cuddie to his mother, 'and if we're no sae bien and comfortable as we were up yonder, yet life's life ony gate, and we're wi' decent kirk-ganging folk o' your ain persuasion, mither; there will be nae quarrelling about that.'

'Of *my* persuasion, hinnie!' said the too-enlightened Mause; 'wae's me for thy blindness and theirs. O, Cuddie, they are but in the court of the Gentiles, and will ne'er win farther ben, I doubt; they are but little better than the prelatists themsells. They wait on the ministry of that blinded man, Peter Poundtext, ance a precious teacher of the Word, but now a backsliding pastor, that has, for the sake of stipend and family maintenance, forsaken the strict path, and gane astray after the black Indulgence. O, my son, had ye but profited by the gospel doctrines ye hae heard in the Glen of Bengonnar, frae the dear Richard Rumbleberry, that sweet youth, who suffered martyrdom in the Grass-market,[3] afore Candlemas! Didna ye hear him say, that Erastianism was as bad as Prelacy, and that the Indulgence was as bad as Erastianism?'

'Heard ever ony body the like o' this!' interrupted Cuddie; 'we'll be driven out o' house and ha' again afore we ken where to turn oursells. Weel, mither, I hae just ae word mair – An I hear ony mair o' your din – afore folk, that is, for I dinna mind your clavers mysell, they aye set me sleeping – but if I hear ony mair din afore folk, as I was saying, about Poundtexts and Rumbleberries, and doctrines and malignants, I'se e'en turn a single sodger mysell, or maybe a sergeant or a captain, if ye plague me the mair, and let Rumbleberry an you gang to the deil thegither. I ne'er gat ony gude by his doctrine, as ye ca't, but a sour fit o' the batts wi' sitting amang the wat moss-hags for four hours at a yoking, and the leddy cured me wi' some hickery-pickery; mair by token, an she had kend how I came by the disorder, she wadna hae been in sic a hurry to mend it.'

Although groaning in spirit over the obdurate and impenitent state, as she thought it, of her son Cuddie, Mause durst neither urge him farther on the topic, nor altogether neglect the warning he had given her. She knew the disposition of her deceased helpmate, whom this surviving pledge of their union greatly resembled, and remembered, that although submitting implicitly in most things to her boast of superior acuteness, he used on certain occasions, when driven to extremity, to be seized with fits of obstinacy, which neither remonstrance, flattery, nor threats, were capable of overpowering. Trembling, therefore, at the very possibility of Cuddie's fulfilling his threat, she put a guard over her tongue, and even when Poundtext was commended in her presence, as an able and fructifying preacher, she had the good sense to suppress the contradiction which thrilled upon her tongue, and to express her sentiments no otherwise than by deep groans, which the hearers charitably construed to flow from a vivid recollection of the more pathetic parts of his homilies. How long she could have repressed her feelings it is difficult to say. An unexpected accident relieved her from the necessity.

The Laird of Milnwood kept up all old fashions which were connected with economy. It was, therefore, still the custom in his house, as it had been universal in Scotland about fifty years before, that the domestics, after having placed the dinner on the table, sate down at the lower end of the board, and partook of the share which was assigned to them, in company with their masters. On the day, therefore, after Cuddie's arrival, being the third from the opening of this narrative, old Robin, who was butler, valet-de-chambre, footman, gardener, and what not, in the house of Milnwood, placed on the table an immense charger of broth, thickened with oatmeal and colewort, in which ocean of liquid was indistinctly discovered, by close observers, two or three short ribs of lean mutton sailing to and fro. Two huge baskets, one of bread made of barley and pease, and one of oatcakes, flanked this standing dish. A large boiled salmon would now-a-days have indicated more liberal house-keeping; but at that period salmon was caught in such plenty in the considerable rivers in Scotland, that instead of being accounted a delicacy, it was generally applied to feed the servants, who are said sometimes to have stipulated that they should not be required to eat a food so luscious and surfeiting in its quality above five times a-week. The large black jack, filled with very small beer of Milnwood's own brewing, was allowed to the company at discretion, as were the bannocks, cakes, and broth; but the mutton was reserved for the heads of the family, Mrs Wilson included : and a measure of ale, somewhat deserving the name, was set apart in a silver tankard for their exclusive use. A huge kebbock, (a cheese, that is, made with ewe-milk mixed with cow's milk,) and a jar of salt butter, were in common to the company.

To enjoy this exquisite cheer, was placed, at the head of the table, the old Laird himself, with his nephew on the one side, and the favourite housekeeper on the other. At a long interval, and beneath the salt of course, sate old Robin, a meagre, half-starved serving-man, rendered cross and cripple by rheumatism, and a dirty drab of a housemaid, whom use had rendered callous to the daily exercitations which her temper underwent at the hands of her master and Mrs Wilson. A barn-man, a white-headed cow-herd boy, with Cuddie the new ploughman and his mother, completed the party. The other labourers belonging to the property resided in their own houses, happy at least in this, that if their cheer was not more delicate than that which we have described, they could eat their fill, unwatched by the sharp, envious grey eyes of Milnwood, which seemed to measure the quantity that each of his dependents swallowed, as closely as if their glances attended each mouthful in its progress from the lips to the stomach. This close inspection was unfavourable to Cuddie, who sustained much prejudice in his new master's opinion, by the silent celerity with which he caused the victuals to disappear before him. And ever and anon Milnwood turned his eyes from the huge feeder to cast indignant glances upon his nephew, whose repugnance to rustic labour was the principal cause of his needing a ploughman, and who had been the direct means of his hiring this very cormorant.

'Pay thee wages, quotha?' said Milnwood to himself, – 'Thou wilt eat in a week the value of mair than thou canst work for in a month.'

These disagreeable ruminations were interrupted by a loud knocking at the outer-gate. It was a universal custom in Scotland, that, when the family was at dinner, the outer-gate of the courtyard, if there was one, and if not, the door of the house itself, was always shut and locked, and only guests of importance, or persons upon urgent business, sought or received admittance at that time.[4] The family of Milnwood were therefore surprised, and, in the unsettled state of the times, something alarmed, at the earnest and repeated knocking with which the gate was now assailed. Mrs Wilson ran in person to the door, and, having reconnoitred those who were so clamorous for admittance, through some secret aperture with which most Scottish door-ways were furnished for the express purpose, she returned wringing her hands in great dismay, exclaiming, 'The red-coats! the red-coats!'

'Robin – Ploughman – what ca' they ye? – Barnsman – Nevoy Harry – open the door, open the door!' exclaimed old Milnwood, snatching up and slipping into his pocket the two or three silver spoons with which the upper end of the table was garnished, those beneath the salt being of goodly horn. 'Speak them fair, sirs – Lord love ye, speak them fair – they winna bide thrawing – we're a' harried – we're a' harried!'

While the servants admitted the troopers, whose oaths and threats already indicated resentment at the delay they had been put to, Cuddie took the opportunity to whisper to his mother, 'Now, ye daft auld carline, mak yoursell deaf – ye hae made us a' deaf ere now – and let me speak for ye. I wad like ill to get my neck raxed for an auld wife's clashes, though ye be our mither.'

'O, hinny, ay; I'se be silent or thou sall come to ill,' was the corresponding whisper of Mause, 'but bethink ye, my dear, them that deny the Word, the Word will deny' –

Her admonition was cut short by the entrance of the Life-Guardsmen, a party of four troopers, commanded by Bothwell.

In they tramped, making a tremendous clatter upon the stone-floor with the iron-shod heels of their large jack-boots, and the clash and clang of their long, heavy, basket-hilted broad-swords. Milnwood and his housekeeper trembled, from well-grounded apprehensions of the system of exaction and plunder carried on during these domiciliary visits. Henry Morton was discomposed with more special cause, for he remembered that he stood answerable to the laws for having harboured Burley. The widow Mause Headrigg, between fear for her son's life and an overstrained and enthusiastic zeal, which reproached her for consenting even tacitly to belie her religious sentiments, was in a strange quandary. The other servants quaked for they knew not well what. Cuddie alone, with the look of supreme indifference and stupidity which a Scottish peasant can at times assume as a mask for considerable shrewdness and craft, continued to swallow large spoonfuls of his broth, to command which he had drawn within his sphere the large vessel that contained it, and helped himself, amid the confusion, to a sevenfold portion.

'What is your pleasure here, gentlemen?' said Milnwood, humbling himself before the satellites of power.

'We come in behalf of the king,' answered Bothwell; 'why the devil did you keep us so long standing at the door?'

'We were at dinner,' answered Milnwood, 'and the door was locked, as is usual in landward towns[5] in this country. I am sure, gentlemen, if I had kend ony servants of our gude king had stood at the door – But wad ye please to drink some ale – or some brandy – or a cup of canary sack, or claret wine?' making a pause between each offer as long as a stingy bidder at an auction, who is loath to advance his offer for a favourite lot.

'Claret for me,' said one fellow.

'I like ale better,' said another, 'provided it is right juice of John Barleycorn.'

'Better never was malted,' said Milnwood; 'I can hardly say sae muckle for the claret. It's thin and cauld, gentlemen.'

'Brandy will cure that,' said a third fellow; 'a glass of brandy to three glasses of wine prevents the curmurring in the stomach.'

'Brandy, ale, sack, and claret? – we'll try them all,' said Bothwell, 'and stick to that which is best. There's good sense in that, if the damn'dest whig in Scotland had said it.'

Hastily, yet with a reluctant quiver of his muscles, Milnwood lugged out two ponderous keys, and delivered them to the governante.

'The housekeeper,' said Bothwell, taking a seat, and throwing himself upon it, 'is neither so young nor so handsome as to tempt a man to follow her to the gauntrees, and devil a one here is there worth sending in her place. – What's this? – meat?' (searching with a fork among the broth, and fishing up a cutlet of mutton) – 'I think I could eat a bit – why, it's as tough as if the devil's dam had hatched it.'

'If there is any thing better in the house, sir,' said Milnwood, alarmed at these symptoms of disapprobation –

'No, no,' said Bothwell, 'it's not worth while, I must proceed to business. – You attend Poundtext, the presbyterian parson, I understand, Mr Morton?'

Mr Morton hastened to slide in a confession and apology.

'By the indulgence of his gracious majesty and the government, for I wad do nothing out of law – I hae nae objection whatever to the establishment of a moderate episcopacy, but only that I am a country-bred man, and the ministers are a hamelier kind of folk, and I can follow their doctrine better; and, with reverence, sir, it's a mair frugal establishment for the country.'

'Well, I care nothing about that,' said Bothwell; 'they are indulged, and there's an end of it; but, for my part, if I were to give the law, never a crop-ear'd cur of the whole pack should bark in a Scotch pulpit. However, I am to obey commands. – There comes the liquor; put it down, my good old lady.'

He decanted about one-half of a quart bottle of claret into a wooden quaigh or bicker, and took it off at a draught.

'You did your good wine injustice, my friend; – it's better than your brandy, though that's good too. Will you pledge me to the king's health?'

'With pleasure,' said Milnwood, 'in ale, – but I never drink claret, and keep only a very little for some honoured friends.'

'Like me, I suppose,' said Bothwell; and then, pushing the bottle to Henry, he said, 'Here, young man, pledge you the king's health.'

Henry filled a moderate glass in silence, regardless of the hints and pushes of his uncle, which seemed to indicate that he ought to have followed his example, in preferring beer to wine.

'Well,' said Bothwell, 'have ye all drank the toast? – What is that old wife about? Give her a glass of brandy, she shall drink the king's health, by' –

'If your honour pleases,' said Cuddie, with great stolidity of aspect, 'this is my mither, stir; and she's as deaf as Corra-linn[6]; we canna mak her hear day nor door; but if your honour pleases, I am ready to drink the king's health for her in as mony glasses of brandy as ye think neshessary.'

'I dare swear you are,' answered Bothwell; 'you look like a fellow that would stick to brandy – help thyself, man; all's free where'er I come. – Tom, help the maid to a comfortable cup, though she's but a dirty jilt neither. Fill round once more – Here's to our noble commander, Colonel Graham of Claverhouse! – What the devil is the old woman groaning for? She looks as very a whig as ever sate on a hill-side – Do you renounce the Covenant, good woman?'

'Whilk Covenant is your honour meaning? Is it the Covenant of Works, or the Covenant of Grace?'[7] said Cuddie, interposing.

'Any covenant; all covenants that ever were hatched,' answered the trooper.

'Mither,' cried Cuddie, affecting to speak as to a deaf person, 'the gentleman wants to ken if ye will renunce the Covenant of Works?'

'With all my heart, Cuddie,' said Mause, 'and pray that my feet may be delivered from the snare thereof.'

'Come,' said Bothwell, 'the old dame has come more frankly off than I expected. Another cup round, and then we'll proceed to business. – You have all heard, I suppose, of the horrid and barbarous murder committed upon the person of the Archbishop of St Andrews, by ten or eleven armed fanatics?'

All started and looked at each other; at length Milnwood himself answered, 'They had heard of some such misfortune, but were in hopes it had not been true.'

'There is the relation published by government, old gentleman; what do you think of it?'

'Think, sir? Wh – wh – whatever the council please to think of it,' stammered Milnwood.

'I desire to have your opinion more explicitly, my friend,' said the dragoon, authoritatively.

Milnwood's eyes hastily glanced through the paper to pick out the strongest expressions of censure with which it abounded, in gleaning which he was greatly aided by their being printed in italics.

'I think it a – bloody and execrable – murder and parricide – devised by hellish and implacable cruelty – utterly abominable, and a scandal to the land.'[8]

'Well said, old gentleman!' said the querist – 'Here's to thee, and I wish you joy of your good principles. You owe me a cup of thanks for having taught you them; nay, thou shalt pledge me in thine own sack – sour ale sits ill upon a loyal stomach. – Now comes your turn, young man; what think you of the matter in hand?'

'I should have little objection to answer you,' said Henry, 'if I knew what right you had to put the question.'

'The Lord preserve us!' said the old housekeeper, 'to ask the like o' that at a trooper, when a' folk ken they do whatever they like through the haill country wi' man and woman, beast and body.'

The old gentleman exclaimed, in the same horror at his nephew's audacity, 'Hold your peace, sir, or answer the gentleman discreetly. Do you mean to affront the king's authority in the person of a sergeant of the Life-Guards?'

'Silence, all of you!' exclaimed Bothwell, striking his hand fiercely on the table – 'Silence, every one of you, and hear me! – You ask me for my right to examine you, sir (to Henry); my cockade and my broadsword are my commission, and a better one than ever Old Nol⁹ gave to his roundheads; and if you want to know more about it, you may look at the act of council empowering his majesty's officers and soldiers to search for, examine, and apprehend suspicious persons; and, therefore, once more, I ask you your opinion of the death of Archbishop Sharpe – it's a new touch-stone we have got for trying people's metal.'

Henry had, by this time, reflected upon the useless risk to which he would expose the family by resisting the tyrannical power which was delegated to such rude hands; he therefore read the narrative over, and replied, composedly, 'I have no hesitation to say, that the perpetrators of this assassination have committed, in my opinion, a rash and wicked action, which I regret the more, as I foresee it will be made the cause of proceedings against many who are both innocent of the deed, and as far from approving it as myself.'

While Henry thus expressed himself, Bothwell, who bent his eyes keenly upon him, seemed suddenly to recollect his features.

'Aha! my friend Captain Popinjay, I think I have seen you before, and in very suspicious company.'

'I saw you once,' answered Henry, 'in the public-house of the town of –.'

'And with whom did you leave that public-house, youngster? – Was it not with John Balfour of Burley, one of the murderers of the Archbishop?'

'I did leave the house with the person you have named,' answered Henry, 'I scorn to deny it; but, so far from knowing him to be a murderer of the primate, I did not even know at the time that such a crime had been committed.'

'Lord have mercy on me, I am ruined! – utterly ruined and undone!' exclaimed Milnwood. 'That callant's tongue will rin the head aff his ain shoulders, and waste my gudes to the very grey cloak on my back!'

'But you knew Burley,' continued Bothwell, still addressing Henry, and regardless of his uncle's interruption, 'to be an inter-communed rebel and traitor, and you knew the prohibition to deal with such persons. You knew, that, as a loyal subject, you were prohibited to reset, supply, or intercommune with this

attainted traitor, to correspond with him by word, writ, or
message, or to supply him with meat, drink, house, harbour, or
victual, under the highest pains – you knew all this, and yet you
broke the law.' (Henry was silent.) 'Where did you part from
him?' continued Bothwell; 'was it in the highway, or did you
give him harbourage in this very house?'

'In this house!' said his uncle; 'he dared not for his neck bring
ony traitor into a house of mine.'

'Dare he deny that he did so?' said Bothwell.

'As you charge it to me as a crime,' said Henry, 'you will
excuse my saying any thing that will criminate myself.'

'O, the lands of Milnwood! – the bonny lands of Milnwood,
that have been in the name of Morton twa hundred years!' exclaimed his uncle; 'they are barking and fleeing, outfield and
infield,[10] haugh and holme!'

'No, sir,' said Henry, 'you shall not suffer on my account. – I
own,' he continued, addressing Bothwell, 'I did give this man a
night's lodging, as to an old military comrade of my father. But
it was not only without my uncle's knowledge, but contrary to
his express general orders. I trust, if my evidence is considered as
good against myself, it will have some weight in proving my
uncle's innocence.'

'Come, young man,' said the soldier, in a somewhat milder
tone, 'you're a smart spark enough, and I am sorry for you; and
your uncle here is a fine old Trojan, kinder, I see, to his guests
than himself, for he gives us wine and drinks his own thin ale –
tell me all you know about this Burley, what he said when you
parted from him, where he went, and where he is likely now to
be found; and, d—n it, I'll wink as hard on your share of the
business as my duty will permit. There's a thousand merks on
the murdering whigamore's head, an I could but light on it –
Come, out with it – where did you part with him?'

'You will excuse my answering that question, sir,' said Morton;
'the same cogent reasons which induced me to afford him hospitality at considerable risk to myself and my friends, would
command me to respect his secret, if, indeed, he had trusted me
with any.'

'So you refuse to give me an answer?' said Bothwell.

'I have none to give,' returned Henry.

'Perhaps I could teach you to find one, by tying a piece of lighted match betwixt your fingers,'[11] answered Bothwell.

'O, for pity's sake,' said old Alison apart to her master, 'gie them siller – it's siller they're seeking – they'll murder Mr Henry, and yoursell next!'

Milnwood groaned in perplexity and bitterness of spirit, and, with a tone as if he was giving up the ghost, exclaimed, 'If twenty p – p – punds would make up this unhappy matter' –

'My master,' insinuated Alison to the sergeant, 'would gie twenty punds sterling' –

'Punds Scotch,[12] ye b—h!' interrupted Milnwood; for the agony of his avarice overcame alike his puritanic precision and the habitual respect he entertained for his housekeeper.

'Punds sterling,' insisted the housekeeper, 'if ye wad hae the gudeness to look ower the lad's misconduct; he's that dour ye might tear him to pieces, and ye wad ne'er get a word out o' him; and it wad do ye little gude, I'm sure, to burn his bonny finger-ends.'

'Why,' said Bothwell, hesitating, 'I don't know – most of my cloth would have the money, and take off the prisoner too; but I bear a conscience, and if your master will stand to your offer, and enter into a bond to produce his nephew, and if all in the house will take the test-oath,[13] I do not know but' –

'O ay, ay, sir,' cried Mrs. Wilson, 'ony test, ony oaths ye please!' And then aside to her master, 'Haste ye away, sir, and get the siller, or they will burn the house about our lugs.'

Old Milnwood cast a rueful look upon his adviser, and moved off, like a piece of Dutch clockwork,[14] to set at liberty his imprisoned angels in this dire emergency. Meanwhile, Sergeant Bothwell began to put the test-oath with such a degree of solemn reverence as might have been expected, being just about the same which is used to this day in his majesty's custom-house.

'You – what's your name, woman?'

'Alison Wilson, sir.'

'You, Alison Wilson, solemnly swear, certify, and declare, that you judge it unlawful for subjects, under pretext of reformation, or any other pretext whatsoever, to enter into Leagues and Covenants' –

Here the ceremony was interrupted by a strife between Cuddie and his mother, which, long conducted in whispers, now became audible.

'Oh, whisht, mither, whisht! they're upon a communing – Oh! whisht, and they'll agree weel eneuch e'enow.'

'I will not whisht, Cuddie,' replied his mother, 'I will uplift my voice and spare not – I will confound the man of sin, even the scarlet man, and through my voice shall Mr Harry be freed from the net of the fowler.'

'She has her leg ower the harrows now,' said Cuddie, 'stop her wha can – I see her cocked up behint a dragoon on her way to the Tolbooth – I find my ain legs tied below a horse's belly[15] – Ay – she has just mustered up her sermon, and there – wi' that grane – out it comes, and we are a' ruined, horse and foot!'

'And div ye think to come here,' said Mause, her withered hand shaking in concert with her keen, though wrinkled visage, animated by zealous wrath, and emancipated, by the very mention of the test, from the restraints of her own prudence, and Cuddie's admonition – 'Div ye think to come here, wi' your soul-killing, saint-seducing, conscience-confounding oaths, and tests, and bands – your snares, and your traps, and your gins? – Surely it is in vain that a net is spread in the sight of any bird.'[16]

'Eh! what, good dame?' said the soldier. 'Here's a whig miracle, egad! the old wife has got both her ears and tongue, and we are like to be driven deaf in our turn. – Go to, hold your peace, and remember whom you talk to, you old idiot.'

'Whae do I talk to! Eh, sirs, ower weel may the sorrowing land ken what ye are. Malignant adherents ye are to the prelates, foul props to a feeble and filthy cause, bloody beasts of prey, and burdens to the earth.'

'Upon my soul,' said Bothwell, astonished as a mastiff-dog might be should a hen-partridge fly at him in defence of her young, 'this is the finest language I ever heard! Can't you give us some more of it?'

'Gie ye some mair o't?' said Mause, clearing her voice with a preliminary cough, 'I will take up my testimony against you ance and again. –Philistines ye are, and Edomites – leopards are ye, and foxes – evening wolves, that gnaw not the bones till the morrow – wicked dogs, that compass about the chosen – thrusting kine, and pushing bulls of Bashan – piercing serpents ye are, and allied baith in name and nature with the great Red Dragon;[17] Revelations, twalfth chapter, third and fourth verses.'

Here the old lady stopped, apparently much more from lack of breath than of matter.

'Curse the old hag!' said one of the dragoons, 'gag her, and take her to head-quarters.'

'For shame, Andrews,' said Bothwell; 'remember the good lady belongs to the fair sex, and uses only the privilege of her tongue. – But, hark ye, good woman, every bull of Bashan and Red Dragon will not be so civil as I am, or be contented to leave you to the charge of the constable and ducking-stool. In the meantime I must necessarily carry off this young man to head-quarters. I cannot answer to my commanding-officer to leave him in a house where I have heard so much treason and fanaticism.'

'See now, mither, what ye hae dune,' whispered Cuddie; 'there's the Philistines, as ye ca' them, are gaun to whirry awa' Mr Henry, and a' wi' your nash-gab, deil be on't!'

'Haud yere tongue, ye cowardly loon,' said the mother, 'and layna the wyte on me; if you and thae thowless gluttons, that are sitting staring like cows bursting on clover, wad testify wi' your hands as I have testified wi' my tongue, they should never harle the precious young lad awa' to captivity.'

While this dialogue passed, the soldiers had already bound and secured their prisoner. Milnwood returned at this instant, and, alarmed at the preparations he beheld, hastened to proffer to Bothwell, though with many a grievous groan, the purse of gold which he had been obliged to rummage out as ransom for his nephew. The trooper took the purse with an air of indifference, weighed it in his hand, chucked it up into the air, and caught it as it fell, then shook his head, and said, 'There's many a merry night in this nest of yellow boys, but d—n me if I dare venture for them – that old woman has spoken too loud, and before all the men too. – Hark ye, old gentleman,' to Milnwood,

'I must take your nephew to head-quarters, so I cannot, in conscience, keep more than is my due as civility-money;' then opening the purse, he gave a gold piece to each of the soldiers, and took three to himself. 'Now,' said he, 'you have the comfort to know that your kinsman, young Captain Popinjay, will be carefully looked after and civilly used; and the rest of the money I return to you.'

Milnwood eagerly extended his hand.

'Only you know,' said Bothwell, still playing with the purse, 'that every landholder is answerable for the conformity and loyalty of his household, and that these fellows of mine are not obliged to be silent on the subject of the fine sermon we have had from that old puritan in the tartan plaid there; and I presume you are aware that the consequences of delation will be a heavy fine before the council.'

'Good sergeant, – worthy captain!' exclaimed the terrified miser, 'I am sure there is no person in my house, to my knowledge, would give cause of offence.'

'Nay,' answered Bothwell, 'you shall hear her give her testimony, as she calls it, herself. – You fellow,' (to Cuddie,) 'stand back, and let your mother speak her mind. I see she's primed and loaded again since her first discharge.'

'Lord! noble sir,' said Cuddie, 'an auld wife's tongue's but a feckless matter to mak sic a fash about. Neither my father nor me ever minded muckle what our mither said.'

'Hold your peace, my lad, while you are well,' said Bothwell; 'I promise you I think you are slyer than you would like to be supposed. – Come, good dame, you see your master will not believe that you can give us so bright a testimony.'

Mause's zeal did not require this spur to set her again on full career.

'Woe to the compliers and carnal self-seekers,' she said, 'that daub over and drown their consciences by complying with wicked exactions, and giving mammon of unrighteousness[18] to the sons of Belial, that it may make their peace with them! It is a sinful compliance, a base confederacy with the Enemy. It is the evil that Menahem did in the sight of the Lord, when he gave a thousand talents to Pul, King of Assyria, that his hand might be with him; Second Kings, feifteen chapter, nineteen verse. It is the evil deed of Ahab, when he sent money to Tiglath-Peleser; see the saame Second Kings, saxteen and aught. And if it was accounted a backsliding even in godly Hezekiah, that he complied with Sennacherib, giving him money, and offering to bear that which was put upon him, (see the saame Second Kings, aughteen chapter, fourteen and feifteen verses,) even so it is with them that in this contumacious and backsliding generation pays localities and fees, and cess[19] and fines, to greedy and unrighteous publicans, and extortions and stipends to hireling curates, (dumb dogs which bark not, sleeping, lying down, loving to slumber,) and gives gifts to be helps and hires to our oppressors and destroyers. They are all like the casters of a lot with them – like the preparing of a table for the troop and the furnishing a drink-offering to the number.'[20]

'There's a fine sound of doctrine for you, Mr Morton! How like you that?' said Bothwell; 'or how do you think the Council will like it? I think we can carry the greatest part of it in our heads without a kylevine pen and a pair of tablets, such as you bring to conventicles. She denies paying cess, I think, Andrews?'

'Yes, by G—,' said Andrews; 'and she swore it was a sin to give a trooper a pot of ale, or ask him to sit down to a table.'

'You hear,' said Bothwell, addressing Milnwood; 'but it's your own affair;' and he proffered back the purse with its diminished contents, with an air of indifference.

Milnwood, whose head seemed stunned by the accumulation of his misfortunes, extended his hand mechanically to take the purse.

'Are ye mad?' said his housekeeper, in a whisper; 'tell them to keep it; – they *will* keep it either by fair means or foul, and it's our only chance to make them quiet.'

'I canna do it, Ailie – I canna do it,' said Milnwood, in the bitterness of his heart. 'I canna part wi' the siller I hae counted sae often ower, to thae blackguards.'

'Then I maun do it mysell, Milnwood,' said the housekeeper, 'or see a' gang wrang thegither. – My master, sir,' she said, addressing Bothwell, 'canna think o' taking back ony thing at the hand of an honourable gentleman like you; he implores ye to pit up the siller, and be as kind to his nephew as ye can, and be favourable in reporting our dispositions to government, and let us tak nae wrang for the daft speeches of an auld jaud,' (here she turned fiercely upon Mause, to indulge herself for the effort which it cost her to assume a mild demeanour to the soldiers,) 'a daft auld whig randy, that ne'er was in the house (foul fa' her) till yesterday afternoon, and that sall ne'er cross the door-stane again an anes I had her out o't.'

'Ay, ay,' whispered Cuddie to his parent, 'e'en sae! I kend we wad be put to our travels again whene'er ye suld get three words spoken to an end. I was sure that wad be the upshot o't, mither.'

'Whisht, my bairn,' said she, 'and dinna murmur at the cross – cross their door-stane! weel I wot I'll ne'er cross their door-stane. There's nae mark on their threshold for a signal that the destroying angel should pass by.[21] They'll get a back-cast o' his hand yet, that think sae muckle o' the creature and sae little o' the Creator – sae muckle o' warld's gear and sae little o' a broken covenant – sae muckle about thae wheen pieces o' yellow muck, and sae little about the pure gold o' the Scripture – sae muckle about their ain friend and kinsman, and sae little about the elect, that are tried wi' hornings, harassings, huntings, searchings, chasings, catchings, imprisonments, torturings, banishments, headings, hangings, dismemberings, and quarterings quick, forby the hundreds forced from their ain habitations to the deserts, mountains, muirs, mosses, moss-flows, and peat-hags, there to hear the word like bread eaten in secret.'

'She's at the Covenant now, sergeant, shall we not have her away?' said one of the soldiers.

'You be d—d!' said Bothwell, aside to him; 'cannot you see she's better where she is, so long as there is a respectable, sponsible, money-broking heritor, like Mr Morton of Milnwood, who has the means of atoning her trespasses? Let the old mother fly to raise another brood, she's too tough to be made any thing of herself – Here,' he cried, 'one other round to Milnwood and his roof-tree, and to our next merry meeting with him! – which I think will not be far distant, if he keeps such a fanatical family.'

He then ordered the party to take their horses, and pressed the best in Milnwood's stable into the king's service to carry the prisoner. Mrs Wilson, with weeping eyes, made up a small parcel of necessaries for Henry's compelled journey, and as she bustled about, took an opportunity, unseen by the party, to slip into his hand a small sum of money. Bothwell and his troopers, in other respects, kept their promise, and were civil. They did not bind their prisoner, but contented themselves with leading his horse between a file of men. They then mounted, and marched off with much mirth and laughter among themselves, leaving the Milnwood family in great confusion. The old Laird himself, overpowered by the loss of his nephew, and the unavailing outlay of twenty pounds sterling, did nothing the whole evening but rock himself backwards and forwards in his great leathern easy-chair, repeating the same lamentation, of 'Ruined on a' sides, ruined on a' sides – harried and undone – harried and undone – body and gudes, body and gudes!'

Mrs Alison Wilson's grief was partly indulged and partly relieved by the torrent of invectives with which she accompanied Mause and Cuddie's expulsion from Milnwood.

'Ill luck be in the graning corse o' thee! the prettiest lad in Clydesdale this day maun be a sufferer, and a' for you and your daft whiggery!'

'Gae wa',' replied Mause; 'I trow ye are yet in the bonds of sin, and in the gall of iniquity,[22] to grudge your bonniest and best in the cause of Him that gave ye a' ye hae – I promise I hae dune as muckle for Mr Harry as I wad do for my ain; for if Cuddie was found worthy to bear testimony in the Grassmarket' –

'And there's gude hope o't,' said Alison, 'unless you and he change your courses.'

'– And if,' continued Mause, disregarding the interruption, ' the bloody Doegs and the flattering Ziphites[23] were to seek to ensnare me with a proffer of his remission upon sinful compliances, I wad persevere, natheless, in lifting my testimony against popery, prelacy, antinomianism, erastianism, lapsarianism, sublapsarianism,[24] and the sins and snares of the times – I wad cry as a woman in labour against the black Indulgence, that has been a stumbling-block to professors – I wad uplift my voice as a powerful preacher.'

'Hout, tout, mither,' cried Cuddie, interfering and dragging her off forcibly, 'dinna deave the gentlewoman wi' your testimony! ye hae preached eneugh for sax days. Ye preached us out o' our canny free-house and gude kale-yard, and out o' this new city o' refuge afore our hinder end was weel hafted in it; and ye hae preached Mr Harry awa to the prison; and ye hae preached twenty punds out o' the Laird's pocket that he likes as ill to quit wi'; and sae ye may haud sae for ae wee while, without preaching me up a ladder and down a tow. Sae, come awa, come awa; the family hae had eneugh o' your testimony to mind it for ae while.'

So saying he dragged off Mause, the words, 'Testimony – Covenant – malignants – indulgence,' still thrilling upon her tongue, to make preparations for instantly renewing their travels in quest of an asylum.

'Ill-fard, crazy, crack-brained gowk, that she is!' exclaimed the housekeeper, as she saw them depart, 'to set up to be sae muckle better than ither folk, the auld besom, and to bring sae muckle distress on a douce quiet family! If it hadna been that I am mair than half a gentlewoman by my station, I wad hae tried my ten nails in the wizen'd hide o' her!'

CHAPTER 9

I am a son of Mars who have been in many wars,
  And show my cuts and scars wherever I come;
This here was for a wench, and that other in a trench,
  When welcoming the French at the sound of the drum.

BURNS[1]

'DON'T be too much cast down,' said Sergeant Bothwell to his prisoner as they journeyed on towards the head-quarters; 'you are a smart pretty lad, and well connected; the worst that will happen will be strapping up for it, and that is many an honest fellow's lot. I tell you fairly your life's within the compass of the law, unless you make submission, and get off by a round fine upon your uncle's estate; he can well afford it.'

'That vexes me more than the rest,' said Henry. 'He parts with his money with regret; and, as he had no concern whatever with my having given this person shelter for a night, I wish to Heaven, if I escape a capital punishment, that the penalty may be of a kind I could bear in my own person.'

'Why, perhaps,' said Bothwell, 'they will propose to you to go into one of the Scotch regiments that are serving abroad. It's no bad line of service; if your friends are active, and there are any knocks going, you may soon get a commission.'

'I am by no means sure,' answered Morton, 'that such a sentence is not the best thing that can happen to me.'

'Why, then, you are no real whig after all?' said the sergeant.

'I have hitherto meddled with no party in the state,' said Henry, 'but have remained quietly at home; and sometimes I have had serious thoughts of joining one of our foreign regiments.'

'Have you?' replied Bothwell; 'why, I honour you for it; I have served in the Scotch French guards[2] myself many a long day; it's the place for learning discipline, d—n me. They never mind what you do when you are off duty; but miss you the roll-call, and see how they'll arrange you – D—n me, if old Captain Montgomery didn't make me mount guard upon the arsenal in my steel-back and breast, plate-sleeves and head-piece, for six hours at once, under so burning a sun, that gad I was baked like a turtle at Port Royale.[3] I swore never to miss answering to Francis Stewart again, though I should leave my hand of cards upon the drum-head – Ah! discipline is a capital thing.'

'In other respects you liked the service?' said Morton.

'*Par excellence*,' said Bothwell; 'women, wine, and wassail, all to be had for little but the asking; and if you find it in your conscience to let a fat priest think he has some chance to convert you, gad he'll help you to these comforts himself, just to gain a little ground in your good affection. Where will you find a crop-eared whig parson will be so civil?'

'Why, nowhere, I agree with you,' said Henry; 'but what was your chief duty?'

'To guard the king's person,' said Bothwell, 'to look after the safety of Louis le Grand, my boy, and now and then to take a turn among the Huguenots (protestants, that is.)[4] And there we had fine scope; it brought my hand pretty well in for the service in this country. But, come, as you are to be a *bon camerado*, as the Spaniards say, I must put you in cash with some of your old uncle's broad-pieces. This is cutter's law;[5] we must not see a pretty fellow want, if we have cash ourselves.'

Thus speaking, he pulled out his purse, took out some of the contents, and offered them to Henry without counting them. Young Morton declined the favour; and, not judging it prudent to acquaint the sergeant, notwithstanding his apparent generosity, that he was actually in possession of some money, he assured him he should have no difficulty in getting a supply from his uncle.

'Well,' said Bothwell, 'in that case these yellow rascals must serve to ballast my purse a little longer. I always make it a rule never to quit the tavern (unless ordered on duty) while my purse is so weighty that I can chuck it over the signpost.[6] When it is so light that the wind blows it back, then, boot and saddle, – we must fall on some way of replenishing. – But what tower is that before us, rising so high upon the steep bank, out of the woods that surround it on every side?'

'It is the tower of Tillietudlem,' said one of the soldiers. 'Old Lady Margaret Bellenden lives there. She's one of the best affected women in the country, and one that's a soldier's friend. When I was hurt by one of the d—d whig dogs that shot at me from behind a fauld-dike, I lay a month there, and would stand such another wound to be in as good quarters again.'

'If that be the case,' said Bothwell, 'I will pay my respects to her as we pass, and request some refreshment for men and horses; I am as thirsty already as if I had drunk nothing at Milnwood. But it is a good thing in these times,' he continued, addressing himself to Henry, 'that the King's soldier cannot pass a house without getting a refreshment. In such houses as Tillie – what d'ye call it? you are served for love; in the houses of the avowed fanatics you help yourself by force; and among the moderate presbyterians and other suspicious persons, you are well treated from fear; so your thirst is always quenched on some terms or other.'

'And you propose,' said Henry, anxiously, 'to go upon that errand up to the tower yonder?'

'To be sure I do,' answered Bothwell. 'How should I be able to report favourably to my officers of the worthy lady's sound principles, unless I know the taste of her sack, for sack she will produce – that I take for granted; it is the favourite consoler of your old dowager of quality, as small claret is the potation of your country laird.'

'Then, for heaven's sake,' said Henry, 'if you are determined to go there, do not mention my name, or expose me to a family that I am acquainted with. Let me be muffled up for the time in one of your soldier's cloaks, and only mention me generally as a prisoner under your charge.'

'With all my heart,' said Bothwell; 'I promised to use you civilly, and I scorn to break my word. – Here, Andrews, wrap a cloak round the prisoner, and do not mention his name, nor where we caught him, unless you would have a trot on a horse of wood.'[7]

They were at this moment at an arched gateway, battlemented and flanked with turrets, one whereof was totally ruinous, excepting the lower story, which served as a cow-house to the peasant, whose family inhabited the turret that remained entire. The gate had been broken down by Monk's soldiers[8] during the civil war, and had never been replaced, therefore presented no obstacle to Bothwell and his party. The avenue, very steep and narrow, and causewayed with large round stones, ascended the side of the precipitous bank in an oblique and zigzag course, now showing now hiding a view of the tower and its exterior bulwarks, which seemed to rise almost perpendicularly above their heads. The fragments of Gothic defences which it exhibited were upon such a scale of strength, as induced Bothwell to exclaim, 'It's well this place is in honest and loyal hands. Egad, if the enemy had it, a dozen of old whigamore wives with their distaffs might keep it against a troop of dragoons, at least if they had half the spunk of the old girl we left at Milnwood. Upon my life,' he continued, as they came in front of the large double tower and its surrounding defences and flankers, 'it is a superb place, founded, says the worn inscription over the gate –

unless the remnant of my Latin has given me the slip – by Sir Ralph de Bellenden in 1350 – a respectable antiquity. I must greet the old lady with due honour, though it should put me to the labour of recalling some of the compliments that I used to dabble in when I was wont to keep that sort of company.'

As he thus communed with himself, the butler, who had reconnoitred the soldiers from an arrow-slit in the wall, announced to his lady, that a commanded party of dragoons, or, as he thought, Life-Guardsmen, waited at the gate with a prisoner under their charge.

'I am certain,' said Gudyill, 'and positive, that the sixth man is a prisoner; for his horse is led, and the two dragoons that are before have their carabines out of their budgets, and rested upon their thighs. It was aye the way we guarded prisoners in the days of the great Marquis.'⁹

'King's soldiers?' said the lady; 'probably in want of refreshment. Go, Gudyill, make them welcome, and let them be accommodated with what provision and forage the Tower can afford. – And stay, tell my gentlewoman to bring my black scarf and manteau. I will go down myself to receive them; one cannot show the King's Life-Guards too much respect in times when they are doing so much for royal authority. And d'ye hear, Gudyill, let Jenny Dennison slip on her pearlings to walk before my niece and me, and the three women to walk behind; and bid my niece attend me instantly.'

Fully accoutred, and attended according to her directions, Lady Margaret now sailed out into the court-yard of her tower with great courtesy and dignity. Sergeant Bothwell saluted the grave and revered lady of the manor with an assurance which had something of the light and careless address of the dissipated men of fashion in Charles the Second's time, and did not at all savour of the awkward or rude manners of a non-commissioned officer of dragoons. His language, as well as his manners, seemed also to be refined for the time and occasion; though the truth was, that, in the fluctuations of an adventurous and profligate life, Bothwell had sometimes kept company much better suited to his ancestry than to his present situation in life. To the lady's request to know whether she could be of service to them, he answered, with a suitable bow, 'That as they had to march some miles farther that night, they would be much accommodated by permission to rest their horses for an hour before continuing their journey.'

'With the greatest pleasure,' answered Lady Margaret; 'and I trust that my people will see that neither horse nor men want suitable refreshment.'

'We are well aware, madam,' continued Bothwell, 'that such has always been the reception, within the walls of Tillietudlem, of those who served the King.'

'We have studied to discharge our duty faithfully and loyally on all occasions, sir,' answered Lady Margaret, pleased with the compliment, 'both to our monarchs and to their followers, particularly to their faithful soldiers. It is not long ago, and it probably has not escaped the recollection of his sacred majesty, now on the throne, since he himself honoured my poor house with his presence, and breakfasted in a room in this castle, Mr Sergeant, which my waiting-gentlewoman shall show you; we still call it the King's room.'

Bothwell had by this time dismounted his party, and committed the horses to the charge of one file, and the prisoner to that of another; so that he himself was at liberty to continue the conversation which the lady had so condescendingly opened.

'Since the King, my master, had the honour to experience your hospitality, I cannot wonder that it is extended to those that serve him, and whose principal merit is doing it with fidelity. And yet I have a nearer relation to his majesty than this coarse red coat would seem to indicate.'

'Indeed, sir? Probably,' said Lady Margaret, 'you have belonged to his household?'

'Not exactly, madam, to his household, but rather to his *house*; a connexion through which I may claim kindred with most of the best families in Scotland, not, I believe, exclusive of that of Tillietudlem.'

'Sir?' said the old lady, drawing herself up with dignity at hearing what she conceived an impertinent jest, 'I do not understand you.'

'It's but a foolish subject for one in my situation to talk of, madam,' answered the trooper; 'but you must have heard of the history and misfortunes of my grandfather Francis Stewart, to whom James I., his cousin-german, gave the title of Bothwell, as my comrades give me the nickname. It was not in the long run more advantageous to him than it is to me.'

'Indeed?' said Lady Margaret, with much sympathy and surprise; 'I have indeed always understood that the grandson of the last Earl was in necessitous circumstances, but I should never have expected to see him so low in the service. With such connexions, what ill fortune could have reduced you' –

'Nothing much out of the ordinary course, I believe, madam,' said Bothwell, interrupting and anticipating the question. 'I have had my moments of good luck like my neighbours – have drunk my bottle with Rochester, thrown a merry main with Buckingham, and fought at Tangiers side by side with Sheffield.[10] But my luck never lasted; I could not make useful friends out of my jolly companions – Perhaps I was not sufficiently aware,' he continued, with some bitterness, 'how much the descendant of the Scottish Stewarts was honoured by being admitted into the convivialities of Wilmot and Villiers.'

'But your Scottish friends, Mr Stewart, your relations here, so numerous and so powerful?'

'Why, ay, my lady,' replied the sergeant, 'I believe some of them might have made me their gamekeeper, for I am a tolerable shot – some of them would have entertained me as their bravo, for I can use my sword well – and here and there was one, who, when better company was not to be had, would have made me his companion, since I can drink my three bottles of wine. – But I don't know how it is – between service and service among my kinsmen, I prefer that of my cousin Charles as the most creditable of them all, although the pay is but poor, and the livery far from splendid.'

'It is a shame, it is a burning scandal!' said Lady Margaret. 'Why do you not apply to his most sacred majesty? he cannot but be surprised to hear that a scion of his august family' –

'I beg your pardon, madam,' interrupted the sergeant, 'I am but a blunt soldier, and I trust you will excuse me when I say, his most sacred majesty is more busy in grafting scions of his own, than with nourishing those which were planted by his grandfather's grandfather.'

'Well, Mr Stewart,' said Lady Margaret, 'one thing you must promise me – remain at Tillietudlem to-night; to-morrow I expect your commanding-officer, the gallant Claverhouse, to whom king and country are so much obliged for his exertions against those who would turn the world upside down. I will speak to him on the subject of your speedy promotion; and I am certain he feels too much, both what is due to the blood which is in your veins, and to the request of a lady so highly distinguished as myself by his most sacred majesty, not to make better provision for you than you have yet received.'

'I am much obliged to your ladyship, and I certainly will remain here with my prisoner, since you request it, especially as it will be the earliest way of presenting him to Colonel Grahame, and obtaining his ultimate orders about the young spark.'

'Who is your prisoner, pray you?' said Lady Margaret.

'A young fellow of rather the better class in this neighbourhood, who has been so incautious as to give countenance to one of the murderers of the primate, and to facilitate the dog's escape.'

'O, fie upon him!' said Lady Margaret; 'I am but too apt to forgive the injuries I have received at the hands of these rogues, though some of them, Mr Stewart, are of a kind not like to be forgotten; but those who would abet the perpetrators of so cruel, and deliberate a homicide on a single man, an old man, and a man of the Archbishop's sacred profession – O fie upon him! If you wish to make him secure, with little trouble to your people, I will cause Harrison, or Gudyill, look for the key of our pit, or principal dungeon. It has not been open since the week after the victory of Kilsythe,[11] when my poor Sir Arthur Bellenden put twenty whigs into it; but it is not more than two stories beneath ground, so it cannot be unwholesome, especially as I rather believe there is somewhere an opening to the outer air.'

'I beg your pardon, madam,' answered the sergeant; 'I daresay the dungeon is a most admirable one; but I have promised to be civil to the lad, and I will take care he is watched, so as to render escape impossible. I'll set those to look after him shall keep him as fast as if his legs were in the boots, or his fingers in the thumbikins.'[12]

'Well, Mr Stewart,' rejoined the lady, 'you best know your own duty. I heartily wish you good evening, and commit you to the care of my steward, Harrison. I would ask you to keep ourselves company, but a – a – a –'

'O, madam, it requires no apology; I am sensible the coarse red coat of King Charles II does and ought to annihilate the privileges of the red blood of King James V.'

'Not with me, I do assure you, Mr Stewart; you do me injustice if you think so. I will speak to your officer to-morrow; and I trust you shall soon find yourself in a rank where there shall be no anomalies to be reconciled.'

'I believe, madam,' said Bothwell, 'your goodness will find itself deceived; but I am obliged to you for your intention, and, at all events, I will have a merry night with Mr Harrison.'

Lady Margaret took a ceremonious leave, with all the respect which she owed to royal blood, even when flowing in the veins of a sergeant of the Life-Guards; again assuring Mr Stewart, that whatever was in the Tower of Tillietudlem was heartily at his service and that of his attendants.

Sergeant Bothwell did not fail to take the lady at her word, and readily forgot the height from which his family had descended, in a joyous carousal, during which Mr Harrison exerted himself to produce the best wine in the cellar, and to excite his guest to be merry by that seducing example, which, in matters of conviviality, goes farther than precept. Old Gudyill associated himself with a party so much to his taste, pretty much as Davy, in the Second Part of Henry the Fourth, mingles in the revels of his master, Justice Shallow.[13] He ran down to the cellar at the risk of breaking his neck, to ransack some private catacomb, known, as he boasted, only to himself, and which never either had, or should, during his superintendence, render forth a bottle of its contents to any one but a real king's friend.

'When the Duke[14] dined here,' said the butler, seating himself at a distance from the table, being somewhat overawed by Bothwell's genealogy, but yet hitching his seat half a yard nearer at every clause of his speech, 'my leddy was importunate to have a bottle of that Burgundy,' – (here he advanced his seat a little,) – 'but I dinna ken how it was, Mr Stewart, I misdoubted him. I jaloused him, sir, no to be the friend to government he pretends : the family are not to lippen to. That auld Duke James lost his heart before he lost his head; and the Worcester man was but wersh parritch, neither gude to fry, boil, nor sup cauld.' (With this witty observation, he completed his first parallel, and commenced a zigzag after the manner of an experienced engineer, in order to continue his approaches to the table.) 'Sae, sir, the faster my leddy cried "Burgundy to his Grace – the auld Burgundy – the choice Burgundy – the Burgundy that came ower in the thirty-nine" – the mair did I say to mysell, Deil a drap gangs down his hause unless I was mair sensible o' his principles; sack and claret may serve him. Na, na, gentlemen, as lang as I hae the trust o' butler in this house o' Tillietudlem, I'll tak it upon me to see that nae disloyal or doubtfu' person is the better o' our binns. But when I can find a true friend to the king and his cause, and a moderate episcopacy; when I find a man, as I say, that will stand by church and crown as I did mysell in my master's life, and all through Montrose's time, I think there's naething in the cellar ower gude to be spared on him.'

By this time he had completed a lodgment in the body of the place, or, in other words, advanced his seat close to the table.

'And now, Mr Francis Stewart of Bothwell, I have the honour to drink your gude health, and a commission t'ye, and much luck may ye have in raking this country clear o' whigs and roundheads, fanatics and Covenanters.'

Bothwell, who, it may well be believed, had long ceased to be very scrupulous in point of society, which he regulated more by his convenience and station in life than his ancestry, readily answered the butler's pledge, acknowledging, at the same time, the excellence of the wine; and Mr Gudyill, thus adopted a regular member of the company, continued to furnish them with the means of mirth until an early hour in the next morning.

CHAPTER 10

Did I but purpose to embark with thee
On the smooth surface of a summer sea,
And would forsake the skiff and make the shore
When the winds whistle and the tempests roar?

PRIOR[1]

WHILE Lady Margaret held, with the high-descended sergeant
of dragoons, the conference which we have detailed in the preceding pages, her granddaughter, partaking in a less degree her
ladyship's enthusiasm for all who were sprung of the blood-royal,
did not honour Sergeant Bothwell with more attention than a
single glance, which showed her a tall powerful person, and a
set of hardy weather-beaten features, to which pride and dissi-
pation had given an air where discontent mingled with the reck-
less gaiety of desperation. The other soldiers offered still less to
detach her consideration; but from the prisoner, muffled and
disguised as he was, she found it impossible to withdraw her
eyes. Yet she blamed herself for indulging a curiosity which
seemed obviously to give pain to him who was its object.

'I wish,' she said to Jenny Dennison, who was the immediate
attendant on her person, 'I wish we knew who that poor fellow is.'

'I was just thinking sae mysell, Miss Edith,' said the waiting
woman, 'but it canna be Cuddie Headrigg, because he's taller
and na sae stout.'

'Yet,' continued Miss Bellenden, 'it may be some poor neighbour, for whom we might have cause to interest ourselves.'

'I can sune learn wha he is,' said the enterprising Jenny, 'if the
sodgers were anes settled and at leisure, for I ken ane o' them
very weel – the best-looking and the youngest o' them.'

'I think you know all the idle young fellows about the
country,' answered her mistress.

'Na, Miss Edith, I am na sae free o' my acquaintance as that,'
answered the fille-de-chambre. 'To be sure, folk canna help kenning the folk by head-mark that they see aye glowring and

looking at them at kirk and market; but I ken few lads to speak to unless it be them o' the family, and the three Steinsons, and Tam Rand, and the young miller, and the five Howisons in Nethersheils, and lang Tam Gilry, and' –

'Pray cut short a list of exceptions which threatens to be a long one, and tell me how you come to know this young soldier,' said Miss Bellenden.

'Lord, Miss Edith, it's Tam Halliday, Trooper Tam, as they ca' him, that was wounded by the hill-folk at the conventicle at Outer-side Muir, and lay here while he was under cure. I can ask him ony thing, and Tam will no refuse to answer me, I'll be caution for him.'

'Try, then,' said Miss Edith, 'if you can find an opportunity to ask him the name of his prisoner, and come to my room and tell me what he says.'

Jenny Dennison proceeded on her errand, but soon returned with such a face of surprise and dismay as evinced a deep interest in the fate of the prisoner.

'What is the matter?' said Edith, anxiously; 'does it prove to be Cuddie, after all, poor fellow?'

'Cuddie, Miss Edith? Na! na! it's nae Cuddie,' blubbered out the faithful fille-de-chambre, sensible of the pain which her news were about to inflict on her young mistress. 'O dear, Miss Edith, it's young Milnwood himsell!'

'Young Milnwood!' exclaimed Edith, aghast in her turn; 'it is impossible – totally impossible! – His uncle attends the clergy-man indulged by law, and has no connexion whatever with the refractory people; and he himself has never interfered in this unhappy dissension; he must be totally innocent, unless he has been standing up for some invaded right.'

'O, my dear Miss Edith,' said her attendant, 'these are not days to ask what's right or what's wrang; if he were as innocent as the new-born infant, they would find some way of making him guilty, if they liked; but Tam Halliday says it will touch his life, for he has been resetting ane o' the Fife gentlemen that killed that auld carle of an Archbishop.'

'His life!' exclaimed Edith, starting hastily up, and speaking with a hurried and tremulous accent, – 'they cannot – they shall not – I will speak for him – they shall not hurt him!'

'O, my dear young leddy, think on your grandmother; think on the danger and the difficulty,' added Jenny; 'for he's kept under close confinement till Claverhouse comes up in the morning, and if he doesna gie him full satisfaction, Tam Halliday says there will be brief wark wi' him – Kneel down – mak ready – present – fire – just as they did wi' auld deaf John Macbriar, that never understood a single question they pat till him, and sae lost his life for lack o' hearing.'[2]

'Jenny,' said the young lady, 'if he should die, I will die with him; there is no time to talk of danger or difficulty – I will put on a plaid, and slip down with you to the place where they have kept him – I will throw myself at the feet of the sentinel, and entreat him, as he has a soul to be saved' –

'Eh, guide us!' interrupted the maid, 'our young leddy at the feet o' Trooper Tam, and speaking to him about his soul, when the puir chield hardly kens whether he has ane or no, unless that he whiles swears by it – that will never do; but what maun be maun be, and I'll never desert a true-love cause – And sae, if ye maun see young Milnwood, though I ken nae gude it will do, but to make baith your hearts the sairer, I'll e'en tak the risk o't, and try to manage Tam Halliday; but ye maun let me hae my ain gate and no speak ae word – he's keeping guard o'er Milnwood in the easter round of the tower.'

'Go, go, fetch me a plaid,' said Edith. 'Let me but see him, and I will find some remedy for his danger – Haste ye, Jenny, as ever ye hope to have good at my hands.'

Jenny hastened, and soon returned with a plaid, in which Edith muffled herself so as completely to screen her face, and in part to disguise her person. This was a mode of arranging the plaid very common among the ladies of that century, and the earlier part of the succeeding one; so much so, indeed, that the venerable sages of the Kirk, conceiving that the mode gave tempting facilities for intrigue, directed more than one act of Assembly against this use of the mantle. But fashion, as usual, proved too strong for authority, and while plaids continued to be worn, women of all ranks occasionally employed them as a sort of muffler or veil.[3] Her face and figure thus concealed, Edith, holding by her attendant's arm, hastened with trembling steps to the place of Morton's confinement.

This was a small study or closet, in one of the turrets, opening upon a gallery in which the sentinel was pacing to and fro; for Sergeant Bothwell, scrupulous in observing his word, and perhaps touched with some compassion for the prisoner's youth and genteel demeanour, had waved the indignity of putting his guard into the same apartment with him. Halliday, therefore, with his carabine on his arm, walked up and down the gallery, occasionally solacing himself with a draught of ale, a huge flagon of which stood upon the table at one end of the apartment, and at other times humming the lively Scottish air,[4]

> 'Between Saint Johnstone and Bonny Dundee,
>   I'll gar ye be fain to follow me.'

Jenny Dennison cautioned her mistress once more to let her take her own way.

'I can manage the trooper weel eneugh,' she said, 'for as rough as he is – I ken their nature weel; but ye maunna say a single word.'

She accordingly opened the door of the gallery just as the sentinel had turned his back from it, and taking up the tune which he hummed, she sung in a coquettish tone of rustic raillery,

> 'If I were to follow a poor sodger lad,
>   My friends wad be angry, my minnie be mad;
>   A laird, or a lord, they were fitter for me,
>   Sae I'll never be fain to follow thee.' –

'A fair challenge, by Jove,' cried the sentinel, turning round, 'and from two at once; but it's not easy to bang the soldier with his bandoleers;' then taking up the song where the damsel had stopt,

> 'To follow me ye weel may be glad,
>   A share of my supper, a share of my bed,
>   To the sound of the drum to range fearless and free,
>   I'll gar ye be fain to follow me.' –

'Come, my pretty lass, and kiss me for my song.'

'I should not have thought of that, Mr Halliday,' answered Jenny, with a look and tone expressing just the necessary degree of contempt at the proposal, 'and, I'se assure ye, ye'll hae but little o' my company unless ye show gentler havings – It wasna to hear that sort o' nonsense that brought me here wi' my friend, and ye should think shame o' yoursell, 'at should ye.'

'Umph! and what sort of nonsense did bring you here then, Mrs Dennison?'

'My kinswoman has some particular business with your prisoner, young Mr Harry Morton, and I am come wi' her to speak till him.'

'The devil you are!' answered the sentinel; 'and pray, Mrs Dennison, how do your kinswoman and you propose to get in? You are rather too plump to whisk through a keyhole, and opening the door is a thing not to be spoke of.'

'It's no a thing to be spoken o', but a thing to be dune,' replied the persevering damsel.

'We'll see about that, my bonny Jenny;' and the soldier resumed his march, humming, as he walked to and fro along the gallery,

> 'Keek into the draw-well,
>   Janet, Janet,
> Then ye'll see your bonny sell,
>   My joe Janet.'[5]

'So ye're no thinking to let us in, Mr Halliday? Weel, weel; gude e'en to you – ye hae seen the last o' me, and o' this bonny die too,' said Jenny, holding between her finger and thumb a splendid silver dollar.

'Give him gold, give him gold,' whispered the agitated young lady.

'Silver's e'en ower gude for the like o' him,' replied Jenny, 'that disna care for the blink o' a bonny lassie's ee – and what's waur, he wad think there was something mair in't than a kinswoman o' mine. My certy! siller's no sae plenty wi' us, let alane gowd.' Having addressed this advice aside to her mistress, she raised her voice, and said, 'My cousin winna stay ony langer, Mr Halliday; sae, if ye please, gude e'en t'ye.'

'Halt a bit, halt a bit,' said the trooper; 'rein up and parley, Jenny. If I let your kinswoman in to speak to my prisoner, you must stay here and keep me company till she come out again, and then we'll all be well pleased you know.'

'The fiend be in my feet then,' said Jenny; 'd'ye think my kinswoman and me are gaun to lose our gude name wi' cracking clavers wi' the like o' you or your prisoner either, without somebody by to see fair play? Hegh, hegh, sirs, to see sic a difference between folk's promises and performance! Ye were aye willing to slight puir Cuddie; but an I had asked him to oblige me in a thing, though it had been to cost his hanging, he wadna hae stude twice about it.'

'D—n Cuddie!' retorted the dragoon, 'he'll be hanged in good earnest, I hope. I saw him to-day at Milnwood with his old puritanical b— of a mother, and if I had thought I was to have had him cast in my dish, I would have brought him up at my horse's tail – we had law enough to bear us out.'

'Very weel, very weel – See if Cuddie winna hae a lang shot at you ane o' thae days, if ye gar him tak the muir wi' sae mony honest folk. He can hit a mark brawly; he was third at the popinjay; and he's as true of his promise as of ee and hand, though he disna mak sic a phrase about it as some acquaintance o' yours – But it's a' ane to me – Come, cousin, we'll awa'.'

'Stay, Jenny; d—n me, if I hang fire more than another when I have said a thing,' said the soldier, in a hesitating tone. 'Where is the sergeant?'

'Drinking and driving ower,' quoth Jenny, 'wi' the Steward and John Gudyill.'

'So, so – he's safe enough – and where are my comrades?' asked Halliday.

'Birling the brown bowl wi' the fowler and the falconer, and some o' the serving folk.'

'Have they plenty of ale?'

'Sax gallons, as gude as e'er was masked,' said the maid.

'Well, then, my pretty Jenny,' said the relenting sentinel, 'they are fast till the hour of relieving guard, and perhaps something later; and so, if you will promise to come alone the next time' —

'Maybe I will, and maybe I winna,' said Jenny; 'but if ye get the dollar, ye'll like that just as weel.'

'I'll be d—n'd if I do,' said Halliday, taking the money, however; 'but it's always something for my risk; for, if Claverhouse hears what I have done, he will build me a horse as high as the Tower of Tillietudlem. But every one in the regiment takes what they can come by; I am sure Bothwell and his blood-royal shows us a good example. And if I were trusting to you, you little jilting devil, I should lose both pains and powder; whereas this fellow,' looking at the piece, 'will be good as far as he goes. So, come, there is the door open for you; do not stay groaning and praying with the young whig now; but be ready, when I call at the door, to start, as if they were sounding "Horse and away." '

So speaking, Halliday unlocked the door of the closet, admitted Jenny and her pretended kinswoman, locked it behind them, and hastily reassumed the indifferent measured step and time-killing whistle of a sentinel upon his regular duty.

The door, which slowly opened, discovered Morton with both arms reclined upon a table, and his head resting upon them in a posture of deep dejection. He raised his face as the door opened, and, perceiving the female figures which it admitted, started up in great surprise. Edith, as if modesty had quelled the courage which despair had bestowed, stood about a yard from the door without having either the power to speak or to advance. All the plans of aid, relief, or comfort, which she had proposed to lay before her lover, seemed at once to have vanished from her recollection, and left only a painful chaos of ideas, with which was mingled a fear that she had degraded herself in the eyes of Morton by a step which might appear precipitate and unfeminine. She hung motionless and almost powerless upon the arm of her attendant, who in vain endeavoured to reassure and inspire her with courage, by whispering, 'We are in now, madam, and we maun mak the best o' our time; for, doubtless, the corporal or the sergeant will gang the rounds, and it wad be a pity to hae the poor lad Halliday punished for his civility.'

Morton, in the meantime, was timidly advancing, suspecting

the truth; for what other female in the house, excepting Edith herself, was likely to take an interest in his misfortunes? and yet afraid, owing to the doubtful twilight and the muffled dress, of making some mistake which might be prejudicial to the object of his affections. Jenny, whose ready wit and forward manners well qualified her for such an office, hastened to break the ice.

'Mr Morton, Miss Edith's very sorry for your present situation, and' –

It was needless to say more; he was at her side, almost at her feet, pressing her unresisting hands, and loading her with a profusion of thanks and gratitude which would be hardly intelligible from the mere broken words, unless we could describe the tone, the gesture, the impassioned and hurried indications of deep and tumultuous feeling, with which they were accompanied.

For two or three minutes, Edith stood as motionless as the statue of a saint which receives the adoration of a worshipper; and when she recovered herself sufficiently to withdraw her hands from Henry's grasp, she could at first only faintly articulate, 'I have taken a strange step, Mr Morton – a step,' she continued with more coherence, as her ideas arranged themselves in consequence of a strong effort, 'that perhaps may expose me to censure in your eyes – But I have long permitted you to use the language of friendship – perhaps I might say more – too long to leave you when the world seems to have left you. How, or why, is this imprisonment? what can be done? can my uncle, who thinks so highly of you – can your own kinsman, Milnwood, be of no use? are there no means? and what is likely to be the event?'

'Be what it will,' answered Henry, contriving to make himself master of the hand that had escaped from him, but which was now again abandoned to his clasp, 'be what it will, it is to me from this moment the most welcome incident of a weary life. To you, dearest Edith – forgive me, I should have said Miss Bellenden, but misfortune claims strange privileges – to you I have owed the few happy moments which have gilded a gloomy existence; and if I am now to lay it down, the recollection of this honour will be my happiness in the last hour of suffering.'

'But is it even thus, Mr Morton?' said Miss Bellenden. 'Have you, who used to mix so little in these unhappy feuds, become so suddenly and deeply implicated, that nothing short of' –

She paused, unable to bring out the word which should have come next.

'Nothing short of my life, you would say?' replied Morton, in a calm, but melancholy tone; 'I believe that will be entirely in the bosoms of my judges. My guards spoke of a possibility of exchanging the penalty for entry into foreign service. I thought I could have embraced the alternative; and yet, Miss Bellenden, since I have seen you once more, I feel that exile would be more galling than death.'

'And is it then true,' said Edith, 'that you have been so desperately rash as to entertain communication with any of those cruel wretches who assassinated the primate?'

'I knew not even that such a crime had been committed,' replied Morton, 'when I gave unhappily a night's lodging and concealment to one of those rash and cruel men, the ancient friend and comrade of my father. But my ignorance will avail me little; for who, Miss Bellenden, save you, will believe it? And, what is worse, I am at least uncertain whether, even if I had known the crime, I could have brought my mind, under all the circumstances, to refuse a temporary refuge to the fugitive.'

'And by whom,' said Edith, anxiously, 'or under what authority, will the investigation of your conduct take place?'

'Under that of Colonel Grahame of Claverhouse, I am given to understand,' said Morton; 'one of the military commission, to whom it has pleased our king, our privy council, and our parliament, that used to be more tenacious of our liberties, to commit the sole charge of our goods and of our lives.'

'To Claverhouse?' said Edith, faintly; 'merciful Heaven, you are lost ere you are tried! He wrote to my grandmother that he was to be here to-morrow morning, on his road to the head of the county, where some desperate men, animated by the presence of two or three of the actors in the primate's murder, are said to have assembled for the purpose of making a stand against the government. His expressions made me shudder, even when I could not guess that – that – a friend' –

'Do not be too much alarmed on my account, my dearest

Edith,' said Henry, as he supported her in his arms; 'Claver-house, though stern and relentless, is, by all accounts, brave, fair, and honourable. I am a soldier's son, and will plead my cause like a soldier. He will perhaps listen more favourably to a blunt and unvarnished defence than a truckling and time-serving judge might do. And, indeed, in a time when justice is, in all its branches, so completely corrupted, I would rather lose my life by open military violence, than be conjured out of it by the hocus-pocus of some arbitrary lawyer, who lends the knowledge he has of the statutes made for our protection, to wrest them to our destruction.'

'You are lost – you are lost, if you are to plead your cause with Claverhouse!' sighed Edith; 'root and branchwork is the mildest of his expressions. The unhappy primate was his intimate friend and early patron.⁶ "No excuse, no subterfuge," said his letter "shall save either those connected with the deed, or such as have given them countenance and shelter, from the ample and bitter penalty of the law, until I shall have taken as many lives in vengeance of this atrocious murder, as the old man had grey hairs upon his venerable head." There is neither ruth nor favour to be found with him.'

Jenny Dennison, who had hitherto remained silent, now ventured, in the extremity of distress which the lovers felt, but for which they were unable to devise a remedy, to offer her own advice.

'Wi' your leddyship's pardon, Miss Edith, and young Mr Morton's, we maunna waste time. Let Milnwood take my plaid and gown; I'll slip them aff in the dark corner, if he'll promise no to look about, and he may walk past Tam Halliday, who is half blind with his ale, and I can tell him a canny way to get out o' the Tower, and your leddyship will gang quietly to your ain room, and I'll row mysell in his grey cloak, and pit on his hat, and play the prisoner till the coast's clear, and then I'll cry in Tam Halliday, and gar him let me out.'

'Let you out?' said Morton; 'they'll make your life answer it.'

'Ne'er a bit,' replied Jenny; 'Tam daurna tell he let ony body in, for his ain sake; and I'll gar him find some other gate to account for the escape.'

'Will you, by G—?' said the sentinel, suddenly opening the door of the apartment; 'if I am half blind, I am not deaf, and you should not plan an escape quite so loud, if you expect to go through with it. Come, come, Mrs Janet – march, troop – quick time – trot, d—n me! – And you, madam kinswoman, – I won't ask your real name, though you were going to play me so rascally a trick, – but I must make a clear garrison; so beat a retreat, unless you would have me turn out the guard.'

'I hope,' said Morton, very anxiously, 'you will not mention this circumstance, my good friend, and trust to my honour to acknowledge your civility in keeping the secret. If you overheard our conversation, you must have observed that we did not accept of, or enter into, the hasty proposal made by this good-natured girl.'

'Oh, devilish good-natured, to be sure,' said Halliday. 'As for the rest, I guess how it is, and I scorn to bear malice, or tell tales, as much as another; but no thanks to that little jilting devil, Jenny Dennison, who deserves a tight skelping for trying to lead an honest lad into a scrape, just because he was so silly as to like her good-for-little chit face.'

Jenny had no better means of justification than the last apology to which her sex trust, and usually not in vain; she pressed her handkerchief to her face, sobbed with great vehemence, and either wept, or managed, as Halliday might have said, to go through the motions wonderfully well.

'And now,' continued the soldier, somewhat mollified, 'if you have any thing to say, say it in two minutes, and let me see your backs turned; for if Bothwell take it into his drunken head to make the rounds half an hour too soon, it will be a black business to us all.'

'Farewell, Edith,' whispered Morton, assuming a firmness he was far from possessing; 'do not remain here – leave me to my fate – it cannot be beyond endurance since you are interested in it. – Good night, good night! – Do not remain here till you are discovered.'

Thus saying, he resigned her to her attendant, by whom she was quietly led and partly supported out of the apartment.

'Every one has his taste, to be sure,' said Halliday; 'but d—n me if I would have vexed so sweet a girl as that is, for all the whigs that ever swore the Covenant.'

When Edith had regained her apartment, she gave way to a burst of grief which alarmed Jenny Dennison, who hastened to administer such scraps of consolation as occurred to her.

'Dinna vex yoursell sae muckle, Miss Edith,' said that faithful attendant; 'wha kens what may happen to help young Milnwood? He's a brave lad, and a bonny, and a gentleman of a good fortune, and they winna string the like o' him up as they do the puir whig bodies that they catch in the muirs, like straps o' onions; maybe his uncle will bring him aff, or maybe your ain grand-uncle will speak a gude word for him – he's weel acquent wi' a' the red-coat gentlemen.'

'You are right, Jenny! you are right,' said Edith, recovering herself from the stupor into which she had sunk; 'this is no time for despair, but for exertion. You must find some one to ride this very night to my uncle's with a letter.'

'To Charnwood, madam? It's unco late, and it's sax miles an' a bittock doun the water; I doubt if we can find man and horse the night, mair especially as they hae mounted a sentinel before the gate. Puir Cuddie! he's gane, puir fallow, that wad hae dune aught in the warld I bade him, and ne'er asked a reason – an' I've had nae time to draw up wi' the new pleugh-lad yet; forby that, they say he's gaun to be married to Meg Murdieson, ill-faur'd cuttie as she is.'

'You *must* find some one to go, Jenny; life and death depend upon it.'

'I wad gang mysell, my leddy, for I could creep out at the window o' the pantry, and speel down by the auld yew-tree weel enough – I hae played that trick ere now. But the road's unco wild, and sae mony red-coats about, forby the whigs, that are no muckle better (the young lads o' them) if they meet a fraim body their lane in the muirs. I wadna stand for the walk – I can walk ten miles by moonlight weel enough.'

'Is there no one you can think of, that, for money or favour, would serve me so far?' asked Edith, in great anxiety.

'I dinna ken,' said Jenny, after a moment's consideration, 'unless it be Guse Gibbie; and he'll maybe no ken the way,

though it's no sae difficult to hit, if he keep the horse-road, and
mind the turn at the Cappercleugh, and dinna drown himsell in
the Whomlekirn-pule, or fa' ower the scaur at the Deil's Loaning, or miss ony o' the kittle steps at the Pass o' Walkwary, or be
carried to the hills by the whigs, or be taen to the tolbooth by the
red-coats.'

'All ventures must be run,' said Edith, cutting short the list
of chances against Goose Gibbie's safe arrival at the end of his
pilgrimage; 'all risks must be run, unless you can find a better
messenger. — Go, bid the boy get ready, and get him out of the
Tower as secretly as you can. If he meets any one, let him say he
is carrying a letter to Major Bellenden of Charnwood, but without mentioning any names.'

'I understand, madam,' said Jenny Dennison; 'I warrant the
callant will do weel eneugh, and Tib the hen-wife will tak care
o' the geese for a word o' my mouth; and I'll tell Gibbie your
leddyship will mak his peace wi' Lady Margaret, and we'll gie
him a dollar.'

'Two, if he does his errand well,' said Edith.

Jenny departed to rouse Goose Gibbie out of his slumbers, to
which he was usually consigned at sundown, or shortly after, he
keeping the hours of the birds under his charge. During her
absence, Edith took her writing materials, and prepared against
her return the following letter, superscribed, For the hands of
Major Bellenden of Charnwood, my much honoured uncle,
These:

'My dear Uncle. — This will serve to inform you I am desirous
to know how your gout is, as we did not see you at the wappen-
schaw, which made both my grandmother and myself very un-
easy. And if it will permit you to travel, we shall be happy to see
you at our poor-house to-morrow at the hour of breakfast, as
Colonel Grahame of Claverhouse is to pass this way on his
march, and we would willingly have your assistance to receive
and entertain a military man of such distinction, who, probably,
will not be much delighted with the company of women. Also,
my dear uncle, I pray you to let Mrs Carefor't, your housekeeper,
send me my double-trimmed paduasoy with the hanging sleeves,

which she will find in the third drawer of the walnut press in the green room, which you are so kind as to call mine. Also, my dear uncle, I pray you to send me the second volume of the Grand Cyrus,[7] as I have only read as far as the imprisonment of Philidaspes upon the seven hundredth and thirty-third page; but, above all, I entreat you to come to us to-morrow before eight of the clock, which, as your pacing nag is so good, you may well do without rising before your usual hour. So, praying to God to preserve your health, I rest your dutiful and loving niece,

'EDITH BELLENDEN.

'*Postscriptum.* A party of soldiers have last night brought your friend, young Mr Henry Morton of Milnwood, hither as a prisoner. I conclude you will be sorry for the young gentleman, and, therefore, let you know this, in case you may think of speaking to Colonel Grahame in his behalf. I have not mentioned his name to my grandmother, knowing her prejudice against the family.'

This epistle being duly sealed and delivered to Jenny, that faithful confidant hastened to put the same in the charge of Goose Gibbie, whom she found in readiness to start from the castle. She then gave him various instructions touching the road, which she apprehended he was likely to mistake, not having travelled it above five or six times, and possessing only the same slender proportion of memory as of judgment. Lastly, she smuggled him out of the garrison through the pantry window into the branchy yew-tree which grew close beside it, and had the satisfaction to see him reach the bottom in safety, and take the right turn at the commencement of his journey. She then returned to persuade her young mistress to go to bed, and to lull her to rest, if possible, with assurances of Gibbie's success in his embassy, only qualified by a passing regret that the trusty Cuddie, with whom the commission might have been more safely reposed, was no longer within reach of serving her.

More fortunate as a messenger than as a cavalier, it was Gibbie's good hap rather than his good management, which, after he had gone astray not oftener than nine times, and given his garments a taste of the variation of each bog, brook, and slough, between Tillietudlem and Charnwood, placed him about daybreak before the gate of Major Bellenden's mansion, having completed a walk of ten miles (for the bittock, as usual, amounted to four) in little more than the same number of hours.

CHAPTER 11

At last comes the troop, by the word of command
Drawn up in our court, where the Captain cries, Stand!

SWIFT[1]

MAJOR BELLENDEN's ancient valet, Gideon Pike as he adjusted his master's clothes by his bedside, preparatory to the worthy veteran's toilet, acquainted him, as an apology for disturbing him an hour earlier than his usual time of rising, that there was an express from Tillietudlem.

'From Tillietudlem?' said the old gentleman, rising hastily in his bed, and sitting bolt upright, – 'Open the shutters, Pike – I hope my sister-in-law is well – furl up the bed-curtain. – What have we all here?' (glancing at Edith's note.) 'The gout? why, she knows I have not had a fit since Candlemas. – The wappen-schaw? I told her a month since I was not to be there. – Paduasoy and hanging sleeves? why, hang the gipsy herself! – Grand Cyrus and Philipdastus? – Philip Devil! – is the wench gone crazy all at once? was it worth while to send an express and wake me at five in the morning for all this trash? – But what says her postscriptum? – Mercy on us!' he exclaimed on perusing it, – 'Pike, saddle old Kilsythe instantly, and another horse for your-self.'

'I hope nae ill news frae the Tower, sir?' said Pike, astonished at his master's sudden emotion.

'Yes – no – yes – that is, I must meet Claverhouse there on some express business; so boot and saddle, Pike, as fast as you can. – O, Lord! what times are these! – the poor lad – my old cronie's son! – and the silly wench sticks it into her postscriptum, as she calls it, at the tail of all this trumpery about old gowns and new romances!'

In a few minutes the good old officer was fully equipped; and having mounted upon his arm-gaunt charger as soberly as Mark Antony[2] himself could have done, he paced forth his way to the Tower of Tillietudlem.

On the road he formed the prudent resolution to say nothing to the old lady (whose dislike to presbyterians of all kinds he knew to be inveterate) of the quality and rank of the prisoner detained within her walls, but to try his own influence with Claverhouse to obtain Morton's liberation.

'Being so loyal as he is, he must do something for so old a cavalier as I am,' said the veteran to himself; 'and if he is so good a soldier as the world speaks of, why, he will be glad to serve an old soldier's son. I never knew a real soldier that was not a frank-hearted, honest fellow; and I think the execution of the laws (though it's a pity they find it necessary to make them so severe) may be a thousand times better intrusted with them than with peddling lawyers and thick-skulled country gentlemen.'

Such were the ruminations of Major Miles Bellenden, which were terminated by John Gudyill (not more than half-drunk) taking hold of his bridle, and assisting him to dismount in the rough-paved court of Tillietudlem.

'Why, John,' said the veteran, 'what devil of a discipline is this you have been keeping? You have been reading Geneva print this morning already.'

'I have been reading the Litany,' said John, shaking his head with a look of drunken gravity, and having only caught one word of the Major's address to him; 'life is short, sir; we are flowers of the field, sir – hiccup – and lilies of the valley.'[3]

'Flowers and lilies? Why, man, such carles as thou and I can hardly be called better than old hemlocks, decayed nettles, or withered rag-weed; but I suppose you think that we are still worth watering.'

'I am an old soldier, sir, I thank Heaven – hiccup' –

'An old skinker, you mean, John. But come, never mind, show me the way to your mistress, old lad.'

John Gudyill led the way to the stone hall, where Lady Margaret was fidgeting about, superintending, arranging, and re-forming the preparations made for the reception of the celebrated Claverhouse, whom one party honoured and extolled as a hero, and another execrated as a bloodthirsty oppressor.

'Did I not tell you,' said Lady Margaret to her principal female attendant – 'did I not tell you, Mysie, that it was my especial pleasure on this occasion to have every thing in the precise order wherein it was upon that famous morning when his most sacred majesty partook of his disjune at Tillietudlem?'

'Doubtless, such were your leddyship's commands, and to the best of my remembrance' – was Mysie answering, when her ladyship broke in with, 'Then wherefore is the venison pasty placed on the left side of the throne, and the stoup of claret upon the right, when ye may right weel remember, Mysie, that his most sacred majesty with his ain hand shifted the pasty to the same side with the flagon, and said they were too good friends to be parted?'

'I mind that weel, madam,' said Mysie; 'and if I had forgot, I have heard your leddyship often speak about that grand morning sin' syne; but I thought every thing was to be placed just as it was when his majesty, God bless him, came into this room, looking mair like an angel than a man, if he hadna been sae black-a-vised.'

'Then ye thought nonsense, Mysie; for in whatever way his most sacred majesty ordered the position of the trenchers and flagons, that, as weel as his royal pleasure in greater matters, should be a law to his subjects, and shall ever be to those of the house of Tillietudlem.'

'Weel, madam,' said Mysie, making the alterations required, 'it's easy mending the error; but if every thing is just to be as his majesty left it, there should be an unco hole in the venison pasty.'

At this moment the door opened.

'Who is that, John Gudyill?' exclaimed the old lady. 'I can speak to no one just now. – Is it you, my dear brother?' she continued, in some surprise, as the Major entered; 'this is a right early visit.'

'Not more early than welcome, I hope, replied Major Bellenden, as he saluted the widow of his deceased brother; 'but I heard by a note which Edith sent to Charnwood about some of her equipage and books, that you were to have Claver'se here this morning, so I thought, like an old fire-lock as I am, that I should like to have a chat with this rising soldier. I caused Pike saddle Kilsythe, and here we both are.'

'And most kindly welcome you are,' said the old lady; 'it is just what I should have prayed you to do, if I had thought there was time. You see I am busy in preparation. All is to be in the same order as when' –

'The king breakfasted at Tillietudlem,' said the Major, who, like all Lady Margaret's friends, dreaded the commencement of that narrative, and was desirous to cut it short, – 'I remember it well; you know I was waiting on his majesty.'

'You were, brother,' said Lady Margaret; 'and perhaps you can help me to remember the order of the entertainment.'

'Nay, good sooth,' said the Major, 'the damnable dinner that Noll[4] gave us at Worcester a few days afterwards drove all your good cheer out of my memory. – But how's this? – you have even the great Turkey-leather elbow-chair, with the tapestry cushions, placed in state.'

'The throne, brother, if you please,' said Lady Margaret, gravely.

'Well, the throne be it, then,' continued the Major. 'Is that to be Claver'se's post in the attack upon the pasty?'

'No, brother,' said the lady; 'as these cushions have been once honoured by accommodating the person of our most sacred Monarch, they shall never, please Heaven, during my life-time, be pressed by any less dignified weight.'

'You should not then,' said the old soldier, 'put them in the way of an honest old cavalier, who has ridden ten miles before breakfast; for, to confess the truth, they look very inviting. But where is Edith?'

'On the battlements of the warder's turret,' answered the old lady, 'looking out for the approach of our guests.'

'Why, I'll go there too; and so should you, Lady Margaret, as soon as you have your line of battle properly formed in the hall here. It's a pretty thing, I can tell you, to see a regiment of horse upon the march.'

Thus speaking, he offered his arm with an air of old-fashioned gallantry, which Lady Margaret accepted with such a courtesy of acknowledgement as ladies were wont to make in Holyrood-house before the year 1642, which, for one while, drove both courtesies and courts out of fashion.

Upon the bartizan of the turret, to which they ascended by many a winding passage and uncouth staircase, they found Edith, not in the attitude of a young lady who watches with fluttering curiosity the approach of a smart regiment of dragoons, but pale, downcast, and evincing, by her countenance, that sleep had not, during the preceding night, been the companion of her pillow. The good old veteran was hurt at her appearance, which, in the hurry of preparation, her grandmother had omitted to notice.

'What is come over you, you silly girl?' he said; 'why, you look like an officer's wife when she opens the News-letter after an action, and expects to find her husband among the killed and wounded. But I know the reason – you will persist in reading these nonsensical romances, day and night, and whimpering for distresses that never existed. Why, how the devil can you believe that Artamines, or what d'ye call him, fought single-handed with a whole battalion? One to three is as great odds as ever fought and won, and I never knew any body that cared to take that, except old Corporal Raddlebanes. But these d—d books put all pretty men's actions out of countenance. I daresay you would think very little of Raddlebanes, if he were alongside of Arta-mines. – I would have the fellows that write such nonsense brought to the picquet for leasing-making.'[5]

Lady Margaret, herself somewhat attached to the perusal of romances, took up the cudgels.

'Monsieur Scuderi,' she said, 'is a soldier, brother; and, as I have heard, a complete one, and so is the Sieur d'Urfé.'[6]

'More shame for them; they should have known better what they were writing about. For my part, I have not read a book these twenty years except my Bible, The Whole Duty of Man, and, of late days, Turner's Pallas Armata, or Treatise on the Ordering of the Pike Exercise,[7] and I don't like *his* discipline much neither. He wants to draw up the cavalry in front of a stand of pikes, instead of being upon the wings. Sure am I, if we had done so at Kilsythe, instead of having our handful of horse on the flanks, the first discharge would have sent them back among our Highlanders. – But I hear the kettle-drums.'

All heads were now bent from the battlements of the turret, which commanded a distant prospect down the vale of the river. The Tower of Tillietudlem stood, or perhaps yet stands, upon the angle of a very precipitous bank, formed by the junction of a considerable brook with the Clyde.[8] There was a narrow bridge of one steep arch, across the brook near its mouth, over which, and along the foot of the high and broken bank, winded the public road; and the fortalice, thus commanding both bridge and pass, had been, in times of war, a post of considerable importance, the possession of which was necessary to secure the communication of the upper and wilder districts of the country with those beneath, where the valley expands, and is more capable of cultivation. The view downwards is of a grand woodland character; but the level ground and gentle slopes near the river form cultivated fields of an irregular shape, interspersed with hedgerow-trees and copses, the enclosures seeming to have been individually cleared out of the forest which surrounds them, and which occupies, in unbroken masses, the steeper declivities and more distant banks. The stream, in colour a clear and sparkling brown, like the hue of the Cairngorm pebbles, rushes through this romantic region in bold sweeps and curves, partly visible and partly concealed by the trees which clothe its banks. With a providence unknown in other parts of Scotland, the peasants have, in most places, planted orchards around their cottages, and the general blossom of the apple-trees at this season of the year gave all the lower part of the view the appearance of a flower-garden.

Looking up the river, the character of the scene was varied considerably for the worse. A hilly, waste, and uncultivated country approached close to the banks; the trees were few, and limited to the neighbourhood of the stream, and the rude moors swelled at a little distance into shapeless and heavy hills, which were again surmounted in their turn by a range of lofty mountains, dimly seen on the horizon. Thus the tower commanded two prospects, the one richly cultivated and highly adorned, the other exhibiting the monotonous and dreary character of a wild and inhospitable moorland.

The eyes of the spectators on the present occasion were attracted to the downward view, not alone by its superior beauty, but because the distant sounds of military music began to be heard from the public high-road which winded up the vale, and announced the approach of the expected body of cavalry. Their glimmering ranks were shortly afterwards seen in the distance, appearing and disappearing as the trees and the windings of the road permitted them to be visible, and distinguished chiefly by the flashes of light which their arms occasionally reflected against the sun. The train was long and imposing, for there were about two hundred and fifty horse upon the march, and the glancing of the swords and waving of their banners, joined to the clang of their trumpets and kettle-drums, had at once a lively and awful effect upon the imagination. As they advanced still nearer and nearer, they could distinctly see the files of those chosen troops following each other in long succession, completely equipped and superbly mounted.

'It's a sight that makes me thirty years younger,' said the old cavalier; 'and yet I do not much like the service that these poor fellows are to be engaged in. Although I had my share of the civil war, I cannot say I had ever so much real pleasure in that sort of service as when I was employed on the Continent, and we were hacking at fellows with foreign faces and outlandish dialect. It's a hard thing to hear a hamely Scotch tongue cry quarter, and be obliged to cut him down just the same as if he called out *miséricorde*. – So, there they come through the Netherwood haugh; upon my word, fine-looking fellows, and capitally mounted. – He that is galloping from the rear of the column must be Claver'se himself; – ay, he gets into the front as they cross the bridge, and now they will be with us in less than five minutes.'

At the bridge beneath the tower the cavalry divided, and the greater part, moving up the left bank of the brook and crossing at a ford a little above, took the road of the Grange, as it was called, a large set of farm-offices belonging to the Tower, where Lady Margaret had ordered preparation to be made for their reception and suitable entertainment. The officers alone, with their colours and an escort to guard them, were seen to take the steep road up to the gate of the Tower, appearing by intervals as they gained the ascent, and again hidden by projections of the bank and of the huge old trees with which it is covered. When they emerged from this narrow path, they found themselves in front of the old Tower, the gates of which were hospitably open for their reception. Lady Margaret, with Edith and her brother-in-law, having hastily descended from their post of observation, appeared to meet and to welcome their guests, with a retinue of domestics in as good order as the orgies of the preceding evening permitted. The gallant young cornet (a relation as well as name-sake of Claverhouse, with whom the reader has been already made acquainted) lowered the standard amid the fanfare of the trumpets, in homage to the rank of Lady Margaret and the charms of her grand-daughter, and the old walls echoed to the flourish of the instruments, and the stamp and neigh of the chargers.

Claverhouse[9] himself alighted from a black horse, the most beautiful perhaps in Scotland. He had not a single white hair upon his whole body, a circumstance which, joined to his spirit and fleetness, and to his being so frequently employed in pursuit of the presbyterian recusants, caused an opinion to prevail among them, that the steed had been presented to his rider by the great Enemy of Mankind, in order to assist him in persecuting the fugitive wanderers. When Claverhouse had paid his respects to the ladies with military politeness, had apologized for the trouble to which he was putting Lady Margaret's family, and had received the corresponding assurances that she could not think any thing an inconvenience which brought within the walls of Til-lietudlem so distinguished a soldier, and so loyal a servant of his sacred majesty; when, in short, all forms of hospitable and polite ritual had been duly complied with, the Colonel requested permission to receive the report of Bothwell, who was now in attendance, and with whom he spoke apart for a few minutes. Major Bellenden took that opportunity to say to his niece, without the hearing of her grandmother, 'What a trifling foolish girl you are, Edith, to send me by express a letter crammed with nonsense about books and gowns, and to slide the only thing I cared a marvedie about into the postscript!'

'I did not know,' said Edith, hesitating very much, 'whether it would be quite – quite proper for me to' –

'I know what you would say – whether it would be right to take any interest in a presbyterian. But I knew this lad's father well. He was a brave soldier; and, if he was once wrong, he was once right too. I must commend your caution, Edith, for having said nothing of this young gentleman's affair to your grand-mother – you may rely on it I shall not – I will take an oppor-tunity to speak to Claver'se. Come, my love, they are going to breakfast. Let us follow them.'

CHAPTER 12

Their breakfast so warm to be sure they did eat,
A custom in travellers mighty discreet.

PRIOR[1]

THE breakfast of Lady Margaret Bellenden no more resembled a modern *déjeûné*, than the great stone-hall at Tillietudlem could brook comparison with a modern drawing-room. No tea, no coffee, no variety of rolls, but solid and substantial viands, – the priestly ham, the knightly sirloin, the noble baron of beef, the princely venison pasty; while silver flagons, saved with difficulty from the claws of the Covenanters, now mantled, some with ale, some with mead, and some with generous wine of various quali-ties and descriptions. The appetites of the guests were in corres-pondence to the magnificence and solidity of the preparation – no piddling – no boy's-play, but that steady and persevering exercise of the jaws which is best learned by early morning hours, and by occasional hard commons.

Lady Margaret beheld with delight the cates which she had provided descending with such alacrity into the persons of her honoured guests, and had little occasion to exercise, with respect to any of the company saving Claverhouse himself, the com-pulsory urgency of pressing to eat, to which, as to the *peine forte et dure*, the ladies of that period were in the custom of subjecting their guests.

But the leader himself, more anxious to pay courtesy to Miss Bellenden, next whom he was placed, than to gratify his appetite, appeared somewhat negligent of the good cheer set before him. Edith heard, without reply, many courtly speeches addressed to her, in a tone of voice of that happy modulation which could alike melt in the low tones of interesting conversation, and rise amid the din of battle, 'loud as a trumpet with a silver sound.' The sense that she was in the presence of the dreadful chief upon whose fiat the fate of Henry Morton must depend – the recollection of the terror and awe which were attached to the very name of the commander, deprived her for some time, not only of the courage to answer, but even of the power of looking upon him. But when, emboldened by the soothing tones of his voice, she lifted her eyes to frame some reply, the person on whom she looked bore, in his appearance at least, none of the terrible attributes in which her apprehensions had arrayed him.

Grahame of Claverhouse was in the prime of life, rather low of stature, and slightly, though elegantly, formed; his gesture, language, and manners, were those of one whose life had been spent among the noble and the gay. His features exhibited even feminine regularity. An oval face, a straight and well-formed nose, dark hazel eyes, a complexion just sufficiently tinged with brown to save it from the charge of effeminacy, a short upper lip, curved upward like that of a Grecian statue, and slightly shaded by small mustachios of light brown, joined to a profusion of long curled locks of the same colour, which fell down on each side of his face, contributed to form such a countenance as limners love to paint and ladies to look upon.

The severity of his character, as well as the higher attributes of undaunted and enterprising valour which even his enemies were compelled to admit, lay concealed under an exterior which seemed adapted to the court or the saloon rather than to the field. The same gentleness and gaiety of expression which reigned in his features seemed to inspire his actions and gestures; and, on the whole, he was generally esteemed, at first sight, rather qualified to be the votary of pleasure than of ambition. But under this soft exterior was hidden a spirit unbounded in daring and in aspiring, yet cautious and prudent as that of Machiavel himself. Profound in politics, and embued, of course, with that disregard for individual rights which its intrigues usually generate, this leader was cool and collected in danger, fierce and ardent in pursuing success, careless of facing death himself, and ruthless in inflicting it upon others. Such are the characters formed in times of civil discord, when the highest qualities, perverted by party spirit, and inflamed by habitual opposition, are too often combined with vices and excesses which deprive them at once of their merit and of their lustre.

In endeavouring to reply to the polite trifles with which Claverhouse accosted her, Edith showed so much confusion, that her grandmother thought it necessary to come to her relief.

'Edith Bellenden,' said the old lady, 'has, from my retired mode of living, seen so little of those of her own sphere, that truly she can hardly frame her speech to suitable answers. A soldier is so rare a sight with us, Colonel Grahame, that unless it be my young Lord Evandale, we have hardly had an opportunity of receiving a gentleman in uniform. And, now I talk of that excellent young nobleman, may I enquire if I was not to have had the honour of seeing him this morning with the regiment?'

'Lord Evandale, madam, was on his march with us,' answered the leader, 'but I was obliged to detach him with a small party to disperse a conventicle of those troublesome scoundrels, who have had the impudence to assemble within five miles of my head-quarters.'

'Indeed,' said the old lady; 'that is a height of presumption to which I would have thought no rebellious fanatics would have ventured to aspire. But these are strange times! There is an evil spirit in the land, Colonel Grahame, that excites the vassals of persons of rank to rebel against the very house that holds and feeds them. There was one of my able-bodied men the other day who plainly refused to attend the wappen-schaw at my bidding. Is there no law for such recusancy, Colonel Grahame?'

'I think I could find one,' said Claverhouse, with great composure, 'if your ladyship will inform me of the name and residence of the culprit.'

'His name,' said Lady Margaret, 'is Cuthbert Headrigg; I can say nothing of his domicile, for ye may weel believe, Colonel Grahame, he did not dwell long in Tillietudlem, but was speedily expelled for his contumacy. I wish the lad no severe bodily injury; but incarceration, or even a few stripes, would be a good example in this neighbourhood. His mother, under whose influence I doubt he acted, is an ancient domestic of this family, which makes me incline to mercy; although,' continued the old lady, looking towards the pictures of her husband and her sons, with which the wall was hung, and heaving, at the same time, a deep sigh, 'I, Colonel Grahame, have in my ain person but little right to compassionate that stubborn and rebellious generation. They have made me a childless widow, and, but for the protection of our sacred sovereign and his gallant soldiers, they would soon deprive me of lands and goods, of hearth and altar. Seven of my tenants, whose joint rent-mail may mount to wellnigh a hundred merks, have already refused to pay either cess or rent, and had the assurance to tell my steward that they would acknowledge neither king nor landlord but who should have taken the Covenant.'

'I will take a course with them – that is, with your ladyship's permission,' answered Claverhouse; 'it would ill become me to neglect the support of lawful authority when it is lodged in such worthy hands as those of Lady Margaret Bellenden. But I must needs say this country grows worse and worse daily, and reduces me to the necessity of taking measures with the recusants that are much more consonant with my duty than with my inclinations. And, speaking of this, I must not forget that I have to thank your ladyship for the hospitality you have been pleased to extend to a party of mine who have brought in a prisoner, charged with having resetted[2] the murdering villain, Balfour of Burley.'

'The house of Tillietudlem,' answered the lady, 'hath ever been open to the servants of his majesty, and I hope that the stones of it will no longer rest on each other when it surceases to be as much at their command as at ours. And this reminds me, Colonel Grahame, that the gentleman who commands the party can hardly be said to be in his proper place in the army, considering whose blood flows in his veins; and if I might flatter myself that any thing would be granted to my request, I would presume to entreat that he might be promoted on some favourable opportunity.'

'Your ladyship means Sergeant Francis Stewart, whom we call Bothwell?' said Claverhouse, smiling. 'The truth is, he is a little too rough in the country, and has not been uniformly so amenable to discipline as the rules of the service require. But to instruct me how to oblige Lady Margaret Bellenden, is to lay down the law to me. - Bothwell,' he continued, addressing the sergeant, who just then appeared at the door, 'go kiss Lady Margaret Bellenden's hand, who interests herself in your promotion, and you shall have a commission the first vacancy.'

Bothwell went through the salutation in the manner prescribed, but not without evident marks of haughty reluctance, and, when he had done so, said aloud, 'To kiss a lady's hand can never disgrace a gentleman; but I would not kiss a man's, save the king's, to be made a general.'

'You hear him,' said Claverhouse, smiling, 'there's the rock he splits upon; he cannot forget his pedigree.'

'I know, my noble colonel,' said Bothwell, in the same tone, 'that *you* will not forget your promise; and then, perhaps, you may permit *Cornet* Stewart to have some recollection of his grandfather, though the *Sergeant* must forget him.'

'Enough of this, sir,' said Claverhouse, in the tone of command which was familiar to him; 'and let me know what you came to report to me just now.'

'My Lord Evandale and his party have halted on the high-road with some prisoners,' said Bothwell.

'My Lord Evandale?' said Lady Margaret. 'Surely, Colonel Grahame, you will permit him to honour me with his society, and to take his poor disjune here, especially considering, that even his most sacred Majesty did not pass the Tower of Tillietudlem without halting to partake of some refreshment.'

As this was the third time in the course of the conversation that Lady Margaret had adverted to this distinguished event, Colonel Grahame, as speedily as politeness would permit, took advantage of the first pause to interrupt the farther progress of the narrative, by saying, 'We are already too numerous a party of guests; but as I know what Lord Evandale will suffer (looking toward Edith) if deprived of the pleasure which we enjoy, I will run the risk of overburdening your ladyship's hospitality. – Bothwell, let Lord Evandale know that Lady Margaret Bellenden requests the honour of his company.'

'And let Harrison take care,' added Lady Margaret, 'that the people and their horses are suitably seen to.'

Edith's heart sprung to her lips during this conversation; for it instantly occurred to her, that, through her influence over Lord Evandale, she might find some means of releasing Morton from his present state of danger, in case her uncle's intercession with Claverhouse should prove ineffectual. At any other time she would have been much averse to exert this influence; for, however inexperienced in the world, her native delicacy taught her the advantage which a beautiful young woman gives to a young man when she permits him to lay her under an obligation. And she would have been the farther disinclined to request any favour of Lord Evandale, because the voice of the gossips in Clydesdale had, for reasons hereafter to be made known, assigned him to her as a suitor, and because she could not disguise from herself that very little encouragement was necessary to realize conjectures which had hitherto no foundation. This was the more to be dreaded, that, in the case of Lord Evandale's making a formal declaration, he had every chance of being supported by the influence of Lady Margaret and her other friends, and that she would have nothing to oppose to their solicitations and authority, except a predilection, to avow which she knew would be equally dangerous and unavailing. She determined, therefore, to wait the issue of her uncle's intercession, and, should it fail, which she conjectured she should soon learn, either from the looks or language of the open-hearted veteran, she would then, as a last effort, make use in Morton's favour of her interest with Lord Evandale. Her mind did not long remain in suspense on the subject of her uncle's application.

Major Bellenden, who had done the honours of the table, laughing and chatting with the military guests who were at that end of the board, was now, by the conclusion of the repast, at liberty to leave his station, and accordingly took an opportunity to approach Claverhouse, requesting from his niece, at the same time, the honour of a particular introduction. As his name and character were well known, the two military men met with expressions of mutual regard; and Edith, with a beating heart, saw her aged relative withdraw from the company, together with his new acquaintance, into a recess formed by one of the arched windows of the hall. She watched their conference with eyes almost dazzled by the eagerness of suspense, and, with observation rendered more acute by the internal agony of her mind, could guess, from the pantomimic gestures which accompanied the conversation, the progress and fate of the intercession in behalf of Henry Morton.

The first expression of the countenance of Claverhouse betokened that open and willing courtesy, which, ere it requires to know the nature of the favour asked, seems to say, how happy the party will be to confer an obligation on the suppliant. But as the conversation proceeded, the brow of that officer became darker and more severe, and his features, though still retaining the expression of the most perfect politeness, assumed, at least to Edith's terrified imagination, a harsh and inexorable character. His lip was now compressed as if with impatience; now curled slightly upward, as if in civil contempt of the arguments urged by Major Bellenden. The language of her uncle, as far as expressed in his manner, appeared to be that of earnest intercession, urged with all the affectionate simplicity of his character, as well as with the weight which his age and reputation entitled him to use. But it seemed to have little impression upon Colonel Grahame, who soon changed his posture, as if about to cut short the Major's importunity, and to break up their conference with a courtly expression of regret, calculated to accompany a positive refusal of the request solicited. This movement brought them so near Edith, that she could distinctly hear Claverhouse say, 'It cannot be, Major Bellenden; lenity, in his case, is altogether beyond the bounds of my commission, though in any thing else I am heartily desirous to oblige you. – And here comes Evandale with news, as I think. – What tidings do you bring us, Evandale?' he continued, addressing the young lord, who now entered in complete uniform, but with his dress disordered, and his boots spattered, as if by riding hard.

'Unpleasant news, sir,' was his reply. 'A large body of whigs are in arms among the hills, and have broken out into actual rebellion. They have publicly burnt the Act of Supremacy, that which established episcopacy, that for observing the martyrdom of Charles I, and some others, and have declared their intention to remain together in arms for furthering the covenanted work of reformation.' [3]

This unexpected intelligence struck a sudden and painful surprise into the minds of all who heard it, excepting Claverhouse.

'Unpleasant news call you them?' replied Colonel Grahame, his dark eyes flashing fire, 'they are the best I have heard these six months. Now that the scoundrels are drawn into a body, we will make short work with them. When the adder crawls into daylight,' he added, striking the heel of his boot upon the floor, as if in the act of crushing a noxious reptile, 'I can trample him to death; he is only safe when he remains lurking in his den or morass. – Where are these knaves?' he continued, addressing Lord Evandale.

'About ten miles off among the mountains, at a place called Loudon-hill,' was the young nobleman's reply. 'I dispersed the conventicle against which you sent me, and made prisoner an old trumpeter of rebellion, – an intercommuned minister, that is to say, – who was in the act of exhorting his hearers to rise and be doing in the good cause, as well as one or two of his hearers who seemed to be particularly insolent; and from some country people and scouts I learned what I now tell you.'

'What may be their strength?' asked his commander.

'Probably a thousand men, but accounts differ widely.'

'Then,' said Claverhouse, 'it is time for us to be up and be doing also – Bothwell, bid them sound to horse.'

Bothwell, who, like the war-horse of scripture,[4] snuffed the battle afar off, hastened to give orders to six negroes, in white dresses richly laced, and having massive silver collars and armlets. These sable functionaries acted as trumpeters, and speedily made the castle and the woods around it ring with their summons.

'Must you then leave us?' said Lady Margaret, her heart sinking under recollection of former unhappy times; 'had ye not better send to learn the force of the rebels? – O, how many a fair face hae I heard these fearfu' sounds call away frae the Tower of Tillietudlem, that my auld een were ne'er to see return to it!'

'It is impossible for me to stop,' said Claverhouse; 'there are rogues enough in this country to make the rebels five times their strength, if they are not checked at once.'

'Many,' said Evandale, 'are flocking to them already, and they give out that they expect a strong body of the indulged presbyterians, headed by young Milnwood, as they call him, the son of the famous old roundhead, Colonel Silas Morton.'

This speech produced a very different effect upon the hearers. Edith almost sunk from her seat with terror, while Claverhouse darted a glance of sarcastic triumph at Major Bellenden, which seemed to imply – 'You see what are the principles of the young man you are pleading for.'

'It's a lie – it's a d—d lie of these rascally fanatics,' said the Major hastily. 'I will answer for Henry Morton as I would for my own son. He is a lad of as good church-principles as any gentleman in the Life-Guards. I mean no offence to any one. He has gone to church service with me fifty times, and I never heard him miss one of the responses in my life. Edith Bellenden can bear witness to it as well as I. He always read on the same Prayer-book with her, and could look out the lessons as well as the curate himself.[5] Call him up; let him be heard for himself.'

'There can be no harm in that,' said Claverhouse, 'whether he be innocent or guilty. – Major Allan,' he said, turning to the officer next in command, 'take a guide, and lead the regiment forward to Loudon-hill by the best and shortest road. Move steadily, and do not let the men blow the horses; Lord Evandale and I will overtake you in a quarter of an hour. Leave Bothwell with a party to bring up the prisoners.'

Allan bowed, and left the apartment, with all the officers, excepting Claverhouse and the young nobleman. In a few minutes the sound of the military music and the clashing of hoofs announced that the horsemen were leaving the castle. The sounds were presently heard only at intervals, and soon died away entirely.

While Claverhouse endeavoured to soothe the terrors of Lady Margaret, and to reconcile the veteran Major to his opinion of Morton, Evandale, getting the better of that conscious shyness which renders an ingenuous youth diffident in approaching the object of his affections, drew near to Miss Bellenden, and accosted her in a tone of mingled respect and interest.

'We are to leave you,' he said, taking her hand, which he pressed with much emotion – 'to leave you for a scene which is not without its dangers. Farewell, dear Miss Bellenden; – let me say for the first, and perhaps the last time, dear Edith ! We part in circumstances so singular as may excuse some solemnity in bidding farewell to one, whom I have known so long, and whom I – respect so highly.'

The manner differing from the words, seemed to express a feeling much deeper and more agitating than was conveyed in the phrase he made use of. It was not in woman to be utterly insensible to his modest and deep-felt expression of tenderness. Although borne down by the misfortunes and imminent danger of the man she loved, Edith was touched by the hopeless and reverential passion of the gallant youth, who now took leave of her to rush into dangers of no ordinary description.

'I hope – I sincerely trust,' she said, 'there is no danger. I hope there is no occasion for this solemn ceremonial – that these hasty insurgents will be dispersed rather by fear than force, and that Lord Evandale will speedily return to be what he must always be, the dear and valued friend of all in this castle.'

'Of all,' he repeated, with a melancholy emphasis upon the word. 'But be it so – whatever is near you is dear and valued to me, and I value their approbation accordingly. Of our success I am not sanguine. Our numbers are so few, that I dare not hope for so speedy, so bloodless, or so safe an end of this unhappy disturbance. These men are enthusiastic, resolute, and desperate, and have leaders not altogether unskilled in military matters. I cannot help thinking that the impetuosity of our Colonel is hurrying us against them rather prematurely. But there are few that have less reason to shun danger than I have.'

Edith had now the opportunity she wished to bespeak the young nobleman's intercession and protection for Henry Morton, and it seemed the only remaining channel of interest by which he could be rescued from impending destruction. Yet she felt at that moment as if, in doing so, she was abusing the partiality and confidence of the lover, whose heart was as open before her, as if his tongue had made an express declaration. Could she with honour engage Lord Evandale in the service of a rival? or could she with prudence make him any request, or lay herself under any obligation to him, without affording ground for hopes which she could never realize? But the moment was too urgent for hesitation, or even for those explanations with which her request might otherwise have been qualified.

'I will but dispose of this young fellow,' said Claverhouse, from the other side of the hall, 'and then, Lord Evandale – I am sorry to interrupt again your conversation – but then we must mount. – Bothwell, why do you not bring up the prisoner? and, hark ye, let two files load their carabines.'

In these words, Edith conceived she heard the death-warrant of her lover. She instantly broke through the restraint which had hitherto kept her silent.

'My Lord Evandale,' she said, 'this young gentleman is a particular friend of my uncle's – your interest must be great with your colonel – let me request your intercession in his favour – it will confer on my uncle a lasting obligation.'

'You overrate my interest, Miss Bellenden,' said Lord Evandale; 'I have been often unsuccessful in such applications, when I have made them on the mere score of humanity.'

'Yet try once again for my uncle's sake.'

'And why not for your own?' said Lord Evandale. 'Will you not allow me to think I am obliging *you* personally in this matter? – Are you so diffident of an old friend that you will not allow him even the satisfaction of thinking that he is gratifying your wishes?'

'Surely – surely,' replied Edith; 'you will oblige me infinitely – I am interested in the young gentleman on my uncle's account – Lose no time, for God's sake!'

She became bolder and more urgent in her entreaties, for she heard the steps of the soldiers who were entering with their prisoner.

'By heaven! then,' said Evandale, 'he shall not die, if I should die in his place! – But will not you,' he said, resuming the hand, which in the hurry of her spirits she had not courage to withdraw, 'will you not grant me one suit, in return for my zeal in your service?'

'Any thing you can ask, my Lord Evandale, that sisterly affection can give.'

'And is this all,' he continued, 'all you can grant to my affection living, or my memory when dead?'

'Do not speak thus, my lord,' said Edith, 'you distress me, and do injustice to yourself. There is no friend I esteem more highly, or to whom I would more readily grant every mark of regard – providing – But' –

A deep sigh made her turn her head suddenly, ere she had well uttered the last word; and, as she hesitated how to frame the exception with which she meant to close the sentence, she became instantly aware she had been overheard by Morton, who, heavily ironed and guarded by soldiers, was now passing behind her in order to be presented to Claverhouse. As their eyes met each other, the sad and reproachful expression of Morton's glance seemed to imply that he had partially heard, and altogether misinterpreted, the conversation which had just passed. There wanted but this to complete Edith's distress and confusion. Her blood, which rushed to her brow, made a sudden revulsion to her heart, and left her as pale as death. This change did not escape the attention of Evandale, whose quick glance easily discovered that there was between the prisoner and the object of his own attachment, some singular and uncommon connexion. He resigned the hand of Miss Bellenden, again surveyed the prisoner with more attention, again looked at Edith, and plainly observed the confusion which she could no longer conceal.

'This,' he said, after a moment's gloomy silence, 'is, I believe, the young gentleman who gained the prize at the shooting match.'

'I am not sure,' hesitated Edith – 'yet – I rather think not,' scarce knowing what she replied.

'It *is* he,' said Evandale, decidedly; 'I know him well. A victor,' he continued, somewhat haughtily, 'ought to have interested a fair spectator more deeply.'

He then turned from Edith, and advancing towards the table at which Claverhouse now placed himself, stood at a little distance, resting on his sheathed broadsword, a silent, but not an unconcerned, spectator of that which passed.

CHAPTER 13

O, my Lord, beware of jealousy!

Othello [1]

To explain the deep effect which the few broken passages of the conversation we have detailed made upon the unfortunate prisoner by whom they were overheard, it is necessary to say something of his previous state of mind, and of the origin of his acquaintance with Edith.

Henry Morton was one of those gifted characters, which possess a force of talent unsuspected by the owner himself. He had inherited from his father an undaunted courage, and a firm and uncompromising detestation of oppression, whether in politics or religion. But his enthusiasm was unsullied by fanatic zeal, and unleavened by the sourness of the puritanical spirit. From these his mind had been freed, partly by the active exertions of his own excellent understanding, partly by frequent and long visits at Major Bellenden's, where he had an opportunity of meeting with many guests whose conversation taught him, that goodness and worth were not limited to those of any single form of religious observance.

The base parsimony of his uncle had thrown many obstacles in the way of his education; but he had so far improved the opportunities which offered themselves, that his instructors as well as his friends were surprised at his progress under such disadvantages. Still, however, the current of his soul was frozen by a sense of dependence, of poverty, above all, of an imperfect and limited education. These feelings impressed him with a

diffidence and reserve which effectually concealed from all but
very intimate friends, the extent of talent and the firmness of
character, which we have stated him to be possessed of. The
circumstances of the times had added to this reserve an air of
indecision and of indifference; for, being attached to neither of
the factions which divided the kingdom, he passed for dull, insensible, and uninfluenced by the feeling of religion or of
patriotism. No conclusion, however, could be more unjust; and
the reasons of the neutrality which he had hitherto professed had
root in very different and most praiseworthy motives. He had
formed few congenial ties with those who were the objects of
persecution, and was disgusted alike by their narrow-minded and
selfish party-spirit, their gloomy fanaticism, their abhorrent condemnation of all elegant studies or innocent exercises, and the
envenomed rancour of their political hatred. But his mind was
still more revolted by the tyrannical and oppressive conduct of
the government, the misrule, license, and brutality of the
soldiery, the executions on the scaffold, the slaughters in the
open field, the free quarters and exactions imposed by military
law, which placed the lives and fortunes of a free people on a
level with Asiatic slaves. Condemning, therefore, each party as
its excesses fell under his eyes, disgusted with the sight of evils
which he had no means of alleviating, and hearing alternative
complaints and exultations with which he could not sympathize,
he would long ere this have left Scotland, had it not been for his
attachment to Edith Bellenden.

The earlier meetings of these young people had been at Charnwood, when Major Bellenden, who was as free from suspicion
on such occasions as Uncle Toby[2] himself, had encouraged their
keeping each other constant company, without entertaining any
apprehension of the natural consequences. Love, as usual in such
cases, borrowed the name of friendship, used her language, and
claimed her privileges. When Edith Bellenden was recalled to
her mother's castle,[3] it was astonishing by what singular and
recurring accidents she often met young Morton in her sequestered walks, especially considering the distance of their
places of abode. Yet it somehow happened that she never expressed the surprise which the frequency of these rencontres

ought naturally to have excited, and that their intercourse assumed gradually a more delicate character, and their meetings began to wear the air of appointments. Books, drawings, letters, were exchanged between them, and every trifling commission, given or executed, gave rise to a new correspondence. Love indeed was not yet mentioned between them by name, but each knew the situation of their own bosom, and could not but guess at that of the other. Unable to desist from an intercourse which possessed such charms for both, yet trembling for its too probable consequences, it had been continued without specific explanation until now, when fate appeared to have taken the conclusion into its own hands.

It followed, as a consequence of this state of things, as well as of the diffidence of Morton's disposition at this period, that his confidence in Edith's return of his affection had its occasional cold fits. Her situation was in every respect so superior to his own, her worth so eminent, her accomplishments so many, her face so beautiful, and her manners so bewitching, that he could not but entertain fears that some suitor more favoured than himself by fortune, and more acceptable to Edith's family than he durst hope to be, might step in between him and the object of his affections. Common rumour had raised up such a rival in Lord Evandale, whom birth, fortune, connexions, and political principles, as well as his frequent visits at Tillietudlem, and his attendance upon Lady Bellenden and her niece at all public places, naturally pointed out as a candidate for her favour. It frequently and inevitably happened, that engagements to which Lord Evandale was a party, interfered with the meeting of the lovers, and Henry could not but mark that Edith either studiously avoided speaking of the young nobleman, or did so with obvious reserve and hesitation.

These symptoms, which, in fact, arose from the delicacy of her own feelings towards Morton himself, were misconstrued by his diffident temper, and the jealousy which they excited was fermented by the occasional observations of Jenny Dennison. This true-bred serving-damsel was, in her own person, a complete country coquette, and when she had no opportunity of teasing her own lovers, used to take some occasional opportunity to torment her young lady's. This arose from no ill-will to Henry Morton, who, both on her mistress's account and his own handsome form and countenance, stood high in her esteem. But then Lord Evandale was also handsome; he was liberal far beyond what Morton's means could afford, and he was a lord, moreover, and, if Miss Edith Bellenden should accept his hand, she would become a baron's lady, and, what was more, little Jenny Dennison, whom the awful housekeeper at Tillietudlem huffed about at her pleasure, would be then Mrs Dennison, Lady Evandale's own woman, or perhaps her ladyship's lady-in-waiting. The impartiality of Jenny Dennison, therefore, did not, like that of Mrs Quickly,[4] extend to a wish that both the handsome suitors could wed her young lady; for it must be owned that the scale of her regard was depressed in favour of Lord Evandale, and her wishes in his favour took many shapes extremely tormenting to Morton; being now expressed as a friendly caution, now as an article of intelligence, and anon as a merry jest, but always tending to confirm the idea, that, sooner or later, his romantic intercourse with her young mistress must have a close, and that Edith Bellenden would, in spite of summer walks beneath the greenwood tree, exchange of verses, of drawings, and of books, end in becoming Lady Evandale.

These hints coincided so exactly with the very point of his own suspicions and fears, that Morton was not long of feeling that jealousy which every one has felt who has truly loved, but to which those are most liable whose love is crossed by the want of friends' consent, or some other envious impediment of fortune. Edith herself, unwittingly, and in the generosity of her own frank nature, contributed to the error into which her lover was in danger of falling. Their conversation once chanced to turn upon some late excesses committed by the soldiery on an occasion when it was said (inaccurately however) that the party was commanded by Lord Evandale. Edith, as true in friendship as in love, was somewhat hurt at the severe strictures which escaped from Morton on this occasion, and which, perhaps, were not the less strongly expressed on account of their supposed rivalry. She entered into Lord Evandale's defence with such spirit as hurt Morton to the very soul, and afforded no small delight to Jenny Dennison, the usual companion of their walks. Edith perceived her error, and endeavoured to remedy it; but the impression was not so easily erased, and it had no small effect in inducing her lover to form that resolution of going abroad, which was disappointed in the manner we have already mentioned.

The visit which he received from Edith during his confinement, the deep and devoted interest which she had expressed in his fate, ought of themselves to have dispelled his suspicions; yet, ingenious in tormenting himself, even this he thought might be imputed to anxious friendship, or, at most, to a temporary partiality, which would probably soon give way to circumstances, the entreaties of her friends, the authority of Lady Margaret, and the assiduities of Lord Evandale.

'And to what do I owe it,' he said, 'that I cannot stand up like a man, and plead my interest in her ere I am thus cheated out of it? – to what, but to the all-pervading and accursed tyranny, which afflicts at once our bodies, souls, estates, and affections! And is it to one of the pensioned cut-throats of this oppressive government that I must yield my pretensions to Edith Bellenden? – I will not, by Heaven! – It is a just punishment on me for being dead to public wrongs, that they have visited me with their injuries in a point where they can be least brooked or borne.'

As these stormy resolutions boiled in his bosom, and while he ran over the various kinds of insult and injury which he had sustained in his own cause and in that of his country, Bothwell entered the tower, followed by two dragoons, one of whom carried handcuffs.

'You must follow me, young man,' said he, 'but first we must put you in trim.'

'In trim!' said Morton. 'What do you mean?'

'Why, we must put on these rough bracelets. I durst not – nay, d—n it, I *durst* do any thing – but I *would* not for three hours' plunder of a stormed town bring a whig before my Colonel without his being ironed. Come, come, young man, don't look sulky about it.'

He advanced to put on the irons; but, seizing the oaken-seat upon which he had rested, Morton threatened to dash out the brains of the first who should approach him.

'I could manage you in a moment, my youngster,' said Bothwell, 'but I had rather you would strike sail quietly.'

Here indeed he spoke the truth, not from either fear or reluctance to adopt force, but because he dreaded the consequences of a noisy scuffle, through which it might probably be discovered that he had, contrary to express orders, suffered his prisoner to pass the night without being properly secured.

'You had better be prudent,' he continued, in a tone which he meant to be conciliatory, 'and don't spoil your own sport. They say here in the castle that Lady Margaret's niece is immediately to marry our young Captain, Lord Evandale. I saw them close together in the hall yonder, and I heard her ask him to intercede for your pardon. She looked so devilish handsome and kind upon him, that on my soul – But what the devil's the matter with you? – You are as pale as a sheet – Will you have some brandy?'

'Miss Bellenden ask my life of Lord Evandale?' said the prisoner, faintly.

'Ay, ay; there's no friend like the women – their interest carries all in court and camp. – Come, you are reasonable now. Ay, I thought you would come round.'

Here he employed himself in putting on the fetters, against which, Morton, thunderstruck by this intelligence, no longer offered the least resistance.

'My life begged of him, and by her ! – ay – ay – put on the irons – my limbs shall not refuse to bear what has entered into my very soul – My life begged by Edith, and begged of Evandale !'

'Ay, and he has power to grant it too,' said Bothwell – 'He can do more with the Colonel than any man in the regiment.'

And as he spoke, he and his party led their prisoner towards the hall. In passing behind the seat of Edith, the unfortunate prisoner heard enough, as he conceived, of the broken expressions which passed between Edith and Lord Evandale, to confirm all that the soldier had told him. That moment made a singular and instantaneous revolution in his character. The depth of despair to which his love and fortunes were reduced, the peril in which his life appeared to stand, the transference of Edith's affections, her intercession in his favour, which rendered her fickleness yet more galling, seemed to destroy every feeling for which he had hitherto lived, but, at the same time, awakened those which had hitherto been smothered by passions more gentle though more selfish. Desperate himself, he determined to support the rights of his country, insulted in his person. His character was for the moment as effectually changed as the appearance of a villa, which, from being the abode of domestic quiet and happiness, is, by the sudden intrusion of an armed force, converted into a formidable post of defence.

We have already said that he cast upon Edith one glance in which reproach was mingled with sorrow, as if to bid her farewell for ever; his next motion was to walk firmly to the table at which Colonel Grahame was seated.

'By what right is it, sir,' said he firmly, and without waiting till he was questioned, – 'By what right is it that these soldiers have dragged me from my family, and put fetters on the limbs of a free man?'

'By my commands,' answered Claverhouse; 'and now I lay my commands on you to be silent and hear my questions.'

'I will not,' replied Morton, in a determined tone, while his boldness seemed to electrify all around him. 'I will know whether I am in lawful custody, and before a civil magistrate, ere the charter of my country shall be forfeited in my person.'

'A pretty springald this, upon my honour!' said Claverhouse.

'Are you mad?' said Major Bellenden to his young friend. 'For God's sake, Henry Morton,' he continued, in a tone between rebuke and entreaty, 'remember you are speaking to one of his majesty's officers high in the service.'

'It is for that very reason, sir,' returned Henry, firmly, 'that I desire to know what right he has to detain me without a legal warrant. Were he a civil officer of the law I should know my duty was submission.'

'Your friend, here,' said Claverhouse to the veteran, coolly, 'is one of those scrupulous gentlemen, who, like the madman in the play, will not tie his cravat without the warrant of Mr Justice

Overdo,[5] but I will let him see, before we part, that my shoulder-knot is as legal a badge of authority as the mace of the Justiciary. So, waving this discussion, you will be pleased, young man, to tell me directly when you saw Balfour of Burley.'

'As I know no right you have to ask such a question,' replied Morton, 'I decline replying to it.'

'You confessed to my sergeant,' said Claverhouse, 'that you saw and entertained him, knowing him to be an intercommuned traitor; why are you not so frank with me?'

'Because,' replied the prisoner, 'I presume you are, from education, taught to understand the rights upon which you seem disposed to trample; and I am willing you should be aware there are yet Scotsmen who can assert the liberties of Scotland.'

'And these supposed rights you would vindicate with your sword, I presume?' said Colonel Grahame.

'Were I armed as you are, and we were alone upon a hill-side, you should not ask me the question twice.'

'It is quite enough,' answered Claverhouse, calmly; 'your language corresponds with all I have heard of you; – but you are the son of a soldier, though a rebellious one, and you shall not die the death of a dog; I will save you that indignity.'

'Die in what manner I may,' replied Morton, 'I will die like the son of a brave man; and the ignominy you mention shall remain with those who shed innocent blood.'

'Make your peace, then, with Heaven, in five minutes' space. – Bothwell, lead him down to the court-yard, and draw up your party.'

The appalling nature of this conversation, and of its result, struck the silence of horror into all but the speakers. But now those who stood round broke forth into clamour and expostulation. Old Lady Margaret, who, with all the prejudices of rank and party, had not laid aside the feelings of her sex, was loud in her intercession.

'O Colonel Grahame,' she exclaimed, 'spare his young blood! Leave him to the law – do not repay my hospitality by shedding men's blood on the threshold of my doors!'

'Colonel Grahame,' said Major Bellenden, 'you must answer this violence. Don't think, though I am old and feckless, that my friend's son shall be murdered before my eyes with impunity. I can find friends that shall make you answer it.'

'Be satisfied, Major Bellenden, I *will* answer it,' replied Claverhouse, totally unmoved; 'and you, madam, might spare me the pain of resisting this passionate intercession for a traitor, when you consider the noble blood your own house has lost by such as he is.'

'Colonel Grahame,' answered the lady, her aged frame trembling with anxiety, 'I leave vengeance to God, who calls it his own. The shedding of this young man's blood will not call back the lives that were dear to me; and how can it comfort me to think that there has maybe been another widowed mother made childless, like mysell, by a deed done at my very door-stane!'

'This is stark madness,' said Claverhouse; 'I *must* do my duty to church and state. Here are a thousand villains hard by in open rebellion, and you ask me to pardon a young fanatic who is enough of himself to set a whole kingdom in a blaze! It cannot be – Remove him, Bothwell.'

She who was most interested in this dreadful decision, had twice strove to speak, but her voice had totally failed her; her mind refused to suggest words, and her tongue to utter them. She now sprung up and attempted to rush forward, but her strength gave way, and she would have fallen flat upon the pavement had she not been caught by her attendant.

'Help!' cried Jenny, – 'Help, for God's sake! my young lady is dying.'

At this exclamation, Evandale, who, during the preceding part of the scene, had stood motionless, leaning upon his sword, now stepped forward, and said to his commanding-officer, 'Colonel Grahame, before proceeding in this matter, will you speak a word with me in private?'

Claverhouse looked surprised, but instantly rose and withdrew with the young nobleman into a recess, where the following brief dialogue passed between them:

'I think I need not remind you Colonel, that when our family interest was of service to you last year in that affair in the privy-council, you considered yourself as laid under some obligation to us?'

'Certainly, my dear Evandale,' answered Claverhouse, 'I am

not a man who forgets such debts; you will delight me by showing how I can evince my gratitude.'

'I will hold the debt cancelled,' said Lord Evandale, 'if you
will spare this young man's life.'

'Evandale,' replied Grahame, in great surprise, 'you are mad –
absolutely mad – what interest can you have in this young spawn
of an old roundhead? – His father was positively the most
dangerous man in all Scotland, cool, resolute, soldierly, and
inflexible in his cursed principles. His son seems his very model;
you cannot conceive the mischief he may do. I know mankind,
Evandale – were he an insignificant, fanatical, country booby,
do you think I would have refused such a trifle as his life to
Lady Margaret and this family? But this is a lad of fire, zeal, and
education – and these knaves want but such a leader to direct
their blind enthusiastic hardiness. I mention this, not as refusing
your request, but to make you fully aware of the possible consequences – I will never evade a promise, or refuse to return an
obligation – if you ask his life, he shall have it.'

'Keep him close prisoner,' answered Evandale, 'but do not be
surprised if I persist in requesting you will not put him to death.
I have most urgent reasons for what I ask.'

'Be it so then,' replied Grahame; – 'but, young man, should you
wish in your future life to rise to eminence in the service of your
king and country, let it be your first task to subject to the public
interest, and to the discharge of your duty, your private passions,
affections, and feelings. These are not times to sacrifice to the
dotage of greybeards, or the tears of silly women, the measures of
salutary severity which the dangers around compel us to adopt.
And remember, that if I now yield this point, in compliance
with your urgency, my present concession must exempt me from
future solicitations of the same nature.'

He then stepped forward to the table, and bent his eyes keenly
on Morton, as if to observe what effect the pause of awful suspense between death and life, which seemed to freeze the bystanders with horror, would produce upon the prisoner himself.
Morton maintained a degree of firmness, which nothing but a
mind that had nothing left upon earth to love or to hope, could
have supported at such a crisis.

'You see him?' said Claverhouse, in a half whisper to Lord Evandale; 'he is tottering on the verge between time and eternity, a situation more appalling than the most hideous certainty; yet his is the only cheek unblenched, the only eye that is calm, the only heart that keeps its usual time, the only nerves that are not quivering. Look at him well, Evandale – If that man shall ever come to head an army of rebels, you will have much to answer for on account of this morning's work.' He then said aloud, 'Young man, your life is for the present safe, through the intercession of your friends – Remove him, Bothwell, and let him be properly guarded, and brought along with the other prisoners.'

'If my life,' said Morton, stung with the idea that he owed his respite to the intercession of a favoured rival, 'if my life be granted at Lord Evandale's request' –

'Take the prisoner away, Bothwell,' said Colonel Grahame, interrupting him; 'I have neither time to make nor to hear fine speeches '

Bothwell forced off Morton, saying, as he conducted him into the court-yard, 'Have you three lives in your pocket, besides the one in your body, my lad, that you can afford to let your tongue run away with them at this rate? Come, come, I'll take care to keep you out of the Colonel's way; for, egad, you will not be five minutes with him before the next tree or the next ditch will be the word. So, come along to your companions in bondage.'

Thus speaking, the sergeant, who, in his rude manner, did not altogether want sympathy for a gallant young man, hurried Morton down to the courtyard, where three other prisones, (two men and a woman,) who had been taken by Lord Evandale, remained under an escort of dragoons.

Meantime, Claverhouse took his leave of Lady Margaret. But it was difficult for the good lady to forgive his neglect of her intercession.

'I have thought till now,' she said, 'that the Tower of Tillietudlem might have been a place of succour to those that are ready to perish, even if they werena sae deserving as they should have been – but I see auld fruit has little savour – our suffering and our services have been of an ancient date.'

'They are never to be forgotten by me, let me assure your

ladyship,' said Claverhouse. 'Nothing but what seemed my sacred duty could make me hesitate to grant a favour requested by you and the Major. Come, my good lady, let me hear you say you have forgiven me, and, as I return to-night, I will bring a drove of two hundred whigs with me, and pardon fifty head of them for your sake.'

'I shall be happy to hear of your success, Colonel,' said Major Bellenden; 'but take an old soldier's advice, and spare blood when battle's over, – and once more let me request to enter bail for young Morton.'

'We will settle that when I return,' said Claverhouse. 'Meanwhile, be assured his life shall be safe.'

During this conversation, Evandale looked anxiously around for Edith; but the precaution of Jenny Dennison had occasioned her mistress being transported to her own apartment.

Slowly and heavily he obeyed the impatient summons of Claverhouse, who, after taking a courteous leave of Lady Margaret and the Major, had hastened to the court-yard. The prisoners with their guard were already on their march, and the officers with their escort mounted and followed. All pressed forward to overtake the main body, as it was supposed they would come in sight of the enemy in little more than two hours.

CHAPTER 14

My hounds may a' rin masterless,
 My hawks may fly frae tree to tree,
My lord may grip my vassal lands,
 For there again maun I never be!

Old Ballad[1]

We left Morton, along with three companions in captivity, travelling in the custody of a small body of soldiers, who formed the rear-guard of the column under the command of Claverhouse, and were immediately under the charge of Sergeant Bothwell. Their route lay towards the hills in which the insurgent presbyterians were reported to be in arms. They had not prosecuted their march a quarter of a mile ere Claverhouse and Evandale galloped past them, followed by their orderly-men, in order to take their proper places in the column which preceded them. No sooner were they past than Bothwell halted the body which he commanded, and disencumbered Morton of his irons.

'King's blood must keep word,' said the dragoon. 'I promised you should be civilly treated as far as rested with me. – Here, Corporal Inglis, let this gentleman ride alongside of the other young fellow who is prisoner; and you may permit them to converse together at their pleasure, under their breath, but take care they are guarded by two files with loaded carabines. If they attempt an escape, blow their brains out. – You cannot call that using you uncivilly,' he continued, addressing himself to Morton, 'it's the rules of war, you know. – And, Inglis, couple up the parson and the old woman,[2] they are fittest company for each other, d—n me; a single file may guard them well enough. If they speak a word of cant or fanatical nonsense, let them have a strapping with a shoulder-belt. There's some hope of choking a silenced parson; if he is not allowed to hold forth, his own treason will burst him.'

Having made this arrangement, Bothwell placed himself at the head of the party, and Inglis, with six dragoons, brought up the rear. The whole then set forward at a trot, with the purpose of overtaking the main body of the regiment.

Morton, overwhelmed with a complication of feelings, was totally indifferent to the various arrangements made for his secure custody, and even to the relief afforded him by his release from the fetters. He experienced that blank and waste of the heart which follows the hurricane of passion, and, no longer supported by the pride and conscious rectitude which dictated his answers to Claverhouse, he surveyed with deep dejection the glades through which he travelled, each turning of which had something to remind him of past happiness and disappointed love. The eminence which they now ascended was that from which he used first and last to behold the ancient tower when approaching or retiring from it; and, it is needless to add, that there he was wont to pause, and gaze with a lover's delight on the battlements, which, rising at a distance out of the lofty wood, indicated the dwelling of her, whom he either hoped soon to meet or had recently parted from. Instinctively he turned his head back to take a last look of a scene formerly so dear to him, and no less instinctively he heaved a deep sigh. It was echoed by a loud groan from his companion in misfortune, whose eyes, moved, perchance, by similar reflections, had taken the same direction. This indication of sympathy, on the part of the captive, was uttered in a tone more coarse than sentimental; it was, however, the expression of a grieved spirit, and so far corresponded with the sigh of Morton. In turning their heads their eyes met, and Morton recognised the stolid countenance of Cuddie Headrigg, bearing a rueful expression, in which sorrow for his own lot was mixed with sympathy for the situation of his companion.

'Hegh, sirs!' was the expression of the ci-devant ploughman of the mains of Tillietudlem; 'it's an unco thing that decent folk should be harled through the country this gate, as if they were a warld's wonder.'

'I am sorry to see you here, Cuddie,' said Morton, who, even in his own distress, did not lose feeling for that of others.

'And sae am I, Mr Henry,' answered Cuddie, 'baith for my-sell and you; but neither of our sorrows will do muckle gude that I can see. To be sure, for me,' continued the captive agriculturist, relieving his heart by talking, though he well knew it was to little purpose, – 'to be sure, for my part, I hae nae right to be here ava', for I never did nor said a word against either king or curate; but my mither, puir body, couldna haud the auld tongue o' her, and we maun baith pay for't, it's like.'

'Your mother is their prisoner likewise?' said Morton, hardly knowing what he said.

'In troth is she, riding ahint ye there like a bride, wi' that auld carle o' a minister that they ca' Gabriel Kettledrummle – Deil that he had been in the inside of a drum or a kettle either, for my share o' him! Ye see, we were nae sooner chased out o' the doors o' Milnwood, and your uncle and the housekeeper bang-ing them to and barring them ahint us, as if we had had the plague on our bodies, than I says to my mother, What are we to do neist? for every hole and bore in the country will be steekit against us, now that ye hae affronted my auld leddy, and gar't the troopers tak up young Milnwood. Sae she says to me, Binna cast doun, but gird yoursell up to the great task o' the day, and gie your testimony like a man upon the mount o' the Covenant.'

'And so I suppose you went to a conventicle?' said Morton.

'Ye sall hear,' continued Cuddie. – 'Aweel, I kendna muckle better what to do, sae I e'en gaed wi' her to an ald daft carline like hersell, and we got some water-broo and bannocks; and mony a weary grace they said, and mony a psalm they sang, or they wad let me win to, for I was amaist famished wi' vexation. Aweel, they had me up in the grey o' the morning, and I behoved to whig awa wi' them, reason or nane, to a great gathering o' their folk at the Miry-sikes; and there this chield, Gabriel Kettledrummle, was blasting awa to them on the hill-side, about lifting up their testimony, nae doubt, and ganging down to the battle of Roman Gilead, or some sic place. Eh, Mr Henry! but the carle gae them a screed o' doctrine! Ye might hae heard him a mile down the wind – He routed like a cow in a fremd loaning. – Weel, thinks I, there's nae place in this country they ca' Roman Gilead[3] – it will be some gate in the west muirlands; and or we win there I'll see to slip awa wi' this mither o' mine, for I winna rin my neck into a tether for ony Kettledrummle in the country side – Aweel,' continued Cuddie, relieving himself by detailing his misfortunes, without being scrupulous concerning the degree of attention which his companion bestowed on his narrative, 'just as I was wearying for the tail of the preaching, cam word that the dragoons were upon us. – Some ran, and some cried, Stand! and some cried, Down wi' the Philistines! – I was at my mither to get her awa sting and ling or the red-coats cam up, but I might as weel hae tried to drive our auld fore-a-hand ox without the goad – deil a step wad she budge. – Weel, after a', the cleugh we were in was strait, and the mist cam thick, and there was good hope the dragoons wad hae missed us if we could hae held our tongues; but, as if auld Kettledrummle himsell hadna made din eneugh to waken the very dead, they behoved a' to skirl up a psalm that ye wad hae heard as far as Lanrick! –

Aweel, to mak a lang tale short, up cam my young Lord Evandale, skelping as fast as his horse could trot, and twenty red-coats
at his back. Twa or three chields wad needs fight, wi' the pistol
and the whinger in the tae hand, and the Bible in the tother, and
they got their crouns weel cloured; but there wasna muckle
skaith dune, for Evandale aye cried to scatter us, but to spare
life.'

'And did you not resist?' said Morton, who probably felt, that,
at that moment, he himself would have encountered Lord Evandale on much slighter grounds.

'Na, truly,' answered Cuddie, 'I keepit aye before the auld
woman, and cried for mercy to life and limb; but twa o' the
red-coats cam up, and ane o' them was gaun to strike my mither
wi' the side o' his broadsword – So I got up my kebbie at them,
and said I wad gie them as gude. Weel, they turned on me, and
clinked at me wi' their swords, and I garr'd my hand keep my
head as weel as I could till Lord Evandale came up, and then I
cried out I was a servant at Tillietudlem – ye ken yoursell he
was aye judged to hae a look after the young leddy – and he
bade me fling down my kent, and sae me and my mither yielded
oursells prisoners. I'm thinking we wad hae been letten slip awa,
but Kettledrummle was taen near us – for Andrew Wilson's naig
that he was riding on had been a dragooner lang syne, and the
sairer Kettledrummle spurred to win awa, the readier the dour
beast ran to the dragoons when he saw them draw up. – Aweel,
when my mother and him forgathered, they set till the sodgers,
and I think they gae them their kale through the reek! Bastards
o' the hure o' Babylon was the best words in their wame. Sae
then the kiln was in a bleeze again, and they brought us a' three
on wi' them to mak us an example, as they ca't.'

'It is most infamous and intolerable oppression!' said Morton,
half speaking to himself; 'here is a poor peaceable fellow, whose
only motive for joining the conventicle was a sense of filial piety,
and he is chained up like a thief or murderer, and likely to die
the death of one, but without the privilege of a formal trial,
which our laws indulge to the worst malefactor! Even to witness
such tyranny, and still more to suffer under it, is enough to make
the blood of the tamest slave boil within him.'

'To be sure,' said Cuddie, hearing, and partly understanding, what had broken from Morton in resentment of his injuries, 'it is no right to speak evil o' dignities – my auld leddy aye said that, as nae doubt she had a gude right to do, being in a place o' dignity hersell; and troth I listened to her very patiently, for she aye ordered a dram, or a sowp kale, or something to us, after she had gien us a hearing on our duties. But deil a dram, or kale, or ony thing else – no sae muckle as a cup o' cauld water – do thae lords at Edinburgh gie us; and yet they are heading and hanging amang us, and trailing us after thae blackguard troopers, and taking our goods and gear as if we were outlaws. I canna say I tak it kind at their hands.'

'It would be very strange if you did,' answered Morton, with suppressed emotion.

'And what I like warst o' a',' continued poor Cuddie, 'is thae ranting red-coats coming amang the lasses, and taking awa our joes. I had a sair heart o' my ain when I passed the Mains down at Tillietudlem this morning about parritch-time, and saw the reek comin' out at my ain lum-head, and kend there was some ither body than my auld mither sitting by the ingle-side. But I think my heart was e'en sairer, when I saw that hellicat trooper, Tam Halliday, kissing Jenny Dennison afore my face. I wonder women can hae the impudence to do sic things; but they are a' for the red-coats. Whiles I hae thought o' being a trooper mysell, when I thought naething else wad gae down wi' Jenny – and yet I'll no blame her ower muckle neither, for maybe it was a' for my sake that she loot Tam touzle her tap-knots that gate.'

'For your sake?' said Morton, unable to refrain from taking some interest in a story which seemed to bear a singular coincidence with his own.

'E'en sae, Milnwood,' replied Cuddie; 'for the puir quean gat leave to come near me wi' speaking the loun fair, (d—n him, that I suld say sae!) and sae she bade me God speed, and she wanted to stap siller into my hand; – I'se warrant it was the tae half o' her fee and bountith, for she wared the ither half on pinners and pearlings to gang to see us shoot yon day at the popinjay.'

'And did you take it, Cuddie?' said Morton.

'Troth did I no, Milnwood; I was sic a fule as to fling it back to her – my heart was ower grit to be behadden to her, when I had seen that loon slavering and kissing at her. But I was a great fule for my pains; it wad hae dune my mither and me some gude, and she'll ware't a' on duds and nonsense.'

There was here a deep and long pause. Cuddie was probably engaged in regretting the rejection of his mistress's bounty, and Henry Morton in considering from what motives, or upon what conditions, Miss Bellenden had succeeded in procuring the interference of Lord Evandale in his favour.

Was it not possible, suggested his awakening hopes, that he had construed her influence over Lord Evandale hastily and unjustly? Ought he to censure her severely, if, submitting to dissimulation for his sake, she had permitted the young nobleman to entertain hopes which she had no intention to realize? Or what if she had appealed to the generosity which Lord Evandale was supposed to possess, and had engaged his honour to protect the person of a favoured rival?

Still, however, the words which he had overheard recurred ever and anon to his remembrance, with a pang which resembled the sting of an adder.

'Nothing that she could refuse him! – was it possible to make a more unlimited declaration of predilection? The language of affection has not, within the limits of maidenly delicacy, a stronger expression. She is lost to me wholly, and for ever; and nothing remains for me now, but vengeance for my own wrongs, and for those which are hourly inflicted on my country.'

Apparently, Cuddie, though with less refinement, was following out a similar train of ideas; for he suddenly asked Morton in a low whisper – 'Wad there be ony ill in getting out o' thae chields' hands an ane could compass it?'

'None in the world,' said Morton; 'and if an opportunity occurs of doing so, depend on it I for one will not let it slip.'

'I'm blythe to hear ye say sae,' answered Cuddie. 'I'm but a puir silly fallow, but I canna think there wad be muckle ill in breaking out by strength o' hand, if ye could mak it ony thing feasible. I am the lad that will ne'er fear to lay on, if it were

come to that; but our auld leddy wad hae ca'd that a resisting o'
the king's authority.'

'I will resist any authority on earth,' said Morton, 'that invades
tyrannically my chartered rights as a freeman; and I am determined I will not be unjustly dragged to a jail, or perhaps a
gibbet, if I can possibly make my escape from these men either by
address or force.'

'Weel, that's just my mind too, aye supposing we hae a feasible
opportunity o' breaking loose. But then ye speak o' a charter;
now these are things that only belang to the like o' you that are
a gentleman, and it mightna bear me through that am but a
husbandman.'

'The charter that I speak of,' said Morton, 'is common to the
meanest Scotchman. It is that freedom from stripes and bondage
which was claimed, as you may read in Scripture, by the Apostle
Paul himself,[4] and which every man who is free-born is called
upon to defend, for his own sake and that of his countrymen.'

'Hegh, sirs!' replied Cuddie, 'it wad hae been lang or my
Leddy Margaret, or my mither either, wad hae fund out sic a
wiselike doctrine in the Bible! The tane was aye graning about
giving tribute to Cæsar,[5] and the tither is as daft wi' her whiggery. I hae been clean spoilt, just wi' listening to twa blethering
auld wives; but if I could get a gentleman that wad let me tak
on to be his servant, I am confident I wad be a clean contrary
creature; and I hope your honour will think on what I am saying,
if ye were ance fairly delivered out o' this house of bondage, and
just take me to be your ain wally-de-shamble.'

'My valet, Cuddie?' answered Morton; 'alas! that would be
sorry preferment, even if we were at liberty.'

'I ken what ye're thinking – that because I am landward-bred,
I wad be bringing ye to disgrace afore folk; but ye maun ken I'm
gay gleg at the uptak; there was never ony thing dune wi' hand
but I learned gay readily, 'septing reading, writing, and cipher-
ing; but there's no the like o' me at the fit-ba', and I can play wi'
the broadsword as weel as Corporal Inglis there. I hae broken his
head or now, for as massy as he's riding ahint us. – And then
ye'll no be gaun to stay in this country?' – said he, stopping and
interrupting himself.

'Probably not,' replied Morton.

'Weel, I carena a boddle. Ye see I wad get my mither bestowed wi' her auld graning tittie, auntie Meg, in the Gallowgate o' Glasgow, and then I trust they wad neither burn her for a witch, or let her fail for fau't o' fude, or hang her up for an auld whig wife; for the provost, they say, is very regardfu' o' sic puir bodies. And then you and me wad gang and pouss our fortunes, like the folk i' the daft auld tales about Jock the Giant-killer and Valentine and Orson;[6] and we wad come back to merry Scotland, as the sang says, and I wad tak to the stilts again, and turn sic furs on the bonny rigs o' Milnwood holms, that it wad be worth a pint but to look at them.'

'I fear,' said Morton, 'there is very little chance, my good friend Cuddie, of our getting back to our old occupation.'

'Hout, stir – hout, stir,' replied Cuddie, 'it's aye gude to keep up a hardy heart – as broken a ship's come to land. – But what's that I hear? never stir, if my auld mither isna at the preaching again! I ken the sough o' her texts, that sound just like the wind blawing through the spence; and there's Kettledrummle setting to wark, too – Lordsake, if the sodgers anes get angry, they'll murder them baith, and us for company!'

Their farther conversation was in fact interrupted by a blatant noise which rose behind them, in which the voice of the preacher emitted, in unison with that of the old woman, tones like the grumble of a bassoon combined with the screaking of a cra ked fiddle. At first, the aged pair of sufferers had been contented to condole with each other in smothered expressions of complaint and indignation; but the sense of their injuries became more pungently aggravated as they communicated with each other, and they became at length unable to suppress their ire.

'Woe, woe, and a threefold woe unto you, ye bloody and violent persecutors!' exclaimed the Reverend Gabriel Kettledrummle – 'Woe, and threefold woe unto you, even to the breaking of seals, the blowing of trumpets, and the pouring forth of vials!'[7]

'Ay – ay – a black cast to a' their ill-fa'ur'd faces, and the outside o' the loof to them at the last day!' echoed the shrill countertenor of Mause, falling in like the second part of a catch.

'I tell you,' continued the divine, 'that your rankings and your ridings – your neighings and your prancings – your bloody, barbarous, and inhuman cruelties – your benumbing, deadening, and debauching the conscience of poor creatures by oaths, soul-damning and self-contradictory, have arisen from earth to Heaven like a foul and hideous outcry of perjury for hastening the wrath to come – hugh! hugh! hugh!'

'And I say,' cried Mause, in the same tune, and nearly at the same time, 'that wi' this auld breath o' mine, and it's sair taen down wi' the asthmatics and this rough trot' –

'Deil gin they would gallop,' said Cuddie, 'wad it but gar her haud her tongue!'

'– Wi' this auld and brief breath,' continued Mause, 'will I testify against the backslidings, defections, defalcations, and declinings of the land – against the grievances and the causes of wrath!'

'Peace, I pr'ythee – Peace, good woman,' said the preacher, who had just recovered from a violent fit of coughing, and found his own anathema borne down by Mause's better wind; 'peace, and take not the word out of the mouth of a servant of the altar. – I say, I uplift my voice and tell you, that before the play is played out – ay, before this very sun gaes down, ye sall learn that neither a desperate Judas, like your prelate Sharpe that's gane to his place; nor a sanctuary-breaking Holofernes, like bloody-minded Claverhouse; nor an ambitious Diotrephes, like the lad Evandale; nor a covetous and warld-following Demas,[8] like him they ca' Sergeant Bothwell, that makes every wife's plack and her meal-ark his ain; neither your carabines, nor your pistols, nor your broadswords, nor your horses, nor your saddles, bridles, surcingles, nose-bags, nor martingales, shall resist the arrows that are whetted and the bow that is bent against you!'

'That shall they never, I trow,' echoed Mause; 'castaways are they ilk ane o' them – besoms of destruction, fit only to be flung into the fire when they have sweepit the filth out o' the Temple – whips of small cords, knotted for the chastisement of those wha like their warldly gudes and gear better than the Cross or the Covenant, but when that wark's done, only meet to mak latchets to the deil's brogues.'

'Fiend hae me,' said Cuddie, addressing himself to Morton, 'if I dinna think our mither preaches as weel as the minister! – But it's a sair pity o' his hoast, for it aye comes on just when he's at the best o't, and that lang routing he made air this morning, is sair again him too – Deil an I care if he wad roar her dumb, and then he wad hae't a' to answer for himsell – It's lucky the road's rough, and the troopers are no taking muckle tent to what they say, wi' the rattling o' the horse's feet; but an we were anes on saft grund, we'll hear news o' a' this.'

Cuddie's conjectures were but too true. The words of the prisoners had not been much attended to while drowned by the clang of horses' hoofs on a rough and stony road; but they now entered upon the moorlands, where the testimony of the two zealous captives lacked this saving accompaniment. And, accordingly, no sooner had their steeds begun to tread heath and green sward, and Gabriel Kettledrummle had again raised his voice with, 'Also I uplift my voice like that of a pelican in the wilderness' –

'And I mine,' had issued from Mause, 'like a sparrow on the house-tops' –[9]

When 'Hollo, ho!' cried the corporal from the rear; 'rein up your tongues, the devil blister them, or I'll clap a martingale on them.'

'I will not peace at the commands of the profane,' said Gabriel.

'Nor I neither,' said Mause, 'for the bidding of no earthly potsherd,[10] though it be painted as red as a brick from the Tower of Babel, and ca' itsell a corporal.'

'Halliday,' cried the corporal, 'hast got never a gag about thee, man? – We must stop their mouths before they talk us all dead.'

Ere any answer could be made, or any measure taken in consequence of the corporal's motion, a dragoon galloped towards Sergeant Bothwell, who was considerably a-head of the party he commanded. On hearing the orders which he brought, Bothwell instantly rode back to the head of his party, ordered them to close their files, to mend their pace, and to move with silence and precaution, as they would soon be in presence of the enemy.

CHAPTER 15

Quantum in nobis, we've thought good
To save the expense of Christian blood,
And try if we, by mediation
Of treaty, and accommodation,
Can end the quarrel, and compose
This bloody duel without blows.

BUTLER[1]

THE increased pace of the party of horsemen soon took away from their zealous captives the breath, if not the inclination, necessary for holding forth. They had now for more than a mile got free of the woodlands, whose broken glades had, for some time, accompanied them after they had left the woods of Tillie-tudlem. A few birches and oaks still feathered the narrow ravines, or occupied in dwarf-clusters the hollow plains of the moor. But these were gradually disappearing; and a wide and waste country lay before them, swelling into bare hills of dark heath, intersected by deep gullies; being the passages by which torrents forced their course in winter, and during summer the disproportioned channels for diminutive rivulets that winded their puny way among heaps of stones and gravel, the effects and tokens of their winter fury; – like so many spendthrifts dwindled down by the consequences of former excesses and extravagance. This desolate region seemed to extend farther than the eye could reach, without grandeur, without even the dignity of mountain wildness, yet striking, from the huge proportion which it seemed to bear to such more favoured spots of the country as were adapted to cultivation, and fitted for the support of man; and thereby impressing irresistibly the mind of the spectator with a sense of the omnipotence of nature, and the comparative inefficacy of the boasted means of amelioration which man is capable of opposing to the disadvantages of climate and soil.

It is a remarkable effect of such extensive wastes, that they impose an idea of solitude even upon those who travel through them in considerable numbers; so much is the imagination affected by the disproportion between the desert around and the party who are traversing it. Thus the members of a caravan of a thousand souls may feel, in the deserts of Africa or Arabia, a sense of loneliness unknown to the individual traveller, whose solitary course is through a thriving and cultivated country.

It was not, therefore, without a peculiar feeling of emotion, that Morton beheld, at the distance of about half a mile, the body of the cavalry to which his escort belonged, creeping up a steep and winding path which ascended from the more level moor into the hills. Their numbers, which appeared formidable when they crowded through narrow roads, and seemed multiplied by appearing partially, and at different points, among the trees, were now apparently diminished by being exposed at once to view, and in a landscape whose extent bore such immense proportion to the columns of horses and men, which, showing more like a drove of black cattle than a body of soldiers, crawled slowly along the face of the hill, their force and their numbers seeming trifling and contemptible.

'Surely,' said Morton to himself, 'a handful of resolute men may defend any defile in these mountains against such a small force as this is, providing that their bravery is equal to their enthusiasm.'

While he made these reflections, the rapid movement of the horsemen who guarded him, soon traversed the space which divided them from their companions; and ere the front of Claverhouse's column had gained the brow of the hill which they had been seen ascending, Bothwell, with his rearguard and prisoners, had united himself, or nearly so, with the main body led by his commander. The extreme difficulty of the road, which was in some places steep, and in others boggy, retarded the progress of the column, especially in the rear; for the passage of the main body, in many instances, poached up the swamps through which they passed, and rendered them so deep, that the last of their followers were forced to leave the beaten path, and find safer passage where they could.

On these occasions, the distresses of the Reverend Gabriel Kettledrummle and of Mause Headrigg, were considerably augmented, as the brutal troopers, by whom they were guarded, compelled them, at all risks which such inexperienced riders were likely to incur, to leap their horses over drains and gullies, or to push them through morasses and swamps.

'Through the help of the Lord I have luppen ower a wall,'[2] cried poor Mause, as her horse was, by her rude attendants, brought up to leap the turf enclosure of a deserted fold, in which feat her curch flew off, leaving her grey hairs uncovered.

'I am sunk in deep mire where there is no standing — I am come into deep waters where the floods overflow me,'[3] exclaimed Kettledrummle, as the charger on which he was mounted plunged up to the saddle-girths in a *well-head*, as the springs are called which supply the marshes, the sable streams beneath spouting over the face and person of the captive preacher.

These exclamations excited shouts of laughter among their military attendants; but events soon occurred which rendered them all sufficiently serious.

The leading files of the regiment had nearly attained the brow of the steep hill we have mentioned, when two or three horsemen, speedily discovered to be a part of their own advanced guard, who had acted as a patrol, appeared returning at full gallop, their horses much blown, and the men apparently in a disordered flight. They were followed upon the spur by five or six riders, well armed with sword and pistol, who halted upon the top of the hill, on observing the approach of the Life-Guards. One or two who had carabines dismounted, and, taking a leisurely and deliberate aim at the foremost rank of the regiment, discharged their pieces, by which two troopers were wounded, one severely. They then mounted their horses, and disappeared over the ridge of the hill, retreating with so much coolness as evidently showed, that, on the one hand, they were undismayed by the approach of so considerable a force as was moving against them, and conscious, on the other, that they were supported by numbers sufficient for their protection. This incident occasioned a halt through the whole body of cavalry; and while Claverhouse himself received the report of his advanced guard, which had been thus driven back upon the main body, Lord Evandale advanced to the top of the ridge over which the enemy's horsemen had retired, and Major Allan, Cornet Grahame, and the other officers, employed themselves in extricating the regiment from the broken ground, and drawing them up on the side of the hill in two lines, the one to support the other.

The word was then given to advance; and in a few minutes the first lines stood on the brow and commanded the prospect on the other side. The second line closed upon them, and also the rear-guard with the prisoners; so that Morton and his companions in captivity could, in like manner, see the form of opposition which was now offered to the farther progress of their captors.

The brow of the hill, on which the royal Life-Guards were now drawn up, sloped downwards (on the side opposite to that which they had ascended) with a gentle declivity, for more than a quarter of a mile, and presented ground, which, though unequal in some places, was not altogether unfavourable for the manœuvres of cavalry, until near the bottom, when the slope terminated in a marshy level, traversed through its whole length by what seemed either a natural gully, or a deep artificial drain, the sides of which were broken by springs, trenches filled with water, out of which peats and turf had been dug, and here and there by some straggling thickets of alders which loved the moistness so well, that they continued to live as bushes, although too much dwarfed by the sour soil and the stagnant bog-water to ascend into trees. Beyond this ditch, or gully, the ground arose into a second heathy swell, or rather hill, near to the foot of which, and as if with the object of defending the broken ground and ditch that covered their front, the body of insurgents appeared to be drawn up with the purpose of abiding battle.

Their infantry was divided into three lines. The first, tolerably provided with fire-arms, were advanced almost close to the verge of the bog, so that their fire must necessarily annoy the royal cavalry as they descended the opposite hill, the whole front of which was exposed, and would probably be yet more fatal if they attempted to cross the morass. Behind this first line was a body of pikemen, designed for their support in case the dragoons should force the passage of the marsh. In their rear was their third line, consisting of countrymen armed with scythes set straight on poles, hay-forks, spits, clubs, goads, fish-spears, and such other rustic implements as hasty resentment had converted into instruments of war. On each flank of the infantry, but a little backward from the bog, as if to allow themselves dry and sound ground whereon to act in case their enemies should force the pass, there was drawn up a small body of cavalry, who were, in general, but indifferently armed, and worse mounted, but full of zeal for the cause, being chiefly either landholders of small property, or farmers of the better class, whose means enabled them to serve on horseback. A few of those who had been engaged in driving back the advanced guard of the royalists, might now be seen returning slowly towards their own squadrons. These were the only individuals of the insurgent army which seemed to be in motion. All the others stood firm and motionless, as the grey stones that lay scattered on the heath around them.

The total number of the insurgents might amount to about a thousand men; but of these there were scarce a hundred cavalry, nor were the half of them even tolerably armed. The strength of their position, however, the sense of their having taken a desperate step, the superiority of their numbers, but, above all, the ardour of their enthusiasm, were the means on which their leaders reckoned, for supplying the want of arms, equipage, and military discipline.

On the side of the hill that rose above the array of battle which they had adopted, were seen the women and even the children, whom zeal, opposed to persecution, had driven into the wilderness. They seemed stationed there to be spectators of the engagement, by which their own fate, as well as that of their parents, husbands, and sons, was to be decided. Like the females of the ancient German tribes,[4] the shrill cries which they raised, when they beheld the glittering ranks of their enemy appear on the brow of the opposing eminence, acted as an incentive to their relatives to fight to the last in defence of that which was dearest to them. Such exhortations seemed to have their full and emphatic effect; for a wild halloo, which went from rank to rank on the appearance of the soldiers, intimated the resolution of the insurgents to fight to the uttermost.

As the horsemen halted their lines on the ridge of the hill, their trumpets and kettle-drums sounded a bold and warlike flourish of menace and defiance, that rang along the waste like the shrill summons of a destroying angel. The wanderers, in answer, united their voices, and sent forth, in solemn modulation, the two first verses of the seventy-sixth Psalm, according to the metrical version of the Scottish Kirk:

> 'In Judah's land God is well known,
>   His name's in Israel great:
> In Salem is his tabernacle,
>   In Zion is his seat.
>
> There arrows of the bow he brake,
>   The shield, the sword, the war.
> More glorious thou than hills of prey,
>   More excellent art far.'

A shout, or rather a solemn acclamation, attended the close of the stanza; and after a dead pause, the second verse was resumed by the insurgents, who applied the destruction of the Assyrians as prophetical of the issue of their own impending contest:—

> 'Those that were stout of heart are spoil'd,
>   They slept their sleep outright;
> And none of those their hands did find,
>   That were the men of might.
>
> When thy rebuke, O Jacob's God,
>   Had forth against them past,
> Their horses and their chariots both
>   Were in a deep sleep cast.'

There was another acclamation, which was followed by the most profound silence.

While these solemn sounds, accented by a thousand voices, were prolonged amongst the waste hills, Claverhouse looked with great attention on the ground, and on the order of battle which the wanderers had adopted, and in which they determined to await the assault.

'The churls,' he said, 'must have some old soldiers with them; it was no rustic that made choice of that ground.'

'Burley is said to be with them for certain,' answered Lord Evandale, 'and also Hackston of Rathillet, Paton of Meadowhead, Cleland,[5] and some other men of military skill.'

'I judged as much,' said Claverhouse, 'from the style in which these detached horsemen leapt their horses over the ditch, as they returned to their position. It was easy to see that there were a few roundheaded troopers among them, the true spawn of the old Covenant. We must manage this matter warily as well as boldly. Evandale, let the officers come to this knoll.'

He moved to a small moss-grown cairn, probably the resting-place of some Celtic chief of other times, and the call of 'Officers to the front,' soon brought them around their commander.

'I do not call you around me, gentlemen,' said Claverhouse, 'in the formal capacity of a council of war, for I will never turn over on others the responsibility which my rank imposes on myself. I only want the benefit of your opinions, reserving to myself, as most men do when they ask advice, the liberty of following my own. – What say you, Cornet Grahame? Shall we attack these fellows who are bellowing yonder? You are youngest and hottest, and therefore will speak first whether I will or no.'

'Then,' said Cornet Grahame, 'while I have the honour to carry the standard of the Life-Guards, it shall never, with my will, retreat before rebels. I say, charge, in God's name and the King's!'

'And what say you, Allan?' continued Claverhouse, 'for Evandale is so modest, we shall never get him to speak till you have said what you have to say.'

'These fellows,' said Major Allan, an old cavalier officer of experience, 'are three or four to one – I should not mind that much upon a fair field, but they are posted in a very formidable strength, and show no inclination to quit it. I therefore think, with deference to Cornet Grahame's opinion, that we should draw back to Tillietudlem, occupy the pass between the hills and the open country, and send for reinforcements to my Lord Ross, who is lying at Glasgow with a regiment of infantry. In this way we should cut them off from the Strath of Clyde, and either compel them to come out of their stronghold, and give us battle on fair terms, or, if they remain here, we will attack them so soon as our infantry has joined us, and enabled us to act with effect among these ditches, bogs, and quagmires.'

'Pshaw!' said the young Cornet, 'what signifies strong ground, when it is only held by a crew of canting, psalm-singing old women?'

'A man may fight never the worse,' retorted Major Allan, 'for honouring both his Bible and Psalter. These fellows will prove as stubborn as steel; I know them of old.'

'Their nasal psalmody,' said the Cornet, 'reminds our Major of the race of Dunbar.' [6]

'Had you been at that race, young man,' retorted Allan, 'you would have wanted nothing to remind you of it for the longest day you have to live.'

'Hush, hush, gentlemen,' said Claverhouse, 'these are untimely repartees. – I should like your advice well, Major Allan, had our rascally patrols (whom I will see duly punished) brought us timely notice of the enemy's numbers and position. But having once presented ourselves before them in line, the retreat of the Life-Guards would argue gross timidity, and be the general signal for insurrection throughout the west. In which case, so far from obtaining any assistance from my Lord Ross, I promise you I should have great apprehensions of his being cut off before we can join him, or he us. A retreat would have quite the same fatal effect upon the king's cause as the loss of a battle – and as to the difference of risk or of safety it might make with respect to ourselves, that, I am sure, no gentleman thinks a moment about. There must be some gorges or passes in the morass through which we can force our way; and, were we once on firm ground, I trust there is no man in the Life-Guards who supposes our squadrons, though so weak in numbers, are unable to trample into dust twice the number of these unpractised clowns. – What say you, my Lord Evandale?'

'I humbly think,' said Lord Evandale, 'that, go the day how it will, it must be a bloody one; and that we shall lose many brave fellows, and probably be obliged to slaughter a great number of these misguided men, who, after all, are Scotchmen and subjects of King Charles as well as we are.'

'Rebels! rebels! and undeserving the name either of Scotchmen or of subjects,' said Claverhouse; 'but come, my lord, what does your opinion point at?'

'To enter into a treaty with these ignorant and misled men,' said the young nobleman.

'A treaty! and with rebels having arms in their hands? Never while I live,' answered his commander.

'At least send a trumpet and flag of truce, summoning them to lay down their weapons and disperse,' said Lord Evandale, 'upon promise of a free pardon – I have always heard, that had that been done before the battle of Pentland hills,[7] much blood might have been saved.'

'Well,' said Claverhouse, 'and who the devil do you think would carry a summons to these headstrong and desperate fanatics? They acknowledge no laws of war. Their leaders, who have been all most active in the murder of the Archbishop of St Andrews, fight with a rope round their necks, and are likely to kill the messenger, were it but to dip their followers in loyal blood, and to make them as desperate of pardon as themselves.'

'I will go myself,' said Evandale, 'if you will permit me. I have often risked my blood to spill that of others, let me do so now in order to save human lives.'

'You shall not go on such an errand, my lord,' said Claverhouse; 'your rank and situation render your safety of too much consequence to the country in an age when good principles are so rare. – Here's my brother's son Dick Grahame, who fears shot or steel as little as if the devil had given him armour of proof against it, as the fanatics say he has given to his uncle.[8] He shall take a flag of truce and a trumpet, and ride down to the edge of the morass to summon them to lay down their arms and disperse.'

'With all my soul, Colonel,' answered the Cornet; 'and I'll tie my cravat on a pike to serve for a white flag – the rascals never saw such a pennon of Flanders lace in their lives before.'

'Colonel Grahame,' said Evandale, while the young officer prepared for his expedition, 'this young gentleman is your nephew and your apparent heir; for God's sake, permit me to go. It was my counsel, and I ought to stand the risk.'

'Were he my only son,' said Claverhouse, 'this is no cause and

no time to spare him. I hope my private affections will never
interfere with my public duty. If Dick Grahame falls, the loss is
chiefly mine; were your lordship to die, the King and country
would be the sufferers. – Come, gentlemen, each to his post. If
our summons is unfavourably received, we will instantly attack;
and, as the old Scottish blazon has it, God shaw the right!'

CHAPTER 16

With many a stout thwack and many a bang,
Hard crab-tree and old iron rang.

Hudibras [1]

CORNET RICHARD GRAHAME descended the hill, bearing in
his hand the extempore flag of truce, and making his managed
horse keep time by bounds and curvets to the tune which he
whistled. The trumpeter followed. Five or six horsemen, having
something the appearance of officers, detached themselves from
each flank of the Presbyterian army, and, meeting in the centre,
approached the ditch which divided the hollow as near as the
morass would permit. Towards this group, but keeping the
opposite side of the swamp, Cornet Grahame directed his horse,
his motions being now the conspicuous object of attention to
both armies; and, without disparagement to the courage of either,
it is probable there was a general wish on both sides that this
embassy might save the risks and bloodshed of the impending
conflict.

When he had arrived right opposite to those, who, by their
advancing to receive his message, seemed to take upon themselves as the leaders of the enemy, Cornet Grahame commanded
his trumpeter to sound a parley. The insurgents having no instrument of martial music wherewith to make the appropriate
reply, one of their number called out with a loud, strong voice,
demanding to know why he approached their leaguer.

'To summon you in the King's name, and in that of Colonel
John Grahame of Claverhouse, specially commissioned by the
right honourable Privy Council of Scotland,' answered the

Cornet, 'to lay down your arms, and dismiss the followers whom ye have led into rebellion, contrary to the laws of God, of the King, and of the country.'

'Return to them that sent thee,' said the insurgent leader, 'and tell them that we are this day in arms for a broken Covenant and a persecuted Kirk; tell them that we renounce the licentious and perjured Charles Stewart, whom you call king, even as he renounced the Covenant, after having once and again sworn to prosecute to the utmost of his power all the ends thereof, really, constantly, and sincerely, all the days of his life, having no enemies but the enemies of the Covenant, and no friends but its friends. Whereas, far from keeping the oath he had called God and angels to witness, his first step, after his incoming into these kingdoms, was the fearful grasping at the prerogative of the Almighty, by that hideous Act of Supremacy, together with his expulsing, without summons, libel, or process of law, hundreds of famous faithful preachers, thereby wringing the bread of life out of the mouth of hungry, poor creatures, and forcibly cramming their throats with the lifeless, saltless, foisonless, lukewarm drammock of the fourteen false prelates, and their sycophantic, formal, carnal, scandalous creature-curates.' [2]

'I did not come to hear you preach,' answered the officer, 'but to know, in one word, if you will disperse yourselves, on condition of a free pardon to all but the murderers of the late Archbishop of St Andrews; or whether you will abide the attack of his majesty's forces, which will instantly advance upon you.'

'In one word, then,' answered the spokesman, 'we are here with our swords on our thighs, as men that watch in the night.[3] We will take one part and portion together, as brethren in righteousness. Whosoever assails us in our good cause, his blood be on his own head. So return to them that sent thee, and God give them and thee a sight of the evil of your ways!'

'Is not your name,' said the Cornet, who began to recollect having seen the person whom he was now speaking with, 'John Balfour of Burley?'

'And if it be,' said the spokesman, 'hast thou aught to say against it?'

'Only,' said the Cornet, 'that, as you are excluded from pardon in the name of the King and of my commanding officer, it is to these country people, and not to you, that I offer it; and it is not with you, or such as you, that I am sent to treat.'

'Thou art a young soldier, friend,' said Burley, 'and scant well learned in thy trade, or thou wouldst know that the bearer of a flag of truce cannot treat with the army but through their officers; and that if he presume to do otherwise, he forfeits his safe conduct.'

While speaking these words, Burley unslung his carabine, and held it in readiness.

'I am not to be intimidated from the discharge of my duty by the menaces of a murderer,' said Cornet Grahame. – 'Hear me, good people; I proclaim, in the name of the King and of my commanding officer, full and free pardon to all, excepting' –

'I give thee fair warning,' said Burley, presenting his piece.

'A free pardon to all,' continued the young officer, still addressing the body of the insurgents – 'to all but' –

'Then the Lord grant grace to thy soul – amen!' said Burley.

With these words he fired, and Cornet Richard Grahame dropped from his horse. The shot was mortal. The unfortunate young gentleman had only strength to turn himself on the ground and mutter forth, 'My poor mother!' when life forsook him in the effort. His startled horse fled back to the regiment at the gallop, as did his scarce less affrightened attendant.

'What have you done?' said one of Balfour's brother officers.

'My duty,' said Balfour, firmly. 'Is it not written, Thou shalt be zealous even to slaying? Let those, who dare, now venture to speak of truce or pardon!' [4]

Claverhouse saw his nephew fall. He turned his eye on Evandale, while a transitory glance of indescribable emotion disturbed, for a second's space, the serenity of his features, and briefly said, 'You see the event.'

'I will avenge him, or die!' exclaimed Evandale; and, putting his horse into motion, rode furiously down the hill, followed by his own troop, and that of the deceased Cornet, which broke down without orders; and, each striving to be the foremost to revenge their young officer, their ranks soon fell into confusion.

These forces formed the first line of the royalists. It was in vain that Claverhouse exclaimed, 'Halt! halt! this rashness will undo us.' It was all that he could accomplish, by galloping along the second line, entreating, commanding, and even menacing the men with his sword, that he could restrain them from following an example so contagious.

'Allan,' he said, as soon as he had rendered the men in some degree more steady, 'lead them slowly down the hill to support Lord Evandale, who is about to need it very much. – Bothwell, thou art a cool and a daring fellow' –

'Ay,' muttered Bothwell, 'you can remember that in a moment like this.'

'Lead ten file up the hollow to the right,' continued his commanding officer, 'and try every means to get through the bog; then form and charge the rebels in flank and rear, while they are engaged with us in front.'

Bothwell made a signal of intelligence and obedience, and moved off with his party at a rapid pace.

Meantime, the disaster which Claverhouse had apprehended, did not fail to take place. The troopers, who, with Lord Evandale, had rushed down upon the enemy, soon found their disorderly career interrupted by the impracticable character of the ground. Some stuck fast in the morass as they attempted to struggle through, some recoiled from the attempt and remained on the brink, others dispersed to seek a more favourable place to pass the swamp. In the midst of this confusion, the first line of the enemy, of which the foremost rank knelt, the second stooped, and the third stood upright, poured in a close and destructive fire that emptied at least a score of saddles, and increased tenfold the disorder into which the horsemen had fallen. Lord Evandale, in the meantime, at the head of a very few well-mounted men, had been able to clear the ditch, but was no sooner across than he was charged by the left body of the enemy's cavalry, who, encouraged by the small number of opponents that had made their way through the broken ground, set upon them with the utmost fury, crying, 'Woe, woe to the uncircumcised Philistines! down with Dagon and all his adherents!' [5]

The young nobleman fought like a lion; but most of his

followers were killed, and he himself could not have escaped the same fate but for a heavy fire of carabines, which Claverhouse, who had now advanced with the second line near to the ditch, poured so effectually upon the enemy, that both horse and foot for a moment began to shrink, and Lord Evandale, disengaged from his unequal combat, and finding himself nearly alone, took the opportunity to effect his retreat through the morass. But notwithstanding the loss they had sustained by Claverhouse's first fire, the insurgents became soon aware that the advantage of numbers and of position were so decidedly theirs, that, if they could but persist in making a brief but resolute defence, the Life-Guards must necessarily be defeated. Their leaders flew through their ranks, exhorting them to stand firm, and pointing out how efficacious their fire must be where both men and horse were exposed to it; for the troopers, according to custom, fired without having dismounted. Claverhouse, more than once, when he perceived his best men dropping by a fire which they could not effectually return, made desperate efforts to pass the bog at various points, and renew the battle on firm ground and fiercer terms. But the close fire of the insurgents, joined to the natural difficulties of the pass, foiled his attempts in every point.

'We must retreat,' he said to Evandale, 'unless Bothwell can effect a diversion in our favour. In the meantime, draw the men out of fire, and leave skirmishers behind these patches of alderbushes to keep the enemy in check.'

These directions being accomplished, the appearance of Bothwell with his party was earnestly expected. But Bothwell had his own disadvantages to struggle with. His detour to the right had not escaped the penetrating observation of Burley, who made a corresponding movement with the left wing of the mounted insurgents, so that when Bothwell, after riding a considerable way up the valley, found a place at which the bog could be passed, though with some difficulty, he perceived he was still in front of a superior enemy. His daring character was in no degree checked by this unexpected opposition.

'Follow me, my lads!' he called to his men; 'never let it be said that we turned our backs before these canting roundheads!'

With that, as if inspired by the spirit of his ancestors, he shouted, 'Bothwell! Bothwell!' and throwing himself into the morass, he struggled through it at the head of his party, and attacked that of Burley with such fury, that he drove them back above a pistol-shot, killing three men with his own hand. Burley, perceiving the consequences of a defeat on this point, and that his men, though more numerous, were unequal to the regulars in using their arms and managing their horses, threw himself across Bothwell's way, and attacked him hand to hand. Each of the combatants was considered as the champion of his respective party, and a result ensued more usual in romance than in real story. Their followers, on either side, instantly paused, and looked on as if the fate of the day were to be decided by the event of the combat between these two redoubted swordsmen. The combatants themselves seemed of the same opinion; for, after two or three eager cuts and pushes had been exchanged, they paused, as if by joint consent, to recover the breath which preceding exertions had exhausted, and to prepare for a duel in which each seemed conscious he had met his match.

'You are the murdering villain, Burley,' said Bothwell, gripping his sword firmly, and setting his teeth close – 'you escaped me once, but' – (he swore an oath too tremendous to be written down) – 'thy head is worth its weight of silver, and it shall go home at my saddle-bow, or my saddle shall go home empty for me.'

'Yes,' replied Burley, with stern and gloomy deliberation, 'I am that John Balfour, who promised to lay thy head where thou shouldst never lift it again; and God do so unto me, and more also, if I do not redeem my word!'

'Then a bed of heather, or a thousand merks!' said Bothwell, striking at Burley with his full force.

'The sword of the Lord and of Gideon!'[6] answered Balfour, as he parried and returned the blow.

There have seldom met two combatants more equally matched in strength of body, skill in the management of their weapons and horses, determined courage, and unrelenting hostility. After exchanging many desperate blows, each receiving and inflicting several wounds, though of no great consequence, they grappled together as if with the desperate impatience of mortal hate, and Bothwell, seizing his enemy by the shoulder-belt, while the grasp of Balfour was upon his own collar, they came headlong to the ground. The companions of Burley hastened to his assistance, but were repelled by the dragoons, and the battle became again general. But nothing could withdraw the attention of the combatants from each other, or induce them to unclose the deadly clasp in which they rolled together on the ground, tearing, struggling, and foaming, with the inveteracy of thorough-bred bull-dogs.

Several horses passed over them in the melée without their quitting hold of each other, until the sword-arm of Bothwell was broken by the kick of a charger. He then relinquished his grasp with a deep and suppressed groan, and both combatants started to their feet. Bothwell's right hand dropped helpless by his side, but his left griped to the place where his dagger hung; it had escaped from the sheath in the struggle, – and, with a look of mingled rage and despair, he stood totally defenceless, as Balfour, with a laugh of savage joy, flourished his sword aloft, and then passed it through his adversary's body. Bothwell received the thrust without falling – it had only grazed on his ribs. He attempted no farther defence, but, looking at Burley with a grin of deadly hatred, exclaimed – 'Base peasant churl, thou hast spilt the blood of a line of kings!'

'Die, wretch! – die!' said Balfour, redoubling the thrust with better aim; and, setting his foot on Bothwell's body as he fell, he a third time transfixed him with his sword. – 'Die, bloodthirsty dog! die as thou hast lived! – die, like the beasts that perish – hoping nothing – believing nothing –'

'And FEARING nothing!' said Bothwell, collecting the last effort of respiration to utter these desperate words, and expiring as soon as they were spoken.

To catch a stray horse by the bridle, throw himself upon it, and rush to the assistance of his followers, was, with Burley, the affair of a moment. And as the fall of Bothwell had given to the insurgents all the courage of which it had deprived his comrades, the issue of this partial contest did not remain long undecided.

Several soldiers were slain, the rest driven back over the morass and dispersed, and the victorious Burley, with his party, crossed it in their turn, to direct against Claverhouse the very manœuvre which he had instructed Bothwell to execute. He now put his troop in order, with the view of attacking the right wing of the royalists; and, sending news of his success to the main body, exhorted them, in the name of Heaven, to cross the marsh, and work out the glorious work of the Lord by a general attack upon the enemy.

Meanwhile, Claverhouse, who had in some degree remedied the confusion occasioned by the first irregular and unsuccessful attack, and reduced the combat in front to a distant skirmish with firearms, chiefly maintained by some dismounted troopers whom he had posted behind the cover of the shrubby copses of alders, which in some places covered the edge of the morass, and whose close, cool, and well-aimed fire greatly annoyed the enemy, and concealed their own deficiency of numbers, – Claverhouse, while he maintained the contest in this manner, still expecting that a diversion by Bothwell and his party might facilitate a general attack, was accosted by one of the dragoons, whose bloody face and jaded horse bore witness he was come from hard service.

'What is the matter, Halliday?' said Claverhouse, for he knew every man in his regiment by name – 'Where is Bothwell?'

'Bothwell is down,' replied Halliday, 'and many a pretty fellow with him.'

'Then the king,' said Claverhouse, with his usual composure, 'has lost a stout soldier. – The enemy have passed the marsh, I suppose?'

'With a strong body of horse, commanded by the devil incarnate that killed Bothwell,' answered the terrified soldier.

'Hush! hush!' said Claverhouse, putting his finger on his lips, 'not a word to any one but me. – Lord Evandale, we must retreat. The fates will have it so. Draw together the men that are dispersed in the skirmishing work. Let Allan form the regiment, and do you two retreat up the hill in two bodies, each halting alternately as the other falls back. I'll keep the rogues in check with the rear-guard, making a stand and facing from time to time. They will be over the ditch presently, for I see their whole line in motion and preparing to cross; therefore lose no time.'

'Where is Bothwell with his party?' said Lord Evandale, astonished at the coolness of his commander.

'Fairly disposed of,' said Claverhouse, in his ear – 'the king has lost a servant, and the devil has got one. But away to business, Evandale – ply your spurs and get the men together. Allan and you must keep them steady. This retreating is new work for us all; but our turn will come round another day.'

Evandale and Allan betook themselves to their task; but ere they had arranged the regiment for the purpose of retreating in two alternate bodies, a considerable number of the enemy had crossed the marsh. Claverhouse, who had retained immediately around his person a few of his most active and tried men, charged those who had crossed in person, while they were yet disordered by the broken ground. Some they killed, others they repulsed into the morass, and checked the whole so as to enable the main body, now greatly diminished, as well as disheartened by the loss they had sustained, to commence their retreat up the hill.

But the enemy's van being soon reinforced and supported, compelled Claverhouse to follow his troops. Never did man, however, better maintain the character of a soldier than he did that day. Conspicuous by his black horse and white feather, he was first in the repeated charges which he made at every favourable opportunity, to arrest the progress of the pursuers, and to cover the retreat of his regiment. The object of aim to every one, he seemed as if he were impassive to their shot. The superstitious fanatics, who looked upon him as a man gifted by the Evil Spirit with supernatural means of defence, averred that they saw the bullets recoil from his jack-boots and buff-coat like hailstones from a rock of granite, as he galloped to and fro amid the storm of the battle. Many a whig that day loaded his musket with a dollar cut into slugs, in order that a silver bullet (such was their belief) might bring down the persecutor of the holy kirk, on whom lead had no power.

'Try him with the cold steel,' was the cry at every renewed

charge – 'powder is wasted on him. Ye might as weel shoot at the Auld Enemy himsell.'[7]

But though this was loudly shouted, yet the awe on the insurgents' minds was such, that they gave way before Claverhouse as before a supernatural being, and few men ventured to cross swords with him. Still, however, he was fighting in retreat, and with all the disadvantages attending that movement. The soldiers behind him, as they beheld the increasing number of enemies who poured over the morass, became unsteady; and, at every successive movement, Major Allan and Lord Evandale found it more and more difficult to bring them to halt and form line regularly, while, on the other hand, their motions in the act of retreating became, by degrees, much more rapid than was consistent with good order. As the retiring soldiers approached nearer to the top of the ridge, from which in so luckless an hour they had descended, the panic began to increase. Every one became impatient to place the brow of the hill between him and the continued fire of the pursuers; nor could any individual think it reasonable that he should be the last in the retreat, and thus sacrifice his own safety for that of others. In this mood, several troopers set spurs to their horses and fled outright, and the others became so unsteady in their movements and formations, that their officers every moment feared they would follow the same example.

Amid this scene of blood and confusion, the trampling of the horses, the groans of the wounded, the continued fire of the enemy, which fell in a succession of unintermitted musketry, while loud shouts accompanied each bullet which the fall of a trooper showed to have been successfully aimed – amid all the terrors and disorders of such a scene, and when it was dubious how soon they might be totally deserted by their dispirited soldiery, Evandale could not forbear remarking the composure of his commanding officer. Not at Lady Margaret's breakfast-table that morning did his eye appear more lively, or his demeanour more composed. He had closed up to Evandale for the purpose of giving some orders, and picking out a few men to reinforce his rear-guard.

'If this bout lasts five minutes longer,' he said, in a whisper, 'our rogues will leave you, my lord, old Allan, and myself, the honour of fighting this battle with our own hands. I must do something to disperse the musketeers who annoy them so hard, or we shall be all shamed. Don't attempt to succour me if you see me go down, but keep at the head of your men; get off as you can, in God's name, and tell the king and the council I died in my duty!'

So saying, and commanding about twenty stout men to follow him, he gave, with this small body, a charge so desperate and unexpected, that he drove the foremost of the pursuers back to some distance. In the confusion of the assault he singled out Burley, and, desirous to strike terror into his followers, he dealt him so severe a blow on the head, as cut through his steel head-piece, and threw him from his horse, stunned for the moment, though unwounded. A wonderful thing it was afterwards thought, that one so powerful as Balfour should have sunk under the blow of a man, to appearance so slightly made as Claverhouse; and the vulgar, of course, set down to supernatural aid the effect of that energy, which a determined spirit can give to a feebler arm. Claverhouse had, in this last charge, however, involved himself too deeply among the insurgents, and was fairly surrounded.

Lord Evandale saw the danger of his commander, his body of dragoons being then halted, while that commanded by Allan was in the act of retreating. Regardless of Claverhouse's disinterested command to the contrary, he ordered the party which he headed to charge down hill and extricate their Colonel. Some advanced with him – most halted and stood uncertain – many ran away. With those who followed Evandale, he disengaged Claverhouse. His assistance just came in time, for a rustic had wounded his horse in a most ghastly manner by the blow of a scythe, and was about to repeat the stroke when Lord Evandale cut him down. As they got out of the press, they looked round them. Allan's division had ridden clear over the hill, that officer's authority having proved altogether unequal to halt them. Evandale's troop was scattered and in total confusion.

'What is to be done, Colonel?' said Lord Evandale.

'We are the last men in the field, I think,' said Claverhouse;

'and when men fight as long as they can, there is no shame in flying. Hector himself would say, "Devil take the hindmost", when there are but twenty against a thousand. – Save yourselves, my lads, and rally as soon as you can. – Come, my lord, we must e'en ride for it.'

So saying, he put spurs to his wounded horse; and the generous animal, as if conscious that the life of his rider depended on his exertions, pressed forward with speed, unabated either by pain or loss of blood.[8] A few officers and soldiers followed him, but in a very irregular and tumultuary manner. The flight of Claverhouse was the signal for all the stragglers, who yet offered desultory resistance, to fly as fast as they could, and yield up the field of battle to the victorious insurgents.

CHAPTER 17

But see! through the fast-flashing lightnings of war,
What steed to the desert flies frantic and far?

CAMPBELL[1]

DURING the severe skirmish of which we have given the details, Morton, together with Cuddie and his mother, and the Reverend Gabriel Kettledrummle, remained on the brow of the hill, near to the small cairn, or barrow, beside which Claverhouse had held his preliminary council of war, so that they had a commanding view of the action which took place in the bottom. They were guarded by Corporal Inglis and four soldiers, who, as may readily be supposed, were much more intent on watching the fluctuating fortunes of the battle, than in attending to what passed among their prisoners.

'If yon lads stand to their tackle,' said Cuddie, 'we'll hae some chance o' getting our necks out o' the brecham again; but I misdoubt them – they hae little skeel o' arms.'

'Much is not necessary, Cuddie,' answered Morton; 'they have a strong position, and weapons in their hands, and are more than three times the number of their assailants. If they cannot fight for their freedom now, they and theirs deserve to lose it for ever.'

'O, sirs,' exclaimed Mause, 'here's a goodly spectacle indeed! My spirit is like that of the blessed Elihu, it burns within me – my bowels are as wine which lacketh vent – they are ready to burst like new bottles.[2] O, that He may look after His ain people in this day of judgment and deliverance! – And now, what ailest thou, precious Mr Gabriel Kettledrummle? I say, what ailest thou, that wert a Nazarite purer than snow, whiter than milk, more ruddy than sulphur,' (meaning, perhaps, sapphires,) – 'I say, what ails thee now, that thou art blacker than a coal, that thy beauty is departed, and thy loveliness withered like a dry potsherd?[3] Surely it is time to be up and be doing, to cry loudly and to spare not, and to wrestle for the puir lads that are yonder testifying with their ain blude and that of their enemies.'

This expostulation implied a reproach on Mr Kettledrummle, who, though an absolute Boanerges,[4] or son of thunder, in the pulpit, when the enemy were afar, and indeed sufficiently contumacious, as we have seen, when in their power, had been struck dumb by the firing, shouts, and shrieks, which now arose from the valley, and – as many an honest man might have been, in a situation where he could neither fight nor fly – was too much dismayed to take so favourable an opportunity to preach the terrors of presbytery, as the courageous Mause had expected at his hand, or even to pray for the successful event of the battle. His presence of mind was not, however, entirely lost, any more than his jealous respect for his reputation as a pure and powerful preacher of the word.

'Hold your peace, woman!' he said, 'and do not perturb my inward meditations and the wrestlings wherewith I wrestle.[5] – But of a verity the shooting of the foemen doth begin to increase! peradventure, some pellet may attain unto us even here. Lo! I will ensconce me behind the cairn, as behind a strong wall of defence.'[6]

'He's but a coward body after a',' said Cuddie, who was himself by no means deficient in that sort of courage which consists in insensibility to danger; 'he's but a daidling coward body. He'll never fill Rumbleberry's bonnet. – Odd! Rumbleberry fought and flyted like a fleeing dragon. It was a great pity, puir man, he couldna cheat the woodie. But they say he gaed singing and rejoicing till't, just as I wad gang to a bicker o' brose, supposing me hungry, as I stand a gude chance to be. – Eh, sirs! yon's an awfu' sight, and yet ane canna keep their een aff frae it!'

Accordingly, strong curiosity on the part of Morton and Cuddie, together with the heated enthusiasm of old Mause, detained them on the spot from which they could best hear and see the issue of the action, leaving to Kettledrummle to occupy alone his place of security. The vicissitudes of combat, which we have already described, were witnessed by our spectators from the top of the eminence, but without their being able positively to determine to what they tended. That the presbyterians defended themselves stoutly was evident from the heavy smoke, which, illumined by frequent flashes of fire, now eddied along the valley, and hid the contending parties in its sulphureous shade. On the other hand, the continued firing from the nearer side of the morass indicated that the enemy persevered in their attack, that the affair was fiercely disputed, and that every thing was to be apprehended from a continued contest in which undisciplined rustics had to repel the assaults of regular troops, so completely officered and armed.

At length horses, whose caparisons showed that they belonged to the Life-Guards, began to fly masterless out of the confusion. Dismounted soldiers next appeared, forsaking the conflict, and straggling over the side of the hill, in order to escape from the scene of action. As the numbers of these fugitives increased, the fate of the day seemed no longer doubtful. A large body was then seen emerging from the smoke, forming irregularly on the hill-side, and with difficulty kept stationary by their officers, until Evandale's corps also appeared in full retreat. The result of the conflict was then apparent, and the joy of the prisoners was corresponding to their approaching deliverance.

'They hae dune the job for anes,' said Cuddie, 'an they ne'er do't again.'

'They flee! – they flee!' exclaimed Mause, in ecstasy. 'O, the truculent tyrants! they are riding now as they never rode before.

O, the false Egyptians – the proud Assyrians – the Philistines –
the Moabites – the Edomites – the Ishmaelites! – The Lord has
brought sharp swords upon them, to make them food for the
fowls of heaven and the beasts of the field.[7] See how the clouds
roll, and the fire flashes ahint them, and goes forth before the
chosen of the Covenant, e'en like the pillar o' cloud and the pillar
o' flame that led the people of Israel out o' the land of Egypt![8]
This is indeed a day of deliverance to the righteous, a day of
pouring out of wrath to the persecutors and the ungodly!'

'Lord save us, mither,' said Cuddie, 'haud the clavering tongue
o' ye, and lie down ahint the cairn, like Kettledrummle, honest
man! The whigamore bullets ken unco little discretion, and will
just as sune knock out the harns o' a psalm-singing auld wife as
a swearing dragoon.'

'Fear naething for me, Cuddie,' said the old dame, transported
to ecstasy by the success of her party; 'fear naething for me! I
will stand, like Deborah, on the tap o' the cairn, and tak up my
sang o' reproach against these men of Harosheth of the Gentiles,
whose horse-hoofs are broken by their prancing.'[9]

The enthusiastic old woman would, in fact, have accomplished
her purpose, of mounting on the cairn, and becoming, as she
said, a sign and a banner to the people, had not Cuddie, with
more filial tenderness than respect, detained her by such force as
his shackled arms would permit him to exert.

'Eh, sirs!' he said, having accomplished this task, 'look out
yonder, Milnwood; saw ye ever mortal fight like the deevil
Claver'se? – Yonder he's been thrice doun amang them, and
thrice cam free aff. – But I think we'll soon be free oursells,
Milnwood. Inglis and his troopers look ower their shouthers
very aften, as if they liked the road ahint them better than the
road afore.'

Cuddie was not mistaken; for, when the main tide of fugitives
passed at a little distance from the spot where they were
stationed, the corporal and his party fired their carabines at
random upon the advancing insurgents, and, abandoning all
charge of their prisoners, joined the retreat of their comrades.
Morton and the old woman, whose hands were at liberty, lost no
time in undoing the bonds of Cuddie and of the clergyman, both

of whom had been secured by a cord tied round their arms above
the elbows. By the time this was accomplished, the rear-guard of
the dragoons, which still preserved some order, passed beneath
the hillock or rising ground which was surmounted by the cairn
already repeatedly mentioned. They exhibited all the hurry and
confusion incident to a forced retreat, but still continued in a
body. Claverhouse led the van, his naked sword deeply dyed with
blood, as were his face and clothes. His horse was all covered
with gore, and now reeled with weakness. Lord Evandale, in
not much better plight, brought up the rear, still exhorting the
soldiers to keep together and fear nothing. Several of the men
were wounded, and one or two dropped from their horses as they
surmounted the hill.

Mause's zeal broke forth once more at this spectacle, while she
stood on the heath with her head uncovered, and her grey hairs
streaming in the wind, no bad representation of a superannuated
bacchante, or Thessalian witch [10] in the agonies of incantation.
She soon discovered Claverhouse at the head of the fugitive
party, and exclaimed with bitter irony, 'Tarry, tarry, ye wha
were aye sae blithe to be at the meetings of the saints, and wad
ride every muir in Scotland to find a conventicle! Wilt thou not
tarry, now thou hast found ane? Wilt thou not stay for one word
mair? Wilt thou na bide the afternoon preaching? [11] – Wae
betide ye!' she said, suddenly changing her tone, 'and cut the
houghs of the creature whase fleetness ye trust in! – Sheugh –
sheugh! – awa wi' ye, that hae spilled sae muckle blude, and
now wad save your ain – awa wi' ye for a railing Rabshakeh, a
cursing Shimei, a bloodthirsty Doeg! [12] – The sword's drawn
now that winna be lang o' o'ertaking ye, ride as fast as ye
will.'

Claverhouse, it may be easily supposed, was too busy to attend
to her reproaches, but hastened over the hill, anxious to get the
remnant of his men out of gun-shot, in hopes of again collecting
the fugitives round his standard. But as the rear of his followers
rode over the ridge, a shot struck Lord Evandale's horse, which
instantly sunk down dead beneath him. Two of the whig horsemen, who were the foremost in the pursuit, hastened up with the
purpose of killing him, for hitherto there had been no quarter

given. Morton, on the other hand, rushed forward to save his life, if possible, in order at once to indulge his natural generosity, and to requite the obligation which Lord Evandale had conferred on him that morning, and under which circumstances had made him wince so acutely. Just as he had assisted Evandale, who was much wounded, to extricate himself from his dying horse, and to gain his feet, the two horsemen came up, and one of them exclaiming, 'Have at the red-coated tyrant!' made a blow at the young nobleman, which Morton parried with difficulty, exclaiming to the rider, who was no other than Burley himself, 'Give quarter to this gentleman, for my sake – for the sake,' he added, observing that Burley did not immediately recognise him, 'of Henry Morton, who so lately sheltered you.'

'Henry Morton?' replied Burley, wiping his bloody brow with his bloodier hand; 'did I not say that the son of Silas Morton would come forth out of the land of bondage, nor be long an indweller in the tents of Ham? Thou art a brand snatched out of the burning – But for this booted apostle of prelacy, he shall die the death! – We must smite them hip and thigh, even from the rising to the going down of the sun. It is our commission to slay them like Amalek, and utterly destroy all they have, and spare neither man nor woman, infant nor suckling;[13] therefore, hinder me not,' he continued, endeavouring again to cut down Lord Evandale, 'for this work must not be wrought negligently.'

'You must not, and you shall not, slay him, more especially while incapable of defence,' said Morton, planting himself before Lord Evandale so as to intercept any blow that should be aimed at him; 'I owed my life to him this morning – my life, which was endangered solely by my having sheltered you; and to shed his blood when he can offer no effectual resistance, were not only a cruelty abhorrent to God and man, but detestable ingratitude both to him and to me.'

Burley paused. – 'Thou art yet,' he said, 'in the court of the Gentiles, and I compassionate thy human blindness and frailty. Strong meat is not fit for babes, nor the mighty and grinding dispensation under which I draw my sword, for those whose hearts are yet dwelling in huts of clay, whose footsteps are tangled in the mesh of mortal sympathies, and who clothe themselves in the righteousness that is as filthy rags. But to gain a soul to the truth is better than to send one to Tophet;[14] therefore I give quarter to this youth, providing the grant is confirmed by the general council of God's army, whom he hath this day blessed with so signal a deliverance. – Thou art unarmed – Abide my return here. I must yet pursue these sinners, the Amalekites, and destroy them till they be utterly consumed from the face of the land, even from Havilah unto Shur.'[15]

So saying, he set spurs to his horse, and continued to pursue the chase.

'Cuddie,' said Morton, 'for God's sake catch a horse as quickly as you can. I will not trust Lord Evandale's life with these obdurate men. – You are wounded, my lord. – Are you able to continue your retreat?' he continued, addressing himself to his prisoner, who, half-stunned by the fall, was but beginning to recover himself.

'I think so,' replied Lord Evandale. 'But is it possible? – Do I owe my life to Mr Morton?'

'My interference would have been the same from common humanity,' replied Morton; 'to your lordship it was a sacred debt of gratitude.'

Cuddie at this instant returned with a horse.

'God-sake, munt – munt, and ride like a fleeing hawk, my lord,' said the good-natured fellow, 'for ne'er be in me, if they arena killing every ane o' the wounded and prisoners!'

Lord Evandale mounted the horse, while Cuddie officiously held the stirrup.

'Stand off, good fellow, thy courtesy may cost thy life. – Mr Morton,' he continued, addressing Henry, 'this makes us more than even – rely on it, I will never forget your generosity – Farewell.'

He turned his horse, and rode swiftly away in the direction which seemed least exposed to pursuit.

Lord Evandale had just rode off, when several of the insurgents, who were in the front of the pursuit, came up, denouncing vengeance on Henry Morton and Cuddie for having aided the escape of a Philistine, as they called the young nobleman.

'What wad ye hae had us to do?' cried Cuddie. 'Had we aught

to stop a man wi' that had twa pistols and a sword? Sudna ye hae come faster up yoursells, instead of flyting at huz?'

This excuse would hardly have passed current; but Kettledrummle, who now awoke from his trance of terror, and was known to, and reverenced by, most of the wanderers, together with Mause, who possessed their appropriate language as well as the preacher himself, proved active and effectual intercessors.

'Touch them not, harm them not,' exclaimed Kettledrummle, in his very best double-bass tones; 'this is the son of the famous Silas Morton, by whom the Lord wrought great things in this land at the breaking forth of the reformation from prelacy, when there was a plentiful pouring forth of the Word and a renewing of the Covenant; a hero and champion of those blessed days, when there was power and efficacy, and convincing and converting of sinners, and heart-exercises, and fellowships of saints, and a plentiful flowing forth of the spices of the garden of Eden.'

'And this is my son Cuddie,' exclaimed Mause, in her turn, 'the son of his father, Judden Headrigg, wha was a douce honest man, and of me, Mause Middlemas, an unworthy professor and follower of the pure gospel, and ane o' your ain folk. Is it not written, "Cut ye not off the tribe of the families of the Kohathites from among the Levites?" Numbers, fourth and aughteenth – O! sirs! dinna be standing here prattling wi' honest folk, when ye suld be following forth your victory with which Providence has blessed ye.'

This party having passed on, they were immediately beset by another, to whom it was necessary to give the same explanation. Kettledrummle, whose fear was much dissipated since the firing had ceased, again took upon him to be intercessor, and grown bold, as he felt his good word necessary for the protection of his late fellow-captives, he laid claim to no small share of the merit of the victory, appealing to Morton and Cuddie, whether the tide of battle had not turned while he prayed on the Mount of Jehovah-Nissi, like Moses, that Israel might prevail over Amalek; but granting them, at the same time, the credit of holding up his hands when they waxed heavy, as those of the prophet were supported by Aaron and Hur.[16] It seems probable that Kettledrummle allotted this part in the success to his companions in adversity, lest they should be tempted to disclose his carnal self-seeking and falling away, in regarding too closely his own personal safety. These strong testimonies in favour of the liberated captives quickly flew abroad, with many exaggerations, among the victorious army. The reports on the subject were various; but it was universally agreed, that young Morton of Milnwood, the son of the stout soldier of the Covenant, Silas Morton, together with the precious Gabriel Kettledrummle, and a singular devout Christian woman, whom many thought as good as himself at extracting a doctrine or an use, whether of terror or consolation, had arrived to support the good old cause, with a reinforcement of a hundred well-armed men from the Middle Ward.[17]

CHAPTER 18

When pulpit, drum ecclesiastic,
Was beat with fist instead of a stick.
        Hudibras[1]

In the meantime, the insurgent cavalry returned from the pursuit, jaded and worn out with their unwonted efforts, and the infantry assembled on the ground which they had won, fatigued with toil and hunger. Their success, however, was a cordial to every bosom, and seemed even to serve in the stead of food and refreshment. It was, indeed, much more brilliant than they durst have ventured to anticipate; for, with no great loss on their part, they had totally routed a regiment of picked men, commanded by the first officer in Scotland, and one whose very name had long been a terror to them. Their success seemed even to have upon their spirits the effect of a sudden and violent surprise, so much had their taking up arms been a measure of desperation rather than of hope. Their meeting was also casual, and they had hastily arranged themselves under such commanders as were remarkable for zeal and courage, without much respect to any other qualities. It followed, from this state of disorganization, that the whole army appeared at once to resolve itself into a general committee for considering what steps were to be taken in consequence of their success, and no opinion could be started so wild that it had not some favourers and advocates. Some proposed they should march to Glasgow, some to Hamilton, some to Edinburgh, some to London. Some were for sending a deputation of their number to London to convert Charles II to a sense of the error of his ways; and others, less charitable, proposed either to call a new successor to the crown, or to declare Scotland a free republic. A free parliament of the nation, and a free assembly of the Kirk, were the objects of the more sensible and moderate of the party. In the meanwhile, a clamour arose among the soldiers for bread and other necessaries, and while all complained of hardship and hunger, none took the necessary measures to procure supplies. In short, the camp of the Covenanters, even in the very moment of success, seemed about to dissolve like a rope of sand, from want of the original principles of combination and union.

Burley, who had now returned from the pursuit, found his followers in this distracted state. With the ready talent of one accustomed to encounter exigences, he proposed, that one hundred of the freshest men should be drawn out for duty – that a small number of those who had hitherto acted as leaders, should constitute a committee of direction until officers should be regularly chosen – and that, to crown the victory, Gabriel Kettledrummle should be called upon to improve the providential success which they had obtained, by a word in season addressed to the army. He reckoned very much, and not without reason, on this last expedient, as a means of engaging the attention of the bulk of the insurgents, while he himself, and two or three of their leaders, held a private council of war, undisturbed by the discordant opinions, or senseless clamour, of the general body.

Kettledrummle more than answered the expectations of Burley. Two mortal hours did he preach at a breathing; and certainly no lungs, or doctrine, excepting his own, could have kept up, for so long a time, the attention of men in such precarious circumstances. But he possessed in perfection a sort of rude and familiar eloquence peculiar to the preachers of that period, which, though it would have been fastidiously rejected by an audience which possessed any portion of taste, was a cake of the right leaven for the palates of those whom he now addressed. His text was from the forty-ninth chapter of Isaiah, 'Even the captives of the mighty shall be taken away, and the prey of the terrible shall be delivered: for I will contend with him that contendeth with thee, and I will save thy children.

'And I will feed them that oppress thee with their own flesh; and they shall be drunken with their own blood, as with sweet wine: and all flesh shall know that I the Lord am thy Saviour and thy Redeemer, the Mighty One of Jacob.'

The discourse which he pronounced upon this subject was divided into fifteen heads, each of which was garnished with seven uses of application, two of consolation, two of terror, two declaring the causes of backsliding and of wrath, and one announcing the promised and expected deliverance.[2] The first part of his text he applied to his own deliverance and that of his companions; and took occasion to speak a few words in praise of young Milnwood, of whom, as of a champion of the Covenant, he augured great things. The second part he applied to the punishments which were about to fall upon the persecuting government. At times he was familiar and colloquial; now he was loud, energetic, and boisterous; – some parts of his discourse might be called sublime, and others sunk below burlesque. Occasionally he vindicated with great animation the right of every freeman to worship God according to his own conscience; and presently he charged the guilt and misery of the people on the awful negligence of their rulers, who had not only failed to establish presbytery as the national religion, but had tolerated sectaries of various descriptions, Papists, Prelatists, Erastians, assuming the name of Presbyterians, Independents, Socinians, and Quakers: all of whom Kettledrummle proposed, by one sweeping act, to expel from the land, and thus re-edify in its integrity the beauty of the sanctuary. He next handled very pithily the doctrine of defensive arms and of resistance to Charles II, observing, that, instead of a nursing father to the Kirk, that monarch had been a nursing father to none but his own bastards.[3] He went at some length through the life and conversation of that

joyous prince, few parts of which, it must be owned, were qualified to stand the rough handling of so uncourtly an orator, who
conferred on him the hard names of Jeroboam, Omri, Ahab,
Shallum, Pekah, and every other evil monarch recorded in the
Chronicles, and concluded with a round application of the
Scripture, 'Tophet is ordained of old; yea, for the KING it is
provided: he hath made it deep and large; the pile thereof is
fire and much wood: the breath of the Lord, like a stream of
brimstone, doth kindle it.'⁴

Kettledrummle had no sooner ended his sermon, and descended from the huge rock which had served him for a pulpit,
than his post was occupied by a pastor of a very different description. The reverend Gabriel was advanced in years, somewhat
corpulent, with a loud voice, a square face, and a set of stupid
and unanimated features, in which the body seemed more to
predominate over the spirit than was seemly in a sound divine.
The youth who succeeded him in exhorting this extraordinary
convocation, Ephraim Macbriar by name, was hardly twenty
years old; yet his thin features already indicated, that a con-
stitution, naturally hectic, was worn out by vigils, by fasts, by
the rigour of imprisonment, and the fatigues incident to a
fugitive life. Young as he was, he had been twice imprisoned for
several months, and suffered many severities, which gave him
great influence with those of his own sect. He threw his faded
eyes over the multitude and over the scene of battle; and a light
of triumph arose in his glance, his pale yet striking features were
coloured with a transient and hectic blush of joy. He folded his
hands, raised his face to heaven, and seemed lost in mental
prayer and thanksgiving ere he addressed the people. When he
spoke, his faint and broken voice seemed at first inadequate to
express his conceptions. But the deep silence of the assembly, the
eagerness with which the ear gathered every word, as the
famished Israelites collected the heavenly manna, had a corresponding effect upon the preacher himself. His words became
more distinct, his manner more earnest and energetic; it seemed
as if religious zeal was triumphing over bodily weakness and
infirmity. His natural eloquence was not altogether untainted
with the coarseness of his sect; and yet, by the influence of a

good natural taste, it was freed from the grosser and more ludicrous errors of his contemporaries; and the language of Scripture, which, in their mouths, was sometimes degraded by misapplication, gave, in Macbriar's exhortation, a rich and solemn effect, like that which is produced by the beams of the sun streaming through the storied representation of saints and martyrs on the Gothic window of some ancient cathedral.

He painted the desolation of the church, during the late period of her distresses, in the most affecting colours. He described her, like Hagar watching the waning life of her infant amid the fountainless desert; like Judah, under her palm-tree, mourning for the devastation of her temple; like Rachel, weeping for her children and refusing comfort.[5] But he chiefly rose into rough sublimity when addressing the men yet reeking from battle. He called on them to remember the great things which God had done for them, and to persevere in the career which their victory had opened.

'Your garments are dyed – but not with the juice of the winepress; your swords are filled with blood,' he exclaimed, 'but not with the blood of goats or lambs; the dust of the desert on which ye stand is made fat with gore, but not with the blood of bullocks, for the Lord hath a sacrifice in Bozrah, and a great slaughter in the land of Idumea. These were not the firstlings of the flock, the small cattle of burnt-offerings, whose bodies lie like dung on the ploughed field of the husbandman; this is not the savour of myrrh, of frankincense, or of sweet herbs, that is steaming in your nostrils; but these bloody trunks are the carcasses of those who held the bow and the lance, who were cruel and would show no mercy, whose voice roared like the sea, who rode upon horses, every man in array as if to battle – they are the carcasses even of the mighty men of war that came against Jacob in the day of his deliverance, and the smoke is that of the devouring fires that have consumed them.[6] And those wild hills that surround you are not a sanctuary planked with cedar and plated with silver; nor are ye ministering priests at the altar, with censers and with torches; but ye hold in your hands the sword, and the bow, and the weapons of death. And yet verily, I say unto you, that not when the ancient Temple was in its first glory was there offered sacrifice more acceptable than that which you have this day presented, giving to the slaughter the tyrant and the oppressor, with the rocks for your altars, and the sky for your vaulted sanctuary, and your own good swords for the instruments of sacrifice. Leave not, therefore, the plough in the furrow – turn not back from the path in which you have entered like the famous worthies of old, whom God raised up for the glorifying of his name and the deliverance of his afflicted people – halt not in the race you are running, lest the latter end should be worse than the beginning. Wherefore, set up a standard in the land; blow a trumpet upon the mountains; let not the shepherd tarry by his sheepfold, or the seedsman continue in the ploughed field; but make the watch strong, sharpen the arrows, burnish the shields, name ye the captains of thousands, and captains of hundreds, of fifties, and of tens; call the footmen like the rushing of winds, and cause the horsemen to come up like the sound of many waters; for the passages of the destroyers are stopped, their rods are burned, and the face of their men of battle hath been turned to flight.[7] Heaven has been with you, and has broken the bow of the mighty; then let every man's heart be as the heart of the valiant Maccabeus, every man's hand as the hand of the mighty Sampson, every man's sword as that of Gideon, which turned not back from the slaughter; for the banner of Reformation is spread abroad on the mountains in its first loveliness, and the gates of hell shall not prevail against it.[8]

'Well is he this day that shall barter his house for a helmet, and sell his garment for a sword, and cast in his lot with the children of the Covenant, even to the fulfilling of the promise; and woe, woe unto him who, for carnal ends and self-seeking, shall withhold himself from the great work, for the curse shall abide with him, even the bitter curse of Meroz, because he came not to the help of the Lord against the mighty.[9] Up, then, and be doing; the blood of martyrs, reeking upon scaffolds, is crying for vengeance; the bones of saints, which lie whitening in the highways, are pleading for retribution; the groans of innocent captives from desolate isles of the sea, and from the dungeons of the tyrants' high places, cry for deliverance; the prayers of persecuted Christians, sheltering themselves in dens and deserts from the sword of their persecutors, famished with hunger, starving with cold, lacking fire, food, shelter, and clothing, because they serve God rather than man – all are with you, pleading, watching, knocking, storming the gates of heaven in your behalf. Heaven itself shall fight for you, as the stars in their courses fought against Sisera.[10] Then whoso will deserve immortal fame in this world, and eternal happiness in that which is to come,[11] let them enter into God's service, and take arles at the hand of his servant, – a blessing, namely, upon him and his household, and his children, to the ninth generation, even the blessing of the promise, for ever and ever! Amen.'

The eloquence of the preacher was rewarded by the deep hum of stern approbation which resounded through the armed assemblage at the conclusion of an exhortation, so well suited to that which they had done, and that which remained for them to do. The wounded forgot their pain, the faint and hungry their fatigues and privations, as they listened to doctrines which elevated them alike above the wants and calamities of the world, and identified their cause with that of the Deity. Many crowded around the preacher, as he descended from the eminence on which he stood, and, clasping him with hands on which the gore was not yet hardened, pledged their sacred vow that they would play the part of Heaven's true soldiers. Exhausted by his own enthusiasm, and by the animated fervour which he had exerted in his discourse, the preacher could only reply, in broken accents, – 'God bless you, my brethren – it is HIS cause. – Stand strongly up and play the men[12] – the worst that can befall us is but a brief and bloody passage to heaven.'

Balfour, and the other leaders, had not lost the time which was employed in these spiritual exercises. Watch-fires were lighted, sentinels were posted, and arrangements were made to refresh the army with such provisions as had been hastily collected from the nearest farm-houses and villages. The present necessity thus provided for, they turned their thoughts to the future. They had dispatched parties to spread the news of their victory, and to obtain, either by force or favour, supplies of what they stood most in need of. In this they had succeeded beyond their hopes, having at one village seized a small magazine of provisions, forage, and ammunition, which had been provided for the royal forces. This success not only gave them relief at the time, but such hopes for the future, that whereas formerly some of their number had begun to slacken in their zeal, they now unanimously resolved to abide together in arms, and commit themselves and their cause to the event of war.

And whatever may be thought of the extravagance or narrow-minded bigotry of many of their tenets, it is impossible to deny the praise of devoted courage to a few hundred peasants, who, without leaders, without money, without magazines, without any fixed plan of action, and almost without arms, borne out only by their innate zeal, and a detestation of the oppression of their rulers, ventured to declare open war against an established government, supported by a regular army and the whole force of three kingdoms.

CHAPTER 19

Why, then, say an old man can do somewhat.

Henry IV Part II[1]

WE must now return to the tower of Tillietudlem, which the march of the Life-Guards, on the morning of this eventful day, had left to silence and anxiety. The assurances of Lord Evandale, had not succeeded in quelling the apprehensions of Edith. She knew him generous, and faithful to his word; but it seemed too plain that he suspected the object of her intercession to be a successful rival; and was it not expecting from him an effort above human nature, to suppose that he was to watch over Morton's safety, and rescue him from all the dangers to which his state of imprisonment, and the suspicions which he had incurred, must repeatedly expose him? She therefore resigned herself to the most heart-rending apprehensions, without admitting, and indeed almost without listening to, the multifarious grounds of consolation which Jenny Dennison brought forward, one after another, like a skilful general who charges with the several divisions of his troops in regular succession.

First, Jenny was morally positive that young Milnwood would come to no harm – then, if he did, there was consolation in the reflection, that Lord Evandale was the better and more appropriate match of the two – then, there was every chance of a battle, in which the said Lord Evandale might be killed, and there wad be nae mair fash about that job – then, if the whigs gat the better, Milnwood and Cuddie might come to the Castle, and carry off the beloved of their hearts by the strong hand.

'For I forgot to tell ye, madam,' continued the damsel, putting her handkerchief to her eyes, 'that puir Cuddie's in the hands of the Philistines as weel as young Milnwood, and he was brought here a prisoner this morning, and I was fain to speak Tam Halliday fair, and fleech him, to let me near the puir creature; but Cuddie wasna sae thankfu' as he needed till hae been neither,' she added, and at the same time changed her tone, and briskly withdrew the handkerchief from her face; 'so I will ne'er waste my een wi' greeting about the matter. There wad be aye enow o' young men left, if they were to hang the tae half o' them.'

The other inhabitants of the Castle were also in a state of dissatisfaction and anxiety. Lady Margaret thought that Colonel Grahame, in commanding an execution at the door of her house, and refusing to grant a reprieve at her request, had fallen short of the deference due to her rank, and had even encroached on her seignorial rights.

'The Colonel,' she said, 'ought to have remembered, brother, that the barony of Tillietudlem has the baronial privilege of pit and gallows; and therefore, if the lad was to be executed on my estate, (which I consider as an unhandsome thing, seeing it is in the possession of females, to whom such tragedies cannot be acceptable,) he ought, at common law, to have been delivered up to my bailie, and justified at his sight.'

'Martial law, sister,' answered Major Bellenden, 'supersedes every other. But I must own I think Colonel Grahame rather deficient in attention to you; and I am not over and above pre-eminently flattered by his granting to young Evandale (I suppose because he is a lord, and has interest with the privy-council) a request which he refused to so old a servant of the king as I am. But so long as the poor young fellow's life is saved, I can comfort myself with the fag-end of a ditty as old as myself.' And therewithal, he hummed a stanza :

> 'And what though winter will pinch severe
>> Through locks of grey and a cloak that's old?
> Yet keep up thy heart, bold cavalier,
>> For a cup of sack shall fence the cold.'

'I must be your guest here to-day, sister. I wish to hear the issue of this gathering on Loudon-hill, though I cannot conceive their standing a body of horse appointed like our guests this morning. – Woe's me, the time has been that I would have liked ill to have sate in biggit wa's waiting for the news of a skirmish to be fought within ten miles of me ! But, as the old song goes,

> ' "For time will rust the brightest blade,
>> And years will break the strongest bow;
> Was ever wight so starkly made,
>> But time and years would overthrow?" '

'We are well pleased you will stay, brother,' said Lady Margaret; 'I will take my old privilege to look after my household, whom this collation has thrown into some disorder, although it is uncivil to leave you alone.'

'O, I hate ceremony as I hate a stumbling horse,' replied the Major. 'Besides, your person would be with me, and your mind with the cold meat and reversionary pasties. – Where is Edith?'

'Gone to her room a little evil-disposed, I am informed, and laid down in her bed for a gliff,' said her grandmother; 'as soon as she wakes, she shall take some drops.'

'Pooh ! pooh ! she's only sick of the soldiers,' answered Major Bellenden. 'She's not accustomed to see one acquaintance led out to be shot, and another marching off to actual service, with some chance of not finding his way back again. She would soon be used to it, if the civil war were to break out again.'

'God forbid, brother !' said Lady Margaret.

'Ay, Heaven forbid, as you say – and, in the meantime, I'll take a hit at trick-track with Harrison.'

'He has ridden out, sir,' said Gudyill, 'to try if he can hear any tidings of the battle.'

'D—n the battle,' said the Major; 'it puts this family as much out of order as if there had never been such a thing in the country before – and yet there was such a place as Kilsythe, John.'

'Ay, and as Tippermuir, your honour,' replied Gudyill, 'where I was his honour my late master's rear-rank man.'

'And Alford, John,' pursued the Major, 'where I commanded the horse; and Innerlochy, where I was the Great Marquis's aid-de-camp; and Auld Earn, and Brig o' Dee.' [2]

'And Philiphaugh, your honour,' said John.

'Umph!' replied the Major; 'the less, John, we say about that matter, the better.'

However, being once fairly embarked on the subject of Montrose's campaigns, the Major and John Gudyill carried on the war so stoutly, as for a considerable time to keep at bay the formidable enemy called Time, with whom retired veterans, during the quiet close of a bustling life, usually wage an unceasing hostility.

It has been frequently remarked, that the tidings of important events fly with a celerity almost beyond the power of credibility, and that reports, correct in the general point, though inaccurate in details, precede the certain intelligence, as if carried by the birds of the air. Such rumours anticipate the reality, not unlike to the 'shadows of coming events', which occupy the imagination of the Highland Seer. Harrison, in his ride, encountered some such report concerning the event of the battle, and turned his horse back to Tillietudlem in great dismay. He made it his first business to seek out the Major, and interrupted him in the midst of a prolix account of the siege and storm of Dundee, with the ejaculation, 'Heaven send, Major, that we do not see a siege of Tillietudlem before we are many days older!'

'How is that, Harrison? – what the devil do you mean?' exclaimed the astonished veteran.

'Troth, sir, there is strong and increasing belief that Claver'se is clean broken, some say killed; that the soldiers are all dispersed, and that the rebels are hastening this way, threatening death and devastation to a' that will not take the Covenant.'

'I will never believe that,' said the Major, starting on his feet – 'I will never believe that the Life-Guards would retreat before rebels; – and yet why need I say that,' he continued, checking himself, 'when I have seen such sights myself? – Send out Pike, and one or two of the servants, for intelligence, and let all the men in the Castle and in the village that can be trusted take up arms. This old tower may hold them play a bit, if it were but victualled and garrisoned, and it commands the pass between the high and low countries. – It's lucky I chanced to be here. – Go, muster men, Harrison. – You, Gudyill, look what provisions you have, or can get brought in, and be ready, if the news be confirmed, to knock down as many bullocks as you have salt for. – The well never goes dry. – There are some old-fashioned guns on the battlements; if we had but ammunition, we should do well enough.'

'The soldiers left some casks of ammunition at the Grange this morning, to bide their return,' said Harrison.

'Hasten, then,' said the Major, 'and bring it into the Castle, with every pike, sword, pistol, or gun, that is within our reach; don't leave so much as a bodkin – Lucky that I was here! – I will speak to my sister instantly.'

Lady Margaret Bellenden was astounded at intelligence so unexpected and so alarming. It had seemed to her that the imposing force which had that morning left her walls, was sufficient to have routed all the disaffected in Scotland, if collected in a body; and now her first reflection was upon the inadequacy of their own means of resistance, to an army strong enough to have defeated Claverhouse and such select troops. 'Woe's me! woe's me!' said she; 'what will all that we can do avail us, brother? – What will resistance do but bring sure destruction on the house, and on the bairn Edith! for, God knows, I thinkna on my ain auld life.'

'Come, sister,' said the Major, 'you must not be cast down; the place is strong, the rebels ignorant and ill-provided : my brother's house shall not be made a den of thieves and rebels while old Miles Bellenden is in it. My hand is weaker than it was, but I thank my old grey hairs that I have some knowledge of war yet. Here comes Pike with intelligence. – What news, Pike? Another Philiphaugh job, eh?'

'Ay, ay,' said Pike, composedly; 'a total scattering. – I thought this morning little gude would come of their newfangled gate of slinging their carabines.'

'Whom did you see? – Who gave you the news?' asked the Major.

'O, mair than half-a-dozen dragoon fellows that are a' on the spur whilk to get first to Hamilton. They'll win the race, I warrant them, win the battle wha like.'

'Continue your preparations, Harrison,' said the alert veteran; 'get your ammunition in, and the cattle killed. Send down to the borough-town for what meal you can gather. We must not lose an instant. – Had not Edith and you, sister, better return to Charnwood, while we have the means of sending you there?'

'No, brother,' said Lady Margaret, looking very pale, but speaking with the greatest composure; 'since the auld house is to be held out, I will take my chance in it. I have fled twice from it in my days, and I have aye found it desolate of its bravest and its bonniest when I returned; sae that I will e'en abide now, and end my pilgrimage in it.'

'It may, on the whole, be the safest course both for Edith and you,' said the Major; 'for the whigs will rise all the way between this and Glasgow, and make your travelling there, or your dwelling at Charnwood, very unsafe.'

'So be it then,' said Lady Margaret; 'and, dear brother, as the nearest blood-relation of my deceased husband, I deliver to you, by this symbol,' – (here she gave into his hand the venerable gold-headed staff of the deceased Earl of Torwood,) – 'the keeping and government and seneschalship of my Tower of Tillietudlem, and the appurtenances thereof, with full power to kill, slay, and damage those who shall assail the same, as freely as I might do myself. And I trust you will so defend it, as becomes a house in which his most sacred majesty has not disdained' –

'Pshaw! sister,' interrupted the Major, 'we have no time to speak about the king and his breakfast just now.'

And, hastily leaving the room, he hurried, with all the alertness of a young man of twenty-five, to examine the state of his garrison, and superintend the measures which were necessary for defending the place.

The Tower of Tillietudlem, having very thick walls, and very narrow windows, having also a very strong court-yard wall, with flanking turrets on the only accessible side, and rising on the other from the very verge of a precipice, was fully capable of defence against any thing but a train of heavy artillery.

Famine or escalade was what the garrison had chiefly to fear. For artillery, the top of the Tower was mounted with some antiquated wall-pieces, and small cannons, which bore the old-fashioned names of culverins, sakers, demi-sakers, falcons, and falconets. These, the Major, with the assistance of John Gudyill, caused to be scaled and loaded, and pointed them so as to command the road over the brow of the opposite hill by which the rebels must advance, causing, at the same time, two or three trees to be cut down, which would have impeded the effect of the artillery when it should be necessary to use it. With the trunks of these trees, and other materials, he directed barricades to be constructed upon the winding avenue which rose to the Tower along the high-road, taking care that each should command the other. The large gate of the court-yard he barricadoed yet more strongly, leaving only a wicket open for the convenience of passage. What he had most to apprehend, was the slenderness of his garrison; for all the efforts of the steward were unable to get more than nine men under arms, himself and Gudyill included, so much more popular was the cause of the insurgents than that of the government. Major Bellenden, and his trusty servant Pike, made the garrison eleven in number, of whom one-half were old men. The round dozen might indeed have been made up, would Lady Margaret have consented that Goose Gibbie should again take up arms. But she recoiled from the proposal, when moved by Gudyill, with such abhorrent re-collection of the former achievements of that luckless cavalier, that she declared she would rather the Castle were lost than that he were to be enrolled in the defence of it. With eleven men, however, himself included, Major Bellenden determined to hold out the place to the uttermost.

The arrangements for defence were not made without the degree of fracas incidental to such occasions. Women shrieked, cattle bellowed, dogs howled, men ran to and fro, cursing and swearing without intermission, the lumbering of the old guns backwards and forwards shook the battlements, the court resounded with the hasty gallop of messengers who went and returned upon errands of importance, and the din of warlike preparation was mingled with the sound of female laments.

Such a Babel of discord might have awakened the slumbers of the very dead, and, therefore, was not long ere it dispelled the abstracted reveries of Edith Bellenden. She sent out Jenny to bring her the cause of the tumult which shook the castle to its very basis; but Jenny, once engaged in the bustling tide, found so much to ask and to hear, that she forgot the state of anxious uncertainty in which she had left her young mistress. Having no pigeon to dismiss in pursuit of information when her raven messenger had failed to return with it, Edith was compelled to venture in quest of it out of the ark of her own chamber into the deluge of confusion which overflowed the rest of the Castle. Six voices speaking at once, informed her, in reply to her first enquiry, that Claver'se and all his men were killed, and that ten thousand whigs were marching to besiege the castle, headed by John Balfour of Burley, young Milnwood, and Cuddie Headrigg. This strange association of persons seemed to infer the falsehood of the whole story, and yet the general bustle in the Castle intimated that danger was certainly apprehended.

'Where is Lady Margaret?' was Edith's second question.

'In her oratory,' was the reply : a cell adjoining to the chapel, in which the good old lady was wont to spend the greater part of the days destined by the rules of the Episcopal Church to devotional observances, as also the anniversaries of those on which she had lost her husband and her children, and, finally, those hours, in which a deeper and more solemn address to Heaven was called for, by national or domestic calamity.

'Where, then,' said Edith, much alarmed, 'is Major Bellenden?'

'On the battlements of the Tower, madam, pointing the cannon,' was the reply.

To the battlements, therefore, she made her way, impeded by a thousand obstacles, and found the old gentleman in the midst of his natural military element, commanding, rebuking, encouraging, instructing, and exercising all the numerous duties of a good governor.

'In the name of God, what is the matter, uncle?' exclaimed Edith.

'The matter, my love?' answered the Major coolly, as, with spectacles on his nose, he examined the position of a gun – 'The matter? Why, – raise her breech a thought more, John Gudyill – the matter? Why, Claver'se is routed, my dear, and the whigs are coming down upon us in force, that's all the matter.'

'Gracious powers!' said Edith, whose eye at that instant caught a glance of the road which ran up the river, 'and yonder they come!'

'Yonder? where?' said the veteran; and, his eyes taking the same direction, he beheld a large body of horsemen coming down the path. 'Stand to your guns, my lads!' was the first exclamation; 'we'll make them pay toll as they pass the heugh. – But stay, stay, these are certainly the Life-Guards.'

'O no, uncle, no,' replied Edith; 'see how disorderly they ride, and how ill they keep their ranks; these cannot be the fine soldiers who left us this morning.'

'Ah, my dear girl!' answered the Major, 'you do not know the difference between men before a battle and after a defeat; but the Life-Guards it is, for I see the red and blue and the King's colours. I am glad they have brought them off, however.'

His opinion was confirmed as the troopers approached nearer, and finally halted on the road beneath the Tower; while their commanding officer, leaving them to breathe and refresh their horses, hastily rode up the hill.

'It is Claverhouse, sure enough,' said the Major; 'I am glad he has escaped, but he has lost his famous black horse. Let Lady Margaret know, John Gudyill; order some refreshments; get oats for the soldiers' horses; and let us to the hall, Edith, to meet him. I surmise we shall hear but indifferent news.'

CHAPTER 20

With careless gesture, mind unmoved,
On rade he north the plain,
His seem in thrang of fiercest strife,
When winner aye the same.

Hardyknute [1]

COLONEL GRAHAME of Claverhouse met the family, assembled in the hall of the Tower, with the same serenity and the same courtesy which had graced his manners in the morning. He had even had the composure to rectify in part the derangement of his dress, to wash the signs of battle from his face and hands, and did not appear more disordered in his exterior than if returned from a morning ride.

'I am grieved, Colonel Grahame,' said the reverend old lady, the tears trickling down her face, 'deeply grieved'.

'And I am grieved, my dear Lady Margaret,' replied Claverhouse, 'that this misfortune may render your remaining at Tillietudlem dangerous for you, especially considering your recent hospitality to the King's troops, and your well-known loyalty. And I came here chiefly to request Miss Bellenden and you to accept my escort (if you will not scorn that of a poor runaway) to Glasgow, from whence I will see you safely sent either to Edinburgh or to Dunbarton Castle, as you shall think best.'

'I am much obliged to you, Colonel Grahame,' replied Lady Margaret; 'but my brother, Major Bellenden, has taken on him the responsibility of holding out this house against the rebels; and, please God, they shall never drive Margaret Bellenden from her ain hearth-stane while there's a brave man that says he can defend it.'

'And will Major Bellenden undertake this?' said Claverhouse hastily, a joyful light glancing from his dark eye as he turned it on the veteran, – 'Yet why should I question it? it is of a piece with the rest of his life. – But have you the means, Major?'

'All, but men and provisions, with which we are ill supplied,' answered the Major.

'As for men,' said Claverhouse, 'I will leave you a dozen or twenty fellows who will make good a breach against the devil. It will be of the utmost service, if you can defend the place but a week, and by that time you must surely be relieved.'

'I will make it good for that space, Colonel,' replied the Major, 'with twenty-five good men and store of ammunition, if we should gnaw the soles of our shoes for hunger; but I trust we shall get in provisions from the country.'

'And, Colonel Grahame, if I might presume a request,' said Lady Margaret, 'I would entreat that Sergeant Francis Stewart might command the auxiliaries whom you are so good as to add to the garrison of our people; it may serve to legitimate his promotion, and I have a prejudice in favour of his noble birth.'

'The sergeant's wars are ended, madam,' said Grahame, in an unaltered tone, 'and he now needs no promotion that an earthly master can give.'

'Pardon me,' said Major Bellenden, taking Claverhouse by the arm, and turning him away from the ladies, 'but I am anxious for my friends; I fear you have other and more important loss. I observe another officer carries your nephew's standard.'

'You are right, Major Bellenden,' answered Claverhouse firmly; 'my nephew is no more. He has died in his duty, as became him.'

'Great God!' exclaimed the Major, 'how unhappy! – the handsome, gallant, high-spirited youth!'

'He was indeed all you say,' answered Claverhouse; 'poor Richard was to me as an eldest son, the apple of my eye, and my destined heir; but he died in his duty, and I – I – Major Bellenden' – (he wrung the Major's hand hard as he spoke) – 'I live to avenge him.'

'Colonel Grahame,' said the affectionate veteran, his eyes filling with tears, 'I am glad to see you bear this misfortune with such fortitude.'

'I am not a selfish man,' replied Claverhouse, 'though the world will tell you otherwise; I am not selfish either in my hopes or fears, my joys or sorrows. I have not been severe for myself, or grasping for myself, or ambitious for myself. The service of my master and the good of the country are what I have tried to aim at. I may, perhaps, have driven severity into cruelty, but I acted for the best; and now I will not yield to my own feelings a deeper sympathy than I have given to those of others.'

'I am astonished at your fortitude under all the unpleasant circumstances of this affair,' pursued the Major.

'Yes,' replied Claverhouse, 'my enemies in the council will lay this misfortune to my charge – I despise their accusations. They will calumniate me to my sovereign – I can repel their charge. The public enemy will exult in my flight – I shall find a time to show them that they exult too early. This youth that has fallen stood betwixt a grasping kinsman and my inheritance, for you know that my marriage-bed is barren; yet, peace be with him! the country can better spare him than your friend Lord Evandale, who, after behaving very gallantly, has, I fear, also fallen.'

'What a fatal day!' ejaculated the Major. 'I heard a report of this, but it was again contradicted; it was added, that the poor young nobleman's impetuosity had occasioned the loss of this unhappy field.'

'Not so, Major,' said Grahame; 'let the living officers bear the blame, if there be any; and let the laurels flourish untarnished on the grave of the fallen. I do not, however, speak of Lord Evandale's death as certain; but killed, or prisoner, I fear he must be. Yet he was extricated from the tumult the last time we spoke together. We were then on the point of leaving the field with a rear-guard of scarce twenty men; the rest of the regiment were almost dispersed.'

'They have rallied again soon,' said the Major, looking from the window on the dragoons, who were feeding their horses and refreshing themselves beside the brook.

'Yes,' answered Claverhouse, 'my blackguards had little temptation either to desert, or to straggle farther than they were driven by their first panic. There is small friendship and scant courtesy between them and the boors of this country; every village they pass is likely to rise on them, and so the scoundrels are driven back to their colours by a wholesome terror of spits, pike-staves, hay-forks, and broomsticks. – But now let us talk about your plans and wants, and the means of corresponding with you. To tell you the truth, I doubt being able to make a long stand at Glasgow, even when I have joined my Lord Ross; for this transient and accidental success of the fanatics will raise the devil through all the western counties.'

They then discussed Major Bellenden's means of defence, and settled a plan of correspondence, in case a general insurrection took place, as was to be expected. Claverhouse renewed his offer to escort the ladies to a place of safety; but, all things considered, Major Bellenden thought they would be in equal safety at Tillie-tudlem.

The Colonel then took a polite leave of Lady Margaret and Miss Bellenden, assuring them, that, though he was reluctantly obliged to leave them for the present in dangerous circumstances, yet his earliest means should be turned to the redemption of his character as a good knight and true, and that they might speedily rely on hearing from or seeing him.

Full of doubt and apprehension, Lady Margaret was little able to reply to a speech so much in unison with her usual expressions and feelings, but contented herself with bidding Claverhouse farewell, and thanking him for the succours which he had promised to leave them. Edith longed to enquire the fate of Henry Morton, but could find no pretext for doing so, and could only hope that it had made a subject of some part of the long private communication which her uncle had held with Claverhouse. On this subject, however, she was disappointed; for the old cavalier was so deeply immersed in the duties of his own office, that he had scarce said a single word to Claverhouse, excepting upon military matters, and most probably would have been equally forgetful, had the fate of his own son, instead of his friend's, lain in the balance.

Claverhouse now descended the bank on which the castle is founded, in order to put his troops again in motion, and Major Bellenden accompanied him to receive the detachment who were to be left in the tower.

'I shall leave Inglis with you,' said Claverhouse, 'for, as I am situated, I cannot spare an officer of rank; it is all we can do, by our joint efforts, to keep the men together. But should any of our missing officers make their appearance, I authorize you to detain them; for my fellows can with difficulty be subjected to any other authority.'

His troops being now drawn up, he picked out sixteen men by name, and committed them to the command of Corporal Inglis, whom he promoted to the rank of sergeant on the spot.

'And hark ye, gentlemen,' was his concluding harangue, 'I leave you to defend the house of a lady, and under the command of her brother, Major Bellenden, a faithful servant to the king. You are to behave bravely, soberly, regularly, and obediently, and each of you shall be handsomely rewarded on my return to relieve the garrison. In case of mutiny, cowardice, neglect of duty, or the slightest excess in the family, the provost-marshal and cord – you know I keep my word for good and evil.'

He touched his hat as he bade them farewell, and shook hands cordially with Major Bellenden.

'Adieu,' he said, 'my stout-hearted old friend! Good luck be with you, and better times to us both.'

The horsemen whom he commanded had been once more reduced to tolerable order by the exertions of Major Allan; and, though shorn of their splendour, and with their gilding all besmirched, made a much more regular and military appearance on leaving, for the second time, the tower of Tillietudlem, than when they returned to it after their rout.

Major Bellenden, now left to his own resources, sent out several videttes, both to obtain supplies of provisions, and especially of meal, and to get knowledge of the motions of the enemy. All the news he could collect on the second subject tended to prove that the insurgents meant to remain on the field of battle for that night. But they, also, had abroad their detachments and advanced guards to collect supplies, and great was the doubt and distress of those who received contrary orders, in the name of the King and in that of the Kirk; the one commanding them to send provisions to victual the Castle of Tillietudlem, and the other enjoining them to forward supplies to the camp of the godly professors of true religion, now in arms for the cause of covenanted reformation, presently pitched at Drumclog, nigh to Loudon-hill. Each summons closed with a denunciation of fire and sword if it was neglected; for neither party could confide so far in the loyalty or zeal of those whom they addressed, as to hope they would part with their property upon other terms. So that the poor people knew not what hand to turn themselves to; and, to say truth, there were some who turned themselves to more than one.

'Thir kittle times will drive the wisest o' us daft,' said Niel Blane, the prudent host of the Howff; 'but I'se aye keep a calm sough. – Jenny, what meal is in the girnel?'

'Four bows o' aitmeal, twa bows o' bear, and twa bows o' pease,' was Jenny's reply.

'Aweel, hinny,' continued Niel Blane, sighing deeply, 'let Bauldy drive the pease and bear meal to the camp at Drumclog – he's a whig, and was the auld gudewife's pleughman – the mashlum bannocks will suit their muirland stamachs weel. He maun say it's the last unce o' meal in the house, or, if he scruples to tell a lie, (as it's no likely he will when it's for the gude o' the house,) he may wait till Duncan Glen, the auld drucken trooper, drives up the aitmeal to Tillietedlum, wi' my dutifu' service to my Leddy and the Major, and I haena as muckle left as will mak my parritch; and if Duncan manage right, I'll gie him a tass o' whisky shall mak the blue low come out at his mouth.'

'And what are we to eat oursells then, father,' asked Jenny, 'when we hae sent awa the haill meal in the ark and the girnel?'

'We maun gar wheat-flour serve us for a blink,' said Niel, in a tone of resignation; 'it's no that ill food, though far frae being sae hearty or kindly to a Scotchman's stamach as the curney aitmeal is; the Englishers live amaist upon't; but, to be sure, the pock-puddings ken nae better.'

While the prudent and peaceful endeavoured, like Niel Blane, to make fair weather with both parties, those who had more public (or party) spirit began to take arms on all sides. The royalists in the country were not numerous, but were respectable from their fortune and influence, being chiefly landed proprietors of ancient descent, who, with their brothers, cousins, and dependents to the ninth generation, as well as their domestic servants, formed a sort of militia, capable of defending their own peel-houses against detached bodies of the insurgents, of resisting their demand of supplies, and intercepting those which were sent to the presbyterian camp by others. The news that the Tower of Tillietudlem was to be defended against the insurgents, afforded great courage and support to these feudal volunteers, who considered it as a stronghold to which they might retreat, in case it should become impossible for them to maintain the desultory war they were now about to wage.

On the other hand, the towns, the villages, the farm-houses, the properties of small heritors, sent forth numerous recruits to the presbyterian interest. These men had been the principal sufferers during the oppression of the time. Their minds were fretted, soured, and driven to desperation, by the various exactions and cruelties to which they had been subjected; and, although by no means united among themselves, either concerning the purpose of this formidable insurrection, or the means by which that purpose was to be obtained, most of them considered it as a door opened by Providence to obtain the liberty of conscience of which they had been long deprived and to shake themselves free of a tyranny, directed both against body and soul. Numbers of these men, therefore, took up arms; and, in the phrase of their time and party, prepared to cast in their lot with the victors of Loudon-hill.

CHAPTER 21

> *Ananias*. I do not like the man: He is a heathen,
> And speaks the language of Canaan truly.
>   *Tribulation*. You must await his calling, and the coming
> Of the good spirit. You did ill to upbraid him.
>   *The Alchemist*[1]

WE return to Henry Morton, whom we left on the field of battle. He was eating, by one of the watch-fires, his portion of the provisions which had been distributed to the army, and musing deeply on the path which he was next to pursue, when Burley suddenly came up to him, accompanied by the young minister, whose exhortation after the victory had produced such a powerful effect.

'Henry Morton,' said Balfour abruptly, 'the council of the army of the Covenant, confiding that the son of Silas Morton can never prove a lukewarm Laodicean, or an indifferent Gallio,[2] in this great day, have nominated you to be a captain of their host, with the right of a vote in their council, and all authority fitting for an officer who is to command Christian men.'

'Mr Balfour,' replied Morton, without hesitation, 'I feel this mark of confidence, and it is not surprising that a natural sense of the injuries of my country, not to mention those I have sustained in my own person, should make me sufficiently willing to draw my sword for liberty and freedom of conscience. But I will own to you, that I must be better satisfied concerning the principles on which you bottom your cause ere I can agree to take a command among you.'

'And can you doubt of our principles,' answered Burley, 'since we have stated them to be the reformation both of church and state, the rebuilding of the decayed sanctuary, the gathering of the dispersed saints, and the destruction of the man of sin?'

'I will own frankly, Mr Balfour,' replied Morton, 'much of this sort of language, which, I observe, is so powerful with others, is entirely lost on me. It is proper you should be aware of this before we commune further together.' (The young clergyman here groaned deeply,) 'I distress you, sir,' said Morton; 'but, perhaps, it is because you will not hear me out. I revere the Scriptures as deeply as you or any Christian can do. I look into them with humble hope of extracting a rule of conduct and a law of salvation. But I expect to find this by an examination of their general tenor, and of the spirit which they uniformly breathe, and not by wresting particular passages from their context, or by the application of Scriptural phrases to circumstances and events with which they have often very slender relation.'

The young divine seemed shocked and thunderstruck with this declaration, and was about to remonstrate.

'Hush, Ephraim!' said Burley, 'remember he is but as a babe in swaddling clothes. – Listen to me, Morton. I will speak to thee in the worldly language of that carnal reason, which is, for the present, thy blind and imperfect guide. What is the object for which thou art content to draw thy sword? Is it not that the

church and state should be reformed by the free voice of a free
parliament, with such laws as shall hereafter prevent the executive government from spilling the blood, torturing and imprison-
ing the persons, exhausting the estates, and trampling upon the
consciences of men, at their own wicked pleasure?'

'Most certainly,' said Morton; 'such I esteem legitimate causes
of warfare, and for such I will fight while I can yield a sword.'

'Nay, but,' said Macbriar, 'ye handle this matter too tenderly;
nor will my conscience permit me to fard or daub over the causes
of divine wrath' –

'Peace, Ephraim Macbriar!' again interrupted Burley.

'I will not peace,' said the young man. 'Is it not the cause of my
Master who hath sent me? Is it not a profane and Erastian destroying of his authority, usurpation of his power, denial of his
name, to place either King or Parliament in his place as the
master and governor of his household, the adulterous husband
of his spouse?'

'You speak well,' said Burley, dragging him aside, 'but not
wisely; your own ears have heard this night in council how this
scattered remnant are broken and divided, and would ye now
make a veil of separation between them? Would ye build a
wall with unslaked mortar? – if a fox go up, it will breach
it.' [3]

'I know,' said the young clergyman, in reply, 'that thou art
faithful, honest, and zealous, even unto slaying; but, believe me,
this worldly craft, this temporizing with sin and with infirmity,
is in itself a falling away; and I fear me Heaven will not honour
us to do much more for His glory, when we seek to carnal
cunning and to a fleshly arm. The sanctified end must be wrought
by sanctified means.'

'I tell thee,' answered Balfour, 'thy zeal is too rigid in this
matter; we cannot yet do without the help of the Laodiceans and
the Erastians; we must endure for a space the indulged in the
midst of the council – the sons of Zeruiah are yet too strong for
us.' [4]

'I tell thee I like it not,' said Macbriar; 'God can work deliverance by a few as well as by a multitude. The host of the
faithful that was broken upon Pentland-hills, paid but the fitting

penalty of acknowledging the carnal interest of that tyrant and oppressor, Charles Stewart.'

'Well, then,' said Balfour, 'thou knowest the healing resolution that the council have adopted, – to make a comprehending declaration, that may suit the tender consciences of all who groan under the yoke of our present oppressors.[5] Return to the council if thou wilt, and get them to recall it, and send forth one upon narrower grounds. But abide not here to hinder my gaining over this youth, whom my soul travails for; his name alone will call forth hundreds to our banners.'

'Do as thou wilt, then,' said Macbriar; 'but I will not assist to mislead the youth, nor bring him into jeopardy of life, unless upon such grounds as will ensure his eternal reward.'

The more artful Balfour then dismissed the impatient preacher, and returned to his proselyte.

That we may be enabled to dispense with detailing at length the arguments by which he urged Morton to join the insurgents, we shall take this opportunity to give a brief sketch of the person by whom they were used, and the motives which he had for interesting himself so deeply in the conversion of young Morton to his cause.

John Balfour of Kinloch, or Burley, for he is designated both ways in the histories and proclamations of that melancholy period, was a gentleman of some fortune, and of good family, in the county of Fife, and had been a soldier from his youth upwards. In the younger part of his life he had been wild and licentious, but had early laid aside open profligacy, and embraced the strictest tenets of Calvinism. Unfortunately, habits of excess and intemperance were more easily rooted out of his dark, saturnine, and enterprising spirit, than the vices of revenge and ambition, which continued, notwithstanding his religious professions, to exercise no small sway over his mind. Daring in design, precipitate and violent in execution, and going to the very extremity of the most rigid recusancy, it was his ambition to place himself at the head of the presbyterian interest.

To attain this eminence among the whigs, he had been active in attending their conventicles, and more than once had commanded them when they appeared in arms, and beaten off the forces sent to disperse them. At length, the gratification of his own fierce enthusiasm, joined, as some say, with motives of private revenge, placed him at the head of that party who assassinated the Primate of Scotland, as the author of the sufferings of the presbyterians. The violent measures adopted by government to revenge this deed, not on the perpetrators only, but on the whole professors of the religion to which they belonged, together with long previous sufferings, without any prospect of deliverance, except by force of arms, occasioned the insurrection, which, as we have already seen, commenced by the defeat of Claverhouse in the bloody skirmish of Loudon-hill.

But Burley, notwithstanding the share he had in the victory, was far from finding himself at the summit which his ambition aimed at. This was partly owing to the various opinions entertained among the insurgents concerning the murder of Archbishop Sharpe. The more violent among them did, indeed, approve of this act as a deed of justice, executed upon a persecutor of God's church through the immediate inspiration of the Deity; but the greater part of the presbyterians disowned the deed as a crime highly culpable, although they admitted, that the Archbishop's punishment had by no means exceeded his deserts. The insurgents differed in another main point, which had been already touched upon. The more warm and extravagant fanatics condemned, as guilty of a pusillanimous abandonment of the rights of the church, those preachers and congregations who were contented, in any manner, to exercise their religion through the permission of the ruling government. This, they said, was absolute Erastianism, or subjection of the church of God to the regulations of an earthly government, and therefore but one degree better than prelacy or popery. – Again, the more moderate party were content to allow the king's title to the throne, and in secular affairs to acknowledge his authority, so long as it was exercised with due regard to the liberties of the subject, and in conformity to the laws of the realm. But the tenets of the wilder sect, called, from their leader Richard Cameron, by the name of Cameronians, went the length of disowning the reigning monarch, and every one of his successors, who should not acknowledge the Solemn League and Covenant. The seeds of disunion were, therefore, thickly sown in this ill-fated party; and Balfour, however enthusiastic, and however much attached to the most violent of those tenets which we have noticed, saw nothing but ruin to the general cause, if they were insisted on during this crisis, when unity was of so much consequence. Hence he disapproved, as we have seen, of the honest, downright, and ardent zeal of Macbriar, and was extremely desirous to receive the assistance of the moderate party of presbyterians in the immediate overthrow of the government, with the hope of being hereafter able to dictate to them what should be substituted in its place.

He was, on this account, particularly anxious to secure the accession of Henry Morton to the cause of the insurgents. The memory of his father was generally esteemed among the presbyterians; and as few persons of any decent quality had joined the insurgents, this young man's family and prospects were such as almost ensured his being chosen a leader. Through Morton's means, as being the son of his ancient comrade, Burley conceived he might exercise some influence over the more liberal part of the army, and ultimately, perhaps, ingratiate himself so far with them, as to be chosen commander-in-chief, which was the mark at which his ambition aimed. He had, therefore, without waiting till any other person took up the subject, exalted to the council the talents and disposition of Morton, and easily obtained his elevation to the painful rank of a leader in this disunited and undisciplined army.

The arguments by which Balfour pressed Morton to accept of this dangerous promotion, as soon as he had gotten rid of his less wary and uncompromising companion, Macbriar, were sufficiently artful and urgent. He did not affect either to deny or to disguise that the sentiments which he himself entertained concerning church government, went as far as those of the preacher who had just left them; but he argued, that when the affairs of the nation were at such a desperate crisis, minute difference of opinion should not prevent those who, in general, wished well to their oppressed country, from drawing their swords in its behalf. Many of the subjects of division, as, for example, that concerning the Indulgence itself, arose, he observed, out of circumstances which would cease to exist, provided their attempt to free the country should be successful, seeing that the presbytery, being in that case triumphant, would need to make no such compromise with the government, and, consequently, with the abolition of the Indulgence all discussion of its legality would be at once ended. He insisted much and strongly upon the necessity of taking advantage of this favourable crisis, upon the certainty of their being joined by the force of the whole western shires, and upon the gross guilt which those would incur, who, seeing the distress of the country, and the increasing tyranny with which it was governed, should, from fear or indifference, withhold their active aid from the good cause.

Morton wanted not these arguments to induce him to join in any insurrection, which might appear to have a feasible prospect of freedom to the country. He doubted, indeed, greatly, whether the present attempt was likely to be supported by the strength sufficient to ensure success, or by the wisdom and liberality of spirit necessary to make a good use of the advantages that might be gained. Upon the whole, however, considering the wrongs he had personally endured, and those which he had seen daily inflicted on his fellow-subjects; meditating also upon the precarious and dangerous situation in which he already stood with relation to the government, he conceived himself, in every point of view, called upon to join the body of presbyterians already in arms.

But while he expressed to Burley his acquiescence in the vote which had named him a leader among the insurgents, and a member of their council of war, it was not without a qualification.

'I am willing,' he said, 'to contribute every thing within my limited power to effect the emancipation of my country. But do not mistake me. I disapprove, in the utmost degree, of the action in which this rising seems to have originated; and no arguments should induce me to join it, if it is to be carried on by such measures as that with which it has commenced.'

Burley's blood rushed to his face, giving a ruddy and dark glow to his swarthy brow.

'You mean,' he said, in a voice which he designed should not betray any emotion – 'You mean the death of James Sharpe?'

'Frankly,' answered Morton, 'such is my meaning.'

'You imagine, then,' said Burley, 'that the Almighty, in times of difficulty, does not raise up instruments to deliver his church from her oppressors? You are of opinion that the justice of an execution consists, not in the extent of the sufferer's crime, or in his having merited punishment, or in the wholesome and salutary effect which that example is likely to produce upon other evil-doers, but hold that it rests solely in the robe of the judge, the height of the bench, and the voice of the doomster? Is not just punishment justly inflicted, whether on the scaffold or the moor? And where constituted judges, from cowardice, or from having cast in their lot with transgressors, suffer them not only to pass at liberty through the land, but to sit in the high places, and dye their garments in the blood of the saints, is it not well done in any brave spirits who shall draw their private swords in the public cause?'

'I have no wish to judge this individual action,' replied Morton, 'further than is necessary to make you fully aware of my principles. I therefore repeat, that the case you have supposed does not satisfy my judgment. That the Almighty, in his mysterious providence, may bring a bloody man to an end deservedly bloody, does not vindicate those who, without authority of any kind, take upon themselves to be the instruments of execution, and presume to call them the executors of divine vengeance.'

'And were we not so?' said Burley, in a tone of fierce enthusiasm. 'Were not we – was not every one who owned the interest of the Covenanted Church of Scotland, bound by that covenant to cut off the Judas who had sold the cause of God for fifty thousand merks a-year?[6] Had we met him by the way as he came down from London, and there smitten him with the edge of the sword, we had done but the duty of men faithful to our cause, and to our oaths recorded in heaven. Was not the execution itself a proof of our warrant? Did not the Lord deliver him into our hands, when we looked out but for one of his inferior tools of persecution? Did we not pray to be resolved how we should act, and was it not borne in on our hearts as if it had been written on them with the point of a diamond, "Ye shall surely take him and slay him?" – Was not the tragedy full half an hour in acting ere the sacrifice was completed, and that in an open heath, and within the patrols of their garrisons – and yet who interrupted the great work? – What dog so much as bayed us during the pursuit, the taking, the slaying, and the dispersing? Then, who will say – who dare say, that a mightier arm than ours was not herein revealed?'

'You deceive yourself, Mr Balfour,' said Morton; 'such circumstances of facility of execution and escape have often attended the commission of the most enormous crimes. – But it is not mine to judge you. I have not forgotten that the way was opened to the former liberation of Scotland by an act of violence which no man can justify, – the slaughter of Cumming by the hand of Robert Bruce;[7] and, therefore, condemning this action, as I do and must, I am not unwilling to suppose that you may have motives vindicating it in your own eyes, though not in mine, or in those of sober reason. I only now mention it, because I desire you to understand, that I join a cause supported by men engaged in open war, which it is proposed to carry on according to the rules of civilized nations, without, in any respect, approving of the act of violence which gave immediate rise to it.'

Balfour bit his lip, and with difficulty suppressed a violent answer. He perceived, with disappointment, that, upon points of principle, his young brother-in-arms possessed a clearness of judgment, and a firmness of mind, which afforded but little hope of his being able to exert that degree of influence over him which he had expected to possess. After a moment's pause, however, he said, with coolness, 'My conduct is open to men and angels. The deed was not done in a corner; I am here in arms to avow it, and care not where, or by whom, I am called on to do so; whether in the council, the field of battle, the place of execution, or the day of the last great trial. I will not now discuss it further with one who is yet on the other side of the veil. But if you will cast in your lot with us as a brother, come with me to the council, who are still sitting, to arrange the future march of the army, and the means of improving our victory.'

Morton arose and followed him in silence; not greatly delighted with his associate, and better satisfied with the general justice of the cause which he had espoused, than either with the measures or the motives of many of those who were embarked in it.

CHAPTER 22

And look how many Grecian tents do stand
Hollow upon this plain – so many hollow factions.

Troilus and Cressida [1]

In a hollow of the hill, about a quarter of a mile from the field of battle, was a shepherd's hut; a miserable cottage, which, as the only enclosed spot within a moderate distance, the leaders of the presbyterian army had chosen for their council-house. Towards this spot Burley guided Morton, who was surprised, as he approached it, at the multifarious confusion of sounds which issued from its precincts. The calm and anxious gravity which it might be supposed would have presided in councils held on such important subjects, and at a period so critical, seemed to have given place to discord wild, and loud uproar, which fell on the ear of their new ally as an evil augury of their future measures. As they approached the door, they found it open indeed, but choked up with the bodies and heads of countrymen, who, though no members of the council, felt no scruple in intruding themselves upon deliberations in which they were so deeply interested. By expostulation, by threats, and even by some degree of violence, Burley, the sternness of whose character maintained a sort of superiority over these disorderly forces, compelled the intruders to retire, and, introducing Morton into the cottage, secured the door behind them against impertinent curiosity. At a less agitating moment, the young man might have been entertained with the singular scene of which he now found himself an auditor and a spectator.

The precincts of the gloomy and ruinous hut were enlightened partly by some furze which blazed on the hearth, the smoke whereof, having no legal vent, eddied around, and formed over the heads of the assembled council a clouded canopy, as opake as their metaphysical theology, through which, like stars through mist, were dimly seen to twinkle a few blinking candles, or rather rushes dipped in tallow, the property of the poor owner of the cottage, which were stuck to the walls by patches of wet clay. This broken and dusky light showed many a countenance elated with spiritual pride, or rendered dark by fierce enthusiasm; and some whose anxious, wandering, and uncertain looks, showed they felt themselves rashly embarked in a cause which they had neither courage nor conduct to bring to a good issue, yet knew not how to abandon, for very shame. They were, indeed, a doubtful and disunited body. The most active of their number were those concerned with Burley in the death of the Primate, four or five of whom had found their way to Loudon-hill, together with other men of the same relentless and uncompromising zeal, who had, in various ways, given desperate and unpardonable offence to the government.

With them were mingled their preachers, men who had spurned at the indulgence offered by government, and preferred assembling their flocks in the wilderness, to worshipping in temples built by human hands, if their doing the latter should be construed to admit any right on the part of their rulers to interfere with the supremacy of the Kirk. The other class of counsellors were such gentlemen of small fortune, and substantial farmers, as a sense of intolerable oppression had induced to take arms and join the insurgents. These also had their clergymen with them, and such divines, having many of them taken advantage of the indulgence,[2] were prepared to resist the measures of their more violent brethren, who proposed a declaration in which they should give testimony against the warrants and instructions for indulgence as sinful and unlawful acts. This delicate question had been passed over in silence in the first draught of the manifestos which they intended to publish, of the reasons of their gathering in arms; but it had been stirred anew during Balfour's absence, and, to his great vexation, he now found that both parties had opened upon it in full cry, Macbriar, Kettledrummle, and other teachers of the wanderers, being at the very spring-tide of polemical discussion with Peter Poundtext, the indulged pastor of Milnwood's parish, who, it seems, had e'en girded himself with a broadsword, but, ere he was called upon to fight for the good cause of presbytery in the field, was manfully defending his own dogmata in the council. It was the din of this conflict, maintained chiefly between Poundtext and Kettledrummle, together with the clamour of their adherents, which had saluted Morton's ears upon approaching the cottage. Indeed, as both the divines were men well gifted with words and lungs, and each fierce, ardent, and intolerant in defence of his own doctrine, prompt in the recollection of texts wherewith they battered each other without mercy, and deeply impressed with the importance of the subject of discussion, the noise of the debate betwixt them fell little short of that which might have attended an actual bodily conflict.

Burley, scandalized at the disunion implied in this virulent strife of tongues, interposed between the disputants, and, by some general remarks on the unseasonableness of discord, a soothing address to the vanity of each party, and the exertion of the authority which his services in that day's victory entitled him to assume, at length succeeded in prevailing upon them to adjourn farther discussion of the controversy. But although Kettledrummle and Poundtext were thus for the time silenced, they continued to eye each other like two dogs, who, having been separated by the authority of their masters while fighting, have retreated, each beneath the chair of his owner, still watching each other's motions, and indicating, by occasional growls, by the erected bristles of the back and ears, and by the red glance of the eye, that their discord is unappeased, and that they only wait the first opportunity afforded by any general movement or commotion in the company, to fly once more at each other's throats.

Balfour took advantage of the momentary pause to present to the council Mr Henry Morton of Milnwood, as one touched with a sense of the evils of the times, and willing to peril goods and life in the precious cause for which his father, the renowned Silas Morton, had given in his time a soul-stirring testimony. Morton was instantly received with the right hand of fellowship by his ancient pastor, Poundtext, and by those among the insurgents who supported the more moderate principles. The others muttered something about Erastianism, and reminded each other in whispers, that Silas Morton, once a stout and worthy servant of the Covenant, had been a backslider in the day when the resolutioners had led the way in owning the authority of Charles Stewart, thereby making a gap whereat the present tyrant was afterwards brought in, to the oppression both of Kirk and country. They added, however, that, on this great day of calling, they would not refuse society with any who should put hand to the plough; and so Morton was installed in his office of leader and counsellor, if not with the full approbation of his colleagues, at least without any formal or avowed dissent. They proceeded, on Burley's motion, to divide among themselves the command of the men who had assembled, and whose numbers were daily increasing. In this partition, the insurgents of Poundtext's parish and congregation were naturally placed under the command of Morton; an arrangement mutually agreeable to both parties, as he was recommended to their confidence, as well by his personal qualities as his having been born among them.

When this task was accomplished, it became necessary to determine what use was to be made of their victory. Morton's heart throbbed high when he heard the Tower of Tillietudlem named as one of the most important positions to be seized upon.[3] It commanded, as we have often noticed, the pass between the more wild and the more fertile country, and must furnish, it was plausibly urged, a stronghold and place of rendezvous to the cavaliers and malignants of the district, supposing the insurgents were to march onward and leave it uninvested. This measure was particularly urged as necessary by Poundtext and those of his immediate followers, whose habitations and families might be exposed to great severities, if this strong place were permitted to remain in possession of the royalists.

'I opine,' said Poundtext, – for, like the other divines of the period, he had no hesitation in offering his advice upon military matters of which he was profoundly ignorant, – 'I opine, that we should take in and raze that stronghold of the woman Lady Margaret Bellenden, even though we should build a fort and raise a mount against it; for the race is a rebellious and a bloody race, and their hand has been heavy on the children of the Covenant, both in the former and the latter times. Their hook hath been in our noses, and their bridle betwixt our jaws.'[4]

'What are their means and men of defence?' said Burley. 'The place is strong; but I cannot conceive that two women can make it good against a host.'

'There is also,' said Poundtext, 'Harrison the steward, and John Gudyill, even the lady's chief butler, who boasteth himself a man of war from his youth upward, and who spread the banner against the good cause with that man of Belial, James Grahame of Montrose.'

'Pshaw!' returned Burley, scornfully, 'a butler!'

'Also, there is that ancient malignant,' replied Poundtext, 'Miles Bellenden of Charnwood, whose hands have been dipped in the blood of the saints.'

'If that,' said Burley, 'be Miles Bellenden, the brother of Sir Arthur, he is one whose sword will not turn back from battle; but he must now be stricken in years.'

'There was word in the country as I rode along,' said another of the council, 'that so soon as they heard of the victory which has been given to us, they caused shut the gates of the tower, and called in men, and collected ammunition. They were ever a fierce and a malignant house.'

'We will not, with my consent,' said Burley, 'engage in a siege which may consume time. We must rush forward, and follow our advantage by occupying Glasgow; for I do not fear that the troops we have this day beaten, even with the assistance of my Lord Ross's regiment, will judge it safe to await our coming.'

'Howbeit,' said Poundtext, 'we may display a banner before the Tower, and blow a trumpet, and summon them to come forth. It may be that they will give over the place into our mercy, though they be a rebellious people. And we will summon the women to come forth of their stronghold, that is, Lady Margaret Bellenden and her grand-daughter, and Jenny Dennison, which is a girl of an ensnaring eye, and the other maids, and we will give them a safe conduct, and send them in peace to the city, even to the town of Edinburgh. But John Gudyill, and Hugh Harrison, and Miles Bellenden, we will restrain with fetters of iron, even as they, in times bypast, have done to the martyred saints.'

'Who talks of safe conduct and of peace?' said a shrill, broken, and overstrained voice, from the crowd.

'Peace, brother Habakkuk,' said Macbriar, in a soothing tone, to the speaker.

'I will not hold my peace,' reiterated the strange and unnatural voice; 'is this a time to speak of peace, when the earth quakes, and the mountains are rent, and the rivers are changed into blood, and the two-edged sword is drawn from the sheath to drink gore as if it were water, and devour flesh as the fire devours dry stubble?'[5]

While he spoke thus, the orator struggled forward to the inner part of the circle, and presented to Morton's wondering eyes a figure worthy of such a voice and such language. The rags of a dress which had once been black, added to the tattered fragments of a shepherd's plaid, composed a covering scarce fit for the purposes of decency, much less for those of warmth or comfort. A long beard, as white as snow, hung down on his breast, and mingled with bushy, uncombed, grizzled hair, which hung in elf-locks around his wild and staring visage. The features seemed to be extenuated by penury and famine, until they hardly retained the likeness of a human aspect. The eyes, grey, wild, and wandering, evidently betokened a bewildered imagination. He held in his hand a rusty sword, clotted with blood, as were his long lean hands, which were garnished at the extremity with nails like eagle's claws.

'In the name of Heaven! who is he?' said Morton, in a whisper to Poundtext, surprised, shocked, and even startled, at this ghastly apparition, which looked more like the resurrection of some cannibal priest, or druid red from his human sacrifice, than like an earthly mortal.

'It is Habakkuk Mucklewrath,' answered Poundtext, in the same tone, 'whom the enemy have long detained in captivity in forts and castles, until his understanding hath departed from him, and, as I fear, an evil demon hath possessed him. Nevertheless, our violent brethren will have it, that he speaketh of the spirit, and that they fructify by his pouring forth.'

Here he was interrupted by Mucklewrath, who cried in a voice that made the very beams of the roof quiver – 'Who talks of peace and safe conduct? who speaks of mercy to the bloody house of the malignants? I say take the infants and dash them against the stones; take the daughters and the mothers of the house and hurl them from the battlements of their trust, that the dogs may fatten on their blood as they did on that of Jezabel, the spouse of Ahab, and that their carcasses may be dung to the face of the field even in the portion of their fathers!'[6]

'He speaks right,' said more than one sullen voice from behind; 'we will be honoured with little service in the great cause, if we already make fair weather with Heaven's enemies.'

'This is utter abomination and daring impiety,' said Morton, unable to contain his indignation. 'What blessing can you expect in a cause, in which you listen to the mingled ravings of madness and atrocity?'

'Hush, young man!' said Kettledrummle, 'and reserve thy censure for that for which thou canst render a reason. It is not for thee to judge into what vessels the spirit may be poured.'

'We judge of the tree by the fruit,'[7] said Poundtext, 'and allow not that to be of divine inspiration that contradicts the divine laws.'

'You forget, brother Poundtext,' said Macbriar, 'that these are the latter days, when signs and wonders shall be multiplied.'

Poundtext stood forward to reply; but, ere he could articulate a word, the insane preacher broke in with a scream that drowned all competition.

'Who talks of signs and wonders? Am not I Habakkuk Mucklewrath, whose name is changed to Magor-Missabib, because I am made a terror unto myself and unto all that are around me?[8] – I heard it – When did I hear it? – Was it not in the Tower of the Bass, that overhangeth the wide wild sea?[9] – And it howled in the winds, and it roared in the billows, and it screamed, and it whistled, and it clanged, with the screams and the clang and the whistle of the sea-birds, as they floated, and flew, and dropped, and dived, on the bosom of the waters. I saw it – Where did I see it? – Was it not from the high peaks of Dunbarton, when I looked westward upon the fertile land, and northward on the wild Highland hills; when the clouds gathered and the tempest came, and the lightnings of heaven flashed in sheets as wide as the banners of an host? – What did I see? – Dead corpses and wounded horses, the rushing together of battle, and garments rolled in blood. – What heard I? – The voice that cried, Slay, slay – smite – slay utterly – let not your eye have pity! slay utterly, old and young, the maiden, the child, and the woman whose head is grey – Defile the house and fill the courts with the slain!'[10]

'We receive the command,' exclaimed more than one of the company. 'Six days he hath not spoken nor broken bread, and now his tongue is unloosed:– We receive the command; as he hath said, so will we do.'

Astonished, disgusted, and horror-struck, at what he had seen and heard, Morton turned away from the circle and left the cottage. He was followed by Burley, who had his eye on his motions.

'Whither are you going?' said the latter, taking him by the arm.

'Any where, – I care not whither; but here I will abide no longer.'

'Art thou so soon weary, young man?' answered Burley. 'Thy hand is but now put to the plough, and wouldst thou already abandon it? Is this thy adherence to the cause of thy father?'

'No cause,' replied Morton, indignantly – 'no cause can prosper, so conducted. One party declares for the ravings of a bloodthirsty madman; another leader is an old scholastic pedant; a third' – he stopped, and his companion continued the sentence – 'Is a desperate homicide, thou wouldst say, like John Balfour of Burley? – I can bear thy misconstruction without resentment. Thou dost not consider, that it is not men of sober and self-seeking minds, who arise in these days of wrath to execute judgment and to accomplish deliverance. Hadst thou but seen the armies of England, during her Parliament of 1640, whose ranks were filled with sectaries and enthusiasts, wilder than the anabaptists of Munster,[11] thou wouldst have had more cause to marvel; and yet these men were unconquered on the field, and their hands wrought marvellous things for the liberties of the land.'

'But their affairs,' replied Morton, 'were wisely conducted, and the violence of their zeal expended itself in their exhortations and sermons, without bringing divisions into their counsels, or cruelty into their conduct. I have often heard my father say so, and protest, that he wondered at nothing so much as the contrast between the extravagance of their religious tenets, and the wisdom and moderation with which they conducted their civil and military affairs. But *our* councils seem all one wild chaos of confusion.'

'Thou must have patience, Henry Morton,' answered Balfour; 'thou must not leave the cause of thy religion and country either for one wild word, or one extravagant action. Hear me. I have already persuaded the wiser of our friends, that the counsellors are too numerous, and that we cannot expect that the Midianites shall, by so large a number, be delivered into our hands.[12] They have hearkened to my voice, and our assemblies will be shortly reduced within such a number as can consult and act together; and in them thou shalt have a free voice, as well as in ordering our affairs of war, and protecting those to whom mercy should be shown – Art thou now satisfied?'

'It will give me pleasure, doubtless,' answered Morton, 'to be the means of softening the horrors of civil war; and I will not leave the post I have taken, unless I see measures adopted at which my conscience revolts. But to no bloody executions after quarter asked, or slaughter without trial, will I lend countenance or sanction; and you may depend on my opposing them, with both heart and hand, as constantly and resolutely, if attempted by our own followers, as when they are the work of the enemy.'

Balfour waved his hand impatiently.

'Thou wilt find,' he said, 'that the stubborn and hard-hearted generation with whom we deal, must be chastised with scorpions ere their hearts be humbled, and ere they accept the punishment of their iniquity. The word is gone forth against them, "I will bring a sword upon you that shall avenge the quarrel of my Covenant."[13] But what is done shall be done gravely, and with discretion, like that of the worthy James Melvin, who executed judgment on the tyrant and oppressor, Cardinal Beaton.'[14]

'I own to you,' replied Morton, 'that I feel still more abhorrent at cold-blooded and premeditated cruelty, than at that which is practised in the heat of zeal and resentment.'

'Thou art yet but a youth,' replied Balfour, 'and hast not learned how light in the balance are a few drops of blood in comparison to the weight and importance of this great national testimony. But be not afraid; thyself shall vote and judge in these matters; it may be we shall see little cause to strive together anent them.'

With this concession Morton was compelled to be satisfied for the present; and Burley left him, advising him to lie down and get some rest, as the host would probably move in the morning.

'And you,' answered Morton, 'do not you go to rest also?'

'No,' said Burley; 'my eyes must not yet know slumber. This is no work to be done lightly; I have yet to perfect the choosing of the committee of leaders, and I will call you by times in the morning to be present at their consultation.'

He turned away, and left Morton to his repose.

The place in which he found himself was not ill adapted for the purpose, being a sheltered nook, beneath a large rock, well protected from the prevailing wind. A quantity of moss with which the ground was overspread, made a couch soft enough for one who had suffered so much hardship and anxiety. Morton wrapped himself in the horseman's cloak which he had still retained, stretched himself on the ground, and had not long indulged in melancholy reflections on the state of the country, and upon his own condition, ere he was relieved from them by deep and sound slumber.

The rest of the army slept on the ground, dispersed in groups, which chose their beds on the fields as they could best find shelter and convenience. A few of the principal leaders held wakeful conference with Burley on the state of their affairs, and some watchmen were appointed who kept themselves on the alert by chanting psalms, or listening to the exercises of the more gifted of their number.

CHAPTER 23

Got with much ease – now merrily to horse.
Henry IV Part I[1]

WITH the first peep of day Henry awoke, and found the faithful Cuddie standing beside him with a portmanteau in his hand.

'I hae been just putting your honour's things in readiness again ye were waking,' said Cuddie, 'as is my duty, seeing ye hae been sae gude as to tak me into your service.'

'I take you into my service, Cuddie?' said Morton, 'you must be dreaming.'

'Na, na, stir,' answered Cuddie; 'didna I say when I was tied on the horse yonder, that if ever ye gat loose I would be your servant, and ye didna say no? and if that isna hiring, I kenna what is. Ye gae me nae arles, indeed, but ye had gien me eneugh before at Milnwood.'

'Well, Cuddie, if you insist on taking the chance of my un-prosperous fortunes' –

'Ou ay, I'se warrant us a' prosper weel eneugh,' answered Cuddie, cheeringly, 'an anes my auld mither was weel putten up. I hae begun the campaigning trade at an end that is easy enough to learn.'

'Pillaging, I suppose?' said Morton, 'for how else could you come by that portmanteau?'

'I wotna if it's pillaging, or how ye ca't,' said Cuddie, 'but it comes natural to a body, and it's a profitable trade. Our folk had tirled the dead dragoons as bare as bawbees before we were loose amaist. – But when I saw the Whigs a' weel yokit by the lugs to Kettledrummle and the other chield, I set off at the lang trot on my ain errand and your honour's. Sae I took up the syke a wee bit, away to the right, where I saw the marks o' mony a horse-foot, and sure eneugh I cam to a place where there had been some clean leatherin', and a' the puir chields were lying there buskit wi' their claes just as they had put them on that morning – naebody had found out that pose o' carcages – and wha suld be in the midst thereof (as my mither says) but our auld acquaintance, Sergeant Bothwell?'

'Ay, has that man fallen?' said Morton.

'Troth has he,' answered Cuddie; 'and his een were open and his brow bent, and his teeth clenched thegither, like the jaws of a trap for foumarts when the spring's doun – I was amaist feared to look at him; however, I thought to hae turn about wi' him, and sae I e'en riped his pouches, as he had dune mony an honester man's; and here's your ain siller again (or your uncle's, which is the same) that he got at Milnwood that unlucky night that made us a' sodgers thegither.'

'There can be no harm, Cuddie,' said Morton, 'in making use of this money, since we know how he came by it; but you must divide with me.'

'Bide a wee, bide a wee,' said Cuddie. 'Weel, and there's a bit ring he had hinging in a black ribbon doun on his breast. I am thinking it has been a love-token, puir fallow – there's naebody sae rough but they hae aye a kind heart to the lasses – and there's a book wi' a wheen papers, and I got twa or three odd things, that I'll keep to mysell, forby.'

'Upon my word, you have made a very successful foray for a beginner,' said his new master.

'Haena I e'en now?' said Cuddie, with great exultation. 'I tauld ye I wasna that dooms stupid, if it cam to lifting things. – And forby, I hae gotten twa gude horse. A feckless loon of a Straven[2] weaver, that has left his loom and his bein house to sit skirling on a cauld hill-side, had catched twa dragoon naigs, and he could neither gar them hup nor wind, sae he took a gowd noble for them baith – I suld hae tried him wi' half the siller, but it's an unco ill place to get change in – Ye'll find the siller's missing out o' Bothwell's purse.'

'You have made a most excellent and useful purchase, Cuddie; but what is that portmanteau?'

'The pockmantle?' answered Cuddie, 'it was Lord Evandale's yesterday, and it's yours the day. I fand it ahint the bush o' broom yonder – ilka dog has its day – Ye ken what the auld sang says,

"Take turn about, mither, quo' Tam o' the Linn."[3]

'And, speaking o' that, I maun gang and see about my mither, puir auld body, if your honour hasna ony immediate commands.'

'But, Cuddie,' said Morton, 'I really cannot take these things from you without some recompense.'

'Hout fie, stir,' answered Cuddie, 'ye suld aye be taking, – for recompense, ye may think about that some other time – I hae seen gay weel to mysell wi' some things that fit me better. What could I do wi' Lord Evandale's braw claes? Sergeant Bothwell's will serve me weel eneugh.'

Not being able to prevail on the self-constituted and dis-interested follower to accept of any thing for himself out of these warlike spoils, Morton resolved to take the first opportunity of returning Lord Evandale's property, supposing him yet to be alive; and, in the meanwhile, did not hesitate to avail himself of Cuddie's prize, so far as to appropriate some changes of linen and other trifling articles amongst those of more value which the portmanteau contained.

He then hastily looked over the papers which were found in Bothwell's pocket-book. These were of a miscellaneous descrip-tion. The roll of his troop, with the names of those absent on furlough, memorandums of tavern-bills, and lists of delinquents who might be made subjects of fine and persecution, first pre-sented themselves, along with a copy of a warrant from the Privy Council to arrest certain persons of distinction therein named. In another pocket of the book were one or two commissions which Bothwell had held at different times, and certificates of his services abroad, in which his courage and military talents were highly praised. But the most remarkable paper was an accurate account of his genealogy, with reference to many documents for establishment of its authenticity; subjoined was a list of the ample possessions of the forfeited Earls of Bothwell, and a particular account of the proportions in which King James VI had be-stowed them on the courtiers and nobility by whose descendants they were at present actually possessed; beneath this list was written, in red letters, in the hand of the deceased, *Haud Immemor*, F. S. E. B. the initials probably intimating Francis Stewart, Earl of Bothwell. To these documents, which strongly painted the character and feelings of their deceased proprietor, were added some which showed him in a light greatly different from that in which we have hitherto presented him to the reader.

In a secret pocket of the book, which Morton did not discover without some trouble, were one or two letters, written in a beautiful female hand. They were dated about twenty years back, bore no address, and were subscribed only by initials. Without having time to peruse them accurately, Morton perceived that they contained the elegant yet fond expressions of female affection directed towards an object whose jealousy they endeavoured to soothe, and of whose hasty, suspicious, and impatient temper, the writer seemed gently to complain. The ink of these manuscripts had faded by time, and, notwithstanding the great care which had obviously been taken for their preservation, they were in one or two places chafed so as to be illegible.

'It matters not,' these words were written on the envelope of that which had suffered most, 'I have them by heart.'

With these letters was a lock of hair wrapped in a copy of verses, written obviously with a feeling, which atoned, in Morton's opinion, for the roughness of the poetry, and the conceits with which it abounded, according to the taste of the period:

> Thy hue, dear pledge, is pure and bright,
> As in that well-remember'd night,
> When first thy mystic braid was wove,
> And first my Agnes whisper'd love.
>   Since then, how often hast thou press'd
> The torrid zone of this wild breast,
> Whose wrath and hate have sworn to dwell
> With the first sin which peopled hell;
> A breast whose blood's a troubled ocean,
> Each throb the earthquake's wild commotion! —
> O, if such clime thou canst endure,
> Yet keep thy hue unstain'd and pure,
> What conquest o'er each erring thought
> Of that fierce realm had Agnes wrought!
> I had not wander'd wild and wide,
> With such an angel for my guide;
> Nor heaven nor earth could then reprove me,
> If she had lived, and lived to love me.
>   Not then this world's wild joys had been
> To me one savage hunting-scene,
> My sole delight the headlong race,
> And frantic hurry of the chase,

To start, pursue, and bring to bay,
Rush in, drag down, and rend my prey,
Then from the carcass turn away;
Mine ireful mood had sweetness tamed,
And soothed each wound which pride inflamed; —
Yes, God and man might now approve me,
If thou hadst lived, and lived to love me!

As he finished reading these lines, Morton could not forbear reflecting with compassion on the fate of this singular and most unhappy being who, it appeared, while in the lowest state of degradation, and almost of contempt, had his recollections continually fixed on the high station to which his birth seemed to entitle him; and, while plunged in gross licentiousness, was in secret looking back with bitter remorse to the period of his youth, during which he had nourished a virtuous, though unfortunate attachment.

'Alas! what are we,' said Morton, 'that our best and most praiseworthy feelings can be thus debased and depraved – that honourable pride can sink into haughty and desperate indifference for general opinion, and the sorrow of blighted affection inhabit the same bosom which license, revenge, and rapine, have chosen for their citadel? But it is the same throughout; the liberal principles of one man sink into cold and unfeeling indifference, the religious zeal of another hurries him into frantic and savage enthusiasm. Our resolutions, our passions, are like the waves of the sea, and, without the aid of Him who formed the human breast, we cannot say to its tides, "Thus far shall ye come, and no farther." '[4]

While he thus moralized, he raised his eyes, and observed that Burley stood before him.

'Already awake?' said that leader – 'It is well, and shows zeal to tread the path before you. – What papers are these?' he continued.

Morton gave him some brief account of Cuddie's successful marauding party, and handed him the pocket-book of Bothwell, with its contents. The Cameronian leader looked with some attention on such of the papers as related to military affairs, or public business; but when he came to the verses, he threw them from him with contempt.

'I little thought,' he said, 'when, by the blessing of God, I passed my sword three times through the body of that arch tool of cruelty and persecution, that a character so desperate and so dangerous could have stooped to an art as trifling as it is profane. But I see that Satan can blend the most different qualities in his well-beloved and chosen agents, and that the same hand which can wield a club or a slaughter-weapon against the godly in the valley of destruction, can touch a tinkling lute, or a gittern, to soothe the ears of the dancing daughters of perdition in their Vanity Fair.' [5]

'Your ideas of duty, then,' said Morton, 'exclude love of the fine arts, which have been supposed in general to purify and to elevate the mind?'

'To me, young man,' answered Burley, 'and to those who think as I do, the pleasures of this world, under whatever name disguised, are vanity, as its grandeur and power are a snare. We have but one object on earth, and that is to build up the temple of the Lord.'

'I have heard my father observe,' replied Morton, 'that many who assumed power in the name of Heaven, were as severe in its exercise, and as unwilling to part with it, as if they had been solely moved by the motives of worldly ambition – But of this another time. Have you succeeded in obtaining a committee of the council to be nominated?'

'I have,' answered Burley. 'The number is limited to six,[6] of which you are one, and I come to call you to their deliberations.'

Morton accompanied him to a sequestered grass-plot, where their colleagues awaited them. In this delegation of authority, the two principal factions which divided the tumultuary army had each taken care to send three of their own number. On the part of the Cameronians, were Burley, Macbriar, and Kettledrummle; and on that of the moderate party, Poundtext, Henry Morton, and a small proprietor, called the Laird of Langcale. Thus the two parties were equally balanced by their representatives in the committee of management, although it seemed likely that those of the most violent opinions were, as is usual in such cases, to possess and exert the greater degree of energy. Their debate, however, was conducted more like men of this world than could have been expected from their conduct on the preceding evening.

After maturely considering their means and situation, and the probable increase of their numbers, they agreed that they would keep their position for that day, in order to refresh their men, and give time to reinforcements to join them, and that, on the next morning, they would direct their march towards Tillietudlem, and summon that stronghold, as they expressed it, of malignancy. If it was not surrendered to their summons, they resolved to try the effect of a brisk assault; and, should that miscarry, it was settled that they should leave a part of their number to blockade the place, and reduce it, if possible, by famine, while their main body should march forward to drive Claverhouse and Lord Ross from the town of Glasgow. Such was the determination of the council of management; and thus Morton's first enterprise in active life was likely to be the attack of a castle belonging to the parent of his mistress, and defended by her relative, Major Bellenden, to whom he personally owed many obligations! He felt fully the embarrassment of his situation, yet consoled himself with the reflection, that his newly-acquired power in the insurgent army would give him, at all events, the means of extending to the inmates of Tillietudlem a protection which no other circumstance could have afforded them; and he was not without hope that he might be able to mediate such an accommodation betwixt them and the presbyterian army, as should secure them a safe neutrality during the war which was about to ensue.

CHAPTER 24

There came a knight from the field of slain,
His steed was drench'd in blood and rain.

FINLAY[1]

WE must now return to the fortress of Tillietudlem and its inhabitants. The morning, being the first after the battle of Loudon-hill, had dawned upon its battlements, and the defenders had already resumed the labours by which they proposed to render the place tenable, when the watchman, who was placed in a high turret, called the Warder's Tower, gave the signal that a horseman was approaching. As he came nearer, his dress indicated an officer of the Life-Guards; and the slowness of his horse's pace, as well as the manner in which the rider stooped on the saddle-bow, plainly showed that he was sick or wounded. The wicket was instantly opened to receive him, and Lord Evandale rode into the court-yard, so reduced by loss of blood, that he was unable to dismount without assistance. As he entered the hall, leaning upon a servant, the ladies shrieked with surprise and terror; for, pale as death, stained with blood, his regimentals soiled and torn, and his hair matted and disordered, he resembled rather a spectre than a human being. But their next exclamation was that of joy at his escape.

'Thank God!' exclaimed Lady Margaret, 'that you are here, and have escaped the hands of the bloodthirsty murderers who have cut off so many of the king's loyal servants!'

'Thank God!' added Edith, 'that you are here and in safety! We have dreaded the worst. But you are wounded, and I fear we have little the means of assisting you.'

'My wounds are only sword-cuts,' answered the young nobleman, as he reposed himself on a seat; 'the pain is not worth mentioning, and I should not even feel exhausted but for the loss of blood. But it was not my purpose to bring my weakness to add to your danger and distress, but to relieve them, if possible. What can I do for you? – Permit me,' he added, addressing Lady Margaret – 'permit me to think and act as your son, my dear madam – as your brother, Edith!'

He pronounced the last part of the sentence with some emphasis, as if he feared that the apprehension of his pretensions as a suitor might render his proffered services unacceptable to Miss Bellenden. She was not insensible to his delicacy, but there was no time for exchange of sentiments.

'We are preparing for our defence,' said the old lady with great dignity; 'my brother has taken charge of our garrison, and, by the grace of God, we will give the rebels such a reception as they deserve.'

'How gladly,' said Evandale, 'would I share in the defence of the Castle! But in my present state, I should be but a burden to you, nay, something worse; for, the knowledge that an officer of the Life-Guards was in the Castle would be sufficient to make these rogues more desperately earnest to possess themselves of it. If they find it defended only by the family, they may possibly march on to Glasgow rather than hazard an assault.'

'And can you think so meanly of us, my lord,' said Edith, with the generous burst of feeling which woman so often evinces, and which becomes her so well, her voice faltering through eagerness, and her brow colouring with the noble warmth which dictated her language – 'Can you think so meanly of your friends, as that they would permit such considerations to interfere with their sheltering and protecting you at a moment when you are unable to defend yourself, and when the whole country is filled with the enemy? Is there a cottage in Scotland whose owners would permit a valued friend to leave it in such circumstances? And can you think we will allow you to go from a castle which we hold to be strong enough for our own defence?'

'Lord Evandale need never think of it,' said Lady Margaret. 'I will dress his wounds myself; it is all an old wife is fit for in war time; but to quit the Castle of Tillietudlem when the sword of the enemy is drawn to slay him, – the meanest trooper that ever wore the king's coat on his back should not do so, much less my young Lord Evandale. – Ours is not a house that ought to brook such dishonour. The tower of Tillietudlem has been too much distinguished by the visit of his most sacred' –

Here she was interrupted by the entrance of the Major.

'We have taken a prisoner, my dear uncle,' said Edith – 'a wounded prisoner, and he wants to escape from us. You must help us to keep him by force.'

'Lord Evandale!' exclaimed the veteran. 'I am as much pleased as when I got my first commission. Claverhouse reported you were killed, or missing at least.'

'I should have been slain, but for a friend of yours,' said Lord Evandale, speaking with some emotion, and bending his eyes on the ground, as if he wished to avoid seeing the impression that what he was about to say would make upon Miss Bellenden. 'I was unhorsed and defenceless, and the sword raised to dispatch me, when young Mr Morton, the prisoner for whom you interested yourself yesterday morning, preserved my life, and furnished me with the means of escaping.'

As he ended the sentence, a painful curiosity overcame his first resolution; he raised his eyes to Edith's face, and imagined he could read in the glow of her cheek and the sparkle of her eye, joy at hearing of her lover's safety and freedom, and triumph at his not having been left last in the race of generosity. Such, indeed, were her feelings; but they were also mingled with admiration of the ready frankness with which Lord Evandale had hastened to bear witness to the merit of a favoured rival, and to acknowledge an obligation which, in all probability, he would rather have owed to any other individual in the world.

Major Bellenden, who would never have observed the emotions of either party, even had they been much more markedly expressed, contented himself with saying, 'Since Henry Morton has influence with these rascals, I am glad he has so exerted it; but I hope he will get clear of them as soon as he can. Indeed, I cannot doubt it. I know his principles, and that he detests their cant and hypocrisy. I have heard him laugh a thousand times at the pedantry of that old presbyterian scoundrel, Poundtext, who, after enjoying the indulgence of the government for so many years, has now, upon the very first ruffle, shown himself in his own proper colours, and set off, with three parts of his crop-eared congregation, to join the host of the fanatics. – But how did you escape after leaving the field, my lord?'

'I rode for my life, as a recreant knight must,' answered Lord Evandale, smiling. 'I took the route where I thought I had least chance of meeting with any of the enemy, and I found shelter for several hours – you will hardly guess where.'

'At Castle Bracklan, perhaps,' said Lady Margaret, 'or in the house of some other loyal gentleman?'

'No, madam. I was repulsed, under one mean pretext or another, from more than one house of that description, for fear of the enemy following my traces; but I found refuge in the cottage of a poor widow, whose husband had been shot within these three months by a party of our corps, and whose two sons are at this very moment with the insurgents.'

'Indeed?' said Lady Margaret Bellenden; 'and was a fanatic woman capable of such generosity? – but she disapproved, I suppose, of the tenets of her family?'

'Far from it, madam,' continued the young nobleman; 'she was in principle a rigid recusant, but she saw my danger and distress, considered me as a fellow-creature, and forgot that I was a cavalier and a soldier. She bound my wounds, and permitted me to rest upon her bed, concealed me from a party of the insurgents who were seeking for stragglers, supplied me with food, and did not suffer me to leave my place of refuge until she had learned that I had every chance of getting to this tower without danger.'

'It was nobly done,' said Miss Bellenden; 'and I trust you will have an opportunity of rewarding her generosity.'

'I am running up an arrear of obligation on all sides, Miss Bellenden, during these unfortunate occurrences,' replied Lord Evandale; 'but when I can attain the means of showing my gratitude, the will shall not be wanting.'

All now joined in pressing Lord Evandale to relinquish his intention of leaving the Castle; but the argument of Major Bellenden proved the most effectual.

'Your presence in the Castle will be most useful, if not absolutely necessary, my lord, in order to maintain, by your authority, proper discipline among the fellows whom Claverhouse has left in garrison here, and who do not prove to be of the most orderly description of inmates; and, indeed, we have the Colonel's authority, for that very purpose, to detain any officer of his regiment who might pass this way.'

'That,' said Lord Evandale, 'is an unanswerable argument, since it shows me that my residence here may be useful, even in my present disabled state.'

'For your wounds, my lord,' said the Major, 'if my sister, Lady Bellenden, will undertake to give battle to any feverish symptom, if such should appear, I will answer that my old campaigner, Gideon Pike, shall dress a flesh-wound with any of the incorporation of Barber-Surgeons. He had enough of practice in Montrose's time, for we had few regularly-bred army chirurgeons, as you may well suppose. – You agree to stay with us, then?'

'My reasons for leaving the Castle,' said Lord Evandale, glancing a look towards Edith, 'though they evidently seemed weighty, must needs give way to those which infer the power of serving you. May I presume, Major, to enquire into the means and plan of defence which you have prepared? or can I attend you to examine the works?'

It did not escape Miss Bellenden, that Lord Evandale seemed much exhausted both in body and mind. 'I think, sir,' she said, addressing the Major, 'that since Lord Evandale condescends to become an officer of our garrison, you should begin by rendering him amenable to your authority, and ordering him to his apartment, that he may take some refreshment ere he enters on military discussions.'

'Edith is right,' said the old lady; 'you must go instantly to bed, my lord, and take some febrifuge, which I will prepare with my own hand; and my lady-in-waiting, Mistress Martha Weddell, shall make some friar's chicken, or something very light. I would not advise wine. – John Gudyill, let the housekeeper make ready the chamber of dais. Lord Evandale must lie down instantly. Pike will take off the dressings, and examine the state of the wounds.'

'These are melancholy preparations, madam,' said Lord Evandale, as he returned thanks to Lady Margaret, and was about to leave the hall, – 'but I must submit to your ladyship's directions; and I trust that your skill will soon make me a more able defender of your castle than I am at present. You must render my body serviceable as soon as you can, for you have no use for my head while you have Major Bellenden.'

With these words he left the apartment.

'An excellent young man, and a modest,' said the Major.

'None of that conceit,' said Lady Margaret, 'that often makes young folk suppose they know better how their complaints should be treated than people that have had experience.'

'And so generous and handsome a young nobleman,' said Jenny Dennison, who had entered during the latter part of this conversation, and was now left alone with her mistress in the hall, the Major returning to his military cares, and Lady Margaret to her medical preparations.

Edith only answered these encomiums with a sigh; but, although silent, she felt and knew better than any one how much they were merited by the person on whom they were bestowed. Jenny, however, failed not to follow up her blow.

'After a', it's true that my lady says – there's nae trusting a presbyterian; they are a' faithless man-sworn louns. Whae wad hae thought that young Milnwood and Cuddie Headrigg wad hae taen on wi' thae rebel blackguards?'

'What do you mean by such improbable nonsense, Jenny?' said her young mistress, very much displeased.

'I ken it's no pleasing for you to hear, madam,' answered Jenny hardily; 'and it's as little pleasant for me to tell; but as gude ye suld ken a' about it sune as syne, for the haill Castle's ringing wi't.'

'Ringing with what, Jenny? Have you a mind to drive me mad?' answered Edith, impatiently.

'Just that Henry Morton of Milnwood is out wi' the rebels, and ane o' their chief leaders.'

'It is a falsehood!' said Edith – 'a most base calumny! and you are very bold to dare to repeat it to me. Henry Morton is incapable of such treachery to his king and country – such cruelty to me – to – to all the innocent and defenceless victims, I mean, who must suffer in a civil war – I tell you he is utterly incapable of it, in every sense.'

'Dear! dear! Miss Edith,' replied Jenny, still constant to her text, 'they maun be better acquainted wi' young men than I am, or ever wish to be, that can tell preceesely what they're capable or no capable o'. But there has been Trooper Tam, and another chield, out in bonnets and grey plaids, like countrymen, to recon- – reconnoitre – I think John Gudyill ca'd it; and they hae been amang the rebels, and brought back word that they had seen young Milnwood mounted on ane o' the dragoon horses that was taen at Loudon-hill, armed wi' swords and pistols, like wha but him, and hand and glove wi' the foremost o' them, and dreeling and commanding the men; and Cuddie at the heels o' him, in ane o' Sergeant Bothwell's laced waistcoats, and a cockit hat with a bab o' blue ribbands at it for the auld cause o' the Coven- ant, (but Cuddie aye liked a blue ribband,) and a ruffled sark, like ony lord o' the land – it sets the like o' him, indeed!'

'Jenny,' said her young mistress hastily, 'it is impossible these men's report can be true; my uncle has heard nothing of it at this instant.'

'Because Tam Halliday,' answered the handmaiden, 'came in just five minutes after Lord Evandale; and when he heard his lordship was in the Castle, he swore (the profane loon!) he would be d—d ere he would make the report, as he ca'd it, of his news to Major Bellenden, since there was an officer of his ain regiment in the garrison. Sae he wad have said naething till Lord Evandale wakened the next morning; only he tauld me about it,' (here Jenny looked a little down,) 'just to vex me about Cuddie.'

'Poh, you silly girl,' said Edith, assuming some courage, 'it is all a trick of that fellow to teaze you.'

'Na, madam, it canna be that, for John Gudyill took the other dragoon (he's an auld hard-favoured man, I wotna his name) into the cellar, and gae him a tass o' brandy to get the news out o' him, and he said just the same as Tam Halliday, word for word; and Mr Gudyill was in sic a rage, that he tauld it a' ower again to us, and says the haill rebellion is owing to the nonsense o' my Leddy and the Major, and Lord Evandale, that begged off young Milnwood and Cuddie yesterday morning, for that, if they had suffered, the country wad hae been quiet – and troth I am muckle o' that opinion mysell.'

This last commentary Jenny added to her tale, in resentment of her mistress's extreme and obstinate incredulity. She was instantly alarmed, however, by the effect which her news produced upon her young lady, an effect rendered doubly violent by the High-church principles and prejudices in which Miss Bellenden had been educated. Her complexion became as pale as a corpse, her respiration so difficult that it was on the point of altogether failing her, and her limbs so incapable of supporting her, that she sunk, rather than sat, down upon one of the seats in the hall, and seemed on the eve of fainting. Jenny tried cold water, burnt feathers, cutting of laces, and all other remedies usual in hysterical cases, but without any immediate effect.

'God forgie me! what hae I done?' said the repentant fille-de-chambre. 'I wish my tongue had been cuttit out! – Wha wad hae thought o' her taking on that way, and a' for a young lad? – O, Miss Edith – dear Miss Edith, haud your heart up about it, it's maybe no true for a' that I hae said – O, I wish my mouth had been blistered! A' body tells me my tongue will do me a mischief some day. What if my Leddy comes? or the Major? – and she's sitting in the throne, too, that naebody has sate in since that weary morning the King was here! – O, what will I do! O, what will become o' us!'

While Jenny Dennison thus lamented herself and her mistress, Edith slowly returned from the paroxysm into which she had been thrown by this unexpected intelligence.

'If he had been unfortunate,' she said, 'I never would have deserted him. I never did so, even when there was danger and disgrace in pleading his cause. If he had died, I would have mourned him – if he had been unfaithful, I would have forgiven him; but a rebel to his King, – a traitor to his country, – the associate and colleague of cut-throats and common stabbers, – the persecutor of all that is noble, – the professed and blasphemous enemy of all that is sacred, – I will tear him from my heart, if my life-blood should ebb in the effort!'

She wiped her eyes, and rose hastily from the great chair, (or throne, as Lady Margaret used to call it,) while the terrified damsel hastened to shake up the cushion, and efface the appearance of any one having occupied that sacred seat; although King Charles himself, considering the youth and beauty as well as the affliction of the momentary usurper of his hallowed chair, would probably have thought very little of the profanation. She then hastened officiously to press her support on Edith, as she paced the hall apparently in deep meditation.

'Tak my arm, madam; better just tak my arm; sorrow maun hae its vent, and doubtless' –

'No, Jenny,' said Edith, with firmness; 'you have seen my weakness, and you shall see my strength.'

'But ye leaned on me the other morning, Miss Edith, when ye were sae sair grieved.'

'Misplaced and erring affection may require support, Jenny – duty can support itself; yet I will do nothing rashly. I will be aware of the reasons of his conduct – and then – cast him off for ever,' was the firm and determined answer of her young lady.

Overawed by a manner of which she could neither conceive

the motive, nor estimate the merit, Jenny muttered between her teeth, 'Odd, when the first flight's ower, Miss Edith taks it as easy as I do, and muckle easier, and I'm sure I ne'er cared half sae muckle about Cuddie Headrigg as she did about young Milnwood. Forby that, it's maybe as weel to hae a friend on baith sides; for, if the whigs suld come to tak the Castle, as it's like they may, when there's sae little victual, and the dragoons wasting what's o't, ou, in that case, Milnwood and Cuddie wad hae the upper hand, and their freendship wad be worth siller – I was thinking sae this morning or I heard the news.'

With this consolatory reflection the damsel went about her usual occupations, leaving her mistress to school her mind as she best might, for eradicating the sentiments which she had hitherto entertained towards Henry Morton.

CHAPTER 25

Once more into the breach – dear friends, once more!
                                                    Henry V [1]

On the evening of this day, all the information which they could procure led them to expect, that the insurgent army would be with early dawn on their march against Tillietudlem. Lord Evandale's wounds had been examined by Pike, who reported them in a very promising state. They were numerous, but none of any consequence; and the loss of blood, as much perhaps as the boasted specific of Lady Margaret, had prevented any tendency to fever; so that, notwithstanding he felt some pain and great weakness, the patient maintained that he was able to creep about with the assistance of a stick. In these circumstances he refused to be confined to his apartment, both that he might encourage the soldiers by his presence, and suggest any necessary addition to the plan of defence, which the Major might be supposed to have arranged upon something of an antiquated fashion of warfare. Lord Evandale was well qualified to give advice on such subjects, having served, during his early youth, both in France and in the Low Countries. There was little or no occasion, however, for altering the preparations already made; and, excepting on the article of provisions, there seemed no reason to fear for the defence of so strong a place against such assailants as those by whom it was threatened.

With the peep of day, Lord Evandale and Major Bellenden were on the battlements again, viewing and re-viewing the state of their preparations, and anxiously expecting the approach of the enemy. I ought to observe, that the report of the spies had now been regularly made and received; but the Major treated the report that Morton was in arms against the government with the most scornful incredulity.

'I know the lad better,' was the only reply he deigned to make; 'the fellows have not dared to venture near enough, and have been deceived by some fanciful resemblance, or have picked up some story.'

'I differ from you, Major,' answered Lord Evandale; 'I think you will see that young gentleman at the head of the insurgents; and, though I shall be heartily sorry for it, I shall not be greatly surprised.'

'You are as bad as Claverhouse,' said the Major, 'who contended yesterday morning down my very throat, that this young fellow, who is as high-spirited and gentleman-like a boy as I have ever known, wanted but an opportunity to place himself at the head of the rebels.'

'And considering the usage which he has received, and the suspicions under which he lies,' said Lord Evandale, 'what other course is open to him? For my own part, I should hardly know whether he deserved most blame or pity.'

'Blame, my lord? – Pity!' echoed the Major, astonished at hearing such sentiments; 'he would deserve to be hanged, that's all; and, were he my own son, I should see him strung up with pleasure – Blame, indeed! But your lordship cannot think as you are pleased to speak?'

'I give you my honour, Major Bellenden, that I have been for some time of opinion, that our politicians and prelates have driven matters to a painful extremity in this country, and have alienated, by violence of various kinds, not only the lower classes, but all those in the upper ranks, whom strong party-feeling, or a desire of court-interest, does not attach to their standard.'

'I am no politician,' answered the Major, 'and I do not under-stand nice distinctions. My sword is the King's, and when he commands, I draw it in his cause.'

'I trust,' replied the young lord, 'you will not find me more backward than yourself, though I heartily wish that the enemy were foreigners. It is, however, no time to debate that matter, for yonder they come, and we must defend ourselves as well as we can.'

As Lord Evandale spoke, the van of the insurgents began to make their appearance on the road which crossed the top of the hill, and thence descended opposite to the Tower. They did not, however, move downwards, as if aware that, in doing so, their columns would be exposed to the fire of the artillery of the place. But their numbers, which at first seemed few, appeared presently so to deepen and concentrate themselves, that, judging of the masses which occupied the road behind the hill from the close-ness of the front which they presented on the top of it, their force appeared very considerable. There was a pause of anxiety on both sides; and, while the unsteady ranks of the Covenanters were agitated, as if by pressure behind, or uncertainty as to their next movement, their arms, picturesque from their variety, glanced in the morning sun, whose beams were reflected from a grove of pikes, muskets, halberds, and battle-axes. The armed mass occupied, for a few minutes, this fluctuating position, until three or four horsemen, who seemed to be leaders, advanced from the front, and occupied the height a little nearer to the Castle. John Gudyill, who was not without some skill as an artilleryman, brought a gun to bear on this detached group.

'I'll flee the falcon,' – (so the small cannon was called,) – 'I'll flee the falcon whene'er your honour gies command; my certie, she'll ruffle their feathers for them!'

The Major looked at Lord Evandale.

'Stay a moment,' said the young nobleman, 'they send us a flag of truce.'

In fact, one of the horsemen at that moment dismounted, and, displaying a white cloth on a pike, moved forward towards the Tower, while the Major and Lord Evandale, descending from the battlement of the main fortress, advanced to meet him as far as the barricade, judging it unwise to admit him within the precincts which they designed to defend. At the same time that the ambassador set forth, the group of horsemen, as if they had anticipated the preparations of John Gudyill for their annoyance, withdrew from the advanced station which they had occupied, and fell back to the main body.

The envoy of the Covenanters, to judge by his mien and manner, seemed fully imbued with that spiritual pride which distinguished his sect. His features were drawn up to a contemptuous primness, and his half-shut eyes seemed to scorn to look upon the terrestial objects around, while, at every solemn stride, his toes were pointed outwards with an air that appeared to despise the ground on which they trode. Lord Evandale could not suppress a smile at this singular figure.

'Did you ever,' said he to Major Bellenden, 'see such an absurd automaton? One would swear it moves upon springs – Can it speak, think you?'

'O, ay,' said the Major; 'that seems to be one of my old acquaintance, a genuine puritan of the right pharisaical leaven. – Stay – he coughs and hems; he is about to summon the Castle with the but-end of a sermon, instead of a parley on the trumpet.'

The veteran, who in his day had had many an opportunity to become acquainted with the manners of these religionists, was not far mistaken in his conjecture; only that, instead of a prose exordium, the Laird of Langcale – for it was no less a personage – uplifted, with a Stentorian voice, a verse of the twenty-fourth Psalm:

> 'Ye gates lift up your heads! ye doors,
>   Doors that do last for aye,
>   Be lifted up' –

'I told you so,' said the Major to Evandale, and then presented himself at the entrance of the barricade, demanding to know for what purpose or intent he made that doleful noise, like a hog in a high wind, beneath the gates of the Castle.

'I come,' replied the ambassador, in a high and shrill voice, and without any of the usual salutations or deferences, – 'I come from the godly army of the Solemn League and Covenant, to speak with two carnal malignants, William Maxwell, called Lord Evandale, and Miles Bellenden of Charnwood.'

'And what have you to say to Miles Bellenden and Lord Evandale?' answered the Major.

'Are you the parties?' said the Laird of Langcale, in the same sharp, conceited, disrespectful tone of voice.

'Even so, for fault of better,' said the Major.

'Then there is the public summons,' said the envoy, putting a paper into Lord Evandale's hand, 'and there is a private letter for Miles Bellenden from a godly youth, who is honoured with leading a part of our host. Read them quickly, and God give you grace to fructify by the contents, though it is muckle to be doubted.'

The summons ran thus: 'We, the named and constituted leaders of the gentlemen, ministers, and others, presently in arms for the cause of liberty and true religion, do warn and summon William Lord Evandale and Miles Bellenden of Charnwood, and others presently in arms, and keeping garrison in the Tower of Tillietudlem, to surrender the said Tower upon fair conditions of quarter, and license to depart with bag and baggage, otherwise to suffer such extremity of fire and sword as belong by the laws of war to those who hold out an untenable post. And so may God defend his own good cause!'

This summons was signed by John Balfour of Burley, as quarter-master-general of the army of the Covenant, for himself, and in name of the other leaders.

The letter to Major Bellenden was from Henry Morton. It was couched in the following language:

'I have taken a step, my venerable friend, which, among many painful consequences, will, I am afraid, incur your very decided disapprobation. But I have taken my resolution in honour and good faith, and with the full approval of my own conscience. I can no longer submit to have my own rights and those of my fellow-subjects trampled upon, our freedom violated, our persons insulted, and our blood spilt, without just cause or legal trial. Providence, through the violence of the oppressors themselves,

seems now to have opened a way of deliverance from this intolerable tyranny, and I do not hold him deserving of the name and
rights of a freeman, who, thinking as I do, shall withhold his
arm from the cause of his country. But God, who knows my
heart, be my witness, that I do not share the angry or violent
passions of the oppressed and harassed sufferers with whom I am
now acting. My most earnest and anxious desire is, to see this
unnatural war brought to a speedy end, by the union of the good,
wise, and moderate of all parties, and a peace restored, which,
without injury to the King's constitutional rights, may substitute
the authority of equal laws to that of military violence, and,
permitting to all men to worship God according to their own
consciences, may subdue fanatical enthusiasm by reason and
mildness, instead of driving it to frenzy by persecution and intolerance.

'With these sentiments, you may conceive with what pain I
appear in arms before the house of your venerable relative, which
we understand you propose to hold against us. Permit me to press
upon you the assurance, that such a measure will only lead to the
effusion of blood – that, if repulsed in the assault, we are yet
strong enough to invest the place, and reduce it by hunger,
being aware of your indifferent preparations to sustain a protracted siege. It would grieve me to the heart to think what
would be the sufferings in such a case, and upon whom they
would chiefly fall.

'Do not suppose, my respected friend, that I would propose to
you any terms which could compromise the high and honourable
character which you have so deservedly won, and so long borne.
If the regular soldiers (to whom I will ensure a safe retreat) are
dismissed from the place, I trust no more will be required than
your parole to remain neuter during this unhappy contest; and
I will take care that Lady Margaret's property, as well as yours,
shall be duly respected, and no garrison intruded upon you. I
could say much in favour of this proposal; but I fear, as I must in
the present instance appear criminal in your eyes, good arguments would lose their influence when coming from an unwel-
come quarter. I will, therefore, break off with assuring you, that
whatever your sentiments may be hereafter towards me, my sense

of gratitude to you can never be diminished or erased; and it would be the happiest moment of my life that should give me more effectual means than mere words to assure you of it. Therefore, although in the first moment of resentment you may reject the proposal I make to you, let that not prevent you from resuming the topic, if future events should render it more acceptable; for whenever, or howsoever, I can be of service to you, it will always afford the greatest satisfaction to

'HENRY MORTON.'

Having read this long letter with the most marked indignation, Major Bellenden put it into the hands of Lord Evandale.

'I would not have believed this,' he said; 'of Henry Morton, if half mankind had sworn it! The ungrateful, rebellious traitor! rebellious in cold blood, and without even the pretext of enthusiasm, that warms the liver of such a crack-brained fop as our friend the envoy there. But I should have remembered he was a presbyterian – I ought to have been aware that I was nursing a wolf-cub, whose diabolical nature would make him tear and snatch at me on the first opportunity. Were Saint Paul on earth again, and a presbyterian, he would be a rebel in three months – it is in the very blood of them.'

'Well,' said Lord Evandale, 'I will be the last to recommend surrender; but, if our provisions fail, and we receive no relief from Edinburgh or Glasgow, I think we ought to avail ourselves of this opening, to get the ladies, at least, safe out of the Castle.'

'They will endure all, ere they would accept the protection of such a smooth-tongued hypocrite,' answered the Major indignantly; 'I would renounce them for relatives were it otherwise. But let us dismiss the worthy ambassador. – My friend,' he said, turning to Langcale, 'tell your leaders, and the mob they have gathered yonder, that, if they have not a particular opinion of the hardness of their own skulls, I would advise them to beware how they knock them against these old walls. And let them send no more flags of truce, or we will hang up the messenger in retaliation of the murder of Cornet Grahame.'

With this answer the ambassador returned to those by whom he had been sent. He had no sooner reached the main body than a murmur was heard among the multitude, and there was raised in front of their ranks an ample red flag, the borders of which were edged with blue. As the signal of war and defiance spread out its large folds upon the morning wind, the ancient banner of Lady Margaret's family, together with the royal ensign, were immediately hoisted on the walls of the Tower, and at the same time, a round of artillery was discharged against the foremost ranks of the insurgents, by which they sustained some loss. Their leaders instantly withdrew them to the shelter of the brow of the hill.

'I think,' said John Gudyill, while he busied himself in re-charging his guns, 'they hae fund the falcon's neb a bit ower hard for them – It's no for nought that the hawk whistles.'

But as he uttered these words, the ridge was once more crowded with the ranks of the enemy. A general discharge of their fire-arms was directed against the defenders upon the battlements. Under cover of the smoke, a column of picked men rushed down the road with determined courage, and, sustaining with firmness a heavy fire from the garrison, they forced their way, in spite of opposition, to the first barricade by which the avenue was de-fended. They were led on by Balfour in person, who displayed courage equal to his enthusiasm; and, in spite of every opposi-tion, forced the barricade, killing and wounding several of the defenders, and compelling the rest to retreat to their second posi-tion. The precautions, however, of Major Bellenden rendered this success unavailing; for no sooner were the Covenanters in posses-sion of the post, than a close and destructive fire was poured into it from the Castle, and from those stations which commanded it in the rear. Having no means of protecting themselves from this fire, or of returning it with effect against men who were under cover of their barricades and defences, the Covenanters were obliged to retreat; but not until they had, with their axes, destroyed the stockade, so as to render it impossible for the defenders to re-occupy it.

Balfour was the last man that retired. He even remained for a short space almost alone, with an axe in his hand, labouring like a pioneer amid the storm of balls, many of which were specially aimed against him. The retreat of the party he commanded was not effected without heavy loss, and served as a severe lesson concerning the local advantages possessed by the garrrison.

The next attack of the Covenanters was made with more caution. A strong party of marksmen, (many of them competitors at the game of the popinjay,) under the command of Henry Morton, glided through the woods where they afforded them the best shelter, and, avoiding the open road, endeavoured, by forcing their way through the bushes and trees, and up the rocks which surrounded it on either side, to gain a position, from which, without being exposed in an intolerable degree, they might annoy the flank of the second barricade, while it was menaced in front by a second attack from Burley. The besieged saw the danger of this movement, and endeavoured to impede the approach of the marksmen, by firing upon them at every point where they showed themselves. The assailants, on the other hand, displayed great coolness, spirit, and judgment, in the manner in which they approached the defences. This was, in a great measure, to be ascribed to the steady and adroit manner in which they were conducted by their youthful leader, who showed as much skill in protecting his own followers as spirit in annoying the enemy.

He repeatedly enjoined his marksmen to direct their aim chiefly upon the red-coats, and to save the others engaged in the defence of the Castle; and, above all, to spare the life of the old Major, whose anxiety made him more than once expose himself in a manner, that, without such generosity on the part of the enemy, might have proved fatal. A dropping fire of musketry now glanced from every part of the precipitous mount on which the Castle was founded. From bush to bush – from crag to crag – from tree to tree, the marksmen continued to advance, availing themselves of branches and roots to assist their ascent, and contending at once with the disadvantages of the ground and the fire of the enemy. At length they got so high on the ascent, that several of them possessed an opportunity of firing into the barricade against the defenders, who then lay exposed to their aim, and Burley, profiting by the confusion of the moment, moved forward to the attack in front. His onset was made with the same

desperation and fury as before, and met with less resistance, the
defenders being alarmed at the progress which the sharp-shooters
had made in turning the flank of their position. Determined to
improve his advantage, Burley, with his axe in his hand, pursued the party whom he had dislodged even to the third and last
barricade, and entered it along with them.

'Kill, kill – down with the enemies of God and his people! –
No quarter – The Castle is ours!' were the cries by which he
animated his friends; the most undaunted of whom followed
him close, whilst the others, with axes, spades, and other implements, threw up earth, cut down trees, hastily labouring to
establish such a defensive cover in the rear of the second barricade as might enable them to retain possession of it, in case the
Castle was not carried by this coup-de-main.

Lord Evandale could no longer restrain his impatience. He
charged with a few soldiers who had been kept in reserve in the
court-yard of the Castle; and, although his arm was in a sling,
encouraged them, by voice and gesture, to assist their companions
who were engaged with Burley. The combat now assumed an air
of desperation. The narrow road was crowded with the followers
of Burley, who pressed forward to support their companions.
The soldiers, animated by the voice and presence of Lord Evandale, fought with fury, their small numbers being in some
measure compensated by their greater skill, and by their possessing the upper ground, which they defended desperately with
pikes and halberds, as well as with the but of the carabines and
their broadswords. Those within the Castle endeavoured to assist
their companions, whenever they could so level their guns as to
fire upon the enemy without endangering their friends. The
sharp-shooters, dispersed around, were firing incessantly on each
object that was exposed upon the battlement. The Castle was
enveloped with smoke, and the rocks rang to the cries of the
combatants. In the midst of this scene of confusion, a singular
accident had nearly given the besiegers possession of the fortress.

Cuddie Headrigg, who had advanced among the marksmen,
being well acquainted with every rock and bush in the vicinity
of the Castle, where he had so often gathered nuts with Jenny
Dennison, was enabled, by such local knowledge, to advance

farther, and with less danger, than most of his companions, excepting some three or four who had followed him close. Now
Cuddie, though a brave enough fellow upon the whole, was by
no means fond of danger, either for its own sake, or for that of
the glory which attends it. In his advance, therefore, he had not,
as the phrase goes, taken the bull by the horns, or advanced in
front of the enemy's fire. On the contrary, he had edged gradually away from the scene of action, and, turning his line of ascent
rather to the left, had pursued it until it brought him under a
front of the Castle different from that before which the parties
were engaged, and to which the defenders had given no attention, trusting to the steepness of the precipice. There was, however, on this point, a certain window belonging to a certain
pantry, and communicating with a certain yew-tree, which grew
out of a steep cleft of the rock, being the very pass through which
Goose Gibbie was smuggled out of the Castle in order to carry
Edith's express to Charnwood, and which had probably, in its
day, been used for other contraband purposes. Cuddie, resting
upon the but of his gun, and looking up at this window, observed
to one of his companions, – 'There's a place I ken weel; mony a
time I hae helped Jenny Dennison out o' the winnock, forby
creeping in whiles mysell to get some daffin, at e'en after the
pleugh was loosed.'

'And what's to hinder us to creep in just now?' said the other,
who was a smart enterprising young fellow.

'There's no muckle to hinder us, an that were a',' answered
Cuddie, 'but what were we to do neist?'

'We'll take the Castle,' cried the other; 'here are five or six o'
us, and a' the sodgers are engaged at the gate.'

'Come awa wi' you, then,' said Cuddie; 'but mind, deil a
finger ye maun lay on Lady Margaret, or Miss Edith, or the auld
Major, or, aboon a', on Jenny Dennison, or ony body but the
sodgers – cut and quarter amang them as ye like, I carena.'

'Ay, ay,' said the other, 'let us once in, and we will make our
ain terms with them a'.'

Gingerly, and as if treading upon eggs, Cuddie began to
ascend the well-known pass, not very willingly; for, besides that
he was something apprehensive of the reception he might meet

with in the inside, his conscience insisted that he was making
but a shabby requital for Lady Margaret's former favours and
protection. He got up, however, into the yew-tree, followed by
his companions, one after another. The window was small, and
had been secured by stancheons of iron; but these had been long
worn away by time, or forced out by the domestics to possess a
free passage for their own occasional convenience. Entrance was
therefore easy, providing there was no one in the pantry, a point
which Cuddie endeavoured to discover before he made the final
and perilous step. While his companions, therefore, were urging
and threatening him behind, and he was hesitating and stretching his neck to look into the apartment, his head became visible
to Jenny Dennison, who had ensconced herself in said pantry
as the safest place in which to wait the issue of the assault. So
soon as this object of terror caught her eye, she set up a hysteric
scream, flew to the adjacent kitchen, and, in the desperate agony
of fear, seized on a pot of kailbrose which she herself had hung
on the fire before the combat began, having promised to Tam
Halliday to prepare his breakfast for him. Thus burdened, she
returned to the window of the pantry, and still exclaiming,
'Murder! murder! – we are a' harried and ravished – the Castle's
taen – tak it amang ye!' she discharged the whole scalding
contents of the pot, accompanied with a dismal yell, upon the
person of the unfortunate Cuddie. However welcome the mess
might have been, if Cuddie and it had become acquainted in a
regular manner, the effects, as administered by Jenny, would
probably have cured him of soldiering for ever, had he been
looking upwards when it was thrown upon him. But, fortunately
for our man of war, he had taken the alarm upon Jenny's first
scream, and was in the act of looking down, expostulating with
his comrades, who impeded the retreat which he was anxious to
commence; so that the steel cap and buff coat which formerly
belonged to Sergeant Bothwell, being garments of an excellent
endurance, protected his person against the greater part of the
scalding brose. Enough, however, reached him to annoy him
severely, so that in the pain and surprise he jumped hastily out of
the tree, oversetting his followers, to the manifest danger of their
limbs, and, without listening to arguments, entreaties, or author-

ity, made the best of his way by the most safe road to the main body of the army whereunto he belonged, and could neither by threats nor persuasion be prevailed upon to return to the attack.

As for Jenny, when she had thus conferred upon one admirer's outward man the viands which her fair hands had so lately been in the act of preparing for the stomach of another, she continued her song of alarm, running a screaming division upon all those crimes, which the lawyers call the four pleas of the crown, namely, murder, fire, rape, and robbery. These hideous exclamations gave so much alarm, and created such confusion within the Castle, that Major Bellenden and Lord Evandale judged it best to draw off from the conflict without the gates, and, abandoning to the enemy all the exterior defences of the avenue, confine themselves to the Castle itself, for fear of its being surprised on some unguarded point. Their retreat was unmolested; for the panic of Cuddie and his companions had occasioned nearly as much confusion on the side of the besiegers, as the screams of Jenny had caused to the defenders.

There was no attempt on either side to renew the action that day. The insurgents had suffered most severely; and, from the difficulty which they had experienced in carrying the barricadoed positions without the precincts of the Castle, they could have but little hope of storming the place itself. On the other hand, the situation of the besieged was dispiriting and gloomy. In the skirmishing they had lost two or three men, and had several wounded; and though their loss was in proportion greatly less than that of the enemy, who had left twenty men dead on the place, yet their small number could much worse spare it, while the desperate attacks of the opposite party plainly showed how serious the leaders were in the purpose of reducing the place, and how well seconded by the zeal of their followers. But, especially, the garrison had to fear for hunger, in case blockade should be resorted to as the means of reducing them. The Major's directions had been imperfectly obeyed in regard to laying in provisions; and the dragoons, in spite of all warning and authority, were likely to be wasteful in using them. It was, therefore, with a heavy heart, that Major Bellenden gave directions for guarding the window through which the Castle had so nearly been surprised, as well as all others which offered the most remote facility for such an enterprise.

CHAPTER 26

– The King hath drawn
The special head of all the land together.

Henry IV Part II[1]

THE leaders of the presbyterian army had a serious consultation upon the evening of the day in which they had made the attack on Tillietudlem. They could not but observe that their followers were disheartened by the loss which they had sustained, and which, as usual in such cases, had fallen upon the bravest and most forward. It was to be feared, that if they were suffered to exhaust their zeal and efforts in an object so secondary as the capture of this petty fort, their numbers would melt away by degrees, and they would lose all the advantages arising out of the present unprepared state of the government. Moved by these arguments, it was agreed that the main body of the army should march against Glasgow, and dislodge the soldiers who were lying in that town. The council nominated Henry Morton, with others, to this last service, and appointed Burley to the command of a chosen body of five hundred men, who were to remain behind, for the purpose of blockading the Tower of Tillietudlem. Morton testified the greatest repugnance to this arrangement.

'He had the strongest personal motives,' he said, 'for desiring to remain near Tillietudlem; and if the management of the siege were committed to him, he had little doubt but that he would bring it to such an accommodation, as, without being rigorous to the besieged, would fully answer the purpose of the besiegers.'

Burley readily guessed the cause of his young colleague's reluctance to move with the army; for, interested as he was in appreciating the characters with whom he had to deal, he had contrived, through the simplicity of Cuddie, and the enthusiasm of old Mause, to get much information concerning Morton's relations with the family of Tillietudlem. He therefore took the advantage of Poundtext's arising to speak to business, as he said, for some short space of time, (which Burley rightly interpreted to mean an hour at the very least,) and seized that moment to withdraw Morton from the hearing of their colleagues, and to hold the following argument with him:

'Thou art unwise, Henry Morton, to desire to sacrifice this holy cause to thy friendship for an uncircumcised Philistine, or thy lust for a Moabitish woman.' [2]

'I neither understand your meaning, Mr Balfour, nor relish your allusions,' replied Morton, indignantly; 'and I know no reason you have to bring so gross a charge, or to use such uncivil language.'

'Confess, however, the truth,' said Balfour, 'and own that there are those within yon dark Tower, over whom thou wouldst rather be watching like a mother over her little ones, than thou wouldst bear the banner of the Church of Scotland over the necks of her enemies.'

'If you mean, that I would willingly terminate this war without any bloody victory, and that I am more anxious to do this than to acquire any personal fame or power, you may be,' replied Morton, 'perfectly right.'

'And not wholly wrong,' answered Burley, 'in deeming that thou wouldst not exclude from so general a pacification thy friends in the garrison of Tillietudlem.'

'Certainly,' replied Morton; 'I am too much obliged to Major Bellenden not to wish to be of service to him, as far as the interest of the cause I have espoused will permit. I never made a secret of my regard for him.'

'I am aware of that,' said Burley; 'but, if thou hadst concealed it, I should, nevertheless, have found out thy riddle. Now, hearken to my words. This Miles Bellenden hath means to subsist his garrison for a month.'

'This is not the case,' answered Morton; 'we know his stores are hardly equal to a week's consumption.'

'Ay, but,' continued Burley, 'I have since had proof, of the strongest nature, that such a report was spread in the garrison by that wily and grey-headed malignant, partly to prevail on the soldiers to submit to a diminution of their daily food, partly to detain us before the walls of his fortress until the sword should be whetted to smite and destroy us.'

'And why was not the evidence of this laid before the council of war?' said Morton.

'To what purpose?' said Balfour. 'Why need we undeceive Kettledrummle, Macbriar, Poundtext, and Langcale, upon such a point? Thyself must own, that whatever is told to them escapes to the host out of the mouth of the preachers at their next holding-forth. They are already discouraged by the thoughts of lying before the fort a week. What would be the consequence were they ordered to prepare for the leaguer of a month?'

'But why conceal it, then, from me? or why tell it me now? and, above all, what proofs have you got of the fact?' continued Morton.

'There are many proofs,' replied Burley; and he put into his hands a number of requisitions sent forth by Major Bellenden, with receipts on the back to various proprietors, for cattle, corn, meal, &c., to such an amount, that the sum total seemed to exclude the possibility of the garrison being soon distressed for provisions. But Burley did not inform Morton of a fact which he himself knew full well, namely, that most of these provisions never reached the garrison, owing to the rapacity of the dragoons sent to collect them, who readily sold to one man what they took from another, and abused the Major's press for stores, pretty much as Sir John Falstaff did that of the King for men.[3]

'And now,' continued Balfour, observing that he had made the desired impression, 'I have only to say, that I concealed this from thee no longer than it was concealed from myself, for I have only received these papers this morning; and I tell it unto thee now, that thou mayest go on thy way rejoicing, and work the great work willingly at Glasgow, being assured that no evil can befall thy friends in the malignant party, since their fort is abundantly victualled, and I possess not numbers sufficient to do more against them than to prevent their sallying forth.'

'And why,' continued Morton, who felt an inexpressible reluctance to acquiesce in Balfour's reasoning – 'why not permit me to remain in the command of this smaller party, and march forward yourself to Glasgow? It is the more honourable charge.'

'And therefore, young man,' answered Burley, 'have I laboured that it should be committed to the son of Silas Morton. I am waxing old, and this grey head has had enough of honour where it could be gathered by danger. I speak not of the frothy bubble which men call earthly fame, but the honour belonging to him that doth not the work negligently. But thy career is yet to run. Thou hast to vindicate the high trust which has been bestowed on thee through my assurance that it was dearly well-merited. At Loudon-hill thou wert a captive, and at the last assault it was thy part to fight under cover, whilst I led the more open and dangerous attack; and, shouldst thou now remain before these walls when there is active service elsewhere, trust me, that men will say, that the son of Silas Morton hath fallen away from the paths of his father.'

Stung by this last observation, to which, as a gentleman and soldier, he could offer no suitable reply, Morton hastily acquiesced in the proposed arrangement. Yet he was unable to divest himself of certain feelings of distrust which he involuntarily attached to the quarter from which he received this information.

'Mr Balfour,' he said, 'let us distinctly understand each other. You have thought it worth your while to bestow particular attention upon my private affairs and personal attachments; be so good as to understand, that I am as constant to them as to my political principles. It is possible, that, during my absence, you may possess the power of soothing or of wounding those feelings. Be assured, that whatever may be the consequences to the issue of our present adventure, my eternal gratitude, or my persevering resentment, will attend the line of conduct you may adopt on such an occasion; and, however young and inexperienced I am, I have no doubt of finding friends to assist me in expressing my sentiments in either case.'

'If there be a threat implied in that denunciation,' replied Burley, coldly and haughtily, 'it had better have been spared. I know how to value the regard of my friends, and despise, from my soul, the threats of my enemies. But I will not take occasion of offence. Whatever happens here in your absence shall be managed with as much deference to your wishes, as the duty I owe to a higher power can possibly permit.'

With this qualified promise Morton was obliged to rest satisfied.

'Our defeat will relieve the garrison,' said he, internally, 'ere they can be reduced to surrender at discretion; and, in case of victory, I already see, from the numbers of the moderate party, that I shall have a voice as powerful as Burley's in determining the use which shall be made of it.'

He therefore followed Balfour to the council, where they found Kettledrummle adding to his *lastly* a few words of practical application. When these were expended, Morton testified his willingness to accompany the main body of the army, which was destined to drive the regular troops from Glasgow. His companions in command were named, and the whole received a strengthening exhortation from the preachers who were present. Next morning, at break of day, the insurgent army broke up from their encampment, and marched towards Glasgow.

It is not our intention to detail at length incidents which may be found in the history of the period. It is sufficient to say, that Claverhouse and Lord Ross, learning the superior force which was directed against them, intrenched, or rather barricadoed themselves, in the centre of the city, where the town-house and old jail were situated, with the determination to stand the assault of the insurgents rather than to abandon the capital of the west of Scotland. The presbyterians made their attack in two bodies, one of which penetrated into the city in the line of the College and Cathedral Church, while the other marched up the Gallowgate, or principal access from the south-east. Both divisions were led by men of resolution, and behaved with great spirit. But the advantages of military skill and situation were too great for their undisciplined valour.

Ross and Claverhouse had carefully disposed parties of their soldiers in houses, at the heads of the streets, and in the entrances of closes, as they are called, or lanes, besides those who were intrenched behind breast-works which reached across the streets. The assailants found their ranks thinned by a fire from invisible opponents, which they had no means of returning with effect. It was in vain that Morton and other leaders exposed their persons with the utmost gallantry, and endeavoured to bring their antagonists to a close action; their followers shrunk from them in every direction. And yet, though Henry Morton was one of the very last to retire, and exerted himself in bringing up the rear, maintaining order in the retreat, and checking every attempt which the enemy made to improve the advantage they had gained by the repulse, he had still the mortification to hear many of those in his ranks muttering to each other, that 'this came of trusting to latitudinarian boys; and that, had honest, faithful Burley led the attack, as he did that of the barricades of Tillietudlem, the issue would have been as different as might be.'

It was with burning resentment that Morton heard these reflections thrown out by the very men who had soonest exhibited signs of discouragement. The unjust reproach, however, had the effect of firing his emulation, and making him sensible that, engaged as he was in a perilous cause, it was absolutely necessary that he should conquer or die.

'I have no retreat,' he said to himself. 'All shall allow – even Major Bellenden – even Edith – that in courage, at least, the rebel Morton was not inferior to his father.'

The condition of the army after the repulse was so undisciplined, and in such disorganization, that the leaders thought it prudent to draw off some miles from the city to gain time for reducing them once more into such order as they were capable of adopting. Recruits, in the meanwhile, came fast in, more moved by the extreme hardships of their own condition, and encouraged by the advantage obtained at Loudon-hill, than deterred by the last unfortunate enterprise. Many of these attached themselves particularly to Morton's division. He had, however, the mortification to see that his unpopularity among the more intolerant part of the Covenanters increased rapidly. The prudence beyond his years, which he exhibited in improving the discipline and arrangement of his followers, they termed a trusting in the arm of flesh, and his avowed tolerance for those of religious sentiments and observances different from his own, obtained him, most unjustly, the nickname of Gallio,[4] who cared for none of those things. What was worse than these misconceptions, the mob of the insurgents, always loudest in applause of those who push political or religious opinions to extremity, and disgusted with such as endeavour to reduce them to the yoke of discipline, preferred avowedly the more zealous leaders, in whose ranks enthusiasm in the cause supplied the want of good order and military subjection, to the restraints which Morton endeavoured to bring them under. In short, while bearing the principal burden of command, (for his colleagues willingly relinquished in his favour every thing that was troublesome and obnoxious in the office of general,) Morton found himself without that authority, which alone could render his regulations effectual.[5]

Yet, notwithstanding these obstacles, he had, during the course of a few days, laboured so hard to introduce some degree of discipline into the army, that he thought he might hazard a second attack upon Glasgow with every prospect of success.

It cannot be doubted that Morton's anxiety to measure himself with Colonel Grahame of Claverhouse, at whose hands he had sustained such injury, had its share in giving motive to his uncommon exertions. But Claverhouse disappointed his hopes; for, satisfied with having the advantage in repulsing the first attack upon Glasgow, he determined that he would not, with the handful of troops under his command, await a second assault from the insurgents, with more numerous and better disciplined forces than had supported their first enterprise. He therefore evacuated the place, and marched at the head of his troops towards Edinburgh. The insurgents of course entered Glasgow without resistance, and without Morton having the opportunity, which he so deeply coveted, of again encountering Claverhouse personally. But, although he had not an opportunity of wiping away the disgrace which had befallen his division of the army of the Covenant, the retreat of Claverhouse, and the possession of Glasgow, tended greatly to animate the insurgent army, and to increase its numbers. The necessity of appointing new officers, of organizing new regiments and squadrons, of making them acquainted with at least the most necessary points of military discipline, were labours, which, by universal consent, seemed to be devolved upon Henry Morton, and which he the more readily undertook, because his father had made him acquainted with the theory of the military art, and because he plainly saw, that, unless he took this ungracious but absolutely necessary labour, it was vain to expect any other to engage in it.

In the meanwhile, fortune appeared to favour the enterprise of the insurgents more than the most sanguine durst have expected. The Privy Council of Scotland, astonished at the extent of resistance which their arbitrary measures had provoked, seemed stupified with terror, and incapable of taking active steps to subdue the resentment which these measures had excited. There were but very few troops in Scotland, and these they drew towards Edinburgh, as if to form an army for protection of the metropolis. The feudal array of the crown vassals in the various counties, was ordered to take the field, and render to the King the military service due for their fiefs. But the summons was very slackly obeyed. The quarrel was not generally popular among the gentry; and even those who were not unwilling themselves to have taken arms, were deterred by the repugnance of their wives, mothers, and sisters, to their engaging in such a cause.

Meanwhile, the inadequacy of the Scottish government to provide for their own defence, or to put down a rebellion of which the commencement seemed so trifling, excited at the English court doubts at once of their capacity, and of the prudence of the severities they had exerted against the oppressed presbyterians. It was, therefore, resolved to nominate to the command of the army of Scotland, the unfortunate Duke of Monmouth,[6] who had by marriage a great interest, large estate, and a numerous following, as it was called, in the southern parts of that kingdom. The military skill which he had displayed on different occasions abroad, was supposed more than adequate to subdue the insurgents in the field; while it was expected that his mild temper, and the favourable disposition which he showed to presbyterians in general, might soften men's minds, and tend to reconcile them to the government. The Duke was, therefore, invested with a commission, containing high powers for settling the distracted affairs of Scotland, and dispatched from London with strong succours to take the principal military command in that country.

CHAPTER 27

- I am bound to Bothwell-hill,
  Where I maun either do or die.

Old Ballad [1]

THERE was now a pause in the military movements on both
sides. The government seemed contented to prevent the rebels
advancing towards the capital, while the insurgents were intent
upon augmenting and strengthening their forces. For this purpose, they established a sort of encampment in the park belonging to the ducal residence at Hamilton,[2] a centrical situation for
receiving their recruits, and where they were secured from any
sudden attack, by having the Clyde, a deep and rapid river, in
front of their position, which is only passable by a long and
narrow bridge, near the castle and village of Bothwell.

Morton remained here for about a fortnight after the attack
on Glasgow, actively engaged in his military duties. He had
received more than one communication from Burley, but they
only stated, in general, that the Castle of Tillietudlem continued
to hold out. Impatient of suspense upon this most interesting
subject, he at length intimated to his colleagues in command his
desire, or rather his intention, – for he saw no reason why he
should not assume a license which was taken by every one else
in this disorderly army, – to go to Milnwood for a day or two to
arrange some private affairs of consequence. The proposal was
by no means approved of; for the military council of the insurgents were sufficiently sensible of the value of his services to fear
to lose them, and felt somewhat conscious of their own inability
to supply his place. They could not, however, pretend to dictate
to him laws more rigid than they submitted to themselves, and
he was suffered to depart on his journey without any direct objection being stated. The Reverend Mr Poundtext took the same
opportunity to pay a visit to his own residence in the neighbourhood of Milnwood, and favoured Morton with his company on
the journey. As the country was chiefly friendly to their cause,

and in possession of their detached parties, excepting here and there the stronghold of some old cavaliering Baron, they travelled without any other attendant than the faithful Cuddie.

It was near sunset when they reached Milnwood, where Poundtext bid adieu to his companions, and travelled forward alone to his own manse, which was situated half a mile's march beyond Tillietudlem. When Morton was left alone to his own reflections, with what a complication of feelings did he review the woods, banks, and fields, that had been familiar to him! His character, as well as his habits, thoughts, and occupations, had been entirely changed within the space of little more than a fortnight, and twenty days seemed to have done upon him the work of as many years. A mild, romantic, gentle-tempered youth, bred up in dependence, and stooping patiently to the control of a sordid and tyrannical relation, had suddenly, by the rod of oppression and the spur of injured feeling, been compelled to stand forth a leader of armed men, was earnestly engaged in affairs of a public nature, had friends to animate and enemies to contend with, and felt his individual fate bound up in that of a national insurrection and revolution. It seemed as if he had at once experienced a transition from the romantic dreams of youth to the labours and cares of active manhood. All that had formerly interested him was obliterated from his memory, excepting only his attachment to Edith; and even his love seemed to have assumed a character more manly and disinterested, as it had become mingled and contrasted with other duties and feelings. As he revolved the particulars of this sudden change, the circumstances in which it originated, and the possible consequences of his present career, the thrill of natural anxiety which passed along his mind was immediately banished by a glow of generous and high-spirited confidence.

'I shall fall young,' he said, 'if fall I must, my motives misconstrued, and my actions condemned, by those whose approbation is dearest to me. But the sword of liberty and patriotism is in my hand, and I will neither fall meanly nor unavenged. They may expose my body, and gibbet my limbs; but other days will come, when the sentence of infamy will recoil against those who may pronounce it. And that Heaven, whose name is so often profaned during this unnatural war, will bear witness to the purity of the motives by which I have been guided.'

Upon approaching Milnwood, Henry's knock upon the gate no longer intimated the conscious timidity of a stripling who has been out of bounds, but the confidence of a man in full possession of his own rights, and master of his own actions, – bold, free, and decided. The door was cautiously opened by his old acquaintance, Mrs Alison Wilson, who started back when she saw the steel cap and nodding plume of the martial visitor.

'Where is my uncle, Alison?' said Morton, smiling at her alarm.

'Lordsake, Mr Harry! is this you?' returned the old lady. 'In troth, ye garr'd my heart loup to my very mouth – But it canna be your ainsell, for ye look taller and mair manly-like than ye used to do.'

'It is, however, my own self,' said Henry, sighing and smiling at the same time; 'I believe this dress may make me look taller, and these times, Ailie, make men out of boys.'

'Sad times indeed!' echoed the old woman; 'and O that you suld be endangered wi' them! but wha can help it? – ye were ill enough guided, and, as I tell your uncle, if ye tread on a worm it will turn.'

'You were always my advocate, Ailie,' said he, and the housekeeper no longer resented the familiar epithet, 'and would let no one blame me but yourself, I am aware of that. – Where is my uncle?'

'In Edinburgh,' replied Alison; 'the honest man thought it was best to gang and sit by the chimley when the reek rase – a vex'd man he's been and a feared – but ye ken the Laird as weel as I do.'

'I hope he has suffered nothing in health?' said Henry.

'Naething to speak of,' answered the housekeeper, 'nor in gudes neither – we fended as weel as we could; and, though the troopers of Tillietudlem took the red cow and auld Hackie, (ye'll mind them weel,) yet they sauld us a gude bargain o' four they were driving to the Castle.'

'Sold you a bargain?' said Morton; 'how do you mean?'

'Ou, they cam out to gather marts for the garrison,' answered the housekeeper; 'but they just fell to their auld trade, and rade through the country couping and selling a' that they gat, like sae mony west-country drovers. My certie, Major Bellenden was laird o' the least share o' what they lifted, though it was taen in his name.'

'Then,' said Morton, hastily, 'the garrison must be straitened for provisions?'

'Stressed eneugh,' replied Ailie – 'there's little doubt o' that.'

A light instantly glanced on Morton's mind.

'Burley must have deceived me – craft as well as cruelty is permitted by his creed.' Such was his inward thought; he said aloud, 'I cannot stay, Mrs Wilson, I must go forward directly.'

'But, oh! bide to eat a mouthfu',' entreated the affectionate housekeeper, 'and I'll mak it ready for you as I used to do afore thae sad days.'

'It is impossible,' answered Morton. – 'Cuddie, get our horses ready.'

'They're just eating their corn,' answered the attendant.

'Cuddie!' exclaimed Ailie; 'what garr'd ye bring that ill-faur'd, unlucky loon alang wi' ye? – It was him and his randie mother began a' the mischief in this house.'

'Tut, tut,' replied Cuddie, 'ye should forget and forgie, mistress. Mither's in Glasgow wi' her tittie, and sall plague ye nae mair; and I'm the Captain's wallie now, and I keep him tighter in thack and rape than ever ye did; – saw ye him ever sae weel put on as he is now?'

'In troth and that's true,' said the old housekeeper, looking with great complacency at her young master, whose mien she thought much improved by his dress. 'I'm sure ye ne'er had a laced cravat like that when ye were at Milnwood; that's nane o' my sewing.'

'Na, na, mistress,' replied Cuddie, 'that's a cast o' my hand – that's ane o' Lord Evandale's braws.'

'Lord Evandale?' answered the old lady, 'that's him that the whigs are gaun to hang the morn, as I hear say.'

'The whigs about to hang Lord Evandale?' said Morton, in the greatest surprise.

'Ay, troth are they,' said the housekeeper. 'Yesterday night he made a sally, as they ca't, (my mother's name was Sally – I wonder they gie Christian folk's names to sic unchristian doings,) – but he made an outbreak to get provisions, and his men were driven back and he was taen, an' the whig Captain Balfour garr'd set up a gallows, and swore, (or said upon his conscience, for they winna swear,) that if the garrison was not gien ower the morn by daybreak, he would hing up the young lord, poor thing, as high as Haman.[3] – These are sair times! – but folk canna help them – sae do ye sit down and tak bread and cheese until better meat's made ready. Ye suldna hae kend a word about it, an I had thought it was to spoil your dinner, hinny.'

'Fed, or unfed,' exclaimed Morton, 'saddle the horses instantly, Cuddie. We must not rest until we get before the Castle.'

And, resisting all Ailie's entreaties, they instantly resumed their journey.

Morton failed not to halt at the dwelling of Poundtext, and summon him to attend him to the camp. That honest divine had just resumed for an instant his pacific habits, and was perusing an ancient theological treatise, with a pipe in his mouth, and a small jug of ale beside him, to assist his digestion of the argument. It was with bitter ill-will that he relinquished these comforts (which he called his studies) in order to recommence a hard ride upon a high-trotting horse. However, when he knew the matter in hand, he gave up, with a deep groan, the prospect of spending a quiet evening in his own little parlour; for he entirely agreed with Morton, that whatever interest Burley might have in rendering the breach between the presbyterians and the government irreconcilable, by putting the young nobleman to death, it was by no means that of the moderate party to permit such an act of atrocity. And it is but doing justice to Mr Poundtext to add, that, like most of his own persuasion, he was decidedly adverse to any such acts of unnecessary violence; besides, that his own present feelings induced him to listen with much complacence to the probability held out by Morton, of Lord Evandale's becoming a mediator for the establishment of peace upon fair and moderate terms. With this similarity of views, they hastened their journey, and arrived about eleven o'clock at night at a small hamlet adjacent to the Castle at Tillietudlem, where Burley had established his head-quarters.

They were challenged by the sentinel, who made his melancholy walk at the entrance of the hamlet, and admitted upon declaring their names and authority in the army. Another soldier kept watch before a house, which they conjectured to be the place of Lord Evandale's confinement, for a gibbet of such great height as to be visible from the battlements of the Castle, was erected before it, in melancholy confirmation of the truth of Mrs Wilson's report.[4] Morton instantly demanded to speak with Burley, and was directed to his quarters. They found him reading the Scriptures, with his arms lying beside him, as if ready for any sudden alarm. He started upon the entrance of his colleagues in office.

'What has brought ye hither?' said Burley, hastily. 'Is there bad news from the army?'

'No,' replied Morton; 'but we understand that there are measures adopted here in which the safety of the army is deeply concerned – Lord Evandale is your prisoner?'

'The Lord,' replied Burley, 'hath delivered him into our hands.'

'And you will avail yourself of that advantage, granted you by Heaven, to dishonour our cause in the eyes of all the world, by putting a prisoner to an ignominious death?'

'If the house of Tillietudlem be not surrendered by daybreak,' replied Burley, 'God do so to me and more also, if he shall not die that death to which his leader and patron, John Grahame of Claverhouse, hath put so many of God's saints.'

'We are in arms,' replied Morton, 'to put down such cruelties, and not to imitate them, far less to avenge upon the innocent the acts of the guilty. By what law can you justify the atrocity you would commit?'

'If thou art ignorant of it,' replied Burley, 'thy companion is well aware of the law which gave the men of Jericho to the sword of Joshua, the son of Nun.'

'But we,' answered the divine, 'live under a better dispensation, which instructeth us to return good for evil, and to pray for those who despitefully use us and persecute us.'[5]

'That is to say,' said Burley, 'that thou wilt join thy grey hairs to his green youth to controvert me in this matter?'

'We are,' rejoined Poundtext, 'two of those to whom, jointly with thyself, authority is delegated over this host, and we will not permit thee to hurt a hair of the prisoner's head. It may please God to make him a means of healing these unhappy breaches in our Israel.'

'I judged it would come to this,' answered Burley, 'when such as thou wert called into the council of the elders.'

'Such as I?' answered Poundtext, – 'And who am I, that you should name me with such scorn? – Have I not kept the flock of this sheep-fold from the wolves for thirty years? Ay, even while thou, John Balfour, wert fighting in the ranks of uncircumcision, a Philistine of hardened brow and bloody hand – Who am I, say'st thou?'

'I will tell thee what thou art, since thou wouldst so fain know,' said Burley. 'Thou art one of those, who would reap where thou hast not sowed, and divide the spoil while others fight the battle – thou art one of those that follow the gospel for the loaves and for the fishes – that love their own manse better than the Church of God, and that would rather draw their stipends under prelatists or heathens, than be a partaker with those noble spirits who have cast all behind them for the sake of the Covenant.'

'And I will tell thee, John Balfour,' returned Poundtext, deservedly incensed, 'I will tell thee what *thou* art. Thou art one of those, for whose bloody and merciless disposition a reproach is flung upon the whole church of this suffering kingdom, and for whose violence and blood-guiltiness, it is to be feared, this fair attempt to recover our civil and religious rights will never be honoured by Providence with the desired success.'

'Gentlemen,' said Morton, 'cease this irritating and unavailing recrimination; and do you, Mr Balfour, inform us, whether it is your purpose to oppose the liberation of Lord Evandale, which appears to us a profitable measure in the present position of our affairs?'

'You are here,' answered Burley, 'as two voices against one;

but you will not refuse to tarry until the united council shall decide upon this matter?'

'This,' said Morton, 'we would not decline, if we could trust the hands in whom we are to leave the prisoner. – But you know well,' he added, looking sternly at Burley, 'that you have already deceived me in this matter.'

'Go to,' said Burley, disdainfully, – 'thou art an idle inconsiderate boy, who, for the black eyebrows of a silly girl, would barter thy own faith and honour, and the cause of God and of thy country.'

'Mr Balfour,' said Morton, laying his hand on his sword, 'this language requires satisfaction.'

'And thou shalt have it, stripling, when and where thou darest,' said Burley; 'I plight thee my good word on it.'

Poundtext, in his turn, interfered to remind them of the madness of quarrelling, and effected with difficulty a sort of sullen reconciliation.

'Concerning the prisoner,' said Burley, 'deal with him as ye think fit. I wash my hands free from all consequences. He is my prisoner, made by my sword and spear, while you, Mr Morton, were playing the adjutant at drills and parades, and you, Mr Poundtext, were warping the Scriptures into Erastianism. Take him unto you, nevertheless, and dispose of him as ye think meet. – Dingwall,' he continued, calling a sort of aid-de-camp, who slept in the next apartment, 'let the guard posted on the malignant Evandale give up their post to those whom Captain Morton shall appoint to relieve them. – The prisoner,' he said, again addressing Poundtext and Morton, 'is now at your disposal, gentlemen. But remember, that for all these things there will one day come a term of heavy accounting.'

So saying, he turned abruptly into an inner apartment, without bidding them good evening. His two visitors, after a moment's consideration, agreed it would be prudent to ensure the prisoner's personal safety, by placing over him an additional guard, chosen from their own parishioners. A band of them happened to be stationed in the hamlet, having been attached, for the time, to Burley's command, in order that the men might be gratified by remaining as long as possible near to their own homes. They were, in general, smart, active young fellows, and were usually called by their companions, the Marksmen of Milnwood. By Morton's desire, four of these lads readily undertook the task of sentinels, and he left with them Headrigg, on whose fidelity he could depend, with instructions to call him, if any thing remarkable happened.

This arrangement being made, Morton and his colleague took possession, for the night, of such quarters as the over-crowded and miserable hamlet could afford them. They did not, however, separate for repose till they had drawn up a memorial of the grievances of the moderate presbyterians,[6] which was summed up with a request of free toleration for their religion in future, and that they should be permitted to attend gospel ordinances as dispensed by their own clergymen, without oppression or molestation. Their petition proceeded to require that a free parliament should be called for settling the affairs of church and state, and for redressing the injuries sustained by the subject; and that all those who either now were, or had been, in arms, for obtaining these ends, should be indemnified. Morton could not but strongly hope that these terms, which comprehended all that was wanted, or wished for, by the moderate party among the insurgents, might, when thus cleared of the violence of fanaticism, find advocates even among the royalists, as claiming only the ordinary rights of Scottish freemen.

He had the more confidence of a favourable reception, that the Duke of Monmouth, to whom Charles had intrusted the charge of subduing this rebellion, was a man of gentle, moderate, and accessible disposition, well known to be favourable to the presbyterians, and invested by the king with full powers to take measures for quieting the disturbances in Scotland. It seemed to Morton, that all that was necessary for influencing him in their favour was to find a fit and sufficiently respectable channel of communication, and such seemed to be opened through the medium of Lord Evandale. He resolved, therefore, to visit the prisoner early in the morning, in order to sound his dispositions to undertake the task of mediator; but an accident happened which led him to anticipate his purpose.

CHAPTER 28

Gie ower your house, lady, he said, –
Gie ower your house to me.

Edom of Gordon[1]

MORTON had finished the revisal and the making out of a fair copy of the paper on which he and Poundtext had agreed to rest as a full statement of the grievances of their party, and the conditions on which the greater part of the insurgents would be contented to lay down their arms; and he was about to betake himself to repose, when there was a knocking at the door of his apartment.

'Enter,' said Morton; and the round bullet-head of Cuddie Headrigg was thrust into the room. 'Come in,' said Morton, 'and tell me what you want. Is there any alarm?'

'Na, stir; but I hae brought ane to speak wi' you.'

'Who is that, Cuddie?' enquired Morton.

'Ane o' your auld acquaintance,' said Cuddie; and, opening the door more fully, he half led, half dragged in a woman, whose face was muffled in her plaid. – 'Come, come ye needna be sae bashfu' before auld acquaintance, Jenny,' said Cuddie, pulling down the veil, and discovering to his master the well-remembered countenance of Jenny Dennison. 'Tell his honour, now – there's a braw lass – tell him what ye were wanting to say to Lord Evandale, mistress.'

'What I was wanting to say,' answered Jenny, 'to his honour himsell the other morning, when I visited him in captivity, ye muckle hash? – D'ye think that folk dinna want to see their friends in adversity, ye dour crowdy-eater?'

This reply was made with Jenny's usual volubility; but her voice quivered, her cheek was thin and pale, the tears stood in her eyes, her hand trembled, her manner was fluttered, and her whole presence bore marks of recent suffering and privation, as well as nervous and hysterical agitation.

'What is the matter, Jenny?' said Morton, kindly. 'You know

how much I owe you in many respects, and can hardly make a request that I will not grant, if in my power.'

'Many thanks, Milnwood,' said the weeping damsel; 'but ye were aye a kind gentleman, though folk say ye hae become sair changed now.'

'What do they say of me?' answered Morton.

'A' body says,' replied Jenny, 'that you and the whigs hae made a vow to ding King Charles aff the throne, and that neither he, nor his posteriors from generation to generation, shall sit upon it ony mair; and John Gudyill threeps ye're to gie a' the church organs to the pipers, and burn the Book o' Common-prayer by the hands of the common hangman, in revenge of the Covenant that was burnt when the king cam hame.'

'My friends at Tillietudlem judge too hastily and too ill of me,' answered Morton. 'I wish to have free exercise of my own religion, without insulting any other; and as to your family, I only desire an opportunity to show them I have the same friendship and kindness as ever.'

'Bless your kind heart for saying sae,' said Jenny, bursting into a flood of tears; 'and they never needed kindness or friendship mair, for they are famished for lack o' food.'

'Good God!' replied Morton, 'I have heard of scarcity, but not of famine! Is it possible? – Have the ladies and the Major' –

'They hae suffered like the lave o' us,' replied Jenny; 'for they shared every bit and sup wi' the whole folk in the Castle – I'm sure my poor een see fifty colours wi' faintness, and my head's sae dizzy wi' the mirligoes that I canna stand my lane.'

The thinness of the poor girl's cheek, and the sharpness of her features, bore witness to the truth of what she said. Morton was greatly shocked.

'Sit down,' he said, 'for God's sake!' forcing her into the only chair the apartment afforded, while he himself strode up and down the room in horror and impatience. 'I knew not of this,' he exclaimed in broken ejaculations, – 'I could not know of it. – Cold-blooded, iron-hearted fanatic – deceitful villain! – Cuddie, fetch refreshments – food – wine, if possible – whatever you can find.'

'Whisky is gude eneugh for her,' muttered Cuddie; 'ane wadna hae thought that gude meal was sae scant amang them, when the quean threw sae muckle gude kail-brose scalding het about my lugs.'

Faint and miserable as Jenny seemed to be, she could not hear the allusion to her exploit during the storm of the Castle, without bursting into a laugh which weakness soon converted into a hysterical giggle. Confounded at her state, and reflecting with horror on the distress which must have been in the Castle, Morton repeated his commands to Headrigg in a peremptory manner; and when he had departed, endeavoured to soothe his visitor.

'You come, I suppose, by the orders of your mistress, to visit Lord Evandale? – Tell me what she desires; her orders shall be my law.'

Jenny appeared to reflect a moment, and then said, 'Your honour is sae auld a friend, I must needs trust to you, and tell the truth.'

'Be assured, Jenny,' said Morton, observing that she hesitated, 'that you will best serve your mistress by dealing sincerely with me.'

'Weel, then, ye maun ken we're starving, as I said before, and have been mair days than ane; and the Major has sworn that he expects relief daily, and that he will not gie ower the house to the enemy till we have eaten up his auld boots, – and they are unco thick in the soles, as ye may weel mind, forby being teugh in the upper-leather. The dragoons, again, they think they will be forced to gie up at last, and they canna bide hunger weel, after the life they led at free quarters for this while bypast; and since Lord Evandale's taen, there's nae guiding them; and Inglis says he'll gie up the garrison to the whigs, and the Major and the leddies into the bargain, if they will but let the troopers gang free themsells.'

'Scoundrels!' said Morton; 'why do they not make terms for all in the Castle?'

'They are fear'd for denial o' quarter to themsells, having dune sae muckle mischief through the country; and Burley has hanged ane or twa o' them already – sae they want to draw their ain necks out o' the collar at hazard o' honest folk's.'

'And you were sent,' continued Morton, 'to carry to Lord Evandale the unpleasant news of the men's mutiny?'

'Just e'en sae,' said Jenny; 'Tam Halliday took the rue, and tauld me a' about it, and gat me out o' the Castle to tell Lord Evandale, if possibly I could win at him.'

'But how can he help you?' said Morton; 'he is a prisoner.'

'Well-a-day, ay,' answered the afflicted damsel; 'but maybe he could mak fair terms for us – or, maybe, he could gie us some good advice – or, maybe, he might send his orders to the dragoons to be civil – or' –

'Or, maybe,' said Morton, 'you were to try if it were possible to set him at liberty?'

'If it were sae,' answered Jenny with spirit, 'it wadna be the first time I hae done my best to serve a friend in captivity.'

'True, Jenny,' replied Morton, 'I were most ungrateful to forget it. But here comes Cuddie with refreshments – I will go and do your errand to Lord Evandale, while you take some food and wine.'

'It willna be amiss ye should ken,' said Cuddie to his master, 'that this Jenny – this Mrs Dennison, was trying to cuittle favour wi' Tam Rand, the miller's man, to win into Lord Evandale's room without ony body kennin'. She wasna thinking, the gipsy, that I was at her elbow.'

'And an unco fright ye gae me when ye cam ahint and took a grip o' me,' said Jenny, giving him a sly twitch with her finger and her thumb – 'if ye hadna been an auld acquaintance, ye daft gomeril' –

Cuddie, somewhat relenting, grinned a smile on his artful mistress, while Morton wrapped himself up in his cloak, took his sword under his arm, and went straight to the place of the young nobleman's confinement. He asked the sentinels if any thing extraordinary had occurred.

'Nothing worth notice,' they said, 'excepting the lass that Cuddie took up, and two couriers that Captain Balfour had dispatched, one to the Reverend Ephraim Macbriar, another to Kettledrummle,' both of whom were beating the drum ecclesiastic[2] in different towns between the position of Burley and the head-quarters of the main army near Hamilton.

'The purpose, I presume,' said Morton, with an affectation of indifference, 'was to call them hither.'

'So I understand,' answered the sentinel, who had spoke with the messengers.

He is summoning a triumphant majority of the council, thought Morton to himself, for the purpose of sanctioning whatever action of atrocity he may determine upon, and thwarting opposition by authority. I must be speedy, or I shall lose my opportunity.

When he entered the place of Lord Evandale's confinement, he found himself ironed, and reclining on a flock bed in the wretched garret of a miserable cottage. He was either in a slumber, or in deep meditation, when Morton entered, and turned on him, when aroused, a countenance so much reduced by loss of blood, want of sleep, and scarcity of food, that no one could have recognized in it the gallant soldier who had behaved with so much spirit at the skirmish of Loudon-hill. He displayed some surprise at the sudden entrance of Morton.

'I am sorry to see you thus, my lord,' said that youthful leader.

'I have heard you are an admirer of poetry,' answered the prisoner; 'in that case, Mr Morton, you may remember these lines, —[3]

> "Stone walls do not a prison make,
>   Or iron bars a cage;
> A free and quiet mind can take
>   These for a hermitage."

But, were my imprisonment less endurable, I am given to expect to-morrow a total enfranchisement.'

'By death?' said Morton.

'Surely,' answered Lord Evandale; 'I have no other prospect. Your comrade, Burley, has already dipped his hand in the blood of men whose meanness of rank and obscurity of extraction might have saved them. I cannot boast such a shield from his vengeance, and I expect to meet its extremity.'

'But Major Bellenden,' said Morton, 'may surrender, in order to preserve your life.'

'Never, while there is one man to defend the battlement, and that man has one crust to eat. I know his gallant resolution, and grieved should I be if he changed it for my sake.'

Morton hastened to acquaint him with the mutiny among the dragoons, and their resolution to surrender the Castle, and put the ladies of the family, as well as the Major, into the hands of the enemy. Lord Evandale seemed at first surprised, and something incredulous, but immediately afterwards deeply affected.

'What is to be done?' he said – 'How is this misfortune to be averted?'

'Hear me, my lord,' said Morton. 'I believe you may not be unwilling to bear the olive branch between our master the King, and that part of his subjects which is now in arms, not from choice, but necessity.'

'You construe me but justly,' said Lord Evandale; 'but to what does this tend?'

'Permit me, my lord' – continued Morton. 'I will set you at liberty upon parole; nay, you may return to the Castle, and shall have a safe conduct for the ladies, the Major, and all who leave it, on condition of its instant surrender. In contributing to bring this about you will only submit to circumstances; for, with a mutiny in the garrison, and without provisions, it will be found impossible to defend the place twenty-four hours longer. Those, therefore, who refuse to accompany your lordship, must take their fate. You and your followers shall have a free pass to Edinburgh, or wherever the Duke of Monmouth may be. In return for your liberty, we hope that you will recommend to the notice of his Grace, as Lieutenant-General of Scotland, this humble petition and remonstrance, containing the grievances which have occasioned this insurrection, a redress of which being granted, I will answer with my head, that the great body of the insurgents will lay down their arms.'

Lord Evandale read over the paper with attention.

'Mr Morton,' he said, 'in my simple judgment, I see little objection that can be made to the measures here recommended; nay, farther, I believe, in many respects, they may meet the private sentiments of the Duke of Monmouth: and yet, to deal frankly with you, I have no hopes of their being granted, unless, in the first place, you were to lay down your arms.'

'The doing so,' answered Morton, 'would be virtually conceding that we had no right to take them up; and that, for one, I will never agree to.'

'Perhaps it is hardly to be expected you should,' said Lord Evandale; 'and yet on that point I am certain the negotiations will be wrecked. I am willing, however, having frankly told you my opinion, to do all in my power to bring about a reconciliation.'

'It is all we can wish or expect,' replied Morton; 'the issue is in God's hands, who disposes the hearts of princes. – You accept, then, the safe conduct?'

'Certainly,' answered Lord Evandale; 'and if I do not enlarge upon the obligation incurred by your having saved my life a second time, believe that I do not feel it the less.'

'And the garrison of Tillietudlem?' said Morton.

'Shall be withdrawn as you propose,' answered the young nobleman. 'I am sensible the Major will be unable to bring the mutineers to reason; and I tremble to think of the consequences, should the ladies and the brave old man be delivered up to this bloodthirsty ruffian, Burley.'

'You are in that case free,' said Morton. 'Prepare to mount on horseback; a few men whom I can trust shall attend you till you are in safety from our parties.'

Leaving Lord Evandale in great surprise and joy at this unexpected deliverance, Morton hastened to get a few chosen men under arms and on horseback, each rider holding the rein of a spare horse. Jenny, who, while she partook of her refreshment, had contrived to make up her breach with Cuddie, rode on the left hand of that valiant cavalier. The tramp of their horses was soon heard under the window of Lord Evandale's prison. Two men, whom he did not know, entered the apartment, disencumbered him of his fetters, and, conducting him down stairs, mounted him in the centre of the detachment. They set out at a round trot towards Tillietudlem.

The moonlight was giving way to the dawn when they approached that ancient fortress, and its dark massive tower had just received the first pale colouring of the morning. The party halted at the Tower barrier, not venturing to approach nearer for fear of the fire of the place. Lord Evandale alone rode up to the gate, followed at a distance by Jenny Dennison. As they approached the gate, there was heard to arise in the court-yard a tumult, which accorded ill with the quiet serenity of a summer dawn. Cries and oaths were heard, a pistol-shot or two were discharged, and every thing announced that the mutiny had broken out. At this crisis Lord Evandale arrived at the gate where Halliday was sentinel. On hearing Lord Evandale's voice, he instantly and gladly admitted him, and that nobleman arrived among the mutinous troopers like a man dropped from the clouds. They were in the act of putting their design into execution, of seizing the place into their own hands, and were about to disarm and overpower Major Bellenden and Harrison, and others of the Castle, who were offering the best resistance in their power.

The appearance of Lord Evandale changed the scene. He seized Inglis by the collar, and, upbraiding him with his villainy, ordered two of his comrades to seize and bind him, assuring the others, that their only chance of impunity consisted in instant submission. He then ordered the men into their ranks. They obeyed. He commanded them to ground their arms. They hesitated; but the instinct of discipline, joined to their persuasion that the authority of their officer, so boldly exerted, must be supported by some forces without the gate, induced them to submit.

'Take away those arms,' said Lord Evandale to the people of the Castle; 'they shall not be restored until these men know better the use for which they are intrusted with them. – And now,' he continued, addressing the mutineers, 'begone! – Make the best use of your time, and of a truce of three hours, which the enemy are contented to allow you. Take the road to Edinburgh, and meet me at the House-of-Muir. I need not bid you beware of committing violence by the way; you will not, in your present condition, provoke resentment for your own sakes. Let your punctuality show that you mean to atone for this morning's business.'

The disarmed soldiers shrunk in silence from the presence of their officer, and, leaving the Castle, took the road to the place of rendezvous, making such haste as was inspired by the fear of meeting with some detached party of the insurgents, whom their present defenceless condition, and their former violence, might inspire with thoughts of revenge. Inglis, whom Evandale destined for punishment, remained in custody. Halliday was praised for his conduct, and assured of succeeding to the rank of the culprit. These arrangements being hastily made, Lord Evandale accosted the Major, before whose eyes the scene had seemed to pass like the change of a dream.

'My dear Major, we must give up the place.'

'Is it even so?' said Major Bellenden. 'I was in hopes you had brought reinforcements and supplies.'

'Not a man – not a pound of meal,' answered Lord Evandale.

'Yet I am blithe to see you,' returned the honest Major; 'we were informed yesterday that these psalm-singing rascals had a plot on your life, and I had mustered the scoundrelly dragoons ten minutes ago in order to beat up Burley's quarters and get you out of limbo, when the dog Inglis, instead of obeying me, broke out into open mutiny. – But what is to be done now?'

'I have, myself, no choice,' said Lord Evandale; 'I am a prisoner, released on parole, and bound for Edinburgh. You and the ladies must take the same route. I have, by the favour of a friend, a safe conduct and horses for you and your retinue – for God's sake make haste – you cannot propose to hold out with seven or eight men, and without provisions – Enough has been done for honour, and enough to render the defence of the highest consequence to government. More were needless, as well as desperate. The English troops are arrived in Edinburgh, and will speedily move upon Hamilton. The possession of Tillietudlem by the rebels will be but temporary.'

'If you think so, my lord,' said the veteran, with a reluctant sigh, – 'I know you only advise what is honourable – if, then, you really think the case inevitable, I must submit; for the mutiny of these scoundrels would render it impossible to man the walls. – Gudyill, let the women call up their mistresses, and all be ready to march – But if I could believe that my remaining in these old walls, till I was starved to a mummy, could do the King's cause the least service, old Miles Bellenden would not leave them while there was a spark of life in his body!'

The ladies, already alarmed by the mutiny, now heard the determination of the Major, in which they readily acquiesced, though not without some groans and sighs on the part of Lady Margaret, which referred, as usual, to the *déjeûné* of his Most Sacred Majesty in the halls which were now to be abandoned to rebels. Hasty preparations were made for evacuating the Castle; and long ere the dawn was distinct enough for discovering objects with precision, the ladies, with Major Bellenden, Harrison, Gudyill, and the other domestics, were mounted on the led horses, and others which had been provided in the neighbourhood, and proceeded towards the north, still escorted by four of the insurgent horsemen. The rest of the party who had accompanied Lord Evandale from the hamlet, took possession of the deserted Castle, carefully forbearing all outrage or acts of plunder. And when the sun arose, the scarlet and blue colours of the Scottish Covenant floated from the Keep of Tillietudlem.

CHAPTER 29

And, to my breast, a bodkin in her hand
Were worth a thousand daggers.

MARLOW[1]

THE cavalcade which left the Castle of Tillietudlem, halted for a few minutes at the small town of Bothwell, after passing the outposts of the insurgents, to take some slight refreshments which their attendants had provided, and which were really necessary to persons who had suffered considerably by want of proper nourishment. They then pressed forward upon the road towards Edinburgh, amid the lights of dawn which were now rising on the horizon. It might have been expected, during the course of the journey, that Lord Evandale would have been frequently by the side of Miss Edith Bellenden. Yet, after his first salutations had been exchanged, and every precaution solicitously adopted which could serve for her accommodation, he rode in the van of the party with Major Bellenden, and seemed to abandon the charge of immediate attendance upon his lovely niece to one of the insurgent cavaliers, whose dark military cloak, with the large flapped hat and feather, which drooped over his face, concealed at once his figure and his features. They rode side by side in silence for more than two miles, when the stranger addressed Miss Bellenden in a tremulous and suppressed voice.

'Miss Bellenden,' he said, 'must have friends wherever she is known; even among those whose conduct she now disapproves. Is there any thing that such can do to show their respect for her, and their regret for her sufferings?'

'Let them learn for their own sakes,' replied Edith, 'to venerate the laws, and to spare innocent blood. Let them return to their allegiance, and I can forgive them all that I have suffered, were it ten times more.'

'You think it impossible, then,' rejoined the cavalier, 'for any one to serve in our ranks, having the weal of his country sincerely at heart, and conceiving himself in the discharge of a patriotic duty?'

'It might be imprudent, while so absolutely in your power,' replied Miss Bellenden, 'to answer that question.'

'Not in the present instance, I plight you the word of a soldier,' replied the horseman.

'I have been taught candour from my birth,' said Edith; 'and, if I am to speak at all, I must utter my real sentiments. God only can judge the heart – men must estimate intentions by actions. Treason, murder by the sword and by gibbet, the oppression of a private family such as ours, who were only in arms for the defence of the established government, and of our own property, are actions which must needs sully all that have accession to them, by whatever specious terms they may be gilded over.'

'The guilt of civil war,' rejoined the horseman – 'the miseries which it brings in its train, lie at the door of those who provoked it by illegal oppression, rather than of such as are driven to arms in order to assert their natural rights as freemen.'

'That is assuming the question,' replied Edith, 'which ought to be proved. Each party contends that they are right in point of principle, and therefore the guilt must lie with them who first drew the sword; as, in an affray, law holds those to be the criminals who are the first to have recourse to violence. '

'Alas!' said the horseman, 'were our vindication to rest there, how easy would it be to show that we have suffered with a patience which almost seemed beyond the power of humanity, ere we were driven by oppression into open resistance! – But I perceive,' he continued, sighing deeply, 'that it is vain to plead before Miss Bellenden a cause which she has already prejudged, perhaps as much from her dislike of the persons as of the principles of those engaged in it.'

'Pardon me,' answered Edith; 'I have stated with freedom my opinion of the principles of the insurgents; of their persons I know nothing – excepting in one solitary instance.'

'And that instance,' said the horseman, 'has influenced your opinion of the whole body?'

'Far from it,' said Edith; 'he is – at least I once thought him – one in whose scale few were fit to be weighed – he is – or he seemed – one of early talent, high faith, pure morality, and warm affections. Can I approve of a rebellion which has made such a man, formed to ornament, to enlighten, and to defend his country, the companion of gloomy and ignorant fanatics, or canting hypocrites, – the leader of brutal clowns, – the brother-in-arms to banditti and highway murderers? – Should you meet such an one in your camp, tell him that Edith Bellenden has wept more over his fallen character, blighted prospects, and dishonoured name, than over the distresses of her own house, – and that she has better endured that famine which has wasted her cheek and dimmed her eye, than the pang of heart which attended the reflection by and through whom these calamities were inflicted.'

As she thus spoke, she turned upon her companion a countenance, whose faded cheek attested the reality of her sufferings, even while it glowed with the temporary animation which accompanied her language. The horseman was not insensible to the appeal; he raised his hand to his brow with the sudden motion of one who feels a pang shoot along his brain, passed it hastily over his face, and then pulled the shadowing hat still deeper on his forehead. The movement, and the feelings which it excited, did not escape Edith, nor did she remark them without emotion.

'And yet,' she said, 'should the person of whom I speak seem to you too deeply affected by the hard opinion of – of – an early friend, say to him, that sincere repentance is next to innocence; – that, though fallen from a height not easily recovered, and the author of much mischief, because gilded by his example, he may still atone in some measure for the evil he has done.'

'And in what manner?' asked the cavalier, in the same suppressed, and almost choked voice.

'By lending his efforts to restore the blessings of peace to his distracted countrymen, and to induce the deluded rebels to lay down their arms. By saving their blood, he may atone for that which has been already spilt; – and he that shall be most active in accomplishing this great end, will best deserve the thanks of this age, and an honoured remembrance in the next.'

'And in such a peace,' said her companion, with a firm voice, 'Miss Bellenden would not wish, I think, that the interests of the people were sacrificed unreservedly to those of the crown?'

'I am but a girl,' was the young lady's reply; 'and I scarce can speak on the subject without presumption. But, since I have gone so far, I will fairly add, I would wish to see a peace which should give rest to all parties, and secure the subjects from military rapine, which I detest as much as I do the means now adopted to resist it.'

'Miss Bellenden,' answered Henry Morton, raising his face, and speaking in his natural tone, 'the person who has lost such a highly-valued place in your esteem, has yet too much spirit to plead his cause as a criminal; and, conscious that he can no longer claim a friend's interest in your bosom, he would be silent under your hard censure, were it not that he can refer to the honoured testimony of Lord Evandale, that his earnest wishes and most active exertions are, even now, directed to the accomplishment of such a peace as the most loyal cannot censure.'

He bowed with dignity to Miss Bellenden, who, though her language intimated that she well knew to whom she had been speaking, probably had not expected that he would justify himself with so much animation. She returned his salute, confused and in silence. Morton then rode forward to the head of the party.

'Henry Morton!' exclaimed Major Bellenden, surprised at the sudden apparition.

'The same,' answered Morton; 'who is sorry that he labours under the harsh construction of Major Bellenden and his family. He commits to my Lord Evandale,' he continued, turning towards the young nobleman, and bowing to him, 'the charge of undeceiving his friends, both regarding the particulars of his conduct and the purity of his motives. Farewell, Major Bellenden – All happiness attend you and yours – May we meet again in happier and better times!'

'Believe me,' said Lord Evandale, 'your confidence, Mr Morton, is not misplaced; I will endeavour to repay the great services I have received from you by doing my best to place your character on its proper footing with Major Bellenden, and all whose esteem you value.'

'I expected no less from your generosity, my lord,' said Morton.

He then called his followers, and rode off along the heath in the direction of Hamilton, their feathers waving and their steel caps glancing in the beams of the rising sun. Cuddie Headrigg alone remained an instant behind his companions to take an affectionate farewell of Jenny Dennison, who had contrived, during this short morning's ride, to re-establish her influence over his susceptible bosom. A straggling tree or two obscured, rather than concealed, their *tête-à-tête*, as they halted their horses to bid adieu.

'Fare ye weel, Jenny,' said Cuddie, with a loud exertion of his lungs, intended perhaps to be a sigh, but rather resembling the intonation of a groan, – 'Ye'll think o' puir Cuddie sometimes – an honest lad that lo'es ye, Jenny; ye'll think o' him now and then?'

'Whiles – at brose-time,' answered the malicious damsel, unable either to suppress the repartee, or the arch smile which attended it.

Cuddie took his revenge as rustic lovers are wont, and as Jenny probably expected, – caught his mistress round the neck, kissed her cheeks and lips heartily, and then turned his horse and trotted after his master.

'Deil's in the fallow,' said Jenny, wiping her lips and adjusting her head-dress, 'he has twice the spunk o' Tam Halliday, after a'. – Coming, my leddy, coming – Lord have a care o' us, I trust the auld leddy didna see us!'

'Jenny,' said Lady Margaret, as the damsel came up, 'was not that young man who commanded the party the same that was captain of the popinjay, and who was afterwards prisoner at Tillietudlem on the morning Claverhouse came there?'

Jenny, happy that the query had no reference to her own little matters, looked at her young mistress, to discover, if possible, whether it was her cue to speak truth or not. Not being able to catch any hint to guide her, she followed her instinct as a lady's maid, and lied.

'I dinna believe it was him, my leddy,' said Jenny, as confidently as if she had been saying her catechism; 'he was a little black man, that.'

'You must have been blind, Jenny,' said the Major: 'Henry Morton is tall and fair, and that youth is the very man.'

'I had ither thing ado than be looking at him,' said Jenny, tossing her head; 'he may be as fair as a farthing candle, for me.'

'Is it not,' said Lady Margaret, 'a blessed escape which we have made, out of the hands of so desperate and bloodthirsty a fanatic?'

'You are deceived, madam,' said Lord Evandale; 'Mr Morton merits such a title from no one, but least from us. That I am now alive, and that you are now on your safe retreat to your friends, instead of being prisoners to a real fanatical homicide, is solely and entirely owing to the prompt, active, and energetic humanity of this young gentleman.'

He then went into a particular narrative of the events with which the reader is acquainted, dwelling upon the merits of Morton, and expatiating on the risk at which he had rendered them these important services, as if he had been a brother instead of a rival.

'I were worse than ungrateful,' he said, 'were I silent on the merits of the man who has twice saved my life.'

'I would willingly think well of Henry Morton, my lord,' replied Major Bellenden; 'and I own he has behaved handsomely to your lordship and to us; but I cannot have the same allowances which it pleases your lordship to entertain for his present courses.'

'You are to consider,' replied Lord Evandale, 'that he has been partly forced upon them by necessity; and I must add, that his principles, though differing in some degree from my own, are such as ought to command respect. Claverhouse, whose know-ledge of men is not to be disputed, spoke justly of him as to his extraordinary qualities, but with prejudice, and harshly, concern-ing his principles and motives.'

'You have not been long in learning all his extraordinary qualities, my lord,' answered Major Bellenden. 'I, who have known him from boyhood, could, before this affair, have said much of his good principles and good-nature; but as to his high talents'—

'They were probably hidden, Major,' replied the generous Lord Evandale, 'even from himself, until circumstances called them forth; and, if I have detected them, it was only because our intercourse and conversation turned on momentous and import-ant subjects. He is now labouring to bring this rebellion to an end, and the terms he has proposed are so moderate, that they shall not want my hearty recommendation.'

'And have you hopes,' said Lady Margaret, 'to accomplish a scheme so comprehensive?'

'I should have, madam, were every whig as moderate as Morton, and every loyalist as disinterested as Major Bellenden. But such is the fanaticism and violent irritation of both parties, that I fear nothing will end this civil war save the edge of the sword.'

It may be readily supposed, that Edith listened with the deepest interest to this conversation. While she regretted that she had expressed herself harshly and hastily to her lover, she felt a conscious and proud satisfaction that his character was, even in the judgment of his noble-minded rival, such as her own affec-tion had once spoke it.

'Civil feuds and domestic prejudices,' she said, 'may render it necessary for me to tear his remembrance from my heart; but it is no small relief to know assuredly, that it is worthy of the place it has so long retained there.'

While Edith was thus retracting her unjust resentment, her lover arrived at the camp of the insurgents, near Hamilton, which he found in considerable confusion. Certain advices had arrived that the royal army, having been recruited from England by a large detachment of the King's Guards, were about to take the field. Fame magnified their numbers and their high state of equipment and discipline, and spread abroad other circumstances, which dismayed the courage of the insurgents. What favour they might have expected from Monmouth, was likely to be intercepted by the influence of those associated with him in command. His lieutenant-general was the celebrated General Thomas Dalzell, who, having practised the art of war in the then barbarous country of Russia, was as much feared for his cruelty and indifference to human life and human sufferings, as respected for his steady loyalty and undaunted valour.[2] This man was second in command to Monmouth, and the horse were commanded by Claverhouse, burning with desire to revenge the death of his nephew, and his defeat at Drumclog. To these accounts was added the most formidable and terrific description of the train of artillery and the cavalry force with which the royal army took the field.[3]

Large bodies, composed of the Highland clans, having in language, religion, and manners, no connexion with the insurgents, had been summoned to join the royal army under their various chieftains; and these Amorites, or Philistines, as the insurgents termed them, came like eagles to the slaughter. In fact, every person who could ride or run at the King's command, was summoned to arms, apparently with the purpose of forfeiting and fining such men of property whom their principles might deter from joining the royal standard, though prudence prevented them from joining that of the insurgent Presbyterians. In short, every rumour tended to increase the apprehension among the insurgents, that the King's vengeance had only been delayed in order that it might fall more certain and more heavy.

Morton endeavoured to fortify the minds of the common people by pointing out the probable exaggeration of these reports, and by reminding them of the strength of their own situation, with an unfordable river in front, only passable by a long and narrow bridge. He called to their remembrance their victory over Claverhouse when their numbers were few, and then much worse disciplined and appointed for battle than now; showed them that the ground on which they lay afforded, by its undulation, and the thickets which intersected it, considerable protection against artillery, and even against cavalry, if stoutly defended; and that their safety, in fact, depended on their own spirit and resolution.

But while Morton thus endeavoured to keep up the courage of the army at large, he availed himself of those discouraging rumours to endeavour to impress on the minds of the leaders the necessity of proposing to the government moderate terms of accommodation, while they were still formidable as commanding an unbroken and numerous army. He pointed out to them, that, in the present humour of their followers, it could hardly be expected that they would engage, with advantage, the well-appointed and regular force of the Duke of Monmouth; and that if they chanced, as was most likely, to be defeated and dispersed, the insurrection in which they had engaged, so far from being useful to the country, would be rendered the apology for oppressing it more severely.

Pressed by these arguments, and feeling it equally dangerous to remain together, or to dismiss their forces, most of the leaders readily agreed, that if such terms could be obtained as had been transmitted to the Duke of Monmouth by the hands of Lord Evandale, the purpose for which they had taken up arms would be, in a great measure, accomplished. They then entered into similar resolutions, and agreed to guarantee the petition and remonstrance which had been drawn up by Morton. On the contrary, there were still several leaders, and those men whose influence with the people exceeded that of persons of more apparent consequence, who regarded every proposal of treaty which did not proceed on the basis of the Solemn League and Covenant of 1640,[4] as utterly null and void, impious, and unchristian. These men diffused their feelings among the multitude, who had little foresight, and nothing to lose, and persuaded many that the timid counsellors who recommended peace upon terms short of the dethronement of the royal family, and the declared independence of the church with respect to the state, were cowardly labourers, who were about to withdraw their hands from the plough, and despicable trimmers, who sought only a specious pretext for deserting their brethren in arms. These contradictory opinions were fiercely argued in each tent of the insurgent army, or rather in the huts or cabins which served in the place of tents. Violence in language often led to open quarrels and blows, and the divisions into which the army of sufferers was rent served as too plain a presage of their future fate.

CHAPTER 30

The curse of growing factions and divisions
Still vex your councils!

Venice Preserved[1]

THE prudence of Morton found sufficient occupation in stemming the furious current of these contending parties, when, two days after his return to Hamilton, he was visited by his friend and colleague, the Reverend Mr Poundtext, flying, as he presently found, from the face of John Balfour of Burley, whom he left not a little incensed at the share he had taken in the liberation of Lord Evandale. When the worthy divine had somewhat recruited his spirits, after the hurry and fatigue of his journey, he proceeded to give Morton an account of what had passed in the vicinity of Tillietudlem after the memorable morning of his departure.

The night march of Morton had been accomplished with such dexterity, and the men were so faithful to their trust, that Burley received no intelligence of what had happened until the morning was far advanced. His first enquiry was, whether Macbriar and Kettledrummle had arrived, agreeably to the summons which he had dispatched at midnight. Macbriar had come, and Kettledrummle, though a heavy traveller, might, he was informed, be instantly expected. Burley then dispatched a messenger to Morton's quarters to summon him to an immediate council. The messenger returned with news that he had left the place. Poundtext was next summoned; but he thinking, as he said himself, that it was ill dealing with fractious folk, had withdrawn to his own quiet manse, preferring a dark ride, though he had been on horseback the whole preceding day, to a renewal in the morning of a controversy with Burley, whose ferocity overawed him when unsupported by the firmness of Morton. Burley's next enquiries were directed after Lord Evandale; and great was his rage when he learned that he had been conveyed away over night by a party of the marksmen of Milnwood, under the immediate command of Henry Morton himself.

'The villain!' exclaimed Burley, addressing himself to Macbriar; 'the base, mean-spirited traitor, to curry favour for himself with the government, hath set at liberty the prisoner taken by my own right hand, through means of whom, I have little doubt, the possession of the place of strength which hath wrought us such trouble, might now have been in our hands!'

'But is it not in our hands?' said Macbriar, looking up towards the Keep of the Castle; 'and are not these the colours of the Covenant that float over its walls?'

'A stratagem – a mere trick,' said Burley, 'an insult over our disappointment, intended to aggravate and embitter our spirits.'

He was interrupted by the arrival of one of Morton's followers, sent to report to him the evacuation of the place, and its occupation by the insurgent forces. Burley was rather driven to fury than reconciled by the news of this success.

'I have watched,' he said – 'I have fought – I have plotted – I have striven for the reduction of this place – I have forborne to seek to head enterprises of higher command and of higher honour – I have narrowed their outgoings, and cut off the springs, and broken the staff of bread within their walls; and when the men were about to yield themselves to my hand, that their sons might be bondsmen, and their daughters a laughing-stock to our whole camp, cometh this youth, without a beard on his chin, and takes it on him to thrust his sickle into the harvest, and to rend the prey from the spoiler! Surely the labourer is worthy of his hire,[2] and the city, with its captives, should be given to him that wins it?'

'Nay,' said Macbriar, who was surprised at the degree of

agitation which Balfour displayed, 'chafe not thyself because of the ungodly. Heaven will use its own instruments; and who knows but this youth' –

'Hush! hush!' said Burley; 'do not discredit thine own better judgment. It was thou that first badest me beware of this painted sepulchre[3] – this lacquered piece of copper, that passed current with me for gold. It fares ill, even with the elect, when they neglect the guidance of such pious pastors as thou. But our carnal affections will mislead us – this ungrateful boy's father was mine ancient friend. They must be as earnest in their struggles as thou, Ephraim Macbriar, that would shake themselves clear of the clogs and chains of humanity.'

This compliment touched the preacher in the most sensible part; and Burley deemed, therefore, he should find little difficulty in moulding his opinions to the support of his own views, more especially as they agreed exactly in their high-strained opinions of church government.

'Let us instantly,' he said, 'go up to the Tower; there is that among the records in yonder fortress, which, well used as I can use it, shall be worth to us a valiant leader and an hundred horsemen.'

'But will such be the fitting aids of the children of the Covenant?' said the preacher. 'We have already among us too many who hunger after lands, and silver and gold, rather than after the Word; it is not by such that our deliverance shall be wrought out.'

'Thou errest,' said Burley; 'we must work by means, and these worldly men shall be our instruments. At all events, the Moabitish woman[4] shall be despoiled of her inheritance, and neither the malignant Evandale, nor the erastian Morton, shall possess yonder castle and lands, though they may seek in marriage the daughter thereof.'

So saying, he led the way to Tillietudlem, where he seized upon the plate and other valuables for the use of the army, ransacked the charter-room, and other receptacles for family papers, and treated with contempt the remonstrances of those who reminded him, that the terms granted to the garrison had guaranteed respect to private property.

Burley and Macbriar, having established themselves in their new acquisition, were joined by Kettledrummle in the course of the day, and also by the Laird of Langcale, whom that active divine had contrived to seduce, as Poundtext termed it, from the pure light in which he had been brought up. Thus united, they sent to the said Poundtext an invitation, or rather a summons, to attend a council at Tillietudlem. He remembered, however, that the door had an iron grate, and the Keep a dungeon, and resolved not to trust himself with his incensed colleagues. He therefore retreated, or rather fled, to Hamilton, with the tidings, that Burley, Macbriar, and Kettledrummle, were coming to Hamilton as soon as they could collect a body of Cameronians sufficient to overawe the rest of the army.

'And ye see,' concluded Poundtext, with a deep sigh, 'that they will then possess a majority in the council; for Langcale, though he has always passed for one of the honest[5] and rational party, cannot be suitably or preceesely termed either fish, or flesh, or gude red-herring – whoever has the stronger party has Langcale.'

Thus concluded the heavy narrative of honest Poundtext, who sighed deeply, as he considered the danger in which he was placed betwixt unreasonable adversaries amongst themselves and the common enemy from without. Morton exhorted him to patience, temper, and composure; informed him of the good hope he had of negotiating for peace and indemnity through means of Lord Evandale, and made out to him a very fair prospect that he should again return to his own parchment-bound Calvin, his evening pipe of tobacco, and his noggin of inspiring ale, providing always he would afford his effectual support and concurrence to the measures which he, Morton, had taken for a general pacification.[6] Thus backed and comforted, Poundtext resolved magnanimously to await the coming of the Cameronians to the general rendezvous.

Burley and his confederates had drawn together a considerable body of these sectaries, amounting to a hundred horse and about fifteen hundred foot, clouded and severe in aspect, morose and jealous in communication, haughty of heart, and confident, as men who believed that the pale of salvation was open for them exclusively; while all other Christians, however slight were the shades of difference of doctrine from their own, were in fact little better than outcasts or reprobates. These men entered the presbyterian camp, rather as dubious and suspicious allies, or possibly antagonists, than as men who were heartily embarked in the same cause, and exposed to the same dangers, with their more moderate brethren in arms. Burley made no private visits to his colleagues, and held no communication with them on the subject of the public affairs, otherwise than by sending a dry invitation to them to attend a meeting of the general council for that evening.

On the arrival of Morton and Poundtext at the place of assembly, they found their brethren already seated. Slight greeting passed between them, and it was easy to see that no amicable conference was intended by those who convoked the council. The first question was put by Macbriar, the sharp eagerness of whose zeal urged him to the van on all occasions. He desired to know by whose authority the malignant, called Lord Evandale, had been freed from the doom of death, justly denounced against him.

'By my authority and Mr Morton's,' replied Poundtext; who, besides being anxious to give his companion a good opinion of his courage, confided heartily in his support, and, moreover, had much less fear of encountering one of his own profession, and who confined himself to the weapons of theological controversy, in which Poundtext feared no man, than of entering into debate with the stern homicide Balfour.

'And who, brother,' said Kettledrummle, 'who gave you authority to interpose in such a high matter?'

'The tenor of our commission,' answered Poundtext, 'gives us authority to bind and to loose. If Lord Evandale was justly doomed to die by the voice of one of our number, he was of a surety lawfully redeemed from death by the warrant of two of us.'

'Go to, go to,' said Burley; 'we know your motives; it was to send that silkworm – that gilded trinket – that embroidered trifle of a lord, to bear terms of peace to the tyrant.'

'It was so,' replied Morton, who saw his companion begin to

flinch before the fierce eye of Balfour – 'it was so; and what then? – Are we to plunge the nation in endless war, in order to pursue schemes which are equally wild, wicked, and unattainable?'

'Hear him!' said Balfour; 'he blasphemeth.'

'It is false,' said Morton; 'they blaspheme who pretend to expect miracles, and neglect the use of the human means with which Providence has blessed them. I repeat it – Our avowed object is the re-establishment of peace on fair and honourable terms of security to our religion and our liberty. We disclaim any desire to tyrannize over those of others.'

The debate would now have run higher than ever, but they were interrupted by intelligence that the Duke of Monmouth had commenced his march towards the west, and was already advanced half way from Edinburgh. This news silenced their divisions for the moment, and it was agreed that the next day should be held as a fast of general humiliation for the sins of the land;[7] that the Reverend Mr Poundtext should preach to the army in the morning, and Kettledrummle in the afternoon; that neither should touch upon any topics of schism or of division, but animate the soldiers to resist to the blood, like brethren in a good cause. This healing overture having been agreed to, the moderate party ventured upon another proposal, confiding that it would have the support of Langcale, who looked extremely blank at the news which they had just received, and might be supposed reconverted to moderate measures. It was to be presumed, they said, that since the King had not intrusted the command of his forces upon the present occasion to any of their active oppressors, but, on the contrary, had employed a nobleman distinguished by gentleness of temper, and a disposition favourable to their cause, there must be some better intention entertained towards them than they had yet experienced. They contended, that it was not only prudent but necessary to ascertain, from a communication with the Duke of Monmouth, whether he was not charged with some secret instructions in their favour. This could only be learned by dispatching an envoy to his army.

'And who will undertake the task?' said Burley, evading a proposal too reasonable to be openly resisted – 'Who will go up to their camp, knowing that John Grahame of Claverhouse hath sworn to hang up whomsoever we shall dispatch towards them, in revenge of the death of the young man his nephew?'

'Let that be no obstacle,' said Morton; 'I will with pleasure encounter any risk attached to the bearer of your errand.'

'Let him go,' said Balfour, apart to Macbriar; 'our councils will be well rid of his presence.'

The motion, therefore, received no contradiction even from those who were expected to have been most active in opposing it; and it was agreed that Henry Morton should go to the camp of the Duke of Monmouth, in order to discover upon what terms the insurgents would be admitted to treat with him. As soon as his errand was made known, several of the more moderate party joined in requesting him to make terms upon the footing of the petition intrusted to Lord Evandale's hands; for the approach of the King's army spread a general trepidation, by no means allayed by the high tone assumed by the Cameronians, which had so little to support it, excepting their own headlong zeal. With these instructions, and with Cuddie as his attendant, Morton set forth towards the royal camp, at all the risks which attend those who assume the office of mediator during the heat of civil discord.

Morton had not proceeded six or seven miles, before he perceived that he was on the point of falling in with the van of the royal forces; and, as he ascended a height, saw all the roads in the neighbourhood occupied by armed men marching in great order towards Bothwell-muir, an open common, on which they proposed to encamp for that evening, at the distance of scarcely two miles from the Clyde, on the farther side of which river the army of the insurgents was encamped. He gave himself up to the first advanced-guard of cavalry which he met, as bearer of a flag of truce, and communicated his desire to obtain access to the Duke of Monmouth. The non-commissioned officer who commanded the party made his report to his superior, and he again to another in still higher command, and both immediately rode to the spot where Morton was detained.

'You are but losing your time, my friend, and risking your life,' said one of them, addressing Morton; 'the Duke of Monmouth will receive no terms from traitors with arms in their hands, and your cruelties have been such as to authorize retaliation of every kind. Better trot your nag back and save his mettle to-day, that he may save your life to-morrow.'

'I cannot think,' said Morton, 'that even if the Duke of Monmouth should consider us as criminals, he would condemn so large a body of his fellow-subjects without even hearing what they have to plead for themselves. On my part I fear nothing. I am conscious of having consented to, or authorized, no cruelty, and the fear of suffering innocently for the crimes of others shall not deter me from executing my commission.'

The two officers looked at each other.

'I have an idea,' said the younger, 'that this is the young man of whom Lord Evandale spoke.'

'Is my Lord Evandale in the army?' said Morton.

'He is not,' replied the officer; 'we left him at Edinburgh, too much indisposed to take the field. – Your name, sir, I presume, is Henry Morton?'

'It is, sir,' answered Morton.

'We will not oppose your seeing the Duke, sir,' said the officer, with more civility of manner; 'but you may assure yourself it will be to no purpose; for, were his Grace disposed to favour your people, others are joined in commission with him who will hardly consent to his doing so.'

'I shall be sorry to find it thus,' said Morton; 'but my duty requires that I should persevere in my desire to have an interview with him.'

'Lumley,' said the superior officer, 'let the Duke know of Mr Morton's arrival, and remind his Grace that this is the person of whom Lord Evandale spoke so highly.'

The officer returned with a message that the General could not see Mr Morton that evening, but would receive him by times in the ensuing morning. He was detained in a neighbouring cottage all night, but treated with civility, and every thing provided for his accommodation. Early on the next morning the officer he had first seen came to conduct him to his audience.

The army was drawn out, and in the act of forming column for march, or attack. The Duke was in the centre, nearly a mile from the place where Morton had passed the night. In riding towards the General, he had an opportunity of estimating the force which had been assembled for the suppression of the hasty and ill-concerted insurrection. There were three or four regiments of English, the flower of Charles's army – there were the Scottish Life-Guards, burning with desire to revenge their late defeat – other Scottish regiments of regulars were also assembled, and a large body of cavalry, consisting partly of gentlemen-volunteers, partly of the tenants of the crown who did military duty for their fiefs. Morton also observed several strong parties of Highlanders drawn from the points nearest to the Lowland frontiers, a people, as already mentioned, particularly obnoxious to the western whigs, and who hated and despised them in the same proportion. These were assembled under their chiefs, and made part of this formidable array. A complete train of field-artillery accompanied these troops; and the whole had an air so imposing, that it seemed nothing short of an actual miracle could prevent the ill-equipped, ill-modelled, and tumultuary army of the insurgents from being utterly destroyed. The officer who accompanied Morton endeavoured to gather from his looks the feelings with which this splended and awful parade of military force had impressed him. But, true to the cause he had espoused, he laboured successfully to prevent the anxiety which he felt from appearing in his countenance, and looked around him on the warlike display as on a sight which he expected, and to which he was indifferent.

'You see the entertainment prepared for you,' said the officers.

'If I had no appetite for it,' replied Morton, 'I should not have been accompanying you at this moment. But I shall be better pleased with a more peaceful regale, for the sake of all parties.'

As they spoke thus, they approached the commander-in-chief, who, surrounded by several officers, was seated upon a knoll commanding an extensive prospect of the distant country, and from which could be easily discovered the windings of the majestic Clyde, and the distant camp of the insurgents on the opposite bank. The officers of the royal army appeared to be surveying the ground, with the purpose of directing an immedi-

ate attack. When Captain Lumley, the officer who accompanied
Morton, had whispered in Monmouth's ear his name and errand,
the Duke made a signal for all around him to retire, excepting
only two general officers of distinction. While they spoke together in whispers for a few minutes before Morton was permitted to advance, he had time to study the appearance of the
persons with whom he was to treat.

It was impossible for any one to look upon the Duke of Monmouth without being captivated by his personal graces and
accomplishments, of which the great High-Priest of all the Nine[8]
afterwards recorded –

> 'Whate'er he did was done with so much ease,
> In him alone 'twas natural to please;
> His motions all accompanied with grace,
> And Paradise was open'd in his face.'

Yet to a strict observer, the manly beauty of Monmouth's face
was occasionally rendered less striking by an air of vacillation
and uncertainty, which seemed to imply hesitation and doubt at
moments when decisive resolution was most necessary.

Beside him stood Claverhouse, whom we have already fully
described, and another general officer whose appearance was
singularly striking. His dress was of the antique fashion of
Charles the First's time, and composed of shamoy leather,
curiously slashed, and covered with antique lace and garniture.
His boots and spurs might be referred to the same distant period.
He wore a breastplate, over which descended a grey beard of
venerable length, which he cherished as a mark of mourning for
Charles the First, having never shaved since that monarch was
brought to the scaffold. His head was uncovered, and almost
perfectly bald. His high and wrinkled forehead, piercing grey
eyes, and marked features, evinced age unbroken by infirmity,
and stern resolution unsoftened by humanity. Such is the outline,
however feebly expressed, of the celebrated General Thomas
Dalzell,[9] a man more feared and hated by the whigs than even
Claverhouse himself, and who executed the same violences
against them out of a detestation of their persons, or perhaps an
innate severity of temper, which Grahame only resorted to on

political accounts, as the best means of intimidating the followers of presbytery, and of destroying that sect entirely.

The presence of these two generals, one of whom he knew by person, and the other by description, seemed to Morton decisive of the fate of his embassy. But, notwithstanding his youth and inexperience, and the unfavourable reception which his proposals seemed likely to meet with, he advanced boldly towards them upon receiving a signal to that purpose, determined that the cause of his country, and of those with whom he had taken up arms, should suffer nothing from being intrusted to him. Monmouth received him with the graceful courtesy which attended even his slightest actions; Dalzell regarded him with a stern, gloomy, and impatient frown; and Claverhouse, with a sarcastic smile and inclination of his head, seemed to claim him as an old acquaintance.

'You come, sir, from these unfortunate people, now assembled in arms,' said the Duke of Monmouth, 'and your name, I believe, is Morton; will you favour us with the purport of your errand?'

'It is contained, my lord,' answered Morton, 'in a paper, termed a Remonstrance and Supplication, which my Lord Evandale has placed, I presume, in your Grace's hands?'

'He has done so, sir,' answered the Duke; 'and I understand, from Lord Evandale, that Mr Morton has behaved in these unhappy matters with much temperance and generosity, for which I have to request his acceptance of my thanks.'

Here Morton observed Dalzell shake his head indignantly, and whisper something into Claverhouse's ear, who smiled in return, and elevated his eyebrows, but in a degree so slight as scarce to be perceptible. The Duke, taking the petition from his pocket, proceeded, obviously struggling between the native gentleness of his own disposition, and perhaps his conviction that the petitioners demanded no more than their rights, and the desire, on the other hand, of enforcing the king's authority, and complying with the sterner opinions of the colleagues in office, who had been assigned for the purpose of controlling as well as advising him.[10]

'There are, Mr Morton, in this paper, proposals, as to the abstract propriety of which I must now waive delivering any opinion. Some of them appear to me reasonable and just; and, although I have no express instructions from the King upon the subject, yet I assure you, Mr Morton, and I pledge my honour, that I will interpose in your behalf, and use my utmost influence to procure you satisfaction from his Majesty. But you must distinctly understand, that I can only treat with supplicants, not with rebels; and, as a preliminary to every act of favour on my side, I must insist upon your followers laying down their arms and dispersing themselves.'

'To do so, my Lord Duke,' replied Morton, undauntedly, 'were to acknowledge ourselves the rebels that our enemies term us. Our swords are drawn for recovery of a birthright wrested from us; your Grace's moderation and good sense has admitted the general justice of our demand, – a demand which would never have been listened to had it not been accompanied with the sound of the trumpet. We cannot, therefore, and dare not, lay down our arms, even on your Grace's assurance of indemnity, unless it were accompanied with some reasonable prospect of the redress of the wrongs which we complain of.'

'Mr Morton,' replied the Duke, 'you are young, but you must have seen enough of the world to perceive, that requests, by no means dangerous or unreasonable in themselves, may become so by the way in which they are pressed and supported.'

'We may reply, my lord,' answered Morton, 'that this disagreeable mode has not been resorted to until all others have failed.'

'Mr Morton,' said the Duke, 'I must break this conference short. We are in readiness to commence the attack; yet I will suspend it for an hour, until you can communicate my answer to the insurgents. If they please to disperse their followers, lay down their arms, and send a peaceful deputation to me, I will consider myself bound in honour to do all I can to procure redress of their grievances; if not, let them stand on their guard and expect the consequences. – I think, gentlemen,' he added, turning to his two colleagues, 'this is the utmost length to which I can stretch my instructions in favour of these misguided persons?'

'By my faith,' answered Dalzell, suddenly, 'and it is a length to which my poor judgment durst not have stretched them, considering I had both the King and my conscience to answer to! But, doubtless, your Grace knows more of the King's private mind than we, who have only the letter of our instructions to look to.'

Monmouth blushed deeply. 'You hear,' he said, addressing Morton, 'General Dalzell blames me for the length which I am disposed to go in your favour.'

'General Dalzell's sentiments, my lord,' replied Morton, 'are such as we expected from him; your Grace's such as we were prepared to hope you might please to entertain. Indeed I cannot help adding, that, in the case of the absolute submission upon which you are pleased to insist, it might still remain something less than doubtful how far, with such counsellors around the King, even your Grace's intercession might procure us effectual relief. But I will communicate to our leaders your Grace's answer to our supplication; and, since we cannot obtain peace, we must bid war welcome as well as we may.'

'Good morning, sir,' said the Duke; 'I suspend the movements of attack for one hour, and for one hour only.[11] If you have an answer to return within that space of time, I will receive it here, and earnestly entreat it may be such as to save the effusion of blood.'

At this moment another smile of deep meaning passed between Dalzell and Claverhouse. The Duke observed it, and repeated his words with great dignity.

'Yes, gentlemen, I said I trusted the answer might be such as would save the effusion of blood. I hope the sentiment neither needs your scorn, nor incurs your displeasure.'

Dalzell returned the Duke's frown with a stern glance, but made no answer. Claverhouse, his lip just curled with an ironical smile, bowed, and said, 'It was not for him to judge the propriety of his Grace's sentiments.'

The Duke made a signal to Morton to withdraw. He obeyed; and, accompanied by his former escort, rode slowly through the army to return to the camp of the non-conformists. As he passed the fine corps of Life-Guards, he found Claverhouse was already at their head. That officer no sooner saw Morton, than he advanced and addressed him with perfect politeness of manner.[12]

'I think this is not the first time I have seen Mr Morton of Milnwood?'

'It is not Colonel Grahame's fault,' said Morton, smiling sternly, 'that he or any one else should be now incommoded by my presence.'

'Allow me at least to say,' replied Claverhouse, 'that Mr Morton's present situation authorizes the opinion I have entertained of him, and that my proceedings at our last meeting only squared to my duty.'

'To reconcile your actions to your duty, and your duty to your conscience, is your business, Colonel Grahame, not mine,' said Morton, justly offended at being thus, in a manner, required to approve of the sentence under which he had so nearly suffered.

'Nay, but stay an instant,' said Claverhouse; 'Evandale insists that I have some wrongs to acquit myself of in your instance. I trust I shall always make some difference between a high-minded gentleman, who, though misguided, acts upon generous principles, and the crazy fanatical clowns yonder, with the bloodthirsty assassins who head them. Therefore, if they do not disperse upon your return, let me pray you instantly come over to our army and surrender yourself, for, be assured, they cannot stand our assault for half an hour. If you will be ruled and do this, be sure to enquire for me. Monmouth, strange as it may seem, cannot protect you – Dalzell will not – I both can and will; and I have promised to Evandale to do so if you will give me an opportunity.'

'I should owe Lord Evandale my thanks,' answered Morton, coldly, 'did not his scheme imply an opinion that I might be prevailed on to desert those with whom I am engaged. For you, Colonel Grahame, if you will honour me with a different species of satisfaction, it is probable, that, in an hour's time, you will find me at the west end of Bothwell Bridge with my sword in my hand.'

'I shall be happy to meet you there,' said Claverhouse, 'but still more so should you think better on my first proposal.'

They then saluted and parted.

'That is a pretty lad, Lumley,' said Claverhouse, addressing himself to the other officer; 'but he is a lost man – his blood be upon his head.'

So saying, he addressed himself to the task of preparation for instant battle.

CHAPTER 31

But, hark! the tent has changed its voice,
There's peace and rest nae langer.

BURNS[1]

The Lowdien Mallisha they
Came with their coats of blew;
Five hundred men from London came,
Claid in a reddish hue.

Bothwell Lines[2]

WHEN Morton had left the well-ordered outposts of the regular army, and arrived at those which were maintained by his own party, he could not but be peculiarly sensible of the difference of discipline, and entertain a proportional degree of fear for the consequences. The same discords which agitated the counsels of the insurgents, raged even among their meanest followers; and their picquets and patrols were more interested and occupied in disputing the true occasion and causes of wrath, and defining the limits of Erastian heresy, than in looking out for and observing the motions of their enemies, though within hearing of the royal drums and trumpets.

There was a guard, however, of the insurgent army, posted at the long and narrow bridge of Bothwell, over which the enemy must necessarily advance to the attack; but, like the others, they were divided and disheartened; and, entertaining the idea that they were posted on a desperate service, they even meditated withdrawing themselves to the main body. This would have been utter ruin; for, on the defence or loss of this pass the fortune of the day was most likely to depend. All beyond the bridge was a plain open field, excepting a few thickets of no great depth, and,

consequently, was ground on which the undisciplined forces of
the insurgents, deficient as they were in cavalry, and totally un-
provided with artillery, were altogether unlikely to withstand the
shock of regular troops.

Morton, therefore, viewed the pass carefully, and formed the
hope, that by occupying two or three houses on the left bank of
the river, with the copse and thickets of alders and hazels that
lined its side, and by blockading the passage itself, and shutting
the gates of a portal, which, according to the old fashion, was
built on the central arch of the bridge of Bothwell, it might be
easily defended against a very superior force. He issued directions accordingly, and commanded the parapets of the bridge,
on the farther side of the portal, to be thrown down, that they
might afford no protection to the enemy when they should
attempt the passage. Morton then conjured the party at this
important post to be watchful and upon their guard, and
promised them a speedy and strong reinforcement. He caused
them to advance videttes beyond the river to watch the progress
of the enemy, which outposts he directed should be withdrawn
to the left bank as soon as they approached; finally, he charged
them to send regular information to the main body of all that
they should observe. Men under arms, and in a situation of
danger, are usually sufficiently alert in appreciating the merit of
their officers. Morton's intelligence and activity gained the
confidence of these men, and with better hope and heart than
before, they began to fortify their position in the manner he
recommended, and saw him depart with three loud cheers.

Morton now galloped hastily towards the main body of the
insurgents, but was surprised and shocked at the scene of confusion and clamour which it exhibited, at the moment when
good order and concord were of such essential consequence.
Instead of being drawn up in line of battle, and listening to the
commands of their officers, they were crowding together in a
confused mass, that rolled and agitated itself like the waves of
the sea, while a thousand tongues spoke, or rather vociferated,
and not a single ear was found to listen. Scandalized at a scene
so extraordinary, Morton endeavoured to make his way through
the press to learn, and, if possible, to remove, the cause of this

so untimely disorder. While he is thus engaged, we shall make the reader acquainted with that which he was some time in discovering.

The insurgents had proceeded to hold their day of humiliation, which, agreeably to the practice of the puritans during the earlier civil war, they considered as the most effectual mode of solving all difficulties, and waiving all discussions. It was usual to name an ordinary week-day for this purpose, but on this occasion the Sabbath itself was adopted, owing to the pressure of the time and the vicinity of the enemy. A temporary pulpit, or tent, was erected in the middle of the encampment; which, according to the fixed arrangement, was first to be occupied by the Reverend Peter Poundtext, to whom the post of honour was assigned, as the eldest clergyman present. But as the worthy divine, with slow and stately steps, was advancing towards the rostrum which had been prepared for him, he was prevented by the unexpected apparition of Habakkuk Mucklewrath, the insane preacher, whose appearance had so much startled Morton at the first council of the insurgents after their victory at Loudon-hill. It is not known whether he was acting under the influence and instigation of the Cameronians, or whether he was merely compelled by his own agitated imagination, and the temptation of a vacant pulpit before him, to seize the opportunity of exhorting so respectable a congregation. It is only certain that he took occasion by the forelock, sprung into the pulpit,[3] cast his eyes wildly round him, and, undismayed by the murmurs of many of the audience, opened the Bible, read forth as his text from the thirteenth chapter of Deuteronomy, 'Certain men, the children of Belial, are gone out from among you, and have withdrawn the inhabitants of their city, saying, let us go and serve other gods, which you have not known;' and then rushed at once into the midst of his subject.

The harangue of Mucklewrath was as wild and extravagant as his intrusion was unauthorized and untimely; but it was provokingly coherent, in so far as it turned entirely upon the very subjects of discord, of which it had been agreed to adjourn the consideration until some more suitable opportunity. Not a single topic did he omit which had offence in it; and, after charging the moderate party with heresy, with crouching to tyranny, with seeking to be at peace with God's enemies, he applied to Morton, by name, the charge that he had been one of those men of Belial, who, in the words of his text, had gone out from amongst them, to withdraw the inhabitants of his city, and to go astray after false gods. To him, and all who followed him, or approved of his conduct, Mucklewrath denounced fury and vengeance, and exhorted those who would hold themselves pure and undefiled to come up from the midst of them.

'Fear not,' he said, 'because of the neighing of horses, or the glittering of breastplates. Seek not aid of the Egyptians, because of the enemy, though they may be numerous as locusts, and fierce as dragons. Their trust is not as our trust, nor their rock as our rock; how else shall a thousand fly before one, and two put ten thousand to the flight! I dreamed it in the visions of the night, and the voice said, 'Habakkuk, take thy fan and purge the wheat from the chaff, that they be not both consumed with the fire of indignation and the lightning of fury.' Wherefore, I say, take this Henry Morton – this wretched Achan, who hath brought the accursed thing among ye, and made himself brethren in the camp of the enemy – take him and stone him with stones, and thereafter burn him with fire, that the wrath may depart from the children of the Covenant. He hath not taken a Babylonish garment, but he hath sold the garment of righteousness to the woman of Babylon – he hath not taken two hundred shekels of fine silver, but he hath bartered the truth, which is more precious than shekels of silver or wedges of gold.' [4]

At this furious charge, brought so unexpectedly against one of their most active commanders, the audience broke out into open tumult, some demanding that there should instantly be a new election of officers,[5] into which office none should hereafter be admitted who had, in their phrase, touched of that which was accursed, or temporized more or less with the heresies and corruptions of the times. While such was the demand of the Cameronians, they vociferated loudly, that those who were not with them were against then,[6] – that it was no time to relinquish the substantial part of the covenanted testimony of the Church, if they expected a blessing on their arms and their cause; and that, in their eyes, a lukewarm Presbyterian was little better than a Prelatist, an Anti-Covenanter, and a Nullifidian.

The parties accused repelled the charge of criminal compliance and defection from the truth with scorn and indignation, and charged their accusers with breach of faith, as well as with wrong-headed and extravagant zeal in introducing such divisions into an army, the joint strength of which could not, by the most sanguine, be judged more than sufficient to face their enemies. Poundtext, and one or two others, made some faint efforts to stem the increasing fury of the factious, exclaiming to those of the other party, in the words of the Patriarch, – 'Let there be no strife, I pray thee, between me and thee, and between thy herdsmen and my herdsmen, for we be brethren.'[7] No pacific overture could possibly obtain audience. It was in vain that even Burley himself, when he saw the dissension proceed to such ruinous lengths, exerted his stern and deep voice, commanding silence and obedience to discipline. The spirit of insubordination had gone forth, and it seemed as if the exhortation of Habakkuk Mucklewrath had communicated a part of his frenzy to all who heard him. The wiser, or more timid part of the assembly, were already withdrawing themselves from the field, and giving up their cause as lost. Others were moderating a harmonious call, as they somewhat improperly termed it, to new officers, and dismissing those formerly chosen, and that with a tumult and clamour worthy of the deficiency of good sense and good order implied in the whole transaction. It was at this moment when Morton arrived in the field and joined the army, in total confusion, and on the point of dissolving itself. His arrival occasioned loud exclamations of applause on the one side, and of imprecation on the other.

'What means this ruinous disorder at such a moment?' he exclaimed to Burley, who, exhausted with his vain exertions to restore order, was now leaning on his sword, and regarding the confusion with an eye of resolute despair.

'It means,' he replied, 'that God has delivered us into the hands of our enemies.'

'Not so,' answered Morton, with a voice and gesture which compelled many to listen; 'it is not God who deserts us, it is we who desert him, and dishonour ourselves by disgracing and betraying the cause of freedom and religion. – Hear me,' he exclaimed, springing to the pulpit which Mucklewrath had been compelled to evacuate by actual exhaustion – 'I bring from the enemy an offer to treat, if you incline to lay down your arms. I can assure you the means of making an honourable defence, if you are of more manly tempers. The time flies fast on. Let us resolve either for peace or war; and let it not be said of us in future days, that six thousand Scottish men in arms had neither courage to stand their ground and fight it out, nor prudence to treat for peace, nor even the coward's wisdom to retreat in good time and with safety. What signifies quarrelling on minute points of church-discipline, when the whole edifice is threatened with total destruction? O, remember, my brethren, that the last and worst evil which God brought upon the people whom he had once chosen – the last and worst punishment of their blindness and hardness of heart, was the bloody dissensions which rent asunder their city, even when the enemy were thundering at its gates!'

Some of the audience testified their feeling of this exhortation, by loud exclamations of applause; others by hooting, and exclaiming – 'To your tents, O Israel!'[8]

Morton, who beheld the columns of the enemy already beginning to appear on the right bank, and directing their march upon the bridge, raised his voice to its utmost pitch, and, pointing at the same time with his hand, exclaimed, – 'Silence your senseless clamours, yonder is the enemy! On maintaining the bridge against him depend our lives, as well as our hope to reclaim our laws and liberties. – There shall at least one Scottishman die in their defence. – Let any one who loves his country follow me!'

The multitude had turned their heads in the direction to which he pointed. The sight of the glittering files of the English Foot-Guards, supported by several squadrons of horse, of the cannon which the artillerymen were busily engaged in planting against the bridge, of the plaided clans who seemed to search for a ford, and of the long succession of troops which were destined to support the attack, silenced at once their clamorous uproar, and struck them with as much consternation as if it were an unexpected apparition, and not the very thing which they ought to have been looking out for. They gazed on each other, and on their leaders, with looks resembling those that indicate the weakness of a patient when exhausted by a fit of frenzy. Yet when Morton, springing from the rostrum, directed his steps towards the bridge, he was followed by about an hundred of the young men who were particularly attached to his command.

Burley turned to Macbriar – 'Ephraim,' he said, 'it is Providence points us the way, through the worldly wisdom of this latitudinarian youth. – He that loves the light, let him follow Burley!'

'Tarry,' replied Macbriar; 'it is not by Henry Morton, or such as he, that our goings-out and our comings-in are to be meted; therefore tarry with us. I fear treachery to the host from this *nullifidian* Achan.[9] – Thou shalt not go with him. Thou art our chariots and our horsemen.'

'Hinder me not,' replied Burley; 'he hath well said that all is lost, if the enemy win the bridge – therefore let me not. Shall the children of this generation be called wiser or braver than the children of the sanctuary?[10] – Array yourselves under your leaders – let us not lack supplies of men and ammunition; and accursed be he who turneth back from the work on this great day!'

Having thus spoken, he hastily marched towards the bridge, and was followed by about two hundred of the most gallant and zealous of his party. There was a deep and disheartened pause when Morton and Burley departed. The commanders availed themselves of it to display their lines in some sort of order, and exhorted those who were most exposed to throw themselves upon their faces to avoid the cannonade which they might presently expect. The insurgents ceased to resist or to remonstrate; but the awe which had silenced their discords had dismayed their courage. They suffered themselves to be formed into ranks with the docility of a flock of sheep, but without possessing, for the time, more resolution or energy; for they experienced a sinking of the heart, imposed by the sudden and imminent approach of the danger which they had neglected to provide against while it was yet distant. They were, however, drawn out with some regularity; and as they still possessed the appearance of an army, their leaders had only to hope that some favourable circumstance would restore their spirits and courage.

Kettledrummle, Poundtext, Macbriar, and other preachers, busied themselves in their ranks, and prevailed on them to raise a psalm. But the superstitious among them observed, as an ill omen, that their song of praise and triumph sunk into 'a quaver of consternation,' and resembled rather a penitentiary stave sung on the scaffold of a condemned criminal, than the bold strain which had resounded along the wild heath of Loudon-hill, in anticipation of that day's victory. The melancholy melody soon received a rough accompaniment; the royal soldiers shouted, the Highlanders yelled, the cannon began to fire on one side, and the musketry on both, and the bridge of Bothwell, with the banks adjacent, were involved in wreaths of smoke.[11]

CHAPTER 32

As e'er ye saw the rain doun fa',
    Or yet the arrow from the bow,
Sae our Scots lads fell even down,
    And they lay slain on every knowe.

Old Ballad[1]

ERE MORTON or Burley had reached the post to be defended, the enemy had commenced an attack upon it with great spirit. The two regiments of Foot-Guards, formed into a close column, rushed forward to the river; one corps, deploying along the right bank, commenced a galling fire on the defenders of the pass, while the other pressed on to occupy the bridge. The insurgents sustained the attack with great constancy and courage; and while part of their number returned the fire across the river, the rest maintained a discharge of musketry upon the further end of the bridge itself, and every avenue by which the soldiers endeavoured to approach it. The latter suffered severely, but still gained ground, and the head of their column was already upon the bridge, when the arrival of Morton changed the scene; and his marksmen, commencing upon the pass a fire as well aimed as it was sustained and regular, compelled the assailants to retire with much loss. They were a second time brought up to the charge, and a second time repulsed with still greater loss, as Burley had now brought his party into action. The fire was continued with the utmost vehemence on both sides, and the issue of the action seemed very dubious.

Monmouth, mounted on a superb white charger, might be discovered on the top of the right bank ⟨ the river, urging, entreating, and animating the exertions of his soldiers. By his orders, the cannon, which had hitherto been employed in annoying the distant main body of the presbyterians, were now turned upon the defenders of the bridge. But these tremendous engines, being wrought much more slowly than in modern times, did not produce the effect of annoying or terrifying the enemy to the extent proposed. The insurgents, sheltered by copsewood along the bank of the river, or stationed in the houses already mentioned, fought under cover, while the royalists, owing to the precautions of Morton, were entirely exposed. The defence was so protracted and obstinate, that the royal generals began to fear it might be ultimately successful. While Monmouth threw himself from his horse, and, rallying the Foot-Guards, brought them on to another close and desperate attack, he was warmly seconded by Dalzell, who, putting himself at the head of a body of Lennox-Highlanders, rushed forward with their tremendous war-cry of Loch-sloy.[2] The ammunition of the defenders of the bridge began to fail at this important crisis; messages, commanding and imploring succours and supplies, were in vain dispatched, one after the other, to the main body of the presbyterian army, which remained inactively drawn up on the open fields in the rear. Fear, consternation, and misrule, had gone abroad among them, and while the post on which their safety depended required to be instantly and powerfully reinforced, there remained none either to command or to obey.

As the fire of the defenders of the bridge began to slacken, that of the assailants increased, and in its turn became more fatal. Animated by the example and exhortations of their generals, they obtained a footing upon the bridge itself, and began to remove the obstacles by which it was blockaded. The portal-gate was broke open, the beams, trunks of trees, and other materials of the barricade, pulled down and thrown into the river. This was not accomplished without opposition. Morton and Burley fought in the very front of their followers, and encouraged them with their pikes, halberds, and partisans, to encounter the bayonets of the Guards, and the broadswords of the Highlanders. But those behind the leaders began to shrink from the unequal combat, and fly singly, or in parties of two or three, towards the main body, until the remainder were, by the mere weight of the hostile column as much as by their weapons, fairly forced from the bridge. The passage being now open, the enemy began to pour over. But the bridge was long and narrow, which rendered the manœuvre slow as well as dangerous; and those who first passed had still to force the houses, from the windows of which the Covenanters continued to fire. Burley and Morton were near each other at this critical moment.

'There is yet time,' said the former, 'to bring down horse to attack them, ere they can get into order; and, with the aid of God, we may thus regain the bridge – hasten thou to bring them down, while I make the defence good with this old and wearied body.'

Morton saw the importance of the advice, and, throwing himself on the horse which Cuddie held in readiness for him behind the thicket, galloped towards a body of cavalry which chanced to be composed entirely of Cameronians. Ere he could speak his errand, or utter his orders, he was saluted by the execrations of the whole body.

'He flies!' they exclaimed – 'the cowardly traitor flies like a hart from the hunters, and hath left valiant Burley in the midst of the slaughter!' [3]

'I do not fly,' said Morton. 'I come to lead you to the attack. Advance boldly, and we shall yet do well.'

'Follow him not! – Follow him not!' – such were the tumultuous exclamations which resounded from the ranks; – 'he hath sold you to the sword of the enemy!'

And while Morton argued, entreated, and commanded in

vain, the moment was lost in which the advance might have been useful; and the outlet from the bridge, with all its defences, being in complete possession of the enemy, Burley and his remaining followers were driven back upon the main body, to whom the spectacle of their hurried and harassed retreat was far from restoring the confidence which they so much wanted.

In the meanwhile, the forces of the King crossed the bridge at their leisure, and, securing the pass, formed in line of battle; while Claverhouse, who, like a hawk perched on a rock, and eyeing the time to pounce on its prey, had watched the event of the action from the opposite bank, now passed the bridge at the head of his cavalry, at full trot, and, leading them in squadrons through the intervals and round the flanks of the royal infantry, formed them in line on the moor, and led them to the charge, advancing in front with one large body, while other two divisions threatened the flanks of the Covenanters. Their devoted army was now in that situation when the slightest demonstration towards an attack was certain to inspire panic. Their broken spirits and disheartened courage were unable to endure the charge of the cavalry, attended with all its terrible accompaniments of sight and sound; – the rush of the horses at full speed, the shaking of the earth under their feet, the glancing of the swords, the waving of the plumes, and the fierce shouts of the cavaliers. The front ranks hardly attempted one ill-directed and disorderly fire, and their rear were broken and flying in confusion ere the charge had been completed; and in less than five minutes the horsemen were mixed with them, cutting and hewing without mercy. The voice of Claverhouse was heard, even above the din of conflict, exclaiming to his soldiers – 'Kill, kill – no quarter – think on Richard Grahame!' The dragoons, many of whom had shared the disgrace of Loudon-hill, required no exhortations to vengeance as easy as it was complete. Their swords drank deep of slaughter among the unresisting fugitives. Screams for quarter were only answered by the shouts with which the pursuers accompanied their blows, and the whole field presented one general scene of confused slaughter, flight, and pursuit.

About twelve hundred[4] of the insurgents who remained in a

body a little apart from the rest, and out of the line of the charge of cavalry, threw down their arms and surrendered at discretion, upon the approach of the Duke of Monmouth at the head of the infantry. That mild-tempered nobleman instantly allowed them the quarter which they prayed for; and, galloping about through the field, exerted himself as much to stop the slaughter as he had done to obtain the victory. While busied in this humane task he met with General Dalzell, who was encouraging the fierce Highlanders and royal volunteers to show their zeal for King and country, by quenching the flame of the rebellion with the blood of the rebels.

'Sheathe your sword, I command you, General!' exclaimed the Duke, 'and sound the retreat. Enough of blood has been shed; give quarter to the King's misguided subjects.'

'I obey your Grace,' said the old man, wiping his bloody sword and returning it to the scabbard; 'but I warn you, at the same time, that enough has *not* been done to intimidate these desperate rebels. Has not your Grace heard that Basil Olifant has collected several gentlemen and men of substance in the west, and is in the act of marching to join them?' [5]

'Basil Olifant?' said the Duke; 'who, or what is he?'

'The next male heir to the last Earl of Torwood. He is disaffected to government from his claim to the estate being set aside in favour of Lady Margaret Bellenden; and I suppose the hope of getting the inheritance has set him in motion.'

'Be his motives what they will,' replied Monmouth, 'he must soon disperse his followers, for this army is too much broken to rally again. Therefore, once more, I command that the pursuit be stopped.'

'It is your Grace's province to command, and to be responsible for your commands,' answered Dalzell, as he gave reluctant orders for checking the pursuit.

But the fiery and vindictive Grahame was already far out of hearing of the signal of retreat, and continued with his cavalry an unwearied and bloody pursuit, breaking, dispersing, and cutting to pieces all the insurgents whom they could come up with. [6]

Burley and Morton were both hurried off the field by the confused tide of fugitives. They made some attempt to defend the streets of the town of Hamilton; but, while labouring to induce the fliers to face about and stand to their weapons, Burley received a bullet which broke his sword-arm.

'May the hand be withered that shot the shot!' he exclaimed, as the sword which he was waving over his head fell powerless to his side. 'I can fight no longer.' [7]

Then turning his horse's head, he retreated out of the confusion. Morton also now saw that the continuing his unavailing efforts to rally the fliers could only end in his own death or captivity, and, followed by the faithful Cuddie, he extricated himself from the press, and, being well mounted, leaped his horse over one or two enclosures, and got into the open country.

From the first hill which they gained in their flight, they looked back, and beheld the whole country covered with their fugitive companions, and with the pursuing dragoons, whose wild shouts and halloo, as they did execution on the groups whom they overtook, mingled with the groans and screams of their victims, rose shrilly up the hill.

'It is impossible they can ever make head again,' said Morton.

'The head's taen aff them, as clean as I wad bite it aff a sybo!' rejoined Cuddie. 'Eh, Lord! see how the broadswords are flashing! war's a fearsome thing. They'll be cunning that catches me at this wark again. – But, for God's sake, sir, let us mak for some strength!'

Morton saw the necessity of following the advice of his trusty squire. They resumed a rapid pace, and continued it without intermission, directing their course towards the wild and mountainous country, where they thought it likely some part of the fugitives might draw together, for the sake either of making defence, or of obtaining terms.

CHAPTER 33

They require
Of Heaven the hearts of lions, breath of tigers,
Yea and the fierceness too.

FLETCHER[1]

EVENING had fallen; and, for the last two hours, they had seen none of their ill-fated companions, when Morton and his faithful attendant gained the moorland, and approached a large and solitary farmhouse, situated in the entrance of a wild glen, far remote from any other habitation.

'Our horses,' said Morton, 'will carry us no farther without rest or food, and we must try to obtain them here, if possible.'

So speaking, he led the way to the house. The place had every appearance of being inhabited. There was smoke issuing from the chimney in a considerable volume, and the marks of recent hoofs were visible around the door. They could even hear the murmuring of human voices within the house. But all the lower windows were closely secured; and when they knocked at the door, no answer was returned. After vainly calling and entreating admittance, they withdrew to the stable, or shed, in order to accommodate their horses, ere they used farther means of gaining admission. In this place they found ten or twelve horses, whose state of fatigue, as well as the military yet disordered appearance of their saddles and accoutrements, plainly indicated that their owners were fugitive insurgents in their own circumstances.

'This meeting bodes luck,' said Cuddie; 'and they hae walth o' beef, that's ae thing certain, for here's a raw hide that has been about the hurdies o' a stot not half an hour syne – it's warm yet.'

Encouraged by these appearances, they returned again to the house, and, announcing themselves as men in the same predicament with the inmates, clamoured loudly for admittance.

'Whoever ye be,' answered a stern voice from the window, after a long and obdurate silence, 'disturb not those who mourn for the desolation and captivity of the land, and search out the causes of wrath and of defection, that the stumbling-blocks may be removed over which we have stumbled.'

'They are wild western whigs,' said Cuddie, in a whisper to his master, 'I ken by their language. Fiend hae me, if I like to venture on them!'

Morton, however, again called to the party within, and insisted on admittance; but, finding his entreaties still disregarded, he opened one of the lower windows, and pushing asunder the shutters, which were but slightly secured, stepped into the large kitchen from which the voice had issued. Cuddie followed him, muttering betwixt his teeth, as he put his head within the window, 'That he hoped there was nae scalding brose on the fire;' and master and servant both found themselves in the company of ten or twelve armed men, seated around the fire, on which refreshments were preparing, and busied apparently in their devotions.

In the gloomy countenances, illuminated by the fire-light, Morton had no difficulty in recognising several of those zealots who had most distinguished themselves by their intemperate opposition to all moderate measures, together with their noted pastor, the fanatical Ephraim Macbriar, and the maniac, Habak-kuk Mucklewrath. The Cameronians neither stirred tongue nor hand to welcome their brethren in misfortune, but continued to listen to the low murmured exercise of Macbriar, as he prayed that the Almighty would lift up his hand from his people, and not make an end in the day of his anger. That they were conscious of the presence of the intruders only appeared from the sullen and indignant glances which they shot at them, from time to time, as their eyes encountered.

Morton, finding into what unfriendly society he had unwittingly intruded, began to think of retreating; but, on turning his head, observed with some alarm, that two strong men had silently placed themselves beside the window, through which they had entered. One of these ominous sentinels whispered to Cuddie, 'Son of that precious woman, Mause Headrigg, do not cast thy lot farther with this child of treachery and perdition – Pass on thy way, and tarry not, for the avenger of blood is behind thee.'

With this he pointed to the window, out of which Cuddie

jumped without hesitation; for the intimation he had received plainly implied the personal danger he would otherwise incur.

'Winnocks are no lucky wi' me,' was his first reflection when he was in the open air; his next was upon the probable fate of his master. 'They'll kill him, the murdering loons, and think they're doing a gude turn! but I'se tak the back road for Hamilton, and see if I canna get some o' our ain folk to bring help in time of needcessity.'

So saying, Cuddie hastened to the stable, and taking the best horse he could find instead of his own tired animal, he galloped off in the direction he proposed.

The noise of his horse's tread alarmed for an instant the devotion of the fanatics. As it died in the distance, Macbriar brought his exercise to a conclusion, and his audience raised themselves from the stooping posture, and louring downward look, with which they had listened to it, and all fixed their eyes sternly on Henry Morton.

'You bend strange countenances on me, gentlemen,' said he, addressing them. 'I am totally ignorant in what manner I can have deserved them.'

'Out upon thee! out upon thee!' exclaimed Mucklewrath, starting up; 'the word that thou hast spurned shall become a rock to crush and to bruise thee; the spear which thou wouldst have broken shall pierce thy side; we have prayed, and wrestled, and petitioned for an offering to atone the sins of the congregation, and lo! the very head of the offence is delivered into our hand. He hath burst in like a thief through the window; he is a ram caught in the thicket, whose blood shall be a drink-offering to redeem vengeance from the church, and the place shall from henceforth be called Jehovah-Jireh, for the sacrifice is provided. Up then, and bind the victim with cords to the horns of the altar!'[2]

There was a movement among the party; and deeply did Morton regret at that moment the incautious haste with which he had ventured into their company. He was armed only with his sword, for he had left his pistols at the bow of his saddle; and, as the whigs were all provided with fire-arms, there was little or no chance of escaping from them by resistance. The interposition, however, of Macbriar protected him for the moment.

'Tarry yet a while, brethren – let us not use the sword rashly, lest the load of innocent blood lie heavy on us. – Come,' he said, addressing himself to Morton, 'we will reckon with thee ere we avenge the cause thou hast betrayed. – Hast thou not,' he continued, 'made thy face as hard as flint against the truth in all the assemblies of the host?'

'He has – he has,' murmured the deep voices of the assistants.

'He hath ever urged peace with the malignants,' said one.

'And pleaded for the dark and dismal guilt of the Indulgence,' said another.

'And would have surrendered the host into the hands of Monmouth,' echoed a third; 'and was the first to desert the honest and manly Burley, while he yet resisted at the pass. I saw him on the moor, with his horse bloody with spurring, long ere the firing had ceased at the bridge.'

'Gentlemen,' said Morton, 'if you mean to bear me down by clamour, and take my life without hearing me, it is perhaps a thing in your power; but you will sin before God and man by the commission of such a murder.'

'I say, hear the youth,' said Macbriar; 'for Heaven knows our bowels have yearned for him, that he might be brought to see the truth, and exert his gifts in its defence. But he is blinded by his carnal knowledge, and has spurned the light when it blazed before him.'

Silence being obtained, Morton proceeded to assert the good faith which he had displayed in the treaty with Monmouth, and the active part he had borne in the subsequent action.

'I may not, gentlemen,' he said, 'be fully able to go the lengths you desire, in assigning to those of my own religion the means of tyrannizing over others; but none shall go farther in asserting our own lawful freedom. And I must needs aver, that had others been of my mind in counsel, or disposed to stand by my side in battle, we should this evening, instead of being a defeated and discordant remnant, have sheathed our weapons in an useful and honourable peace, or brandished them triumphantly after a decisive victory.'

'He hath spoken the word,' said one of the assembly – 'he hath avowed his carnal self-seeking and Erastianism; let him die the death!'

'Peace yet again,' said Macbriar, 'for I will try him further. – Was it not by thy means that the malignant Evandale twice escaped from death and captivity? Was it not through thee that Miles Bellenden and his garrison of cut-throats were saved from the edge of the sword?'

'I am proud to say, that you have spoken the truth in both instances,' replied Morton.

'Lo! you see,' said Macbriar, 'again hath his mouth spoken it. – And didst thou not do this for the sake of a Midianitish woman,[3] one of the spawn of prelacy, a toy with which the arch-enemy's trap is baited? Didst thou not do all this for the sake of Edith Bellenden?'

'You are incapable,' answered Morton, boldly, 'of appreciating my feelings towards that young lady; but all that I have done I would have done had she never existed.'

'Thou art a hardy rebel to the truth,' said another dark-brow'd man; 'and didst thou not so act, that, by conveying away the aged woman, Margaret Bellenden, and her grand-daughter, thou mightest thwart the wise and godly project of John Balfour of Burley for bringing forth to battle Basil Olifant, who had agreed to take the field if he were insured possession of these women's worldly endownments?'

'I never heard of such a scheme,' said Morton, 'and therefore I could not thwart it. – But does your religion permit you to take such uncreditable and immoral modes of recruiting?'

'Peace,' said Macbriar, somewhat disconcerted; 'it is not for thee to instruct tender professors, or to construe Covenant obligations. For the rest, you have acknowledged enough of sin and sorrowful defection, to draw down defeat on a host, were it as numerous as the sands on the sea-shore. And it is our judgment, that we are not free to let you pass from us safe and in life, since Providence hath given you into our hands at the moment that we prayed with godly Joshua,[4] saying, "What shall we say when Israel turneth their backs before their enemies?" – Then camest thou, delivered to us as it were by lot, that thou mightest sustain the punishment of one that hath wrought folly in Israel. There-fore, mark my words. This is the Sabbath, and our hand shall not be on thee to spill thy blood upon this day; but, when the twelfth hour shall strike, it is a token that thy time on earth hath run! Wherefore improve thy span, for it flitteth fast away. - Seize on the prisoner, brethren, and take his weapon.'⁵

The command was so unexpectedly given, and so suddenly executed by those of the party who had gradually closed behind and around Morton, that he was overpowered, disarmed, and a horse-girth passed round his arms, before he could offer any effectual resistance. When this was accomplished, a dead and stern silence took place. The fanatics ranged themselves around a large oaken table, placing Morton amongst them bound and helpless, in such a manner as to be opposite to the clock which was to strike his knell. Food was placed before them, of which they offered their intended victim a share; but, it will readily be believed, he had little appetite. When this was removed, the party resumed their devotions. Macbriar, whose fierce zeal did not perhaps exclude some feelings of doubt and compunction, began to expostulate in prayer, as if to wring from the Deity a signal that the bloody sacrifice they proposed was an acceptable service. The eyes and ears of his hearers were anxiously strained, as if to gain some sight or sound which might be converted or wrested into a type of approbation, and ever and anon dark looks were turned on the dial-plate of the time-piece, to watch its progress towards the moment of execution.

Morton's eye frequently took the same course, with the sad reflection, that there appeared no possibility of his life being expanded beyond the narrow segment which the index had yet to travel on the circle until it arrived at the fatal hour. Faith in his religion, with a constant unyielding principle of honour, and the sense of conscious innocence, enabled him to pass through this dreadful interval with less agitation than he himself could have expected, had the situation been prophesied to him. Yet there was a want of that eager and animating sense of right which sup-ported him in similar circumstances, when in the power of Claverhouse. Then he was conscious, that, amid the spectators, were many who were lamenting his condition, and some who applauded his conduct. But now, among these pale-eyed and ferocious zealots, whose hardened brows were soon to be bent, not merely with indifference, but with triumph, upon his execution, – without a friend to speak a kindly word, or give a look either of sympathy or encouragement, – awaiting till the sword destined to slay him crept out of the scabbard gradually, and as it were by strawbreadths, and condemned to drink the bitterness of death drop by drop, – it is no wonder that his feelings were less composed than they had been on any former occasion of danger. His destined executioners, as he gazed around them, seemed to alter their forms and features, like spectres in a feverish dream; their figures became larger, and their faces more disturbed; and, as an excited imagination predominated over the realities which his eyes received, he could have thought himself surrounded rather by a band of demons than of human beings; the walls seemed to drop with blood, and the light tick of the clock thrilled on his ear with such loud, painful distinctness, as if each sound were the prick of a bodkin inflicted on the naked nerve of the organ.

It was with pain that he felt his mind wavering, while on the brink between this and the future world. He made a strong effort to compose himself to devotional exercises, and unequal, during that fearful strife of nature, to arrange his own thoughts into suitable expressions, he had, instinctively, recourse to the petition for deliverance and for composure of spirit which is to be found in the Book of Common Prayer of the Church of England.[6] Macbriar, whose family were of that persuasion, instantly recognised the words, which the unfortunate prisoner pronounced half aloud.

'There lacked but this,' he said, his pale cheek kindling with resentment, 'to root out my carnal reluctance to see his blood spilt. He is a prelatist, who has sought the camp under the disguise of an Erastian, and all, and more than all, that has been said of him must needs be verity. His blood be on his head, the deceiver! – let him go down to Tophet, with the ill-mumbled mass which he calls a prayer-book, in his right hand!'

'I take up my song against him!' exclaimed the maniac. 'As the sun went back on the dial ten degrees for intimating the recovery of holy Hezekiah,[7] so shall it now go forward, that the wicked may be taken away from among the people, and the Covenant established in its purity.'

He sprang to a chair with an attitude of frenzy, in order to anticipate the fatal moment by putting the index forward; and several of the party began to make ready their slaughter-weapons for immediate execution, when Mucklewrath's hand was arrested by one of his companions.

'Hist!' he said – 'I hear a distant noise.'

'It is the rushing of the brook over the pebbles,' said one.

'It is the sough of the wind among the bracken,' said another.

'It is the galloping of horse,' said Morton to himself, his sense of hearing rendered acute by the dreadful situation in which he stood; 'God grant they may come as my deliverers!'

The noise approached rapidly, and became more and more distinct.

'It is horse,' cried Macbriar. 'Look out and descry who they are.'

'The enemy are upon us!' cried one who had opened the window, in obedience to his order.

A thick trampling and loud voices were heard immediately round the house. Some rose to resist, and some to escape; the doors and windows were forced at once, and the red coats of the troopers appeared in the apartment.

'Have at the bloody rebels! – Remember Cornet Grahame!' was shouted on every side.

The lights were struck down, but the dubious glare of the fire enabled them to continue the fray. Several pistol-shots were fired; the whig who stood next to Morton received a shot as he was rising, stumbled against the prisoner, whom he bore down with his weight, and lay stretched above him a dying man. This accident probably saved Morton from the damage he might otherwise have received in so close a struggle, where fire-arms were discharged and sword-blows given for upwards of five minutes.

'Is the prisoner safe?' exclaimed the well-known voice of Claverhouse; 'look about for him, and dispatch the whig dog who is groaning there.'

Both orders were executed. The groans of the wounded man

were silenced by a thrust with a rapier, and Morton, disencumbered of his weight, was speedily raised and in the arms of
the faithful Cuddie, who blubbered for joy when he found that
the blood with which his master was covered had not flowed from
his own veins. A whisper in Morton's ear, while his trusty
follower relieved him from his bonds, explained the secret of the
very timely appearance of the soldiers.

'I fell into Claverhouse's party when I was seeking for some o'
our ain folk to help ye out o' the hands of the whigs, sae being
atween the deil and the deep sea, I e'en thought it best to bring
him on wi' me, for he'll be wearied wi' felling folk the night,
and the morn's a new day, and Lord Evandale awes ye a day in
ha'arst; and Monmouth gies quarter, the dragoons tell me, for
the asking. Sae haud up your heart, an I'se warrant we'll do a'
weel eneugh yet.' [8]

CHAPTER 34

Sound, sound the clarion, fill the fife!
To all the sensual world proclaim,
One crowded hour of glorious life
Is worth an age without a name.

Anonymous[1]

WHEN the desperate affray had ceased, Claverhouse commanded
his soldiers to remove the dead bodies, to refresh themselves and
their horses, and prepare for passing the night at the farm-house,
and for marching early in the ensuing morning. He then turned
his attention to Morton, and there was politeness, and even kindness, in the manner in which he addressed him.

'You would have saved yourself risk from both sides, Mr
Morton, if you had honoured my counsel yesterday morning with
some attention; but I respect your motives. You are a prisoner-of-
war at the disposal of the king and council, but you shall be
treated with no incivility; and I will be satisfied with your parole
that you will not attempt an escape.'

When Morton had passed his word to that effect, Claverhouse bowed civilly, and, turning away from him, called for his sergeant-major.

'How many prisoners, Halliday, and how many killed?'

'Three killed in the house, sir, two cut down in the court, and one in the garden – six in all; four prisoners.'

'Armed or unarmed?' said Claverhouse.

'Three of them armed to the teeth,' answered Halliday; 'one without arms – he seems to be a preacher.'

'Ay – the trumpeter to the long-ear'd rout, I suppose,' replied Claverhouse, glancing slightly round upon his victims, 'I will talk with him to-morrow. Take the other three down to the yard, draw out two files, and fire upon them; and, d'ye hear, make a memorandum in the orderly book of three rebels taken in arms and shot, with the date and name of the place – Drumshinnel, I think, they call it. – Look after the preacher till to-morrow; as he was not armed, he must undergo a short examination. Or better, perhaps, take him before the Privy Council; I think they should relieve me of a share of this disgusting drudgery. – Let Mr Morton be civilly used, and see that the men look well after their horses; and let my groom wash Wildblood's shoulder with some vinegar, the saddle has touched him a little.'

All these various orders, – for life and death, the securing of his prisoners, and the washing his charger's shoulder, – were given in the same unmoved and equable voice, of which no accent or tone intimated that the speaker considered one direction as of more importance than another.

The Cameronians, so lately about to be the willing agents of a bloody execution, were now themselves to undergo it. They seemed prepared alike for either extremity, nor did any of them show the least sign of fear, when ordered to leave the room for the purpose of meeting instant death. Their severe enthusiasm sustained them in that dreadful moment, and they departed with a firm look and in silence, excepting that one of them, as he left the apartment, looked Claverhouse full in the face, and pronounced, with a stern and steady voice, – 'Mischief shall haunt the violent man!'[2] to which Grahame only answered by a smile of contempt.

They had no sooner left the room than Claverhouse applied

himself to some food, which one or two of his party had hastily provided, and invited Morton to follow his example, observing, it had been a busy day for them both. Morton declined eating; for the sudden change of circumstances – the transition from the verge of the grave to a prospect of life, had occasioned a dizzy revulsion in his whole system. But the same confused sensation was accompanied by a burning thirst, and he expressed his wish to drink.

'I will pledge you, with all my heart,' said Claverhouse; 'for here is a black jack full of ale, and good it must be, if there be good in the country, for the whigs never miss to find it out. – My service to you, Mr Morton,' he said, filling one horn of ale for himself, and handing another to his prisoner.

Morton raised it to his head, and was just about to drink, when the discharge of carabines beneath the window, followed by a deep and hollow groan, repeated twice or thrice, and more faint at each interval, announced the fate of the three men who had just left them. Morton shuddered, and set down the untasted cup.

'You are but young in these matters, Mr Morton,' said Claverhouse, after he had very composedly finished his draught; 'and I do not think the worse of you as a young soldier for appearing to feel them acutely. But habit, duty, and necessity, reconcile men to every thing.'

'I trust,' said Morton, 'they will never reconcile me to such scenes as these.'

'You would hardly believe,' said Claverhouse in reply, 'that, in the beginning of my military career, I had as much aversion to seeing blood spilt as ever man felt; it seemed to me to be wrung from my own heart; and yet, if you trust one of those whig fellows, he will tell you I drink a warm cup of it every morning before I breakfast.[3] But in truth, Mr Morton, why should we care so much for death, light upon us or around us whenever it may? Men die daily – not a bell tolls the hour but it is the death-note of some one or other; and why hesitate to shorten the span of others, or take over-anxious care to prolong our own? It is all a lottery – when the hour of midnight came, you were to die – it has struck, you are alive and safe, and the lot has fallen on those fellows who were to murder you. It is not the expiring pang that is worth thinking of in an event that must happen one day, and may befall us on any given moment – it is the memory which the soldier leaves behind him, like the long train of light that follows the sunken sun – that is all which is worth caring for, which distinguishes the death of the brave or the ignoble. When I think of death, Mr Morton, as a thing worth thinking of, it is in the hope of pressing one day some well-fought and hard-won field of battle, and dying with the shout of victory in my ear – *that* would be worth dying for, and more, it would be worth having lived for!'

At the moment when Grahame delivered these sentiments, his eye glancing with the martial enthusiasm which formed such a prominent feature in his character, a gory figure, which seemed to rise out of the floor of the apartment, stood upright before him, and presented the wild person and hideous features of the maniac so often mentioned. His face, where it was not covered with blood-streaks, was ghastly pale, for the hand of death was on him. He bent upon Claverhouse eyes, in which the grey light of insanity still twinkled, though just about to flit for ever, and exclaimed, with his usual wildness of ejaculation, 'Wilt thou trust in thy bow and in thy spear, in thy steed and in thy banner? And shall not God visit thee for innocent blood? – Wilt thou glory in thy wisdom, and in thy courage, and in thy might? And shall not the Lord judge thee? – Behold the princes, for whom thou hast sold thy soul to the destroyer, shall be removed from their place, and banished to other lands, and their names shall be a desolation, and an astonishment, and a hissing, and a curse. And thou, who hast partaken of the wine-cup of fury, and hast been drunken and mad because thereof,[4] the wish of thy heart shall be granted to thy loss, and the hope of thine own pride shall destroy thee. I summon thee, John Grahame, to appear before the tribunal of God, to answer for this innocent blood, and the seas besides which thou hast shed.'

He drew his right hand across his bleeding face, and held it up to heaven as he uttered these words, which he spoke very loud, and then added more faintly, 'How long, O Lord, holy and true, dost thou not judge and avenge the blood of thy saints!'[5]

As he uttered the last word, he fell backwards without an

attempt to save himself, and was a dead man ere his head touched the floor.

Morton was much shocked at this extraordinary scene, and the prophecy of the dying man, which tallied so strangely with the wish which Claverhouse had just expressed; and he often thought of it afterwards when that wish seemed to be accomplished. Two of the dragoons who were in the apartment, hardened as they were, and accustomed to such scenes, showed great consternation at the sudden apparition, the event, and the words which preceded it. Claverhouse alone was unmoved. At the first instant of Mucklewrath's appearance, he had put his hand to his pistol, but on seeing the situation of the wounded wretch, he immediately withdrew it, and listened with great composure to his dying exclamation.

When he dropped, Claverhouse asked, in an unconcerned tone of voice – 'How came the fellow here? – Speak, you staring fool!' he added, addressing the nearest dragoon, 'unless you would have me think you such a poltroon as to fear a dying man.'

The dragoon crossed himself, and replied with a faltering voice, – 'That the dead fellow had escaped their notice when they removed the other bodies, as he chanced to have fallen where a cloak or two had been flung aside, and covered him.'

'Take him away now, then, you gaping idiot, and see that he does not bite you, to put an old proverb to shame. – This is a new incident, Mr Morton, that dead men should rise and push us from our stools. I must see that my blackguards grind their swords sharper; they used not to do their work so slovenly. – But we have had a busy day; they are tired, and their blades blunted with their bloody work; and I suppose you, Mr Morton, as well as I, are well disposed for a few hours' repose.'

So saying, he yawned, and taking a candle which a soldier had placed ready, saluted Morton courteously, and walked to the apartment which had been prepared for him.

Morton was also accommodated, for the evening, with a separate room. Being left alone, his first occupation was the returning thanks to Heaven for redeeming him from danger, even through the instrumentality of those who seemed his most dangerous enemies; he also prayed sincerely for the Divine assistance in guiding his course through times which held out so many dangers and so many errors. And having thus poured out his spirit in prayer before the Great Being who gave it, he betook himself to the repose which he so much required.

CHAPTER 35

The charge is prepared, the lawyers are met,
The judges all ranged – a terrible show!

Beggar's Opera[1]

So deep was the slumber which succeeded the agitation and embarrassment of the preceding day, that Morton hardly knew where he was when it was broken by the tramp of horses, the hoarse voice of men, and the wild sound of the trumpets blowing the réveillé. The sergeant-major immediately afterwards came to summon him, which he did in a very respectful manner, saying the General (for Claverhouse now held that rank)[2] hoped for the pleasure of his company upon the road. In some situations an intimation is a command, and Morton considered that the present occasion was one of these. He waited upon Claverhouse as speedily as he could, found his own horse saddled for his use, and Cuddie in attendance. Both were deprived of their fire-arms, though they seemed, otherwise, rather to make part of the troop than of the prisoners; and Morton was permitted to retain his sword, the wearing which was, in those days, the distinguishing mark of a gentleman. Claverhouse seemed also to take pleasure in riding beside him, in conversing with him, and in confounding his ideas when he attempted to appreciate his real character. The gentleness and urbanity of that officer's general manners, the high and chivalrous sentiments of military devotion which he occasionally expressed, his deep and accurate insight into the human bosom, demanded at once the approbation and the wonder of those who conversed with him; while, on the other hand, his cold indifference to military violence and cruelty seemed altogether inconsistent with the social, and even admirable qualities which he displayed. Morton could not help, in his heart, contrasting him with Balfour of Burley; and so deeply did the idea impress him, that he dropped a hint of it as they rode together at some distance from the troop.

'You are right,' said Claverhouse, with a smile; 'you are very right – we are both fanatics; but there is some distinction between the fanaticism of honour and that of dark and sullen superstition.'

'Yet you both shed blood without mercy or remorse,' said Morton, who could not suppress his feelings.

'Surely,' said Claverhouse, with the same composure; 'but of what kind? – There is a difference, I trust, between the blood of learned and reverend prelates and scholars, of gallant soldiers and noble gentlemen, and the red puddle that stagnates in the veins of psalm-singing mechanics, crack-brained demagogues, and sullen boors; – some distinction, in short, between spilling a flask of generous wine, and dashing down a can full of base muddy ale?'

'Your distinction is too nice for my comprehension,' replied Morton. 'God gives every spark of life – that of the peasant as well as of the prince; and those who destroy his work recklessly or causelessly, must answer in either case. What right, for example, have I to General Grahame's protection now, more than when I first met him?'

'And narrowly escaped the consequences, you would say?' answered Claverhouse – 'why, I will answer you frankly. Then I thought I had to do with the son of an old roundheaded rebel, and the nephew of a sordid presbyterian laird; now I know your points better, and there is that about you which I respect in an enemy as much as I like in a friend. I have learned a good deal concerning you since our first meeting, and I trust that you have found that my construction of the information has not been unfavourable to you.'

'But yet,' said Morton –

'But yet,' interrupted Grahame, taking up the word, 'you would say you were the same when I first met you that you are now? True; but then, how could I know that? though, by the by, even my reluctance to suspend your execution may show you how high your abilities stood in my estimation.'

'Do you expect, General,' said Morton, 'that I ought to be particularly grateful for such a mark of your esteem?'

'Poh! poh! you are critical,' returned Claverhouse. 'I tell you I thought you a different sort of person. Did you ever read Froissart?' [3]

'No,' was Morton's answer.

'I have half a mind,' said Claverhouse, 'to contrive you should have six months' imprisonment in order to procure you that pleasure. His chapters inspire me with more enthusiasm than even poetry itself. And the noble canon, with what true chivalrous feeling he confines his beautiful expressions of sorrow to the death of the gallant and high-bred knight, of whom it was a pity to see the fall, such was his loyalty to his king, pure faith to his religion, hardihood towards his enemy, and fidelity to his lady-love! – Ah, benedicite! how he will mourn over the fall of such a pearl of knighthood, be it on the side he happens to favour, or on the other. But, truly, for sweeping from the face of the earth some few hundreds of villain churls, who are born but to plough it, the high-born and inquisitive historian has marvellous little sympathy, – as little, or less, perhaps, than John Grahame of Claverhouse.'

'There is one ploughman in your possession, General, for whom,' said Morton, 'in despite of the contempt in which you hold a profession which some philosophers have considered as useful as that of a soldier, I would humbly request your favour.'

'You mean,' said Claverhouse, looking at a memorandum book, 'one Hatherick – Hedderick – or – or – Headrigg. Ay, Cuthbert, or Cuddie Headrigg – here I have him. O, never fear him, if he will be but tractable. The ladies of Tillietudlem made interest with me on his account some time ago. He is to marry their waiting-maid, I think. He will be allowed to slip off easy, unless his obstinacy spoils his good fortune.'

'He has no ambition to be a martyr, I believe,' said Morton.

' 'Tis the better for him,' said Claverhouse. 'But, besides, although the fellow had more to answer for, I should stand his friend, for the sake of the blundering gallantry which threw him into the midst of our ranks last night, when seeking assistance for you. I never desert any man who trusts me with such implicit confidence. But, to deal sincerely with you, he has been long in our eye. – Here, Halliday; bring me up the black book.'⁴

The sergeant, having committed to his commander this ominous record of the disaffected, which was arranged in alphabetical order, Claverhouse, turning over the leaves as he rode on, began to read names as they occurred.

'Gumblegumption, a minister, aged 50, indulged, close, sly, and so forth – Pooh! pooh! – He – He – I have him here – Heathercat; outlawed – a preacher – a zealous Cameronian – keeps a conventicle among the Campsie hills – Tush! – O, here is Headrigg – Cuthbert; his mother a bitter puritan – himself a simple fellow – like to be forward in action, but of no genius for plots – more for the hand than the head, and might be drawn to the right side, but for his attachment to' – (Here Claverhouse looked at Morton, and then shut the book and changed his tone.) 'Faithful and true are words never thrown away upon me, Mr Morton. You may depend on the young man's safety.'

'Does it not revolt a mind like yours,' said Morton, 'to follow a system which is to be supported by such minute enquiries after obscure individuals?'

'You do not suppose *we* take the trouble?' said the General, haughtily. 'The curates, for their own sakes, willingly collect all these materials for their own regulation in each parish; they know best the black sheep of the flock. I have had your picture for three years.'

'Indeed?' replied Morton. 'Will you favour me by imparting it?'

'Willingly,' said Claverhouse; 'it can signify little, for you cannot avenge yourself on the curate, as you will probably leave Scotland for some time.'

This was spoken in an indifferent tone. Morton felt an involuntary shudder at hearing words which implied a banishment from his native land; but ere he answered, Claverhouse proceeded to read, 'Henry Morton, son of Silas Morton, Colonel of horse for the Scottish Parliament, nephew and apparent heir of Morton of Milnwood – imperfectly educated, but with spirit beyond his years – excellent at all exercises – indifferent to forms of religion, but seems to incline to the presbyterian – has high-flown and dangerous notions about liberty of thought and speech, and hovers between a latitudinarian and an enthusiast. Much admired and followed by the youth of his own age – modest, quiet, and unassuming in manner, but in his heart peculiarly bold and intractable. He is – Here follow three red crosses, Mr Morton, which signify triply dangerous. You see how important a person you are. – But what does this fellow want?'

A horseman rode up as he spoke, and gave a letter. Claverhouse glanced it over, laughed scornfully, bade him tell his master to send his prisoners to Edinburgh, for there was no answer; and, as the man turned back, said contemptuously to Morton – 'Here is an ally of yours deserted from you, or rather, I should say, an ally of your good friend Burley – Hear how he sets forth – "*Dear Sir*," (I wonder when we were such intimates,) "may it please your Excellency to accept my humble congratulations on the victory" – hum – hum – "blessed his Majesty's army. I pray you to understand I have my people under arms to take and intercept all fugitives, and have already several prisoners," and so forth. Subscribed Basil Olifant – You know the fellow by name, I suppose?'

'A relative of Lady Margaret Bellenden,' replied Morton, 'is he not?'

'Ay,' replied Grahame, 'and heir-male of her father's family, though a distant one, and moreover a suitor to the fair Edith, though discarded as an unworthy one; but, above all, a devoted admirer of the estate of Tillietudlem, and all thereunto belonging.'

'He takes an ill mode of recommending himself,' said Morton, suppressing his feelings, 'to the family at Tillietudlem, by corresponding with our unhappy party.'

'O, this precious Basil will turn cat in pan with any man!' replied Claverhouse. 'He was displeased with the government, because they would not overturn in his favour a settlement of the late Earl of Torwood, by which his lordship gave his own estate to his own daughter; he was displeased with Lady Margaret, because she avowed no desire for his alliance, and with the pretty Edith, because she did not like his tall ungainly person. So he held a close correspondence with Burley, and raised his followers with the purpose of helping him, providing always he needed no help, that is, if you had beat us yesterday. And now the rascal pretends he was all the while proposing the King's service, and, for aught I know, the council will receive his pretext for current coin, for he knows how to make friends among them – and a dozen scores of poor vagabond fanatics will be shot, or hanged, while this cunning scoundrel lies hid under the double cloak of loyalty, well-lined with the fox-fur of hypocrisy.'

With conversation on this and other matters they beguiled the way, Claverhouse all the while speaking with great frankness to Morton, and treating him rather as a friend and companion than as a prisoner; so that, however uncertain of his fate, the hours he passed in the company of this remarkable man were so much lightened by the varied play of his imagination, and the depth of his knowledge of human nature, that since the period of his becoming a prisoner of war, which relieved him at once from the cares of his doubtful and dangerous station among the insurgents, and from the consequences of their suspicious resentment, his hours flowed on less anxiously than at any time since his having commenced actor in public life. He was now, with respect to his fortune, like a rider who has flung his reins on the horse's neck, and, while he abandoned himself to circumstances, was at least relieved from the task of attempting to direct them. In this mood he journeyed on, the number of his companions being continually augmented by detached parties of horse who came in from every quarter of the country, bringing with them, for the most part, the unfortunate persons who had fallen into their power. At length they approached Edinburgh.

'Our council,' said Claverhouse, 'being resolved, I suppose, to testify by their present exultation the extent of their former terror, have decreed a kind of triumphal entry to us victors and our captives; but as I do not quite approve the taste of it, I am willing to avoid my own part in the show, and, at the same time, to save you from yours.'

So saying, he gave up the command of the forces to Allan, (now a Lieutenant-colonel,) and, turning his horse into a by-lane, rode into the city privately, accompanied by Morton and two or three servants. When Claverhouse arrived at the quarters which he usually occupied in the Canongate, he assigned to his prisoner a small apartment, with an intimation, that his parole confined him to it for the present.

After about a quarter of an hour spent in solitary musing on the strange vicissitudes of his late life, the attention of Morton was summoned to the window by a great noise in the street beneath. Trumpets, drums, and kettle-drums, contended in noise with the shouts of a numerous rabble, and apprised him that the royal cavalry were passing in the triumphal attitude which Claverhouse had mentioned. The magistrates of the city, attended by their guard of halberds, had met the victors with their welcome at the gate of the city, and now preceded them as a part of the procession. The next object was two heads borne upon pikes; and before each bloody head were carried the hands of the dismembered sufferers, which were, by the brutal mockery of those who bore them, often approached towards each other as if in the attitude of exhortation or prayer. These bloody trophies belonged to two preachers who had fallen at Bothwell Bridge. After them came a cart led by the executioner's assistant, in which were placed Macbriar, and other two prisoners, who seemed of the same profession. They were bareheaded, and strongly bound, yet looked around them with an air rather of triumph than dismay, and appeared in no respect moved either by the fate of their companions, of which the bloody evidences were carried before them, or by dread of their own approaching execution, which these preliminaries so plainly indicated.

Behind these prisoners, thus held up to public infamy and derision, came a body of horse, brandishing their broadswords, and filling the wide street with acclamations, which were answered by the tumultuous outcries and shouts of the rabble, who, in every considerable town, are too happy in being permitted to huzza for any thing whatever which calls them together. In the rear of these troopers came the main body of the prisoners, at the head of whom were some of their leaders, who were treated with every circumstance of inventive mockery and insult. Several were placed on horseback with their faces to the animal's tail; others were chained to long bars of iron, which they were obliged to support in their hands, like the galley-slaves in

Spain when travelling to the port where they are to be put on shipboard. The heads of others who had fallen were borne in triumph before the survivors, some on pikes and halberds, some in sacks, bearing the names of the slaughtered persons labelled on the outside. Such were the objects who headed the ghastly procession, who seemed as effectually doomed to death as if they wore the *sanbenitos* of the condemned heretics in an *auto-da-fe*.[5]

Behind them came on the nameless crowd to the number of several hundreds, some retaining under their misfortunes a sense of confidence in the cause for which they suffered captivity, and were about to give a still more bloody testimony; others seemed pale, dispirited, dejected, questioning in their own minds their prudence in espousing a cause which Providence seemed to have disowned, and looking about for some avenue through which they might escape from the consequences of their rashness. Others there were who seemed incapable of forming an opinion on the subject, or of entertaining either hope, confidence, or fear, but who, foaming with thirst and fatigue, stumbled along like over-driven oxen, lost to every thing but their present sense of wretchedness, and without having any distinct idea whether they were led to the shambles or to the pasture. These unfortunate men were guarded on each hand by troopers, and behind them came the main body of the cavalry, whose military music resounded back from the high houses on each side of the street, and mingled with their own songs of jubilee and triumph, and the wild shouts of the rabble.

Morton felt himself heart-sick while he gazed on the dismal spectacle, and recognised in the bloody heads, and still more miserable and agonized features of the living sufferers, faces which had been familiar to him during the brief insurrection. He sunk down in a chair in a bewildered and stupified state, from which he was awakened by the voice of Cuddie.

'Lord forgie us, sir!' said the poor fellow, his teeth chattering like a pair of nut-crackers, his hair erect like boar's bristles, and his face as pale as that of a corpse – 'Lord forgie us, sir! we maun instantly gang before the Council! – O Lord, what made them send for a puir bodie like me, sae mony braw lords and gentles! – and there's my mither come on the lang tramp frae Glasgow to see to gar me testify, as she ca's it, that is to say, confess and be hanged; but deil tak me if they mak sic a guse o' Cuddie, if I can do better. But here's Claverhouse himsell – the Lord preserve and forgie us, I say anes mair!'

'You must immediately attend the Council Mr Morton,' said Claverhouse, who entered while Cuddie spoke, 'and your servant must go with you. You need be under no apprehension for the consequences to yourself personally. But I warn you that you will see something that will give you much pain, and from which I would willingly have saved you, if I had possessed the power. My carriage waits us – shall we go?'

It will be readily supposed that Morton did not venture to dispute this invitation, however unpleasant. He rose and accompanied Claverhouse.

'I must apprise you,' said the latter, as he led the way down stairs, 'that you will get off cheap; and so will your servant, provided he can keep his tongue quiet.'

Cuddie caught these last words to his exceeding joy.

'Deil a fear o' me,' said he, 'an my mither disna pit her finger in the pie.'

At that moment his shoulder was seized by old Mause, who had contrived to thrust herself forward into the lobby of the apartment.

'O, hinny, hinny!' said she to Cuddie, hanging upon his neck, 'glad and proud, and sorry and humbled am I, a' in ane and the same instant, to see my bairn ganging to testify for the truth gloriously with his mouth in council, as he did with his weapon in the field!'

'Whisht, whisht, mither!' cried Cuddie impatiently. 'Odd, ye daft wife, is this a time to speak o' thae things? I tell ye I'll testify naething either ae gate or another. I hae spoken to Mr Poundtext, and I'll tak the declaration, or whate'er they ca' it, and we're a' to win free off if we do that – he's gotten life for himsell and a' his folk, and that's a minister for my siller; I like nane o' your sermons that end in a psalm at the Grassmarket.'[6]

'O, Cuddie, man, laith wad I be they suld hurt ye,' said old Mause, divided grievously between the safety of her son's soul and that of his body; 'but mind, my bonny bairn, ye hae battled for the faith, and dinna let the dread o' losing creature-comforts withdraw ye frae the gude fight.'

'Hout tout, mither,' replied Cuddie, 'I hae fought e'en ower muckle already, and, to speak plain, I'm wearied o' the trade. I hae swaggered wi' a' thae arms, and muskets, and pistols, buff-coats, and bandoliers, lang eneugh, and I like the pleugh-paidle a hantle better. I ken naething suld gar a man fight, (that's to say, when he's no angry,) by and out-taken the dread o' being hanged or killed if he turns back.'

'But, my dear Cuddie,' continued the persevering Mause, 'your bridal garment – Oh, hinny, dinna sully the marriage garment!'[7]

'Awa, awa, mither,' replied Cuddie; 'dinna ye see the folks waiting for me? – Never fear me – I ken how to turn this far better than ye do – for ye're bleezing awa about marriage, and the job is how we are to win by hanging.'

So saying, he extricated himself out of his mother's embraces, and requested the soldiers who took him in charge to conduct him to the place of examination without delay. He had been already preceded by Claverhouse and Morton.

CHAPTER 36

My native land, good night!

LORD BYRON[1]

THE Privy Council of Scotland, in whom the practice since the union of the crowns vested great judicial powers, as well as the general superintendence of the executive department, was met in the ancient dark Gothic room, adjoining to the House of Parliament in Edinburgh, when General Grahame entered and took his place amongst the members at the council table.

'You have brought us a leash of game to-day, General,' said a nobleman of high place amongst them.[2] 'Here is a craven to confess – a cock of the game to stand at bay – and what shall I call the third, General?'

'Without further metaphor, I will entreat your Grace to call him a person in whom I am specially interested,' replied Claver-house.

'And a whig into the bargain?' said the nobleman, lolling out a tongue which was at all times too big for his mouth, and accommodating his coarse features to a sneer, to which they seemed to be familiar.

'Yes, please your Grace, a whig; as your Grace was in 1641,' replied Claverhouse, with his usual appearance of imperturbable civility.

'He has you there, I think, my Lord Duke,' said one of the Privy Councillors.

'Ay, ay,' returned the Duke, laughing, 'there's no speaking to him since Drumclog – but come, bring in the prisoners – and do you, Mr Clerk, read the record.'

The clerk read forth a bond, in which General Grahame of Claverhouse and Lord Evandale entered themselves securities, that Henry Morton, younger of Milnwood, should go abroad and remain in foreign parts, until his Majesty's pleasure was further known, in respect of the said Henry Morton's accession to the late rebellion, and that under penalty of life and limb to the said Henry Morton, and of ten thousand marks to each of his securities.

'Do you accept of the King's mercy upon these terms, Mr Morton?' said the Duke of Lauderdale, who presided in the Council.

'I have no other choice, my lord,' replied Morton.

'Then subscribe your name in the record.'

Morton did so without reply, conscious that, in the circum-stances of his case, it was impossible for him to have escaped more easily. Macbriar, who was at the same instant brought to the foot of the council-table, bound upon a chair, for his weak-ness prevented him from standing, beheld Morton in the act of what he accounted apostasy.

'He hath summed his defection by owning the carnal power of the tyrant!' he exclaimed, with a deep groan – 'A fallen star! – a fallen star!'

'Hold your peace, sir,' said the Duke, 'and keep your ain breath to cool your ain porridge – ye'll find them scalding hot, I promise you. – Call in the other fellow, who has some common sense. One sheep will leap the ditch when another goes first.'

Cuddie was introduced unbound, but under the guard of two halberdiers, and placed beside Macbriar at the foot of the table. The poor fellow cast a piteous look around him, in which were mingled awe for the great men in whose presence he stood, and compassion for his fellow-sufferers, with no small fear of the personal consequences which impended over himself. He made his clownish obeisances with a double portion of reverence, and then awaited the opening of the awful scene.

'Were you at the battle of Bothwell Brigg?' was the first question which was thundered in his ears.

Cuddie meditated a denial, but had sense enough, upon reflection, to discover that the truth would be too strong for him; so he replied, with true Caledonian indirectness of response, 'I'll no say but it may be possible that I might hae been there.'

'Answer directly, you knave – yes, or no? – You know you were there.'

'It's no for me to contradict your Lordship's Grace's honour,' said Cuddie.

'Once more, sir, were you there? – yes, or no?' said the Duke, impatiently.

'Dear stir,' again replied Cuddie, 'how can ane mind preceesely where they hae been a' the days o' their life?'

'Speak out, you scoundrel,' said General Dalzell, 'or I'll dash your teeth out with my dudgeon-haft! – Do you think we can stand here all day to be turning and dodging with you, like greyhounds after a hare?'[3]

'Aweel, then,' said Cuddie, 'since naething else will please ye, write down that I cannot deny but I was there.'

'Well, sir,' said the Duke, 'and do you think that the rising upon that occasion was rebellion or not?'

'I'm no just free to gie my opinion, stir,' said the cautious captive, 'on what might cost my neck; but I doubt it will be very little better.'

'Better than what?'

'Just than rebellion, as your honour ca's it,' replied Cuddie.

'Well, sir, that's speaking to the purpose,' replied his Grace.

'And are you content to accept of the King's pardon for your guilt as a rebel, and to keep the church, and pray for the King?'

'Blithely, stir,' answered the unscrupulous Cuddie; 'and drink his health into the bargain, when the ale's gude.'

'Egad,' said the Duke, 'this is a hearty cock. – What brought you into such a scrape, mine honest friend?'

'Just ill example, stir,' replied the prisoner, 'and a daft auld jaud of a mither, wi' reverence to your Grace's honour.'

'Why, God-a-mercy, my friend,' replied the Duke, 'take care of bad advice another time; I think you are not likely to commit treason on your own score. – Make out his free pardon, and bring forward the rogue in the chair.'

Macbriar was then moved forward to the post of examination.

'Were you at the battle of Bothwell Bridge?' was, in like manner, demanded of him.

'I was,' answered the prisoner, in a bold and resolute tone.

'Were you armed?'

'I was not – I went in my calling as a preacher of God's word, to encourage them that drew the sword in His cause.'

'In other words, to aid and abet the rebels?' said the Duke.

'Thou hast spoken it,' replied the prisoner.

'Well, then,' continued the interrogator, 'let us know if you saw John Balfour of Burley among the party? – I presume you know him?'

'I bless God that I do know him,' replied Macbriar; 'he is a zealous and a sincere Christian.'

'And when and where did you last see this pious personage?' was the query which immediately followed.

'I am here to answer for myself,' said Macbriar, in the same dauntless manner, 'and not to endanger others.'

'We shall know,' said Dalzell, 'how to make you find your tongue.'

'If you can make him fancy himself in a conventicle,' answered Lauderdale, 'he will find it without you. – Come, laddie, speak while the play is good – you're too young to bear the burden will be laid on you else.'

'I defy you,' retorted Macbriar. 'This has not been the first of my imprisonments or of my sufferings; and, young as I may be,

I have lived long enough to know how to die when I am called upon.'

'Ay, but there are some things which must go before an easy death, if you continue obstinate,' said Lauderdale, and rung a small silver bell which was placed before him on the table.

A dark crimson curtain, which covered a sort of niche, or Gothic recess in the wall, rose at the signal, and displayed the public executioner, a tall, grim, and hideous man, having an oaken table before him, on which lay thumb-screws, and an iron case, called the Scottish boot, used in those tyrannical days to torture accused persons. Morton, who was unprepared for this ghastly apparition, started when the curtain arose, but Macbriar's nerves were more firm. He gazed upon the horrible apparatus with much composure; and if a touch of nature called the blood from his cheek for a second, resolution sent it back to his brow with greater energy.

'Do you know who that man is?' said Lauderdale, in a low, stern voice, almost sinking into a whisper.

'He is, I suppose,' replied Macbriar, 'the infamous executioner of your bloodthirsty commands upon the persons of God's people. He and you are equally beneath my regard; and, I bless God, I no more fear what he can inflict than what you can command. Flesh and blood may shrink under the sufferings you can doom me to, and poor frail nature may shed tears, or send forth cries; but I trust my soul is anchored firmly on the rock of ages.'

'Do your duty,' said the Duke to the executioner.

The fellow advanced, and asked, with a harsh and discordant voice, upon which of the prisoner's limbs he should first employ his engine.

'Let him choose for himself,' said the Duke; 'I should like to oblige him in any thing that is reasonable.'

'Since you leave it to me,' said the prisoner, stretching forth his right leg, 'take the best – I willingly bestow it in the cause for which I suffer.'[4]

The executioner, with the help of his assistants, enclosed the leg and knee within the tight iron boot, or case, and then placing a wedge of the same metal between the knee and the edge of the machine, took a mallet in his hand, and stood waiting for farther orders. A well-dressed man, by profession a surgeon, placed himself by the other side of the prisoner's chair, bared the prisoner's arm, and applied his thumb to the pulse in order to regulate the torture according to the strength of the patient. When these preparations were made, the President of the Council repeated with the same stern voice the question, 'When and where did you last see John Balfour of Burley?'

The prisoner, instead of replying to him, turned his eyes to heaven as if imploring Divine strength, and muttered a few words, of which the last were distinctly audible, 'Thou hast said thy people shall be willing in the day of thy power!'[5]

The Duke of Lauderdale glanced his eye around the council as if to collect their suffrages, and, judging from their mute signs, gave on his own part a nod to the executioner, whose mallet instantly descended on the wedge, and, forcing it between the knee and the iron boot, occasioned the most exquisite pain, as was evident from the flush which instantly took place on the brow and on the cheeks of the sufferer. The fellow then again raised his weapon, and stood prepared to give a second blow.

'Will you yet say,' repeated the Duke of Lauderdale, 'where and when you last parted from Balfour of Burley?'

'You have my answer,' said the sufferer resolutely, and the second blow fell. The third and fourth succeeded; but at the fifth, when a larger wedge had been introduced, the prisoner set up a scream of agony.

Morton, whose blood boiled within him at witnessing such cruelty, could bear no longer, and, although unarmed and himself in great danger, was springing forward, when Claverhouse, who observed his emotion, withheld him by force, laying one hand on his arm and the other on his mouth, while he whispered, 'For God's sake, think where you are!'

This movement, fortunately for him, was observed by no other of the councillors, whose attention was engaged with the dreadful scene before them.

'He is gone,' said the surgeon – 'he has fainted, my Lords, and human nature can endure no more.'

'Release him,' said the Duke; and added, turning to Dalzell, 'He will make an old proverb good, for he'll scarce ride to-day, though he has had his boots on. I suppose we must finish with him?'

'Ay, dispatch his sentence, and have done with him; we have plenty of drudgery behind.'

Strong waters and essences were busily employed to recall the senses of the unfortunate captive; and, when his first faint gasps intimated a return of sensation, the Duke pronounced sentence of death upon him, as a traitor taken in the act of open rebellion, and adjudged him to be carried from the bar to the common place of execution, and there hanged by the neck; his head and hands to be stricken off after death, and disposed of according to the pleasure of the Council,[6] and all and sundry his movable goods and gear escheat and inbrought to his Majesty's use.

'Doomster,' he continued, 'repeat the sentence to the prisoner.'

The office of Doomster was in those days, and till a much later period, held by the executioner *in commendam*, with his ordinary functions.[7] The duty consisted in reciting to the unhappy criminal the sentence of the law as pronounced by the judge, which acquired an additional and horrid emphasis from the recollection, that the hateful personage by whom it was uttered was to be the agent of the cruelties he denounced. Macbriar had scarce understood the purport of the words as first pronounced by the Lord President of the Council; but he was sufficiently recovered to listen and to reply to the sentence when uttered by the harsh and odious voice of the ruffian who was to execute it, and at the last awful words, 'And this I pronounce for doom,' he answered boldly – 'My Lords, I thank you for the only favour I looked for, or would accept at your hands, namely, that you have sent the crushed and maimed carcass, which has this day sustained your cruelty, to this hasty end. It were indeed little to me whether I perish on the gallows or in the prison-house; but if death, following close on what I have this day suffered, had found me in my cell of darkness and bondage, many might have lost the sight how a Christian man can suffer in the good cause. For the rest, I forgive you, my Lords, for what you have appointed and I have sustained – And why should I not? – Ye send me to a happy exchange – to the company of angels and the spirits of the just, for that of frail dust and ashes – Ye send me from darkness into day – from mortality to immortality – and, in a word, from earth to heaven! – If the thanks, therefore, and pardon of a dying man can do you good, take them at my hand, and may your last moments be as happy as mine!'

As he spoke thus, with a countenance radiant with joy and triumph, he was withdrawn by those who had brought him into the apartment, and executed within half an hour, dying with the same enthusiastic firmness which his whole life had evinced.

The Council broke up, and Morton found himself again in the carriage with General Grahame.

'Marvellous firmness and gallantry!' said Morton, as he reflected upon Macbriar's conduct; 'what a pity it is that with such self-devotion and heroism should have been mingled the fiercer features of his sect!'

'You mean,' said Claverhouse, 'his resolution to condemn you to death? – To that he would have reconciled himself by a single text; for example, "And Phinehas arose and executed judgment",[8] or something to the same purpose. – But wot ye where you are now bound, Mr Morton?'

'We are on the road to Leith, I observe,' answered Morton. 'Can I not be permitted to see my friends ere I leave my native land?'

'Your uncle,' replied Grahame, 'has been spoken to, and declines visiting you. The good gentleman is terrified, and not without some reason, that the crime of your treason may extend itself over his lands and tenements – he sends you, however, his blessing, and a small sum of money. Lord Evandale continues extremely indisposed. Major Bellenden is at Tillietudlem putting matters in order. The scoundrels have made great havoc there with Lady Margaret's muniments of antiquity, and have desecrated and destroyed what the good lady called the Throne of his most Sacred Majesty. Is there any one else whom you would wish to see?'

Morton sighed deeply as he answered, 'No – it would avail nothing. – But my preparations, – small as they are, some must be necessary.'

'They are all ready for you,' said the General. 'Lord Evandale has anticipated all you wish. Here is a packet from him with letters of recommendation for the court of the Stadtholder Prince of Orange, to which I have added one or two. I made my first campaigns under him, and first saw fire at the battle of Seneff.[9] There are also bills of exchange for your immediate wants, and more will be sent when you require it.'

Morton heard all this and received the parcel with an astounded and confused look, so sudden was the execution of the sentence of banishment.

'And my servant?' he said.

'He shall be taken care of, and replaced, if it be practicable, in the service of Lady Margaret Bellenden; I think he will hardly neglect the parade of the feudal retainers, or go a-whigging a second time. – But here we are upon the quay, and the boat waits you.'

It was even as Claverhouse said. A boat waited for Captain Morton, with the trunks and baggage belonging to his rank. Claverhouse shook him by the hand, and wished him good fortune, and a happy return to Scotland in quieter times.

'I shall never forget,' he said, 'the gallantry of your behaviour to my friend Evandale, in circumstances when many men would have sought to rid him out of their way.'

Another friendly pressure, and they parted. As Morton descended the pier to get into the boat, a hand placed in his a letter folded up in very small space. He looked round. The person who gave it seemed much muffled up; he pressed his finger upon his lip, and then disappeared among the crowd. The incident awakened Morton's curiosity; and when he found himself on board of a vessel bound for Rotterdam, and saw all his companions of the voyage busy making their own arrangements, he took an opportunity to open the billet thus mysteriously thrust upon him. It ran thus:– 'Thy courage on the fatal day when Israel fled before his enemies, hath, in some measure, atoned for thy unhappy owning of the Erastian interest. These are not days for Ephraim to strive with Israel.[10] – I know thy heart is with the daughter of the stranger. But turn from that folly; for in exile, and in flight, and even in death itself, shall my hand be heavy against that bloody and malignant house, and Providence hath given me the means of meting unto them with their own measure of ruin and confiscation. The resistance of their stronghold was the main cause of our being scattered at Bothwell Bridge, and I have bound it upon my soul to visit it upon them. Wherefore, think of her no more, but join with our brethren in banishment, whose hearts are still towards this miserable land to save and to relieve her. There is an honest remnant in Holland whose eyes are looking out for deliverance. Join thyself unto them like the true son of the stout and worthy Silas Morton, and thou wilt have good acceptance among them for his sake and for thine own working. Shouldst thou be found worthy again to labour in the vineyard, thou wilt at all times hear of my incomings and out-goings, by enquiring after Quintin Mackell of Irongray, at the house of that singular Christian woman, Bessie Maclure, near to the place called the Howff, where Niel Blane entertaineth guests. So much from him who hopes to hear again from thee in brotherhood, resisting unto blood, and striving against sin. Meanwhile, possess thyself in patience. Keep thy sword girded, and thy lamp burning, as one that wakes in the night; for He who shall judge the Mount of Esau, and shall make false professors as straw, and malignants as stubble, will come in the fourth watch with garments dyed in blood, and the house of Jacob shall be for spoil, and the house of Joseph for fire. I am he that hath written it, whose hand hath been on the mighty in the waste field.'[11]

This extraordinary letter was subscribed J. B. of B.; but the signature of these initials was not necessary for pointing out to Morton that it could come from no other than Burley. It gave him new occasion to admire the indomitable spirit of this man, who, with art equal to his courage and obstinacy, was even now endeavouring to re-establish the web of conspiracy which had been so lately torn to pieces. But he felt no sort of desire, in the present moment, to sustain a correspondence which must be perilous, or to renew an association, which, in so many ways, had been nearly fatal to him. The threats which Burley held out against the family of Bellenden, he considered as a mere expression of his spleen on account of their defence of Tillietudlem; and nothing seemed less likely than that, at the very moment of their party being victorious, their fugitive and distressed adversary could exercise the least influence over their fortunes.

Morton, however, hesitated for an instant, whether he should not send the Major or Lord Evandale intimation of Burley's threats. Upon consideration, he thought he could not do so without betraying his confidential correspondence; for to warn them of his menaces would have served little purpose, unless he had given them a clew to prevent them, by apprehending his person; while, by doing so, he deemed he should commit an ungenerous breach of trust to remedy an evil which seemed almost imaginary. Upon mature consideration, therefore, he tore the letter, having first made a memorandum of the name and place where the writer was to be heard of, and threw the fragments into the sea.

While Morton was thus employed the vessel was unmoored, and the white sails swelled out before a favourable north-west wind. The ship leaned her side to the gale, and went roaring through the waves, leaving a long and rippling furrow to track her course. The city and port from which he had sailed became undistinguishable in the distance; the hills by which they were surrounded melted finally into the blue sky, and Morton was separated for several years from the land of his nativity.

CHAPTER 37

Whom does time gallop withal?

As You Like it[1]

IT is fortunate for tale-tellers that they are not tied down like theatrical writers to the unities of time and place, but may conduct their personages to Athens and Thebes at their pleasure, and bring them back at their convenience. Time, to use Rosalind's simile, has hitherto paced with the hero of our tale; for, betwixt Morton's first appearances as a competitor for the popinjay, and his final departure for Holland, hardly two months elapsed. Years, however, glided away ere we find it possible to resume the thread of our narrative, and Time must be held to have galloped over the interval. Craving, therefore, the privilege of my cast, I entreat the reader's attention to the continuation of the narrative, as it starts from a new era, being the year immediately subsequent to the British Revolution.[2]

Scotland had just begun to repose from the convulsion occasioned by a change of dynasty, and, through the prudent tolerance of King William, had narrowly escaped the horrors of a protracted civil war. Agriculture began to revive;[3] and men, whose minds had been disturbed by the violent political concussions, and the general change of government in church and state, had begun to recover their ordinary temper, and to give the usual attention to their own private affairs in lieu of discussing those of the public. The Highlanders alone resisted the newly-established order of things, and were in arms in a considerable body under the Viscount of Dundee, whom our readers have hitherto known by the name of Grahame of Claverhouse. But the usual state of the Highlands was so unruly, that their being more or less disturbed was not supposed greatly to affect the general tranquillity of the country, so long as their disorders were confined within their own frontiers. In the Lowlands, the Jacobites, now the undermost party, had ceased to expect any immediate advantage by open resistance, and were, in their turn, driven to hold private meetings, and form associations for mutual defence, which the government termed treason, while *they* cried out persecution.

The triumphant whigs, while they re-established presbytery as the national religion, and assigned to the General Assemblies of the Kirk their natural influence, were very far from going the lengths which the Cameronians and more extravagant portion of the non-conformists under Charles and James loudly demanded. They would listen to no proposal for re-establishing the Solemn League and Covenant; and those who had expected to find in King William a zealous Covenanted Monarch, were grievously disappointed when he intimated, with the phlegm peculiar to his country, his intention to tolerate all forms of religion which were consistent with the safety of the state. The principles of indulgence thus espoused and gloried in by the government, gave great offence to the more violent party, who condemned them as diametrically contrary to Scripture; for which narrow-spirited doctrine they cited various texts, all, as it may well be supposed, detached from their context, and most of them derived from the charges given to the Jews in the Old Testament dispensation, to extirpate idolaters out of the promised land. They also murmured highly against the influence assumed by secular persons in exercising the rights of patronage, which they termed a rape upon the chastity of the Church. They censured and condemned as Erastian many of the measures, by which government after the Revolution showed an inclination to interfere with the management of the Church, and they positively refused to take the oath of allegiance to King William and Queen Mary, until they should, on their part, have sworn to the Solemn League and Covenant, the Magna Charta, as they termed it, of the Presbyterian Church.

This party, therefore, remained grumbling and dissatisfied, and made repeated declarations against defections and causes of wrath, which, had they been prosecuted as in the two former reigns, would have led to the same consequence of open rebellion. But as the murmurers were allowed to hold their meetings uninterrupted, and to testify as much as they pleased against Socinianism, Erastianism, and all the compliances and defections of the time, their zeal, unfanned by persecution, died gradually away, their numbers became diminished, and they sunk into the scattered remnant of serious, scrupulous, and harmless enthusiasts, of whom Old Mortality, whose legends have afforded the groundwork of my tale, may be taken as no bad representative. But in the years which immediately succeeded the Revolution, the Cameronians continued a sect strong in numbers and vehement in their political opinions, whom government wished to discourage, while they prudently temporized with them. These men formed one violent party in the state; and the Episcopalian and Jacobite interest, notwithstanding their ancient and national animosity, yet repeatedly endeavoured to intrigue among them, and avail themselves of their discontents, to obtain their assistance in recalling the Stewart family. The Revolutionary government, in the meanwhile, was supported by the great bulk of the Lowland interest, who were chiefly disposed to a moderate presbytery, and formed in a great measure the party, who, in the former oppressive reigns, were stigmatized by the Cameronians, for having exercised that form of worship under the declaration of Indulgence issued by Charles II. Such was the state of parties in Scotland immediately subsequent to the Revolution.

It was on a delightful summer evening, that a stranger, well mounted, and having the appearance of a military man of rank, rode down a winding descent which terminated in view of the romantic ruins of Bothwell Castle and the river Clyde, which winds so beautifully between rocks and woods to sweep around the towers formerly built by Aymer de Valence.[4] Bothwell Bridge was at a little distance, and also in sight. The opposite field, once the scene of slaughter and conflict, now lay as placid and quiet as the surface of a summer lake. The trees and bushes, which grew around in romantic variety of shade, were hardly seen to stir under the influence of the evening breeze. The very murmur of the river seemed to soften itself into unison with the stillness of the scene around.

The path, through which the traveller descended, was occasionally shaded by detached trees of great size, and elsewhere by the hedges and boughs of flourishing orchards, now laden with summer fruits.

The nearest object of consequence was a farmhouse, or, it might be, the abode of a small proprietor, situated on the side of a sunny bank, which was covered by apple and pear trees. At the foot of the path which led up to this modest mansion was a small cottage, pretty much in the situation of a porter's lodge, though obviously not designed for such a purpose. The hut seemed comfortable, and more neatly arranged than is usual in Scotland. It had its little garden, where some fruit-trees and bushes were mingled with kitchen herbs; a cow and six sheep fed in a paddock hard by; the cock strutted and crowed, and summoned his family around him before the door; a heap of brushwood and turf, neatly made up, indicated that the winter fuel was provided; and the thin blue smoke which ascended from the straw-bound chimney, and winded slowly out from among the green trees, showed that the evening meal was in the act of being made ready. To complete the little scene of rural peace and comfort, a girl of

about five years old was fetching water in a pitcher from a beautiful fountain of the purest transparency, which bubbled up at
the root of a decayed old oak-tree, about twenty yards from the
end of the cottage.

The stranger reined up his horse, and called to the little
nymph, desiring to know the way to Fairy-Knowe. The child
set down her water-pitcher, hardly understanding what was said
to her, put her fair flaxen hair apart on her brows, and opened
her round blue eyes with the wondering, 'What's your wull?'
which is usually a peasant's first answer, if it can be called one,
to all questions whatever.

'I wish to know the way to Fairy-Knowe.'

'Mammie, mammie,' exclaimed the little rustic, running towards the door of the hut, 'come out and speak to the gentleman.'

Her mother appeared, – a handsome young country-woman,
to whose features, originally sly and espiegle in expression, matrimony had given that decent matronly air which peculiarly marks
the peasant's wife of Scotland. She had an infant in one arm,
and with the other she smoothed down her apron, to which
hung a chubby child of two years old. The elder girl, whom the
traveller had first seen, fell back behind her mother as soon as
she appeared, and kept that station, occasionally peeping out to
look at the stranger.

'What was your pleasure, sir?' said the woman, with an air of
respectful breeding, not quite common in her rank of life, but
without any thing resembling forwardness.

The stranger looked at her with great earnestness for a
moment, and then replied, 'I am seeking a place called Fairy-
Knowe, and a man called Cuthbert Headrigg. You can probably
direct me to him?'

'It's my gudeman, sir,' said the young woman, with a smile of
welcome; 'will you alight, sir, and come into our puir dwelling?
– Cuddie, Cuddie,' – (a white-headed rogue of four years appeared at the door of the hut) – 'Rin awa, my bonny man, and
tell your father a gentleman wants him. – Or, stay – Jenny, ye'll
hae mair sense – rin ye awa and tell him; he's down at the Four-

acres Park. – Winna ye light down and bide a blink, sir? – Or
would ye take a mouthfu' o' bread and cheese, or a drink o' ale,
till our gudeman comes? It's gude ale, though I shouldna say sae
that brews it; but ploughman-lads work hard, and maun hae
something to keep their hearts abune by ordinar, sae I aye pit a
gude gowpin o' maut to the browst.'

As the stranger declined her courteous offers, Cuddie, the
reader's old acquaintance, made his appearance in person. His
countenance still presented the same mixture of apparent dullness with occasional sparkles, which indicated the craft so often
found in the clouted shoe. He looked on the rider as on one
whom he never had before seen; and, like his daughter and wife,
opened the conversation with the regular query, 'What's your
wull wi' me, sir?'

'I have a curiosity to ask some questions about this country,'
said the traveller, 'and I was directed to you as an intelligent
man who can answer them.'

'Nae doubt, sir,' said Cuddie, after a moment's hesitation –
'But I would first like to ken what sort of questions they are. I
hae had sae mony questions speered at me in my day, and in sic
queer ways, that if ye kend a', ye wadna wonder at my jalousing
a' thing about them. My mother gar'd me learn the Single
Carritch,[5] whilk was a great vex; then I behoved to learn about
my godfathers and godmothers to please the auld leddy; and
while I jumbled them thegether and pleased nane o' them; and
when I cam to man's yestate, cam another kind o' questioning in
fashion, that I liked waur than Effectual Calling;[6] and the "did
promise and vow" of the tane were yokit to the end o' the tother.
Sae ye see, sir, I aye like to hear questions asked before I answer
them.'

'You have nothing to apprehend from mine, my good friend;
they only relate to the state of the country.'

'Country?' replied Cuddie; 'ou, the country's weel eneugh, an
it werena that dour deevil, Claver'se, (they ca' him Dundee now,)
that's stirring about yet in the Highlands, they say, wi' a' the
Donalds, and Duncans, and Dugalds, that ever wore bottom-
less breeks, driving about wi' him, to set things asteer again, now
we hae gotten them a' reasonably weel settled. But Mackay [7] will

pit him down, there's little doubt o' that; he'll gie him his fairing, I'll be caution for it.'

'What makes you so positive of that, my friend?' asked the horseman.

'I heard it wi' my ain lugs,' answered Cuddie, 'foretauld to him by a man that had been three hours stane dead, and came back to this earth again just to tell him his mind. It was at a place they ca' Drumshinnel.'

'Indeed?' said the stranger; 'I can hardly believe you, my friend.'

'Ye might ask my mither, then, if she were in life,' said Cuddie; 'it was her explained it a' to me, for I thought the man had only been wounded. At ony rate, he spake of the casting out of the Stewarts by their very names, and the vengeance that was brewing for Claver'se, and his dragoons. They ca'd the man Habakkuk Mucklewrath; his brain was a wee ajee, but he was a braw preacher for a' that.'

'You seem,' said the stranger, 'to live in a rich and peaceful country.'

'It's no to compleen o', sir, an we get the crap weel in,' quoth Cuddie; 'but if ye had seen the blude rinnin' as fast on the tap o' that brigg yonder as ever the water ran below it, ye wadna hae thought it sae bonnie a spectacle.'

'You mean the battle some years since? – I was waiting upon Monmouth that morning, my good friend, and did see some part of the action,' said the stranger.

'Then ye saw a bonny stour,' said Cuddie, 'that sall serve me for fighting a' the days o' my life. – I judged ye wad be a trooper, by your red scarlet lace-coat and your looped hat.'

'And which side were you upon, my friend?' continued the inquisitive stranger.

'Aha, lad?' retorted Cuddie, with a knowing look, or what he designed for such – 'there's nae use in telling that, unless I kend wha was asking me.'

'I commend your prudence, but it is unnecessary; I know you acted on that occasion as servant to Henry Morton.'

'Ay!' said Cuddie, in surprise, 'how came ye by that secret? – No that I need care a bodle about it, for the sun's on our side o' the hedge now. I wish my master were living to get a blink o't.'

'And what became of him?' said the rider.

'He was lost in the vessel gaun to that weary Holland – clean lost, and a' body perished, and my poor master amang them. Neither man nor mouse was ever heard o' mair.' Then Cuddie uttered a groan.

'You had some regard for him, then?' continued the stranger.

'How could I help it? – His face was made of a fiddle, as they say, for a' body that looked on him liked him. And a braw soldier he was. O, an ye had but seen him down at the brigg there, fleeing about like a fleeing dragon to gar folk fight that had unco little will till't! There was he and that sour whigamore they ca'd Burley – if twa men could hae won a field, we wadna hae gotten our skins paid that day.'

'You mention Burley – Do you know if he yet lives?'

'I kenna muckle about him. Folk say he was abroad, and our sufferers wad hold no communion wi' him, because o' his having murdered the archbishop. Sae he cam hame ten times dourer than ever, and broke aff wi' mony o' the presbyterians; and, at this last coming of the Prince of Orange, he could get nae countenance nor command for fear of his deevilish temper, and he hasna been heard of since; only some folk say, that pride and anger hae driven him clean wud.'

'And – and,' said the traveller, after considerable hesitation, – 'do you know any thing of Lord Evandale?'

'Div I ken ony thing o' Lord Evandale? – Div I no? Is not my young leddy up by yonder at the house, that's as gude as married to him?'

'And are they not married, then?' said the rider, hastily.

'No; only what they ca' betrothed – me and my wife were witnesses – it's no mony months bypast – it was a lang courtship – few folk kend the reason by Jenny and mysell. But will ye no light down? I downa bide to see ye sitting up there, and the clouds are casting up thick in the west ower Glasgow-ward, and maist skeily folk think that bodes rain.'

In fact, a deep black cloud had already surmounted the setting sun; a few large drops of rain fell, and the murmurs of distant thunder were heard.

'The deil's in this man,' said Cuddie to himself; 'I wish he would either light aff or ride on, that he may quarter himsell in Hamilton or the shower begin.'

But the rider sate motionless on his horse for two or three moments after his last question, like one exhausted by some uncommon effort. At length, recovering himself, as if with a sudden and painful effort, he asked Cuddie, 'if Lady Margaret Bellenden still lived.'

'She does,' replied Cuddie, 'but in a very sma' way. They hae been a sad changed family since thae rough times began; they hae suffered eneugh first and last – and to lose the auld Tower and a' the bonny barony and the holms that I hae pleughed sae often, and the Mains, and my kale-yard, that I suld hae gotten back again, and a' for naething, as a body may say, but just the want o' some bits of sheep-skin that were lost in the confusion of the taking of Tillietudlem.'

'I have heard something of this,' said the stranger, deepening his voice, and averting his head. 'I have some interest in the family, and would willingly help them if I could. Can you give me a bed in your house to-night, my friend?'

'It's but a corner of a place, sir,' said Cuddie, 'but we'se try, rather than ye suld ride on in the rain and thunner; for, to be free wi' ye, sir, I think ye seem no that ower weel.'

'I am liable to a dizziness,' said the stranger, 'but it will soon wear off.'

'I ken we can gie ye a decent supper, sir,' said Cuddie; 'and we'll see about a bed as weel as we can. We wad be laith a stranger suld lack what we have, though we are jimply provided for in beds rather; for Jenny has sae mony bairns, (God bless them and her,) that troth I maun speak to Lord Evandale to gie us a bit eik, or outshot o' some sort, to the onstead.'

'I shall be easily accommodated,' said the stranger, as he entered the house.

'And ye may rely on your naig being weel sorted,' said Cuddie; 'I ken weel what belangs to suppering a horse, and this is a very gude ane.'

Cuddie took the horse to the little cow-house, and called to his wife to attend in the meanwhile to the stranger's accommodation.

The officer entered, and threw himself on a settle at some distance from the fire, and carefully turning his back to the little lattice window. Jenny, or Mrs Headrigg, if the reader pleases, requested him to lay aside the cloak, belt, and flapped hat, which he wore upon his journey, but he excused himself under pretence of feeling cold; and, to divert the time till Cuddie's return, he entered into some chat with the children, carefully avoiding, during the interval, the inquisitive glances of his landlady.

CHAPTER 38

What tragic tears bedim the eye!
What deaths we suffer ere we die!
Our broken friendships we deplore,
And loves of youth that are no more.
                                        LOGAN[1]

CUDDIE soon returned, assuring the stranger, with a cheerful voice, 'that the horse was properly suppered up, and that the gudewife should make a bed up for him at the house, mair purpose-like and comfortable than the like o' them could gie him.'

'Are the family at the house?' said the stranger, with an interrupted and broken voice.

'No, stir; they're awa wi' a' the servants – they keep only twa now-a-days, and my gudewife there has the keys and the charge, though she's no a fee'd servant. She has been born and bred in the family, and has a' trust and management. If they were there, we behovedna to take sic freedom without their order; but when they are awa, they will be weel pleased we serve a stranger gentleman. Miss Bellenden wad help a' the haill warld, an her power were as gude as her will; and her grandmother, Leddy Margaret, has an unco respect for the gentry, and she's no ill to the poor bodies neither – And now, wife, what for are ye no getting forrit wi' the sowens?'

'Never mind, lad,' rejoined Jenny, 'ye sall hae them in gude time; I ken weel that ye like your brose het.'

Cuddie fidgeted, and laughed with a peculiar expression of intelligence at this repartee, which was followed by a dialogue of little consequence betwixt his wife and him, in which the stranger took no share. At length he suddenly interrupted them by the question – 'Can you tell me when Lord Evandale's marriage takes place?'

'Very soon, we expect,' answered Jenny, before it was possible for her husband to reply; 'it wad hae been ower afore now, but for the death o' auld Major Bellenden.'

'The excellent old man!' said the stranger; 'I heard at Edinburgh he was no more – Was he long ill?'

'He couldna be said to haud up his head after his brother's wife and his niece were turned out o' their ain house; and he had himsell sair borrowing siller to stand the law – but it was in the latter end o' King James's days – and Basil Olifant, who claimed the estate, turned a papist to please the managers,[2] and then naething was to be refused him; sae the law gaed again the leddies at last, after they had fought a weary sort o' years about it; and, as I said before, the Major ne'er held up his head again. And then cam the pitting awa o' the Stewart line; and, though he had but little reason to like them, he couldna brook that, and it clean broke the heart o' him, and creditors cam to Charnwood and cleaned out a' that was there – he was never rich, the gude auld man, for he dow'd na see ony body want.'

'He was indeed,' said the stranger, with a faltering voice, 'an admirable man – that is, I have heard that he was so. – So the ladies were left without fortune, as well as without a protector?'

'They will neither want the tane nor the tother while Lord Evandale lives,' said Jenny; 'he has been a true friend in their griefs – E'en to the house they live in is his lordship's; and never man, as my auld gudemother used to say, since the days of the patriarch Jacob, served sae lang and sae sair for a wife as gude Lord Evandale has dune.'

'And why,' said the stranger, with a voice that quivered with emotion, 'why was he not sooner rewarded by the object of his attachment?'

'There was the lawsuit to be ended,' said Jenny readily, 'forby many other family arrangements.'

'Na, but,' said Cuddie, 'there was another reason forby; for the young leddy' –

'Whisht, haud your tongue, and sup your sowens,' said his wife; 'I see the gentleman's far frae weel, and downa eat our coarse supper – I wad kill him a chicken in an instant.'

'There is no occasion,' said the stranger; 'I shall want only a glass of water, and to be left alone.'

'You'll gie yoursell the trouble then to follow me,' said Jenny, lighting a small lantern, 'and I'll show you the way.'

Cuddie also proffered his assistance; but his wife reminded him, 'That the bairns would be left to fight thegither, and coup ane anither into the fire,' so that he remained to take charge of the menage.

His wife led the way up a little winding path, which, after threading some thickets of sweetbrier and honeysuckle, conducted to the back-door of a small garden. Jenny undid the latch, and they passed through an old-fashioned flowergarden, with its clipped yew hedges and formal parterres, to a glass-sashed door, which she opened with a master-key, and lighting a candle, which she placed upon a small work-table, asked pardon for leaving him there for a few minutes, until she prepared his apartment. She did not exceed five minutes in these preparations; but, when she returned, was startled to find that the stranger had sunk forward with his head upon the table, in what she at first apprehended to be a swoon. As she advanced to him, however, she could discover by his short-drawn sobs that it was a paroxysm of mental agony. She prudently drew back until he raised his head, and then showing herself, without seeming to have observed his agitation, informed him, that his bed was prepared. The stranger gazed at her a moment, as if to collect the sense of her words. She repeated them, and only bending his head, as an indication that he understood her, he entered the apartment, the door of which she pointed out to him. It was a small bedchamber, used, as she informed him, by Lord Evandale when a guest at Fairy-Knowe, connecting, on one side, with a little china-cabinet, which opened to the garden, and on the other, with a saloon, from which it was only separated by a thin wainscot partition. Having wished the stranger better health and good rest, Jenny descended as speedily as she could to her own mansion.

'O, Cuddie!' she exclaimed to her helpmate as she entered, 'I doubt we're ruined folk!'

'How can that be? What's the matter wi' ye?' returned the imperturbed Cuddie, who was one of those persons who do not easily take alarm at any thing.

'Wha d'ye think yon gentleman is? – O, that ever ye suld hae asked him to light here!' exclaimed Jenny.

'Why, wha the muckle deil d'ye say he is? There's nae law against harbouring and intercommunicating now,' said Cuddie, 'sae, whig or tory, what need we care wha he be?'

'Ay, but it's ane will ding Lord Evandale's marriage ajee yet, if it's no the better looked to,' said Jenny; 'it's Miss Edith's first joe, your ain auld maister, Cuddie.'

'The deil, woman!' exclaimed Cuddie, starting up, 'trow ye that I am blind? I wad hae kend Mr Harry Morton amang a hunder.'

'Ay, but, Cuddie lad,' replied Jenny, 'though ye are no blind, ye are no sae notice-taking as I am.'

'Weel, what for needs ye cast that up to me just now? or what did ye see about the man that was like our Maister Harry?'

'I will tell ye,' said Jenny; 'I jaloused his keeping his face frae us, and speaking wi' a made-like voice, sae I e'en tried him wi' some tales o' lang syne, and when I spake o' the brose, ye ken, he didna just laugh – he's ower grave for that now-a-days – but he gae a gledge wi' his ee that I kend he took up what I said. And a' his distress is about Miss Edith's marriage, and I ne'er saw a man mair taen down wi' true love in my days – I might say man or woman – only I mind how ill Miss Edith was when she first gat word that him and you (ye muckle graceless loon) were coming against Tillietudlem wi' the rebels. – But what's the matter wi' the man now?'

'What's the matter wi' me, indeed!' said Cuddie, who was again hastily putting on some of the garments he had stripped himself of, 'am I no gaun up this instant to see my maister?'

'Atweel, Cuddie, ye are gaun nae sic gate,' said Jenny, coolly and resolutely.

'The deil's in the wife!' said Cuddie; 'd'ye think I am to be John Tamson's man,[3] and maistered by women a' the days o' my life?'

'And whase man wad ye be? And wha wad ye hae to maister ye but me, Cuddie, lad?' answered Jenny. 'I'll gar ye comprehend in the making of a hay-band. Naebody kens that this young gentleman is living but oursells, and frae that he keeps himsell up sae close, I am judging that he's purposing, if he fand Miss Edith either married, or just gaun to be married, he wad just slide awa easy, and gie them nae mair trouble. But if Miss Edith kend that he was living, and if she were standing before the very minister wi' Lord Evandale when it was tauld to her, I'se warrant she wad say No when she suld say Yes.'

'Weel,' replied Cuddie, 'and what's my business wi' that? if Miss Edith likes her auld joe better than her new ane, what for suld she no be free to change her mind like other folk? – Ye ken, Jenny, Halliday aye threeps he had a promise frae yoursell.'

'Halliday's a liar, and ye're naething but a gomeril to hearken till him, Cuddie. And then for this leddy's choice, lack-a-day! – ye may be sure a' the gowd Mr Morton has is on the outside o' his coat, and how can he keep Leddy Margaret and the young leddy?'

'Isna there Milnwood?' said Cuddie. 'Nae doubt, the auld laird left his housekeeper the life-rent, as he heard nought o' his nephew; but it's but speaking the auld wife fair, and they may a' live brawly thegither, Leddy Margaret and a'.'

'Hout tout, lad,' replied Jenny, 'ye ken them little to think leddies o' their rank wad set up house wi' auld Ailie Wilson, when they're maist ower proud to take favours frae Lord Evandale himsell. Na, na, they maun follow the camp, if she tak Morton.'

'That wad sort ill wi' the auld leddy, to be sure,' said Cuddie; 'she wad hardly win ower a lang day in the baggage-wain.'

'Then sic a flyting as there wad be between them, a' about whig and tory,' continued Jenny.

'To be sure,' said Cuddie, 'the auld leddy's unco kittle in thae points.'

'And then, Cuddie,' continued his helpmate, who had reserved her strongest argument to the last, 'if this marriage wi' Lord Evandale is broken off, what comes o' our ain bit free house, and the kale-yard, and the cow's grass? – I trow that baith us and thae bonny bairns will be turned on the wide warld!'

Here Jenny began to whimper – Cuddie writhed himself this way and that way, the very picture of indecision. At length he broke out, 'Weel, woman, canna ye tell us what we suld do, without a' this din about it?'

'Just do naething at a',' said Jenny. 'Never seem to ken ony thing about this gentleman, and for your life say a word that he suld hae been here, or up at the house! – An I had kend, I wad hae gien him my ain bed, and sleepit in the byre or he had gane up by: but it canna be helpit now. The neist thing's to get him cannily awa the morn, and I judge he'll be in nae hurry to come back again.'

'My puir maister!' said Cuddie; 'and maun I no speak to him, then?'

'For your life, no,' said Jenny; 'ye're no obliged to ken him; and I wadna hae tauld ye, only I feared ye wad ken him in the morning.'

'Aweel,' said Cuddie, sighing heavily, 'I'se awa to pleugh the outfield then; for, if I am no to speak to him, I wad rather be out o' the gate.'

'Very right, my dear hinny,' replied Jenny; 'naebody has better sense than you when ye crack a bit wi' me ower your affairs, but ye suld ne'er do ony thing aff hand out o' your ain head.'

'Ane wad think it's true,' quoth Cuddie; 'for I hae aye had some carline or quean or another, to gar me gang their gate instead o' my ain. There was first my mither,' he continued, as he undressed and tumbled himself into bed – 'then there was Leddy Margaret didna let me ca' my soul my ain – then my mither and her quarrelled, and pu'ed me twa ways at anes, as if ilk ane had an end o' me, like Punch and the Deevil⁴ rugging about the Baker at the fair – and now I hae gotten a wife,' he murmured in continuation, as he stowed the blankets around his person, 'and she's like to tak the guiding o' me a' thegither.'

'And amna I the best guide ye ever had in a' your life?' said

Jenny, as she closed the conversation by assuming her place beside her husband, and extinguishing the candle.

Leaving this couple to their repose, we have next to inform the reader, that, early on the next morning, two ladies on horseback, attended by their servants, arrived at the house of Fairy-Knowe, whom, to Jenny's utter confusion, she instantly recognised as Miss Bellenden, and Lady Emily Hamilton, a sister of Lord Evandale.

'Had I no better gang to the house to put things to rights?' said Jenny, confounded with this unexpected apparition.

'We want nothing but the pass-key,' said Miss Bellenden; 'Gudyill will open the windows of the little parlour.'

'The little parlour's locked, and the lock's spoiled,' answered Jenny, who recollected the local sympathy between that apartment and the bedchamber of her guest.

'In the red parlour, then,' said Miss Bellenden, and rode up to the front of the house, but by an approach different from that through which Morton had been conducted.

All will be out, thought Jenny, unless I can get him smuggled out of the house the back way.

So saying, she sped up the bank in great tribulation and uncertainty.

'I had better hae said at ance there was a stranger there,' was her next natural reflection. 'But then they wad hae been for asking him to breakfast. O, safe us! what will I do? – And there's Gudyill walking in the garden, too!' she exclaimed internally on approaching the wicket – 'and I daurna gang in the back way till he's aff the coast. O, sirs! what will become of us?'

In this state of perplexity she approached the *ci-devant* butler, with the purpose of decoying him out of the garden. But John Gudyill's temper was not improved by his decline in rank and increase in years. Like many peevish people, too, he seemed to have an intuitive perception as to what was most likely to teaze those whom he conversed with; and, on the present occasion, all Jenny's efforts to remove him from the garden served only to root him in it as fast as if he had been one of the shrubs. Unluckily, also, he had commenced florist during his residence at Fairy-Knowe, and, leaving all other things to the charge of Lady

Emily's servant, his first care was dedicated to the flowers, which he had taken under his special protection, and which he propped, dug, and watered, prosing all the while upon their respective merits to poor Jenny, who stood by him trembling, and almost crying, with anxiety, fear, and impatience.

Fate seemed determined to win a match against Jenny this unfortunate morning. As soon as the ladies entered the house, they observed that the door of the little parlour, the very apartment out of which she was desirous of excluding them on account of its contiguity to the room in which Morton slept, was not only unlocked, but absolutely ajar. Miss Bellenden was too much engaged with her own immediate subjects of reflection to take much notice of the circumstance, but, desiring the servant to open the window-shutters, walked into the room along with her friend.

'He is not yet come,' she said. 'What can your brother possibly mean? – Why express so anxious a wish that we should meet him here? And why not come to Castle-Dinnan, as he proposed? I own, my dear Emily, that, even engaged as we are to each other, and with the sanction of your presence, I do not feel that I have done quite right in indulging him.'

'Evandale was never capricious,' answered his sister; 'I am sure he will satisfy us with his reasons, and if he does not, I will help you to scold him.'

'What I chiefly fear,' said Edith, 'is his having engaged in some of the plots of this fluctuating and unhappy time. I know his heart is with that dreadful Claverhouse and his army, and I believe he would have joined them ere now but for my uncle's death, which gave him so much additional trouble on our account. How singular that one so rational and so deeply sensible of the errors of the exiled family, should be ready to risk all for their restoration!'

'What can I say?' answered Lady Emily; 'it is a point of honour with Evandale. Our family have always been loyal – he served long in the Guards – the Viscount of Dundee was his commander and his friend for years – he is looked on with an evil eye by many of his own relations, who set down his inactivity to the score of want of spirit. You must be aware, my dear Edith, how often family connexions, and early predilections, influence our actions more than abstract arguments. But I trust Evandale will continue quiet, though, to tell you truth, I believe you are the only one who can keep him so.'

'And how is it in my power?' said Miss Bellenden.

'You can furnish him with the Scriptural apology for not going forth with the host, – "he has married a wife, and therefore cannot come".' [5]

'I have promised,' said Edith, in a faint voice; 'but I trust I shall not be urged on the score of time.'

'Nay,' said Lady Emily, 'I will leave Evandale (and here he comes) to plead his own cause.'

'Stay, stay, for God's sake!' said Edith, endeavouring to detain her.

'Not I, not I,' said the young lady, making her escape; 'the third person makes a silly figure on such occasions. When you want me for breakfast, I will be found in the willow-walk by the river.'

As she tripped out of the room, Lord Evandale entered – 'Good-morrow, brother, and good-by till breakfast-time,' said the lively young lady; 'I trust you will give Miss Bellenden some good reasons for disturbing her rest so early in the morning.'

And so saying, she left them together, without waiting a reply.

'And now, my lord,' said Edith, 'may I desire to know the meaning of your singular request to meet you here at so early an hour?'

She was about to add, that she hardly felt herself excusable in having complied with it; but, upon looking at the person whom she addressed, she was struck dumb by the singular and agitated expression of his countenance, and interrupted herself to exclaim – 'For God's sake, what is the matter?'

'His Majesty's faithful subjects have gained a great and most decisive victory near Blair of Athole;[6] but, alas! my gallant friend, Lord Dundee' –

'Has fallen?' said Edith, anticipating the rest of his tidings.

'True – most true – he has fallen in the arms of victory, and not a man remains of talents and influence sufficient to fill up his loss in King James's service. This, Edith, is no time for temporizing with our duty. I have given directions to raise my followers, and I must take leave of you this evening.'

'Do not think of it, my lord,' answered Edith; 'your life is essential to your friends; do not throw it away in an adventure so rash. What can your single arm, and the few tenants or servants who might follow you, do against the force of almost all Scotland, the Highland clans only excepted?'

'Listen to me, Edith,' said Lord Evandale. 'I am not so rash as you may suppose me, nor are my present motives of such light importance as to affect only those personally dependent on myself. The Life-Guards, with whom I served so long, although new-modelled and new-officered by the Prince of Orange, retain a predilection for the cause of their rightful master; and' – (and here he whispered as if he feared even the walls of the apartment had ears) – 'when my foot is known to be in the stirrup, two regiments of cavalry have sworn to renounce the usurper's service, and fight under my orders.[7] They delayed only till Dundee should descend into the Lowlands; – but, since he is no more, which of his successors dare take that decisive step, unless encouraged by the troops declaring themselves! Meantime, the zeal of the soldiers will die away. I must bring them to a decision while their hearts are glowing with the victory their old leader has obtained, and burning to avenge his untimely death.'

'And will you, on the faith of such men as you know these soldiers to be,' said Edith, 'take a part of such dreadful moment?'

'I will,' said Lord Evandale – 'I must; my honour and loyalty are both pledged for it.'

'And all for the sake,' continued Miss Bellenden, 'of a prince, whose measures, while he was on the throne, no one could condemn more than Lord Evandale?'

'Most true,' replied Lord Evandale; 'and as I resented, even during the plenitude of his power, his innovations on church and state, like a freeborn subject, I am determined I will assert his real rights, when he is in adversity, like a loyal one. Let courtiers and sycophants flatter power and desert misfortune; I will neither do the one nor the other.'

'And if you are determined to act what my feeble judgment

must still term rashly, why give yourself the pain of this untimely meeting?'

'Were it not enough to answer,' said Lord Evandale, 'that, ere rushing on battle, I wished to bid adieu to my bethrothed bride? – surely it is judging coldly of my feelings, and showing too plainly the indifference of your own, to question my motive for a request so natural.'

'But why in this place, my lord?' said Edith – 'and why with such peculiar circumstances of mystery?'

'Because,' he replied, putting a letter into her hand, 'I have yet another request, which I dare hardly proffer, even when prefaced by these credentials.'

In haste and terror Edith glanced over the letter, which was from her grandmother.

'My dearest childe,' such was its tenor in style and spelling, 'I never more deeply regretted the reumatizm, which disqualified me from riding on horseback, than at this present writing, when I would most have wished to be where this paper will soon be, that is at Fairy-Knowe, with my poor dear Willie's only child. But it is the will of God I should not be with her, which I conclude to be the case, as much for the pain I now suffer, as because it hath now not given way either to cammomile poultices or to decoxion of wild mustard, wherewith I have often relieved others. Therefore, I must tell you, by writing instead of word of mouth, that, as my young Lord Evandale is called to the present campaign, both by his honour and his duty, he hath earnestly solicited me that the bonds of holy matrimony be knitted before his departure to the wars between you and him, in implement of the indenture formerly entered into for that effeck, whereuntill as I see no raisonable objexion, so I trust that you, who have been always a good and obedient childe, will not devize any which has less than raison. It is trew that the contrax of our house have heretofore been celebrated in a manner more befitting our Rank, and not in private, and with few witnesses, as a thing done in a corner. But it has been Heaven's own freewill, as well as those of the kingdom where we live, to take away from us our estate, and from the King his throne. Yet I trust He will yet restore the rightful heir to the throne, and turn his heart to the true Protestant Episcopal faith, which I have the better right to expect to see even with my old eyes, as I have beheld the royal family when they were struggling as sorely with masterful usurpers and rebels as they are now; that is to say, when his most sacred Majesty, Charles the Second of happy memory, honoured our poor house of Tillietudlem, by taking his *disjune* therein,' &c. &c. &c.

We will not abuse the reader's patience by quoting more of Lady Margaret's prolix epistle. Suffice it to say, that it closed by laying her commands on her grandchild to consent to the solemnization of her marriage without loss of time.

'I never thought till this instant,' said Edith, dropping the letter from her hand, 'that Lord Evandale would have acted ungenerously.'

'Ungenerously, Edith!' replied her lover. 'And how can you apply such a term to my desire to call you mine, ere I part from you perhaps for ever?'

'Lord Evandale ought to have remembered,' said Edith, 'that when his perseverance, and, I must add, a due sense of his merit and of the obligations we owed him, wrung from me a slow consent that I would one day comply with his wishes, I made it my condition, that I should not be pressed to a hasty accomplishment of my promise; and now he avails himself of his interest with my only remaining relative, to hurry me with precipitate and even indelicate importunity. There is more selfishness than generosity, my lord, in such eager and urgent solicitation.'

Lord Evandale, evidently much hurt, took two or three turns through the apartment ere he replied to this accusation; at length he spoke – 'I should have escaped this painful charge, durst I at once have mentioned to Miss Bellenden my principal reason for urging this request. It is one which she will probably despise on her own account, but which ought to weigh with her for the sake of Lady Margaret. My death in battle must give my whole estate to my heirs of entail; my forfeiture as a traitor, by the usurping government, may vest it in the Prince of Orange, or some Dutch favourite. In either case, my venerable friend and betrothed bride must remain unprotected and in poverty. Vested with the rights and provisions of Lady Evandale, Edith will find, in the power of supporting her aged parent, some consolation for having condescended to share the titles and fortunes of one who does not pretend to be worthy of her.'

Edith was struck dumb by an argument which she had not expected, and was compelled to acknowledge, that Lord Evandale's suit was urged with delicacy as well as with consideration.

'And yet,' she said, 'such is the waywardness with which my heart reverts to former times, that I cannot' (she burst into tears) 'suppress a degree of ominous reluctance at fulfilling my engagement upon such a brief summons.'

'We have already fully considered this painful subject,' said Lord Evandale; 'and I hoped, my dear Edith, your own enquiries, as well as mine, had fully convinced you that these regrets were fruitless.'

'Fruitless indeed!' said Edith, with a deep sigh, which, as if by an unexpected echo, was repeated from the adjoining apartment. Miss Bellenden started at the sound, and scarcely composed herself upon Lord Evandale's assurances, that she had heard but the echo of her own respiration.

'It sounded strangely distinct,' she said, 'and almost ominous; but my feelings are so harassed that the slightest trifle agitates them.'

Lord Evandale eagerly attempted to soothe her alarm, and reconcile her to a measure, which, however hasty, appeared to him the only means by which he could secure her independence. He urged his claim in virtue of the contract, her grandmother's wish and command, the propriety of insuring her comfort and independence, and touched lightly on his own long attachment, which he had evinced by so many and such various services. These Edith felt the more the less they were insisted upon; and at length, as she had nothing to oppose to his ardour, excepting a causeless reluctance, which she herself was ashamed to oppose against so much generosity, she was compelled to rest upon the impossibility of having the ceremony performed upon such hasty notice, at such a time and place. But for all this Lord Evandale was prepared, and he explained, with joyful alacrity, that the former chaplain of his regiment was in attendance at the Lodge with a faithful domestic, once a non-commissioned officer in the same corps; that his sister was also possessed of the secret; and that Headrigg and his wife might be added to the list of witnesses, if agreeable to Miss Bellenden. As to the place, he had chosen it on very purpose. The marriage was to remain a secret, since Lord Evandale was to depart in disguise very soon after it was solemnized, a circumstance which, had their union been public, must have drawn upon him the attention of the government, as being altogether unaccountable, unless from his being engaged in some dangerous design. Having hastily urged these motives and explained his arrangements, he ran, without waiting for an answer, to summon his sister to attend his bride, while he went in search of the other persons whose presence was necessary.

When Lady Emily arrived, she found her friend in an agony of tears, of which she was at some loss to comprehend the reason, being one of those damsels who think there is nothing either wonderful or terrible in matrimony, and joining with most who knew him in thinking, that it could not be rendered peculiarly alarming by Lord Evandale being the bridegroom. Influenced by these feelings, she exhausted in succession all the usual arguments for courage, and all the expressions of sympathy and condolence ordinarily employed on such occasions. But when Lady Emily beheld her future sister-in-law deaf to all those ordinary topics of consolation – when she beheld tears follow fast and without intermission down cheeks as pale as marble – when she felt that the hand which she pressed in order to enforce her arguments turned cold within her grasp, and lay, like that of a corpse, insensible and unresponsive to her caresses, her feelings of sympathy gave way to those of hurt pride and pettish displeasure.

'I must own,' she said, 'that I am something at a loss to understand all this, Miss Bellenden. Months have passed since you agreed to marry my brother, and you have postponed the fulfilment of your engagement from one period to another, as if you had to avoid some dishonourable or highly disagreeable connexion. I think I can answer for Lord Evandale, that he will seek no woman's hand against her inclination; and, though his sister, I may boldly say, that he does not need to urge any lady further than her inclinations carry her. You will forgive me, Miss

Bellenden; but your present distress augurs ill for my brother's future happiness, and I must needs say, that he does not merit all these expressions of dislike and dolour, and that they seem an odd return for an attachment which he has manifested so long, and in so many ways.'

'You are right, Lady Emily,' said Edith, drying her eyes, and endeavouring to resume her natural manner, though still betrayed by her faltering voice and the paleness of her cheeks – 'You are quite right – Lord Evandale merits such usage from no one, least of all from her whom he has honoured with his regard. But if I have given way, for the last time, to a sudden and irresistible burst of feeling, it is my consolation, Lady Emily, that your brother knows the cause; that I have hid nothing from him, and that he at least is not apprehensive of finding in Edith Bellenden a wife undeserving of his affection. But still you are right, and I merit your censure for indulging for a moment fruitless regret and painful remembrances. It shall be so no longer; my lot is cast with Evandale, and with him I am resolved to bear it. Nothing shall in future occur to excite his complaints, or the resentment of his relations; no idle recollections of other days shall intervene to prevent the zealous and affectionate discharge of my duty; no vain illusions recall the memory of other days' –

As she spoke these words, she slowly raised her eyes, which had before been hidden by her hand, to the latticed window of her apartment, which was partly open, uttered a dismal shriek, and fainted. Lady Emily turned her eyes in the same direction, but saw only the shadow of a man, which seemed to disappear from the window, and, terrified more by the state of Edith than by the apparition she had herself witnessed, she uttered shriek upon shriek for assistance. Her brother soon arrived with the chaplain and Jenny Dennison, but strong and vigorous remedies were necessary ere they could recall Miss Bellenden to sense and motion. Even then her language was wild and incoherent.

'Press me no farther,' she said to Lord Evandale; 'it cannot be – Heaven and earth – the living and the dead, have leagued themselves against this ill-omened union. Take all I can give – my sisterly regard – my devoted friendship. I will love you as a sister, and serve you as a bondswoman, but never speak to me more of marriage.'

The astonishment of Lord Evandale may easily be conceived.

'Emily,' he said to his sister, 'this is your doing – I was accursed when I thought of bringing you here – some of your confounded folly has driven her mad!'

'On my word, brother,' answered Lady Emily, 'you're sufficient to drive all the women in Scotland mad. Because your mistress seems much disposed to jilt you, you quarrel with your sister who has been arguing in your cause, and had brought her to a quiet hearing, when, all of a sudden, a man looked in at a window, whom her crazed sensibility mistook either for you or some one else, and has treated us gratis with an excellent tragic scene.'

'What man? What window?' said Lord Evandale, in impatient displeasure. 'Miss Bellenden is incapable of trifling with me; – and yet what else could have' –

'Hush! hush!' said Jenny, whose interest lay particularly in shifting further enquiry; 'for Heaven's sake, my lord, speak low, for my lady begins to recover.'

Edith was no sooner somewhat restored to herself than she begged, in a feeble voice, to be left alone with Lord Evandale. All retreated, Jenny with her usual air of officious simplicity, Lady Emily and the chaplain with that of awakened curiosity. No sooner had they left the apartment than Edith beckoned Lord Evandale to sit beside her on the couch; her next motion was to take his hand, in spite of his surprised resistance, to her lips; her last was to sink from her seat and to clasp his knees.

'Forgive me, my lord!' she exclaimed – 'Forgive me! – I must deal most untruly by you, and break a solemn engagement. You have my friendship, my highest regard, my most sincere gratitude – You have more; you have my word and my faith – But, O, forgive me, for the fault is not mine – you have not my love, and I cannot marry you without a sin!'

'You dream, my dearest Edith!' said Evandale, perplexed in the utmost degree, – 'you let your imagination beguile you; this is but some delusion of an over-sensitive mind; the person whom you preferred to me has been long in a better world, where your unavailing regret cannot follow him, or, if it could, would only diminish his happiness.'

'You are mistaken, Lord Evandale,' said Edith, solemnly. 'I am not a sleep-walker, or a madwoman. No – I could not have believed from any one what I have seen. But, having seen him, I must believe mine own eyes.'

'Seen *him?* – seen whom?' asked Lord Evandale, in great anxiety.

'Henry Morton,' replied Edith, uttering these two words as if they were her last, and very nearly fainting when she had done so.

'Miss Bellenden,' said Lord Evandale, 'you treat me like a fool or a child; if you repent your engagement to me,' he continued, indignantly, 'I am not a man to enforce it against your inclination; but deal with me as a man, and forbear this trifling.'

He was about to go on, when he perceived, from her quivering eye and pallid cheek, that nothing less than imposture was intended, and that by whatever means her imagination had been so impressed, it was really disturbed by unaffected awe and terror. He changed his tone, and exerted all his eloquence in endeavouring to soothe and extract from her the secret cause of such terror.

'I saw him!' she repeated – 'I saw Henry Morton stand at that window, and look into the apartment at the moment I was on the point of abjuring him for ever. His face was darker, thinner, and paler than it was wont to be; his dress was a horseman's cloak, and hat looped down over his face; his expression was like that he wore on that dreadful morning when he was examined by Claverhouse at Tillietudlem. Ask your sister, ask Lady Emily, if she did not see him as well as I. – I know what has called him up – he came to upbraid me, that, while my heart was with him in the deep and dead sea, I was about to give my hand to another. My lord, it is ended between you and me – be the consequences what they will, *she* cannot marry whose union disturbs the repose of the dead.'[8]

'Good heaven!' said Evandale, as he paced the room, half mad himself with surprise and vexation, 'her fine understanding must be totally overthrown, and that by the effort which she has made to comply with my ill-timed, though well-meant, request. Without rest and attention her health is ruined for ever.'

At this moment the door opened, and Halliday, who had been Lord Evandale's principal personal attendant since they both left the Guards on the Revolution, stumbled into the room with a countenance as pale and ghastly as terror could paint it.

'What is the matter next, Halliday?' cried his master, starting up. 'Any discovery of the' –

He had just recollection sufficient to stop short in the midst of the dangerous sentence.

'No, sir,' said Halliday, 'it is not that, nor any thing like that; but I have seen a ghost!'

'A ghost! you eternal idiot!' said Lord Evandale, forced altogether out of his patience. 'Has all mankind sworn to go mad in order to drive me so? – What ghost, you simpleton?'

'The ghost of Henry Morton, the whig captain at Bothwell Bridge,' replied Halliday. 'He passed by me like a fire-flaught when I was in the garden!'

'This is mid-summer madness,' said Lord Evandale, 'or there is some strange villainy afloat. – Jenny, attend your lady to her chamber, while I endeavour to find a clew to all this.'

But Lord Evandale's enquiries were in vain. Jenny, who might have given (had she chosen) a very satisfactory explanation, had an interest to leave the matter in darkness; and interest was a matter which now weighed principally with Jenny, since the possession of an active and affectionate husband in her own proper right had altogether allayed her spirit of coquetry. She had made the best use of the first moments of confusion hastily to remove all traces of any one having slept in the apartment adjoining to the parlour, and even to erase the mark of footsteps beneath the window, through which she conjectured Morton's face had been seen, while attempting, ere he left the garden, to gain one look at her whom he had so long loved, and was now on the point of losing for ever. That he had passed Halliday in the garden was equally clear; and she learned from her elder boy, whom she had employed to have the stranger's horse saddled and ready for his departure, that he had rushed into the stable, thrown the child a broad gold piece, and, mounting his horse, had ridden with fearful rapidity down towards the Clyde. The secret was, therefore, in their own family, and Jenny was resolved it should remain so.

'For, to be sure,' she said, 'although her lady and Halliday kend Mr Morton by broad daylight, that was nae reason I suld own to kenning him in the gloaming and by candlelight, and him keeping his face frae Cuddie and me a' the time.'

So she stood resolutely upon the negative when examined by Lord Evandale. As for Halliday, he could only say, that as he entered the garden-door, the supposed apparition met him walk- ing swiftly, and with a visage on which anger and grief appeared to be contending.

'He knew him well,' he said, 'having been repeatedly guard upon him, and obliged to write down his marks of stature and visage in case of escape. And there were few faces like Mr Morton's.' But what should make him haunt the country where he was neither hanged nor shot, he, the said Halliday, did not pretend to conceive.

Lady Emily confessed she had seen the face of a man at the window, but her evidence went no farther. John Gudyill de- poned *nil novit in causa*. He had left his gardening to get his morning dram just at the time when the apparition had taken place. Lady Emily's servant was waiting orders in the kitchen, and there was not another being within a quarter of a mile of the house.

Lord Evandale returned perplexed and dissatisfied in the highest degree, at beholding a plan which he thought necessary not less for the protection of Edith in contingent circumstances, than for the assurance of his own happiness, and which he had brought so very near perfection, thus broken off without any apparent or rational cause. His knowledge of Edith's character set her beyond the suspicion of covering any capricious change of determination by a pretended vision. But he would have set the apparition down to the influence of an overstrained imagin- ation, agitated by the circumstances in which she had so sud- denly been placed, had it not been for the coinciding testimony of Halliday, who had no reason for thinking of Morton more

than any other person, and knew nothing of Miss Bellenden's
vision when he promulgated his own. On the other hand, it
seemed in the highest degree improbable that Morton, so long
and so vainly sought after, and who was, with such good reason,
supposed to be lost when the Vryheid of Rotterdam went down
with crew and passengers, should be alive and lurking in this
country, where there was no longer any reason why he should
not openly show himself, since the present government favoured
his party in politics. When Lord Evandale reluctantly brought
himself to communicate these doubts to the chaplain, in order to
obtain his opinion, he could only obtain a long lecture on demonology, in which, after quoting Delrio, and Burthoog, and
De L'Ancre,[9] on the subject of apparitions, together with sundry
civilians and common lawyers on the nature of testimony, the
learned gentleman expressed his definite and determined opinion
to be, either that there had been an actual apparition of the
deceased Henry Morton's spirit, the possibility of which he was,
as a divine and a philosopher, neither fully prepared to admit or
to deny; or else, that the said Henry Morton, being still *in
rerum natura*, had appeared in his proper person that morning;
or, finally, that some strong *deceptio visus*, or striking similitude
of person, had deceived the eyes of Miss Bellenden and of
Thomas Halliday. Which of these was the most probable hypo-
thesis, the Doctor declined to pronounce, but expressed himself
ready to die in the opinion that one or other of them had occasioned that morning's disturbance.

Lord Evandale soon had additional cause for distressful
anxiety. Miss Bellenden was declared to be dangerously ill.

'I will not leave this place,' he exclaimed, 'till she is pronounced to be in safety. I neither can nor ought to do so; for
whatever may have been the immediate occasion of her illness,
I gave the first cause for it by my unhappy solicitation.'

He established himself, therefore, as a guest in the family,
which the presence of his sister as well as of Lady Margaret
Bellenden, (who, in despite of her rheumatism, caused herself
to be transported thither when she heard of her grand-daughter's
illness,) rendered a step equally natural and delicate. And thus
he anxiously awaited, until, without injury to her health, Edith

could sustain a final explanation ere his departure on his expedition.

'She shall never,' said the generous young man, 'look on her engagement with me as the means of fettering her to a union, the idea of which seems almost to unhinge her understanding.'

CHAPTER 39

> Ah, happy hills! ah, pleasing shades!
>   Ah, fields beloved in vain!
> Where once my careless childhood stray'd,
>   A stranger yet to pain.
>
> *Ode on a distant prospect of Eton College*[1]

It is not by corporal wants and infirmities only that men of the most distinguished talents are levelled, during their life-time, with the common mass of mankind. There are periods of mental agitation when the firmest of mortals must be ranked with the weakest of his brethren; and when, in paying the general tax of humanity, his distresses are even aggravated by feeling that he transgresses, in the indulgence of his grief, the rules of religion and philosophy, by which he endeavours in general to regulate his passions and his actions. It was during such a paroxysm that the unfortunate Morton left Fairy-Knowe. To know that his long-loved and still-beloved Edith, whose image had filled his mind for so many years, was on the point of marriage to his early rival, who had laid claim to her heart by so many services, as hardly left her a title to refuse his addresses, bitter as the intelligence was, yet came not as an unexpected blow.

During his residence abroad he had once written to Edith. It was to bid her farewell for ever, and to conjure her to forget him. He had requested her not to answer his letter, yet he half hoped, for many a day, that she might transgress his injunction. The letter never reached her to whom it was addressed, and Morton, ignorant of its miscarriage, could only conclude himself laid aside and forgotten, according to his own self-denying request. All that he had heard of their mutual relations since his return to Scotland, prepared him to expect that he could only look upon Miss Bellenden as the betrothed bride of Lord Evandale; and, even if freed from the burden of obligation to the latter, it would still have been inconsistent with Morton's generosity of disposition to disturb their arrangements, by attempting the assertion of a claim, proscribed by absence, never sanctioned by the consent of friends, and barred by a thousand circumstances of difficulty. Why then did he seek the cottage which their broken fortunes had now rendered the retreat of Lady Margaret Bellenden and her grand-daughter? He yielded, we are under the necessity of acknowledging, to the impulse of an inconsistent wish, which many might have felt in his situation.

Accident apprized him, while travelling towards his native district, that the ladies, near whose mansion he must necessarily pass, were absent; and learning that Cuddie and his wife acted as their principal domestics, he could not resist pausing at their cottage, to learn, if possible, the real progress which Lord Evandale had made in the affections of Miss Bellenden – alas! no longer his Edith. This rash experiment ended as we have related, and he parted from the house of Fairy-Knowe, conscious that he was still beloved by Edith, yet compelled, by faith and honour, to relinquish her for ever. With what feelings he must have listened to the dialogue between Lord Evandale and Edith, the greater part of which he involuntarily overheard, the reader must conceive, for we dare not attempt to describe them. An hundred times he was tempted to burst upon their interview, or to exclaim aloud – 'Edith, I yet live!' – and as often the recollection of her plighted troth, and of the debt of gratitude which he owed Lord Evandale, (to whose influence with Claverhouse he justly ascribed his escape from torture and from death,) withheld him from a rashness which might indeed have involved all in further distress, but gave little prospect of forwarding his own happiness. He repressed forcibly these selfish emotions, though with an agony which thrilled his every nerve.

'No, Edith!' was his internal oath, 'never will I add a thorn to thy pillow – That which Heaven has ordained, let it be; and let me not add, by my selfish sorrows, one atom's weight to the burden thou hast to bear. I was dead to thee when thy resolution was adopted; and never – never shalt thou know that Henry Morton still lives!'

As he formed this resolution, diffident of his own power to keep it, and seeking that firmness in flight which was every moment shaken by his continuing within hearing of Edith's voice, he hastily rushed from his apartment by the little closet and the sashed door which led to the garden.

But firmly as he thought his resolution was fixed, he could not leave the spot where the last tones of a voice so beloved still vibrated on his ear, without endeavouring to avail himself of the opportunity which the parlour window afforded, to steal one last glance at the lovely speaker. It was in this attempt, made while Edith seemed to have her eyes unalterably bent upon the ground, that Morton's presence was detected by her raising them suddenly. So soon as her wild scream made this known to the unfortunate object of a passion so constant, and which seemed so ill-fated, he hurried from the place as if pursued by the furies. He passed Halliday in the garden without recognising, or even being sensible that he had seen him, threw himself on his horse, and, by a sort of instinct rather than recollection, took the first by-road in preference to the public route to Hamilton.

In all probability this prevented Lord Evandale from learning that he was actually in existence; for the news that the Highlanders had obtained a decisive victory at Killiecrankie, had occasioned an accurate look-out to be kept, by order of the Government, on all the passes, for fear of some commotion among the Lowland Jacobites. They did not omit to post sentinels on Bothwell Bridge, and as these men had not seen any traveller pass westward in that direction, and as, besides, their comrades stationed in the village of Bothwell were equally positive that none had gone eastward, the apparition, in the existence of which Edith and Halliday were equally positive, became yet more mysterious in the judgment of Lord Evandale, who was finally inclined to settle in the belief, that the heated and disturbed imagination of Edith had summoned up the phantom she stated herself to have seen, and that Halliday had, in some unaccountable manner, been infected by the same superstition.

Meanwhile, the by-path which Morton pursued, with all the speed which his vigorous horse could exert, brought him in a very few seconds to the brink of the Clyde, at a spot marked with the feet of horses, who were conducted to it as a watering-place. The steed, urged as he was to the gallop, did not pause a single instant, but, throwing himself into the river, was soon beyond his depth. The plunge which the animal made as his feet quitted the ground, with the feeling that the cold water rose above his sword-belt, were the first incidents which recalled Morton, whose movements had been hitherto mechanical, to the necessity of taking measures for preserving himself and the noble animal which he bestrode. A perfect master of all manly exercises, the management of a horse in water was as familiar to him as when upon a meadow. He directed the animal's course somewhat down the stream towards a low plain, or holm, which seemed to promise an easy egress from the river. In the first and second attempt to get on shore, the horse was frustrated by the nature of the ground, and nearly fell backwards on his rider. The instinct of self-preservation seldom fails, even in the most desperate circumstances, to recall the human mind to some degree of equipoise, unless when altogether distracted by terror, and Morton was obliged to the danger in which he was placed for complete recovery of his self-possession. A third attempt, at a spot more carefully and judiciously selected, succeeded better than the former, and placed the horse and his rider in safety upon the farther and left-hand bank of the Clyde.

'But whither,' said Morton, in the bitterness of his heart, 'am I now to direct my course? or rather, what does it signify to which point of the compass a wretch so forlorn betakes himself? I would to God, could the wish be without a sin, that these dark waters had flowed over me, and drowned my recollection of that which was, and that which is!'

The sense of impatience, which the disturbed state of his feelings had occasioned, scarcely had vented itself in these violent expressions, ere he was struck with shame at having given way to such a paroxysm. He remembered how signally the life which he now held so lightly in the bitterness of his disappointment, had been preserved through the almost incessant perils which had beset him since he entered upon his public career.

'I am a fool!' he said, 'and worse than a fool, to set light by that existence which Heaven has so often preserved in the most marvellous manner. Something there yet remains for me in this world, were it only to bear my sorrows like a man, and to aid those who need my assistance. What have I seen, – what have I heard, but the very conclusion of that which I knew was to happen? They' – (he durst not utter their names even in soliloquy) – 'they are embarrassed and in difficulties. She is stripped of her inheritance, and he seems rushing on some dangerous career, with which, but for the low voice in which he spoke, I might have become acquainted. Are there no means to aid or to warn them?'

As he pondered upon this topic, forcibly withdrawing his mind from his own disappointment, and compelling his attention to the affairs of Edith and her betrothed husband, the letter of Burley, long forgotten, suddenly rushed on his memory, like a ray of light darting through a mist.

'Their ruin must have been his work,' was his internal conclusion. 'If it can be repaired, it must be through his means, or by information obtained from him. I will search him out. Stern, crafty, and enthusiastic as he is, my plain and downright rectitude of purpose has more than once prevailed with him. I will seek him out, at least; and who knows what influence the information I may acquire from him may have on the fortunes of those, whom I shall never see more, and who will probably never learn that I am now suppressing my own grief, to add, if possible, to their happiness.'

Animated by these hopes, though the foundation was but slight, he sought the nearest way to the high-road; and as all the tracks through the valley were known to him since he hunted through them in youth, he had no other difficulty than that of surmounting one or two enclosures, ere he found himself on the road to the small burgh where the feast of the popinjay had been celebrated. He journeyed in a state of mind sad indeed and dejected, yet relieved from its earlier and more intolerable state of anguish; for virtuous resolution and manly disinterestedness seldom fail to restore tranquility even where they cannot create happiness. He turned his thoughts with strong effort upon the means of discovering Burley, and the chance there was of extracting from him any knowledge which he might possess favourable to her in whose cause he interested himself, and at length formed the resolution of guiding himself by the circumstances in which he might discover the object of his quest, trusting, that, from Cuddie's account of a schism betwixt Burley and his brethren of the presbyterian persuasion, he might find him less rancorously disposed against Miss Bellenden, and inclined to exert the power which he asserted himself to possess over her fortunes, more favourably than heretofore.

Noontide had passed away, when our traveller found himself in the neighbourhood of his deceased uncle's habitation of Milnwood. It rose among glades and groves that were chequered with a thousand early recollections of joy and sorrow, and made upon Morton that mournful impression, soft and affecting, yet, withal, soothing, which the sensitive mind usually receives from a return to the haunts of childhood and early youth, after having experienced the vicissitudes and tempests of public life. A strong desire came upon him to visit the house itself.

Old Alison, he thought, will not know me, more than the honest couple whom I saw yesterday. I may indulge my curiosity, and proceed on my journey, without her having any knowledge of my existence. I think they said my uncle had bequeathed to her my family mansion – well – be it so. I have enough to sorrow for, to enable me to dispense with lamenting such a disappointment as that; and yet methinks he has chosen an odd successor in my grumbling old dame, to a line of respectable, if not distinguished, ancestry. Let it be as it may, I will visit the old mansion at least once more.

The house of Milnwood, even in its best days, had nothing cheerful about it, but its gloom appeared to be doubled under the auspices of the old housekeeper. Every thing, indeed, was in repair; there were no slates deficient upon the steep grey roof, and no panes broken in the narrow windows. But the grass in the court-yard looked as if the foot of man had not been there for years; the doors were carefully locked, and that which admitted to the hall seemed to have been shut for a length of time, since the spiders had fairly drawn their webs over the door-way and the staples. Living sight or sound there was none, until, after much knocking, Morton heard the little window, through which it was usual to reconnoitre visitors, open with much caution. The face of Alison, puckered with some score of wrinkles, in addition to those with which it was furrowed when Morton left Scotland, now presented itself, enveloped in a *toy*, from under the protection of which some of her grey tresses had escaped in a manner more picturesque than beautiful, while her shrill tremulous voice demanded the cause of the knocking.

'I wish to speak an instant with one Alison Wilson who resides here,' said Henry.

'She's no at hame the day,' answered Mrs Wilson, *in propria persona*, the state of whose headdress, perhaps, inspired her with this direct mode of denying herself; 'and ye are but a mislear'd person to speer for her in sic a manner. Ye might hae had an M under your belt for *Mistress* Wilson of Milnwood.'

'I beg pardon,' said Morton, internally smiling at finding in old Ailie the same jealousy of disrespect which she used to exhibit upon former occasions – 'I beg pardon; I am but a stranger in this country, and have been so long abroad, that I have almost forgotten my own language.'

'Did ye come frae foreign parts?' said Ailie; 'then maybe ye may hae heard of a young gentleman of this country that they ca' Henry Morton?'

'I have heard,' said Morton, 'of such a name in Germany.'

'Then bide a wee bit where ye are, friend – or stay – gang round by the back o' the house, and ye'll find a laigh door; it's on the latch, for it's never barred till sunset. Ye'll open't – and tak care ye dinna fa' ower the tub, for the entry's dark – and then ye'll turn to the right, and then ye'll haud straught forward, and then ye'll turn to the right again, and ye'll tak heed o' the cellar stairs, and then ye'll be at the door o' the little kitchen – it's a' the kitchen that's at Milnwood now – and I'll come down t'ye, and whate'er ye wad say to Mistress Wilson ye may very safely tell it to me.'

A stranger might have had some difficulty, notwithstanding the minuteness of the directions supplied by Ailie, to pilot himself in safety through the dark labyrinth of passages that led from the back-door to the little kitchen, but Henry was too well acquainted with the navigation of these straits to experience danger, either from the Scylla which lurked on one side in shape of a bucking tub, or the Charybdis[2] which yawned on the other in the profundity of a winding cellar-stair. His only impediment arose from the snarling and vehement barking of a small cocking spaniel, once his own property, but which, unlike to the faithful Argus,[3] saw his master return from his wanderings without any symptom of recognition.

'The little dogs and all!' said Morton to himself, on being disowned by his former favourite. 'I am so changed, that no breathing creature that I have known and loved will now acknowledge me!'

At this moment he had reached the kitchen, and soon after the tread of Alison's high heels, and the pat of the crutch-handled cane, which served at once to prop and to guide her footsteps, were heard upon the stairs, an annunciation which continued for some time ere she fairly reached the kitchen.

Morton had, therefore, time to survey the slender preparations for housekeeping, which were now sufficient in the house of his ancestors. The fire, though coals are plenty in that neighbourhood, was husbanded with the closest attention to economy of fuel, and the small pipkin, in which was preparing the dinner of the old woman and her maid-of-all-work, a girl of twelve years old, intimated, by its thin and watery vapour, that Ailie had not mended her cheer with her improved fortune.

When she entered, the head which nodded with self-importance – the features in which an irritable peevishness, acquired by habit and indulgence, strove with a temper naturally affectionate and goodnatured – the coif – the apron – the blue checked gown, were all those of old Ailie; but laced pinners, hastily put on to meet the stranger, with some other trifling articles of decoration, marked the difference between Mrs Wilson, life-rentrix of Milnwood, and the housekeeper of the late proprietor.

'What were ye pleased to want wi' Mrs Wilson, sir? – I am Mrs Wilson,' was her first address; for the five minutes time which she had gained for the business of the toilette, entitled her, she conceived, to assume the full merit of her illustrious name, and shine forth on her guest in unchastened splendour. Morton's sensations, confounded between the past and present, fairly confused him so much, that he would have had difficulty in answering her, even if he had known well what to say. But as he had not determined what character he was to adopt while concealing that which was properly his own, he had an additional reason for remaining silent. Mrs Wilson, in perplexity, and with some apprehension, repeated her question.

'What were ye pleased to want wi' me, sir? Ye said ye kend Mr Harry Morton?'

'Pardon me, madam,' answered Henry; 'it was of one Silas Morton I spoke.'

The old woman's countenance fell.

'It was his father then ye kent o', the brother o' the late Milnwood? Ye canna mind him abroad, I wad think – he was come hame afore ye were born. I thought ye had brought me news of poor Maister Harry.'

'It was from my father I learned to know Colonel Morton,' said Henry; 'of the son I know little or nothing; rumour says he died abroad on his passage to Holland.'

'That's ower like to be true,' said the old woman with a sigh, 'and mony a tear it's cost my auld een. His uncle, poor gentleman, just sough'd awa wi' it in his mouth. He had been gieing me preceeze directions anent the bread, and the wine, and the brandy, at his burial, and how often it was to be handed round the company, (for, dead or alive, he was a prudent, frugal, painstaking man,) and then he said, said he, "Ailie," (he aye ca'd me Ailie, we were auld acquaintance,) "Ailie, take ye care and haud the gear weel thegither; for the name of Morton of Milnwood's gane out like the last sough of an auld sang." And sae he fell o' ae dwam into another, and ne'er spak a word mair, unless it were something we cou'dna mak out, about a dipped candle being gude eneugh to see to dee wi". – He cou'd ne'er bide to see a moulded ane, and there was ane, by ill luck, on the table.'

While Mrs Wilson was thus detailing the last moments of the old miser, Morton was pressingly engaged in diverting the assiduous curiosity of the dog, which, recovered from his first surprise, and combining former recollections, had, after much snuffing and examination, begun a course of capering and jumping upon the stranger which threatened every instant to betray him. At length, in the urgency of his impatience, Morton could not forbear exclaiming, in a tone of hasty impatience, 'Down, Elphin! Down, sir!'

'Ye ken our dog's name,' said the old lady, struck with great and sudden surprise – 'ye ken our dog's name, and it's no a common ane. And the creature kens you too,' she continued, in a more agitated and shriller tone – 'God guide us! it's my ain bairn!'

So saying, the poor old woman threw herself around Morton's neck, clung to him, kissed him as if he had been actually her child, and wept for joy. There was no parrying the discovery, if he could have had the heart to attempt any further disguise. He returned the embrace with the most grateful warmth, and answered –

'I do indeed live, dear Ailie, to thank you for all your kindness, past and present, and to rejoice that there is at least one friend to welcome me to my native country.'

'Friends!' exclaimed Ailie, 'ye'll hae mony friends – ye'll hae mony friends; for ye will hae gear, hinny – ye will hae gear. Heaven mak ye a gude guide o't! But, eh, sirs!' she continued, pushing him back from her with her trembling hand and shrivelled arm, and gazing in his face as if to read, at more convenient distance, the ravages which sorrow rather than time had made on his face – 'Eh, sirs! ye're sair altered, hinny; your face is turned pale, and your een are sunken, and your bonny red-and-white cheeks are turned a' dark and sun-burnt. O, weary on the wars! mony's the comely face they destroy. – And when cam ye here, hinny? And where hae ye been? – And what hae ye been doing? – And what for did ye na write to us? – And how cam ye to pass yoursell for dead? – And what for did ye come creepin' to your ain house as if ye had been an unco body, to gie poor auld Ailie sic a start?' she concluded, smiling through her tears.

It was some time ere Morton could overcome his own emotion so as to give the kind old woman the information which we shall communicate to our readers in the next Chapter.

CHAPTER 40

Aumerle that was,
But that is gone for being Richard's friend;
And, madam, you must call him Rutland now.

Richard II[1]

THE scene of explanation was hastily removed from the little kitchen to Mrs Wilson's own matted room; the very same which she had occupied as housekeeper, and which she continued to retain. 'It was,' she said, 'better secured against sifting winds than the hall, which she had found dangerous to her rheumatisms, and it was more fitting for her use than the late Milnwood's apartment, honest man, which gave her sad thoughts;' and as for the great oak parlour, it was never opened but to be aired, washed, and dusted, according to the invariable practice of the family, unless upon their most solemn festivals. In the matted room, therefore, they were settled, surrounded by pickle-pots and conserves of all kinds, which the *ci-devant* housekeeper continued to compound, out of mere habit, although neither she herself, nor any one else, ever partook of the comfits which she so regularly prepared.

Morton, adapting his narrative to the comprehension of his auditor, informed her briefly of the wreck of the vessel and the loss of all hands, excepting two or three common seamen, who had early secured the skiff, and were just putting off from the vessel when he leaped from the deck into their boat, and unexpectedly, as well as contrary to their inclination, made himself partner of their voyage and of their safety. Landed at Flushing, he was fortunate enough to meet with an old officer who had been in service with his father. By his advice, he shunned going immediately to the Hague, but forwarded his letters to the court of the Stadtholder.[2]

'Our Prince,' said the veteran, 'must as yet keep terms with his father-in-law, and with your King Charles; and to approach him in the character of a Scottish malecontent would render it imprudent for him to distinguish you by his favour. Wait, therefore, his orders, without forcing yourself on his notice; observe the strictest prudence and retirement; assume for the present a different name; shun the company of the British exiles; and, depend upon it, you will not repent your prudence.'

The old friend of Silas Morton argued justly. After a considerable time had elapsed, the Prince of Orange, in a progress through the United States, came to the town where Morton, impatient at his situation and the incognito which he was obliged to observe, still continued, nevertheless, to be a resident. He had an hour of private interview assigned, in which the Prince expressed himself highly pleased with his intelligence, his prudence, and the liberal view which he seemed to take of the factions of his native country, their motives and their purposes.

'I would gladly,' said William, 'attach you to my own person, but that cannot be without giving offence in England. But I will do as much for you, as well out of respect for the sentiments you have expressed, as for the recommendations you have brought me. Here is a commission in a Swiss regiment at present in garrison in a distant province, where you will meet few or none of your countrymen. Continue to be Captain Melville, and let the name of Morton sleep till better days.'

'Thus began my fortune,' continued Morton; 'and my services have, on various occasions, been distinguished by his Royal Highness, until the moment that brought him to Britain as our political deliverer. His commands must excuse my silence to my few friends in Scotland; and I wonder not at the report of my death, considering the wreck of the vessel, and that I found no occasion to use the letters of exchange with which I was furnished by the liberality of some of them, a circumstance which must have confirmed the belief that I had perished.'

'But, dear hinny,' asked Mrs Wilson, 'did ye find nae Scotch body at the Prince of Oranger's court that kend ye? I wad hae thought Morton o' Milnwood was kend a' through the country.'

'I was purposely engaged in distant service,' said Morton, 'until a period when few, without as deep and kind a motive of interest as yours, Ailie, would have known the stripling Morton in Major-General Melville.'

'Malville was your mother's name,' said Mrs Wilson; 'but Morton sounds far bonnier in my auld lugs. And when ye tak up the lairdship, ye maun tak the auld name and designation again.'

'I am like to be in no haste to do either the one or the other, Ailie, for I have some reasons for the present to conceal my being alive from every one but you; and as for the lairdship of Milnwood, it is in as good hands.'

'As gude hands, hinny!' re-echoed Ailie; 'I'm hopefu' ye are no meaning mine? The rents and the lands are but a sair fash to me. And I'm ower failed to tak a helpmate, though Wylie Mactrickit the writer [3] was very pressing, and spak very civilly; but I'm ower auld a cat to draw that strae before me. He canna williwhaw me as he's dune mony a ane. And then I thought aye ye wad come back, and I wad get my pickle meal and my soup milk, and keep a' things right about ye as I used to do in your puir uncle's time, and it wad be just pleasure eneugh for me to see ye thrive and guide the gear canny — Ye'll hae learned that in Holland, I'se warrant, for they're thrifty folk there, as I hear tell. — But ye'll be for keeping rather a mair house than puir auld Milnwood that's gane; and, indeed, I would approve o' your eating butcher-meat maybe as aften as three times a-week — it keeps the wind out o' the stamack.'

'We will talk of all this another time,' said Morton, surprised at the generosity upon a large scale, which mingled in Ailie's thoughts and actions with habitual and sordid parsimony, and at the odd contrast between her love of saving and indifference to self-acquisition. 'You must know,' he continued, 'that I am in this country only for a few days on some special business of importance to the government, and therefore, Ailie, not a word of having seen me. At some other time I will acquaint you fully with my motives and intentions.'

'E'en be it sae, my jo,' replied Ailie, 'I can keep a secret like my neighbours; and weel auld Milnwood kend it, honest man, for he tauld me where he keepit his gear, and that's what maist folk like to hae as private as possibly may be. — But come awa wi' me, hinny, till I show ye the oak-parlour how grandly it's keepit, just as if ye had been expected hame every day — I loot naebody sort it but my ain hands. It was a kind o' divertisement to me, though whiles the tear wan into my ee, and I said to mysell, what needs I fash wi' grates, and carpets, and cushions, and the muckle brass candlesticks, ony mair? for they'll ne'er come hame that aught it rightfully.'

With these words she hauled him away to this *sanctum sanctorum*, the scrubbing and cleaning whereof was her daily employment, as its high state of good order constituted the very pride of her heart. Morton, as he followed her into the room, underwent a rebuke for not "dighting his shune", which showed that Ailie had not relinquished her habits of authority. On entering the oak-parlour, he could not but recollect the feelings of solemn awe with which, when a boy, he had been affected at his occasional and rare admission to an apartment, which he then supposed had not its equal save in the halls of princes. It may be readily supposed, that the worked-worsted chairs, with their short ebony legs and long upright backs, had lost much of their influence over his mind; that the large brass andirons seemed diminished in splendour; that the green worsted tapestry appeared no masterpiece of the Arras loom; and that the room looked, on the whole, dark, gloomy, and disconsolate. Yet there were two objects, 'The counterfeit presentment of two brothers,' which, dissimilar as those described by Hamlet,[4] affected his mind with a variety of sensations. One full-length portrait represented his father, in complete armour, with a countenance indicating his masculine and determined character; and the other set forth his uncle, in velvet and brocade, looking as if he were ashamed of his own finery, though entirely indebted for it to the liberality of the painter.

'It was an idle fancy,' Ailie said, 'to dress the honest auld man in thae expensive fal-lalls that he ne'er wore in his life, instead o' his douce Raploch grey, and his band wi' the narrow edging.'

In private, Morton could not help being much of her opinion; for any thing approaching to the dress of a gentleman sate as ill on the ungainly person of his relative, as an open or generous expression would have done on his mean and money-making features. He now extricated himself from Ailie to visit some of his haunts in the neighbouring wood, while her own hands made an addition to the dinner she was preparing; an incident no otherwise remarkable than as it cost the life of a fowl, which, for any event of less importance than the arrival of Henry Morton, might have cackled on to a good old age, ere Ailie could have been guilty of the extravagance of killing and dressing it. The meal was seasoned by talk of old times, and by the plans which Ailie laid out for futurity, in which she assigned her young master all the prudential habits of her old one, and planned out the dexterity with which she was to exercise her duty as governante. Morton let the old woman enjoy her day-dreams and castle-building during moments of such pleasure, and deferred, till some fitter occasion, the communication of his purpose again to return and spend his life upon the Continent.

His next care was to lay aside his military dress, which he considered likely to render more difficult his researches after Burley. He exchanged it for a grey doublet and cloak, formerly his usual attire at Milnwood, and which Mrs Wilson produced from a chest of walnut-tree, wherein she had laid them aside, without forgetting carefully to brush and air them from time to time. Morton retained his sword and fire-arms, without which few persons travelled in those unsettled times. When he appeared in his new attire, Mrs Wilson was first thankful 'that they fitted him sae decently, since, though he was nae fatter, yet he looked mair manly than when he was taen frae Milnwood.'

Next she enlarged on the advantage of saving old clothes to be what she called 'beet-masters to the new', and was far advanced in the history of a velvet cloak belonging to the late Milnwood, which had first been converted to a velvet doublet, and then into a pair of breeches, and appeared each time as good as new, when Morton interrupted her account of its transmigration to bid her good-by.

He gave, indeed, a sufficient shock to her feelings, by expressing the necessity he was under of proceeding on his journey that evening.

'And where are ye gaun? — And what wad ye do that for? — And whar wad ye sleep but in your ain house, after ye hae been sae mony years frae hame?'

'I feel all the unkindness of it, Ailie, but it must be so; and that was the reason that I attempted to conceal myself from you, as I suspected you would not let me part from you so easily.'

'But whar are ye gaun, then?' said Ailie, once more. 'Saw e'er mortal een the like o' you, just to come ae moment, and flee awa like an arrow out of a bow the neist?'

'I must go down,' replied Morton, 'to Niel Blane the Piper's Howff; he can give me a bed, I suppose?'

'A bed? — I'se warrant can he,' replied Ailie, 'and gar ye pay weel for't into the bargain. Laddie, I daresay ye hae lost your wits in thae foreign parts, to gang and gie siller for a supper and a bed, and might hae baith for naething, and thanks t'ye for accepting them.'

'I assure you, Ailie,' said Morton, desirous to silence her re-monstrances, 'that this is a business of great importance, in which I may be a great gainer, and cannot possibly be a loser.'

'I dinna see how that can be, if ye begin by gieing maybe the feck o' twal shillings Scots for your supper; but young folks are aye venturesome, and think to get siller that way. My puir auld master took a surer gate, and never parted wi' it when he had anes gotten't.'

Persevering in his desperate resolution, Morton took leave of Ailie, and mounted his horse to proceed to the little town, after exacting a solemn promise that she would conceal his return until she again saw or heard from him.

I am not very extravagant, was his natural reflection, as he trotted slowly towards the town; but were Ailie and I to set up house together, as she proposes, I think my profusion would break the good old creature's heart before a week were out.

CHAPTER 41

Where's the jolly host
You told me of? 'T has been my custom ever
To parley with mine host.

Lover's Progress [1]

MORTON reached the borough town without meeting with any
remarkable adventure, and alighted at the little inn. It had
occurred to him more than once, while upon his journey, that his
resumption of the dress which he had worn while a youth,
although favourable to his views in other respects, might render
it more difficult for him to remain *incognito*. But a few years of
campaigns and wandering had so changed his appearance, that
he had great confidence that in the grown man, whose brows
exhibited the traces of resolution and considerate thought, none
would recognize the raw and bashful stripling who won the
game of the popinjay. The only chance was, that here and there
some whig, whom he had led to battle, might remember the
Captain of the Milnwood Marksmen; but the risk, if there was
any, could not be guarded against.

The Howff seemed full and frequented as if possessed of all its
old celebrity. The person and demeanour of Niel Blane, more
fat and less civil than of yore, intimated that he had increased
as well in purse as in corpulence; for in Scotland a landlord's
complaisance for his guests decreases in exact proportion to his
rise in the world. His daughter had acquired the air of a dex-
terous bar-maid, undisturbed by the circumstances of love and
war, so apt to perplex her in the exercise of her vocation. Both
showed Morton the degree of attention which could have been
expected by a stranger travelling without attendants, at a time
when they were particularly the badges of distinction. He took
upon himself exactly the character his appearance presented, –
went to the stable and saw his horse accommodated, – then
returned to the house, and, seating himself in the public room,
(for to request one to himself, would, in those days, have been

thought an overweening degree of conceit,) he found himself in the very apartment in which he had some years before celebrated his victory at the game of the popinjay, a jocular preferment which led to so many serious consequences.

He felt himself, as may well be supposed, a much-changed man since that festivity; and yet, to look around him, the groups assembled in the Howff seemed not dissimilar to those which the same scene had formerly presented. Two or three burghers husbanded their 'dribbles o' brandy'; two or three dragoons lounged over their muddy ale, and cursed the inactive times that allowed them no better cheer. Their Cornet did not, indeed, play at backgammon with the curate in his cassock, but he drank a little modicum of *aqua mirabilis* [2] with the grey-cloaked presbyterian minister. The scene was another, and yet the same, differing only in persons, but corresponding in general character.

Let the tide of the world wax or wane as it will, Morton thought, as he looked around him, enough will be found to fill the places which chance renders vacant; and, in the usual occupations and amusements of life, human beings will succeed each other, as leaves upon the same tree, with the same individual difference and the same general resemblance.

After pausing a few minutes, Morton, whose experience had taught him the readiest mode of securing attention, ordered a pint of claret, and, as the smiling landlord appeared with the pewter measure foaming fresh from the tap, (for bottling wine was not then in fashion,) he asked him to sit down and take a share of the good cheer. This invitation was peculiarly acceptable to Niel Blane, who, if he did not positively expect it from every guest not provided with better company, yet received it from many, and was not a whit abashed or surprised at the summons. He sat down, along with his guest, in a secluded nook near the chimney; and while he received encouragement to drink by far the greater share of the liquor before them, he entered at length, as a part of his expected functions, upon the news of the country, – the births, deaths, and marriages, – the change of property, – the downfall of old families, and the rise of new. But politics, now the fertile source of eloquence, mine host did not care to mingle in his theme; and it was only in answer to a question of

Morton, that he replied with an air of indifference, 'Um! ay! we aye hae sodgers amang us, mair or less. There's a wheen German horse down at Glasgow yonder; they ca' their commander Wittybody, or some sic name, though he's as grave and grewsome an auld Dutchman as e'er I saw.'

'Wittenbold, perhaps?' said Morton; 'an old man, with grey hair and short black moustaches – speaks seldom?'

'And smokes for ever,' replied Niel Blane. 'I see your honour kens the man. He may be a very gude man too, for aught I see, that is, considering he is a sodger and a Dutchman; but if he were ten generals, and as mony Wittybodies, he has nae skill in the pipes; he gar'd me stop in the middle of Torphichen's Rant, the best piece o' music that ever bag gae wind to.'

'But these fellows,' said Morton, glancing his eye towards the soldiers that were in the apartment, 'are not of his corps?'

'Na, na, these are Scotch dragoons,' said mine host; 'our ain auld caterpillars; these were Claver'se's lads a while syne, and wad be again, maybe, if he had the lang ten [3] in his hand.'

'Is there not a report of his death?' enquired Morton.

'Troth is there,' said the landlord; 'your honour is right – there is sic a fleeing rumour; but, in my puir opinion, it's lang or the deil die. I wad hae the folks here look to themsells. If he makes an outbreak, he'll be doun frae the hielands or I could drink this glass – and whare are they then? A' thae hell-rakers o' dragoons wad be at his whistle in a moment. Nae doubt they're Willie's men e'en now, as they were James's a while syne – and reason good – they fight for their pay; what else hae they to fight for? They hae neither lands nor houses, I trow. There's ae gude thing o' the change, or the Revolution, as they ca' it, – folks may speak out afore thae birkies now, and nae fear o' being hauled awa to the guard-house, or having the thumikins screwed on your finger-ends, just as I wad drive the screw through a cork.'

There was a little pause, when Morton, feeling confident in the progress he had made in mine host's familiarity, asked, though with the hesitation proper to one who puts a question on the answer to which rests something of importance, – 'Whether Blane knew a woman in that neighbourhood, called Elisabeth Maclure?'

'Whether I ken Bessie Maclure?' answered the landlord, with

a landlord's laugh – 'How can I *but* ken my ain wife's – (haly be her rest!) – my ain wife's first gudeman's sister, Bessie Maclure? an honest wife she is, but sair she's been trysted wi' misfortunes, – the loss o' twa decent lads o' sons, in the time o' the persecution, as they ca' it now-a-days; and doucely and decently she has borne her burden, blaming nane, and condemning nane. If there's an honest woman in the world, it's Bessie Maclure. And to lose her twa sons, as I was saying, and to hae dragoons clinked down on her for a month bypast – for, be whig or tory uppermost, they aye quarter thae loons on victuallers, – to lose, as I was saying' –

'This woman keeps an inn, then?' interrupted Morton.

'A public, in a puir way,' replied Blane, looking round at his own superior accommodations – 'a sour browst o' sma' ale that she sells to folk that are ower drouthy wi' travel to be nice; but naething to ca' a stirring trade or a thriving change-house.'

'Can you get me a guide there?' said Morton.

'Your honour will rest here a' the night? – ye'll hardly get accommodation at Bessie's,' said Niel, whose regard for his deceased wife's relative by no means extended to sending company from his own house to hers.

'There is a friend,' answered Morton, 'whom I am to meet with there, and I only called here to take a stirrup-cup and enquire the way.'

'Your honour had better,' answered the landlord, with the perseverance of his calling, 'send some ane to warn your friend to come on here.'

'I tell you, landlord,' answered Morton impatiently, 'that will not serve my purpose; I must go straight to this woman Maclure's house, and I desire you to find me a guide.'

'Aweel, sir, ye'll choose for yoursell, to be sure,' said Niel Blane, somewhat disconcerted; 'but deil a guide ye'll need, if ye gae doun the water for twa mile or sae, as gin ye were bound for Milnwoodhouse, and then tak the first broken disjasked-looking road that makes for the hills – ye'll ken't by a broken ash-tree that stands at the side o' a burn just where the roads meet; and then travel out the path – ye canna miss Widow Maclure's public, for deil another house or hauld is on the road for ten lang Scots miles, and that's worth twenty English. I am sorry your honour would think o' gaun out o' my house the night. But my wife's gude-sister is a decent woman, and it's no lost that a friend gets.'

Morton accordingly paid his reckoning and departed. The sunset of the summer day placed him at the ash-tree, where the path led up towards the moors.

'Here,' he said to himself, 'my misfortunes commenced; for just here, when Burley and I were about to separate on the first night we ever met, he was alarmed by the intelligence, that the passes were secured by soldiers lying in wait for him. Beneath that very ash sate the old woman who apprized him of his danger. How strange that my whole fortunes should have become inseparably interwoven with that man's, without any thing more on my part, than the discharge of an ordinary duty of humanity! Would to Heaven it were possible I could find my humble quiet and tranquillity of mind, upon the spot where I lost them!'

Thus arranging his reflections betwixt speech and thought, he turned his horse's head up the path.

Evening lowered around him as he advanced up the narrow dell which had once been a wood, but was now a ravine divested of trees, unless where a few, from their inaccessible situation on the edge of precipitous banks, or clinging among rocks and huge stones, defied the invasion of men and of cattle, like the scattered tribes of a conquered country, driven to take refuge in the barren strength of its mountains. These too, wasted and decayed, seemed rather to exist than to flourish, and only served to indicate what the landscape had once been. But the stream brawled down among them in all its freshness and vivacity, giving the life and animation which a mountain rivulet alone can confer on the barest and most savage scenes, and which the inhabitants of such a country miss when gazing even upon the tranquil winding of a majestic stream through plains of fertility, and beside palaces of splendour. The track of the road followed the course of the brook, which was now visible, and now only to be distinguished by its brawling heard among the stones, or in the clefts of the rocks, that occasionally interrupted its course.

'Murmurer that thou art,' said Morton, in the enthusiasm of his reverie, — 'why chafe with the rocks that stop thy course for a moment? There is a sea to receive thee in its bosom; and there is an eternity for man when his fretful and hasty course through the vale of time shall be ceased and over. What thy petty fuming is to the deep and vast billows of a shoreless ocean, are our cares, hopes, fears, joys, and sorrows, to the objects which must occupy us through the awful and boundless succession of ages!'

Thus moralizing, our traveller passed on till the dell opened, and the banks, receding from the brook, left a little green vale, exhibiting a croft, or small field, on which some corn was growing, and a cottage, whose walls were not above five feet high, and whose thatched roof, green with moisture, age, house-leek, and grass, had in some places suffered damage from the encroachment of two cows, whose appetite this appearance of verdure had diverted from their more legitimate pasture. An ill-spelt and worse-written inscription intimated to the traveller that he might here find refreshment for man and horse; — no unacceptable intimation, rude as the hut appeared to be, considering the wild path he had trod in approaching it, and the high and waste mountains which rose in desolate dignity behind this humble asylum.

It must indeed have been, thought Morton, in some such spot as this, that Burley was likely to find a congenial confident.

As he approached, he observed the good dame of the house herself, seated by the door; she had hitherto been concealed from him by a huge alder bush.

'Good evening, mother,' said the traveller. 'Your name is Mistress Maclure?'

'Elizabeth Maclure, sir, a poor widow' was the reply.

'Can you lodge a stranger for a night?'

'I can, sir, if he will be pleased with the widow's cake and the widow's cruize.' [4]

'I have been a soldier, good dame,' answered Morton, 'and nothing can come amiss to me in the way of entertainment.'

'A sodger, sir?' said the old woman, with a sigh, 'God send ye a better trade!'

'It is believed to be an honourable profession, my good dame. I hope you do not think the worse of me for having belonged to it?'

'I judge no one, sir,' replied the woman, 'and your voice sounds like that of a civil gentleman; but I hae witnessed sae muckle ill wi' sodgering in this puir land, that I am e'en content that I can see nae mair o't wi' these sightless organs.'

As she spoke thus, Morton observed that she was blind.

'Shall I not be troublesome to you, my good dame?' said he, compassionately; 'your infirmity seems ill calculated for your profession.'

'Na, sir,' answered the old woman; 'I can gang about the house readily eneugh; and I hae a bit lassie to help me, and the dragoon lads will look after your horse when they come hame frae their patrol, for a sma' matter; they are civiller now than lang syne.'

Upon these assurances, Morton alighted.

'Peggy, my bonny bird,' continued the hostess, addressing a little girl of twelve years old, who had by this time appeared, 'tak the gentleman's horse to the stable, and slack his girths, and tak aff the bridle, and shake down a lock o' hay before him, till the dragoons come back. — Come this way, sir,' she continued; 'ye'll find my house clean, though it's a puir ane.'

Morton followed her into the cottage accordingly.

CHAPTER 42

Then out and spake the auld mother,
    And fast her tears did fa —
'Ye wadna be warn'd, my son Johnie,
    Frae the hunting to bide awa!'

                                                    Old Ballad[1]

WHEN he entered the cottage, Morton perceived that the old hostess had spoken truth. The inside of the hut belied its outward appearance, and was neat, and even comfortable, especially the inner apartment, in which the hostess informed her guest that he was to sup and sleep. Refreshments were placed before him, such as the little inn afforded; and, though he had small occasion for them, he accepted the offer, as the means of maintaining some discourse with the landlady. Notwithstanding her blindness, she was assiduous in her attendance, and seemed, by a sort of instinct, to find her way to what she wanted.

'Have you no one but this pretty little girl to assist you in waiting on your guests?' was the natural question.

'None, sir,' replied his old hostess: 'I dwell alone, like the widow of Zarephath.[2] Few guests come to this puir place; and I haena custom eneugh to hire servants. I had anes twa fine sons that lookit after a' thing – But God gives and takes away – His name be praised!' she continued, turning her clouded eyes towards Heaven – "I was anes better off, that is, warldly speaking, even since I lost them; but that was before this last change.'

'Indeed!' said Morton, 'and yet you are a presbyterian, my good mother?'

'I am, sir; praised be the light that showed me the right way,' replied the landlady.

'Then, I should have thought,' continued the guest, 'the Revolution would have brought you nothing but good.'

'If,' said the old woman, 'it has brought the land gude, and freedom of worship to tender consciences, it's little matter what it has brought to a puir blind worm like me.'

'Still,' replied Morton, 'I cannot see how it could possibly injure you.'

'It's a lang story, sir,' answered his hostess, with a sigh. 'But ae night, sax weeks or thereby afore Bothwell Brigg, a young gentleman stopped at this puir cottage, stiff and bloody with wounds, pale and dune out wi' riding, and his horse sae weary he couldna drag ae foot after the other, and his foes were close ahint him, and he was ane o' our enemies – What could I do, sir? – You that's a sodger will think me but a silly auld wife – but I fed him, and relieved him, and keepit him hidden till the pursuit was ower.'

'And who,' said Morton, 'dares disapprove of your having done so?'

'I kenna,' answered the blind woman – 'I gat ill-will about it amang some o' our ain folk. They said I should hae been to him what Jael was to Sisera [3] – But weel I wot I had nae divine com-

mand to shed blood, and to save it was baith like a woman and a
Christian. – And then they said I wanted natural affection, to
relieve ane that belanged to the band that murdered my twa
sons.'

'That murdered your two sons?'

'Ay, sir; though maybe ye'll gie their deaths another name –
The tane fell wi' sword in hand, fighting for a broken national
Covenant; the tother – O, they took him and shot him dead on
the green before his mother's face ! – My auld een dazzled when
the shots were looten off, and, to my thought, they waxed weaker
and weaker ever since that weary day – and sorrow, and heart-
break, and tears that would not be dried, might help on the
disorder. But, alas ! betraying Lord Evandale's young blood to
his enemies' sword wad ne'er hae brought my Ninian and Johnie
alive again.' [4]

'Lord Evandale?' said Morton, in surprise; 'Was it Lord
Evandale whose life you saved?'

'In troth, even his,' she replied. 'And kind he was to me after,
and gae me a cow and calf, malt, meal, and siller, and nane durst
steer me when he was in power. But we live on an outside bit of
Tillietudlem land, and the estate was sair plea'd between Leddy
Margaret Bellenden and the present Laird, Basil Olifant, and
Lord Evandale backed the auld leddy for love o' her daughter
Miss Edith, as the country said, ane o' the best and bonniest lasses
in Scotland. But they behuved to gie way, and Basil gat the
Castle and land, and on the back o' that came the Revolution,
and wha to turn coat faster than the laird? for he said he had
been a true whig a' the time, and turned papist only for fashion's
sake. And then he got favour, and Lord Evandale's head was
under water; for he was ower proud and manfu' to bend to
every blast o' wind, though mony a ane may ken as weel as me,
that be his ain principles as they might, he was nae ill friend to
our folk when he could protect us, and far kinder than Basil
Olifant, that aye keepit the cobble head doun the stream. But he
was set by and ill looked on, and his word ne'er asked; and
then Basil, wha's a revengefu' man, set himsell to vex him in a'
shapes, and especially by oppressing and despoiling the auld
blind widow, Bessie Maclure, that saved Lord Evandale's life,

and that he was sae kind to. But he's mistaen, if that's his end; for it will be lang or Lord Evandale hears a word frae me about the selling my kye for rent or e'er it was due, or the putting the dragoons on me when the country's quiet, or ony thing else that will vex him — I can bear my ain burden patiently, and warld's loss is the least part o't.'

Astonished and interested at this picture of patient, grateful, and high-minded resignation, Morton could not help bestowing an execration upon the poor-spirited rascal who had taken such a dastardly course of vengeance.

'Dinna curse him, sir,' said the old woman; 'I have heard a good man say, that a curse was like a stone flung up to the heavens, and maist like to return on the head that sent it. But if ye ken Lord Evandale, bid him look to himsell, for I hear strange words pass atween the sodgers that are lying here, and his name is often mentioned; and the tane o' them has been twice up at Tillietudlem. He's a kind of favourite wi' the Laird, though he was in former times ane o' the maist cruel oppressors ever rade through a country (out-taken Sergeant Bothwell) — they ca' him Inglis.' [5]

'I have the deepest interest in Lord Evandale's safety,' said Morton, 'and you may depend on my finding some mode to apprize him of these suspicious circumstances: And, in return, my good friend, will you indulge me with another question? Do you know any thing of Quintin Mackell of Irongray?'

'Do I know *whom*?' echoed the blind woman, in a tone of great surprise and alarm.

'Quintin Mackell of Irongray,' repeated Morton; 'is there any thing so alarming in the sound of that name?'

'Na, na,' answered the woman with hesitation, 'but to hear him asked after by a stranger and a sodger — Gude protect us, what mischief is to come next!'

'None by my means, I assure you,' said Morton; 'the subject of my enquiry has nothing to fear from me, if, as I suppose, this Quintin Mackell is the same with John Bal —'

'Do not mention his name,' said the widow, pressing his lips with her fingers. 'I see you have his secret and his pass-word, and I'll be free wi' you. But, for God's sake, speak lound and

low. In the name of Heaven, I trust ye seek him not to his hurt!
— Ye said ye were a sodger?'

'I said truly; but one he has nothing to fear from. I commanded a party at Bothwell Bridge.'

'Indeed?' said the woman. 'And verily there is something in
your voice I can trust. Ye speak prompt and readily, and like an
honest man.'

'I trust I am so,' said Morton.

'But nae displeasure to you, sir, in thae waefu' times,' continued Mrs Maclure, 'the hand of brother is against brother, and
he fears as mickle almaist frae this government, as e'er he did
frae the auld persecutors.'

'Indeed?' said Morton, in a tone of enquiry; 'I was not aware
of that. But I am only just now returned from abroad.'

'I'll tell ye,' said the blind woman, first assuming an attitude
of listening that showed how effectually her powers of collecting
intelligence had been transferred from the eye to the ear; for, instead of casting a glance of circumspection around, she stooped
her face, and turned her head slowly around, in such a manner as
to ensure that there was not the slightest sound stirring in the
neighbourhood, and then continued: 'I'll tell ye. Ye ken how he
has laboured to raise up again the Covenant, burned, broken,
and buried in the hard hearts and selfish devices of this stubborn
people. Now, when he went to Holland, far from the countenance and thanks of the great, and the comfortable fellowship of
the godly, both whilk he was in right to expect, the Prince of
Orange wad show him no favour, and the ministers no godly
communion. This was hard to bide for ane that had suffered and
done mickle — ower mickle, it may be — but why suld I be a
judge? He came back to me and to the auld place o' refuge that
had often received him in his distresses, mair especially before
the great day of victory at Drumclog, for I sall ne'er forget how
he was bending hither of a' nights in the year on that e'ening
after the play when young Milnwood wan the popinjay; but I
warned him off for that time.'

'What!' exclaimed Morton, 'it was you that sat in your red
cloak by the high-road, and told him there was a lion in the
path?'

'In the name of Heaven! wha are ye?' said the old woman, breaking off her narrative in astonishment. 'But be wha ye may,' she continued, resuming it with tranquillity, 'ye can ken nae-thing waur o' me than that I hae been willing to save the life o' friend and foe.'

'I know no ill of you, Mrs Maclure, and I mean no ill by you – I only wished to show you that I know so much of this person's affairs, that I might be safely intrusted with the rest. Proceed, if you please, in your narrative.'

'There is a strange command in your voice,' said the blind woman, 'though its tones are sweet. I have little mair to say. The Stewarts hae been dethroned, and William and Mary reign in their stead, but nae mair word of the Covenant than if it were a dead letter. They hae taen the indulged clergy, and an Erastian General Assembly of the ance pure and triumphant Kirk of Scotland, even into their very arms and bosoms. Our faithfu' champions o' the testimony agree e'en waur wi' this than wi' the open tyranny and apostasy of the persecuting times, for souls are hardened and deadened, and the mouths of fasting multitudes are crammed wi' fizenless bran instead of the sweet word in season; and many an hungry, starving creature, when he sits down on a Sunday forenoon to get something that might warm him to the great work, has a dry clatter o' morality driven about his lugs, and' –

'In short,' said Morton, desirous to stop a discussion which the good old woman, as enthusiastically attached to her religious profession as to the duties of humanity, might probably have indulged longer – 'In short, you are not disposed to acquiesce in this new government, and Burley is of the same opinion?'

'Many of our brethren, sir, are of belief we fought for the Covenant, and fasted, and prayed, and suffered for that grand national league, and now we are like neither to see nor hear tell of that which we suffered, and fought, and fasted, and prayed for. And anes it was thought something might be made by bringing back the auld family on a new bargain and a new bottom, as, after a', when King James went awa, I understand the great quarrel of the English against him was in behalf of seven un-hallowed prelates;[6] and sae, though ae part of our people were free to join wi' the present model, and levied an armed regiment under the Yerl of Angus,[7] yet our honest friend, and others that stude up for purity of doctrine and freedom of conscience, were determined to hear the breath o' the Jacobites before they took part again them, fearing to fa' to the ground like a wall built with unslaked mortar, or from sitting between twa stools.'

'They chose an odd quarter,' said Morton, 'from which to expect freedom of conscience and purity of doctrine.'

'O, dear sir!' said the landlady, 'the natural day-spring rises in the east, but the spiritual day-spring may rise in the north, for what we blinded mortals ken.'

'And Burley went to the north to seek it?' replied the guest.

'Truly ay, sir; and he saw Claver'se himsell, that they ca' Dundee now.'

'What!' exclaimed Morton, in amazement; 'I would have sworn that meeting would have been the last of one of their lives.'

'Na, na, sir; in troubled times, as I understand,' said Mrs Maclure, 'there's sudden changes — Montgomery, and Ferguson,[8] and mony ane mair that were King James's greatest faes, are on his side now — Claver'se spake our friend fair, and sent him to consult with Lord Evandale. But then there was a break-off, for Lord Evandale wadna look at, hear, or speak wi' him; and now he's anes wud and aye waur, and roars for revenge again Lord Evandale, and will hear nought of ony thing but burn and slay — and O thae starts o' passion! they unsettle his mind, and gie the Enemy sair advantages.'

'The enemy?' said Morton; 'What enemy?'

'What enemy? Are ye acquainted familiarly wi' John Balfour o' Burley, and dinna ken that he has had sair and frequent combats to sustain against the Evil One? Did ye ever see him alone but the Bible was in his hand, and the drawn sword on his knee? did ye never sleep in the same room wi' him, and hear him strive in his dreams with the delusions of Satan? O, ye ken little o' him, if ye have seen him only in fair daylight, for nae man can put the face upon his doleful visits and strifes that he can do. I hae seen him, after sic a strife of agony, tremble, that an infant might hae held him, while the hair on his brow was drapping as fast as ever my puir thatched roof did in a heavy rain.'

As she spoke, Morton began to recollect the appearance of Burley during his sleep in the hay-loft at Milnwood, the report of Cuddie that his senses had become impaired, and some whispers current among the Cameronians, who boasted frequently of Burley's soul-exercises, and his strifes with the foul fiend; which several circumstances led him to conclude that this man himself was a victim to those delusions, though his mind, naturally acute and forcible, not only disguised his superstition from those in whose opinion it might have discredited his judgment, but by exerting such a force as is said to be proper to those afflicted with epilepsy, could postpone the fits which it occasioned until he was either freed from superintendence, or surrounded by such as held him more highly on account of these visitations. It was natural to suppose, and could easily be inferred from the narrative of Mrs Maclure, that disappointed ambition, wrecked hopes, and the downfall of the party which he had served with such desperate fidelity, were likely to aggravate enthusiasm into temporary insanity. It was, indeed, no uncommon circumstance in those singular times, that men like Sir Harry Vane, Harrison, Overton,[9] and others, themselves slaves to the wildest and most enthusiastic dreams, could, when mingling with the world, conduct themselves not only with good sense in difficulties, and courage in dangers, but with the most acute sagacity and determined valour. The subsequent part of Mrs Maclure's information confirmed Morton in these impressions.

'In the grey of the morning,' she said, 'my little Peggy sall show ye the gate to him before the sodgers are up. But ye maun let his hour of danger, as he ca's it, be ower, afore ye venture on him in his place of refuge. Peggy will tell ye when to venture in. She kens his ways weel, for whiles she carries him some little helps that he canna do without to sustain life.'

'And in what retreat then,' said Morton, 'has this unfortunate person found refuge?'

'An awesome place,' answered the blind woman, 'as ever living creature took refuge in. They ca' it the Black Linn of Linklater —it's a doleful place; but he loves it abune a' others, because he has sae often been in safe hiding there; and it's my belief he prefers it to a tapestried chamber and a down bed. But ye'll see't. I hae seen it mysell mony a day syne. I was a daft hempie lassie then, and little thought what was to come o't — Wad ye choose ony thing, sir, ere ye betake yoursell to your rest, for ye maun stir wi' the first dawn o' the grey light?'

'Nothing more, my good mother,' said Morton; and they parted for the evening.

Morton recommended himself to Heaven, threw himself on the bed, heard, between sleeping and waking, the trampling of the dragoon horses at the riders' return from their patrol, and then slept soundly after such painful agitation.

CHAPTER 43

The darksome cave they enter, where they found
The accursed man, low sitting on the ground,
Musing full sadly in his sullen mind.
SPENSER[1]

As the morning began to appear on the mountains, a gentle knock was heard at the door of the humble apartment in which Morton slept, and a girlish treble voice asked him from without, 'If he wad please gang to the Linn or the folk raise?'

He arose upon the invitation, and, dressing himself hastily, went forth and joined his little guide. The mountain maid tript lightly before him, through the grey haze, over hill and moor. It was a wild and varied walk, unmarked by any regular or distinguishable track, and keeping, upon the whole, the direction of the ascent of the brook, though without tracing its windings. The landscape, as they advanced, became waster and more wild, until nothing but heath and rock encumbered the side of the valley.

'Is the place still distant?' said Morton.

'Nearly a mile off,' answered the girl. 'We'll be there belive.'

'And do you often go this wild journey, my little maid?'

'When grannie sends me wi' milk and meal to the Linn,' answered the child.

'And are you not afraid to travel so wild a road alone?'

'Hout na, sir,' replied the guide; 'nae living creature wad touch sic a bit thing as I am, and grannie says we need never fear ony thing else when we are doing a gude turn.'

'Strong in innocence as in triple mail!' said Morton to himself, and followed her steps in silence.

They soon came to a decayed thicket, where brambles and thorns supplied the room of the oak and birches of which it had once consisted. Here the guide turned short off the open heath, and, by a sheep-track, conducted Morton to the brook. A hoarse and sullen roar had in part prepared him for the scene which presented itself, yet it was not to be viewed without surprise and even terror. When he emerged from the devious path which conducted him through the thicket, he found himself placed on a ledge of flat rock, projecting over one side of a chasm not less than a hundred feet deep, where the dark mountain-stream made a decided and rapid shoot over the precipice, and was swallowed up by a deep, black, yawning gulf. The eye in vain strove to see the bottom of the fall; it could catch but one sheet of foaming uproar and sheer descent, until the view was obstructed by the projecting crags which enclosed the bottom of the waterfall, and hid from sight the dark pool which received its tortured waters; far beneath, at the distance of perhaps a quarter of a mile, the eye caught the winding of the stream as it emerged into a more open course. But, for that distance, they were lost to sight as much as if a cavern had been arched over them; and indeed the steep and projecting ledges of rock through which they wound their way in darkness, were very nearly closing and over-roofing their course.

While Morton gazed at this scene of tumult, which seemed, by the surrounding thickets and the clefts into which the waters descended, to seek to hide itself from every eye, his little attendant, as she stood beside him on the platform of rock which commanded the best view of the fall, pulled him by the sleeve, and said, in a tone which he could not hear without stooping his ear near the speaker, 'Hear till him! Eh! hear till him!'

Morton listened more attentively, and out of the very abyss into which the brook fell, and amidst the tumultuary sounds of the cataract, thought he could distinguish shouts, screams, and even articulate words, as if the tortured demon of the stream had been mingling his complaints with the roar of his broken waters.

'This is the way,' said the little girl: 'follow me, gin ye please, sir, but tak tent to your feet"; and, with the daring agility which custom had rendered easy, she vanished from the platform on which she stood, and, by notches and slight projections in the rock, scrambled down its face into the chasm which it overhung. Steady, bold, and active, Morton hesitated not to follow her; but the necessary attention to secure his hold and footing in a descent where both foot and hand were needful for security, prevented him from looking around him, till, having descended nigh twenty feet, and being sixty or seventy above the pool which received the fall, his guide made a pause, and he again found himself by her side in a situation that appeared equally romantic and precarious. They were nearly opposite to the waterfall, and in point of level situated at about one-quarter's depth from the point of the cliff over which it thundered, and three-fourths of the height above the dark, deep, and restless pool which received its fall. Both these tremendous points, the first shoot, namely, of the yet unbroken stream, and the deep and sombre abyss into which it was emptied, were full before him, as well as the whole continuous stream of billowy froth, which, dashing from the one, was eddying and boiling in the other. They were so near this grand phenomenon that they were covered with its spray, and wellnigh deafened by the incessant roar. But crossing in the very front of the fall, and at scarce three yards distance from the cataract, an old oak-tree, flung across the chasm in a manner that seemed accidental, formed a bridge of fearfully narrow dimensions and uncertain footing. The upper end of the tree rested on the platform on which they stood – the lower or up-rooted extremity extended behind a projection on the opposite side, and was secured, Morton's eye could not discover where. From behind the same projection glimmered a strong red light, which, glancing in the waves of the falling water, and tinging them partially with crimson, had a strange preternatural and sinister effect when contrasted with the beams of the rising sun, which glanced on the first broken waves of the fall, though even its meridian splendour could not gain the third of its full depth. When he had looked around him for a moment, the girl again pulled his sleeve, and pointing to the oak and the projecting point beyond it, (for hearing speech was now out of the question,) indicated that there lay his farther passage.

Morton gazed at her with surprise; for, although he well knew that the persecuted presbyterians had in the preceeding reigns sought refuge among dells and thickets, caves and cataracts, – in spots the most extraordinary and secluded – although he had heard of the champions of the Covenant, who had long abidden beside Dobs-linn on the wild heights of Polmoodie, and others who had been concealed in the yet more terrific cavern called Creehope-linn, in the parish of Closeburn,² yet his imagination had never exactly figured out the horrors of such a residence, and he was surprised how the strange and romantic scene which he now saw had remained concealed from him, while a curious investigator of such natural phenomena. But he readily conceived, that, lying in a remote and wild district, and being destined as a place of concealment to the persecuted preachers and professors of non-conformity, the secret of its existence was carefully preserved by the few shepherds to whom it might be known.

As, breaking from these meditations, he began to consider how he should traverse the doubtful and terrific bridge, which, skirted by the cascade, and rendered wet and slippery by its constant drizzle, traversed the chasm above sixty feet from the bottom of the fall, his guide, as if to give him courage, tript over and back without the least hesitation. Envying for a moment the little bare feet which caught a safer hold of the rugged side of the oak than he could pretend to with his heavy boots, Morton nevertheless resolved to attempt the passage, and, fixing his eye firm on a stationary object on the other side, without allowing his head to become giddy, or his attention to be distracted by the flash, the foam, and the roar of the waters around him, he strode steadily and safely along the uncertain bridge, and reached the mouth of a small cavern on the farther side of the torrent. Here he paused; for a light, proceeding from a fire of red-hot charcoal, permitted him to see the interior of the cave, and enabled him to contemplate the appearance of its inhabitant, by whom he himself could

not be so readily distinguished, being concealed by the shadow
of the rock. What he observed would by no means have encouraged a less determined man to proceed with the task which
he had undertaken.

Burley, only altered from what he had been formerly by the
addition of a grisly beard, stood in the midst of the cave, with
his clasped Bible in one hand, and his drawn sword in the other.
His figure, dimly ruddied by the light of the red charcoal, seemed
that of a fiend in the lurid atmosphere of Pandemonium, and his
gestures and words, as far as they could be heard, seemed equally
violent and irregular. All alone, and in a place of almost un-
approachable seclusion, his demeanour was that of a man who
strives for life and death with a mortal enemy. 'Ha! ha! – there
– there!' he exclaimed, accompanying each word with a thrust,
urged with his whole force against the impassible and empty air
– 'Did I not tell thee so? – I have resisted, and thou fleest from
me! – Coward as thou art – come in all thy terrors – come with
mine own evil deeds, which render thee most terrible of all –
there is enough betwixt the boards of this book to rescue me! –
What mutterest thou of grey hairs? – It was well done to slay
him – the more ripe the corn the readier for the sickle. – Art
gone? – I have ever known thee but a coward – ha! ha! ha!'

With these wild exclamations he sunk the point of his sword,
and remained standing still in the same posture, like a maniac
whose fit is over.

'The dangerous time is by now,' said the little girl who had
followed; 'it seldom lasts beyond the time that the sun's ower
the hill; ye may gang in and speak wi' him now. I'll wait for
you at the other side of the linn; he canna bide to see twa folk
at anes.'

Slowly and cautiously, and keeping constantly upon his guard,
Morton presented himself to the view of his old associate in
command.

'What! comest thou again when thine hour is over?' was his
first exclamation; and flourishing his sword aloft, his countenance assumed an expression in which ghastly terror seemed
mingled with the rage of a demoniac.

'I am come, Mr Balfour,' said Morton, in a steady and composed tone, 'to renew an acquaintance which has been broken off since the fight of Bothwell Bridge.'

As soon as Burley became aware that Morton was before him in person, – an idea which he caught with marvellous celerity, – he at once exerted that mastership over his heated and enthusiastic imagination, the power of enforcing which was a most striking part of his extraordinary character. He sunk his swordpoint at once, and as he stole it composedly into the scabbard, he muttered something of the damp and cold which sent an old soldier to his fencing exercise, to prevent his blood from chilling. This done, he proceeded in the cold determined manner which was peculiar to his ordinary discourse.

'Thou hast tarried long, Henry Morton, and hast not come to the vintage before the twelfth hour has struck.[3] Art thou yet willing to take the right hand of fellowship, and be one with those who look not to thrones or dynasties, but to the rule of Scripture, for their directions?'

'I am surprised,' said Morton, evading the direct answer to his question, 'that you should have known me after so many years.'

'The features of those who ought to act with me are engraved on my heart,' answered Burley; 'and few but Silas Morton's son durst have followed me into this my castle of retreat. Seest thou that drawbridge of Nature's own construction?' he added, pointing to the prostrate oak-tree – 'one spurn of my foot, and it is overwhelmed in the abyss below, bidding foemen on the farther side stand at defiance, and leaving enemies on this at the mercy of one, who never yet met his equal in single fight.'

'Of such defences,' said Morton, 'I should have thought you would now have had little need.'

'Little need?' said Burley impatiently – 'What little need, when incarnate fiends are combined against me on earth, and Sathan himself – But it matters not,' added he, checking himself – 'Enough that I like my place of refuge – my cave of Adullam,[4] and would not change its rude ribs of limestone rock for the fair chambers of the castle of the Earls of Torwood, with their broad bounds and barony. Thou, unless the foolish fever-fit be over, mayst think differently.'

'It was of those very possessions I came to speak,' said Morton; 'and I doubt not to find Mr Balfour the same rational and reflecting person which I knew him to be in times when zeal disunited brethren.'

'Ay?' said Burley; 'indeed? – Is such truly your hope? – wilt thou express it more plainly?'

'In a word then,' said Morton, 'you have exercised, by means at which I can guess, a secret, but most prejudicial influence over the fortunes of Lady Margaret Bellenden and her granddaughter, and in favour of that base, oppressive apostate, Basil Olifant, whom the law, deceived by thy operations, has placed in possession of their lawful property.'

'Sayest thou?' said Balfour.

'I do say so,' replied Morton; 'and face to face you will not deny what you have vouched by your handwriting.'

'And suppose I deny it not?' said Balfour, 'and suppose that thy eloquence were found equal to persuade me to retrace the steps I have taken on matured resolve, what will be thy need? Dost thou still hope to possess the fair-haired girl, with her wide and rich inheritance?'

'I have no such hope,' answered Morton calmly.

'And for whom, then, hast thou ventured to do this great thing, to seek to rend the prey from the valiant, to bring forth food from the den of the lion, and to extract sweetness from the maw of the devourer? – For whose sake hast thou undertaken to read this riddle, more hard than Samson's?'[5]

'For Lord Evandale's and that of his bride,' replied Morton firmly. 'Think better of mankind, Mr Balfour, and believe there are some who are willing to sacrifice their happiness to that of others.'

'Then, as my soul liveth,' replied Balfour, 'thou art, to wear beard, and back a horse, and draw a sword, the tamest and most gall-less puppet that ever sustained injury unavenged. What! thou wouldst help that accursed Evandale to the arms of the woman that thou lovest? – thou wouldst endow them with wealth and with heritages, and thou think'st that there lives another man, offended even more deeply than thou, yet equally cold-livered and mean-spirited, crawling upon the face of the earth, and hast dared to suppose that one other to be John Balfour?'

'For my own feelings,' said Morton composedly, 'I am answerable to none but Heaven – To you, Mr Balfour, I should suppose it of little consequence whether Basil Olifant or Lord Evandale possess these estates.'

'Thou art deceived,' said Burley; 'both are indeed in outer darkness, and strangers to the light, as he whose eyes have never been opened to the day. But this Basil Olifant is a Nabal – a Demas [6] – a base churl, whose wealth and power are at the disposal of him who can threaten to deprive him of them. He became a professor because he was deprived of these lands of Tillietudlem – he turned a papist to obtain possession of them – he called himself an Erastian, that he might not again lose them, and he will become what I list while I have in my power the document that may deprive him of them. These lands are a bit between his jaws and a hook in his nostrils,[7] and the rein and the line are in my hands to guide them as I think meet; and his they shall therefore be, unless I had assurance of bestowing them on a sure and sincere friend. But Lord Evandale is a malignant, of heart like flint, and brow like adamant; the goods of the world fall on him like leaves on the frost-bound earth, and unmoved he will see them whirled off by the first wind. The heathen virtues of such as he are more dangerous to us than the sordid cupidity of those, who, governed by their interest, must follow where it leads, and who, therefore, themselves the slaves of avarice, may be compelled to work in the vineyard, were it but to earn the wages of sin.'

'This might have been all well some years since,' replied Morton; 'and I could understand your argument, although I could never acquiesce in its justice. But at this crisis it seems useless to you to persevere in keeping up an influence which can no longer be directed to an useful purpose. The land has peace, liberty, and freedom of conscience – and what would you more?'

'More!' exclaimed Burley, again unsheathing his sword, with a vivacity which nearly made Morton start; 'look at the notches upon that weapon; they are three in number, are they not?'

'It seems so,' answered Morton; 'but what of that?'

'The fragment of steel that parted from this first gap, rested on the skull of the perjured traitor, who first introduced Episcopacy into Scotland; – this second notch was made in the rib-bone of an impious villain, the boldest and best soldier that upheld the prelatic cause at Drumclog; – this third was broken on the steel head-piece of the captain who defended the Chapel of Holyrood [8] when the people rose at the Revolution. I cleft him to the teeth through steel and bone. It has done great deeds this little weapon, and each of these blows was a deliverance to the church. This sword,' he said, again sheathing it, 'has yet more to do – to weed out this base and pestilential heresy of Erastianism – to vindicate the true liberty of the Kirk in her purity – to restore the Covenant in its glory, – then let it moulder and rust beside the bones of its master.' [9]

'You have neither men nor means, Mr Balfour, to disturb the government as now settled,' argued Morton; 'the people are in general satisfied, excepting only the gentlemen of the Jacobite interest; and surely you would not join with those who would only use you for their own purposes?'

'It is they,' answered Burley, 'that should serve ours. I went to the camp of the malignant Claver'se, as the future King of Israel sought the land of the Philistines;[10] I arranged with him a rising, and, but for the villain Evandale, the Erastians ere now had been driven from the west – I could slay him,' he added, with a vindictive scowl, 'were he grasping the horns of the altar!' He then proceeded in a calmer tone: 'If thou, son of mine ancient comrade, wert suitor for thyself to this Edith Bellenden, and wert willing to put thy hand to the great work with zeal equal to thy courage, think not I would prefer the friendship of Basil Olifant to thine; thou shouldst then have the means that this document (he produced a parchment) affords, to place her in possession of the lands of her fathers. This have I longed to say to thee ever since I saw thee fight the good fight so strongly at the fatal Bridge. The maiden loved thee, and thou her.'

Morton replied firmly, 'I will not dissemble with you, Mr Balfour, even to gain a good end. I came in hopes to persuade you to do a deed of justice to others, not to gain any selfish end of my own. I have failed – I grieve for your sake, more than for the loss which others will sustain by your injustice.'

'You refuse my proffer, then?' said Burley, with kindling eyes.

'I do,' said Morton. 'Would you be really, as you are desirous to be thought, a man of honour and conscience, you would, regardless of all other considerations, restore that parchment to Lord Evandale, to be used for the advantage of the lawful heir.'

'Sooner shall it perish !' said Balfour; and, casting the deed into the heap of red charcoal beside him, pressed it down with the heel of his boot.

While it smoked, shrivelled, and crackled in the flames, Morton sprung forward to snatch it, and Burley catching hold of him, a struggle ensued. Both were strong men, but although Morton was much the more active and younger of the two, yet Balfour was the most powerful, and effectually prevented him from rescuing the deed until it was fairly reduced to a cinder. They then quitted hold of each other, and the enthusiast, rendered fiercer by the contest, glared on Morton with an eye expressive of frantic revenge.

'Thou hast my secret,' he exclaimed; 'thou must be mine, or die !'

'I contemn your threats,' said Morton; 'I pity you, and leave you.'

But, as he turned to retire, Burley stept before him, pushed the oak-trunk from its resting place, and, as it fell thundering and crashing into the abyss beneath, drew his sword, and cried out, with a voice that rivalled the roar of the cataract and the thunder of the falling oak, – 'Now thou art at bay ! – fight – yield, or die !' and standing in the mouth of the cavern, he flourished his naked sword.

'I will not fight with the man that preserved my father's life,' said Morton; – 'I have not yet learned to say the words, I yield; and my life I will rescue as I best can.'

So speaking, and ere Balfour was aware of his purpose, he sprung past him, and exerting that youthful agility of which he possessed an uncommon share, leaped clear across the fearful chasm which divided the mouth of the cave from the projecting rock on the opposite side, and stood there safe and free from his incensed enemy. He immediately ascended the ravine, and, as he turned, saw Burley stand for an instant aghast with astonishment, and then, with the frenzy of disappointed rage, rush into the interior of his cavern.

It was not difficult for him to perceive that this unhappy man's mind had been so long agitated by desperate schemes, and sudden disappointments, that it had lost its equipoise, and that there was now in his conduct a shade of lunacy, not the less striking, from the vigour and craft with which he pursued his wild designs. Morton soon joined his guide, who had been terrified by the fall of the oak. This he represented as accidental; and she assured him in return, that the inhabitant of the cave would experience no inconvenience from it, being always provided with materials to construct another bridge.

The adventures of the morning were not yet ended. As they approached the hut, the little girl made an exclamation of surprise at seeing her grandmother groping her way towards them, at a greater distance from her home than she could have been supposed capable of travelling.

'O, sir, sir!' said the old woman, when she heard them approach, 'gin e'er ye loved Lord Evandale, help now, or never! – God be praised that left my hearing when he took my poor eye-sight! – Come this way – this way – And O! tread lightly. – Peggy, hinny, gang saddle the gentleman's horse, and lead him cannily ahint the thorny shaw, and bide him there.'

She conducted him to a small window, through which, himself unobserved, he could see two dragoons seated at their morning draught of ale, and conversing earnestly together.

'The more I think of it,' said the one, 'the less I like it, Inglis; Evandale was a good officer, and the soldier's friend; and though we were punished for the mutiny at Tillietudlem, yet, by —, Frank, you must own we deserved it.'

'D—n seize me, if I forgive him for it, though!' replied the other; 'and I think I can sit in his skirts now.'

'Why, man, you should forget and forgive – Better take the

start with him along with the rest, and join the ranting High-landers. We have all eat King James's bread.'

'Thou art an ass; the start, as you call it, will never happen; the day's put off. Halliday's seen a ghost, or Miss Bellenden's fallen sick of the pip, or some blasted nonsense or another; the thing will never keep two days longer, and the first bird that sings out will get the reward.'

'That's true, too,' answered his comrade; 'and will this fel-low – this Basil Olifant, pay handsomely?'

'Like a prince, man,' said Inglis; 'Evandale is the man on earth whom he hates worst, and he fears him, besides, about some law business, and were he once rubbed out of the way, all, he thinks, will be his own.'

'But shall we have warrants and force enough?' said the other fellow. 'Few people here will stir against my lord, and we may find him with some of our own fellows at his back.'

'Thou'rt a cowardly fool, Dick,' returned Inglis; 'he is living quietly down at Fairy-Knowe to avoid suspicion. Olifant is a magistrate, and will have some of his own people that he can trust along with him. There are us two, and the Laird says he can get a desperate fighting whig fellow, called Quintin Mackell, that has an old grudge at Evandale.'

'Well, well, you are my officer, you know,' said the private, with true military conscience, 'and if any thing is wrong' –

'I'll take the blame,' said Inglis. 'Come, another pot of ale, and let us to Tillietudlem. – Here, blind Bess! why, where the devil has the old hag crept to?'

'Delay them as long as you can,' whispered Morton, as he thrust his purse into the hostess's hand; 'all depends on gaining time.'

Then, walking swiftly to the place where the girl held his horse ready, 'To Fairy-Knowe? – no; alone I could not protect them. – I must instantly to Glasgow. Wittenbold, the comman-dant there, will readily give me the support of a troop, and procure me the countenance of the civil power. I must drop a caution as I pass. – Come, Moorkopf,' he said, addressing his horse as he mounted him, – 'this day must try your breath and speed.'

CHAPTER 44

Yet could he not his closing eyes withdraw,
Though less and less of Emily he saw;
So, speechless for a little space he lay,
Then grasp'd the hand he held, and sigh'd his soul away.

Palamon and Arcite[1]

THE indisposition of Edith confined her to bed during the eventful day on which she had received such an unexpected shock from the sudden apparition of Morton. Next morning, however, she was reported to be so much better, that Lord Evandale resumed his purpose of leaving Fairy-Knowe. At a late hour in the forenoon, Lady Emily entered the apartment of Edith with a peculiar gravity of manner. Having received and paid the compliments of the day, she observed it would be a sad one for her, though it would relieve Miss Bellenden of an encumbrance – 'My brother leaves us today, Miss Bellenden.'

'Leaves us!' exclaimed Edith in surprise; 'for his own house, I trust?'

'I have reason to think he meditates a more distant journey,' answered Lady Emily; 'he has little to detain him in this country.'

'Good Heaven!' exclaimed Edith, 'why was I born to become the wreck of all that is manly and noble! What can be done to stop him from running headlong on ruin? I will come down instantly – Say that I implore he will not depart until I speak with him.'

'It will be in vain, Miss Bellenden; but I will execute your commission;' and she left the room as formally as she had entered it, and informed her brother, Miss Bellenden was so much recovered as to propose coming down stairs ere he went away.

'I suppose,' she added pettishly, 'the prospect of being speedily released from our company has wrought a cure on her shattered nerves.'

'Sister,' said Lord Evandale, 'you are unjust if not envious.'

'Unjust I may be, Evandale, but I should not have dreamt,' glancing her eye at a mirror, 'of being thought envious without better cause – But let us go to the old lady; she is making a feast in the other room, which might have dined all your troop when you had one.'

Lord Evandale accompanied her in silence to the parlour, for he knew it was in vain to contend with her prepossessions and offended pride. They found the table covered with refreshments, arranged under the careful inspection of Lady Margaret.

'Ye could hardly weel be said to breakfast this morning, my Lord Evandale, and ye maun e'en partake of a small collation before ye ride, such as this poor house, whose inmates are so much indebted to you, can provide in their present circumstances. For my ain part, I like to see young folk take some refection before they ride out upon their sports or their affairs, and I said as much to his most Sacred Majesty when he breakfasted at Tillietudlem in the year of grace sixteen hundred and fifty-one; and his most Sacred Majesty was pleased to reply, drinking to my health at the same time in a flagon of Rhenish wine, "Lady Margaret, ye speak like a Highland oracle." These were his Majesty's very words; so that your lordship may judge whether I have not good authority to press young folk to partake of their vivers.'

It may be well supposed that much of the good lady's speech failed Lord Evandale's ears, which were then employed in listening for the light step of Edith. His absence of mind on this occasion, however natural, cost him very dear. While Lady Margaret was playing the kind hostess, a part she delighted and excelled in, she was interrupted by John Gudyill, who, in the natural phrase for announcing an inferior to the mistress of a family, said, 'There was ane wanting to speak to her leddyship.'

'Ane! what ane? Has he nae name? Ye speak as if I kept a shop, and was to come at every body's whistle.'

'Yes, he has a name,' answered John, 'but your leddyship likes ill to hear't.'

'What is it, you fool?'

'It's Calf-Gibbie, my leddy,' said John, in a tone rather above the pitch of decorous respect, on which he occasionally trespassed, confiding in his merit as an ancient servant of the family, and a faithful follower of their humble fortunes – 'It's Calf-Gibbie, an your leddyship will hae't, that keeps Edie Henshaw's kye down yonder at the Brigg-end – that's him that was Guse-Gibbie at Tillietudlem, and gaed to the wappinshaw, and that' –

'Hold your peace, John,' said the old lady, rising in dignity; 'you are very insolent to think I wad speak wi' a person like that. Let him tell his business to you or Mrs Headrigg.'

'He'll no hear o' that, my leddy; he says, them that sent him bade him gie the thing to your leddyship's ain hand direct, or to Lord Evandale's, he wots na whilk. But, to say the truth, he's far frae fresh, and he's but an idiot an he were.'

'Then turn him out,' said Lady Margaret, 'and tell him to come back to-morrow when he is sober. I suppose he comes to crave some benevolence, as an ancient follower o' the house.'

'Like eneugh, my leddy, for he's a' in rags, poor creature.'

Gudyill made another attempt to get at Gibbie's commission, which was indeed of the last importance, being a few lines from Morton to Lord Evandale, acquainting him with the danger in which he stood from the practices of Olifant, and exhorting him either to instant flight, or else to come to Glasgow and surrender himself, where he could assure him of protection. This billet, hastily written, he intrusted to Gibbie, whom he saw feeding his herd beside the bridge, and backed with a couple of dollars his desire that it might instantly be delivered into the hand to which it was addressed.

But it was decreed that Goose-Gibbie's intermediation, whether as an emissary, or as a man-at-arms, should be unfortunate to the family of Tillietudlem. He unluckily tarried so long at the ale-house, to prove if his employer's coin was good, that, when he appeared at Fairy-Knowe, the little sense which nature had given him was effectually drowned in ale and brandy, and instead of asking for Lord Evandale, he demanded to speak with Lady Margaret, whose name was more familiar to his ear. Being refused admittance to her presence, he staggered away with the letter undelivered, perversely faithful to Morton's instructions in the only point in which it would have been well had he departed from them.

A few minutes after he was gone, Edith entered the apartment. Lord Evandale and she met with mutual embarrassment, which Lady Margaret, who only knew in general that their union had been postponed by her grand-daughter's indisposition, set down to the bashfulness of a bride and bridegroom, and, to place them at ease, began to talk to Lady Emily on indifferent topics. At this moment, Edith, with a countenance as pale as death, muttered, rather than whispered, to Lord Evandale, a request to speak with him. He offered his arm, and supported her into the small anteroom, which, as we have noticed before, opened from the parlour. He placed her in a chair, and, taking one himself, awaited the opening of the conversation.

'I am distressed, my lord,' were the first words she was able to articulate, and those with difficulty; 'I scarce know what I would say, or how to speak it.'

'If I have any share in occasioning your uneasiness,' said Lord Evandale mildly, 'you will soon, Edith, be released from it.'

'You are determined then, my lord,' she replied, 'to run this desperate course with desperate men, in spite of your own better reason – in spite of your friends' entreaties – in spite of the almost inevitable ruin which yawns before you?'

'Forgive me, Miss Bellenden; even your solicitude on my account must not detain me when my honour calls. My horses stand ready saddled, my servants are prepared, the signal for rising will be given so soon as I reach Kilsyth – If it is my fate that calls me, I will not shun meeting it. It will be something,' he said, taking her hand, 'to die deserving your compassion, since I cannot gain your love.'

'O, my lord, remain!' said Edith, in a tone which went to his heart; 'time may explain the strange circumstance which has shocked me so much; my agitated nerves may recover their tranquillity. O, do not rush on death and ruin! remain to be our prop and stay, and hope every thing from time!'

'It is too late, Edith,' answered Lord Evandale; 'and I were most ungenerous could I practise on the warmth and kindliness of your feelings towards me. I know you cannot love me; nervous distress, so strong as to conjure up the appearance of the dead or absent, indicates a predilection too powerful to give way to friendship and gratitude alone. But were it otherwise, the die is now cast.'

As he spoke thus, Cuddie burst into the room, terror and haste in his countenance. 'O, my lord, hide yoursell! they hae beset the outlets o' the house,' was his first exclamation.

'They? Who?' said Lord Evandale.

'A party of horse, headed by Basil Olifant,' answered Cuddie.

'O, hide yourself, my lord!' echoed Edith, in an agony of terror.

'I will not, by Heaven!' answered Lord Evandale. 'What right has the villain to assail me, or stop my passage? I will make my way, were he backed by a regiment; tell Halliday and Hunter to get out the horses – And now, farewell, Edith!' He clasped her in his arms, and kissed her tenderly; then, bursting from his sister, who, with Lady Margaret, endeavoured to detain him, rushed out and mounted his horse.

All was in confusion – the women shrieked and hurried in consternation to the front windows of the house, from which they could see a small party of horsemen, of whom two only seemed soldiers. They were on the open ground before Cuddie's cottage, at the bottom of the descent from the house, and showed caution in approaching it, as if uncertain of the strength within.

'He may escape, he may escape!' said Edith; 'O, would he but take the by-road!'

But Lord Evandale, determined to face a danger which his high spirit undervalued, commanded his servants to follow him, and rode composedly down the avenue. Old Gudyill ran to arm himself, and Cuddie snatched down a gun which was kept for the protection of the house, and, although on foot, followed Lord Evandale. It was in vain his wife, who had hurried up on the alarm, hung by his skirts, threatening him with death by the sword or halter for meddling with other folk's matters.

'Haud your peace, ye b——,' said Cuddie, 'and that's braid Scotch, or I wotna what is; is it ither folk's matters to see Lord Evandale murdered before my face?' and down the avenue he marched. But considering on the way that he composed the whole infantry, as John Gudyill had not appeared, he took his vantage ground behind the hedge, hammered his flint, cocked his piece, and, taking a long aim at Laird Basil, as he was called, stood prompt for action.

As soon as Lord Evandale appeared, Olifant's party spread themselves a little, as if preparing to enclose him. Their leader stood fast, supported by three men, two of whom were dragoons, the third in dress and appearance a countryman, all well armed. But the strong figure, stern features, and resolved manner of the third attendant, made him seem the most formidable of the party; and whoever had before seen him could have no difficulty in recognising Balfour of Burley.

'Follow me,' said Lord Evandale to his servants, 'and if we are forcibly opposed, do as I do.' He advanced at a hand gallop towards Olifant, and was in the act of demanding why he had thus beset the road, when Olifant called out, 'Shoot the traitor!' and the whole four fired their carabines upon the unfortunate nobleman. He reeled in the saddle, advanced his hand to the holster, and drew a pistol, but, unable to discharge it, fell from his horse mortally wounded. His servants had presented their carabines. Hunter fired at random; but Halliday, who was an intrepid fellow, took aim at Inglis, and shot him dead on the spot. At the same instant, a shot, from behind the hedge, still more effectually avenged Lord Evandale, for the ball took place in the very midst of Basil Olifant's forehead, and stretched him lifeless on the ground. His followers, astonished at the execution done in so short a time, seemed rather disposed to stand inactive, when Burley, whose blood was up with the contest, exclaimed, 'Down with the Midianites!' and attacked Halliday sword in hand. At this instant the clatter of horses' hoofs was heard, and a party of horse, rapidly advancing on the road from Glasgow, appeared on the fatal field. They were foreign dragoons, led by the Dutch commandant Wittenbold, accompanied by Morton and a civil magistrate.

A hasty call to surrender, in the name of God and King William, was obeyed by all except Burley, who turned his horse and attempted to escape. Several soldiers pursued him by command of their officer, but, being well mounted, only the two headmost seemed likely to gain on him. He turned deliberately twice, and discharging first one of his pistols, and then the other, rid himself of the one pursuer by mortally wounding him, and of the other by shooting his horse, and then continued his flight to Bothwell Bridge, where, for his misfortune, he found the gates shut and guarded. Turning from thence, he made for a place where the river seemed passable, and plunged into the stream, the bullets from the pistols and carabines of his pursuers whizzing around him. Two balls took effect when he was past the middle of the stream, and he felt himself dangerously wounded. He reined his horse round in the midst of the river, and returned towards the bank he had left, waving his hand, as if with the purpose of intimating that he surrendered. The troopers ceased firing at him accordingly, and awaited his return, two of them riding a little way into the river to seize and disarm him. But it presently appeared that his purpose was revenge, not safety. As he approached the two soldiers, he collected his remaining strength, and discharged a blow on the head of one, which tumbled him from his horse. The other dragoon, a strong muscular man, had in the meanwhile laid hands on him. Burley, in requital, grasped his throat, as a dying tiger seizes his prey, and both, losing the saddle in the struggle, came headlong into the river, and were swept down the stream. Their course might be traced by the blood which bubbled up to the surface. They were twice seen to rise, the Dutchman striving to swim, and Burley clinging to him in a manner that showed his desire that both should perish. Their corpses were taken out about a quarter of a mile down the river. As Balfour's grasp could not have been unclenched without cutting off his hands, both were thrown into a hasty grave, still marked by a rude stone, and a ruder epitaph.*

*Gentle reader, I did request of mine honest friend Peter Proudfoot, travelling merchant, known to many of this land for his faithful and just dealings, as well in muslins and cambrics as in small wares, to procure me on his next peregrinations to the vicinage, a copy of the Epitaphion alluded to. And, according to his report, which I see no ground to discredit, it runneth thus:

> Here lyes ane saint to prelates surly,
> Being John Balfour, sometime of Burley,
> Who stirred up to vengeance take,
> For Solemn League and Cov'nant's sake,

While the soul of this stern enthusiast flitted to its account, that of the brave and generous Lord Evandale was also released. Morton had flung himself from his horse upon perceiving his situation, to render his dying friend all the aid in his power. He knew him, for he pressed his hand, and, being unable to speak, intimated by signs his wish to be conveyed to the house. This was done with all the care possible, and he was soon surrounded by his lamenting friends. But the clamorous grief of Lady Emily was far exceeded in intensity by the silent agony of Edith. Unconscious even of the presence of Morton, she hung over the dying man; nor was she aware that Fate, who was removing one faithful lover, had restored another as if from the grave, until Lord Evandale, taking their hands in his, pressed them both affectionately, united them together, raised his face, as if to pray for a blessing on them, and sunk back and expired in the next moment.

> Upon the Magus-Moor in Fife,
> Did tak James Sharpe the apostate's life;
> By Dutchman's hands was hacked and shot,
> Then drowned in Clyde near this saam spot.[2]

CONCLUSION

I HAD determined to wave the task of a concluding chapter, leaving to the reader's imagination the arrangements which must necessarily take place after Lord Evandale's death. But as I was aware that precedents are wanting for a practice, which might be found convenient both to readers and compilers, I confess myself to have been in a considerable dilemma, when fortunately I was honoured with an invitation to drink tea with Miss Martha Buskbody, a young lady who has carried on the profession of mantua-making at Gandercleugh and in the neighbourhood, with great success, for about forty years. Knowing her taste for narratives of this description, I requested her to look over the loose sheets the morning before I waited on her, and enlighten me by the experience which she must have acquired in reading through the whole stock of three circulating libraries, in Gandercleugh and the two next market-towns. When, with a palpitating heart, I appeared before her in the evening, I found her much disposed to be complimentary.

'I have not been more affected,' said she, wiping the glasses of her spectacles, 'by any novel, excepting the Tale of Jemmy and Jenny Jessamy,[1] which is indeed pathos itself; but your plan of omitting a formal conclusion will never do. You may be as harrowing to our nerves as you will in the course of your story, but, unless you had the genius of the author of Julia de Roubigné,[2] never let the end be altogether overclouded. Let us see a glimpse of sunshine in the last chapter; it is quite essential.'

'Nothing would be more easy for me, madam, than to comply with your injunctions; for, in truth, the parties in whom you have had the goodness to be interested, did live long and happily, and begot sons and daughters."

'It is unnecessary, sir,' she said, with a slight nod of reprimand, 'to be particular concerning their matrimonial comforts. But what is your objection to let us have, in a general way, a glimpse of their future felicity?'

'Really, madam,' said I, 'you must be aware, that every volume of a narrative turns less and less interesting as the author draws to a conclusion; just like your tea, which, though excellent hyson, is necessarily weaker and more insipid in the last cup. Now, as I think the one is by no means improved by the luscious lump of half-dissolved sugar usually found at the bottom of it, so I am of opinion that a history, growing already vapid, is but dully crutched up by a detail of circumstances which every reader must have anticipated, even though the author exhaust on them every flowery epithet in the language.'

'This will not do, Mr Pattieson,' continued the lady, 'you have, as I may say, basted up your first story very hastily and clumsily at the conclusion; and, in my trade, I would have cuffed the youngest apprentice who had put such a horrid and bungled spot of work out of her hand. And if you do not redeem this gross error by telling us all about the marriage of Morton and Edith, and what became of the other personages of the story, from Lady Margaret down to Goose-Gibbie, I apprize you, that you will not be held to have accomplished your task handsomely.'

'Well, madam,' I replied, 'my materials are so ample, that I think I can satisfy your curiosity, unless it descend to very minute circumstances indeed.'

'First then,' said she, 'for that is most essential, – Did Lady Margaret get back her fortune and her castle?'

'She did, madam, and in the easiest way imaginable, as heir, namely, to her worthy cousin, Basil Olifant, who died without a will; and thus, by his death, not only restored, but even augmented, the fortune of her, whom, during his life, he had pursued with the most inveterate malice. John Gudyill, reinstated in his dignity, was more important than ever; and Cuddie, with rapturous delight, entered upon the cultivation of the mains of Tillietudlem, and the occupation of his original cottage. But, with the shrewd caution of his character, he was never heard to boast of having fired the lucky shot which repossessed his lady and himself in their original habitations. "After a'," he said to Jenny, who was his only confidant, "auld Basil Olifant was my leddy's cousin, and a grand gentleman; and though he was acting again the law, as I understand, for he ne'er showed ony warrant, or required Lord Evandale to surrender, and though I mind killing him nae mair than I wad do a muircock, yet it's just as weel to keep a calm sough about it." He not only did so, but ingeniously enough countenanced a report that old Gudyill had done the deed, which was worth many a gill of brandy to him from the old butler, who, far different in disposition from Cuddie, was much more inclined to exaggerate than suppress his exploits of manhood. The blind widow was provided for in the most comfortable manner, as well as the little guide to the Linn; and' –

'But what is all this to the marriage – the marriage of the principal personages?' interrupted Miss Buskbody, impatiently tapping her snuff-box.

'The marriage of Morton and Miss Bellenden was delayed for several months, as both went into deep mourning on account of Lord Evandale's death. They were then wedded.'

'I hope, not without Lady Margaret's consent, sir?' said my fair critic. 'I love books which teach a proper deference in young persons to their parents. In a novel the young people may fall in love without their countenance, because it is essential to the necessary intricacy of the story, but they must always have the benefit of their consent at last. Even old Delville received Cecilia,[3] though the daughter of a man of low birth.'

'And even so, madam,' replied I, 'Lady Margaret was pre-vailed on to countenance Morton, although the old Covenanter, his father, stuck sorely with her for some time. Edith was her only hope, and she wished to see her happy; Morton, or Melville Morton, as he was more generally called, stood so high in the reputation of the world, and was in every other respect such an eligible match, that she put her prejudice aside, and consoled herself with the recollection, that marriage went by destiny, as was observed to her, she said, by his most Sacred Majesty, Charles the Second of happy memory, when she showed him the portrait of her grandfather Fergus, third Earl of Torwood, the handsomest man of his time, and that of Countess Jane, his second lady, who had a hump-back and only one eye. This was his Majesty's observation, she said, on one remarkable morning when he deigned to take his *disjune*' –

'Nay,' said Miss Buskbody, again interrupting me, 'if she brought such authority to countenance her acquiescing in a misalliance, there was no more to be said. – And what became of old Mrs What's her name, the housekeeper?'

'Mrs Wilson, madam?' answered I; 'she was perhaps the happiest of the party; for once-a-year, and not oftener, Mr and Mrs Melville Morton dined in the great wainscotted-chamber in solemn state, the hangings being all displayed, the carpet laid down, and the huge brass-candlestick set on the table, stuck round with leaves of laurel. The preparing the room for this yearly festival employed her mind for six months before it came about, and the putting matters to rights occupied old Alison the other six, so that a single day of rejoicing found her business for all the year round.'

'And Niel Blane?' said Miss Buskbody.

'Lived to a good old age, drank ale and brandy with guests of all persuasions, played whig or jacobite tunes as best pleased his customers, and died worth as much money as married Jenny to a cock laird. I hope, ma'am, you have no other enquiries to make, for really' –

'Goose-Gibbie, sir?' said my persevering friend; 'Goose-Gibbie, whose ministry was fraught with such consequences to the personages of the narrative?'

'Consider, my dear Miss Buskbody, – (I beg pardon for the familiarity,) – but pray consider, even the memory of the renowned Scheherazade,[4] that Empress of Tale-tellers, could not preserve every circumstance. I am not quite positive as to the fate of Goose-Gibbie, but am inclined to think him the same with one Gilbert Dudden, alias Calf-Gibbie, who was whipped through Hamilton for stealing poultry.'

Miss Buskbody now placed her left foot on the fender, crossed her right leg over her knee, lay back on the chair, and looked towards the ceiling. When I observed her assume this contemplative mood, I concluded she was studying some farther cross-examination, and therefore took my hat and wished her a hasty good-night, ere the Demon of Criticism had supplied her with any more queries. In like manner, gentle Reader, returning you my thanks for the patience which has conducted you thus far, I take the liberty to withdraw myself from you for the present.

THE END OF OLD MORTALITY

PERORATION

It was mine earnest wish, most courteous Reader, that the 'Tales of my Landlord' should have reached thine hands in one entire succession of tomes, or volumes. But as I sent some few more manuscript quires, containing the continuation of these most pleasing narratives, I was apprised, somewhat unceremoniously, by my publisher, that he did not approve of novels (as he injuriously called these real histories) extending beyond four volumes, and, if I did not agree to the first four being published separately, he threatened to decline the article. (O, ignorance! as if the vernacular article of our mother English were capable of declension!) Whereupon, somewhat moved by his remonstrances, and more by heavy charges for print and paper, which he stated to have been already incurred, I have resolved that these four volumes shall be the heralds or avant-couriers of the Tales which are yet in my possession, nothing doubting that they will be eagerly devoured, and the remainder anxiously demanded, by the unanimous voice of a discerning public. I rest, esteemed Reader, thine as thou shalt construe me,

JEDEDIAH CLEISHBOTHAM

GANDERCLEUGH, *Nov.* 15, 1816.

APPENDIX A

THE remarkable person, called by the title of Old Mortality, was well known in Scotland about the end of the last century. His real name was Robert Paterson.[1] He was a native, it is said, of the parish of Closeburn, in Dumfries-shire, and probably a mason by profession – at least educated to the use of the chisel. Whether family dissensions, or the deep and enthusiastic feeling of supposed duty, drove him to leave his dwelling, and adopt the singular mode of life in which he wandered, like a palmer, through Scotland, is not known. It could not be poverty, however, which prompted his journeys, for he never accepted any thing beyond the hospitality which was willingly rendered him, and when that was not proffered, he always had money enough to provide for his own humble wants. His personal appearance, and favourite, or rather sole occupation, are accurately described in the preliminary chapter of the following work.

It is about thirty years since, or more, that the author met this singular person in the churchyard of Dunnottar, when spending a day or two with the late learned and excellent clergyman, Mr Walker, the minister of that parish, for the purpose of a close examination of the ruins of the Castle of Dunnottar, and other subjects of antiquarian research in that neighbourhood. Old Mortality chanced to be at the same place, on the usual business of his pilgrimage; for the castle of Dunnottar, though lying in the anti-covenanting district of the Mearns, was, with the parish churchyard, celebrated for the oppressions sustained there by the Cameronians in the time of James II.

It was in 1685, when Argyle[2] was threatening a descent upon Scotland, and Monmouth was preparing to invade the west of England, that the Privy Council of Scotland, with cruel precaution, made a general arrest of more than a hundred persons in the southern and western provinces, supposed, from their religious principles, to be inimical to Government, together with many women and children. These captives were driven northward like a flock of bullocks, but with less precaution to provide for their wants, and finally penned up in a subterranean dungeon in the Castle of Dunnottar, having a window opening to the front of a precipice which overhangs the German Ocean. They had suffered not a little on the journey, and were much hurt both at the scoffs of the northern prelatists, and the mocks, gibes, and contemptuous tunes played by the fiddlers and pipers who had come from every quarter as they passed, to triumph over the revilers of their calling. The repose which the melancholy dungeon afforded them, was any thing but undisturbed. The guards made them pay for every indulgence, even that of water; and when some of the prisoners resisted a demand so unreasonable, and insisted on their right to have this necessary of life untaxed, their keepers emptied the water on the prison floor, saying, 'If they were obliged to bring water for the canting whigs, they were not bound to afford them the use of bowls or pitchers gratis.'

In this prison, which is still termed the Whig's Vault, several died of the diseases incidental to such a situation; and others broke their limbs, and incurred fatal injury, in desperate attempts to escape from their stern prison-house. Over the graves of these unhappy persons, their friends, after the Revolution, erected a monument with a suitable inscription.

This peculiar shrine of the Whig martyrs is very much honoured by their descendants, though residing at a great distance from the land of their captivity and death. My friend, the Rev. Mr Walker, told me, that being once upon a tour in the south of Scotland, probably about forty years since, he had the bad luck to involve himself in the labyrinth of passages and tracks which cross, in every direction, the extensive waste called Lochar Moss, near Dumfries, out of which it is scarcely possible for a stranger to extricate himself; and there was no small difficulty in procuring a guide, since such people as he saw were engaged in digging their peats – a work of paramount necessity, which will hardly brook interruption. Mr Walker could, therefore, only procure unintelligible directions in the southern brogue, which differs widely from that of the Mearns. He was beginning to think himself in a serious dilemma, when he stated his case to a farmer of rather the better class, who was employed, as the others, in digging his winter fuel. The old man at first made the same excuse with those who had already declined acting as the traveller's guide; but perceiving him in great perplexity, and paying the respect due to his profession, 'You are a clergyman, sir?' he said. Mr Walker assented. 'And I observe from your speech, that you are from the north?' – 'You are right, my good friend,' was the reply. 'And may I ask if you have ever heard of a place called Dunnottar?' – 'I ought to know something about it, my friend,' said Mr Walker, 'since I have been several years the minister of the parish.' – 'I am glad to hear it,' said the Dumfriesian, 'for one of my near relations lies buried there, and there is, I believe, a monument over his grave. I would give half of what I am aught, to know if it is still in existence.' – 'He was one of those who perished in the Whig's Vault at the castle?' said the minister; 'for there are few south-landers besides lying in our churchyard, and none, I think, having monuments.' – 'Even sae – even sae,' said the old Cameronian, for such was the farmer. He then laid down his spade, cast on his coat, and heartily offered to see the minister out of the moss, if he should lose the rest of the *day's dargue*. Mr Walker was able to requite him amply, in his opinion, by reciting the epitaph, which he remembered by heart. The old man was enchanted with finding the memory of his grandfather or great-grandfather faithfully recorded amongst the names of brother sufferers; and rejecting all other offers of recompense, only requested, after he had guided Mr Walker to a safe and dry road, that he would let him have a written copy of the inscription.

It was whilst I was listening to this story, and looking at the monument referred to, that I saw Old Mortality engaged in his daily task of cleaning and repairing the ornaments and epitaphs upon the tomb. His appearance and equipment were exactly as described in the Novel. I was very desirous to see something of a person so singular, and expected to have done so, as he took up his quarters with the hospitable and liberal-spirited minister. But though Mr Walker invited him up after dinner to partake of a glass of spirits and water, to which he was supposed not to be very averse, yet he would not speak frankly upon the subject of his occupation. He was in bad humour, and had, according to his phrase, no freedom for conversation with us.

His spirit had been sorely vexed by hearing, in a certain Aberdonian kirk, the psalmody directed by a pitch-pipe, or some similar instrument, which was to Old Mortality the abomination of abominations. Perhaps, after all, he did not feel himself at ease with his company; he might suspect the questions asked by a north-country minister and a young barrister to savour more of idle curiosity than profit. At any rate, in the phrase of John Bunyan, Old Mortality went on his way, and I saw him no more.

The remarkable figure and occupation of this ancient pilgrim was recalled to my memory by an account transmitted by my friend Mr Joseph Train, supervisor of excise at Dumfries, to whom I owe many obligations of a similar nature. From this, besides some other circumstances, among which are those of the old man's death, I learned the particulars described in the text. I am also informed, that the old palmer's family, in the third generation, survives, and is highly respected both for talents and worth.

While these sheets were passing through the press, I received the following communication from Mr Train, whose undeviating kindness had, during the intervals of laborious duty, collected its materials from an indubitable source.

'In the course of my periodical visits to the Glenkens, I have become intimately acquainted with Robert Paterson, a son of Old Mortality, who lives in the little village of Balmaclellan; and although he is now in the 70th year of his age, preserves all the vivacity of youth – has a most retentive memory, and a mind stored with information far above what could be expected from a person in his station of life. To him I am indebted for the following particulars relative to his father, and his descendants down to the present time.

'Robert Paterson, *alias* Old Mortality, was the son of Walter Paterson and Margaret Scott, who occupied the farm of Haggisha, in the parish of Hawick, during nearly the first half of the eighteenth century. Here Robert was born, in the memorable year 1715.

'Being the youngest son of a numerous family, he, at an early age, went to serve with an elder brother, named Francis, who rented, from Sir John Jardine of Applegarth, a small tract in Comcockle Moor, near Lochmaben. During his residence there, he became acquainted with Elizabeth Gray, daughter of Robert Gray, gardener to Sir John Jardine, whom he afterwards married. His wife had been, for a considerable time, a cook-maid to Sir Thomas Kirkpatrick of Closeburn, who procured for her husband, from the Duke of Queensberry, an advantageous lease of the freestone quarry of Gatelowbrigg, in the parish of Morton. Here he built a house, and had as much land as kept a horse and cow. My informant cannot say, with certainty, the year in which his father took up his residence at Gatelowbrigg, but he is sure it must have been only a short time prior to the year 1746, as, during the memorable frost in 1740, he says his mother still resided in the service of Sir Thomas Kirkpatrick. When the Highlanders were returning from England on their route to Glasgow, in the year 1745-6, they plundered Mr Paterson's house at Gatelowbrigg, and carried him a prisoner as far as Glenbuck, merely because he said to one of the straggling army, that their retreat might have been easily foreseen, as the strong arm of the Lord was evidently raised, not only against the bloody and wicked house of Stewart, but against all who attempted to support the abominable heresies of the Church of Rome. From this circumstance it appears that Old Mortality had, even at that early period of his life, imbibed the religious enthusiasm by which he afterwards became so much distinguished.

'The religious sect called Hill-men, or Cameronians, was at that time much noted for austerity and devotion, in imitation of Cameron, their founder, of whose tenets Old Mortality became a most strenuous supporter. He made frequent journeys into Galloway to attend their conventicles, and occasionally carried with him gravestones from his quarry at Gatelowbrigg, to keep in remembrance the righteous whose dust had been gathered to their fathers. Old Mortality was not one of those religious devotees, who, although one eye is seemingly turned towards heaven, keep the other steadfastly fixed on some sublunary object. As his enthusiasm increased, his journeys into Galloway became more frequent; and he gradually neglected even the common prudential duty of providing for his offspring. From about the year 1758, he neglected wholly to return from Galloway to his wife and five children at Gatelowbrigg, which induced her to send her eldest son Walter, then only twelve years of age, to Galloway, in search of his father. After traversing nearly the whole of that extensive district, from the Nick of Benncorie to the Fell of Barullion, he found him at last working on the Cameronian monuments, in the old kirkyard of Kirkchrist, on the west side of the Dee, opposite the town of Kirkcudbright. The little wanderer used all the influence in his power to induce his father to return to his family; but in vain. Mrs Paterson sent even some of her female children into Galloway in search of their father, for the same purpose of persuading him to return home; but without any success. At last, in the summer of 1768, she removed to the little upland village of Balmaclellan, in the Glenkens of Galloway, where, upon the small pittance derived from keeping a little school, she supported her numerous family in a respectable manner.

'There is a small monumental stone in the farm of the Caldon, near the House of the Hill, in Wigtonshire, which is highly venerated as being the first erected, by Old Mortality, to the memory of several persons who fell at that place in defence of their religious tenets in the civil war, in the reign of Charles Second.*

'From the Caldon, the labours of Old Mortality, in the course of time, spread over nearly all the Lowlands of Scotland. There are few churchyards in Ayrshire, Galloway, or Dumfries-shire, where the work of his chisel is not yet to be seen. It is easily distinguished from the work of any other artist by the primitive rudeness of the emblems of death, and of the inscriptions which

---

* 'The house was stormed by a Captain Orchard or Urquhart, who was shot in the attack.'

adorn the ill-formed blocks of his erection. This task of repairing and erecting gravestones, practised without fee or reward, was the only ostensible employment of this singular person for upwards of forty years. The door of every Cameronian's house was indeed open to him at all times when he chose to enter, and he was gladly received as an inmate of the family; but he did not invariably accept of these civilities, as may be seen by the following account of his frugal expenses, found, amongst other little papers, (some of which I have likewise in my possession,) in his pocket-book after his death.

'Gatehouse of Fleet, 4th February, 1796.

ROBERT PATERSON *debtor to* MARGARET CHRYSTALE.

To drye Lodginge for seven weeks,	—	—	—	—	L.0 4 1
To Four Auchlet of Ait Meal,	—	—	—	—	0 3 4
To 6 Lippies of Potatoes,	—	—	—	—	0 1 3
To Lent Money at the time of Mr Reid's Sacrament,	—				0 6 0
To 3 Chappins of Yell with Sandy the Keelman,*				—	0 0 9

L.0 15 5

Received in part, — — — — 0 10 0

Unpaid, — — — — L.0 5 5

'This statement shows the religious wanderer to have been very poor in his old age; but he was so more by choice than through necessity, as at the period here alluded to, his children were all comfortably situated, and were most anxious to keep their father at home, but no entreaty could induce him to alter his erratic way of life. He travelled from one churchyard to another, mounted on his old white pony, till the last day of his existence, and died, as you have described, at Bankhill, near Lockerby, on the 14th February, 1801, in the 86th year of his age. As soon as his body was found, intimation was sent to his sons at Balmaclellan; but from the great depth of the snow at that time, the letter communicating the particulars of his death was so long detained by the way, that the remains of the pilgrim were interred before any of his relations could arrive at Bankhill.

* 'A well-known humorist, still alive, popularly called by the name of Old Keelybags, who deals in the keel or chalk with which farmers mark their flocks.'

'The following is an exact copy of the account of his funeral expenses, – the original of which I have in my possession:–

'Memorandum of the Funral Charges of Robert Paterson, who dyed at Bankhill on the 14th day of February, 1801,

To a Coffon, –	–	–	–	–	–	–	–	L.o 12	0
To Munting for do.	–	–	–	–	–	–	–	0 2	8
To a Shirt for him, –	–	–	–	–	–	–	–	0 5	6
To a pair of Cotten Stockings, –	–	–	–	–	–		0 2	0
To Bread at the Founral, –	–	–	–	–	–	–	0 2	6
To Chise at ditto, –	–	–	–	–	–	–	–	0 3	0
To 1 pint Rume, –	–	–	–	–	–	–	–	0 4	6
To 1 pint Whiskie, –	–	–	–	–	–	–	–	0 4	0
To a man going to Annan, –	–	–	–	–	–	0 2	0
To the grave diger, –	–	–	–	–	–	–	0 1	0
To Linnen for a sheet for him, –	–	–	–	–	–	0 2	8

	L.2 1 10
Taken off him when dead, – –	1 7 6
	L.o 14 4

'The above account is authenticated by the son of the deceased.

'My friend was prevented by indisposition from even going to Bankhill to attend the funeral of his father, which I regret very much, as he is not aware in what churchyard he was interred.

'For the purpose of erecting a small monument to his memory, I have made every possible enquiry, wherever I thought there was the least chance of finding out where Old Mortality was laid; but I have done so in vain, as his death is not registered in the session-book of any of the neighbouring parishes. I am sorry to think, that in all probability, this singular person, who spent so many years of his lengthened existence in striving with his chisel and mallet to perpetuate the memory of many less deserving than himself, must remain even without a single stone to mark out the resting place of his mortal remains.

'Old Mortality had three sons, Robert, Walter, and John; the former, as has been already mentioned, lives in the village of

Balmaclellan, in comfortable circumstances, and is much respected by his neighbours. Walter died several years ago, leaving behind him a family now respectably situated in this point. John went to America in the year 1776, and, after various turns of fortune, settled at Baltimore.'

Old Nol himself is said to have loved an innocent jest. (See Captain Hodgson's Memoirs.[3]) Old Mortality somewhat resembled the Protector in this turn to festivity. Like Master Silence,[4] he had been merry twice and once in his time; but even his jests were of a melancholy and sepulchral nature, and sometimes attended with inconvenience to himself, as will appear from the following anecdote:—

The old man was at one time following his wonted occupation of repairing the tombs of the martyrs, in the churchyard of Girthon, and the sexton of the parish was plying his kindred task at no small distance. Some roguish urchins were sporting near them, and by their noisy gambols disturbing the old men in their serious occupation. The most petulant of the juvenile party were two or three boys, grandchildren of a person well known by the name of Cooper Climent. This artist enjoyed almost a monopoly in Girthon and the neighbouring parishes, for making and selling ladles, caups, bickers, bowls, spoons, cogues, and trenchers, formed of wood, for the use of the country people. It must be noticed, that notwithstanding the excellence of the Cooper's vessels, they were apt, when new, to impart a reddish tinge to whatever liquor was put into them, a circumstance not uncommon in like cases.

The grandchildren of this dealer in wooden work took it into their head to ask the sexton, what use he could possibly make of the numerous fragments of old coffins which were thrown up in opening new graves. 'Do you not know,' said Old Mortality, 'that he sells them to your grandfather, who makes them into spoons, trenchers, bickers, bowies, and so forth?' At this assertion, the youthful group broke up in great confusion and disgust, on reflecting how many meals they had eaten out of dishes which, by Old Mortality's account, were only fit to be used at a banquet of witches or of ghoules. They carried the tidings home, when many a dinner was spoiled by the loathing which the intelligence imparted; for the account of the materials was supposed to explain the reddish tinge which, even in the days of the Cooper's fame, had seemed somewhat suspicious. The ware of Cooper Climent was rejected in horror, much to the benefit of his rivals the muggers, who dealt in earthenware. The man of cutty-spoon and ladle saw his trade interrupted, and learned the reason, by his quondam customers coming upon him in wrath to return the goods which were composed of such unhallowed materials, and demand repayment of their money. In this disagreeable predicament, the forlorn artist cited Old Mortality into a court of justice, where he proved that the wood he used in his trade was that of the staves of old wine-pipes bought from smugglers, with whom the country then abounded, a circumstance which fully accounted for their imparting a colour to their contents. Old Mortality himself made the fullest declaration, that he had no other purpose in making the assertion, than to check the petulance of the children. But it is easier to take away a good name than to restore it. Cooper Climent's business continued to languish, and he died in a state of poverty.

APPENDIX B

Two Ballads from *The Minstrelsy of the Scottish Border*

These ballads are given as printed in the collected *Poetical Works of Sir Walter Scott, Bart.*, volume 2, 1833, pp. 222–5 and pp. 237–40.

Loudon, or Loudoun Hill had been the scene of a victory by Robert Bruce over the English in 1307. It is near Drumclog, and the two names are used interchangeably for the later battle.

THE
BATTLE OF LOUDON HILL

You'l marvel when I tell ye o'
    Our noble Burly, and his train;
When last he march'd up through the land,
    Wi' sax-and-twenty Westland men.

Than they I ne'er o' braver heard,
    For they had a' baith wit and skill;
They proved right well, as I heard tell,
    As they cam up o'er Loudon Hill.

Weel prosper a' the gospel lads,
    That are into the west countrie;
Aye wicked Claver'se to demean,
    And aye an ill deid may he die!

For he's drawn up i' battle rank,
    An' that baith soon an' hastilie;
But they wha live till simmer come,
    Some bludie days for this will see.

But up spak cruel Claver'se, then,
    Wi' hastie wit, an' wicked skill;

'Gae fire on yon Westlan' men;
  I think it is my sov'reign's will.' –

But up bespake his Cornet, then,
  'It's be wi' nae consent o' me !
I ken I'll ne'er come back again,
  An' mony mae as weel as me.

'There is not ane of a' yon men,
  But wha is worthy other three;
There is na ane amang them a',
  That in his cause will stap to die.

'An' as for Burly, him I knaw;
  He's a man of honour, birth, and fame;
Gie him a sword into his hand,
  He'll fight thysell an' other ten.' –

But up spake wicked Claver'se, then,
  I wat his heart it raise fu' hie !
And he has cried that a' might hear,
  'Man, ye hae sair deceived me.

'I never ken'd the like afore,
  Na, never since I came frae hame,
That you sae cowardly here suld prove,
  An' yet come of a noble Græme.' –

But up bespake his Cornet, then,
  'Since that it is your honour's will,
Mysell shall be the foremost man,
  That shall gie fire on Loudon Hill –

'At your command I'll lead them on,
  But yet wi' nae consent o' me;
For weel I ken I'll ne'er return,
  And mony mae as weel as me.' –

Then up he drew in battle rank;
   I wat he had a bonny train!
But the first time that bullets flew,
   Aye he lost twenty o' his men.

Then back he came the way he gaed,
   I wat right soon and suddenly!
He gave command amang his men,
   And sent them back, and bade them flee.

Then up came Burly, bauld an' stout,
   Wi's little train o' Westland men;
Wha mair than either aince or twice
   In Edinburgh confined had been.

They hae been up to London sent,
   An' yet they're a' come safely down;
Sax troop o' horsemen they hae beat,
   And chased them into Glasgow town.

THE

BATTLE OF BOTHWELL BRIDGE

'O, billie, billie, bonny billie,
   Will ye go to the wood wi' me?
We'll ca' our horse hame masterless,
   An' gar them trow slain men are we.' –

'O no, O no!' says Earlstoun,
   'For that's the thing that mauna be;
For I am sworn to Bothwell Hill,
   Where I maun either gae or die.' –

So Earlstoun rose in the morning,
   An' mounted by the break o' day;

An' he has joined our Scottish lads,
    As they were marching out the way.

'Now, farewell, father, and farewell, mother,
    And fare ye weel, my sisters three;
An' fare ye weel, my Earlstoun,
    For thee again I'll never see !' –

So they're awa' to Bothwell Hill,
    An' waly they rode bonnily !
When the Duke o' Monmouth saw them comin',
    He went to view their company.

'Ye're welcome, lads,' the Monmouth said,
    'Ye're welcome, brave Scots lads, to me;
And sae are you, brave Earlstoun.
    The foremost o' your company !

'But yield your weapons ane an a';
    O yield your weapons, lads, to me;
For gin ye'll yield your weapons up,
    Ye'se a' gae hame to your country.' –

Out then spak a Lennox lad,
    And waly but he spoke bonnily !
'I winna yield my weapons up,
    To you nor nae man that I see.' –

Then he set up the flag o' red.
    A' set about wi' bonny blue;
'Since ye'll no cease, and be at peace,
    See that ye stand by ither true.' –

They stell'd[1] their cannons on the height,
    And showr'd their shot down in the howe;
An' beat our Scots lads even down,
    Thick they lay slain on every knowe.

As e'er you saw the rain down fa',
   Or yet the arrow frae the bow, –
Sae our Scottish lads fell even down,
   An' they lay slain on every knowe.

'O hold your hand,' then Monmouth cry'd,
   'Gie quarters to yon men for me!' –
But wicked Claver'se swore an oath,
   His Cornet's death revenged sud be.

'O hold your hand,' then Monmouth cry'd,
   'If onything you'll do for me;
Hold up your hand, you cursed Græme,
   Else a rebel to our King ye'll be.' –

Then wicked Claver'se turn'd about,
   I wot an angry man was he;
And he has lifted up his hat,
   And cry'd, 'God bless his Majesty!' –

Than he's awa' to London town,
   Aye e'en as fast as he can dree;
Fause witnesses he has wi' him ta'en,
   And ta'en Monmouth's head frae his body.

Alang the brae, beyond the brig,
   Mony brave man lies cauld and still;
But lang we'll mind, and sair we'll rue,
   The bloody battle of Bothwell Hill.

APPENDIX C

EXTRACT FROM A REVIEW OF *Tales of My Landlord*
IN *Quarterly Review*, April 1817

THIS is an extract from the review of *Tales of My Landlord* published in the (tory) *Quarterly Review* of January 1817 and organized by Scott himself even before he had learnt of the (whig) M'Crie's assault. The entire review takes up fifty pages in volume XVI of the periodical (pp. 430–80). The section reproduced here is the final one, from midway in p. 470 onwards.

Martin Lightfoot, in 'Scott's Self-Review: Manuscript and Other Evidence', *Nineteenth Century Fiction*, vol. 23, no. 2, September 1968, argues that the first thirty-five pages are by Scott, that William Gifford, a famous critic of the day, wrote the next five pages or so, and that Scott's old friend William Erskine, using material supplied to him by Scott, actually wrote the whole passage reproduced here except for a final coda by Scott himself.

The special interest of this extract is that (through Erskine or not) it gives us Scott's own defence of his own essential accuracy.

The paragraph preceding this extract ends with a promise to deal with 'the historical portraits with which the author has presented us':

Most of the group are drawn in harsh colours, and yet the truth of the resemblances, when illustrated by historical documents, will scarcely be disputed, except by those staunch partizans whose religious or political creed is the sole gauge for estimating the good or bad qualities of the characters of past ages. To such men an extensive knowledge of history is only the means of further perversion of its truth. The portraits of their favourites (as Queen Elizabeth is said to have required of her own) must be drawn without shadow, and the objects of their political antipathy be blackened, horned, hoofed, and clawed ere they will acknowledge the likeness of either. But if we are to idolize the memory of deceased men of worth and piety of our own persuasion, as if they had not been fallible mortals, it is in vain that we are converted from paganism, which transformed deceased heroes into deities; and if we damn utterly the characters and motives of those who stood in opposition to their opinions, we have gained little by leaving the Church of Rome, in whose creed heresy includes every other possible guilt.

The most prominent portrait, historically considered, is that of John Grahame, of Claverhouse, afterwards Viscount of Dundee; and its accurate resemblance can hardly be disputed, though those who only look at his cruelty towards the Presbyterians will consider his courage, talents, high spirit, and loyal devotion to an unfortunate master, as ill associated with such evil attributes. They who study his life will have some reason to think that a mistaken opinion of the absolute obedience due by an officer to his superiors, joined to unscrupulous ambition, was the ruling principle of many of his worst actions. Yet he was not uniformly so ruthless as he is painted in the Tales. In some cases he interceded for the life of those whom he was ordered to put to death; and particularly, he pleaded hard with Sir James Johnstone, of Westerhall, for the life of one Hyslop, shot on Eskdale moor. It appears also, from his correspondence with Lord Lithgow, that he was attentive to his prisoners, as he apologizes for not bringing one of them, who laboured under a disease rendering it painful for him to be on horseback. From the following anecdote it would seem that his activity against the Whigs did not always correspond with the wishes of those in power :

'The Thesr. Queensberry having taken some disgust at Claverhouse, *for not being so active against the Whigs as he ought*, (they having killed two men, and made one Mr Shaw, a minister, swear never to preach under bishops,) orders his brother, Colonel Douglas, to take two hundred men of his regiment and attack the rebels. But having one day with a party of his men met with as many of the rebels in a house, they killed two of his men and Captain Urquhart Meldrum's brother, and was near being shot himself, had not a Whig's carabine misgiven, (the more pity, considering what a vile traitor the Colonel after proved to King James VII.), that Douglas therefore shot the said Whig, January, 1685.' – *Fountainhall's M S. Diary.*

Something is also to be given to the exaggeration of political and polemical hatred. For example, John Brown of Muirkirk is, in Wodrow's history, said to have been shot by Claverhouse with his own hand. But in the Life of Peden,[1] which gives a minute and interesting account of this execution, the particulars whereof the author had from the unfortunate widow, we are expressly told that Brown was shot by a file of soldiers, Claverhouse looking on and commanding. Enough will, however, remain, after every possible deduction, to stigmatize Claverhouse during this earlier part of his military career, as a fierce and savage officer; the ready executioner of the worst commands of his superiors; forgetting that no officer is morally justifiable in the execution of cruelty and oppression, however the commands of his superiors may be his warrant in an earthly court of justice : for the alternative of surrendering his commission being at all times in his power, he who voluntarily continues in a service where such things are exacted at his hand, cannot be judged otherwise than as one who prefers professional advancement and private interest to good faith, justice, and honour. But there are circumstances in Grahame's subsequent conduct which have gilded over cruelties that, we shall presently shew, belonged as much to the age as to the man, and they have been glossed over, if not extenuated, by the closing scenes of his life.

During the general desertion of James II Claverhouse, then Viscount of Dundee, remained inalienably firm to his benefactor. In his personal expenses he had been a rigid economist, but he was profuse of his fortune when it could aid the cause of his misguided prince. When James had disbanded his army, and was about to take the last and desperate step of leaving Britain, Claverhouse withstood it. He maintained, that the army, though disembodied, was not so dispersed but that they could be again assembled; and he offered to collect them under the king's standard, and to give battle to the Dutch.[2] Disappointed in this enterprize by the pusillanimity of the king, he did not desert his sinking cause. He fought his cause in the convention of estates in Scotland; and finally retreating to the Highlands, raised the clans in his defence. No name is yet so loved and venerated among the Highlanders as that of Dundee, and the influence which he had been able to acquire over the minds of this keen-spirited and aboriginal race is of itself sufficient to prove his talents. Sir John Dalrymple has idly represented him as studying their ancient poetry, and heating his enthusiasm with their ancient traditions. The truth is, that Dundee did not even understand their language, and never learned above a few words of it. His ascendancy over them was acquired by his superior talents and the art which he possessed of managing minds inferior to his own. He fell in the moment of a most decided victory, gained over troops superior to his own in number, in equipment, in military skill, in every thing but the valour and activity of the soldiers and the military talents of the general. Few men have left to posterity a character so strikingly varied. It is not shaded – it is not even chequered – it is on the one side purely heroic, on the other, cruel, savage and sanguinary. The old story of the gold and silver shield is but a type of the character of Claverhouse; and partizans on either side may assail or defend his character with as good faith as the knights in the fable. The minstrels have not been silent on the occasion, and the censure of the amiable Grahame may be well contrasted with the classical epitaph of Pitcairn.

Claverhouse is the only cavalier of importance upon whom our author has dwelt, though he has touched slightly on Sir John Dalzell[3] and the Duke of Lauderdale. Among the Covenanters, the character of Balfour is most prominent. This man (for he actually existed) was a gentleman by birth, and brother-in-law to Hackstorne of Rathillet, an enthusiast of another and more unmixed mould. In point of religious observances he did not act up to the strictness of his sect, but he atoned for such negligence by his military enterprize and unsparing cruelty. This we learn from Howie, whose work we have already quoted; and at the same time we become acquainted with what the honest man considered as the criterion of a soldier of the Covenant.

'He joined with the more faithful part of our late sufferers, and although he was by some reckoned none of the most religious, yet he was always zealous and honest-hearted, courageous in every enterprize, and a brave soldier, *seldom any escaping that came in his hands.*' – *Scottish Worthies*, p. 563.

From another passage we gain something of his personal appearance, which seems to have been as unattractive as his proceedings were ruthless.

'At that meeting at Loudon Hill, dispersed May 5th, 1681, it is said that he disarmed one of Duke Hamilton's men with his own hand, taking a pair of fine pistols belonging to the duke from his saddle, telling him to tell his master, he would keep them till meeting. Afterwards, when the Duke asked his man, What he was like? he told him he was a little man, squint eyed, and of a very fierce aspect; the Duke said, he knew who it was, and withal prayed that he might never see his face, for if he should, he was sure he would not live long.' – Ibidem.

Burley appears to have been wounded in the battle of Bothwell Bridge, for he was heard to execrate the hand which had fired the shot. He fled to Holland, where his company was shunned by such of the Scottish fugitives as had their religious zeal qualified by moral considerations, and he was refused the communion by the Scottish congregation. He is said to have accompanied Argyle in his unfortunate attempt, along with one Fleming, also an assassin of the Archbishop. And finally, he joined the expedition of the Prince of Orange, but died before the disembarkation; an event to which Mr Howie fondly ascribes the limitation of the revenge which would otherwise have been taken on the persecutors of the Lord's people and cause in Scotland.

'It is said he (Balfour) obtained liberty from the prince for that purpose, but died at sea before their arrival in Scotland. Whereby that design was never accomplished, and so the land was never purged by the blood of them who had shed innocent blood, according to the law of the Lord, Gen. ix. 6. *Whoso sheddeth man's blood, by man shall his blood be shed.*' – *Scottish Worthies, ibidem.*

It will hardly be alleged that our author has greatly misrepresented this singular character. On the contrary, he appears to have imputed to Burley, as the prime motive of his actions, a deep though regulated spirit of enthusiasm, which, from Howie's account, he seems not to have in reality possessed, and so far has rendered him more interesting and terrible, than if he had been painted as the thorough-going, bloody-minded ruffian, with little religion and less mercy, in which character he figures among the Scottish Worthies.

Admitting, however, that these portraits are sketched with spirit and effect, two questions arise of much more importance than any thing affecting the merits of the novels – namely, whether it is safe or prudent to imitate, in a fictitious narrative, and often with a view to a ludicrous effect, the scriptural style of the zealots of the seventeenth century; and secondly, whether the recusant presbyterians, collectively considered, do not carry too reverential and sacred a character to be treated by an unknown author with such insolent familiarity.

On the first subject, we frankly own we have great hesitation. It is scarcely possible to ascribe scriptural expressions to hypocritical or extravagant characters without some risk of mischief, because it will be apt to create an habitual association between the expression and the ludicrous manner in which it is used, unfavourable to the reverence due to the sacred text. And it is no defence to state that this is an error inherent in the plan of the novel. Bourdaloue, a great authority, extends this restriction still farther, and denounces all attempts to unmask hypocrisy by raillery, because in doing so the satirist is necessarily compelled to expose to ridicule the religious vizard of which he has divested him. Yet even against such authority it may be stated, that ridicule is the friend both of religion and virtue, when directed against those who assume their garb, whether from hypocrisy or fanaticism. The satire of Butler, not always decorous in these particulars, was yet eminently useful in stripping off their borrowed gravity and exposing to public ridicule the affected fanaticism of the times in which he lived. It may also be remembered, that in the days of Queen Anne a number of the Camisars or Huguenots of Dauphiné arrived as refugees in England, and became distinguished by the name of the French prophets. The fate of these enthusiasts in their own country had been somewhat similar to that of the Covenanters. Like them, they used to assemble in the mountains and desolate places, to the amount of many hundreds, in arms, and like them they were hunted and persecuted by the military. Like them, they were enthusiasts, though their enthusiasm assumed a character more decidedly absurd. The fugitive Camisars who came to London had convulsion-fits, prophesied, made converts, and attracted the public attention by an offer to raise the dead. The English minister, instead of fine and imprisonment and other inflictions which might have placed them in the rank and estimation of martyrs, and confirmed in their faith their numerous disciples, encouraged a dramatic author to bring out a farce on the subject which, though neither very witty nor very delicate, had the good effect of laughing the French prophets out of their audience and putting a stop to an inundation of nonsense which could not have failed to disgrace the age in which it appeared. The Camisars subsided into their ordinary vocation of psalmodic whiners, and no more was heard of their sect or their miracles. It would be well if all folly of the kind could be so easily quelled : for enthusiastic nonsense, whether of this day or of those which have passed away, has no more title to shelter itself under the veil of religion than a common pirate to be protected by the reverence due to an honoured and friendly flag.

Still, however, we must allow that there is great delicacy and hesitation to be used in employing the weapon of ridicule on any point connected with religion. Some passages occur in the work before us for which the writer's sole apology must be the uncontroulable disposition to indulge the peculiarity of his vein of humour – a temptation which even the saturnine John Knox was unable to resist either in narrating the martyrdom of his friend Wisheart or the assassination of his enemy Beatson,[4] and in the impossibility of resisting which his learned and accurate biographer has rested his apology for this mixture of jest and earnest.

'There are writers,' he says, (rebutting the charge of Hume against Knox), 'who can treat the most sacred subjects with a levity bordering on profanity. Must we at once pronounce them profane, and is nothing to be set down to the score of natural temper inclining them to wit and humour? The pleasantry which Knox has mingled with his narrative of his (Cardinal Beatson's) death and burial is unseasonable and unbecoming. But it is to be imputed not to any pleasure which he took in describing a bloody scene, but to the strong propensity which he had to indulge his vein of humour. Those who have read his history with attention must have perceived that he is not able to check this even on very serious occasions.' – *Macrie's Life of Knox*, p. 147.

Indeed Dr Macrie himself has given us a striking instance of the indulgence which the Presbyterian clergy, even of the strictest persuasion, permit to the *vis comica*. After describing a polemical work as 'ingeniously constructed and occasionally enlivened with strokes of humour,' he transfers, to embellish his own pages, (for we can discover no purpose of edification which the tale serves,) a ludicrous parody made by an ignorant parish-priest on certain words of a Psalm, too sacred to be here quoted. Our own innocent pleasantry cannot, in this instance, be quite reconciled with that of the learned biographer of John Knox, but we can easily conceive that his authority may be regarded in Scotland as decisive of the extent to which a humorist may venture in exercising his wit upon scriptural expressions without incurring censure even from her most rigid divines.

It may however be a very different point how far the author is entitled to be acquitted upon the second point of indictment. To use too much freedom with things sacred is a course much more easily glossed over than that of exposing to ridicule the persons of any particular sect. Every one knows the reply of the great Prince of Condé to Louis XIV, when this monarch, expressed his surprize at the clamour excited by Molière's Tartuffe, while a blasphemous farce called *Scaramouche Hermite* was performed without giving any scandal : 'C'est parceque Scaramouche ne jouoit que le ciel et la religion, dont les dévots se soucioient beaucoup moins que d'eux-mêmes.' We believe, therefore, the best service we can do our author in the present case is to shew that the odious part of his satire applies only to that fierce and unreasonable set of extra-presbyterians, whose zeal, equally absurd and cruel, afforded pretexts for the severities inflicted on non-conformists without exception, and gave the greatest scandal and offence to the wise, sober, enlightened, and truly pious among the Presbyterians.

The principal difference betwixt the Cameronians and the rational presbyterians has been already touched upon. It may be summed in a very few words.

After the restoration of Charles II episcopacy was restored in Scotland, upon the unanimous petition of the Scottish parliament. Had this been accompanied with a free toleration of the presbyterians, whose consciences preferred a different mode of church-government, we do not conceive there would have been any wrong done to that ancient kingdom. But instead of this, the most violent means of enforcing conformity were resorted to without scruple, and the ejected presbyterian clergy were persecuted by penal statutes and prohibited from the exercise of their ministry. These rigours only made the people more anxiously seek out and adhere to the silenced preachers. Driven from the churches, they held conventicles in houses. Expelled from cities and the mansions of men, they met on the hills and deserts like the French huguenots. Assailed with arms, they repelled force by force. The severity of the rulers, instigated by the episcopal clergy, increased with the obstinacy of the recusants, until the latter, in 1666, assumed arms for the purpose of asserting their right to worship God in their own way. They were defeated at Pentland; and in 1669 a gleam of common sense and justice seems to have beamed upon the Scottish councils of Charles. They granted what was called an *indulgence* (afterwards repeatedly renewed) to the presbyterian clergy, assigned them small stipends, and permitted them to preach in such deserted churches as should be assigned to them by the Scottish Privy Council. This 'indulgence,' though clogged with harsh conditions and frequently renewed or capriciously recalled, was still an acceptable boon to the wiser and better part of the presbyterian clergy, who considered it as an opening to the exercise of their ministry under the lawful authority, which they continued to acknowledge. But fiercer and more intractable principles were evinced by the younger ministers of that persuasion. They considered the submitting to exercise their ministry under the control of any visible authority as absolute erastianism, a desertion of the great invisible and divine Head of the church, and a line of conduct which could only be defended, says one of their tracts, by nullifidians, time-servers, infidels, or the Archbishop of Canterbury. They held up to ridicule and abhorrence such of their brethren as considered mere toleration as a boon worth accepting. Every thing, according to these fervent divines, which fell short of re-establishing presbytery as the sole and predominating religion, all that did not imply a full restoration of the Solemn League and Covenant, was an imperfect and unsound composition between God and mammon, episcopacy and prelacy. The following extracts from a printed sermon by one of them, on the subject of 'soul-confirmation,' will at once exemplify the contempt and scorn with which these high-flyers regarded their more sober-minded brethren, and serve as a specimen of the homely eloquence with which they excited their followers. The reader will probably be of opinion that it is worthy of Kettledrummle himself, and will serve to clear Mr Jedediah Cleishbotham of the charge of exaggeration.

'There is many folk that has a face to the religion that is in fashion, and there is many folk, they have ay a face to the old company, they have a face for godly folk, and they have a face for persecutors of godly folk, and they will be daddies bairns and minnies bairns both; they will be *prelates* bairns and they will be *malignants* bairns and they will be the people of God's bairns. And what think ye of that bastard temper? Poor Peter had a trial of this soupleness, but God made Paul an instrument to take him by the neck and shake it from him: And O that God would take us by the neck and shake our soupleness from us.

'Therefore you that keeps only your old job-trot, and does not mend your pace, you will not wone at *soul-confirmation*, there is a whine (i.e. *a few*) old job-trot, and does not mend your pace, you will not wone at *soul-confirmation*, there is a whine old job-trot ministers among us, a whine old job-trot professors, they have their own pace, and faster they will not go; O therefore they could never wine to *soul-confirmation* in the mettere of God. And our old job-trot ministers is turned *curates*, and our old job-trot professors is joined with them, and now this way God has turned them inside out, and has made it manifest and when their heart is hanging upon this braw, I will not give a gray groat for them and their profession both.

'The devil has the ministers and professors of Scotland, now in a sive, and O as he sifts, and O as he riddles, and O as he rattles, and O the chaff he gets; And I fear there be more chaff nor there be good corn, and that will be found among us or all be done: but the *soul-confirmed* man leaves ever the devil at two more, and he has ay the matter gadged, and leaves ay the devil in the lee side, – Sirs O work in the day of the cross.'

The more moderate presbyterian ministers saw with pain and resentment the lower part of their congregation, who had least to lose by taking desperate courses, withdrawn from their flocks, by their more zealous pretenders to purity of doctrine, while they themselves were held up to ridicule, old jog trot professors and chaff-winnowed out and flung away by Satan. They charged the Cameronian preachers with leading the deluded multitude to slaughter at Bothwell, by prophesying a certainty of victory, and dissuading them from accepting the amnesty offered by Monmouth. 'All could not avail,' says Mr Law, himself a presbyterian minister, 'with M'Cargill, Kidd, Douglas, and other witless men amongst them, to hearken to any proposals of peace. Among others that Douglas, sitting on his horse, and preaching to the confused multitude, told them that they would come to terms with them, and like a drone was always droning on these terms with them: "they would give us a half Christ, but we will have a whole Christ," and such like impertinent speeches as these, good enough to feed those that are served with wind and not with the sincere milk of the word of God.' Law also censures these irritated and extravagant enthusiasts, not only for intending to overthrow the government, but as binding themselves to kill all that would not accede to their opinion, and he gives several instances of such cruelty being exercised by them, not only upon straggling soldiers whom they shot by the way or surprized in their quarters, but upon those who, having once joined them, had fallen away from their principles. Being asked why they committed these cruelties in cold blood, they answered, 'they were obliged to do it by their sacred bond.' Upon these occasions they practised great cruelties, mangling the bodies of their victims that each man might have his share of the guilt. In these cases the Cameronians imagined themselves the direct and inspired executioners of the vengeance of heaven. Nor did they lack the usual incentives of enthusiasm. Peden and others among them set up a claim to the gift of prophecy, though they seldom foretold any thing to the purpose. They detected witches, had bodily encounters with the enemy of mankind in his own shape, or could discover him as, lurking in the disguise of a raven, he inspired the rhetoric of a Quaker's meeting. In some cases, celestial guardians kept guard over their field-meetings. At a conventicle held on the Lomond-hills, the Rev Mr Blacader was credibly assured, under the hands of four honest men, that at the time the meeting was disturbed by the soldiers, some women who had remained at home, 'clearly perceived as the form of a tall man, majestic-like, stand in the air in stately posture with the one leg, as it were, advanced before the other, standing above the people all the time of the soldiers shooting.' Unluckily this great vision of the Guarded Mount did not conclude as might have been expected. The divine sentinel left his post too soon, and the troopers fell upon the rear of the audience, plundered and stripped many, and made eighteen prisoners.

But we have no delight to dwell either upon the atrocities or absurdities of a people whose ignorance and fanaticism were rendered frantic by persecution. It is enough for our present purpose to observe that the present Church of Scotland, which comprizes so much sound doctrine and learning, and has produced so many distinguished characters, is the legitimate representative of the indulged clergy of the days of Charles II settled however upon a comprehensive basis. That after the revolution, it should have succeeded episcopacy as the national religion, was natural and regular, because it possessed all the sense, learning, and moderation fit for such a change, and because among its followers were to be found the only men of property and influence who acknowledged presbytery. But the Cameronians continued long as a separate sect, though their preachers were bigoted and ignorant, and their hearers were gleaned out of the lower ranks of the peasantry. Their principle, so far as it was intelligible, asserted that paramount species of presbyterian church-government which was established in the year 1648, and they continued to regard the established church as erastian and time-serving, because they prudently remained silent upon certain abstract and delicate topics, where there might be some collision between the absolute liberty asserted by the church and the civil government of the state. The Cameronians, on the contrary, disowned all kings and government whatsoever, which should not take the Solemn League and Covenant; and long retained hopes of re-establishing that great national engagement, a bait which was held out to them by all those who wished to disturb the government during the reign of William and Anne, as is evident from the Memoirs of Ker of Kersland, and the Negotiations of Colonel Hooke with the jacobites and disaffected of the year.

A party so wild in their principles, so vague and inconsistent in their views, could not subsist long under a free and unlimited toleration. They continued to hold their preachings on the hills, but they lost much of their zeal when they were no longer liable to be disturbed by dragoons, sheriffs, and lieutenants of Militia. – The old fable of the Traveller's Cloak was in time verified, and the fierce sanguinary zealots of the days of Claverhouse sunk into such quiet and peaccable enthusiasts as Howie of Lochgoin, or Old Mortality himself. It is, therefore, upon a race of sectaries who have long ceased to exist, that Mr Jedediah Cleishbotham has charged all that is odious, and almost all that is ridiculous, in his fictitious narrative; and we can no more suppose any moderate presbyterian involved in the satire, than we should imagine that the character of Hampden stood committed by a little raillery on the person of Ludovic Claxton, the Muggletonian. If, however, there remain any of those sectaries who, confining the beams of the Gospel to the Goshen of their own obscure synagogue, and with James Mitchell, the intended assassin, giving their sweeping testimony against prelacy and popery, The Whole Duty of Man and bordles, promiscuous dancing and the Common Prayer-book, and all the other enormities and backslidings of the time, may perhaps be offended at this idle tale, we are afraid they will receive their answer in the tone of the revellers to Malvolio, who, it will be remembered, was something a kind of Puritan : 'Doest thou think because thou art virtuous, there shall be no more cakes and ale? – Aye, by Saint Anne, and ginger will be hot in the mouth too.'[5]

We intended here to conclude this long article, when a strong report reached us of certain transatlantic confessions, which, if genuine, (though of this we know nothing,) assign a different author to these volumes, than the party suspected by our Scottish correspondents. Yet a critic may be excused seizing upon the nearest suspicious person, on the principle happily expressed by Claverhouse, in a letter to the Earl of Linlithgow. He had been, it seems, in search of a gifted weaver, who used to hold forth at conventicles: 'I sent to seek the webster, (weaver) they brought in his *brother* for him: though he maybe cannot preach like his brother, I doubt not but he is as well principled as he, wherefore I thought it would be no great fault to give him the trouble to go jail with the rest.'[6]

NOTES

NOTES

I INCORPORATE Scott's own notes, supplied for the 1830 edition, with my own. The ones with titles were situated (clumsily) at the ends of the relevant chapters; the others appeared as footnotes to the text.

I must record here, warmly, my debts to two scholars without whose work my own annotations would not have been so full, and my thanks for their kindness in giving me freedom to draw on it. Alexander Welsh's edition of the novel for Riverside Editions (Boston, 1966) in particular pointed out to me numerous biblical allusions I would otherwise have missed, and James Anderson's doctorate thesis for Edinburgh University on 'Scott and History' directed me to Scott's historical sources in great detail. Dr Anderson also saw these notes in draft and suggested several improvements. It would seem pedantic to indicate each place where I have been assisted, but I have acknowledged several specific pieces of help.

Life is short, I have not usually felt moved to annotate Scott's handling of costume and manners; nor can I pretend to have seen daylight through the curious legal and genealogical fog surrounding the Bellenden family. And if these notes had exhausted every literary allusion and every biblical, historical and topographical reference in the novel they might have been twice as long. I have, however, made rather long historical notes at certain places to illustrate Scott's play with his sources. The key to my references will be found in the Bibliography.

The mottoes at the heads of chapters display very interestingly, I think, the sorts of literature Scott himself had found inspiring and memorable. His debt to Shakespeare's comedies and histories and his wide knowledge of seventeenth-century plays and poetry are especially germane to the success of this novel.

Like the biblical quotations, and, indeed, several historical references, the mottoes show how amazing Scott's memory was. He quotes time and again with enough general accuracy to make it an easy business to track the original down, but with particular slips which make it quite clear that he didn't bother to consult his bookshelf.

GENERAL NOTE ON SOURCES OF
LOCALITIES AND CHARACTERS

In Chapter 37 Scott makes an important point about the transition from violent past to civil present by setting the scene of Cuddie's domestic prosperity so close to the battlefield of Bothwell Bridge. But otherwise he was, for good reasons, reluctant to tie his episodes to actual localities, except where history insisted on them.

The 'royal borough' which Scott refuses to name (p. 72) can, in fact, only be Lanark, the sole royal burgh in the Upper Ward of Clydesdale and the only town in the area garrisoned in 1679. Lanark is not far from Craignethan Castle (originally Draffen or Draphane) which is set in superb wooded scenery near the junction of Nethan Water with the Clyde, and which was, in the sixteenth century, the seat of the Evandale branch of the great Hamilton family. When Scott first visited it in 1799, he was staying at Bothwell as a guest of Lord Douglas, and he was so delighted by the ruined buildings set on a steep hump above a deep gorge that his kind host pressed on him the lifetime use of a small house he owned within the walls. No one who sees Craignethan with the novel fresh in his mind can doubt that Scott drew most of his inspiration for Tillietudlem from it.

But Craignethan isn't actually on the Clyde. The literal-minded Aiton (90) pointed out that the ruins of Orbiston Castle commanded a view of woodlands and fine holmes to front and hills to rear, like Tillietudlem, and unlike Craignethan. Nor are the buildings at Craignethan anything like as old as the inscription over Tillietudlem's gate would seem to make some of those in the novel; it was built by Sir James Hamilton of Finnart early in the sixteenth century. What Scott's synthesizing imagination has provided for us is a medieval castle, in a setting as beautiful as that of Craignethan, and rather similar to it, but extending into a wider landscape which symbolizes a contrast between the impoverished but heroic past – that 'inhospitable moorland' – and the 'richly cultivated and highly adorned' culture of the Regency. This contrast provides the commanding theme of all the Scottish Waverley novels. Tillietudlem stands at a moment of junction and in a place of transition.

When Burley's paranoia and ambition drive him into isolation, his character becomes assimilated with 'inhospitable' elemental grandeur. The Black Linn has various prototypes in the hills above Moffat and around Loch Skene which Scott had visited (for instance) in 1802 on the same trip on which he recovered the three Covenanting ballads which went into the *Minstrelsy*. This wild area was a prime refuge for hunted Covenanters.

The way in which Scott creates characters often corresponds to that in which he arranges scenery. He synthesizes, drawing his material almost always from within the area he describes and the period of history he deals with. (Even the name 'Tillietudlem' has been explained as an echo of 'Gillytudlem', the name of a ravine near Lanark; and the David Olifard who founded the lordship of Bothwell under Malcolm IV was an ancestor of the family of 'Olifant'.)

As for 'Morton', there is a parish of that name in the south-west, and there was at Bothwell Bridge a 'moderate' minister named Andrew Morton (see the note to p. 282). We may find it hard to believe that a very young man with literary tastes could have played an heroic military role among dour bigots at that period. Yet William Cleland, only about eighteen at the time, was a daring commander of foot at Drumclog and then an officer again at Bothwell Bridge, and he wrote verse which displays no mighty talent, but reveals a lively mind and even a hint of a 'romantic' temperament. (See the note to p. 214). Alexander Gordon of Earlstoun, whom Scott supposed to be the hero of the ballad about Bothwell Bridge which he put into the *Minstrelsy* (see Appendix B) must certainly have been in his mind as he created Morton's role. Scott had noted (*Minstrelsy* 2:234–6) 'He was not a Cameronian but of the more moderate class of Presbyterians, whose sole object was freedom of conscience, and relief from oppressive laws against nonconformists. He joined the insurgents shortly after the skirmish at Loudon Hill. He appears to have been active in forwarding the supplication sent to the Duke of Monmouth.' And those who think that Jenny Dennison's suggestion (p. 161) that Morton should slip into her plaid and gown and get free is merely a typical piece of Scott's romantic twaddling, should note that Earlstoun escaped after the battle by 'flying into a house at Hamilton, belonging to one of his tenants, and disguising himself in female attire.'

But the gentleman marked out in the sources as the secular leader of the rebels was Robert Hamilton, a 'Cameronian' extremist. While one or two elements in Morton's story seem to have been borrowed from him, more of him seems to have gone into Scott's Burley. The canting, sectarian, self-justifying style of Hamilton's letters (see *Faithful Contendings*) gives some basis for Burley's completely humourless speeches. Burley's switch of course at Bothwell is more dignified than that which the sources attribute to Hamilton, who at one moment signed the 'moderate' supplication to Monmouth, though before and after rejecting all compromise.

There was little hard fact about Burley to inhibit Scott from synthesis; we can add nothing to his own notes, except that Scott knew, though he doesn't cite it, Wodrow's judgement (2 : 32) ... 'I cannot find that this gentleman had ever any great character for religion among those that knew him; and such were the accounts of him when abroad, that the reverend ministers of the Scots congregation at Rotterdam would never allow him to communicate with them.' Scott's Burley *does* maintain a 'character for religion', though his secular ambitions are clearly adumbrated, and Scott must have thought of Montgomery of Skelmorlie and even Ferguson 'the Plotter' (see note to p. 456) in framing his general conception of him.

The prominent role at Drumclog assigned to Burley in the ballad is not accorded him elsewhere. Hackston is presented as the hero (with Cleland) of that skirmish, and Hackston is the leader of the valiant defence of Bothwell Bridge. But the Covenanting sources had an interest in building up Hackston, who hadn't actually struck at Sharp and had been 'martyred' at the scaffold in 1680, and so was a more attractive subject for hagiography – folk tradition, extolling Burley, may have just as much truth on its side.

The actual Balfour, born about 1640, could hardly have fought at Marston Moor four years later. Scott makes Burley function as the typical Covenanting soldier of a period of fifty years of history, and, as his notes show, draws inspiration in this from the veteran Captain John Paton, who had indeed fought in the Civil Wars of 1638–51, and again at the Pentland Rising of 1666, before he brought his scarred sword to Bothwell Bridge; he was probably in his seventies when captured and executed in 1684, and Howie (*Scots Worthies* 414–27) builds him up to epic status – suggesting that he slew, on one occasion, eighteen 'malignants' with his own hand.

Burley's epic adversary Bothwell is a more blatant composite. The real Francis Stewart didn't fight and fall at Drumclog, though his friend Creichton (35) assigns him a pretty prominent part at Bothwell Bridge. Scott builds up the scant outline by adapting language from the Restoration plays he knew so well, having edited John Dryden, and by giving him much of the devil-may-care, honest-roguery of Creichton himself; while at least a single touch is drawn from one of those memoirs of seventeenth-century mercenaries out of which Scott soon afterwards constructed the wholly different character of Dugald Dalgetty.

Bothwell's name, chiming oddly with that of the battle, also evokes the tragedy of Mary Queen of Scots and the later odd doings of the 'Warlock Earl of Bothwell' – its presence in the novel thus increases the range of past violence within our view. 'Evandale' or 'Avendale' was the name of the valley of Avon Water in which Drumclog is found. There had been at one time 'Lord Evandales', though the title was not in use in 1679. Scott owned the manuscript memoirs of one 'Lady Margaret' Cuninghame, written in 1608 and recording her ill-treatment by her husband the Master of Evandale. But the nice lilt of the name suits in the novel its nice fictional owner. Why he should be a Maxwell (296) and his sister a Hamilton (414), Scott alone knew.

'Bellenden' is a more complicated case. Personal associations would certainly affect Scott's naming of his characters. – 'Alison Wilson', as it happens, was the name of the elderly housekeeper at his grand-parents' farm where Scott stayed as a boy. 'Bellenden' was the war-cry of the Scotts of Buccleuch, the novelist's own clan. He had had occasion to remember it late in 1815 when arranging a football match between the parish of Ettrick, backed by the Duke of Buccleuch, and that of Yarrow, backed by himself. He thought of this occasion, as his letters make clear, as a kind of wappenschaw, and he went to much trouble to display the banner of Buccleuch, which had 'Bellenden' on one side. (*Letters* 4 : 125, 128)

So the old 'malignants' are rewarded with a name not only attractive in itself (suggesting 'belle') but also one very close indeed to Scott's antiquarian heart. Yet for students of the period in which the novel is set, its resonance is very different. Lord Bellenden (d. 1671) was a privy councillor of Scotland in the 1660s, a member of Lauderdale's faction, 'noted for his violent and overbearing manners at the treasury board meetings, especially when, as was the case, his own accounts as treasurer-depute were called in question, or when any matter of precedence was in dispute.' (*DNB*) And Sir William Bellenden (or Ballantyne) was a notorious coadjutor with Sir James Turner in the oppression of the south-west which provoked the Pentland Rising. His illegal exactions had been so blatant that he was banished from Scotland in 1668.

But of course the Royalists are more politely named than the Covenanters. There is a Gudyill (good-ale) to balance a Poundtext,

and a Raddlebanes to balance a Rumbleberry, but really Inglis or
Halliday should be called 'Slaughtermen' or 'Blindrunk' to counter-
poise the unfortunate Kettledrummle. While M'Crie was right (363)
in pointing out that Scott 'must have had his eye upon Mr John
King', the captured preacher whom Claverhouse actually took with
him to Drumclog, his complaint that Kettledrummle's preaching is
nothing like King's speech before his execution misses the mark,
because even this minor character is synthetic, and one of his actions (see the note for p. 229) seems to have been borrowed from another preacher, Gabriel Sempill, whose Christian name Scott copies.

An alien element has certainly intruded into the novel through the
Old Testament names which Scott gives to his still more extreme
preachers. M'Crie (349) protested, shrewdly, that 'he borrowed this
from the English plays written in derision of the Puritans'. Such
names weren't common even in England. In Scotland, only the
ultra-extremist sect of Gibbites, which appeared in the 1680s and
which scandalized the Covenanters themselves, seems to have gone
in for Biblical names, and the martyrologies give no basis at all for
Scott's 'Ephraim' or 'Habbakuk' in their long rolls of Johns, James,
and Williams.

But Macbriar itself is a real, though uncommon, name. (Howie's
Judgements (33–4), presents a 'cruel persecutor' called M'Bryar.) Of
course, Scott must have chosen it as an apt one for a sharp-spined
extremist, but it's not a joke name in the Ben Jonson manner.
Macbriar has distinguished prototypes. M'Crie noted (413) that the
idea of his sermon was borrowed from one of Cameron's, and also
pointed out the obvious parallel with Hugh M'Kail, a consumptive
preacher aged only twenty-five who was tortured with the boot and
executed after the Pentland Rising – Burnet (1 : 237) gives an admir-
ing account of his courage. Also, the frail James Renwick (1662–88),
who was, like Macbriar but unlike M'Kail, an out-and-out extremist,
must have been in Scott's mind.

Nor is Mucklewrath quite the creature of neo-classical imagination (vatic, 'sublime') that he seems at first sight. His name is one
version of McIlwraith, a pretty common one, and Scott had already
given it to a minor character in *Waverley*. There was more than one
Covenanting 'martyr' who bore it. Defoe (250–52) gives an unsupported and probably fictitious story that 'Matthew Mekellwraith'
was shot at once on Claverhouse's orders merely for running across
the street in front of his soldiers. This is in piquant conflict, if one
thinks about it, with the inscription on a stone in Colmonell Churchyard (Hewison 554):

I MATTHEW M'ILWRAITH IN THIS PARISH OF COLMONELL
BY BLOODY CLAVERHOUSE I FELL
WHO DID COMMAND THAT I SHOULD DIE
FOR OWNING COVENANTED PRESBYTERY...

While no mad preacher (except the later, un-bloodthirsty Gibb) crops up in the sources, Mucklewrath's prophetic style has a precedent in Alexander Peden (d.1686), hero of a biography by Patrick Walker which Scott had probably known since childhood. Peden was imprisoned, like Mucklewrath, on the Bass Rock (1674–7) but afterwards showed much flair for keeping out of trouble – he wasn't at Bothwell Bridge, but instead was a good many miles away impressing those near him by his prophecies of bloody defeat. He was no sword-swinging militant, and his familiar manner of addressing God in moments of danger – 'cast the lap of thy cloak o'er old Sandy and thir poor things, and save us this one time' – has, alas, no echoes in *Old Mortality*. But when Walker (1:65–6) sets him preaching in Ireland one hears a less Scriptural Mucklewrath:

Pack and let us go to Scotland, pack and let us go to Scotland. Let us flee from one devouring sword and go to another: the poor honest lads in Scotland are running upon the hills and have little either meat or drink but cold and hunger; and the bloody enemy are pursuing them, and murdering them wherever they find them: their blood is running like water upon scaffolds and fields: rise, let us go and take part with them; for we fear they bar us out of heaven. Oh secure Ireland, a dreadful day is coming upon thee within a few years, that they shall ride many miles and shall not see a reeking house in thee: oh hunger, hunger in Derry, many a black and pale face shall be in thee . . .

EDITOR'S NOTES AND SCOTT'S NOTES

INTRODUCTION TO TALES OF MY LANDLORD

1. (p. 51) *Burns*: from Robert Burns's poem 'On the Late Captain Grose's Peregrinations Thro' Scotland', a tribute to an antiquarian.

2. (p. 51) *Gandercleugh*: 'Gandy', according to *SND*, means 'to talk in a blustering, boastful or pert fashion... Hence *gandier*, a vain, boastful person'. A 'gander' of course is a male goose. A 'cleugh' is a narrow gorge or chasm with high rocky sides, or a crag rock.

3. (p. 52) *Ithacus*: Odysseus. The Roman poet is Horace (*Ars Poetica*).

4. (p. 52) *Zoilus*: a philosopher of Amphipolis, 4th c. B.C., whose severe comments on Homer made him a byword for stiff critics.

5. (p. 52) *General Assembly*: of the Church of Scotland – its highest court.

6. (p. 55) *Mr Robert Carey*: this is more likely to be Jedediah's slip than Scott's. The elegy on Donne which is quoted, is by Thomas Carew (*c.* 1594–1640). Scott himself had edited in 1808 the lively memoirs of Robert Carey, Earl of Monmouth (1560–1639)

7. (p. 55) *Mirthful Man*: John Ballantyne.

8. (p. 56) *Dean of St Patrick's*: Jonathan Swift.

CHAPTER I

1. (p. 59) *Langhorne*: the Rev. John Langhorne (1735–79), whose *Poetical Works* appeared in 1766. This quotation comes from 'The Wall-Flower', the seventh of his 'Fables of Flora'.

2. (p. 61) *the battle of Pentland Hills*: fought at Rullion Green, near Edinburgh, on the 28 November 1666, where the defeat by Sir Thomas Dalzell of a force of western whigs terminated the so-called 'Pentlands Rising'.

3. (p. 62) *Hampden ... Hooper ... Latimer*: John Hampden (?1595–1643) was a leader of the English Commons in their struggle with Charles I. John Hooper (d. 1555) and Hugh Latimer (*c.* 1490–1555) were defiant Protestants martyred by Queen Mary.

4. (p. 62) *native sycamore*: 'native' only in a rather diluted sense:

Acer Pseudoplatanus, though growing in Britain by the sixteenth century, was introduced from continental Europe.

5. (p. 65) *Cameronian*: by the time of the fictional Peter Pattieson, this term would be applied to the members of the sect of Reformed Presbyterians, originally so named in 1743. These people inherited, or claimed to inherit, the principles of the followers of Richard Cameron (d. 1680) and Donald Cargill (d. 1681), extremists who, like Burley and Macbriar in this novel, attacked the Indulgence and defied the authority of the King. But Scott's use of the term is rather loose and problematical. The extremist party had certainly formed by 1679, whipped up by exiled ideologists in Holland, but Cameron himself emerged as its leader only briefly, in the period *after* Bothwell Bridge, at which he was not present. Following Cameron's death in battle at Aird's Moss and Cargill's capture and execution, the party, left without a qualified preacher, formed a Union of Correspondence to link their various secret societies (hence the term "Society People"). The gifted and attractive James Renwick returned from Holland to lead them from 1683 to his execution in 1688. After the Glorious Revolution they split; one section was happy to form the famous Cameronian Regiment in order to help defend the new régime, and only a vestige, probably rather less important than Scott suggests in Chapter 37, continued to remain outside the Church of Scotland. Known sometimes as 'McMillanites' after John McMillan, who became their preacher in 1706, they gave no more serious trouble to the authorities.

Patrick Walker (1:241) says emphatically that the word Cameronian was 'very little to be heard of until the Revolution', and Scott would not have found it in contemporary sources, where the extremists at Bothwell Bridge style themselves the 'honest party'. He uses it as shorthand. Burley and Macbriar represent both the triumphant murderous zealots of Philiphaugh in 1645 and the small band who held out in the 1680s under Cameron, Cargill and Renwick. The term 'Cameronian' is meant to convey 'extremist, militant, anti-Erastian, intolerant'.

6. (p. 65) *Maxim of Solomon*: see Proverbs 13:24.

7. (p. 66) *The only true whigs*: this term, applied from 1689 to the party in Britain who supported the Glorious Revolution, had first been used in Scotland following the so-called 'Whiggamore Raid' on Edinburgh in 1648, when insurgents from the radical southwest seized the capital. Burnet (1:43) says that it arose because men from that area coming up to buy corn in the summer drove their horses on with the 'word Whiggam'. Hence, it would seem, a local

nickname for the south-westerners became applied, first to Scots Presbyterians in general, then to the dominant party in eighteenth-century England.

8. (p. 66) *Mr Peden*: Alexander Peden (*c.* 1626–86), a famous outlawed field-preacher.

9. (p. 66) *1677*: the old man's memory errs. Though the so-called 'Highland Host' which was sent in to take up free quarters in the disloyal south-west was commissioned in December 1677, it didn't invade that unlucky area until February 1678, when 6,000 Highlanders from the gaelic-speaking clans and also 3,000 militiamen from the Lowlands settled down to spoil and pillage for about a month. The idea was to force the local nobles and gentry to sign bonds for the loyal behaviour of all persons residing on their lands.

10. (p. 69) *nonjuring bishop*: since the Presbyterian Church system was established in Scotland from 1689 on, in that country the bishops of the Episcopal Church were Nonconformists.

11. (p. 69) *Earlshall*: Captain Andrew Bruce of Earls' Hall, commissioned jointly with Claverhouse as Sheriff-Depute in Galloway in 1679, and later Claverhouse's Lieutenant when the king's new regiment of horse in Scotland was set up in 1682. A notorious hunter of men, who commanded the party which defeated and slew Richard Cameron in 1680.

12. (p. 70) *Dryden*: John Dryden (1631–1700), the major English poet, whose works Scott had edited, by 1808, on a grand scholarly scale.

13. (p. 70) *our only Scottish tragedy*: the long-famous blank verse drama *Douglas* (1756) by John Home (1722–1808). These lines are spoken by Lady Randolph in Act I.

CHAPTER 2

1. (p. 70) *Douglas*: see the note immediately above. This quotation comes from the opening of Act IV, i. (*Lord Randolph* 'The Danes are landed: we must beat them back/Or live the slaves of Denmark'. *Lady Randolph* 'Dreadful times!')

2. (p. 72) *popinjay* (Scott's note):

Festival of the Popinjay

The Festival of the Popinjay is still, I believe, practised at Maybole, in Ayrshire. The following passage in the history of the Somerville family, suggested the scenes in the text. The author of that curious manuscript thus celebrates his father's demeanour at such an assembly.

'Having now passed his infancie, in the tenth year of his age, he was by his grandfather putt to the grammar school, ther being then att the toune of Delserf a very able master that taught the grammar, and fitted boyes for the colledge. Dureing his educating in this place, they had then a custome every year to solemnize the first Sunday of May with danceing about a May-pole, fyreing of pieces, and all manner of ravelling then in use. Ther being at that tyme feu or noe merchants in this pettie village, to furnish necessaries for the schollars sports, this youth resolves to provide himself elsewhere, so that he may appear with the bravest. In order to this, by break of day he ryses and goes to Hamiltoune, and there bestowes all the money that for a long tyme before he had gotten from his freinds, or had other-wayes purchased, upon ribbones of diverse colours, a new hatt and gloves. But in nothing he bestowed his money more liberallie than upon gunpowder, a great quantitie whereof he buyes for his owne use, and to supplie the wantes of his comerades; thus furnished with these commodities, but an empty purse, he returnes to Delserf by seven a clock, (haveing travelled that Sabbath morning above eight myles), puttes on his cloathes, and new hatt, flying with ribbones of all culloures; and in this equipage, with his little phizie (fusee) upon his shoulder, he marches to the church yaird, where the May-pole was sett up, and the solemnitie of that day was to be kept. There first at the foot-ball he equalled any one that played; but in handleing his piece, in chargeing and dischargeing, he was so ready, and shott so near the marke, that he farre surpassed all his fellow schollars, and became a teacher of that art to them before the thretteenth year of his oune age. And really, I have often admired his dexterity in this, both at the exercizeing of his soulders, and when for recreatione. I have gone to the gunning with him when I was but a stripeling myself; and albeit that passetyme was the exercize I delighted most in, yet could I never attaine to any perfectione comparable to him. This dayes sport being over, he had the applause of all the spectatores, the kynd-nesse of his fellow-condisciples, and the favour of the whole inhabi-tants of that little village.'

[Scott had edited J. Somerville, *Memorie of the Somervilles*, and published it in two volumes in 1815].

3. (p. 72) *puritanism* : Scott imports, here and elsewhere, an English term into Scottish history, and M'Crie (339–46) takes immense and paranoiac exception to his use of it. Earlier (273) M'Crie objects that even precise preachers of the period countenanced exercises and

pastimes then normal. But Scott clearly took his idea from the 'puritanical' comments of Patrick Walker, and from the tone of other sources. And Smout (78–81) applies the term without inhibition.

4. (p. 74) *episcopalian ... commination*: the Bellendens are, as is made clear later, 'High Church', though the 'episcopalian' system established at the restoration wasn't. Anyway, the Bellendens use the Book of Common Prayer (q.v.) in which Harrison knows the 'commination', a string of curses against sinners.

5. (p. 74) *Kilsythe and Tippermoor*: victories won by Montrose's Royalist forces in 1644–5. See p. 19.

6. (p. 75) *Worcester*: where Cromwell defeated Charles II and his Scottish supporters on 3 September 1651.

7. (p. 76) *Calprenede and Scuderi*: Gauthier de Costes de La Calprenède (1614–63) and Madeleine de Scudéry (1607–1701), French writers of the period.

8. (p. 77) *Cyrus, Cleopatra*: Madeleine de Scudéry published in ten volumes (1649–53) *Artamène ou le Grand Cyrus*, dealing with the love of Cyrus for Mandane, princess of Media, and this enormous tale was very popular in Britain, *Cléopâtre* (1647–56) is by La Calprenède.

CHAPTER 3

1. (p. 77) *Pleasures of Hope*: a once famous poem published in 1799 by Thomas Campbell (1777–1844), an important Scottish Romantic. Scott misquotes Part 2, 181–2.

2. (p. 80) *Malvolio ... imaginary retinue*: see Shakespeare's *Twelfth Night*, II, v. Note that the comparison tends to mock this Duke, in his fatuous carriage, who must be assumed to be the then Duke of Hamilton, clearly referred to later in the novel.

3. (p. 81) *Dunbar and Inverkeithing*: at Dunbar on 3 September 1650 a Scottish army purged of non-Covenanting elements, but supporting Charles II, was defeated by Cromwell. The battle of Inverkeithing, 20 July 1651, was another defeat for pro-Stuart Scots forces at the hands of one of Cromwell's lieutenants. At both, Silas Morton could have fought for the king *and* for Scotland *and* for the Covenants.

4. (p. 81) *Marston-Moor and Philiphaugh*: but at Marston Moor on 2 July 1644 Scots fought for the victorious Parliamentary forces *against* Charles I, and the Scots cavalry under David Leslie charged decisively. David Leslie surprised and routed Montrose at Philiphaugh on 13 September 1645, and Lady Margaret's husband was clearly one

of the royalists put to death by the victors after the battle, when the Covenanting ministers bayed for blood. Scott thinks of the name as two words, because 'haugh' is common by itself.

5. (p. 83) *Orlando*: the hero of Ludovico Ariosto's poem *Orlando Furioso* (1532) a romantic epic lavish with incident, and a favourite of Scott when he was a boy.

CHAPTER 4

1. (p. 84) *Elegy on Habbie Simpson*: from 'The Life and Death of the Piper of Kilbarchan or The Epitaph of Habbie Simpson', but somewhat misquoted. This mock-elegy is the most important Scottish poem of the seventeenth century, which is saying very little, and its stanza, though not invented by the author Sir Robert Sempill of Beltrees (*c.* 1595–*c.* 1660), and much used later by Burns, is still called 'Standard Habbie'.

2. (p. 85) *Gaius*: see Romans 16:23.

3. (p. 85) *curate*: the term always applied to the Episcopalians brought in, largely from the conservative north-east, to take the place of the ministers deprived for not accepting the 1662 settlement of the church. Few bodies of men have attracted more abuse. Burnet in a famous passage (1:158) wrote 'They were the worst preachers I ever heard: They were ignorant to a reproach: And many of them were openly vitious.'

4. (p. 87) *the celebrated John Grahame of Claverhouse's regiment of Life-Guards*: Claverhouse was not in fact commissioned as Colonel of the king's new regiment of horse in Scotland until December 1682, and was not very 'celebrated' at the time in which the novel is set. See the present editor's introduction.

5. (p. 88) *James VI*: Scott's slip for James V– (Scott's note):

Sergeant Bothwell

The history of the restless and ambitious Francis Stewart, Earl of Bothwell, makes a considerable figure in the reign of James VI of Scotland, and First of England. After being repeatedly pardoned for acts of treason, he was at length obliged to retire abroad, where he died in great misery. Great part of his forfeited estate was bestowed on Walter Scott, first Lord of Buccleuch, and on the first Earl of Roxburghe.

Francis Stewart, son of the forfeited Earl, obtained from the favour of Charles I, a decree arbitral, appointing the two noblemen, grantees of his father's estate, to restore the same, or make some compensation for retaining it. The barony of Crichton, with its beautiful castle, was surrendered by the curators of Francis, Earl of Buccleuch, but he retained the far more extensive property in Liddesdale. James Stewart also, as appears from writings in the author's possession, made an advantageous composition with the Earl of Roxburghe. 'But,' says the satirical Scotstarvet, '*male parta pejus dilabuntur*; for he never brooked them, (enjoyed them,) nor was any thing the richer, since they accrued to his creditors, and are now in the possession of Dr Seaton. His eldest son Francis became a trooper in the late war; as for the other brother John, who was Abbot of Coldingham, he also disponed all that estate, and now has nothing, but lives on the charity of his friends.' *

Francis Stewart, who had been a trooper during the great Civil War, seems to have received no preferment, after the Restoration, suited to his high birth, though, in fact, third cousin to Charles II. Captain Crichton, the friend of Dean Swift, who published his Memoirs, found him a private gentleman in the King's Life-Guards. At the same time this was no degrading condition; for Fountainhall records a duel fought between a Life-Guardsman and an officer in the militia, because the latter had taken upon him to assume superior rank as an officer, to a gentleman private in the Life-Guards. The Life-Guards man was killed in the rencontre, and his antagonist was executed for murder.

The character of Bothwell, except in relation to the name, is entirely ideal.

6. (p. 89) *colt foaled of an acorn*: see Scott's note to p. 541.

7. (p. 91) *Rabshakehs*: this loud-mouthed officer of Sennacherib, King of Assyria, who 'rails' at the people of Jerusalem in 2 Kings 18, was a byword among the Covenanters.

8. (p. 93) *swords and daggers* (Scott's note):

The general account of this act of assassination is to be found in all histories of the period. A more particular narrative may be found in the words of one of the actors, James Russell, in the Appendix to Kirkton's History of the Church of Scotland, published by Charles Kirkpatrick Sharpe, Esquire, 4to, Edinburgh, 1817.

9. (p. 93) *enmity* (Scott's note):

One Carmichael, sheriff-depute in Fife, who had been active in en-

---

* The Staggering State of the Scots Statesmen for one hundred years, by Sir John Scot of Scotstarvet. Edinburgh, 1754. P. 154.

forcing the penal measures against non-conformists. He was on the moors hunting, but receiving accidental information that a party was out in quest of him, he returned home, and escaped the fate designed for him, which befell his patron the Archbishop.

10. (p. 93) *into their hands* (Scott's note):

Murderers of Archbishop Sharpe

The leader of this party was David Hackston, of Rathillet, a gentleman of ancient birth and good estate. He had been profligate in his younger days, but having been led from curiosity to attend the conventicles of the nonconforming clergy, he adopted their principles in the fullest extent. It appears, that Hackston had some personal quarrel with Archbishop Sharpe, which induced him to decline the command of the party when the slaughter was determined upon, fearing his acceptance might be ascribed to motives of personal enmity. He felt himself free in conscience, however, to be present; and when the archbishop, dragged from his carriage, crawled towards him on his knees for protection, he replied coldly, 'Sir, I will never lay a finger on you.' It is remarkable that Hackston, as well as a shepherd who was also present, but passive, on the occasion, were the only two of the party of assassins who suffered death by the hands of the executioner.

On Hackston refusing the command, it was by universal suffrage conferred on John Balfour of Kinloch, called Burley, who was Hackston's brother-in-law. He is described 'as a little man, squint-eyed, and of a very fierce aspect' – 'He was,' adds the same author, 'by some reckoned none of the most religious; yet he was always reckoned zealous and honest-hearted, courageous in every enterprise, and a brave soldier, seldom any escaping that came into his hands. He was the principal actor in killing that arch-traitor to the Lord and his church, James Sharpe.'*

CHAPTER 5

1. (p. 94) *James Duff*: these lines cannot be found in *A Collection of Poems, Songs, &c. Chiefly Scottish* by James Duff (Perth 1816) and seem remote from the sub-Burnsian vein of this very minor poet. Perhaps Scott invented them, or misattributed them.

2. (p. 94) *He that is mighty ... wheat from the chaff*: cf. Matthew 3 : 11–12 and Luke 3 : 16–17.

* See Scottish Worthies. 8vo. Leith, 1816. Page 522.

3. (p. 95) *indulgence ... the proffered terms*: 'The first indulgence (June 1669) resulted in the restoration of forty-two presbyterian ministers to their parishes, and a second, in 1672, allowed some ninety more of them to preach; these indulged ministers served under certain restrictions, but were not obliged to renounce their preference for presbyterian government. One result of the indulgences was to split the presbyterians: while the more moderate ministers accepted the indulgences, and many of the gentry welcomed the return of their old pastors, opposition was stimulated by ministers who had been banished to Holland after 1662, and hatred of the indulgences was instilled into the lower orders.' (Donaldson 369). It will be seen that Scott's view, here and elsewhere in the novel, is exactly that of our leading modern authority.

4. (p. 95) *children of light*: cf. John 12:35–6.

5. (p. 95) *I must necessarily be guided ... family*: the left-wing M'Crie's outburst is worth quoting. 'This is passive obedience with a witness! to the utter prostration of the rights of conscience, and leading to all the extent of the wicked principle of Hobbes!' (345).

6. (p. 95) *golden-calf of Bethel ... cast upon the waters*: see 1 Kings 12:25–33 and Exodus 32:20.

7. (p. 96) *lion in the path*: cf. Proverbs 22:13; 26:13. And 1 Peter 5:8 'Be sober, be vigilant; because your adversary the devil, as a roaring lion, walketh about, seeking whom he may devour.'

8. (p. 96) *Hamilton and Dingwall*: it is odd that these real people are mentioned here and then forgotten. William Dingwall, one of Sharpe's murderers, actually fell at Drumclog. Sir Robert Hamilton (1650–1701) with Burley, Hackston and several score others published the Rutherglen Declaration on 29 May 1679, and he led the rebels at Drumclog, and again at Bothwell Bridge, where his strange behaviour did much to ensure defeat. He fled to Holland and, returning after the Revolution, became leader of the 'rump' of 'Cameronian' extremists, and was imprisoned in 1692–3. Scott transfers elements of his role to Morton, and of his personality to Burley.

The 'Dingwall' who figures as 'a sort of aid-de-camp' to Burley later (p. 320) *may* be meant for one of Sharpe's murderers, though his subordinate position makes this seem doubtful. If he were, it would be a slip, since Dingwall would by this time be dead.

9. (p. 97) *intercommuned persons*: in August 1675 the authorities issued 'letters of intercommuning' against a list of nearly a hundred diehard conventiclers, later extended. These people were put under boycott or ostracism, since those who consorted with them were liable to be prosecuted as 'art and part with them'.

10. (p. 97) *tabernacle . . . cedar*: cf. Song of Solomon 8 : 9.

11. (p. 97) *Longmarston-Moor*: another name for Marston Moor where the battle was fought in 1644.

12. (p. 98) *Resolutioners and Protesters*: the former took their name from the resolutions passed by the moderate majority in the commission of the General Assembly in December 1650 and May 1651 which recognised Charles II as King of Scots and effectively suspended the Act of Classes; the latter rejected the authority of these resolutions, and eschewed government 'after a carnal manner, by plurality of votes'.

13. (p. 101) *Duke . . . London*: James, first Duke of Hamilton (b. 1606) executed by the English for treason in 1649.

14. (p. 102) *every member of it* (Scott's note):

A masculine retainer of this kind, having offended his master extremely, was commanded to leave his service instantly. 'In troth and that will I not,' answered the domestic; 'if your honour disna ken when ye hae a gude servant, I ken when I hae a gude master, and go away I will not.' On another occasion of the same nature, the master said, 'John, you and I shall never sleep under the same roof again;' to which John replied, with much *naïveté*, 'Whare the deil can your honour be ganging?'

CHAPTER 6

1. (p. 102) *Shakspeare*: from *2 Henry IV*, I, i.

2. (p. 102) *kettledrums* (Scott's note):

Regimental music is never played at night. But who can assure us that such was not the custom in Charles the Second's time? Till I am well-informed on this point, the kettle-drums shall clash on, as adding something to the picturesque effect of the night march.

3. (p. 105) *Jeremiah . . . mire*: see Jeremiah 38 : 6.

4. (p. 106) *malignants*: from 1642 on, a jargon-word, or smearword, for all those who disagreed with the Covenanters or with Presbyterian dominance.

5. (p. 106) *Westport*: a gate of the city of Edinburgh.

6. (p. 106) *words of the prophet*: Jeremiah 8 : 15–16.

7. (p. 106) *put my hand to the plough*: see Luke 9 : 62.

8. (p. 107) *like bubbles . . . stream*: a quotation from Shakespeare's *1 Henry IV*, II, iii.

9. (p. 107) *Judas*: Archbishop Sharpe. Donaldson (370–71) tells us

that Sharpe 'had never been a fervent covenanter and during the Cromwellian period had emerged as a leader of the resolutioners. In the critical months of 1660 he was in London as a representative of that party, and with his background he found it congenial enough to give way to the drift towards episcopacy. His compliance brought him the primacy, but to many he was a Judas who had betrayed the cause.' This is putting it mildly. Kirkton (84) accused Sharpe of atheism and of strangling his illegitimate child with his own hands, and believed the tale, credited also by his murderers (hence, no doubt, their frantic brutality) that he had been given proof against shot by Satan. By his own account (Kirkton 416–18) James Russell, after the murderers had stopped Sharpe's coach on Magus Moor, 'desired the bishop to come forth, Judas'.

Even the kindest modern accounts can make Sharpe seem no better than an unscrupulous and fawning, if able, politician. Scott would seem to have accepted Burnet's plausible view that Sharpe was guilty of double-dealing, zeal for oppression, cruelty and cowardice.

10. (p. 107) *a priest of Baal ... Brook Kishon*: in I Kings 18:40 the prophet Elijah slays the prophets of Baal at the Brook Kishon.

11. (p. 109) *both God and Mammon*: Matthew 6:24 and Luke 16:13.

12. (p. 109) *sons of God ... flood*: see Genesis 6:1–4.

13. (p. 109) *An heavy yoke ... time of rest*: from the apocryphal book Ecclesiasticus, Chapter 40. Burley quotes the passage with general accuracy but with inexact detail.

14. (p. 110) *Ruthvens ... Lesleys ... Monroes ... Gustavus Adolphus*: it is typical of Morton's 'moderation' and appreciation of the military virtues wherever found that he should admire Patrick Ruthven, later Earl of Brentford (*c.* 1573–1651) at one time Commander-in-Chief of Charles I's army. Two Leslies, or Lesleys – Alexander (*c.* 1580–1661) and David (d. 1682) – also played a prominent part in the Civil Wars after serving, like Ruthven, under Gustavus Adolphus (1594–1632) the Protestant King of Sweden. The Monroe, or Monro, most in Morton's mind was probably Colonel Robert, author of *Monro his Expedition ...* (1637) a book which Scott drew on when creating Dugald Dalgetty in *A Legend of Montrose* and for Bothwell's experience of guard duty on p. 143 of this novel. But there were other Monroes – perhaps 20,000 or 30,000 Scots altogether served Gustavus Adolphus in a civil or military capacity, and scores attained high rank. (cf. Mitchison 183). Altogether 100,000 or more Scots, perhaps a tenth of the total population, left the country in the seventeenth century.

NOTES 535

15. (p. 113) *battle of Lutzen*: in Saxony. Gustavus Adolphus was killed there in 1632, though the Swedes won. *The Margrave* 'probably refers to Duke Bernard of Saxe-Weimar'. (Welsh).

CHAPTER 7

1. (p. 115) *As You Like It*: spoken by Adam in II, iii.

2. (p. 117) *Malcolm Canmore*: Malcolm III ('Bighead') King of Scots from 1058 to 1093.

3. (p. 118) *kindly tenants*: Smout (137–8) makes clear that the class of kindly tenants, 'roughly analogous to the copyholders in England' who had had 'what amounted to customary (but unwritten) rights of heritable tenure' were probably 'almost extinct by 1600 in all but a few localities'. The situation of Tillietudlem is to this extent untypical and 'old fashioned', though Lady Margaret's high-handed behaviour is not. See Mitchison (296).

4. (p. 118) *Nebuchadnezzar . . . plain o' Dura*: see Daniel 3.

5. (p. 119) *sixteen hundred and forty-twa*: the year in which the English parliament began its war against the King. As Dr Anderson points out to me, Lady Margaret seems to forget that the Scots themselves rebelled in 1638 – Montrose included.

6. (p. 119) *new-fangled machine*: (Scott's note).

Probably something similar to the barn-fanners now used for winnowing corn, which were not, however, used in their present shape until about 1730. They were objected to by the more rigid sectaries on their first introduction, upon such reasoning as that of honest Mause in the text.

7. (p. 120) *windle-straes and sandy lavrocks*: (Scott's note).

'Bent-grass and sand-larks'. [Scott knowingly gives to Lady Margaret a famous remark of Lauderdale's. As he relates in *Tales of a Grandfather*, when Lauderdale was told in 1678 'that the oppression of the Highlanders and of the soldiery' whom he had sent into the south west 'would totally interrupt the produce of agriculture, he replied, "it were better that the west bore nothing but windle-straws and sandy-laverocks than that it should bear rebels to the King".']

8. (p. 122) *Saint Johnstone's tippit*: hangman's noose or rope. Saint Johnstone is another name for Perth, from where men rode (according to an old tale) with ropes around their necks, in 1559, symbolizing their determination to hang deserters from the cause of the Reformation.

9. (p. 122) *son of the righteous ... text*: Psalms 37:25.

CHAPTER 8

1. (p. 123) *Twelfth Night*: Maria in II, iii – grievously misquoted.

2. (p. 123) *tartan plaid*: in 1679, poor people in the Lowlands dressed in plaids as did those in the Highlands, and there was nothing specially Gaelic about the 'tartan' patterns used. See R. M. D. Grange, *A Short History of The Scottish Dress* (Burke's Peerage, 1966). The notion that particular patterns appertained to particular clans seems to have derived from enterprising weavers of the late eighteenth-century.

3. (p. 125) *the Grassmarket*: in Edinburgh, the place of public execution.

4. (p. 128) *at that time* (Scott's note in text):
This was a point of high etiquette. (Scott's note at end of chapter.)

Locking the Doors during Dinner

The custom of keeping the door of a house or chateau locked during the time of dinner, probably arose from the family being anciently assembled in the hall at that meal, and liable to surprise. But it was in many instances continued as a point of high etiquette, of which the following is an example:

A considerable landed proprietor in Dumfries-shire, being a bachelor, without near relations, and determined to make his will, resolved previously to visit his two nearest kinsmen, and decide which should be his heir, according to the degree of kindness with which he should be received. Like a good clansman, he first visited his own chief, a baronet in rank, descendant and representative of one of the oldest families in Scotland. Unhappily the dinner-bell had rung, and the door of the castle had been locked before his arrival. The visitor in vain announced his name and requested admittance; but his chief adhered to the ancient etiquette, and would on no account suffer the doors to be unbarred. Irritated at this cold reception, the old Laird rode on to Sanquhar Castle, then the residence of the Duke of Queensberry, who no sooner heard his name, than, knowing well he had a will to make, the drawbridge dropped, and the gates flew open – the table was covered anew – his grace's bachelor and intestate kinsman was received with the utmost attention and respect; and it is scarcely necessary to add, that upon his death some years after, the visitor's considerable landed property went to augment the domains of the Ducal House of Queensberry. This happened about the end of the seventeenth century.

5. (p. 129) *landward towns* (Scott's note):

The Scots retain the use of the word *town* in its comprehensive Saxon meaning, as a place of habitation. A mansion or a farm house, though solitary, is called *the town*. A *landward town* is a dwelling situated in the country.

6. (p. 131) *Corra-linn*: one of the upper falls of the Clyde, near Lanark.

7. (p. 131) *Covenant of Works ... Covenant of Grace*: A. O. J. Cockshutt (145) comments: 'To Mause the Covenant of Works is the Arminian or Catholic doctrine of salvation by works as well as faith. It denies total depravity, irresistible grace and all the glory and terror of the Calvinist tradition... For Bothwell "covenant" is no more than a word used as a badge... The comedy reflects dignity only on Mause, and casts the stigma of brutal, unthinking oppression upon Bothwell... We see Scott going beyond and behind the classic Augustan statements about theological fanaticism, recovering the human content of formulae supposed to be dead.'

See the Shorter Catechism of the Westminster Confession of Faith, that used by Scottish Presbyterians: 'Q.20. Did God leave all mankind to perish in the estate of sin and misery? – A. God having, out of his mere good pleasure, from all eternity, elected some to everlasting life, did enter into a covenant of grace, to deliver them out of the estate of sin and misery, and to bring them into an estate of salvation by a Redeemer.'

It is likely that Scott, reared in this faith as a child, did indeed take this formula seriously. But the episode is derived from Defoe (247–8), as the *Quarterly Review* makes plain. A soldier, meeting a countryman on the road whom he suspects is a Covenanting rebel, is offered by Defoe as an exceptional instance of good nature amidst so much persecution. He doesn't want to hurt the man, so he questions him in such a way as to leave him plenty of scope for evasion:

'*Sold*: ... Now I have e'en but ane question more, and ye and Ise tak a drink together. *Will ye renounce the Covenant?*
C. Man: Nay, but now I mun speir at you too, and ye like. There are twa Covenants, Man, which of them do you mean? ... There's the Covenant of Works, Man, and the Covenant of Grace.

Sold: Fou' fa me and I ken, Man; but e'en renounce ane of them, and I am satisfy'd.

C. Man: With au my heart, Sir; indeed I renounce the Covenant of Works with au my heart.'

8. (p. 132) *bloody ... scandal to the land*: cf. Wodrow (2: appendix xi) where he prints a proclamation issued by the authorities on 4 May 1679 'for Discovery of the Murderers of the Archbishop of St Andrews'. Among the phrases there, Milnwood's eye seems to fall on these: 'horrid and bloody murder ... barbarous and inhumane assassination and parricide ... such bloody and execrable attempts ... a spirit of hellish and insatiable cruelty ... the scandal of all government.' But either his eyes are letting him down or Scott is quoting from memory. (I am indebted for this note to Anderson.)

9. (p. 133) *Old Nol*: Oliver Cromwell.

10. (p. 134) *outfield and infield*: Smout (118) says of seventeenth-century Scotland: 'It is probably true that everywhere the arable land was divided into two types, "infield" and "outfield", the terms being descriptive not of separate field areas but of types of ground that often lay in intermingled blocks. Infield, perhaps normally only a quarter or less of the total tillable area, was fertile enough to bear grain crops year after year without ever enjoying a fallow break. Outfield was poorer land that could only be farmed by alternating several years of fallow with several years of oats.'

11. (p. 135) *lighted match betwixt your fingers*: Wodrow (2:77) reports the case of Anna Mitchel (*sic*), who was tortured to reveal the whereabouts of her husband, said to have been at Bothwell Bridge. The soldiers 'bound her, and put kindled matches 'twixt her fingers'. The same page would have shown Scott the story of a man who lent his plough to someone the soldiers said had been at Bothwell Bridge, and had fourteen soldiers quartered on him for some days until he gave them £50 to save his house from being 'plundered'. But Creichton (25) gives a more obvious precedent for the bribe offered in terror by Milnwood in this scene, when he tells us he 'lived plentifully a twelvemonth' on the money given him by the frightened acquaintances of a fine lady whom he caught attending a conventicle.

12. (p. 135) *Punds Scotch*: the Scots pound was worth only one-twelfth of a pound sterling; that is, 1s 8d.

13. (p. 135) *test-oath*: this is misleading. While Bothwell could have imposed an oath of allegiance, the famous Test Oath, used as a

main instrument against the Presbyterians of the south-west in the so-called 'Killing Time', was not introduced until 1681.

14. (p. 135) *Dutch clock-work*: cheap, and not elegant, clock-work. The so-called Dutch clocks were wooden ones from Germany, within the purchasing power of ordinary people, and attractive to the parsimonious.

15. (p. 136) *legs tied below a horse's belly*: a way of treating captured whigs, mentioned in Wodrow (2 : 141).

16. (p. 136) *Surely it is in vain ... any bird*: Proverbs 1 : 17.

17. (p. 137) *evening wolves ... bulls of Bashan ... Red Dragon*: the Red Dragon is indeed in Revelation 12 : 3–4; Mause's references are always correct. For evening wolves see Zephaniah 3 : 3; and for bulls of Bashan see Psalm 22. James Russell, one of Sharpe's murderers, in a proclamation which he pinned up on the door of the parish church of Kettle in Fife in 1681 referred to the king as 'Charles Stewart, a bull of Bashan' and added 'all his associats are bulls and keyn of Bashan' (Kirkton, 399). It was a Covenanting by-word.

18. (p. 138) *mammon of unrighteousness*: Luke 16 : 9.

19. (p. 139) *cess*: a land tax. The conventiclers strongly objected to the acts passed to raise money in order to suppress them; in June 1678 Parliament had approved the raising by 'cess' of a sum of £1,800,000 to go to supply forces to put down conventicles. *Ahab*, above, is an error for Ahaz.

20. (p. 139) *dumb dogs ... table for the troop ... number*: the phrase 'dumb dogs', from Isaiah 56 : 10 was, according to Burnet (1 : 282) applied by the disgusted people of the south-west to the ministers who accepted the Indulgence of 1669, and who were nick-named 'King's Curates' as opposed to the Episcopalian 'Bishop's Curates'. And James Nisbet, in his dying testimony (*Cloud* 369) while denouncing 'all Cess and Locality', quotes the passage (Isaiah 65 : 11) in which those who forsake the lord and prepare a table for the troop are consigned 'to the slaughter'.

21. (p. 140) *mark on their threshold ... pass by*: see Exodus 12.

22. (p. 141) *bonds of sin ... gall of iniquity*: a misquotation of Acts 8 : 23.

23. (p. 141) *Doegs ... Ziphites*: Doeg in 1 Samuel 22 slays four-score and five priests of the Lord. The people of Ziph in 1 Samuel 23 and 26 try to betray the fugitive David to Saul.

24. (p. 141) *antinomianism ... sublapsarianism*: Antinomianism is the heresy of those Christians who believe themselves exempt from

moral laws. Erastianism (from Thomas Erastus, 1524–83, a Swiss theologian) is the doctrine that the ecclesiastical power should be subordinated to the supremacy of the state. Sublapsarians were Calvinists holding the view that God's election of some to everlasting life was consequent to his prescience of the fall of man; their opponents on this point were 'supralapsarians'. The *OED* does not recognize Mause's word 'lapsarian': nor does the *SND*.

<h3 style="text-align:center">CHAPTER 9</h3>

1. (p. 142) *Burns*: from 'The Jolly Beggars' by Robert Burns (1759–96).

2. (p. 143) *Scotch French guards*: these originated in 1418, when the Scots sent men across to help the French against the English; the Scots Guard became the trusted personal bodyguard of the French king. In the course of time this outfit became mainly French in personnel, but thousands of Scots served the French in the Thirty Years War and revived the tradition of the 'auld alliance'.

3. (p. 143) *Port Royale*: Anderson points out that Bothwell's account of guard duty here is borrowed from *Monro his Expedition* ... (1637) where Robert Monro, a soldier of fortune, describes himself enduring such torment for *nine* hours. 'Port Royale' may be 'Port Royal des Champs' the famous centre of French Jansenism; a convent where from 1664–9 and again from 1679 the nuns were persecuted for their religious dissidence. How they baked their turtles there, I don't know (but Dr Anderson suggests to me that Bothwell must be referring to Port Royal in Jamaica).

4. (p. 144) *Louis le Grand ... Huguenots ... that is*: Louis XIV persecuted the Huguenots severely for twenty-four years before finally revoking the Edict of Nantes, under which they had been 'tolerated', in 1685.

5. (p. 144) *cutter's law*: 'cutter' means a bully, a bravo, a highway robber, a cut-throat. *OED* cites an example from Scott's *Woodstock* – 'I see, sir, you understand cutter's law – when one tall fellow has coin, another must not be thirsty.' The notion would appeal to Scott because he enjoyed observing the ethical codes obtaining in the underworld and finding in them sources of redemption for his roguish characters.

6. (p. 144) *chuck it over the signpost* (Scott's note):

A Highland laird, whose peculiarities live still in the recollection of his countrymen, used to regulate his residence at Edinburgh in the following manner: Every day he visited the Water-gate, as it is called, of the Canongate, over which is extended a wooden arch. Specie being then the general currency, he threw his purse over the gate, and as long as it was heavy enough to be thrown over, he continued his round of pleasure in the metropolis; when it was too light, he thought it time to retire to the Highlands. Query — How often would he have repeated this experiment at Temple Bar?

7. (p. 145) *horse of wood* (Scott's note):

Wooden Mare

The punishment of riding the wooden mare was, in the days of Charles and long after, one of the various and cruel modes of enforcing military discipline. In front of the old guard-house in the High Street of Edinburgh, a large horse of this kind was placed, on which now and then, in the more ancient times, a veteran might be seen mounted, with a firelock tied to each foot, atoning for some small offence.

There is a singular work, entitled Memoirs of Prince William Henry, Duke of Gloucester, (son of Queen Anne,) from his birth to his ninth year, in which Jenkin Lewis, an honest Welshman in attendance on the royal infant's person, is pleased to record that his Royal Highness laughed, cried, crow'd, and said *Gig* and *Dy*, very like a babe of plebeian descent. He had also a premature taste for the discipline as well as the show of war, and had a corps of twenty-two boys, arrayed with paper caps and wooden swords. For the maintenance of discipline in this juvenile corps, a wooden horse was established in the Presence-chamber, and was sometimes employed in the punishment of offences not strictly military. Hughes, the Duke's tailor, having made him a suit of clothes which were too tight, was appointed, in an order of the day issued by the young prince, to be placed on this penal steed. The man of remnants, by dint of supplication and mediation, escaped from the penance, which was likely to equal the inconveniences of his brother artist's equestrian trip to Brentford. But an attendant named Weatherley, who had presumed to bring the young Prince a toy, (after he had discarded the use of them,) was actually mounted on the wooden horse without a saddle, with his face to the tail, while he was plied by four servants of the household with syringes and squirts, till he had a thorough wetting. 'He was a waggish fellow,' says Lewis, 'and would not lose any thing for the joke's sake when he was putting his tricks upon others, so he was obliged to submit cheerfully to what was inflicted upon him, being at our mercy to play him off well, which we did accordingly.' Amid much such nonsense, Lewis's book shows that this poor child, the heir of the British monarchy, who died when he was eleven years old, was, in truth, of promising parts, and of a good disposition. The volume, which rarely occurs, is an octavo, published in 1789, the editor being Dr Philip Hayes of Oxford.

[I can't identify the allusion to the tailor's trip to Brentford. I wonder if Scott has a muddled memory of Cowper's well known comic poem 'John Gilpin'.]

8. (p. 145) *Monk's soldiers*: presumably in 1650–51, when General George Monk first entered Scotland as one of Cromwell's lieutenants and played an important part in capturing fortresses. He was Commander-in-Chief in Scotland in 1651–2 and again from 1654 to 1660, when he advanced into England and restored Charles II.

9. (p. 146) *the great Marquis*: Montrose.

10. (p. 148) *Rochester ... Buckingham ... Sheffield*: famous courtiers, and also men of real talent. The dissipated John Wilmot, 2nd Earl of Rochester (1647–80) was a great poet; and George Villiers, 2nd Duke of Buckingham (1628–87) and John Sheffield, 1st Duke of Buckingham and Normanby (1648–1721) were both considerable men of letters. Since Sheffield's expedition to save Tangier from the Moors did not take place until 1680, Scott is guilty here of a minor anachronism.

11. (p. 149) *Kilsythe*: Montrose's victory at Kilsythe on 15 August 1645 made him, briefly, master of all Scotland.

12. (p. 150) *boots ... thumbikins*: instruments of torture peculiar to Scotland and to this period. We will see the 'boots' in operation in Chapter 36. Though he had a spurious authority in Patrick Walker (1 : 51), Scott is wrong to suggest that the 'thumbikins', or thumbscrews, were already in use at this time; it can be shown (notes to Walker 2 : 130–31) that they were introduced as 'a new inventione and ingyne' in July 1684. Mitchison (270) pleads on behalf of the Scottish Privy Council that they used torture only fifteen times in the twenty-eight years of the restored monarchy, and seems to draw on Burnet's point that the Council members would 'almost all offer to run away' rather than witness it as they were compelled to do. But Burnet (1 : 583) is trying to point up the callousness, by contrast, of James II, who looked on with curiosity and 'unmoved indifference', and is perhaps no more to be relied on here than anywhere else. In fact, the use of torture in Scotland at this period surely marks out the régime as one particularly vicious and severe.

13. (p. 150) *Davy ... Shallow*: in V, iii.

14. (p. 150) *the Duke ... Duke James ... the Worcester man*: Gudyill's view of three successive Dukes of Hamilton is far from unique in stressing their shiftiness. James, first Duke of Hamilton (1606–49) showed what Mathieson (2 : 65) calls a 'cautious, half-hearted and time serving spirit' as Charles I's chief agent in treating with the Covenanters after 1638, and Charles himself imprisoned him for double-dealing between 1643–6. However, he led the Scottish royalist army of Engagers which was ignominiously defeated at Preston in 1648, and was executed by the English for treason. The 'Worcester man' is the second Duke, his brother William, who died of his wounds after the Battle of Worcester, 1651. William Douglas (1634–94) received the title via his wife, and is 'the Duke' in the novel. He emerged as the leader of the party which opposed Lauderdale, and while ready on occasion to persecute Whigs, his large land holdings in the south-west put him in a tricky position – in 1678 he was the most prominent of those who refused to sign a bond for the good behaviour of their tenants, and had the 'Highland Host' quartered on them. In 1689 he emerged as a leading supporter of William III. Burnet (1 : 103) calls him 'mutinous when out of power and imperious in it'.

CHAPTER 10

1. (p. 152) *Prior*: from 'Henry and Emma' by Matthew Prior (1664–1721), an important English poet. Scott omits a couplet in the middle.

2. (p. 154) *lost his life for lack o' hearing*: as does a man in one of Defoe's atrocity stories cited against Claverhouse (Defoe 252).

3. (p. 155) *a sort of muffler or veil* (Scott's note):

Concealment of an individual, while in public or promiscuous society, was then very common. In England, where no plaids were worn, the ladies used vizard masks for the same purpose, and the gallants drew the skirts of their cloaks over the right shoulder, so as to cover part of the face. This is repeatedly alluded to in Pepys's Diary.

4. (p. 155) *the lively Scottish air*: related, perhaps, to that on which Scott founded his own heroic song about Claverhouse, 'Bonnie Dundee', written in 1825 (*Journal* 45). He seems to have been the first to transfer the epithet from the town to the man.

5. (p. 156) *My Joe Janet*: for the full text see *Scotish Songs*, vol. 1 (1794), edited by Joseph Ritson, pp. 173–5.

6. (p. 161) *root and branchwork . . . early patron*: 'root and branch-work' means extermination, and as Welsh points out Claverhouse must use it sardonically 'since it was made famous in the seventeenth century by the bill to destroy the power of the bishops in 1641. The metaphor was borrowed from Malachi 4:1.' As for the notion that Claverhouse had a personal debt of gratitude and friendship to Sharpe, Scott had only flimsy warrant for this (see Terry, 11–12), and M'Crie (315–16) with laboured irony but much insight, accuses him of having put it in so as to give Claverhouse a motive for his later sever-ities which the reader can condone.

7. (p. 165) *the Grand Cyrus*: *Artamène ou le Grand Cyrus* by Madeleine de Scudéry, published in ten volumes, 1649–53.

CHAPTER II

1. (p. 166) *Swift*: from 'The Grand Question debated whether Hamilton's Bawn should be turned into a Barrack or a Malt-House' by Jonathan Swift (1667–1745).

2. (p. 167) *Mark Antony*: cf. *Antony and Cleopatra*, I, v.

3. (p. 167) *Geneva Print . . . lilies of the valley*: the Major makes a complicated pun. As Welsh points out 'discipline' makes him think of the Calvinist (Genevan) *Book of Discipline*. 'Geneva print' was the kind of type used in the 'Geneva Bible', an English translation first published in 1560. Gudyill's eyes are presumably red like those of a man who has been perusing old print. But we must fear that Scott is also punning on 'Geneva', meaning a spirit distilled from grain and flavoured with juniper, the later 'gin'. This would probably be anachronistic, as *OED* dates this usage no earlier than 1706. Gudyill retorts by invoking the Litany in the Book of Common Prayer of the Church of England. But his remark about 'flowers of the field' echoes not the Litany but Psalm 103, and also the Order for the Burial of the Dead found elsewhere in that Book.

4. (p. 169) *Noll*: Oliver Cromwell.

5. (p. 170) *Artamines . . . leasing-making* (Scott's note):

Romances of the Seventeenth Century

As few, in the present age, are acquainted with the ponderous folios to which the age of Louis XIV gave rise, we need only say, that they combine the dullness of the metaphysical courtship with all the im-probabilities of the ancient Romance of Chivalry. Their character will be most easily learned from Boileau's Dramatic Satire, or Mrs Lennox's Female Quixote.

[The work by Nicolas Boileau-Despréaux (1636–1711) to which Scott alludes here is presumably his *Dialogue des héros de romans.* Mrs Charlotte Lennox (1720–1804) published her novel *The Female Quixote* in 1752.

Artamenes, properly so spelt, is the assumed name of the Grand Cyrus in the romance. 'Leasing-making', in Scottish law, means spreading seditious calumny about the sovereign, and also applies to rumour-mongering in general. The 'picquet' or picket was a stake with a sharp top used in the seventeenth century in a military punishment where the offenders had to stand with one foot on the point while partially suspended by the opposite arm. His remark displays a certain callousness in the Major.]

6. (p. 170) *Monsieur Scuderi ... Sieur d'Urfé*: both gentlemen, however, were dead. Madeleine de Scudéry's brother, a prolific dramatist, had helped her with her romances. Honoré d'Urfé (1567–1625) had written a vast prose romance *L'Astrée* published between 1607 and 1628.

7. (p. 170) *The Whole Duty of Man ... Pike Exercise* (Scott's note):

Sir James Turner

Sir James Turner was a soldier of fortune, bred in the civil wars. He was intrusted with a commission to levy the fines imposed by the Privy Council for non-conformity, in the district of Dumfries and Galloway. In this capacity he vexed the country so much by his exactions, that the people rose and made him prisoner, and then proceeded in arms towards Mid-Lothian, where they were defeated at Pentland Hills, in 1666. Besides his treatise on the Military Art, Sir James Turner wrote several other works; the most curious of which is his Memoirs of his own Life and Times, which has just been printed, under the charge of the Bannatyne Club.

[The other work the major mentions would have been equally obnoxious to the Covenanters. It was published anonymously in 1658 and was extremely popular for more than a century. But the Covenanting preacher Kirkton complained 'that it was so far from being the whole duty of man, that it was not half of the duty of man; for his thoughts were, that the whole duty of man consisted in receiving Christ; and in all this book there was never a word of Christ, either as to receiving or employing him in any thing whatsoever.' The curates and their followers are said to have liked the book. (Kirkton xv).]

8. (p. 171) *The Tower of Tillietudlem ... Clyde* (Scott's note):

The Castle of Tillietudlem is imaginary; but the ruins of Craig-nethan Castle, situated on the Nethan, about three miles from its junction with the Clyde, have something of the character of the description in the text.

9. (p. 173) *Claverhouse* (Scott's note):

John Grahame of Claverhouse

This remarkable person united the seemingly inconsistent qualities of courage and cruelty, a disinterested and devoted loyalty to his prince, with a disregard of the rights of his fellow-subjects. He was the unscrupulous agent of the Scottish Privy Council in executing the merciless severities of the government in Scotland during the reigns of Charles II and James II; but he redeemed his character by the zeal with which he asserted the cause of the latter monarch after the Revolution, the military skill with which he supported it at the battle of Killiecrankie, and by his own death in the arms of victory.

It is said by tradition, that he was very desirous to see, and be introduced to, a certain Lady Elphinstoun, who had reached the advanced age of one hundred years and upwards. The noble matron, being a stanch whig, was rather unwilling to receive Claver'se, (as he was called from his title,) but at length consented. After the usual compliments, the officer observed to the lady, that having lived so much beyond the usual term of humanity, she must in her time have seen many strange changes. 'Hout na, sir,' said Lady Elphinstoun, 'the world is just to end with me as it began. When I was entering life, there was ane Knox deaving us a' wi' his *clavers*, and now I am ganging out, there is ane Claver'se deaving us a' wi' his *knocks*.'

Clavers signifying in common parlance, idle chat, that double pun does credit to the ingenuity of a lady of a hundred years old.

CHAPTER 12

1. (p. 174) *Prior*: from 'Down-Hall' by Matthew Prior (1664–1721).

2. (p. 177) *resetted*: (Scott's note): i.e. received or harboured.

3. (p. 181) *a large body of whigs ... covenanted work of reformation*: in the chronology of the novel, we have reached 8 May 1679. But the action reported by Evandale here corresponds to the 'Ruther-glen Declaration' of the 29 May, when Robert Hamilton and some four-score conventiclers of the anti-indulgence party rode into this small royal burgh near Glasgow, fixed a declaration to the market cross and burnt various acts, though not, according to Wodrow (2:44–5) 'that for observing the martyrdom of Charles I'. What they

did burn was an Act making 29 May itself a day of rejoicing and thanksgiving for Charles II's birth and restoration. The Act of Supremacy, which they also burnt, had been passed by the Scottish Parliament in November 1669 and accorded the King supreme authority over all persons and in all causes ecclesiastical.

4. (p. 181) *war horse of scripture*: see Job 39 : 19–25 for the famous horse who 'saith among the trumpets, Ha ha; and he smelleth the battle afar off, the thunder of the captains, and the shouting.'

5. (p. 182) *same Prayer-book ... the curate himself*: the reader would be misled by Scott if he thought that this and other passages showed the established Episcopalian Church in Scotland after 1662 to be identical with the English Church in its worship. Although the Prayer Book was 'used by individual ministers in public worship and by many clergy and laity in their private devotions, there was no compulsory liturgy, but the reading of the scriptures in church, the doxology, the Lord's Prayer and the Apostles' Creed were reintroduced.' (Donaldson 364). The church attended by Edith and Morton is therefore exceptional. Scott is at his usual work of sharpening contrasts.

CHAPTER 13

1. (p. 186) *Othello*: Scott misquotes Iago in III, iii.

2. (p. 187) *Uncle Toby*: the lovably eccentric old soldier in Laurence Sterne's great novel *Tristram Shandy* (1759–67).

3. (p. 187) *her mother's castle*: a slip for 'her grandmother's castle'.

4. (p. 189) *Mrs Quickly ... her young lady*: see *Merry Wives of Windsor*, III, iv, where three suitors are in fact named.

5. (p. 192) *Mr Justice Overdo*: in Ben Jonson's play *Bartholomew Fair*, IV, i (1614).

CHAPTER 14

1. (p. 197) *Old Ballad*: 'Jamie Telfer of the Fair Dodhead', which Scott had printed in his *Minstrelsy* (Child 190). However, Scott himself had interpolated this particular stanza.

2. (p. 198) *couple up ... old woman*: according to Wodrow (2 : 46), Claverhouse, marching towards Drumclog did take his prisoners with him 'bound two and two of them together'. It is hard to understand exactly what Scott means us to see; it emerges in the next chapter that the two old people have separate horses.

3. (p. 200) *Roman Gilead*: Ramoth-Gilead. See I Kings 22. King

Ahab died at this place fighting the Syrians. Cf. Walker (1 : 186) where the preacher John Semple in 1648 tells the army of Engagers marching towards Preston and defeat – 'Go ye up to Ramoth Gilead and prosper; but, if ye prosper in the way that ye are going, God never spake by me . . .'

4. (p. 204) *Apostle Paul himself* : see Acts 22, where Paul, by asserting his rights as a free-born Roman citizen, avoids a scourging.

5. (p. 204) *tribute to Caesar* : see Matthew 22 : 17–21.

6. (p. 205) *Jock the Giantkiller . . . Valentine and Orson* : Jack the Giantkiller is the familiar folk-tale hero. Valentine and Orson are the subject of an early French romance. The story, dealing with two brothers, appeared in English first about 1550. Scott owned a chapbook version of it (Melville Clark 59) and knew the ballad presenting it in Percy's *Reliques*.

7. (p. 205) *breaking of seals . . . vials* : Kettledrummle invokes the apocalypse as described in Revelation 5–11, 15 and 16.

8. (p. 206) *Judas . . . Holofernes . . . Diotrephes . . . Demas* : Holofernes was Nebuchadnezzar's general, the villain slain by Judith in the apocryphal book. Diotrephes, more obscurely, is a man mentioned in 3 John 9 who 'loveth to have the pre-eminence.' Demas is the fellow-disciple of Paul's whose desertion he reports in 2 Timothy 4 : 10 – 'For Demas hath forsaken me, having loved this present world.' As Scott must have known, in Howie's *Judgements* (38) Sharpe, all alone, is accused of 'the ambition of Diotrephes, the covetousness of Demas, the treachery of Judas, the apostacy of Julian, and the cruelty of Nero.'

9. (p. 207) *pelican . . . sparrow on the housetops* : Psalms 102:6–7.

10. (p. 207) *earthly potsherd* : cf. Isaiah 45 : 9.

CHAPTER 15

1. (p. 208) slightly misquoted from *Hudibras* Part I, canto i, 721–6, (1662) the famous satirical mock-epic by Samuel Butler (1613–80).

2. (p. 210) *Through . . . luppen over a wall* : cf. Psalms 18 : 29 – 'By my God have I leaped over a wall.'

3. (p. 210) *Sunk in deep mire . . . overflow me* : cf. Psalms 69 : 2. M'Crie took furious exception to these ejaculations by Mause and Kettledrummle (368–9) and now David Craig (183–4) finds them 'grossly implausible'. Craig suggests that Scott is perhaps thinking of the dying words of the English puritan, Major-General Harrison – 'By God I have leapt over a wall, by God I have run thro' a troop, and by God I will go through this death, and He will make it easy to

me.' Very likely, since Scott was interested enough in Harrison to make him an important character in *Woodstock*. But when Craig goes on to argue that 'this fine formal utterance is merely out of keeping when put into the farm woman's mouth, at such a juncture; it is ludicrous in the wrong way', he seems to be off the mark. The phrases are Biblical. One of M'Crie's objections is, indeed, that Kettledrummle's words come from a passage often quoted in the New Testament with reference to Jesus. It seems to me that Mause is in an understandable state of excitement and religious exaltation in which this quotation from the Bible comes aptly to her lips, and that this is both moving and pitiful. Kettledrummle is a professional, who mustn't allow himself to be beaten by an amateur, and his outburst is pompous and ludicrous. I find neither 'implausible'.

4. (p. 212) *females of the ancient German tribes*: as described in Tacitus's *Germania* (A.D. 98). See the Penguin Classic's translation, p. 107. And cf., the notes to p. 232 and the interesting description of landscape on p. 448.

5. (p. 214) *Hackston ... Paton ... Cleland*: Hackston, like Burley, was indeed with the rebels at Drumclog. So was William Cleland (*c*. 1661–89), who was a leader of the foot, though he had hardly yet had a chance to earn the reputation for military skill which he consolidated only by his death in gallant battle against vast odds with the new-formed Cameronian Regiment, successfully defending Dunkeld against the Jacobites in 1689. This very minor poet is, as I suggest in my general note, perhaps a prototype for Morton. Captain John Paton of Meadowhead is much more clearly a prototype for Burley. Scott knew his life from Howie. He had fought on the Continent and in the Civil Wars of the 1640s, then at Rullion Green in 1666. But he wasn't at Drumclog; he joined the rebels later, in time for Bothwell Bridge.

6. (p. 215) *race of Dunbar*: 'race' presumably because in 1650 the Scots, defeated by Cromwell, fled so fast. Allan fought in an army purged of non-Covenanting elements, alongside Morton's father. But Allan, like Morton's father, is fictitious.

7. (p. 216) *battle of Pentland Hills*: or 'Rullion Green', in November 1666; the end of the 'Pentland Rising'.

8. (p. 216) *my brother's son ... his uncle* (Scott's note):

Cornet Grahame

There was actually a young cornet of the Life-Guards named Grahame, and probably some relation of Claverhouse, slain in the skirmish of Drumclog. In the old ballad on the Battle of Bothwell Bridge, Claverhouse is said to have continued the slaughter of the fugitives in revenge of this gentleman's death.

> 'Haud up your hand', then Monmouth said;
> 'Gie quarters to these men for me';
> But bloody Claver'se swore an oath,
> His kinsman's death avenged should be.

The body of this young man was found shockingly mangled after the battle, his eyes pulled out, and his features so much defaced, that it was impossible to recognise him. The Tory writers say that this was done by the Whigs; because, finding the name Grahame wrought in the young gentleman's neckcloth, they took the corpse for that of Claver'se himself. The Whig authorities give a different account, from tradition, of the cause of Cornet Grahame's body being thus mangled. He had, say they, refused his own dog any food on the morning of the battle, affirming, with an oath, that he should have no breakfast but upon the flesh of the Whigs. The ravenous animal, it is said, flew at his master as soon as he fell, and lacerated his face and throat.

These two stories are presented to the reader, leaving it to him to judge whether it is most likely that a party of persecuted and insurgent fanatics should mangle a body supposed to be that of their chief enemy, in the same manner as several persons present at Drumclog had shortly before treated the person of Archbishop Sharpe; or that a domestic dog should, for want of a single breakfast, become so ferocious as to feed on his own master, selecting his body from scores that were lying around, equally accessible to his ravenous appetite.

[Scott ignores the likeliest explanation; that the whigs, who had no special reason to execrate Claverhouse in 1679, left the body alone and that it was trampled on by horses. The story about the dog is told by Russell (Kirkton 442); the story of the Whigs mangling the body is found in Creichton (31) and the *Memoirs of Dundee* (9–10). The latter source avers that the Cornet was a relation of Claverhouse. There was indeed a *Robert* Graham commissioned Cornet in Claverhouse's troop in September 1678, and this man seems to have fallen at Drumclog; but if he was a kinsman, the relationship was more remote than the novel suggests. Claverhouse's only brother David never married at all, while Claverhouse, in spite of his remark on p. 254 of this novel, was unmarried in 1679. See Terry (56–7).]

CHAPTER 16

1. (p. 217) *Hudibras*: from Samuel Butler's *Hudibras*, Part I, canto ii, 831–2; but misquoted.

2. (p. 218) *Charles Stewart ... fourteen false prelates ... creature-curates*: Charles had indeed signed both the Covenants in 1650, and later renounced them; but it is untrue of Burley to say that his 'first step' at the Restoration was to introduce the Act of Supremacy (see note to p. 181), which was passed in 1669. The fourteen false prelates were those occupying the fourteen sees of Scotland since 1662.

3. (p. 218) *swords ... night*: cf. Song of Solomon 3 : 8.

4. (p. 219) *truce or pardon*: Scott directed readers at this point to his note on Cornet Grahame printed on p. 549 above.

5. (p. 220) *Dagon ... adherents*: Dagon, with the face and hands of a man and the tail of a fish, was the national god of the Philistines, as the Bible makes plain.

6. (p. 222) *The sword ... Gideon*: see Judges 7 : 18.

7. (p. 226) *Auld Enemy himself* (Scott's note):

Proof against Shot given by Satan

The belief of the Covenanters that their principal enemies, and Claverhouse in particular, had obtained from the Devil a charm which rendered them proof against leaden bullets, led them to pervert even the circumstances of his death. Howie of Lochgoin, after giving some account of the battle of Killiecrankie, adds:

'The battle was very bloody, and by Mackay's third fire, Claverhouse fell, of whom historians give little account; but it has been said for certain, that his own waiting-servant, taking a resolution to rid the world of this truculent bloody monster, and knowing he had proof of lead, shot him with a silver button he had before taken off his own coat for that purpose. However, he fell, and with him Popery, and King James's interest in Scotland.' – *God's Judgment on Persecutors*, p. xxxix.

Original note. – 'Perhaps some may think this anent proof of a shot a paradox, and be ready to object here, as formerly, concerning Bishop Sharpe and Dalziel – "How can the Devil have or give a power to save life?"&c. Without entering upon the thing in its reality, I shall only observe, 1st, That it is neither in his power, or of his nature, to be a saviour of men's lives; he is called Apollyon the destroyer. 2d, That even in this case he is said only to give enchantment against one kind of metal, and this does not save life: for the lead would not take Sharpe or Claverhouse's lives, yet steel and silver would do it; and for Dalziel, though he died not on the field, he did not escape the arrows of the Almighty.' – *Ibidem*.

[Scott cites the Leith (1816) edition of Howie here; it is p. 52 in the 1797 edition.]

8. (p. 228) *loss of blood* (Scott's note):

Claverhouse's Charger

It appears, from the letter of Claverhouse afterwards quoted, that the horse on which he rode at Drumclog was not black, but sorrel. The author has been misled as to the colour by the many extraordinary traditions current in Scotland concerning Claverhouse's famous black charger, which was generally believed to have been a gift to its rider from the Author of Evil, who is said to have performed the Cæsarean operation upon its dam. This horse was so fleet, and its rider so expert, that they are said to have outstripped and *coted*, or turned, a hare upon the Bran-Law, near the head of Moffat Water, where the descent is so precipitous, that no merely earthly horse could keep its feet, or merely mortal rider could keep the saddle.

There is a curious passage in the testimony of John Dick, one of the suffering Presbyterians, in which the author, by describing each of the persecutors by their predominant qualities or passions, shows how little their best-loved attributes would avail them in the great day of judgment. When he introduces Claverhouse, it is to reproach him with his passion for horses in general, and for that steed in particular, which was killed at Drumclog, in the manner described in the text:

'As for that bloodthirsty wretch, Claverhouse, how thinks he to shelter himself that day? Is it possible the pitiful thing can be so mad as to think to secure himself by the fleetness of his horse, (a creature he has so much respect for, that he regarded more the loss of his horse at Drumclog, than all the men that fell there, and sure there fell prettier men on either side than himself?) No, sure – could he fall upon a chemist that could extract the spirit out of all the horses in the world, and infuse them into his one, though he were on that horse never so well mounted, he need not dream of escaping.' – *The Testimony to the Doctrine, Worship, Discipline, and Government of the Church of Scotland, &c. as it was left in write by that truly pious and eminently faithful, and now glorified Martyr, Mr John Dick. To which is added, his last Speech and Behaviour on the Scaffold, on 5th March*, 1684, *which day he sealed this testimony.* 57 pp. 4to. No year or place of publication.

The reader may perhaps receive some farther information on the subject of Cornet Grahame's death and the flight of Claverhouse, from the following Latin lines, a part of a poem entitled, *Bellum Bothuellianum*, by Andrew Guild, which exists in manuscript in the Advocates' Library:

> Mons est occiduus, surgit qui celsus in oris,
> (Nomine Loudunum) fossis puteisque profundis
> Quot scatet hic tellus, et aprico gramine tectus:
> Huc collecta (ait), numeroso milite cincta,
> Turba ferox, matres, pueri, innuptæque puellæ,
> Quam parat egregia Græmus dispersere turma.
> Venit et primo campo discedere cogit;
> Post hos et alios, cœno provolvit inerti;
> At numerosa cohors, campum dispersa per omnem,
> Circumfusa, ruit; turmasque, indagine captas,
> Aggreditur; virtus non hic, nec profuit ensis;
> Corripuere fugam, viridi sed gramine tectis,
> Precipitata perit, fossis, pars ultima, quorum
> Cornipedes hæsere luto, sessore rejecto:
> Tum rabiosa cohors, misereri nescia, stratos
> Invadit laceratque viros: hic signifer, eheu!
> Trajectus globulo, Græmus, quo fortior alter,
> Inter Scotigenas fuerat, nec justior ullus:
> Hunc manibus rapuere feris, faciemque virilem
> Fœdarunt, lingua, auriculis, manibusque resectis,
> Aspera diffuso spargentes saxa cerebro:
> Vix dux ipse fuga salvo, namque exta trahebat
> Vulnere tardatus sonipes generosus hiante:
> Insequitur clamore cohors fanatica, namque
> Crudelis semper timidus, si vicerit unquam.
>
> *M S. Bellum Bothuellianum*

[Guild's MS, of about a dozen pages, is held by the National Library of Scotland, and seems to be contemporary with the events which it describes. There is little point in giving a complete translation of this passage; in any case, the transcription which Scott uses is not always accurate. Guild is, in effect, a propagandist for the cavalier side, presenting the difficulty of the ground and the fact that the troopers are outnumbered as excuses for their defeat. He has Cornet Grahame, the bravest and justest of the Scots, shot, then seized by the Covenanters who cut out his tongue, cut off his ears and his hands, and scatter his brains over the rocks. Claverhouse barely escapes, with his horse dragging its entrails from a gaping wound.

I am grateful to Mr Francis Cairns for helping me over my lack of Latin. He points out that the style of the poet, as one would expect in his period, is highly derivative from ancient authors.]

CHAPTER 17

1. (p. 228) *Campbell*: from 'Lochiel's Warning' by Thomas Campbell (1777–1844), printed in *Gertrude of Wyoming ... and Other Poems* (1809).

2. (p. 229) *Elihu ... New Bottles*: see Job 32 : 19.

3. (p. 229) *Nazarite ... potsherd*: cf., Lamentations 4 : 7–8 and Psalms 22 : 15.

4. (p. 229) *Boanerges*: see Mark 3 : 17.

5. (p. 229) *wrestlings ... wrestle*: cf., Genesis 30 : 8.

6. (p. 229) *I will ... defence*: as Anderson points out, Sir James Turner (184–5) reports, at the Battle of Rullion Green, 1666, Mr Welch and Mr Gabriel Sempill, two preachers, going to take up a safe vantage point which the captured Turner and his guards had just quit, 'behind the little riseing of a ground'. He comments, 'I thought both of them had provided indifferentlie well for their oune safetie.'

7. (p. 231) *fowls of heaven ... beasts of the field*: cf. Psalms 79 : 2.

8. (p. 231) *pillar o' cloud ... Egypt*: see Exodus 13 : 21–2.

9. (p. 231) *Deborah ... prancing*: see Judges 4 and 5.

10. (p. 232) *bacchante ... Thessalian witch*: the bacchantes of the classical world were priestesses of Bacchus who, as in Euripides' great play, were noted for wild, orgiastic behaviour. Thessaly, anciently a part of Greece, was notorious for the superstition of its people and for their addiction to the study of magic. These are two out of several references whereby Scott seeks to give the Covenanters on the moor the character of a wild tribe, and to associate their behaviour strongly with pre-Christian religions. cf. note 9 above and note 4 to Chapter 15.

11. (p. 232) *Tarry, tarry ... the afternoon preaching*: Scott in the *Minstrelsy* (2 : 218) attributes remarks like these to the preacher, King whom Claverhouse had captured and brought with him, and who 'hollowed to the flying commander, "to halt, and to take his prisoner with him"; or, as others say, "to stay, and take the afternoon's preaching".' cf. Creichton (32).

12. (p. 232) *Rabshakeh ... Shimei ... Doeg*: baddies from the Old Testament. See 2 Kings 18, 2 Samuel 16 and 1 Samuel 21 and 22.

13. (p. 233) *indweller ... Ham ... Amalek ... suckling*: a speech

which shows how soaked in the Bible Scott's memory must have been. It combines references to Psalms 78:51; Zechariah 3:2; Judges 15:8; Psalms 50:1 and 1 Samuel 15:3. But the phrase *booted apostle* comes from Howie's *Judgements* (43) where Thomas Kennoway, the trooper who recaptured the preacher King after Bothwell Bridge, is denounced as a 'booted apostle for the propagation of episcopacy'.

14. (p. 234) *Tophet*: a place mentioned in the Old Testament where human sacrifices were offered. See Isaiah 30:33 and Jeremiah 7:31–2.

15. (p. 234) *Amalekites . . . Shur*: see 1 Samuel 15:7.

16. (p. 235) *Mount of Jehovah-Nissi . . . Aaron and Hur*: see Exodus 17.

17. (p. 236) *Middle Ward* (Scott's note):

Skirmish at Drumclog

This affair, the only one in which Claverhouse was defeated, or the insurgent Cameronians successful, was fought pretty much in the manner mentioned in the text. The Royalists lost about thirty or forty men. The commander of the Presbyterian, or rather Covenanting party, was Mr Robert Hamilton, of the honourable House of Preston, brother of Sir William Hamilton, to whose title and estate he afterwards succeeded; but, according to his biographer, Howie of Lochgoin, he never took possession of either, as he could not do so without acknowledging the right of King William (an uncovenanted monarch) to the crown. Hamilton had been bred by Bishop Burnet, while the latter lived at Glasgow; his brother, Sir Thomas, having married a sister of that historian. 'He was then,' says the Bishop, 'a lively, hopeful young man; but getting into that company, and into their notions, he became a crack-brained enthusiast.'

Several well-meaning persons have been much scandalized at the manner in which the victors are said to have conducted themselves towards the prisoners at Drumclog. But the principle of these poor fanatics, (I mean the high-flying, or Cameronian party,) was to obtain not merely toleration for their church, but the same supremacy which Presbytery had acquired in Scotland after the treaty of Rippon, betwixt Charles I and his Scottish subjects, in 1640.

The fact is, that they conceived themselves a chosen people, sent forth to extirpate the heathen, like the Jews of old, and under a similar charge to show no quarter.

The historian of the Insurrection of Bothwell makes the following explicit avowal of the principles on which their General acted:—

'Mr Hamilton discovered a great deal of bravery and valour, both in the conflict with, and pursuit of, the enemy; but when he and some other were pursuing the enemy, others flew too greedily upon the spoil, small as it was, instead of pursuing the victory; and some, without Mr Hamilton's knowledge, and directly contrary to his express command, gave five of those bloody enemies quarter, and then let them go; this greatly grieved Mr Hamilton when he saw some of Babel's brats spared, after that the Lord had delivered them into their hands, that they might dash them against the stones. Psalm cxxxvii, 9. In his own account of this, he reckons the sparing of these enemies, and letting them go, to be among their first steppings aside, for which he feared that the Lord would not honour them to do much more for him; and says, that he was neither for taking favours from, nor giving favours to, the Lord's enemies.' See *A true and impartial Account of the persecuted Presbyterians in Scotland, their being in arms, and defeat at Bothwell Brigg, in* 1679, *by William Wilson, late Schoolmaster in the parish of Douglas.* The reader who would authenticate the quotation, must not consult any other edition than that of 1697; for somehow or other the publisher of the last edition has omitted this remarkable part of the narrative.

Sir Robert Hamilton himself felt neither remorse nor shame for having put to death one of the prisoners after the battle with his own hand, which appears to have been a charge against him, by some whose fanaticism was less exalted than his own.

'As for that accusation they bring against me of killing that poor man (as they call him) at Drumclog, I may easily guess that my accusers can be no other but some of the house of Saul or Shimei, or some such risen again to espouse that poor gentleman (Saul) his quarrel against honest Samuel, for his offering to kill that poor man Agag, after the king's giving him quarter. But I, being to command that day, gave out the word that no quarter should be given; and returning from pursuing Claverhouse, one or two of these fellows were standing in the midst of a company of our friends, and some were debating for quarter, others against it. None could blame me to decide the controversy, and I bless the Lord for it to this day. There were five more that without my knowledge got quarter, who were brought to me after we were a mile from the place as having got quarter, which I reckoned among the first steppings aside; and seeing that spirit amongst us at that time, I then told it to some that were with me, (to my best remembrance, it was honest old John Nisbet,) that I feared the Lord would not honour us to do much more for him. I shall only say this, – I desire to bless his holy name, that since ever he helped me to set my face to his work, I never had, nor would take, a favour from enemies, either on right or left hand, and desired to give as few.'

The preceding passage is extracted from a long vindication of his own conduct, sent by Sir Robert Hamilton, 7th December, 1685, addressed to the anti-Popish, anti-Prelatic, anti-Erastian, anti-sectarian true Presbyterian remnant of the Church of Scotland; and the substance is to be found in the work or collection, called, 'Faithful Contendings Displayed, collected and transcribed by John Howie'.

As the skirmish of Drumclog has been of late the subject of some enquiry, the reader may be curious to see Claverhouse's own account of the affair, in a letter to the Earl of Linlithgow, written immediately after the action. This gazette, as it may be called, occurs in the volume called Dundee's Letters, printed by Mr Smythe of Methven, as a contribution to the Bannatyne Club. The original is in the library of the Duke of Buckingham. Claverhouse, it may be observed, spells like a chambermaid.

'FOR THE EARLE OF LINLITHGOW
[Commander-in-Chief of King Charles II's forces in Scotland]

Glaskow, Jun. the 1, 1679

'MY LORD, — Upon Saturday's night, when my Lord Rosse came into this place, I marched out, and because of the insolency that had been done tue nights before at Ruglen, I went thither and inquyred for the names. So soon as I got them, I sent our partys to sease on them, and found not only three of those rogues, but also ane intercomend minister called King. We had them at Strevan about six in the morning yesterday, and resolving to convey them to this, I thought that we might make a little tour to see if we could fall upon a conventicle; which we did, little to our advantage; for when we came in sight of them, we found them drawn up in batell, upon a most adventageous ground, to which there was no coming but through mosses and lakes. They wer not preaching, and had got away all there women and shildring. They consisted of four battaillons of foot, and all well armed with fusils and pitchforks, and three squadrons of horse. We sent both partys to skirmish, they of foot and we of dragoons; they run for it, and sent down a battaillon of foot against them; we sent threescore of dragoons, who made them run again shamfully; but in end they percaiving that we had the better of them in skirmish, they resolved a generall engadgment, and

imediatly advanced with there foot, the horse folowing; they came
throght the lotche; the greatest body of all made up against my
troupe; we keeped our fyre till they wer within ten pace of us: they
recaived our fyr, and advanced to shok; the first they gave us
broght down the Coronet Mr Crafford and Captain Bleith, besides
that with a pitchfork they made such an openeing in my rone horse's
belly, that his guts hung out half an elle, and yet he caryed me af an
myl; which so discoraged our men, that they sustained not the shok,
but fell into disorder. There horse took the occasion of this, and
purseued us so hotly that we had no tym to rayly. I saved the
standarts, but lost on the place about aight or ten men, besides
wounded; but the dragoons lost many mor. They ar not com esily
af on the other side, for I sawe severall of them fall befor we cam to
the shok. I mad the best retraite the confusion of our people would
suffer, and I am now laying with my Lord Rosse. The toun of
Streven drew up as we was making our retrait, and thoght of a pass
to cut us off, but we took courage and fell to them, made them run,
leaving a dousain on the place. What these rogues will dou yet I
know not, but the contry was flocking to them from all hands. This
may be counted the begining of the rebellion, in my opinion.

'I am, my lord,

'Your lordship's most humble servant,

'J. GRAHAME

'My lord, I am so wearied, and so sleapy, that I have wryton this
very confusedly.'

[Scott's assurance that the battle was fought 'pretty much in the
manner mentioned in the text' seems to have satisfied the great
G. M. Young (92–3) who says, praising Scott's sense of place, that
'in his narrative of Drumclog . . . Scott set an example and a standard
which some of his successors, professed historians, may have reached,
but none, I think, has ever surpassed'.

It depends what you want from a historian. Scott makes the battle
take place on 8 May instead of 1 June. He gives Claverhouse about
250 horse; Terry (52–9) says he certainly had less than 150. The
account given in Claverhouse's letter accords on main details with
that given by Russell (Kirkton 441–3). Neither, of course, describes
Cornet Grahame's death, or Bothwell's flanking movement, or the
single combat between Bothwell and Burley, because these episodes
are wholly imaginary and are designed to raise a trivial little
skirmish which Claverhouse should never have been fool enough to

fight into an epic occasion on which Claverhouse's dignity is awesomely enhanced. Aiton (92–4) also accuses Scott (with what seems to the tourist's eye like justice) of making the area around Drumclog seem much wilder than it actually was, though in fairness to Scott it should be said that his sources aren't very specific on local details.

C'est magnifique, but it's hardly *scholarly* 'history', even if one accepts the disappearance of Hamilton, Hackston, Russell, Cleland, etc. etc. from the cast. I would suggest that it is instead the most remarkable instance which anyone is likely to find of the epic mode transported with success into 'English' prose fiction.]

CHAPTER 18

1. (p. 236) *Hudibras*: Part I, canto I, 11–12; from Samuel Butler's mock-epic.

2. (p. 238) *Fifteen heads ... deliverance*: M'Crie took exception to Scott's account of Kettledrummle's preaching, but if one allows for Scott's genteel descriptive jargon, it seems fair enough. See Howie's *Collection of Very Valuable Sermons*, appended to *Faithful Contendings*.

3. (p. 238) *nursing father ... bastards*: Anderson points out that Kettledrummle is mocking the term 'nursing father' very commonly used by ecclesiastical right-wingers in the seventeenth century to denote the king's relationship to the church.

4. (p. 239) *Tophet ... kindle it*: Isaiah 30:33.

5. (p. 240) *Hagar ... Judah ... Rachel ... Comfort*: for Hagar see Genesis 21 and for Rachel see Jeremiah 31:15 and Matthew 2:18. Judah under her palm tree is perhaps an imaginative touch of Macbriar's own. (But Dr Anderson points out to me that *Deborah*, the prophetess [Judges 4:5] dwelt under a palm tree.)

6. (p. 240) *Your swords are filled ... consumed them*: combines references to, or echoes of, Isaiah 34:6–7 and 63:1–4 and Jeremiah 6:23 and 50:42 as well as others which might no doubt be traced. If 'Jacob' is taken as a synonym for 'Israel', Exodus 14 is loosely evoked.

7. (p. 241) *passages of the destroyers ... turned to flight*: cf. Jeremiah 51:32, where the 'rods' are 'reeds'.

8. (p. 241) *Maccabeus ... Samson ... Gideon ... gates of hell ... against them*: the final reference is to Matthew 16:18. Judas Maccabeus, in the Apocrypha, leads the Jews in revolt against their Graeco-Syrian oppressors. Samson is the strong man who fights the

Philistines in Judges 13–16, while Gideon, in Judges 6–8, leads Israel against the Midianites.

9. (p. 241) *curse of Meroz . . . mighty*: see Judges 5 : 23.

10. (p. 242) *Sisera*: yet another reference to Judges 5.

11. (p. 242) *Then whoso will deserve immortal fame in this world, and eternal happiness in that which is to come . . .*: M'Crie (365) points out, quite rightly, that this is not in accordance with Covenanting doctrine, which stresses the impossibility of man *deserving* anything. But Macbriar, brought up in the Church of England (see p. 373) is, surely, a well-drawn example of the strained extremism of the convert, and his slip here helps to deepen Scott's portrayal.

12. (p. 242) *stand up strongly . . . men*: cf. I Corinthians 16 : 13.

CHAPTER 19

1. (p. 243) *Henry IV Part II*: Silence, in V, iii.

2. (p. 246) *Kilsythe . . . Tippermuir . . . Alford . . . Innerlochy . . . Auld Earn . . . Brig o' Dee*: also *Philiphaugh* and *Dundee* a little later. All these names refer to battles in Montrose's campaigns of 1644–5, which is clear enough. What is not so clear to the general reader is that Major Bellenden is, on this showing, as die-hard as Balfour. He stuck with Montrose until he defeated Argyll at Inverlochy in February 1645. At this point, according to Scott's own account in *Tales,* 'of all his Lowland adherents, the old Earl of Airlie and his sons alone remained' and Montrose was otherwise left with Highlanders and Irish, in the bitter winter, and with little hope of success.

CHAPTER 20

1. (p. 252) *Hardyknute*: a ballad (Scott's favourite in extreme youth) 'first published in 1719, presumably written by Lady Elizabeth Wardlaw, and reprinted in several eighteenth-century collections.' (Welsh).

CHAPTER 21

1. (p. 258) *The Alchemist*: Ben Jonson's play (1610). Scott quotes from III, i, omitting no fewer than twenty-nine lines between Ananias's speech and Tribulation's reply.

2. (p. 259) *Laodicean . . . Gallio*: for the accusation of lukewarmness against the early church at Laodicea see Revelation 3 : 14–16 – 'because thou art lukewarm, and neither cold nor hot, I will spue

thee out of my mouth.' The reference to Gallio is one Scott would have found in Patrick Walker (1:175) and elsewhere. He must be aware of its irony. The Covenanters oddly chose to deprecate, implicitly, the indifference to 'words and names' shown by the Roman proconsul in Achaia, Gallio (see Acts 18) even though this saved the Apostle Paul. When the Jews brought Paul to judgement, Gallio who 'cared for none of these things' drove them away.

3. (p. 260) *if a fox ... breach it*: cf. Nehemiah 4:3.

4. (p. 260) *sons of Zeruiah ... strong for us*: cf. 2 Samuel 3:39. Scott makes Burley use here a text applied by Sir Henry Vane, the English Independent, (according to Scott's own account in *Tales*) when he told his own party to temporize their opposition to Presbytery since the English parliament needed the help of the Scots.

5. (p. 261) *the healing resolution ... present oppressors*: Scott here attributes to the 'Cameronian' Burley support, or pretended support, for a declaration actually pressed for and made by the 'moderates' or 'Erastians' led by the preacher Welch.

6. (p. 265) *Judas ... fifty thousand merks a year*: Burley exaggerates Sharpe's salary, if Scott is right in saying in QR that it was £1,000.

7. (p. 266) *Cumming ... Bruce*: 'Red Comyn', John Comyn, was sacrilegiously murdered by Robert Bruce in a church in 1306. Bruce hurried to Scone and had himself crowned King of Scotland, and thereafter led his successful fight to wrest Scotland from the control of the English crown.

CHAPTER 22

1. (p. 267) *Troilus and Cressida*: from Ulysses' famous speech in I, iii.

2. (p. 268) *such divines ... indulgence*: a major departure from fact. As Rait says (23), there is no evidence that any Indulged minister joined the rising.

3. (p. 270) *Tower of Tillietudlem ... to be seized upon*: no long siege of the kind described in the novel took place in the rising of 1679 (or, indeed, in that of 1666), though Wodrow indicates (2:267) that some Covenanters took Hawick Castle before going on to Bothwell Bridge.

4. (p. 271) *Hook in our noses ... jaws*: cf. 2 Kings 19:28 and Isaiah 37:29.

5. (p. 272) *the earth quakes ... dry stubble*: 'The speech contains some distant echoes of Nahum 1:5–10.' (Welsh).

6. (p. 273) *dogs may fatten ... portion of their fathers*: see 2 Kings 9:10 and 9:30–7.

7. (p. 273) *We judge ... by the fruit*: cf. Matthew 7:15–20.

8. (p. 273) *whose name is changed to Magor-Missabib ... around me*: see Jeremiah 20:3–4. It is no doubt a sign of Mucklewrath's madness that he equates himself with one Pashur, an enemy of God's prophet Jeremiah. Howie, *Judgements* (iv) more aptly applies the text when he admits that his pages haven't captured *all* the wicked persecutors so as to make them 'a Magor Missabib, a wonder unto themselves and others'.

9. (p. 273) *Tower of the Bass ... wild sea*: see a work by various hands, including Thomas M'Crie Jnr, *The Bass Rock* (Edinburgh 1848). The Bass is an islet a mile in circumference and rising 420 feet above sea level, a great haunt of gannets, set in the Firth of Forth about 1¼ miles from the coast of East Lothian. *The Bass Rock* names thirty-nine 'martyrs' who were imprisoned on this unattractive spot between 1671 and 1687, including the prophetic Peden, a prototype for one feature of Mucklewrath. See Walker 1:49–50.

10. (p. 274) *Slay, slay ... slain*: cf. Ezekiel 9:5–7.

11. (p. 274) *Anabaptists of Munster*: for a full account of the practices of the Anabaptists who took over the north-west German town of Munster in 1534–5 and established a communist theocracy under a 'king', John of Leyden, who took a harem of fifteen wives, see chapter 12 of Norman Cohn's *The Pursuit of the Millennium* (Paladin, 1970). *Jus Populi Vindicatum* (2) indignantly rejects the comparison drawn by an episcopalian apologist between the Pentland risers of 1666 and what *JPV* itself calls 'the irrational, furious, and brutish rabble of Anabaptists who followed Knipperdoling and John of Leyden.'

12. (p. 275) *Midianites ... hands*: see Judges 7:7.

13. (p. 275) *scorpions ... sword ... Covenant*: see 1 Kings 12:11, 14 and, for the direct quotation, Leviticus 26:25.

14. (p. 275) *James Melvin ... Cardinal Beaton*: David Beaton, Cardinal Archbishop of St Andrews (1494–1546), a great politician and persecutor of reformers, was murdered by a party led by John Leslie, in revenge for the burning of the reformer Wishart. James *Melville* actually despatched Beaton, invoking Wishart's death as he did so. See John Knox's *History of the Reformation in Scotland* (ed. W. C. Dickinson, Nelson, 1949) vol. I, pp. 77–8.

CHAPTER 23

1. (p. 277) *Henry IV, Part I*: spoken by Hal in II, ii.

2. (p. 278) *Straven*: the village of Strathaven, near Drumclog, commonly so abbreviated.

3. (p. 278) *Take turn about ... Tam o' the Linn*: Tam o' the Linn, hero of many such humorous verses, is a distant descendant of Tam Lin or Tamlane the elfin knight in the great ballad. (Child 39).

4. (p. 281) *Thus far ... and no farther*: see Job 38 : 11.

5. (p. 282) *Vanity Fair*: Burley somehow keeps well up with the latest books. The English field-preacher John Bunyan (1628–88) published *Pilgrim's Progress*, with its memorable Vanity Fair, in 1678. It wasn't published in Scotland until 1681, going into a second edition there in 1684. (Hewison 547).

6. (p. 282) *committee of the council ... limited to six*: Scott is no doubt prompted to this device by a small committee referred to by Hamilton in *Faithful Contendings* (194). On the day before the battle of Bothwell Bridge, with the row raging between moderates and extremists, the moderates suggested 'that two gentlemen, and a minister of each party, should confer a little in the business' of submitting a supplication to Monmouth. 'Mr Andrew Morton' was the minister on the moderate side. It will be seen that Scott reverses the pattern, so as to make the ministers dominant, as they were in the army which lost at Dunbar in 1650, and to play down the fact that a good number of gentlemen were on the rebels' side at Bothwell Bridge, so that Morton wouldn't have been as isolated as he is made to appear in the novel.

CHAPTER 24

1. (p. 283) *Finlay*: Scott improves by misquotation two lines from 'Dirge' printed in *Wallace ... and other Poems* by John Finlay, (Glasgow 1804).

CHAPTER 25

1. (p. 292) *Henry V*: III, i.

CHAPTER 26

1. (p. 305) *Henry IV, Part II*: actually from 1 *Henry IV*, IV, iv.

2. (p. 306) *Moabitish woman*: see Numbers 25 : 1 and Deuteronomy 23 : 3, etc.

3. (p. 307) *Falstaff ... men*: see 2 *Henry IV*, III, ii.

4. (p. 310) *Gallio*: see Acts 18, and the note to p. 259 above.

5. (p. 311) *his regulations effectual* (Scott's note):

These feuds, which tore to pieces the little army of insurgents, turned merely on the point whether the king's interest or royal authority was to be owned or not, and whether the party in arms were to be contented with a free exercise of their own religion, or insist upon the re-establishment of Presbytery in its supreme authority, and with full power to predominate over all other forms of worship. The few country gentlemen who joined the insurrection, with the most sensible part of the clergy, thought it best to limit their demands to what it might be possible to attain. But the party who urged these moderate views were termed by the more zealous bigots, the Erastian party, men, namely, who were willing to place the church under the influence of the civil government, and therefore they accounted them, 'a snare upon Mizpah, and a net spread upon Tabor.' See the Life of Sir Robert Hamilton in the Scottish Worthies, and his account of the Battle of Bothwell-bridge, *passim*.

6. (p. 312) *Duke of Monmouth*: it is worth knowing that this famous man was, after a fashion, a fellow-clansman of the author of the novel. The natural son of Charles II and of Lucy Walters, he was born in 1649 and given the title Duke of Monmouth in 1663. In the same year he acquired the surname 'Scott' and the title Duke of Buccleuch when he married Anne Scott, Countess of Buccleuch. Having early fallen out with James, Duke of York, he put his considerable weight behind the cause of Protestant dissent. After his father's death, he led a brief uprising in south-west England on behalf of his own claim to the crown. He was defeated at Sedgemoor and executed in July 1685. Scott makes it seem here as if Monmouth arrived in Scotland some time in May. In fact, he only reached Edinburgh on 18 June.

CHAPTER 27

1. (p. 313) *Old Ballad*: this is from 'The Battle of Bothwell Bridge' (Child 206) which Scott had printed in the *Minstrelsy*, though three words here are different from those in his own text.

2. (p. 313) *park ... at Hamilton*: Scott simplifies a complicated story here. In fact, between Drumclog (1 June) and Bothwell Bridge (22 June), the rebel army quartered itself for short periods on nine or

ten different places. According to Wilson's account, it would seem to have spent only eight nights at Hamilton.

3. (p. 317) *Haman*: see Esther 7:9–10.

4. (p. 318) *Mrs Wilson's report* (Scott's note):

The Cameronians had suffered persecution, but it was without learning mercy. We are informed by Captain Crichton, that they had set up in their camp a huge gibbet, or gallows, having many hooks upon it, with a coil of new ropes lying beside it, for the execution of such royalists as they might make prisoners. Guild, in his *Bellum Bothuellianum*, describes this machine particularly.

[See Creichton (38–9). Blackader (249) mentions a gallows which stood on the battlefield. Modern authorities suggest that it stood there before the rebels gathered on that spot. It is odd that Scott should accept so uncritically what seems to be, at best, an eager misunderstanding on the part of the Royalists; again, he is probably thinking of Philiphaugh, and associating the rebels of 1679 with the zealots of 1645 who had law on their side.]

5. (p. 318) *law ... sword of Joshua ... better dispensation ... persecute us*: in this exchange, Burley evokes the moment in the Old Testament where the Lord gives the city of Jericho into Joshua's hands and the children of Israel slaughter all its people 'both men and women, young and old ... with the edge of the sword.' See Joshua 6. Poundtext responds by citing the Sermon on the Mount; see Matthew 5:44.

6. (p. 321) *a memorial of the grievances of the moderate presbyterians*: besides the confusingly-named 'Hamilton Declaration', which claimed to speak for all the rebels, which was railroaded through by the moderates and published on 13 June 1679, and which is printed in Wodrow (2: appendix XXV), Scott knew of a paper declaring their principles drawn up by moderates in Edinburgh and conveyed to the West Country army, where Welch and his followers are said to have welcomed it. With its ravings about the Popish Plot, in which it claims that many members of the Scottish Privy Council are implicated, this gives one a most unfavourable impression of the real-life Poundtexts. (See Wodrow 2:59–61). However, the declaration entrusted here to Evandale plays in effect the same role as the supplication sent by the rebels to Monmouth. Wodrow prints (2:65–6) what he says may only be a draft. This *'Humbly sheweth*, that whereas we the Presbyterians of the Church and Kingdom of Scotland, being, by a long continued tract of violence and oppression upon us, in our lives, liberty, fortune and conscience, and without all hope of remedy, cut off from all access of petitioning, and that by an

act of Parliament, and discharged to pour out our just grievances and complaints; and our lives being made so bitter by cruel bondage, as death seemed more eligible than life, the causes whereof we have partly mentioned in our Declaration; and being, by an unavoidable necessity, driven unto the fields in arms, in our own innocent self-defence ...' And it goes on to ask Monmouth to give safe conduct to envoys who will 'lay open our heart in this matter' to him. It seems 'the free exercise of religion' was an additional demand with which the envoys were eventually entrusted, as were a 'free parliament' and a 'free general assembly' and an indemnification for all who were, or had been, in arms. Scott would be on absolutely solid historical ground if he hadn't made Morton call for a *Parliament* to settle the affairs of the *Church*.

CHAPTER 28

1. (p. 322) *Edom of Gordon*: the important ballad. (Child 178.)

2. (p. 325) *beating the drum ecclesiastic*: i.e. preaching. See the quotation from *Hudibras* which opens Chapter 18.

3. (p. 326) *these lines*: Evandale himself doesn't remember them too well; he misquotes quite severely the best known lines from 'To Althea, From Prison' by the gifted and important 'cavalier poet', Richard Lovelace (1618–56/7); a most appropriately idealistic author for Evandale to have thought of.

CHAPTER 29

1. (p. 331) *Marlow*: neither Professor Welsh nor I can find these lines in the works of Christopher Marlowe (1564–93), and their rhythm is not Marlovian. Perhaps Scott invented them.

2. (p. 338) *Dalzell ... valour*: Scott's portrait of Sir Thomas Dalzell (or Dalziel, or Dalyell) accords closely with his sources. He was born around 1599 and was already a veteran when he fought for Charles II at Worcester, in 1651, and then in the Highland Rising in favour of the King in 1654. He then became a general under Tsar Alexis of Muscovy. Returning at the King's request in 1665, he commanded at the defeat of the Pentland Rising and became notorious for his brutality in the mopping-up operations – Burnet says (1:238), 'He threatened to spit men, and to roast them.' Dalzell seems to have felt slighted when Monmouth was made commander in 1679. He refused to serve under him and (as Scott knew very well – see his *Quarterly Review*), wasn't at Bothwell Bridge. But he became Commander-in-

Chief of the royal forces in Scotland later in the same year, and held the position till his death in 1685.

Scott makes him present where he wasn't in order to have both the most notorious diabolical 'persecutors' on hand to overrule the clement Monmouth and to slaughter the rebels afterwards.

3. (p. 338) *royal army . . . field* (Scott's note):

Royal Army at Bothwell Bridge

A Cameronian muse was awakened from slumber on this doleful occasion, and gave the following account of the muster of the royal forces, in poetry nearly as melancholy as the subject:

> They marched east through Lithgow-town
>> For to enlarge their forces;
> And sent for all the north-country
>> To come, both foot and horses.
>
> Montrose did come and Athole both,
>> And with them many more;
> And all the Highland Amorites
>> That had been there before.
>
> The Lowdien Mallisha* they
>> Came with their coats of blew;
> Five hundred men from London came,
>> Claid in a reddish hue.
>
> When they were assembled one and all,
>> A full brigade were they;
> Like to a pack of hellish hounds,
>> Roreing after their prey.
>
> When they were all provided well,
>> In armour and amonition,
> Then thither wester did they come,
>> Most cruel of intention.

The royalists celebrated their victory in stanzas of equal merit. Specimens of both may be found in the curious collection of Fugitive Scottish Poetry, principally of the Seventeenth Century, printed for the Messrs Laing, Edinburgh.

*Lothian Militia.

4. (p. 339) *1640*: This should be 1643.

CHAPTER 30

1. (p. 340) *Venice Preserved*: IV, 263–4 of the play by Thomas Otway (1652–85).

2. (p. 341) *labourer ... hire*: see Luke, 10:7.

3. (p. 342) *painted sepulchre*: Matthew 23:27–8.

4. (p. 342) *Moabitish woman*: see I Kings 11:1–8 and Nehemiah 13:23–7, etc.

5. (p. 343) *honest*: Scott here makes the 'moderate' Poundtext use the term habitually applied in his sources by the 'extremist' party to themselves.

6. (p. 343) *general pacification* (Scott's note):

Moderate Presbyterians

The author does not, by any means, desire that Poundtext should be regarded as a just representation of the moderate presbyterians, among whom were many ministers whose courage was equal to their good sense and sound views of religion. Were he to write the tale anew, he would probably endeavour to give the character a higher turn. It is certain, however, that the Cameronians imputed to their opponents in opinion concerning the Indulgence, or others of their strained and fanatical notions, a disposition not only to seek their own safety, but to enjoy themselves. Hamilton speaks of three clergymen of this description as follows:

'They pretended great zeal against the Indulgence; but alas! that was all their practice, otherwise being but very gross, which I shall but hint at in short. When great Cameron and those with him were taking many a cold blast and storm in the fields and among the cot-houses in Scotland, these three had for the most part their residence in Glasgow, where they found good quarter and a full table, which I doubt not but some bestowed upon them from real affection to the Lord's cause; and when these three were together, their greatest work was who should make the finest and sharpest roundel, and breathe the quickest jests upon one another, and to tell what valiant acts they were to do, and who could laugh loudest and most heartily among them; and when at any time they came out to the country, whatever other things they had, they were careful each of them to have a great flask of brandy with them, which was very heavy to some, particularly to Mr Cameron, Mr Cargill, and Henry Hall – I shall name no more.' – *Faithful Contendings*, p. 198.

7. (p. 345) *day ... of general humiliation ... land*: this was *not* agreed. It was exactly what the 'extremists' could *not* get the 'moderates' to accept. Once again, Scott is introducing detail typical of the theocratic 1640s into his account of 1679. (See Wodrow 2:57).

8. (p. 349) *great High-Priest of all the Nine*: John Dryden. Scott goes on to quote famous lines from Dryden's satire, *Absalom and*

Achitophel (1681), in which Monmouth himself figures as 'Absalom'.

9. (p. 349) *General Thomas Dalzell* (Scott's note):

General Dalzell, usually called Tom Dalzell

In Crichton's Memoirs, edited by Swift, where a particular account of this remarkable person's dress and habits is given, he is said never to have worn boots. The following account of his rencounter with John Paton of Meadowhead, showed, that in action at least he wore pretty stout ones, unless the reader be inclined to believe in the truth of his having a charm, which made him proof against lead.

'Dalzell,' says Paton's biographer, 'advanced the whole left wing of his army on Colonel Wallace's right. Here Captain Paton behaved with great courage and gallantry. Dalzell, knowing him in the former wars, advanced upon him himself, thinking to take him prisoner. Upon his approach, each presented his pistol. On their first discharge, Captain Paton, perceiving his pistol ball to hop upon Dalzell's *boots*, and knowing what was the cause, (he having proof,) put his hand in his pocket for some small pieces of silver he had there for the purpose, and put one of them into his other pistol. But Dalzell, having his eye upon him in the meanwhile, retired behind his own man, who by that means was slain.'

['Paton's biographer' is John Howie, *Scots Worthies* (414–27).]

10. (p. 350) *the Duke ... advising him*: the plausible Burnet says (1:472) that Lauderdale had contrived that the King should give Monmouth orders not to treat with the rebels but 'fall on them immediately'. The less plausible Blackader says he has 'heard' that Monmouth had 'an ample commission to hear grievances, and redress them ... But the prelatick party and council, when he came, pushed him forward to fight and suppress them only by violence ...' (242–3). But Terry (74–5) can find no hard evidence for the suggestion that Monmouth's natural mildness was overridden by his instructions, or by his advisers. The preacher Hume and the Laird of Kaitloch (or alternatively 'Murdoch') came across to see him with the moderate supplication after skirmishing had started at Bothwell Bridge. Monmouth said he would treat with the Whigs only if they laid down their arms. According to Blackader's hearsay (245) Monmouth would have given a more favourable answer, but 'several Scots noblemen did so stir up and instigate the duke, that they dissuaded him from hearkening, or granting them any cessation, but presently to fall on with force, unless they should cast down their arms, and render themselves at mercy, within the space of half an hour, or an hour at most.'

11. (p. 352) *one hour only*: Blackader (above) says 'an hour at most'. Wodrow (2:66) says Monmouth sent the ambassadors back to their friends and told them to bring him word within 'half an hour at farthest' whether they would accept quarter on condition they laid down their arms; 'and *at the same time* he gave orders to his army to advance towards Bothwell Bridge'. Creichton (36) makes it seem as if Monmouth used the time spent on parley to beat the unsuspecting rebels to the draw, talking moderately to the envoys while bringing down his field-pieces; as soon as the negotiations ended, he says, a ferocious fire opened up. As the reader will see, Scott soars easily above the conflict and confusion of these sources by making Monmouth suspend movements of attack for one hour, a thing which none of them suggest he did, though an obscure passage in Russell (Kirkton 466) may be interpreted to mean that he gave them half an hour. However, Scott perhaps had another authority. Terry's account of the business (74–6), is probably as sound as can be got. Hume and Murdoch go back with Monmouth's reply that the rebels must lay down their arms. Hamilton retorts 'and hang next'. Monmouth meanwhile goes on to complete his arrangements for attack. The rebels beat a second parley. The officers sent to find out what they have decided, learn only that they want to know what terms of accommodation Monmouth has brought from England. Monmouth of course won't tell them. Hume and Murdoch withdraw again. Battle begins.

12. (p. 352) *That officer ... manner*: Scott was perhaps thinking of an odd passage in Wodrow (2:66) where Claverhouse 'having some Jealousy' of Hume and 'Kaitloch', who were in disguise, watched them 'upon their return, and having got some hint of them, saluted them by their names.' (This is pointed out by Terry, 75).

CHAPTER 31

1. (p. 354) *Burns*: from Robert Burns' 'The Holy Fair'.

2. (p. 354) *Bothwell Lines*: for a longer quotation from this curious doggerel poem, attributed to William Wilson, the author of a prose account of the Battle, see Scott's note to p. 338. The whole thing is printed in David Laing (ed.), *Various Pieces of Fugitive Scottish Poetry* (Edinburgh, 1825).

3. (p. 356) *sprung into the pulpit*: according to Russell (Kirkton 459–60) something very like this happened on Sunday 15 June, while the army was racked by debates. But the aggressor was a *'moderate'*. 'Mr Hume thrust Mr Douglas from the place where he was going to

preach, and preached himself, crying up the king's lawful authority, and the accepting of all persons to the army.'

4. (p. 357) *Their trust ... flight ... take thy fan ... fire ... gold*: cf. Deuteronomy 32:30–31, 37 and Matthew 3:12. *Achan* was a Covenanting byword; Wilson (11) applies it to one Weir of Greenridge, whose presence in the Whig army was a bone of contention because he had fought under Dalzell at Rullion Green in 1666, and (13) denounces Welch and his followers as a 'sad company of Achans'. Achan, at the destruction of Jericho, in Joshua 7 steals some spoil, including a '*goodly Babylonish garment*'. He is stoned and burnt to death, after his crime has angered the Lord so much that He lets the children of Israel be defeated by the men of Ai. For *the woman of Babylon*, cf. Psalm 137; Isaiah 47, and Revelation 18. Babylon is the symbol of wicked luxury, and the words written against it in the Bible are very suitable for contexts where class hatred is being fanned. Finally *shekels of silver* and *wedges of gold* are among the spoils stolen by Achan: see Joshua 7:21.

5. (p. 357) *new election of officers*: it was in fact the *moderates*, once they found themselves numerically predominant, who made this demand on the day before the battle, hoping to oust the extremist officers whom they had found in charge (Wodrow 2:64–5). But Scott is thinking of the purging of the Scottish Army before Dunbar in 1650.

6. (p. 357) *those who were not with them were against them*: cf. Matthew 12:30 and Luke 11:23.

7. (p. 358) *Patriarch ... brethren*: the words, slightly misquoted, are spoken by Abram to his nephew Lot in Genesis 13:8.

8. (p. 359) *To your tents, O Israel*: I Kings 12:16.

9. (p. 360) *Achan*: see note 4 above.

10. (p. 360) *children of this generation ... sanctuary*: cf. Luke 16:8.

11. (p. 361) *the cannon began to fire ... wreaths of smoke*: it seems pointless to measure Scott's account of the battle detail by detail against what 'actually happened', when the details of the battle are anyway somewhat uncertain. See Terry (76–8) for a scholarly account of the action. No authority or source casts the slightest doubt on the main point which Scott makes; that the rebels were confused and bitterly divided before and even during the battle, and that once the brave men defending the bridge had had to fall back, complete rout followed with terrible swiftness. But the roles assigned to Morton, Burley, and Dalzell on the field of battle are all imaginary.

CHAPTER 32

1. (p. 361) *Old Ballad*: 'Bothwell Bridge', from the *Minstrelsy*, again.

2. (p. 362) *Loch-sloy* (Scott's note):
This was the slogan or war-cry of the MacFarlanes, taken from a lake near the head of Loch Lomond, in the centre of their ancient possessions on the western banks of that beautiful inland sea.

3. (p. 363) *He flies ... slaughter*: Scott adapts hints from Wodrow (2:66–7). According to this account, Hackston and the others defending the bridge send back for more ammunition. Hamilton in turn orders them to quit the bridge and retire to the main body. Then, according to Hackston himself, with the Royal Army already across the bridge, 'upon a sudden the cry rose from the troops and the companies on all hands that their leaders were gone, which, *adds he*, were the men who were inclined to the Indulgence, either flying or seeking a parley with the enemy.' As Wodrow points out, the moderates, contrariwise, blamed Hamilton and the extremists for being 'soonest out of the field'

4. (p. 364) *twelve hundred*: this is the figure given in Wodrow (2:67). Perhaps 800 rebels were killed.

5. (p. 365) *Basil Olifant ... marching to join them*: Scott adapts two hints from Wodrow who mentions (2:64) the 'accession of a good many gentlemen of some note' on the day *before* the battle, and says that William Gordon of Earlstoun, coming up to join the whigs on the day of the battle, was slain by English dragoons. But Basil Olifant is a wholly fictional figure, and no such person was leading several gentlemen forward on the day of the battle itself.

6. (p. 365) *Sheathe your sword ... unwearied and bloody pursuit ... come up with*: Terry (79–82) can find no justification for Scott's making Claverhouse play this prominent and vindictive role at Bothwell Bridge, or for suggesting that Monmouth was in the least backward in pursuit of the rebels. Yet the sources chorus out Scott's tale.

With greater or lesser colour and emphasis, Wodrow (2:67–70), Burnet (1:473) and Law (151) present a merciful Monmouth restraining terrible slaughter. Creichton (37) depicts a cowardly Monmouth whose orders not to pursue the flying rebels are ignored. The whig Blackader (248–9) and the tory *Memoirs of Dundee* (14) concur with Wodrow in emphasizing the bloodthirstiness of Claverhouse. Blackader says he disobeyed orders to retreat, while the memorialist gloats over the slaughter. 'Drum-Clog and the Archbishop of St Andrews

murder, were sufficiently reveng'd that day; and if Clavers and
Oglethorp had been left to their own discretion, they had put an end
to that rebellious crowd; and purg'd the nation of much superfluous
and corrupted blood.'

Of course, the whig writers were anxious to praise Monmouth, and
the tories were anxious to show him as backward and ineffectual in
the battle. It may be, as Terry suggests, that the fact that Monmouth
halted most of his force after about a mile and sent Claverhouse and
Oglethorp to keep up the pursuit with a detachment of cavalry, explained the traditional notion which found its way into ballads as
well as books; such a sight might be misinterpreted.

7. (p. 366) *May the hand . . . no longer* (Scott's note):
This incident, and Burley's exclamation, are taken from the records.

[Not exactly, perhaps. What Burley actually called out, according
to a witness, when he had received a shot, was, 'the devil cut off the
hands that gave it'. (Kirkton 474). This would be too 'low' for
Scott's epic figure.]

CHAPTER 33

1. (p. 367) *Fletcher*: from *Two Noble Kinsmen*, V, i, by John
Fletcher (1579–1625) and William Shakespeare. This scene is now
usually attributed to Shakespeare.

2. (p. 369) *thief through the window . . . ram . . . Jehovah–Jireh . . .
horns of the altar*: for the thief cf. John 10: 1–10. Mucklewrath then
compares Morton with the ram offered up by Abraham in Genesis
22: 13–14 instead of his son Isaac, at the place he called Jehovah–Jireh.
The final command is similar to Psalms 118: 27.

3. (p. 371) *Midianitish woman*: see Numbers 25: 6–8.

4. (p. 371) *godly Joshua*: see Joshua 7: 8.

5. (p. 372) *Seize on the prisoner . . . weapon*: no 'moderate' leader
appears, from the sources, to have been so treated by 'extremists'
after Bothwell Bridge. But the 'extremist' leader Hamilton believed
that his life had been plotted against by a company of moderates
'who after the break at Bothwell, sat down in the Old Clachan at
Galloway' (*Faithful Contendings* 188).

6. (p. 373) *Book of Common Prayer of the Church of England*: see
the note to p. 182. And for an earlier sign of Macbriar's un-
Presbyterian background, see the note to p. 242. Scott used the Book
of Common Prayer in his own household (Johnson 297).

7. (p. 374) *Hezekiah*: see Isaiah 38:8.
8. (p. 375) *weel eneugh yet* (Scott's note):

NOTE TO CHAPTER XXV

The principal incident of the foregoing Chapter was suggested by an
occurrence of a similar kind, told me by a gentleman, now deceased,
who held an important situation in the Excise, to which he had been
raised by active and resolute exertions in an inferior department.
When employed as a supervisor on the coast of Galloway, at a time
when the immunities of the Isle of Man rendered smuggling almost
universal in that district, this gentleman had the fortune to offend
highly several of the leaders in the contraband trade, by his zeal in
serving the revenue.

This rendered his situation a dangerous one, and, on more than
one occasion, placed his life in jeopardy. At one time in particular,
as he was riding after sunset on a summer evening, he came suddenly
upon a gang of the most desperate smugglers in that part of the
country. They surrounded him, without violence, but in such a
manner as to show that it would be resorted to if he offered resistance, and gave him to understand he must spend the evening with
them, since they had met so happily. The officer did not attempt
opposition, but only asked leave to send a country lad to tell his wife
and family that he should be detained later than he expected. As he
had to charge the boy with this message in the presence of the
smugglers, he could found no hope of deliverance from it, save what
might arise from the sharpness of the lad's observation, and the
natural anxiety and affection of his wife. But if his errand should be
delivered and received literally, as he was conscious the smugglers
expected, it was likely that it might, by suspending alarm about his
absence from home, postpone all search after him till it might be
useless. Making a merit of necessity, therefore, he instructed and
dispatched his messenger, and went with the contraband traders,
with seeming willingness, to one of their ordinary haunts. He sat
down at table with them, and they began to drink and indulge
themselves in gross jokes, while, like Mirabel in the 'Inconstant',
their prisoner had the heavy task of receiving their insolence as wit,
answering their insults with good-humour, and withholding from
them the opportunity which they sought of engaging him in a
quarrel, that they might have a pretence for misusing him. He succeeded for some time, but soon became satisfied it was their purpose
to murder him outright, or else to beat him in such a manner as

scarce to leave him with life. A regard for the sanctity of the Sabbath evening, which still oddly subsisted among these ferocious men, amidst their habitual violation of divine and social law, prevented their commencing their intended cruelty until the Sabbath should be terminated. They were sitting around their anxious prisoner, muttering to each other words of terrible import, and watching the index of a clock, which was shortly to strike the hour at which, in their apprehension, murder would become lawful, when their intended victim heard a distant rustling like the wind among withered leaves. It came nearer, and resembled the sound of a brook in flood chafing within its banks; it came nearer yet, and was plainly distinguished as the galloping of a party of horse. The absence of her husband, and the account given by the boy of the suspicious appearance of those with whom he had remained, had induced Mrs — to apply to the neighbouring town for a party of dragoons, who thus providentially arrived in time to save him from extreme violence, if not from actual destruction.

[*The Inconstant* (1702) is a play by George Farquhar (1678–1707).]

CHAPTER 34

1. (p. 375) *Anonymous*: these famous lines, sometimes attributed to Scott himself, are in fact long identified as by Thomas Osbert Mordaunt (1730–1809) and come from a poem which appeared in *The Bee* magazine (Edinburgh) 12 October 1791.

2. (p. 376) *Mischief shall haunt the violent man*: with 'hunt' instead of 'haunt', this saying is applied by both Walker (2:57) and Howie (*Judgements* 45) to the man-hunter James Irvine of Bonshaw who captured the preacher Cargill in 1681. (Irvine, as they were glad to record, was stabbed to death by a comrade of his.) cf. Psalms 140:11 and 7:16.

3. (p. 377) *before I breakfast* (Scott's note):

The author is uncertain whether this was ever said of Claverhouse. But it was currently reported of Sir Robert Grierson of Lagg, another of the persecutors, that a cup of wine placed in his hand turned to clotted blood.

4. (p. 378) *Wilt thou trust in thy bow ... Behold the princes ... mad because thereof*: cf. Psalms 44:6; Hosea 1:7 and Jeremiah 25:15–18.

5. (p. 378) *How long ... saints*: Revelation 6:10.

CHAPTER 35

1. (p. 380) *Beggars Opera*: by John Gay (1685–1732). In the famous entertainment of 1728, the robber Macheath sings this song in III, xi, to the tune of 'Bonnie Dundee'.

2. (p. 380) *General*: Claverhouse was not promoted Colonel until 1682, and only became a Major-General in 1686.

3. (p. 382) *Froissart*: Jean Froissart (c. 1337–c. 1410), the French chronicler. Sir John Dalrymple, in his *Memoirs of Great Britain . . .*, of which Scott owned the third (1790) edition, claimed (Pt 2, Bk 2, 73) that 'Dundee had inflamed his mind from his earliest youth, by the perusal of ancient poets, historians, and orators, with the love of the great actions they praise and describe.' But Terry (12) says that Dalrymple 'follows tradition rather than fact'.

4. (p. 383) *black book*: this record seems to correspond in character to the so-called Porteous (portable) Rolls framed after Bothwell Bridge (Wodrow 2 : 91–2).

5. (p. 387) *auto da fe* (Scott's note):

David Hackston of Rathillet, who was wounded and made prisoner in the skirmish of Air's-Moss, in which the celebrated Cameron fell, was, on entering Edinburgh, 'by order of the Council, received by the Magistrates at the Watergate, and set on a horse's bare back with his face to the tail, and the other three laid on a goad of iron, and carried up the street, Mr Cameron's hand being on a halberd before them.'

[Scott quotes Howie, *Scots Worthies* (370).]
6. (p. 388) *Grassmarket* (Scott's note):

Then the place of public execution.

7. (p. 389) *bridal garment . . . marriage garment*: see Isaiah 61 : 10 and Matthew 22 : 1–14. For a post-Freudian age, the implications of this jargon are intriguing. According to *Cloud* (489) when the drums beat the first warning of his imminent execution, the field-preacher Renwick said to those around him, ' "Let us be glad and rejoice, for the marriage of the Lamb is come"; and I can say, in some measure, "The bride, the Lamb's wife, hath made herself ready." And, till dinner was over, he enlarged upon the parallel of a marriage, and invited all of them to come to the wedding, meaning his execution.' Most of the 1,400 or so Covenanters who were taken to Edinburgh after Bothwell Bridge and there imprisoned, did in fact 'tak the declaration', as Cuddie puts it, pledging themselves never to rise in arms again, and were released. (Mathieson, 281–2.)

CHAPTER 36

1. (p. 389) *Lord Byron*: from canto i of *Childe Harold's Pilgrimage* (1812) by George Gordon, Lord Byron (1788–1824), the other very major Scottish writer of the day.

2. (p. 389) *a nobleman of high place amongst them*: John Maitland, 2nd Earl and 1st Duke of Lauderdale (1616–82). A leading Coven-anter in the early 1640s, he was one of the Lords who negotiated the Engagement with Charles I in 1647, and he was imprisoned as a Royalist from 1651–60. From 1660 to 1680 he was Charles II's Secretary for Scottish Affairs. But he seems to have been in London in the period in which this novel is set, and he certainly wasn't at the trials of the prisoners from Bothwell Bridge. Lauderdale was indeed a renegade, and he was profoundly and inventively corrupt, but his immense learning and deep patriotism might have been ex-pected to appeal to Scott. We must wonder whether Scott's hostile attitude, here and in the *Tales*, was influenced by his well-attested fury against the then Duke of Lauderdale who in 1810 attacked, in the House of Lords, a nifty piece of jobbery whereby Scott had secured for his feckless brother Tom an official sinecure. (See Johnson 330–31.) But the big tongue is from Burnet (1 : 101–2) who also notes Lauderdale's rough manners and his unpleasant sense of humour.

3. (p. 391) *greyhounds after a hare* (Scott's note):

The General is said to have struck one of the captive whigs, when under examination, with the hilt of his sabre, so that the blood gushed out. The provocation for this unmanly violence was, that the prisoner had called the fierce veteran 'a Muscovy beast, who used to roast men'. Dalzell had been long in the Russian service, which in those days was no school of humanity.

4. (p. 393) *for which I suffer* (Scott's note):
This was the reply actually made by James Mitchell when subjected to the torture of the boot, for an attempt to assassinate Archbishop Sharpe.

5. (p. 394) *Thou hast said ... power*: see Psalms 110 : 3. John Kid, a preacher actually put to death after Bothwell Bridge, was tortured first with the boots. See Wodrow (2 : 84).

6. (p. 395) *pleasure of the Council* (Scott's note):

The pleasure of the Council respecting the relics of their victims was often as savage as the rest of their conduct. The heads of the preachers were frequently exposed on pikes between their two hands, the palms displayed as in the attitude of prayer. When the celebrated Richard Cameron's head was exposed in this manner, a spectator bore testimony to it as that of one who lived praying and preaching, and died praying and fighting.

[See Walker 1.234.]

7. (p. 395) *Doomster ... functions* (Scott's note):

See a note on the subject of this office in the Heart of Mid-Lothian.

[Not worth space here.]

8. (p. 396) *And Phinehas arose and executed judgement*: see Psalms 106:30, referring to Numbers 25:1–15, a passage referred to also on p. 306 and p. 371. Claverhouse had good reason to think of this particular text. Cited in *Naphtali* (1667) by a Covenanting writer, it provided subject matter for a whole chapter in the Episcopalian reply, *The Survey of Naphtali. Jus Populi Vindicatum* (1669) retorts with another whole chapter. It explains (409) that Phineas (sic) executed judgement on an 'Israelitish prince and his Midianitish whore, to stay the plague and judgement of God, which was broken out on the whole congregation, because of their defection to Midianitish whore-dome and idolatry.' But the writer concludes (426) 'I would not have the reader to think, that I do look upon that example of Phineas as a binding precedent in all times to all persons, unless it be every way so circumstantiated as it was then.' Scott must have noticed this controversy, and he must certainly have seen the place where Howie (*Judgements* 39) applies the text to the murder of Sharpe.

9. (p. 397) *Prince of Orange ... Seneff*: [Scott believed (see his *Tales*) that Claverhouse had rescued William at the battle of Seneff in 1674, and had remounted him on his own horse, when the Prince's had been slain under him.] Scott's own note at this point reads:

August 1674. Claverhouse greatly distinguished himself in this action, and was made Captain.

[Scott got this story from *Memoirs of Dundee* (4–5). It is all wrong, though Claverhouse may have saved William's life in some later battle. He did not receive promotion in William's service until November 1676, when he became Captain of Horse. (See Terry 18–23, 29.)]

10. (p. 397) *Ephraim ... Israel*: cf. Judges 12:1–6 and Isaiah 11:13.

11. (p. 398) *Keep thy sword girded ... in the waste field*: there are references here to Obadiah 1:8–9 and 1:18, and more distantly to Matthew 14:25 – and probably others.

CHAPTER 37

1. (p. 399) *As You Like it*: III, ii; misquoted.

2. (p. 400) *the year immediately subsequent to the British Revolution*: we are now in the summer of 1689: to be precise, in July 1689, since Dundee fell at Killiecrankie on 17 July, and news of his death arrives on p. 416.

3. (p. 400) *Agriculture began to revive*: Scott's enthusiasm for the Revolution leads him far astray. Generally speaking, in a country poised always on the brink of famine arising from the failure of the oat crop, the whole period from 1660 to 1695 was remarkably good – there were only four bad seasons, and grain prices were otherwise unusually low. Then, between 1695 and 1699 came 'King William's Ill Years' – four years of bad harvest, a murrain among the cattle, and the worst famine for a century, with (it is said) a third or a half of the population dying or emigrating in some districts. See Smout (143–5) and cf. Mitchison (294).

4. (p. 402) *Bothwell Castle … Aymer de Valence*: Bothwell Castle dates from the late thirteenth century and was at one time occupied by Aymer de Valence (d. 1324) Earl of Pembroke, an English governor of Scotland. *One* of the towers was traditionally known as the Valence tower.

5. (p. 404) *Single Carritch*: the Shorter Catechism of the Westminster Assembly, used by Scottish Presbyterians.

6. (p. 404) *Effectual Calling*: a phrase in the Shorter Catechism: 'Effectual calling is the work of God's Spirit, whereby, convincing us of our sin and misery, enlightening our minds in the knowledge of Christ, and renewing our wills, he doth persuade and enable us to embrace Jesus Christ, freely offered to us in the gospel.'

7. (p. 404) *Mackay*: Major General Hugh Mackay, who opposed Dundee as the Williamite commander at Killiecrankie, had previously stalked him for weeks through the Highlands.

CHAPTER 38

1. (p. 408) *Logan*: from 'Ode On the Death of a Young Lady' by a minor Scottish poet, Rev. John Logan (1748–88).

2. (p. 409) *managers*: the word Wodrow uses to refer to the highest authorities in Edinburgh, the King's chief servants in Scotland who manned the Committee for Public Affairs and sat on the Privy Council.

3. (p. 412) *John Tamson's man*: according to *SND*, 'a henpecked

husband, a proverbial expression found in O.Sc. from *c.* 1500 and of uncertain origin.'

4. (p. 413) *Punch and the Deevil*: the well-known puppet character, originating in Italy, had reached London by 1662, so Cuddie might well have seen a version of his adventures at a local fair.

5. (p. 416) *He has married a wife, and therefore cannot come*: see Luke 14:20.

6. (p. 416) *near Blair of Athole*: i.e. at Killiecrankie.

7. (p. 417) *The Life-Guards ... fight under my orders*: there really was a plot afoot to swing a regiment over to Dundee, in which Lord Kilsyth was involved, along with Scott's source Captain Creichton. Mackay learnt about it before anything could come of it, and the leaders were imprisoned. See Creichton (82–7).

8. (p. 424) *repose of the dead* (Scott's note):

Supposed Apparition of Morton

This incident is taken from a story in the History of Apparitions written by Daniel Defoe, under the assumed name of Morton. To abridge the narrative, we are under the necessity of omitting many of those particular circumstances which give the fictions of this most ingenious author such a lively air of truth.

A gentleman married a lady of family and fortune, and had one son by her, after which the lady died. The widower afterwards united himself in a second marriage; and his wife proved such a very step-mother to the heir of the first marriage, that, discontented with his situation, he left his father's house, and set out on distant travels. His father heard from him occasionally, and the young man for some time drew regularly for certain allowances which were settled upon him. At length, owing to the instigation of his mother-in-law, one of his draughts was refused, and the bill returned dishonoured.

After receiving this affront, the youth drew no bills, and wrote no more letters, nor did his father know in what part of the world he was. The stepmother seized the opportunity to represent the young man as deceased, and to urge her husband to settle his estate anew upon her children, of whom she had several. The father for a length of time positively refused to disinherit his son, convinced as he was, in his own mind, that he was still alive.

At length, worn out by his wife's importunities, he agreed to execute the new deeds, if his son did not return within a year.

During the interval, there were many violent disputes between the husband and wife, upon the subject of the family settlements. In the midst of one of these altercations, the lady was startled by seeing a hand at a casement of the window; but as the iron hasps, according to the ancient fashion, fastened in the inside, the hand seemed to essay the fastenings, and being unable to undo them, was immediately withdrawn. The lady, forgetting the quarrel with her husband, exclaimed that there was some one in the garden. The husband rushed out, but could find no trace of any intruder, while the walls of the garden seemed to render it impossible for any such to have made his escape. He therefore taxed his wife with having fancied that which she supposed she saw. She maintained the accuracy of her sight; on which her husband observed, that it must have been the devil, who was apt to haunt those who had evil consciences. This tart remark brought back the matrimonial dialogue to its original current. 'It was no devil,' said the lady, 'but the ghost of your son come to tell you he is dead, and that you may give your estate to your bastards, since you will not settle it on the lawful heirs.' – 'It was my son,' said he, 'come to tell me that he is alive, and ask you how you can be such a devil as to urge me to disinherit him;' with that he started up and exclaimed, 'Alexander, Alexander! if you are alive, show yourself, and do not let me be insulted every day with being told you are dead.'

At these words, the casement which the hand had been seen at, opened of itself, and his son Alexander looked in with a full face, and, staring directly on the mother with an angry countenance, cried, 'Here!' and then vanished in a moment.

The lady, though much frightened at the apparition, had wit enough to make it serve her own purpose; for, as the spectre appeared at her husband's summons, she made affidavit that he had a familiar spirit who appeared when he called it. To escape from this discreditable charge, the poor husband agreed to make the new settlement of the estate in the terms demanded by the unreasonable lady.

A meeting of friends was held for that purpose, the new deed was executed, and the wife was about to cancel the former settlement by tearing the seal, when on a sudden they heard a rushing noise in the parlour in which they sat, as if something had come in at the door of the room which opened from the hall, and then had gone through the room towards the garden-door, which was shut; they were all surprised at it, for the sound was very distinct, but they saw nothing.

This rather interrupted the business of the meeting, but the persevering lady brought them back to it. 'I am not frightened,' said she, 'not I. – Come,' said she to her husband, haughtily, 'I'll cancel the old writings if forty devils were in the room;' with that she took up one of the deeds, and was about to tear off the seal. But the *double-ganger*, or *Eidolon*, of Alexander, was as pertinacious in guarding the rights of his principal, as his stepmother in invading them.

The same moment she raised the paper to destroy it, the casement flew open, though it was fast in the inside just as it was before, and the shadow of a body was seen as standing in the garden without, the face looking into the room, and staring directly at the woman with a stern and angry countenance. 'HOLD!' said the spectre, as if speaking to the lady, and immediately closed the window and vanished. After this second interruption, the new settlement was cancelled by the consent of all concerned, and Alexander, in about four or five months after, arrived from the East Indies, to which he had gone four years before from London in a Portuguese ship. He could give no explanation of what had happened, excepting that he dreamed his father had written him an angry letter, threatening to disinherit him. – *The History and Reality of Apparitions*, chap. viii.

[Coleman O. Parsons, in his *Witchcraft and Demonology in Scott's Fiction* (Oliver & Boyd, 1964) remarks sensibly: 'Since the events in *Old Mortality* take place in the latter half of the seventeenth century, Edith Bellenden's belief that her lover's spirit has returned to rebuke her is not surprising.']

9. (p. 427) *Delrio ... Burthoog ... De L'Ancre*: real scholars who really wrote relevant books – Martin Antoine Del Rio (1551–1608), Richard Burthogge (1637–98) and Pierre de Lancre (died *c.* 1630). (Welsh.)

CHAPTER 39

1. (p. 428) *Ode on a distant prospect of Eton College*: by Thomas Gray (1716–71).

2. (p. 435) *Scylla ... Charybdis*: two whirlpools opposite each other in the sea between Italy and Sicily, which are referred to in Homer's *Odyssey* 12:85, and are an ancient and modern byword.

3. (p. 435) *Argus*: the dog of Odysseus, who knew his master after an absence of twenty years. If Drumclog recalls the *Iliad*, Scott is nudging us hard in this paragraph to remember Homer's other great work, but the effect is mock-heroic; Morton doesn't live any more on the epic level, which the Glorious Revolution has, indeed, rendered obsolete.

CHAPTER 40

1. (p. 438) *Richard II*: V, ii.

2. (p. 439) *Stadtholder*: another title of the Prince of Orange.

3. (p. 440) *writer*: in Scotland, this denotes the equivalent of the English attorney or solicitor.

4. (p. 441) *Hamlet*: see III, iv.

CHAPTER 41

1. (p. 444) *Lover's Progress*: from III, i, of the play by John Fletcher (1579–1625), adapted by Philip Massinger and produced in 1623.

2. (p. 445) *aqua mirabilis*: the *OED* cites Johnson: 'The wonderful water, prepared of cloves, galangals, cubebs, mace, cardomums, nutmegs, ginger, and spirit of wine, digested twenty-four hours, then distilled.'

3. (p. 446) *the lang ten*: the ten of trumps in the Scottish card-game 'catch-the-ten', in which the main object is to take the trick containing it.

4. (p. 449) *widow's cake and the widow's cruize*: see I Kings 17 : 8–16.

CHAPTER 42

1. (p. 450) *Old Ballad*: from 'Johnie of Breadislee', a version of 'Johnie Cock' (Child 114), printed in the *Minstrelsy*.

2. (p. 451) *widow of Zarephath*: the poor woman who put up the prophet Elijah in I Kings 17. A striking image of pious poverty.

3. (p. 451) *Jael . . . Sisera*: there have already been several references in the novel to the story, told in Judges 4, of how Sisera, a great enemy of the people of Israel for twenty years, is finally defeated by Barak. He flees and takes shelter in the tent of Jael, the wife of a man at peace with Sisera's people. While he is asleep, Jael drives a nail through his temples with a hammer. She is an apt heroine of revolution; she is also an ugly precedent for treacherous murder.

4. (p. 452) *My auld een dazzled . . . alive again*: Scott has taken touches for Bessie Maclure from two separate women mentioned in Patrick Walker's famous, debatable story (1 : 84–6) of how Claverhouse had John Brown of Priesthill, 'the Christian Carrier', slain summarily in front of his wife in the 'Killing Time'. This tale shows Walker's style at its best; Scott compares it in his notes to the *Minstrelsy* (2 : 241) to 'the beautiful book of Ruth'. Brown's wife sat weeping over her husband. The first person to come to her was one

Jean Brown, who had lost a husband in the Pentland Rising, a son killed at Drumclog, and another son shot by the soldiers when taken. Walker goes on: 'The said Isabel Weir (i.e. Mrs Brown) sitting upon her husband's gravestone, told me, that, before that, she could see no blood but she was in danger to faint, and yet was helped to be a witness to all this without either fainting or confusion, except, when the shotts were let off, her eyes dazled.'

5. (p. 453) *Inglis* (Scott's note):

The deeds of a man, or rather a monster, of this name, are recorded upon the tombstone of one of those martyrs which it was Old Mortality's delight to repair. I do not remember the name of the murdered person, but the circumstances of the crime were so terrible to my childish imagination, that I am confident the following copy of the Epitaph will be found nearly correct, although I have not seen the original for forty years at least.

> This martyre was by Peter Inglis shot,
> By birth a tiger rather than a Scot;
> Who, that his hellish offspring might be seen,
> Cut off his head, then kick'd it o'er the green;
> Thus was the head which was to wear the croun,
> A foot-ball made by a profane dragoon.

In Dundee's Letters, Captain Inglish, or Inglis, is repeatedly mentioned as commanding a troop of horse.

[Scott's quotation is indeed 'nearly correct' – *Cloud* (592) gives 'monstrous extract' instead of 'hellish offspring'. But he doesn't make it clear that the sources refer to two different Inglis's – the football player is defined in *Cloud* (546) as the son of Captain Inglis.
Dundee's Letters refers to the Bannatyne Club edition of 1826.]

6. (p. 455) *seven unhallowed prelates*: seven bishops petitioned James II and VII to withdraw the order that his second Declaration of Indulgence, granting toleration to dissenters, of May 1688, should be read in every church. They were sent to the Tower and tried for seditious libel, but in June were found not guilty, having become symbols of resistance to the King.

7. (p. 456) *Yerl of Angus*: James Douglas, Earl of Angus (d. 1692) had William Cleland (see the note to p. 214) as his Lieutenant-Colonel in the newly formed regiment, which became known as the 'Cameronian Regiment', and was, initially at least, equipped with ministers and elders as well as officers.

8. (p. 456) *Montgomery and Ferguson*: it is slightly anachronistic

for Mrs Maclure to speak of Sir James Montgomery of Skelmorlie (d. 1694) as a known ally of James in July 1689. This prominent Presbyterian, annoyed at not being given higher office by William, didn't plot with the Jacobites until a little later.

He was associated with Robert Ferguson, 'The Plotter' (d. 1714), originally from Aberdeen but resident in England from c. 1655. Involved in the Rye House Plot, he was later chaplain to Monmouth's army in 1685. Like Montgomery, he expected greater reward from William than he got, and intrigued with James's court in France.

9. (p. 457) *Sir Harry Vane, Harrison, Overton*: all prominent English servants of the Commonwealth – Sir Harry Vane the Younger (1613–62), Thomas Harrison (1606–60), and Robert Overton (born c. 1609).

CHAPTER 43

1. (p. 458) *Spenser*: from *The Faerie Queene*, Bk. I, canto ix, St. 35, by Edmund Spenser (c. 1552–99).

2. (p. 461) *Closeburn* (Scott's note):

The Retreats of the Covenanters

The severity of persecution often drove the sufferers to hide themselves in dens and caves of the earth, where they had not only to struggle with the real dangers of damp, darkness, and famine, but were called upon, in their disordered imaginations, to oppose the infernal powers by whom such caverns were believed to be haunted. A very romantic scene of rocks, thickets and cascades, called Creehope Linn, on the estate of Mr Menteath of Closeburn, is said to have been the retreat of some of these enthusiasts, who judged it safer to face the apparitions by which the place was thought to be haunted, than to expose themselves to the rage of their mortal enemies.

Another remarkable encounter betwixt the Foul Fiend and the champions of the Covenant, is preserved in certain rude rhymes, not yet forgotten in Ettrick Forest. Two men, it is said, by name Halbert Dobson and David Dun, constructed for themselves a place of refuge in a hidden ravine of a very savage character, by the side of a considerable waterfall, near the head of Moffat water. Here, concealed from human foes, they were assailed by Satan himself, who came upon them grinning and making mouths, as if trying to frighten them, and disturb their devotions. The wanderers, more incensed than astonished at this supernatural visitation, assailed their ghostly visitor, buffeted him soundly with their Bibles, and compelled him at length to change himself into the resemblance of a pack of dried hides, in which shape he rolled down the cascade. The shape which he assumed was probably designed to excite the cupidity of the assailants, who, as Souters of Selkirk, might have been disposed to attempt something to save a package of good leather. Thus,

'Hab Dab and David Din,
Dang the Deil ower Dabson's Linn.'

The popular verses recording this feat, to which Burns seems to have been indebted for some hints in his Address to the Deil, may be found in the Minstrelsy of the Scottish Border, vol. ii.

It cannot be matter of wonder to any one at all acquainted with human nature, that superstition should have aggravated, by its horrors, the apprehensions to which men of enthusiastic character were disposed by the gloomy haunts to which they had fled for refuge.

3. (p. 463) *vintage ... struck*: cf. Matthew 20: 1–16.

4. (p. 463) *Cave of Adullam*: in I Samuel 22. Burley compares himself to the fugitive, future, King David.

5. (p. 464) *riddle ... Samson's*: see Judges 14: 12–14.

6. (p. 465) *Nabal ... Demas*: Nabal in I Samuel 25 insults King David but dies of fright. Demas, a worldling, deserts St Paul in 2 Timothy 4: 10.

7. (p. 465) *bit ... nostrils*: cf. 2 Kings 19: 28 and Isaiah 37: 29.

8. (p. 466) *Chapel of Holyrood*: Burley's capacity for epic encounter is prodigious. During the Revolution, on 17 December 1688, a mob, including many Westland whigs, rose in Edinburgh and attacked Holyrood Palace, where James VII had installed a Catholic Chapel Royal in the nave of the abbey of Holyrood, and a Jesuit school and a Catholic printing press in the Palace itself. The troops there, commanded by Captain Wallace, couldn't defend it, and the chapel was sacked. I can find no mention, however, of the captain being 'cleft to the teeth' by a Cameronian aged seventy or over.

9. (p. 466) *bones of its master* (Scott's note):

Predictions of the Covenanters

The sword of Captain John Paton of Meadowhead, a Cameronian famous for his personal prowess, bore testimony to his exertions in the cause of the Covenant, and was typical of the oppressions of the times. 'This sword of short shabble' (*sciabla*, Italian) 'yet remains,' says Mr Howie of Loch Goin. 'It was then by his progenitors' (meaning descendants, a rather unusual use of the word) 'counted to have twenty-eight gaps in its edge; which made them afterwards observe, that there were just as many years in the time of the persecution as there were steps or broken pieces in the edge thereof.' – *Scottish Worthies*, edit, 1797, p. 419.

The persecuted party, as their circumstances led to their placing a due and sincere reliance on heaven, when earth was scarce permitted to bear them, fell naturally into enthusiastic credulity, and, as they imagined, direct contention with the powers of darkness, so they conceived some amongst them to be possessed of a power of prediction, which, though they did not exactly call it inspired prophecy, seems to have approached, in their opinion, very nearly to it. The subject of these predictions was generally of a melancholy nature; for it is during such times of blood and confusion that

'Pale-eyed prophets whisper fearful change.'

The celebrated Alexander Peden was haunted by the terrors of a French invasion, and was often heard to exclaim, 'Oh, the Monzies, the French Monzies,' (for Monsieurs, doubtless,) 'how they run! How long will they run? Oh Lord, cut their houghs, and stay their running!' He afterwards declared, that French blood would run thicker in the waters of Ayr and Clyde than ever did that of the Highlandmen. Upon another occasion, he said he had been made to see the French marching with their armies through the length and breadth of the land in the blood of all ranks, up to the bridle reins, and that for a burned, broken, and buried covenant.

Gabriel Semple also prophesied. In passing by the house of Kenmure, to which workmen were making some additions, he said, 'Lads, you are very busy enlarging and repairing that house, but it will be burned like a crow's nest in a misty May morning;' which accordingly came to pass, the house being burned by the English forces in a cloudy May morning. Other instances might be added, but these are enough to show the character of the people and times.

[For Peden's 'monzies' see Walker (1 : 91–2). Scott carelessly tells of Gabriel Sempill the story Walker relates of John Semple (1 : 188).]

10. (p. 466) *King of Israel … Philistines*: see I Samuel 27 : 1–7. Burley again compares himself with David.

CHAPTER 44

1. (p. 470) *Palamon and Arcite*: Bk 3, 840–43 of John Dryden's rendering of Chaucer's *Knight's Tale*. Welsh notes too subtly for

paraphrase here the significant resemblances between this story and Scott's tale of gallant rivalry between Morton and Evandale.

2. (p. 477) *this saam spot* (Scott's note):

John Balfour, called Burley

The return of John Balfour of Kinloch, called Burley, to Scotland, as well as his violent death in the manner described, is entirely fictitious. He was wounded at Bothwell Bridge, when he uttered the execration transferred to the text, not much in unison with his religious pretentions. He afterwards escaped to Holland, where he found refuge, with other fugitives of that disturbed period. His biographer seems simple enough to believe that he rose high in the Prince of Orange's favour, and observes, 'That having still a desire to be avenged upon those who persecuted the Lord's cause and people in Scotland, it is said he obtained liberty from the Prince for that purpose, but died at sea before his arrival in Scotland; whereby that design was never accomplished, and so the land was never cleansed by the blood of them who had shed innocent blood, according to the law of the Lord, Gen. ix, 6, *Whoso sheddeth man's blood, by man shall his blood be shed.*' – *Scottish Worthies*, p. 522.

It was reserved for this historian to discover, that the moderation of King William, and his prudent anxiety to prevent that perpetuating of factious quarrels, which is called in modern times Reaction, were only adopted in consequences of the death of John Balfour, called Burley.

The late Mr Wemyss of Wemyss Hall, in Fifeshire, succeeded to Balfour's property in late times, and had several accounts, papers, articles of dress, &c. which belonged to the old homicide.

His name seems still to exist in Holland or Flanders; for in the Brussels papers of 28th July, 1828, Lieutenant-Colonel Balfour de Burleigh is named Commandant of the troops of the King of the Netherlands in the West Indies.

CONCLUSION

1. (p. 478) *Jemmy and Jenny Jessamy*: a novel published in 1753 by Eliza Haywood (*c.* 1693–1756).

2. (p. 478) *Julia de Roubigné*: a novel (1777) by the Scottish writer Henry Mackenzie (1745–1831).

3. (p. 480) *Delville ... Cecilia*: characters in *Cecilia*, a novel by Fanny Burney (1752–1840) published in 1782.

4. (p. 481) *Scheherezade*: who told tales for the thousand and one nights – the 'Arabian Nights'.

NOTES TO APPENDIX A

INTRODUCTION TO

OLD MORTALITY

FROM THE 1830 EDITION

1. (p. 485) *Robert Paterson*: see W. S. Crockett's *The Scott Originals* (1912) pp. 170–83 for a few further details about Paterson (1716–1801).

2. (p. 485) *Argyle*: Archibald Campbell, 9th Earl (1629–85). Condemned to death for treason when he refused to take the Test Oath brought in by legislation of 1681, he escaped abroad and returned in 1685 to make an abortive attempt at rebellion against James VII. He was then executed.

3. (p. 493) *Captain Hodgson's Memoirs*: edited by Scott from the seventeenth-century MS in 1806 and published by Constable, in a volume of *Original Memoirs, Written during the Great Civil War*.

4. (p. 493) *Silence*: 2 *Henry IV*, V, iii.

NOTES TO APPENDIX C

EXTRACT FROM A REVIEW OF

TALES OF MY LANDLORD
IN *QUARTERLY REVIEW*, APRIL 1817

1. (p. 502) *Life of Peden*: by Patrick Walker.

2. (p. 502) *battle to the Dutch*: (original note), see Macpherson's State Papers.

3. (p. 503) *Sir John Dalzell*: a slip for 'Sir Thomas'. I would suggest that this too-obvious error rather tends to confirm that Scott himself didn't write this passage.

4. (p. 506) *Beatson*: should be 'Beaton'. See the note to p. 275.

5. (p. 512) *in the mouth too*: *Twelfth Night*, II, iii.

6. (p. 513) *with the rest*: the joking here must surely be Scott's own, reflecting his characteristic love of tongue-in-cheek mystification. It alludes to a rumour current since the publication of *Waverley* itself, that the new Scottish novels were the work of Scott's brother Tom, who was in Canada. (Hence 'transatlantic confessions'.) See Johnson (456–8, 558.)

BIBLIOGRAPHY AND GLOSSARY

BIBLIOGRAPHY

The list below gives, by alphabetical order of abbreviated titles, books referred to in the introduction and notes to this volume.

The biographies listed, by Johnson and Lockhart, are the standard works of reference. For shorter, stimulating views of the man see John Buchan, *Sir Walter Scott* (Cassell, 1933) and David Daiches, *Sir Walter Scott and His World* (Thames & Hudson, 1971).

An excellent short critical survey is by Thomas Crawford, *Scott* (Oliver & Boyd, 1965). The most influential modern interpretations of Scott's work are found in Georg Lukacs, *The Historical Novel* (Penguin, 1969); David Daiches, *Literary Essays* (Oliver & Boyd, 1967) and Alexander Welsh, *The Hero of the Waverley Novels* (New Haven, Conn., 1963). Welsh has many important things to say about *Old Mortality* in particular, and Cockshutt, Craig and Gordon, among the books listed below, also offer interesting standpoints on the novel.

AITON: William Aiton, *A History of the Rencounter at Drumclog...*, Hamilton, 1821. (Attempts to correct Scott's history.)

ANDERSON: James Anderson, 'Sir Walter Scott and History', Edinburgh University Ph.D. Thesis, 1965.

BLACKADER: Andrew Crichton, *Memoirs of Rev. John Blackader*, Edinburgh, 1823. (Prints important memoirs by a field-preacher already known to Scott in MS.)

BRINTON: Crane Brinton, *The Political Ideas of the English Romanticists*, Oxford, 1926.

BURNET: Gilbert Burnet, *History of His Own Time*, vol. 1, London, 1724.

CLOUD: *A Cloud of Witnesses*, Rev. J. H. Thomson (ed.), Edinburgh, 1871. (Convenient reprint of an important collection of Covenanting 'testimonies' published in 1714.)

COCKSHUTT: A. O. J. Cockshutt, *The Achievement of Walter Scott*, Collins, 1969.

COWAN: I. B. Cowan, 'The Covenanters: A Revision Article', *Scottish Historical Review*, vol. XLVII, 1968. (Indispensable review of what other scholars have written.)

CRAIG: David Craig, *Scottish Literature and the Scottish People*, Chatto & Windus, 1961.

CREICHTON: 'Memoirs of Captain John Creichton...' (1731), re-printed in Sir Walter Scott (ed.), *The Works of Jonathan Swift D.D.*, vol. XII, 2nd edition, Edinburgh, 1824. (Originally 1814. Swift 'ghosted' Creichton's memoirs.)

DEFOE: (Daniel Defoe), *Memoirs of the Church of Scotland*, London, 1717.

DNB: The Dictionary of National Biography.

DONALDSON: Gordon Donaldson, *Scotland: James V to James VII*, Oliver & Boyd, 1965.

FAITHUL CONTENDINGS: *Faithful Contendings Displayed*, com-piled by Michael Shields, John Howie (ed.), Glasgow, 1780. (A col-lection of 'Cameronian' documents and sermons.)

GORDON: R. C. Gordon, *Under Which King?*, Oliver & Boyd, 1969.

HAZLITT: William Hazlitt, *The Spirit of the Age*, London, 1825.

HEWISON: J. K. Hewison, *The Covenanters*, vol. 2, Glasgow, 1913. (A standard work still, alas; bigotted but scholarly enough to be use-ful.)

HOWIE, *Scots Worthies*: John Howie, *Bibliographia Scoticana or ... Scots Worthies*, 3rd edition, Glasgow, 1797. (The most useful edition of this hagiographical collection. Bound with *Judgements* and Wilson, below.)

HOWIE, *Judgements*: John Howie, *The Judgement and Justice of God Exemplified*. (An appendix on persecutors bound with *Scots Worthies*, above.)

JOHNSON: Edgar Johnson, *Sir Walter Scott – The Great Unknown*, Hamish Hamilton, 1970.

JOURNAL: *The Journal of Sir Walter Scott*, W. E. K. Anderson (ed.), Oxford, 1972.

Jus Populi Vindicatum: (Sir James Stewart of Goodtrees), *Jus Populi Vindicatum ...*, 1669. (Covenanting tract of immense length.)

KIRKTON: Rev. James Kirkton, *The Secret and True History of the Church of Scotland, from the Restoration to the year 1678*, ed. from the MS by C. K. Sharpe, Edinburgh, 1817. (Includes Russell, below, as an appendix. Scott, Sharpe's friend, knew both MSS.)

LAW: Rev. Robert Law, *Memorialls ...* (1638–84), ed. from the MS by C. K. Sharpe, Edinburgh, 1818. (Memoirs, already known to Scott, by a 'moderate' minister.)

Letters: The Letters of Sir Walter Scott, Sir H. J. C. Grierson (ed.), 12 vols., London, 1932–7.

LOCKHART: J. G. Lockhart, *Memoirs of the Life of Sir Walter Scott*, 7 vols., Edinburgh, 1837–8.

LUKACS: Georg Lukacs, *Writer and Critic*, Merlin Press, 1970.

M'CRIE: Thomas M'Crie, *Miscellaneous Writings*, Edinburgh, 1841. (Reprints his review of *Tales of My Landlord* from the *Christian Instructor*, 1817.)

MATHIESON: W. L. Mathieson, *Politics and Religion*, Glasgow, 1902. (Still one of the soundest books to survey the Covenanters.)

MELVILLE CLARK: Arthur Melville Clark, *Sir Walter Scott: The Formative Years*, W. Blackwood, 1969. (Very useful on Scott's taste and range in reading.)

Memoirs ...: *Memoirs of the Lord Viscount Dundee* ... by 'An Officer of the Army', London, 1718.

Minstrelsy: Sir Walter Scott, *Minstrelsy of the Scottish Border*, in *Poetical Works* ..., vols. 1–4, Edinburgh, 1833.

MITCHISON: Rosalind Mitchison, *A History of Scotland*, Methuen, 1970.

NAPIER: Mark Napier, *Memorials and Letters illustrative of the Life and Times of John Graham of Claverhouse, Viscount Dundee*, vol. I, Edinburgh, 1859.

OED: *The Oxford English Dictionary*.

QR: (Sir Walter Scott), Review of Sharpe's edition of Kirkton (above) in *Quarterly Review*, vol. XVIII, 1818.

Quarterly: Unsigned review by Scott and others of *Tales of My Landlord* in *Quarterly Review*, vol. XVII, 1817.

RAIT: Robert Rait, 'Walter Scott and Thomas M'Crie', in *Sir Walter Scott Today*, Sir H. J. C. Grierson (ed.), London, 1932.

RUSSELL: 'An Account of the Murder of Archbishop Sharp by James Russell, an Actor Therein', edited by C. K. Sharpe from an MS known to Scott and appended to Kirkton, above.

SMOUT: T. C. Smout, *A History of the Scottish People 1560–1830*, 2nd edition, Collins, 1972. (A splendid book.)

SND: *The Scottish National Dictionary*.

Tales: Sir Walter Scott, *Tales of a Grandfather*, Edinburgh, 1828.

TERRY: C. S. Terry, *John Graham of Claverhouse Viscount of Dundee*, London, 1905.

THOMPSON: E. P. Thompson, *The Making of the English Working Class*, Penguin, 1968. (Though concerned with England, this gives much of the political and social context within which Scott himself consciously wrote.)

TREVOR-ROPER: Hugh Trevor-Roper, 'Sir Walter Scott and History', *Listener*, vol. 86, 19 August 1971.

TURNER: Sir James Turner, *Memoirs of His Own Life and Times 1632–1670*, Edinburgh, 1829.

WALKER: Patrick Walker, *Six Saints of the Covenant*, D. Hay

Fleming (ed.), 2 vols., London, 1901. (Originally separate pamphlets, 1724–32. This is a most useful modern edition.)

WELSH: Sir Walter Scott, *Old Mortality*, Alexander Welsh (ed.), Boston, Mass., 1966.

WILSON: William Wilson, 'A True and Impartial Relation of the Persecuted Presbyterians in Scotland; their Rising in Arms, and Defeat at Bothwel-Bridge 1679', appended to Howie, *Scots Worthies*, above. (Written in 1751.)

WODROW: Robert Wodrow, *The History of the Sufferings of the Church of Scotland, from the Restoration to the Revolution*, 2 vols., Edinburgh, 1721–2.

YOUNG: G. M. Young, 'Scott and the Historians', in *Sir Walter Scott Lectures 1940–1948*, introd. W. L. Renwick, Edinburgh, 1950. (Disappointing.)

I would like to take this chance to thank the Librarian of Edinburgh University for giving me permission to use that valuable library, and the staff of the National Library of Scotland, whose helpfulness makes that such a splendid place to work in.

GLOSSARY

This includes, beside Scottish words, certain Latin and French expressions, and some obsolete terms common to Scots and English.

a' : all
a'body : everybody
aboon, abune : above
abulyiements : accoutrements
abune by ordinar : above the ordinary
adhuc in pendente : still pending
ae : one
aff : off
afore : before
again : against, until
ahint : behind
ain : own
aitmeal : oatmeal
ajee : awry
amaist : almost
amna : am not
an : if, suppose
ance : once
ance wud and aye waur : in a furious passion
ane : one
anent : regarding
anes : once
anither : another
ark : meal-chest
arles : money given to bind a bargain
asteer : in confusion
atweel, aweel : well
atween : between
auchlet : two stones weight, or a peck measure

aucht : eight; *or* owed, possessed of
auld : old
ava' : at all
awa' : away
awe : to owe
awe a day in har'st : to owe a good turn
awsome : awful, terrible

bab : tassel, bunch
back-cast : a back-stroke
baff : blow, bang, a heavy thump
bag : the bagpipes
bailie : magistrate
bairn : a child
baith : both
bang : to beat
bannock : a flat round cake, usually of barley or pease-meal
barking and fleeing : on the verge of bankruptcy
barouche : a sort of four-wheeled carriage used from *c.* 1805
batts : colic
bawbee : halfpenny
bear : a kind of barley
bedral : a beadle, a grave-digger
beetmaster : a substitute
behadden : beholden, under an obligation
beild : shelter
belive : speedily

ben: inner apartment; *or* intimate, well cared-for

bennison: blessing

besom: a jade

bestial: the whole of the cattle, horses, sheep etc. on a farm

bicker: a wooden bowl or dish

bide: to wait, to suffer

bien: well provided

biggit wa's: built walls, i.e. houses

bilbo: a sword noted for the temper and elasticity of its blade

binna: be not

birkies: lively fellows

birling: drinking

bit: small, little

bittock: a little bit

black-a-vised: dark in complexion

black fishers: night poachers of fish who would spear salmon by torchlight

blate: backward

blawing in a woman's lug: flattering her

bleeze: a blaze; *also* to brag

blethering: foolish talking

blink: a twinkling, a glimpse

blithe, blythe: glad, happy, pleasant

blude, bluid: blood

boddle, bodle: a copper coin worth one-sixth of an English penny

bole: a square aperture

bonny: pretty

bountith: reward

bow: a boll, containing the sixteenth part of a chalder, which is itself an obsolete dry measure

bowies: tubs, milk-pails

bracken: fern

branks: a sort of wooden muzzle, used as a bridle

braw: fine, splendid

brawly: cleverly

braws: fine clothes

brecham: a working horse's collar

breeks: breeches

breering: showing above ground

brickle: difficult, brittle

brigg: a bridge

brogue: the Highland shoe, of untanned hide

broo: the juice of meat; *also* favourable opinion

brose: a dish made by pouring boiling water or milk on oatmeal

brose-time: suppertime

browst: brewing

budget: a carabine socket

buskit: dressed

by and out-taken: over and above and excepting

byre: cowhouse

ca': to call; *ca' the plough*: to work the plough

callant: lad

calm sough: keep quiet, say little or nothing

Candlemas: 2 February

canna: cannot; *canna hear day nor door*: as deaf as a post

cannily: cautiously, prudently

canny: skilful, prudent

carabine: a kind of firearm,

shorter than the musket, but larger than a pistol

carcage: a carcass

carena: care not

carle: fellow, gruff old man

carline: an old woman, a witch

cast: fate; *cast o' a cart*: lift in a cart

cat in pan, to turn: change sides from motives of interest

cateran: Highland robber

cauld: cold

caup: a cup, a wooden bowl

caution: security

certie: conscience; *by my certie*: a kind of oath equivalent to troth

chainzie: chain

chancy: lucky

change-house: tavern or inn where horses are changed on a journey

chappins: quarts

chiel, chield: young fellow

chimley-neuk: chimney-corner

clachan: a hamlet

claes: clothes

clashes: scandal, tittle-tattle

clatter: tattle

clavers: foolish talk; *to claver*: talk foolishly

clean wud: quite mad

cleugh: ravine, hollow

clinked: struck

clinked down: quartered

cloured: dinted

clow-gillieflower: clove-gillyflower

coal; a cauld coal to blaw at: an unprofitable task

cobble-head: the head of a short flat-bottomed rowing boat used for crossing rivers etc.

cockernony: the gathering up of a young woman's hair in a snood

cock-laird: petty landowner, yeoman

cogues: round wooden vessels for holding milk, liquor etc.

compleen: complain

corse: body

couldna: could not

coup: a bowl; *also* to barter, to turn over

crack a bit: talk a little

cracking clavers: talking and boasting

crap: the produce of the ground

creel: a basket

cronie: intimate friend

crook a houg to fyke: descriptive of the motions of dancing

crowdy: meal and milk mixed in a cold state

cuittle favour: curry favour

curch: woman's cap

curmurring: grumbling

curney: round

cuttie: an unchaste woman

cutty spoon: short-handled spoon

daffin', daffing: frivolous conversation

daft: silly, crack-brained

daidling: trifling

dargue: a set quantity of work

daur: to dare

daurna: dare not

deave: to deafen

deceptio visus: deception of the sight

deer-hair: the scaly-stalked club-rush, *scirpus caespitosus*

deil: the devil

delation: a denouncement

denty: dandy

dichting, dighting: sifting or separating the corn from the chaff

didna: did not

die: a toy, a gewgaw

dikeside, dykeside: side of the stone-wall fence

ding: to knock

dinna, disna: do not

dirdum: scolding, row

disjasked, disjaskit: downcast-looking, decayed-looking

disjune: breakfast

div: do

doo, dow: a dove

dooms: absolutely

door-cheek: side of the door

douce: sedate, quiet

doudling: dandling

doun: down

dour: stubborn

dow: dove

dow'd na: did not like

downa: cannot

downa bide: cannot bear, don't like

downsitting: without rising, the session of a court

drammock: a thick raw mixture of meal and water

drave: drove

dree'd: endured

driving ower: passing or whiling away the time

drouthy: thirsty

drucken: drunken

dry-stane dyke: an unmortared wall

duds: clothes

dung: knocked about

dwam: swoon

ee: eye

een: eyes

e'en: evening; even

e'enow: presently, at present

eident: hard-working, diligent

eik: addition

eneuch, eneugh, enow: enough

enow: just now

espiegle: frolicsome, roguish

ewhow: ah! alas!

fa': fall

fairing: a drubbing; *also* deserts

fal-lalls: finery

fallow: a fellow

fand: found

fard: colour, paint

farther ben: more favoured

fash: ado, trouble

fauld: a fold; *fauld-dike*: wall of a fold

faured: favoured

fause: false

faut: fault

fau't; 'fau't o' fude': want of food

feared: afraid

febrifuge: a medicine to cure fever

feck: part

feckless: feeble

fee: wages; *fee'd*: paid

fended: provided

fire-flaught: lightning

fit-ba': football

fizzenless: insipid

flaught: flitter

flee: to fly

fleech: cajole

flit: to remove

flyte: to scold, inveigh against

foisonless: insipid

forby: besides

fore-a-hand: first in order

foregathered: met

forgie: forgive

forrit: forward

foul fa' ye: ill befall you!

foumarts: polecats

frae: from

fraim, fremd: strange

friar's chicken: a kind of broth made with veal and chicken and with beaten eggs added

fule: a fool

fund: found

fur: a furrow

fusee: a light musket

gad: iron bar

gae: go; *also*, gave

Galloway: small, strong horse

gane: gone

gang: go

gar: make, force; *garr'd*: compelled

gat: got

gate: way

gaun: going

gauntrees: wooden frames supporting casks in a cellar

gay, gey: very

gear: money, property, goods, cattle

gentles: gentlefolk

gie: give

gilpy: a frolicsome person

gin: if

girnel: meal-chest

gledge: a side-glance

gleg: ready, sharp, on the alert

gliff: a short time

gloaming: twilight

glower: gaze

goadsman: driver of a team of oxen

gomeril, gomeral: blockhead

gowd: gold

gowk: goose, blockhead

gowpin: handful

graith: to put on military accoutrements

gramoches: long gaiters or leggings of cloth or leather

grane: groan, to groan

greeting: weeping

grewsome: frightful

grit: great

grund: ground

gude: good; God

gudeman: husband, head of the household

gudewife: wife, used also to denote the head of the female portion of a household

guide: manage

guse: goose, fool

ha'arst: harvest

hae: have

haena: have not

hae't: have it

haft: to fix or settle

haill: whole

halbert: a kind of combination of spear and battle-axe, mounted on a handle five to seven feet long

hamely: homely, home-like, familiar

hantle: great many, great deal

harle: to drag

harns: brains

harried: plundered

harrows; to have one's legs o'er the harrows: to break loose

hash: big blockhead

haud: to hold, to have

hauld: a habitation

haugh: a meadow

hause: throat

havings: behaviour, demeanour

hay band: rope of twisted hay used to bind up a truss or bundle of hay

hellicat: half-witted

hempie: giddy

heugh: a dell; *also* a crag

hickery-pickery: mixture

hill-folk: open-air conventiclers

hinder-end: extremity

hinny: honey

hoast: cough

hoddin-grey: cloth having the natural colour of wool, worn by the peasantry

holm, holme: level ground beside a stream

horn: a vessel for holding liquor

horning; letter of horning: a letter in which a debtor is charged to pay the debt for which he is prosecuted, or perform the obligation within a certain time under the pain of rebellion. cf. 'To put to the horn', to proclaim an outlaw

houghs: the hams

houseleek: a plant, *sempervivum tectorum*

howe: hollow

howff: a retreat, a haunt

humle-cow: a cow without horns

hunder: a hundred

hurcheon: hedgehog

hurdies: buttocks

hure: whore

huz: us

ilka: each, every

ilka-days: weekdays

ill-faured, ill-faurd, ill-fard: ill-favoured, plain-looking

ill-guide: to ill-treat

in commendam: (held) in charge or trust

ingle-nook: chimney-corner

in rerum natura: in the physical world

intercommune: to have intercourse with people proclaimed rebels

i'se: I shall

isna: is not

ither: other

jalouse: suspect

jaud: jade

jenny-flection: genuflexion

jimply: sparingly, scantily

jo, joe: sweetheart

justify: to punish with death

kail, kale: a sort of cabbage; *also* the broth made from it

kail-brose: a pottage of meal made with the scum of broth

kail-worm: caterpillar

kail through the reek: a sound scolding

kail-yard: a vegetable garden

kaisar: Caesar, emperor

kebbie: a stick

kebbock: a cheese
keek: peep
ken: to know; *kend*: knew; *kenda*: didn't know; *kenna, kensna*: know(s) not
kent: cudgel, rough walking stick
kittle: difficult
knapping: uttering smartly; talking, chattering; affecting to speak fine English
knowe: hillock
kye: cows
kylevine pen: lead pencil
laddie: a boy
laigh: low
laird: landed proprietor
laith: loath
landau: a four-wheeled carriage, in use from the eighteenth century, the top of which, being made in two parts, could be closed or thrown open
lane: lone, alone; *his lane, her lane, my lane* etc.: by himself, etc.
lang: long
lassock: little girl
lave: rest, remainder
lawing: reckoning
leasing-making: seditious talking
leatherin': beating, drubbing
leggins: leggings
letten: allowed
lick: a blow
lift: to carry off by theft
linn: a cataract, a waterfall
lippen: rely upon, trust to
lippie: the fourth part of a peck
loaning: an opening between fields of corn, near, or leading to, the homestead, left uncultivated, for the sake of driving the cattle homewards
locality: a requisition, generally of forage for military purposes, made proportionately to the valued rent on the landowners of a parish
lock: a handful
loof: the palm of the hand
loon: a lad, a low or lazy person
loot: let, allow
lound: quiet
lounder: a stunning blow
loup: to leap
low: a flame
lug: the ear
lum: a chimney
lum-head: chimney-pot
luppen: leaped

mains: farm attached to a mansion house; cf. demesne
mair: more
maist: most
malt; when the malt begins to get aboon the meal: when one gets drunk
man-sworn: perjured
march-dyke: boundary wall
mart: a fatted cow
martingale: strap to prevent a horse from rearing or throwing back his head
marvedie: a Spanish copper coin of little value
masked: brewed
mashlum: mixed grain
massy: full of self-importance
maun: must
maunder: incoherent talk
maunna: must not

maut: malt

mawkin: hare

meal-ark: meal-chest

Mearns: Kincardineshire

mensfu': modest, mannerly

merk: a Scottish coin, valued at 1s 1½d of English money

mickle: much

minched pies: mince-pies

mind: remember

mirligoes: dizziness, megrims in the head

mislear'd: ill-bred, ill-taught

mistaen: mistaken

mony: many

monzies: monsieurs

moor-pout: moor-fowl

morn, the: tomorrow

moss-flow: a boggy place

moss-hags: pits and sloughs in a mire or bog

muck: dung

muckle: much

muir: moor

murgeons: violent gestures, twistings of the body, antics

mutchkin: an English pint

na, nae: no, not

nae broo o': no liking for

naething: nothing

naig: a nag

nash-gab: insolent or trashy talk

natheless: nevertheless

neb: nose

needed till hae been: should have been

needna: need not

neist: next

neuk: a nook, a corner

nevoy: nephew

night, the: tonight

nil novit in causa: knew nothing about the case

noble: English coin, worth one-third or one-half of a pound sterling; Scottish coin worth about 6½d. sterling

onstead: the buildings on a farm

ony: any

or: before

ordinar, by: in an uncommon way

o't: of it

outshot: a projection in a building

out-taken: excepting

ower: over

owsen: oxen

paduasoy: silk of Padua; a lady's habit

paid: beaten

parritch: porridge

pat: a pot

pearlings: a species of lace made of thread or silk

peat-hag: a hollow in moss left after digging peats

peine forte et dure: 'severe and hard punishment', formerly inflicted on persons arraigned for felony who refused to plead; pressing to death

penny-fee: wage

phraise: fine speech

pickle: a small quantity

piddling: trifling; eating and drinking without the least relish

pinners: women's caps with two long flaps, one on each side, pinned on and hanging down *pit*: to put

pit and gallows: a privilege formerly conferred on a baron, of having on his ground a pit for drowning women and a gallows for hanging men, convicted of theft

plack: a copper coin of very little value

plenishing: providing

pleugh: a plough

pleugh-paidle: a plough staff

poached: broke

pockmantle: a portmanteau

pock-puddings: bag-puddings, a terms of abuse applied to the English

pose: deposit

pouss: push

pouther: powder

prent: print

pretty: fine, smart, spirited

pu': pull

puir: poor

pule: a pool

pund Scots: worth 1s 8d English money

putten: put

putten up: provided for

quaigh: a small and shallow drinking cup with two ears

queans: girls, young women

rade: rode

randy: a scold

raploch: coarse, undyed home-spun woollen cloth

rase: rose

raxed: stretched

redd: to clear up

redder: peacemaker

reek: smoke

reiving: thieving

reset: to harbour

rigs: ridges

rin: run

riped: searched

round: to whisper

rout: to bellow, roar

row: to roll

rue; to take the rue: to repent of a proposal or bargain

rugging: pulling roughly

sae: so

sair: sore

sair travailed: wearied, worn out

sall: shall

sark: shirt

saul: the soul

sauld: sold

saut: salt

scaff and raff: riff-raff, mob

scaur: an overhanging bank

screed: a long tirade

seena: see not

set: to suit, to become one; *also* to beset

shaw: wood

sheeling-hill: a mound where the oats were winnowed

short by the head: short of money

shouther: the shoulder

shune: shoes

sic: such

siller: money

single sodger: private soldier

skaith: harm, damage

skeel: skill

skeily: skilful

skellies: squints

skelp: to thrash the bottom with an open hand; *also* to move quickly

skinker: one who draws, pours out or serves liquor

skirl: shrill cry

skirl-in-the-pan: sop in the pan

sma' : small

sma' browst: small ale

sodger: a soldier, to soldier

somegate: somehow

sorning: exacting food and lodging

sort: to arrange, to supply; *also* as noun, a term applied to persons or things when the number is rather small

sough: sigh, sound, note; *calm sough*: an easy mind, a still tongue; *soughed awa'*: died gently

soup, sowp: a sip, small amount of liquid

sowens: a Scottish food consisting of farinaceous matter extracted from the bran or husks of oats

spak: spoke

spang: to spring

speel: climb

speer: ask, inquire

spence: a pantry, the inner apartment

springald: a youth, young man

spunk: mettle, activity, spirit

stamach: stomach

stane: stone

stap: to push, to cram

starkly: strongly

staw: to surfeit

steekit: closed

steer: to disturb

stell'd: planted

stilt: the handle of a plough

sting and ling: wholly, entirely

stir: sir

stot: a bullock between two and three years old

stoup: a measure

stour: stern

strae: straw

stressed: distressed, inconvenienced

stude: hesitated

sud, suld: should; *suldna*: should not

sune as syne: now as afterwards

sweal: swing

sybo: onion

syke: a streamlet dry in summer

syne: since, afterwards

tae, tane: one

ta'en: taken

tak on: to engage

tangs: tongs

tap-knots: knot of ribbons worn in a woman's cap or bonnet

tass: cup, glass

tauld: told

tawpie: an awkward girl, a foolish woman

tent: care, attention

teugh: tough

thack: thatch

thack and rape: snug and comfortable

thae: these, those

theeking: showing above ground

thegither: together

thir: these

thowless: useless

thrapple: throat

thrang: busy

thrawing: twisting

threep: to aver strongly

thriftless: unprofitable, worthless

tilbury: a light, open two-wheeled carriage, fashionable in Scott's day

till: to

till't: to it

tirled: stripped

tither: the other

tittie: sister

tolbooth: goal

tother: the other

touzle: to dishevel, put in disorder

tow: a rope

toy: a woman's close linen or wool cap, with flaps coming down to the shoulders

trick track: an old variety of backgammon

troupe dorée: 'gilded troop', used ironically

trow: to believe, to think, to guess

trysted: visited or met by appointment

twa: two

twall: twelve

umquhile: deceased, late

unco: very, particularly, prodigious, terrible; *also* strange

unco body: stranger

uptak, uptake: to understand, to comprehend

videttes: mounted sentries placed in advance of the out-posts of an army to observe the movements of the enemy

vivers: food, provisions

wad: would; *wadna*: would not

wae: sorry

wallie: valet; *wally de shamble*: valet de chambre

walth: plenty, abundance

wame: belly

wan: got, reached

wappenschaw, wappinschaw: a periodical review or muster of the men under arms within a particular district

wared: spent

warse: worse

warst: worst

wasna: was not

wat: wet

water broo: water-gruel

waught: quaff, hearty draught

waur: worse

weans: children

wee: little

wee ajee: a bit awry

weel: well

weir: war

wersh: tasteless

we'se: we shall

wha, whae: who

what for: why

wheen: few, number of

whiles: sometimes

whilk: which

whilly-wha's: wheedling talk, cajoling; *whilliewhae*: to cajole

whinger: a short-sword, a hanger

whirry: to whirl

whistl: hush!

whomlekirn pule: a pool where

churns were plunged in for washing

wi : with

win : to get

win by : get past, escape

win ower : to get over

window-bole : the part of a cottage window filled by a wooden blind

winna : will not

winnock : window

wizened : withered

woodie : gallows

wot : to know

wotna : know not

wow! : an exclamation of surprise

wud : mad

wull : will; *what's yer wull?* : what is your pleasure?

wunna : will not

wyte : blame

yaird : a garden

yerl : earl

yestate : estate

yill, yell : ale

yoking : the time that a horse is in the yoke

yokit : yoked